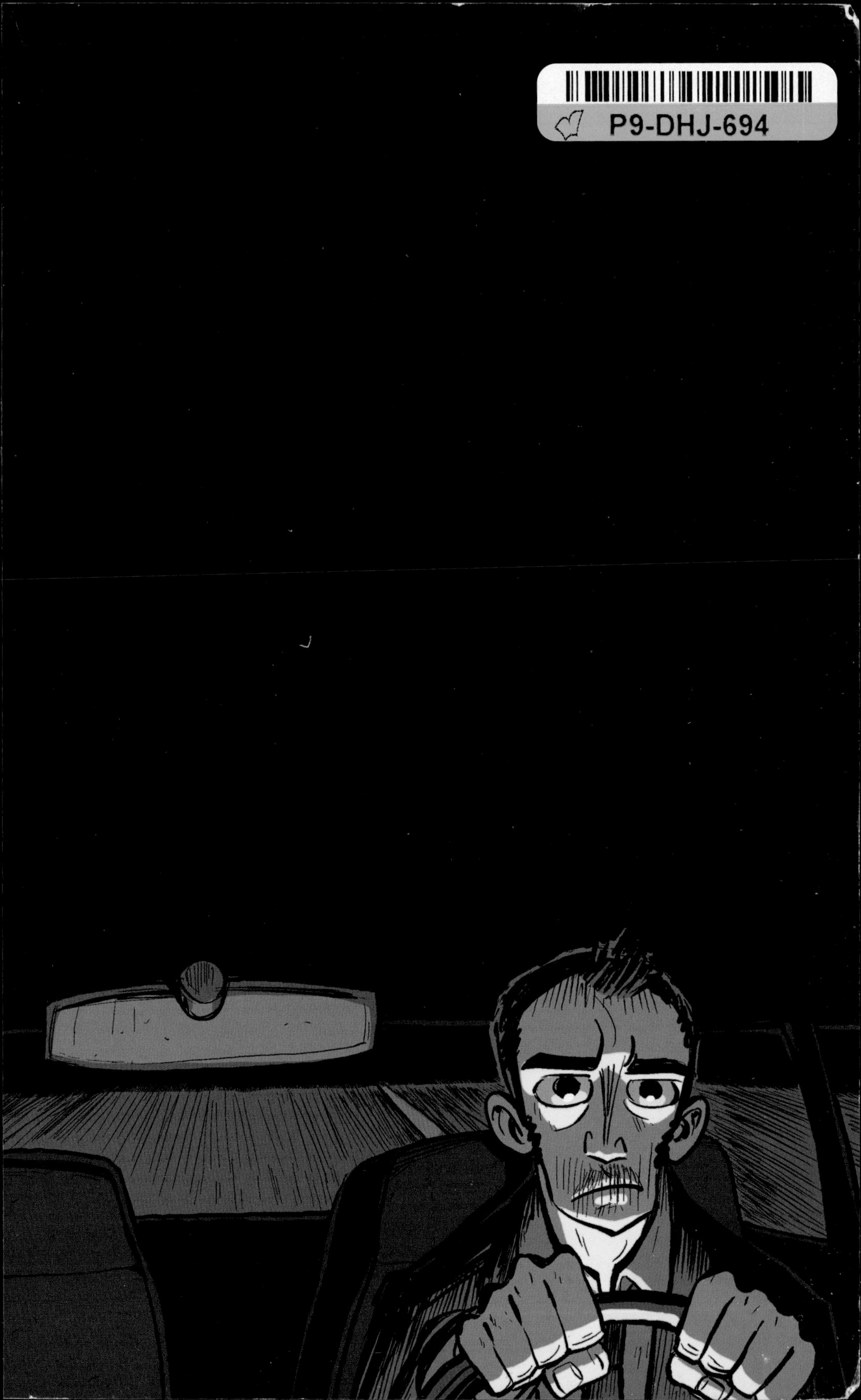

CREATED, WRITTEN, AND DRAWN BY
DOUG TENNAPEL

LEAD COLORISTS
KATHERINE GARNER
TOM RHODES

ASSISTANT COLORISTS
MATT LASKODI, AARON CRAYNE, WES SCOG, RICK RANDOLPH,
KENNY HITT, ETHAN NICOLLE, ERIC BRANSCUME, DIRK ERIK
SCHULZ, SEAN MCGOWAN, AND DAVID KOWALYK

BOOK DESIGN BY
PHIL FALCO

EDITED BY
ADAM RAU AND DAVID SAYLOR

CREATIVE DIRECTOR
DAVID SAYLOR

graphix

An Imprint of

◼ SCHOLASTIC

New York Toronto London Auckland Sydney
Mexico City New Delhi Hong Kong

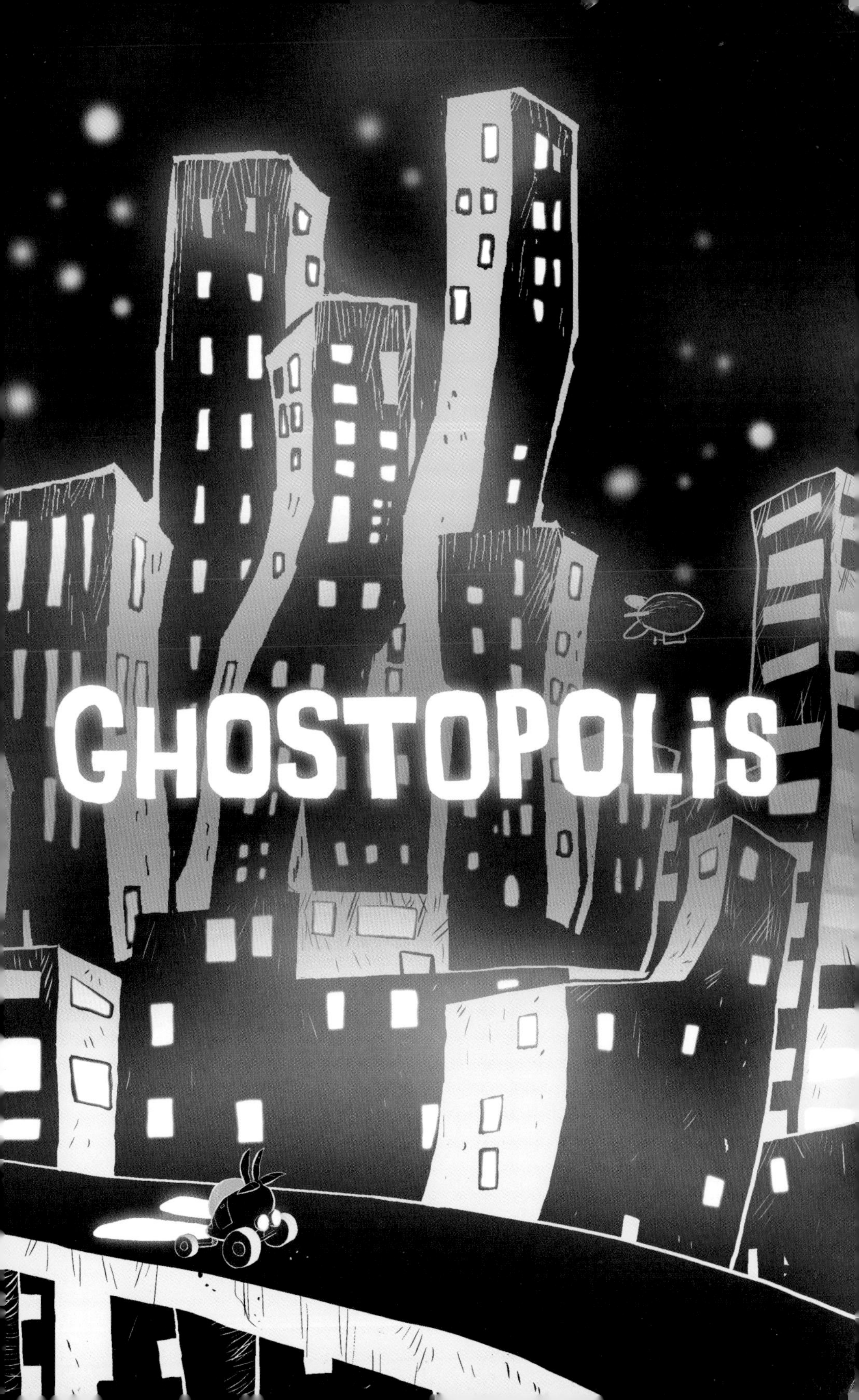
GHOSTOPOLIS

FOR DR. MICHAEL WARD

All rights reserved. Published by Graphix, a division of Scholastic Inc., *Publishers since 1920*. SCHOLASTIC and associated logos are trademarks and/or registered trademarks of Scholastic Inc. No part of this publication may be reproduced, stored in a retrieval system, or transmitted in any form or by any means, electronic, mechanical, photocopying, recording, or otherwise, without written permission of the publisher. For information regarding permission, write to Scholastic Inc., Attention: Permissions Department, 557 Broadway, New York, NY 10012.

Library of Congress Cataloging-in-Publication Data Available

ISBN 978-0-545-21027-0 (hardcover)
ISBN 978-0-545-21028-7 (paperback)

10 9 8 7 6 5 4 3 2   10 11 12 13 14
Printed in Singapore   46

First edition, July 2010

This book was drawn digitally using Manga Studio EX 4.

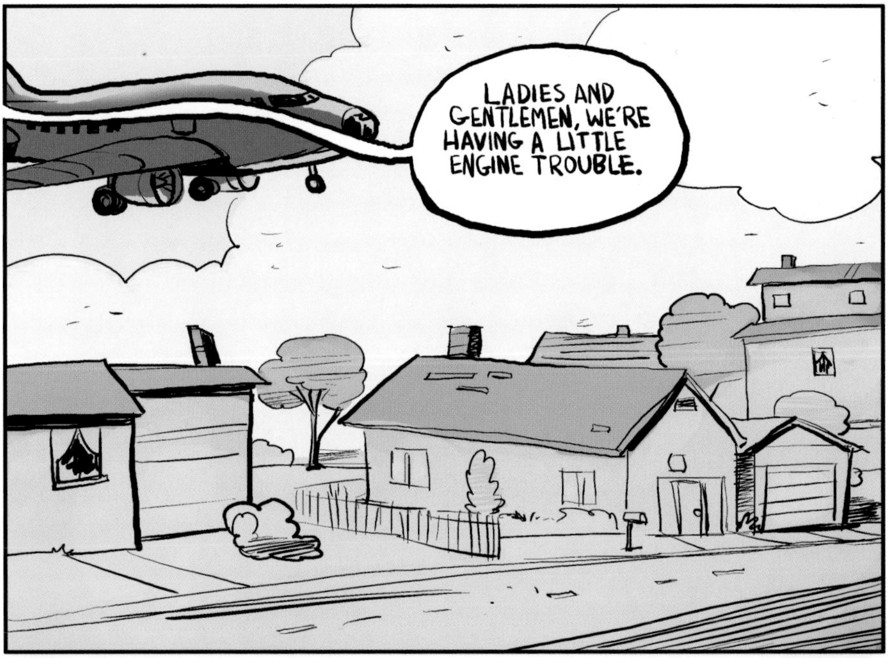
LADIES AND GENTLEMEN, WE'RE HAVING A LITTLE ENGINE TROUBLE.

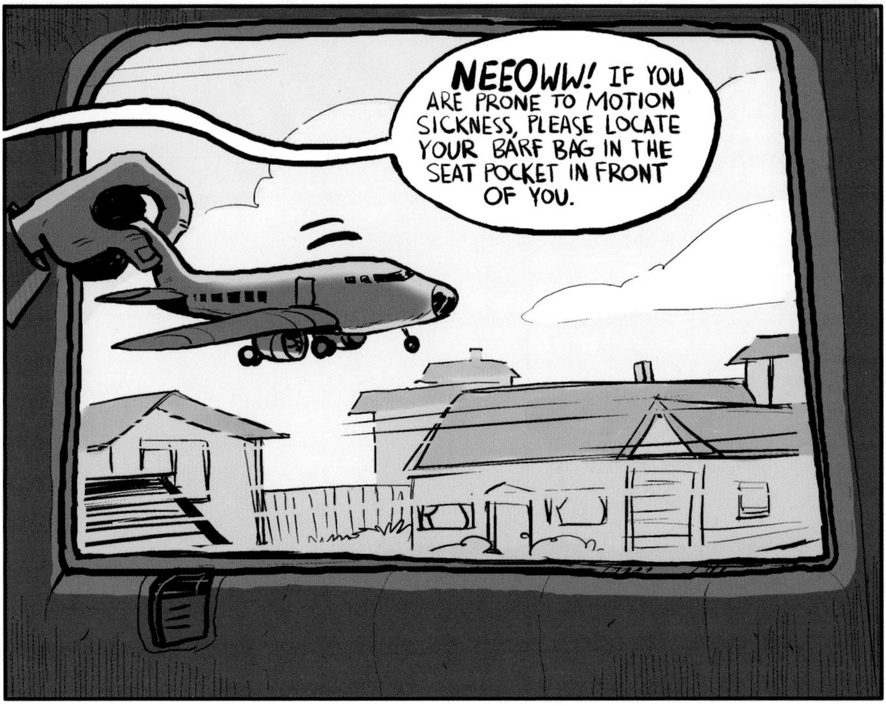
NEEOWW! IF YOU ARE PRONE TO MOTION SICKNESS, PLEASE LOCATE YOUR BARF BAG IN THE SEAT POCKET IN FRONT OF YOU.

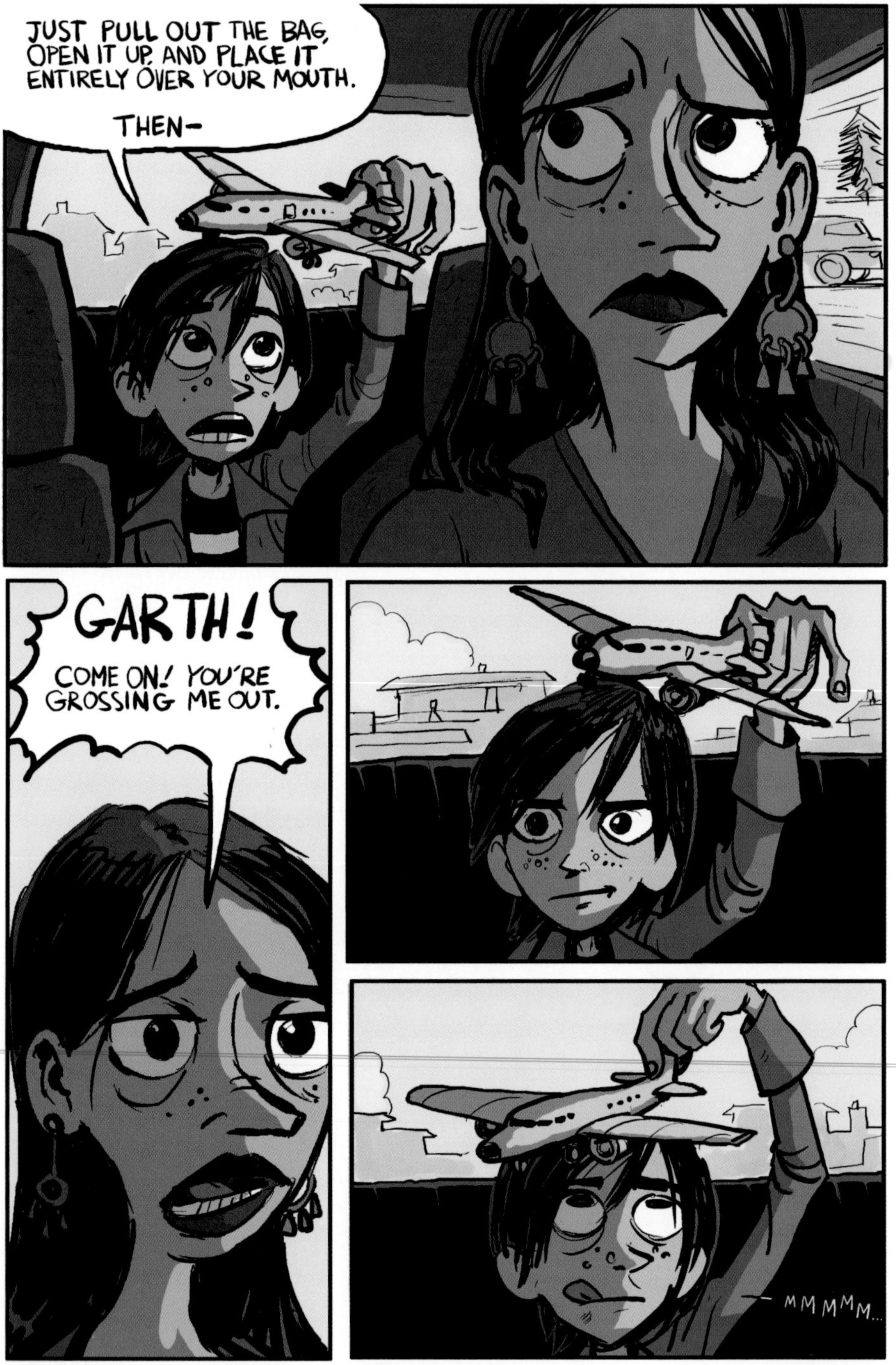
JUST PULL OUT THE BAG, OPEN IT UP, AND PLACE IT ENTIRELY OVER YOUR MOUTH.
THEN-
GARTH!
COME ON! YOU'RE GROSSING ME OUT.
MMMMM...

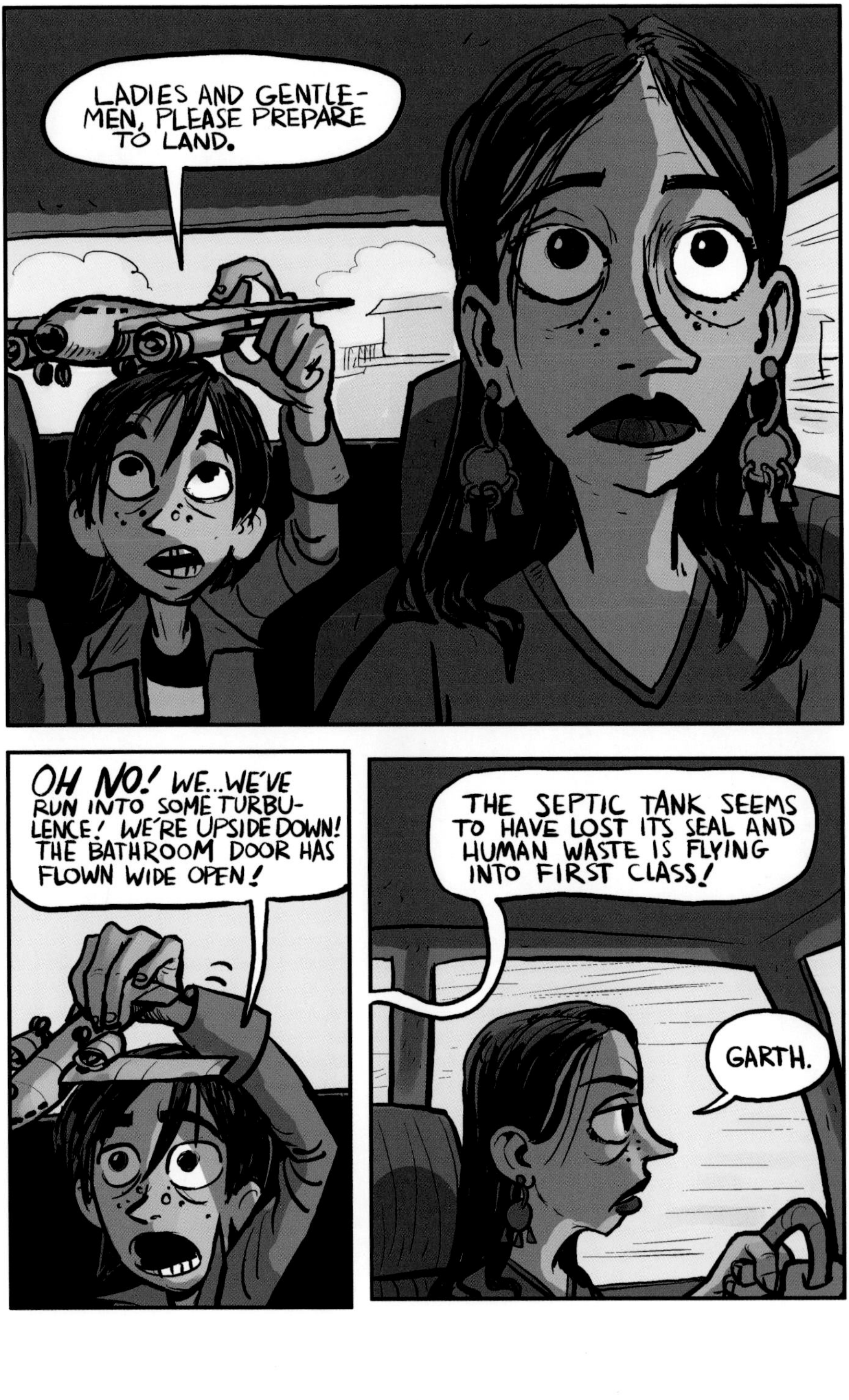
LADIES AND GENTLE-MEN, PLEASE PREPARE TO LAND.
OH NO! WE...WE'VE RUN INTO SOME TURBULENCE! WE'RE UPSIDE DOWN! THE BATHROOM DOOR HAS FLOWN WIDE OPEN!
THE SEPTIC TANK SEEMS TO HAVE LOST ITS SEAL AND HUMAN WASTE IS FLYING INTO FIRST CLASS!
GARTH.

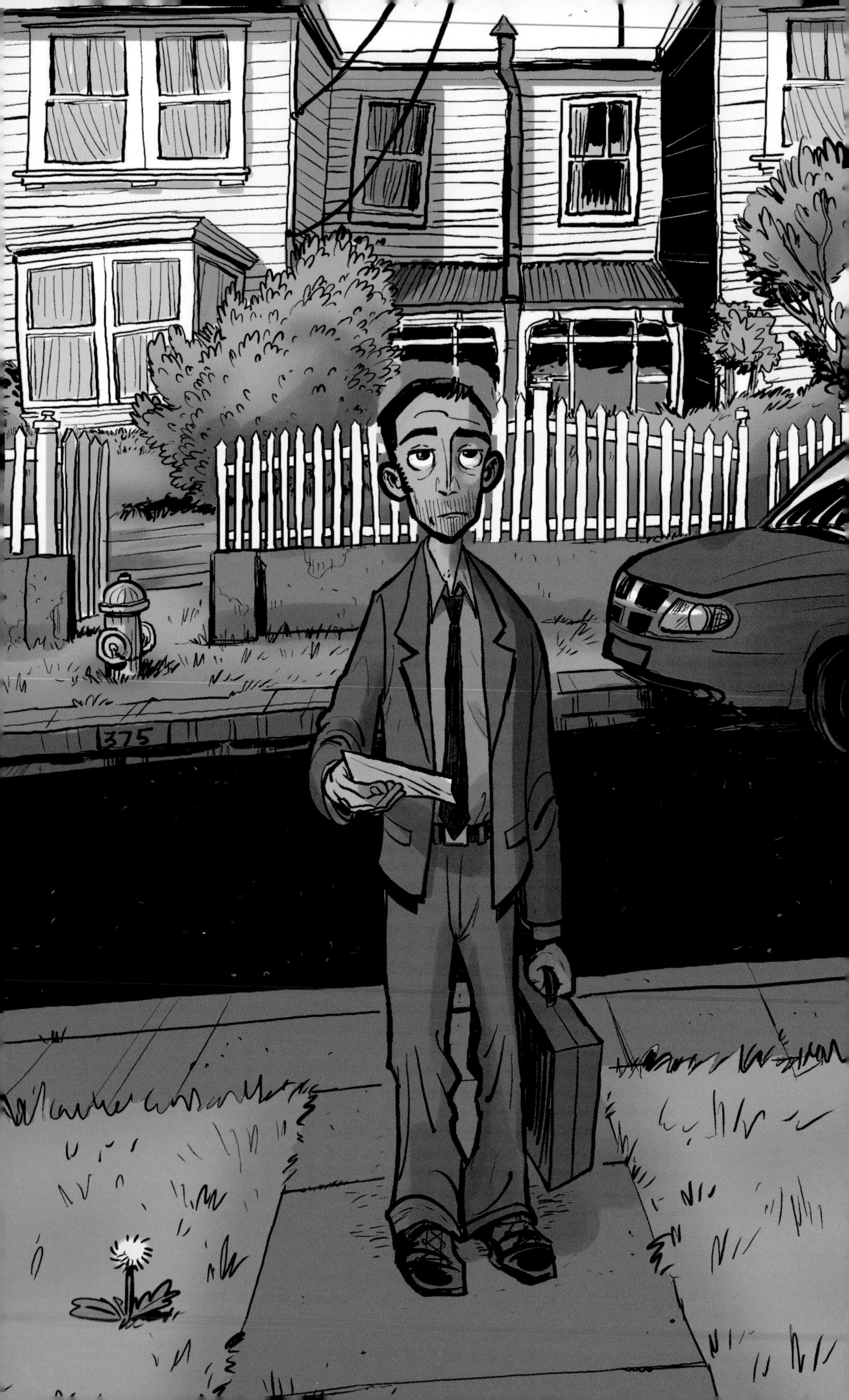
375

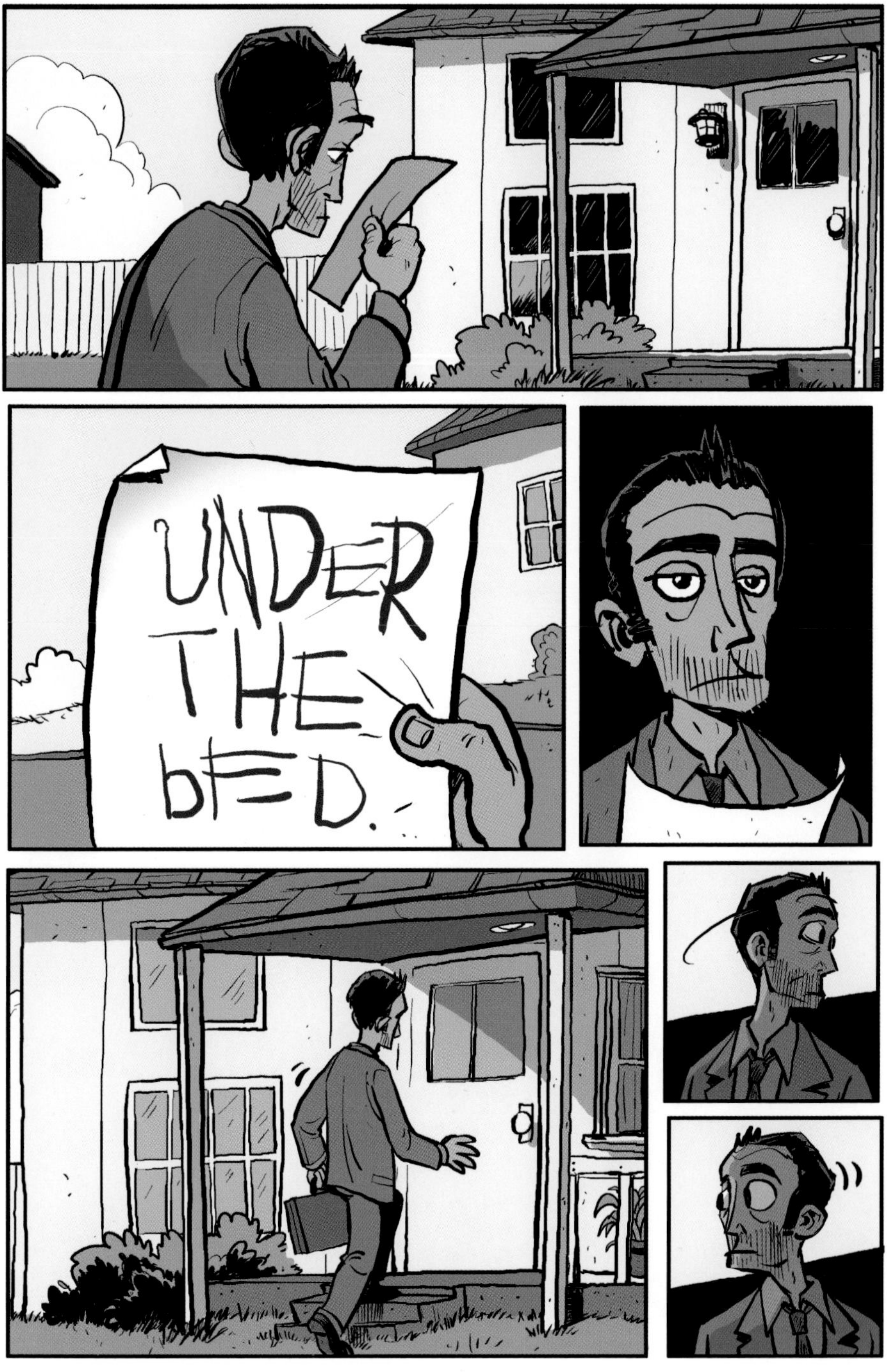
UNDER THE bED.

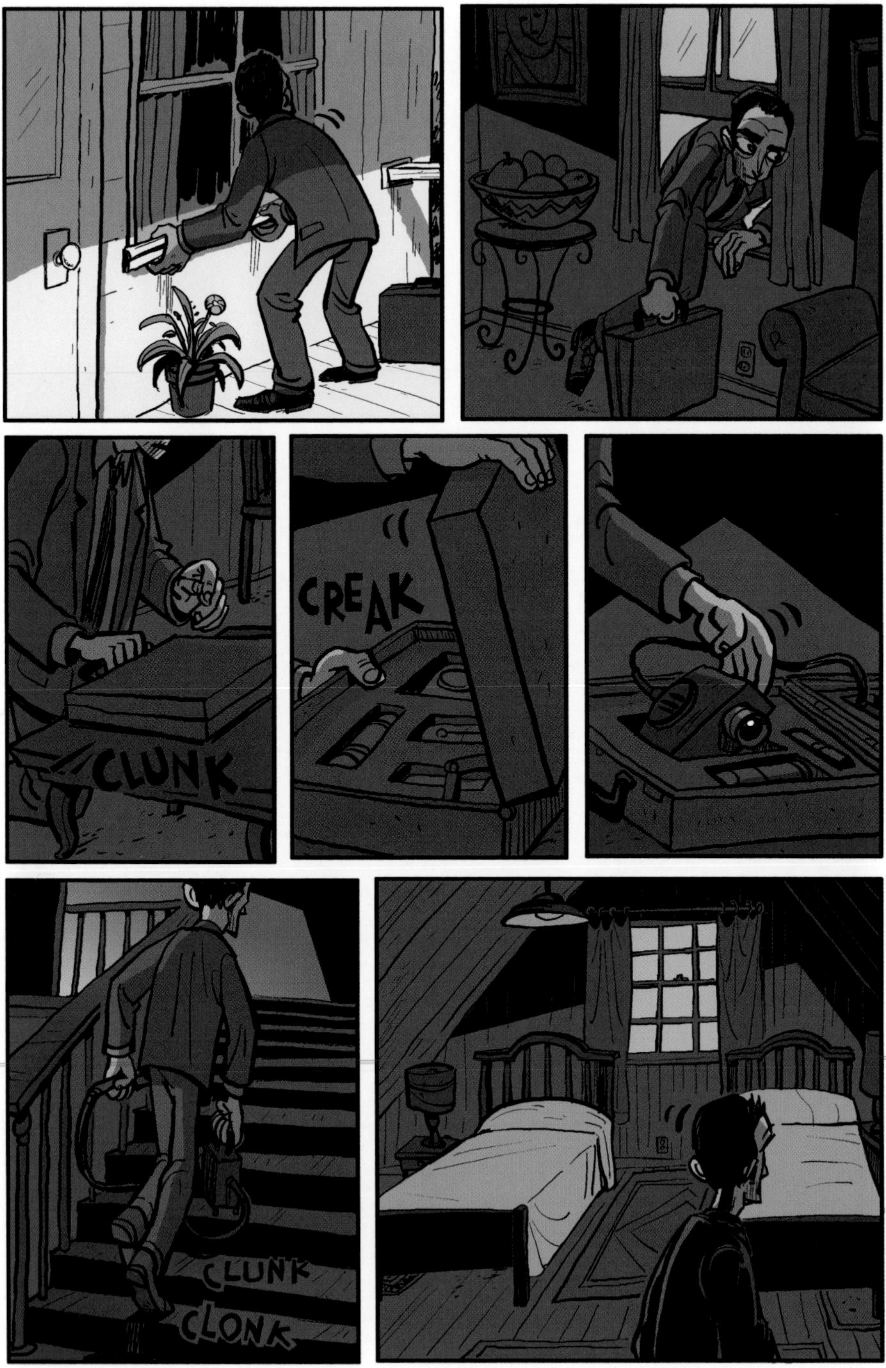
CLUNK
CREAK
CLUNK
CLONK

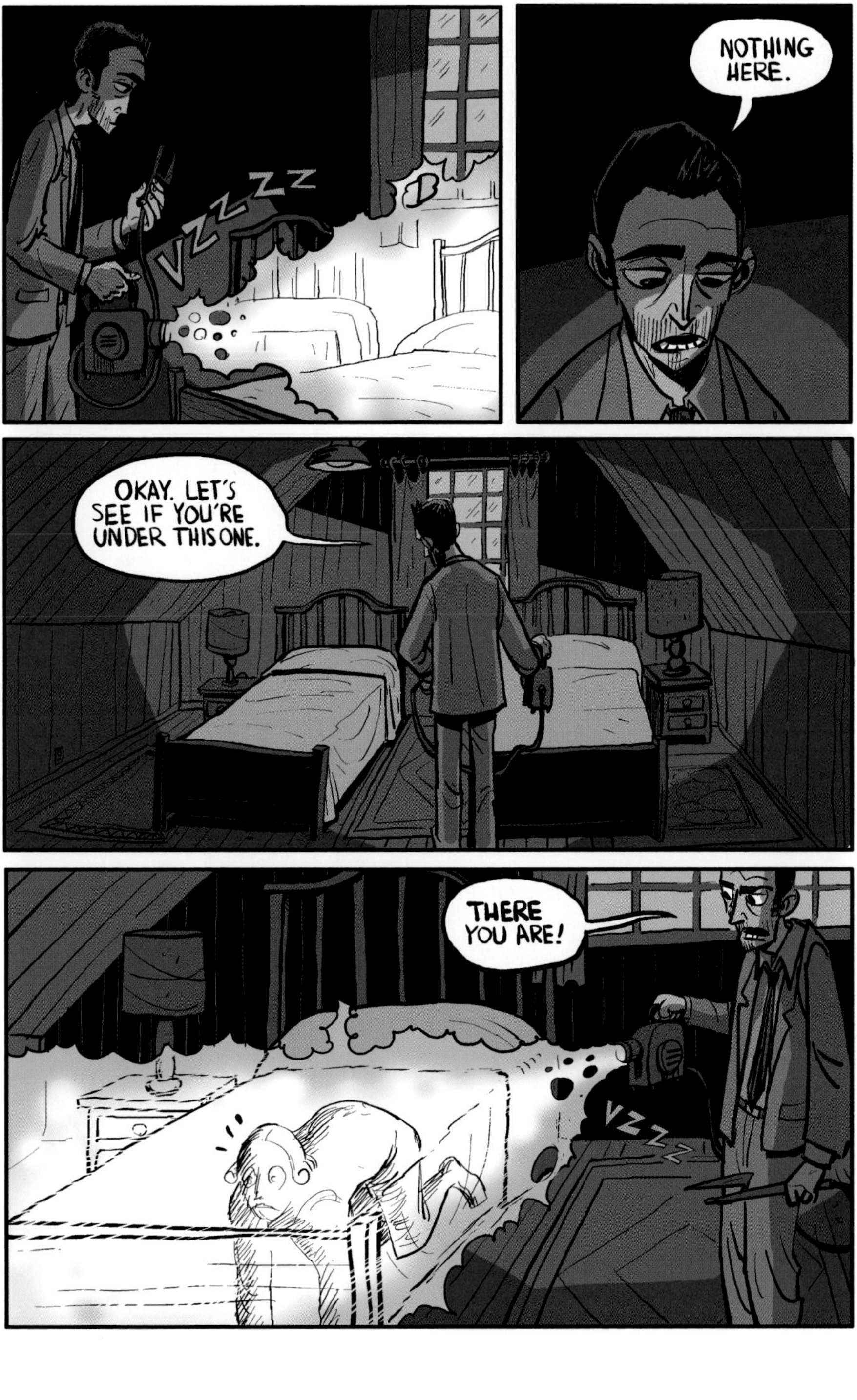
VZZZZZ
NOTHING HERE.
OKAY. LET'S SEE IF YOU'RE UNDER THIS ONE.
THERE YOU ARE!
VZZZ

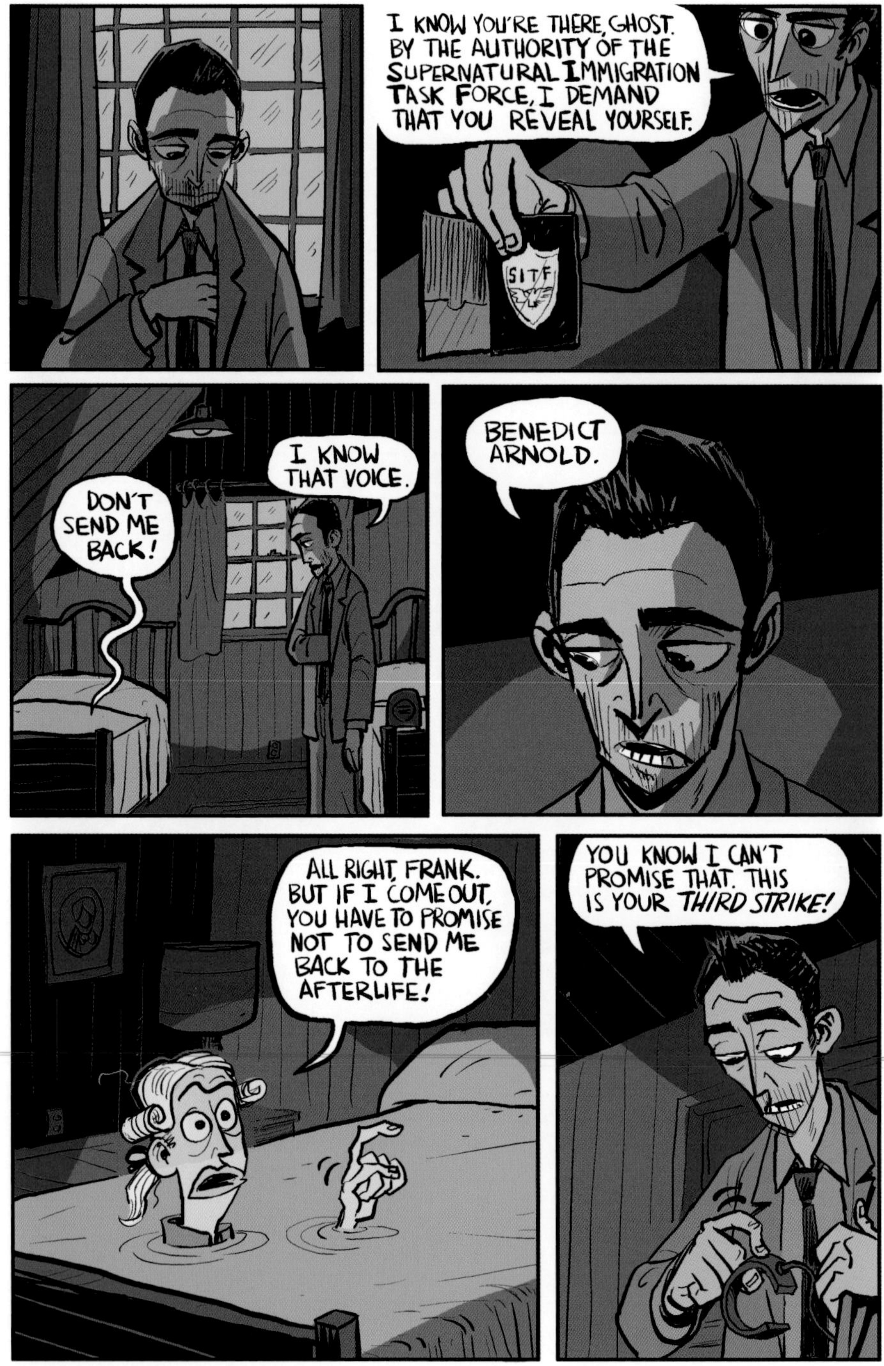
I KNOW YOU'RE THERE, GHOST. BY THE AUTHORITY OF THE SUPERNATURAL IMMIGRATION TASK FORCE, I DEMAND THAT YOU REVEAL YOURSELF.
SITF
DON'T SEND ME BACK!
I KNOW THAT VOICE.
BENEDICT ARNOLD.
ALL RIGHT, FRANK. BUT IF I COME OUT, YOU HAVE TO PROMISE NOT TO SEND ME BACK TO THE AFTERLIFE!
YOU KNOW I CAN'T PROMISE THAT. THIS IS YOUR *THIRD STRIKE!*

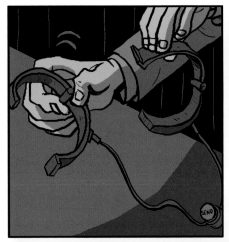

NO! NOT THE PLASMA CUFFS!

CLICK

HOLD STILL!

ONE MORE SET. THIS WON'T HURT A BIT.

CLICK

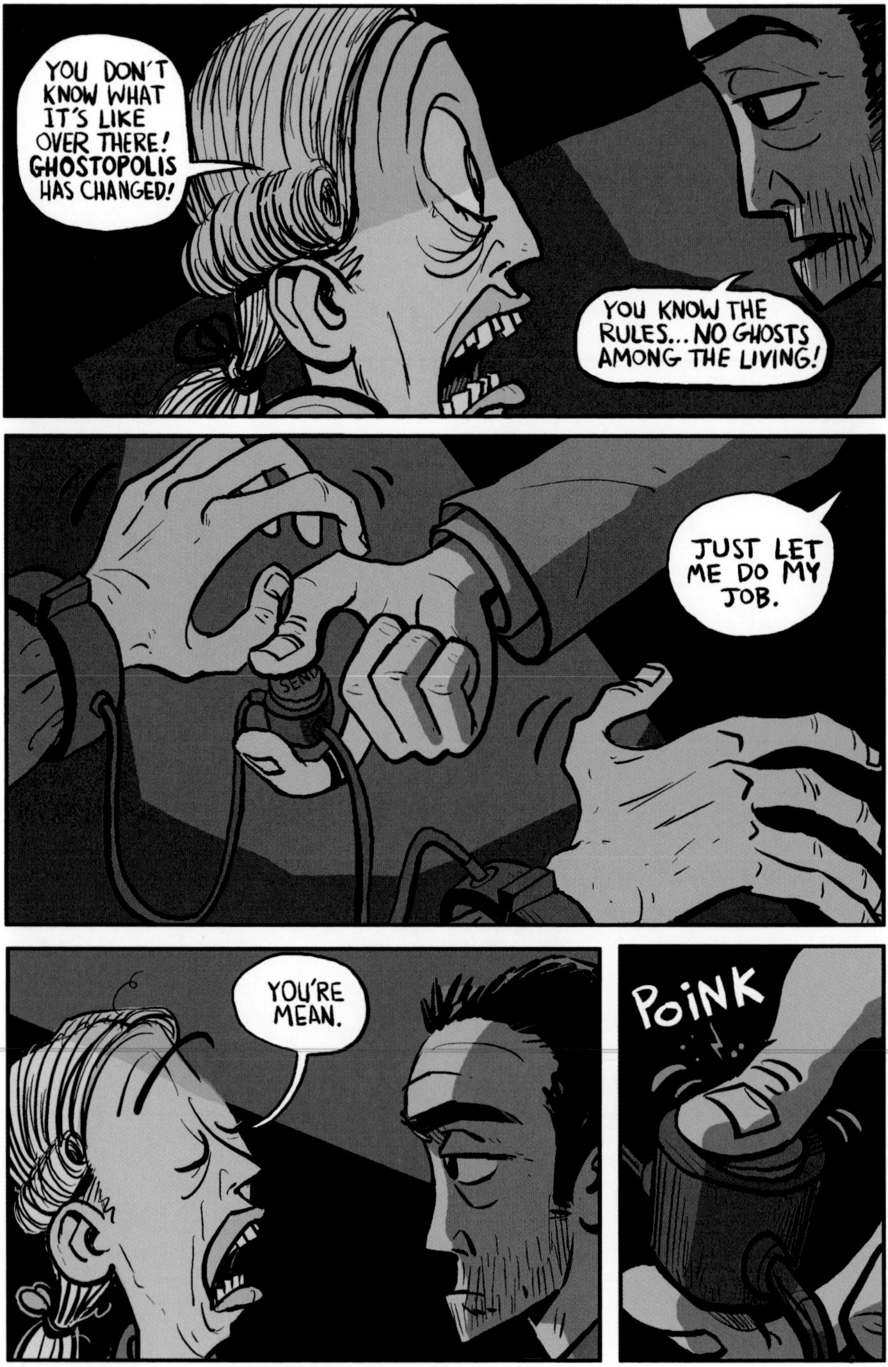
YOU DON'T KNOW WHAT IT'S LIKE OVER THERE! GHOSTOPOLIS HAS CHANGED!
YOU KNOW THE RULES... NO GHOSTS AMONG THE LIVING!
SEND
JUST LET ME DO MY JOB.
YOU'RE MEAN.
POINK

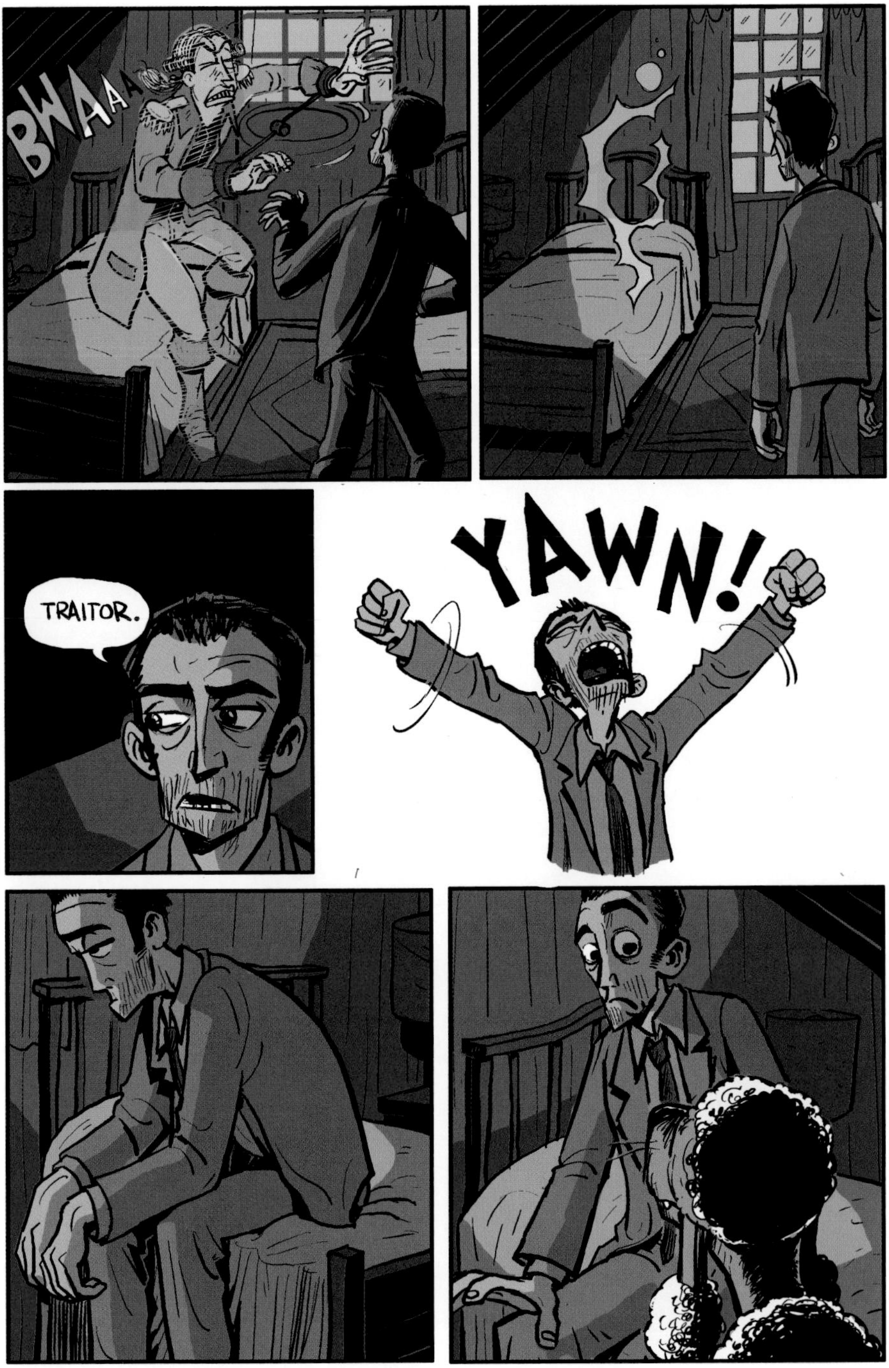
BWAAAA
TRAITOR.
YAWN!

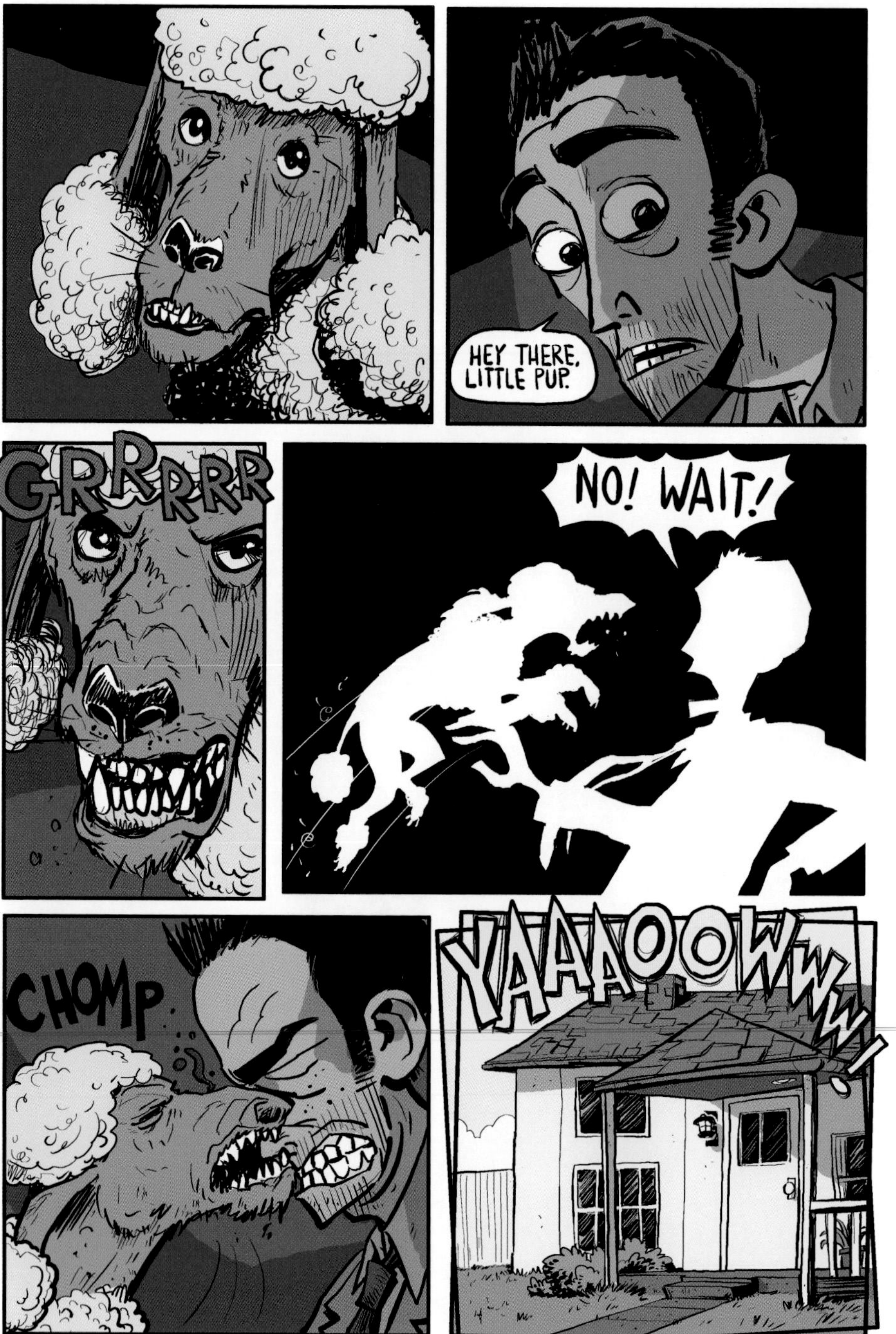
HEY THERE, LITTLE PUP.
GRRRRRR
NO! WAIT!
CHOMP
YAAAOOWWW!

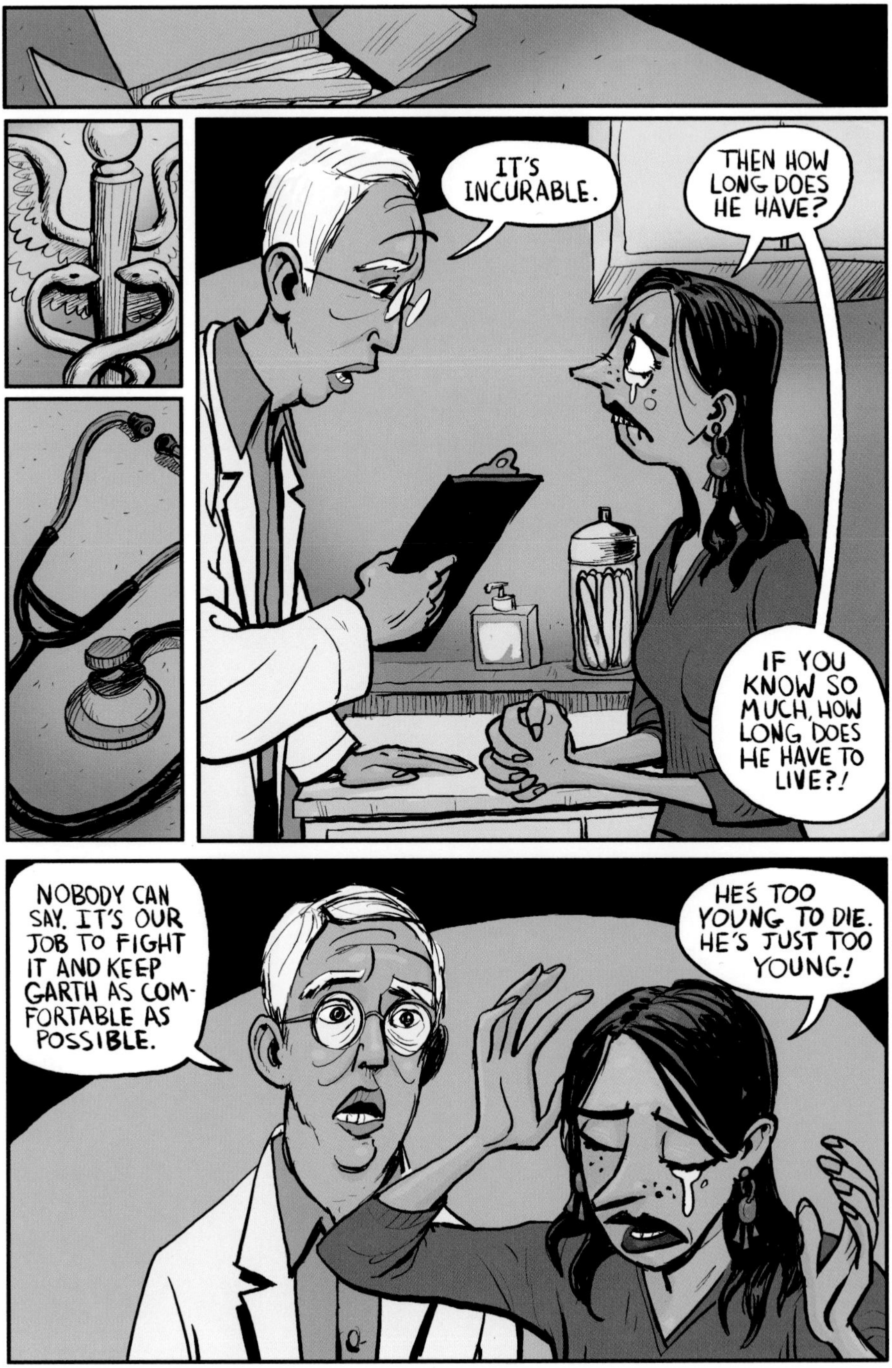
IT'S INCURABLE.
THEN HOW LONG DOES HE HAVE?
IF YOU KNOW SO MUCH, HOW LONG DOES HE HAVE TO LIVE?!
NOBODY CAN SAY. IT'S OUR JOB TO FIGHT IT AND KEEP GARTH AS COMFORTABLE AS POSSIBLE.
HE'S TOO YOUNG TO DIE. HE'S JUST TOO YOUNG!

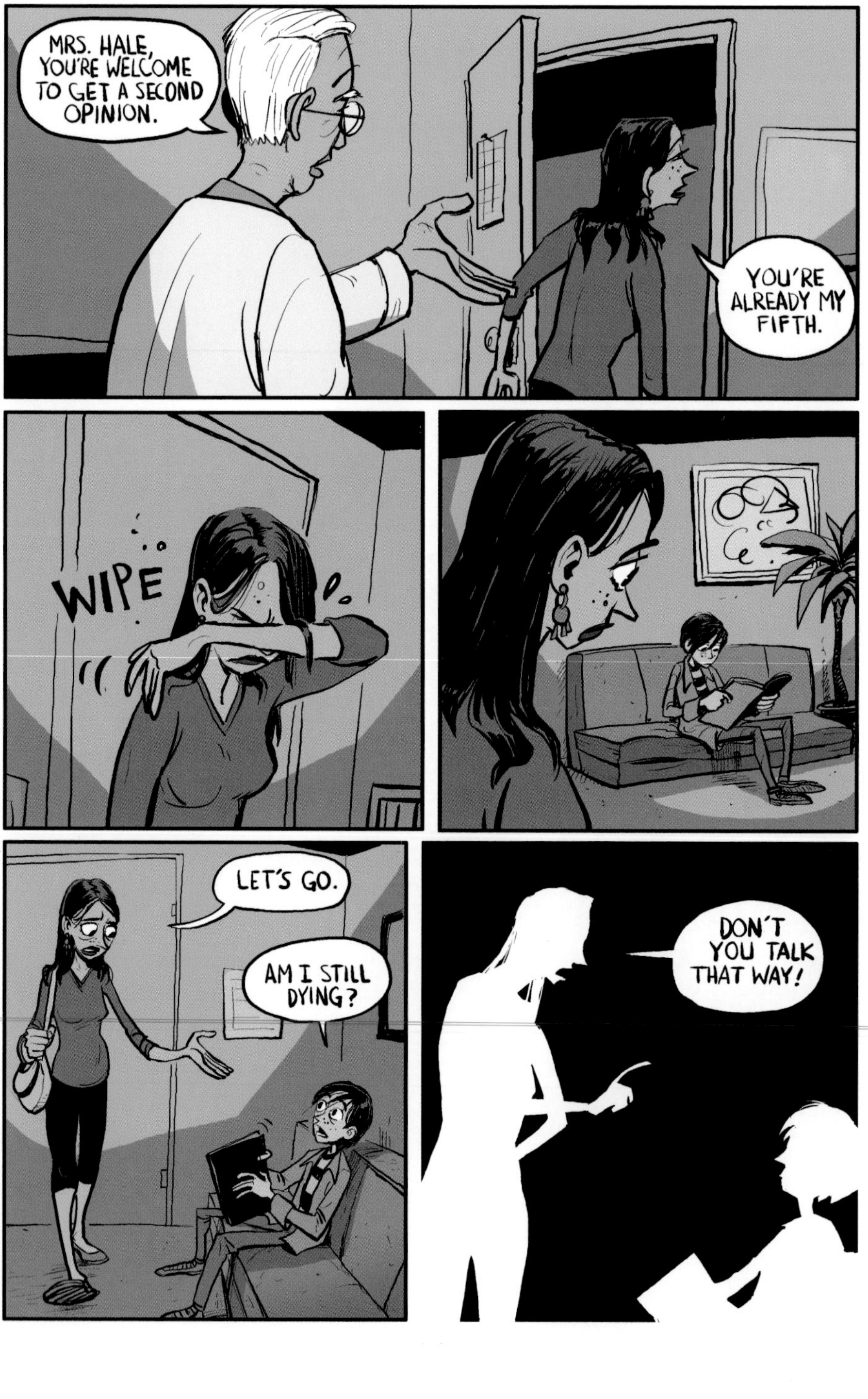
MRS. HALE, YOU'RE WELCOME TO GET A SECOND OPINION.
YOU'RE ALREADY MY FIFTH.
WIPE
LET'S GO.
AM I STILL DYING?
DON'T YOU TALK THAT WAY!

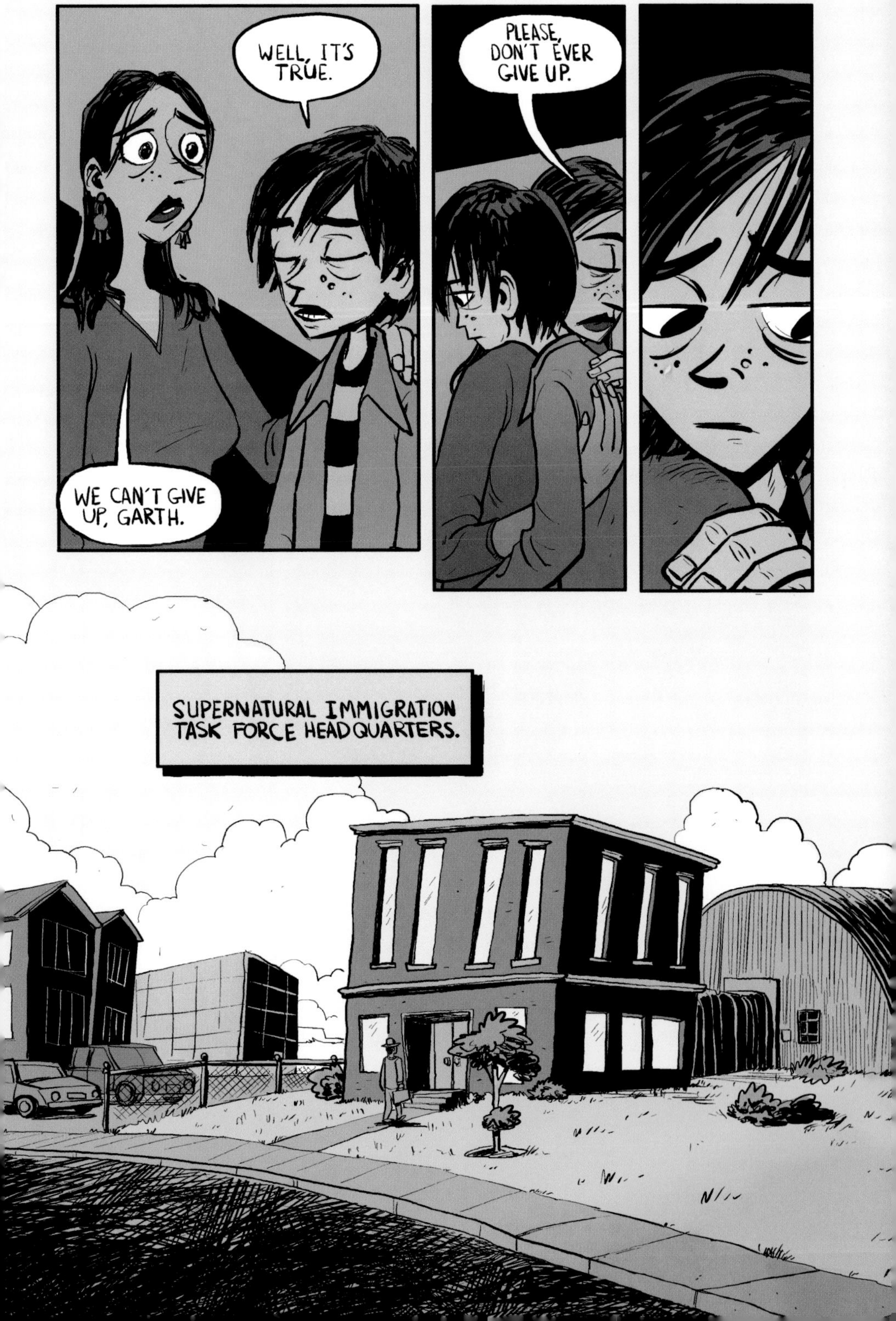
WELL, IT'S TRUE.
WE CAN'T GIVE UP, GARTH.
PLEASE, DON'T EVER GIVE UP.
SUPERNATURAL IMMIGRATION TASK FORCE HEADQUARTERS.

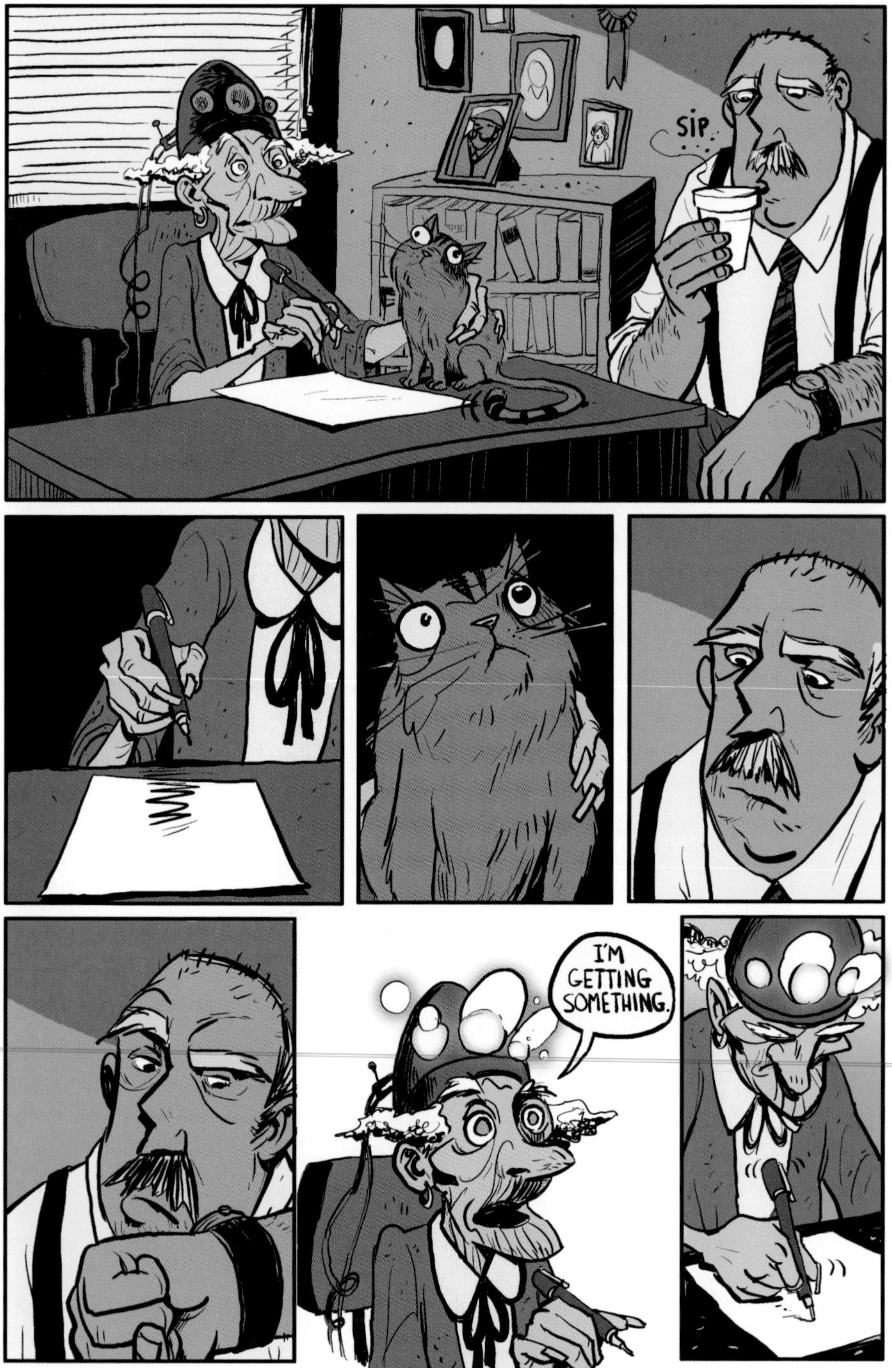
SIP
I'M GETTING SOMETHING.

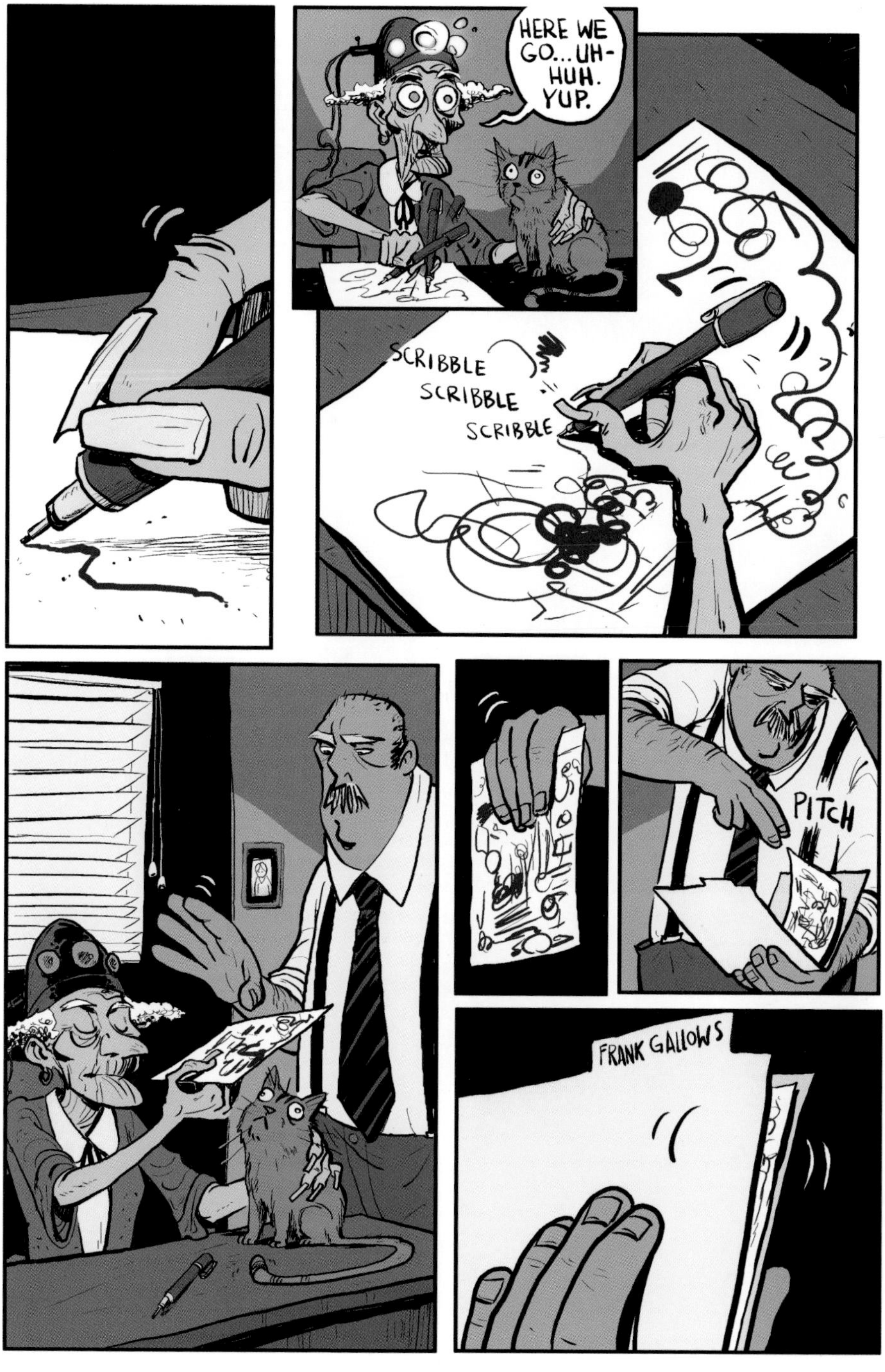
HERE WE GO...UH-HUH. YUP.
SCRIBBLE
SCRIBBLE
SCRIBBLE
PITCH
FRANK GALLOWS

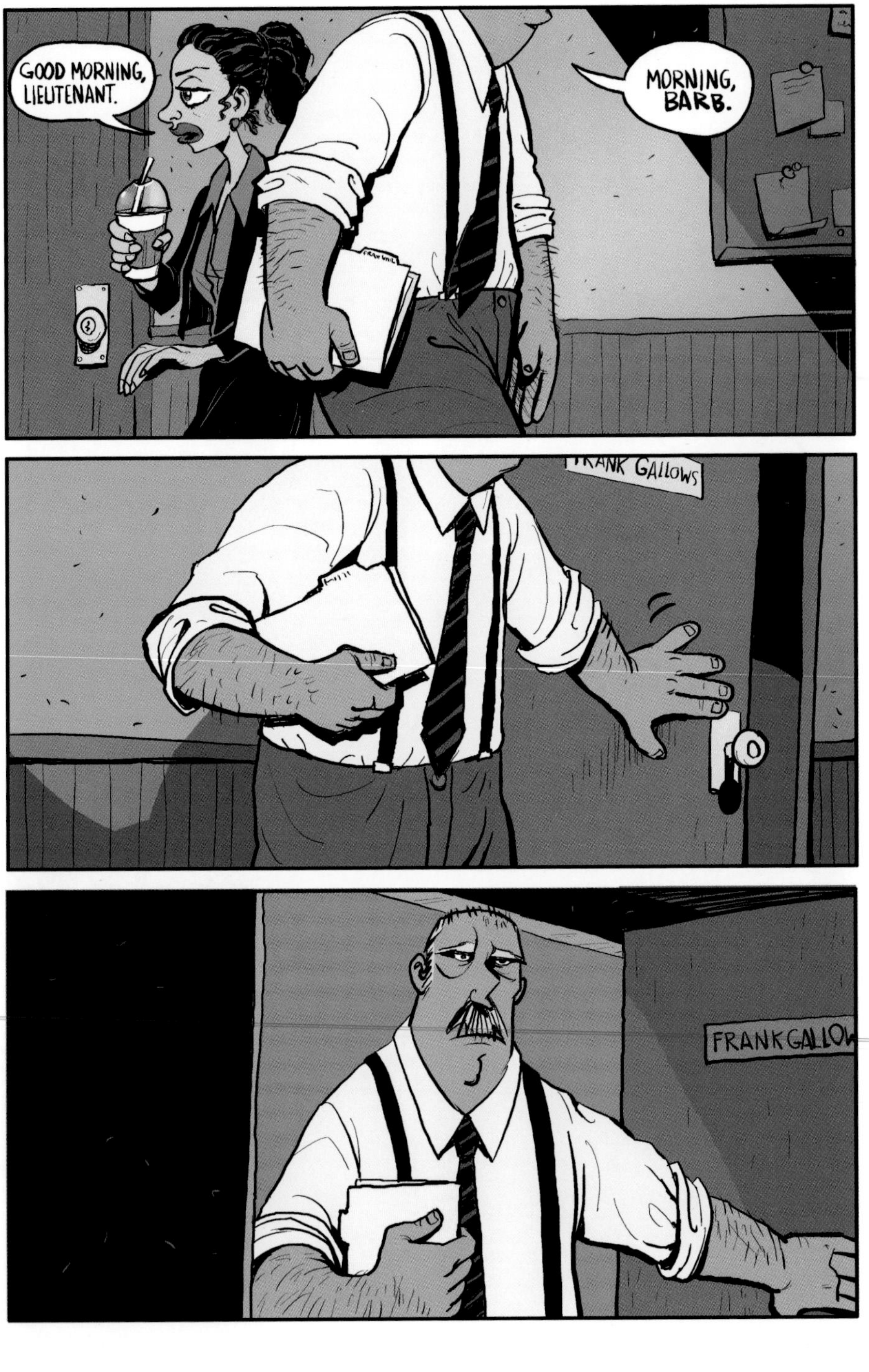
GOOD MORNING, LIEUTENANT.
MORNING, BARB.
FRANK GALLOWS
FRANKGALLOW

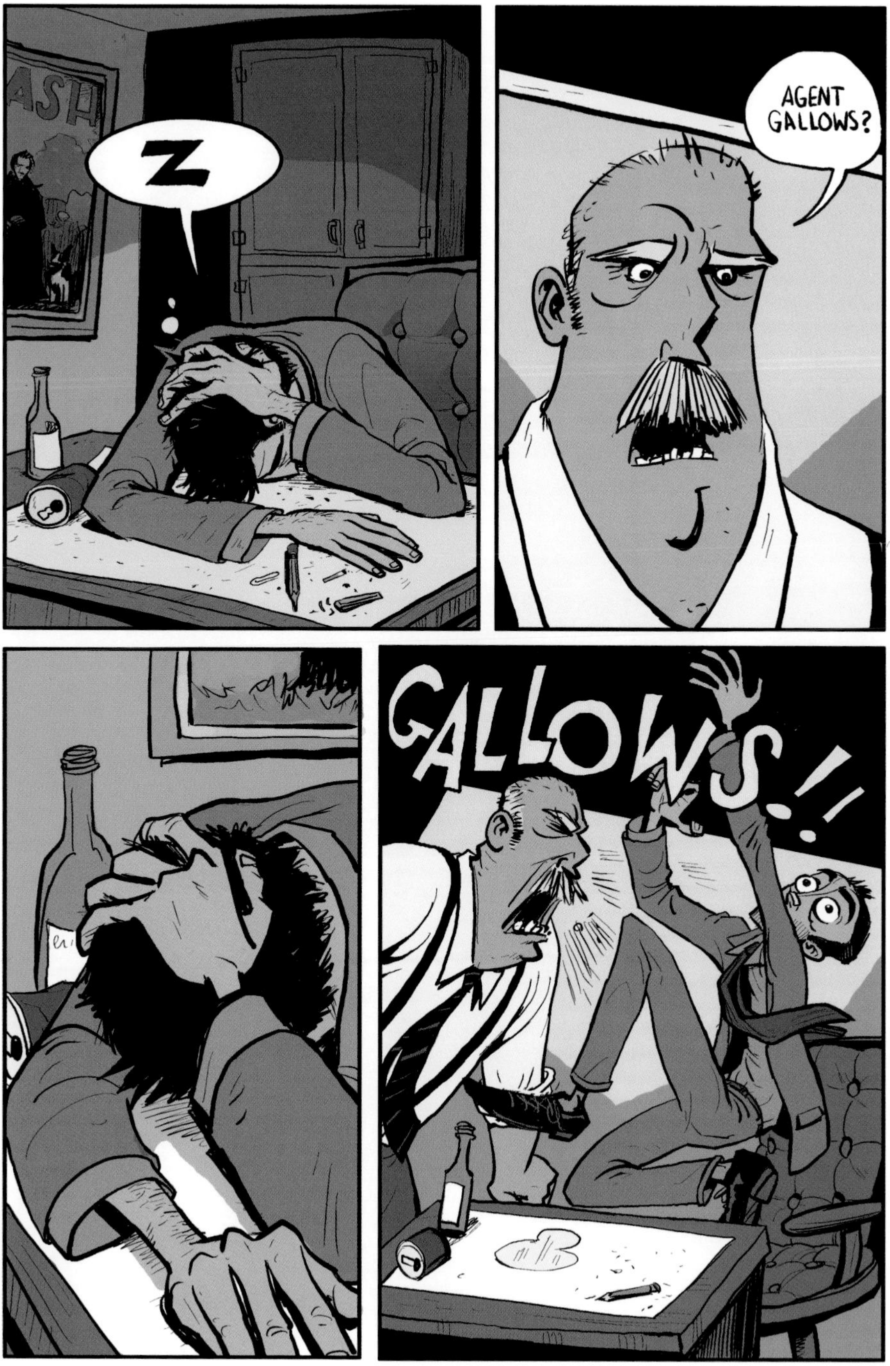
Z
AGENT GALLOWS?
GALLOWS!!

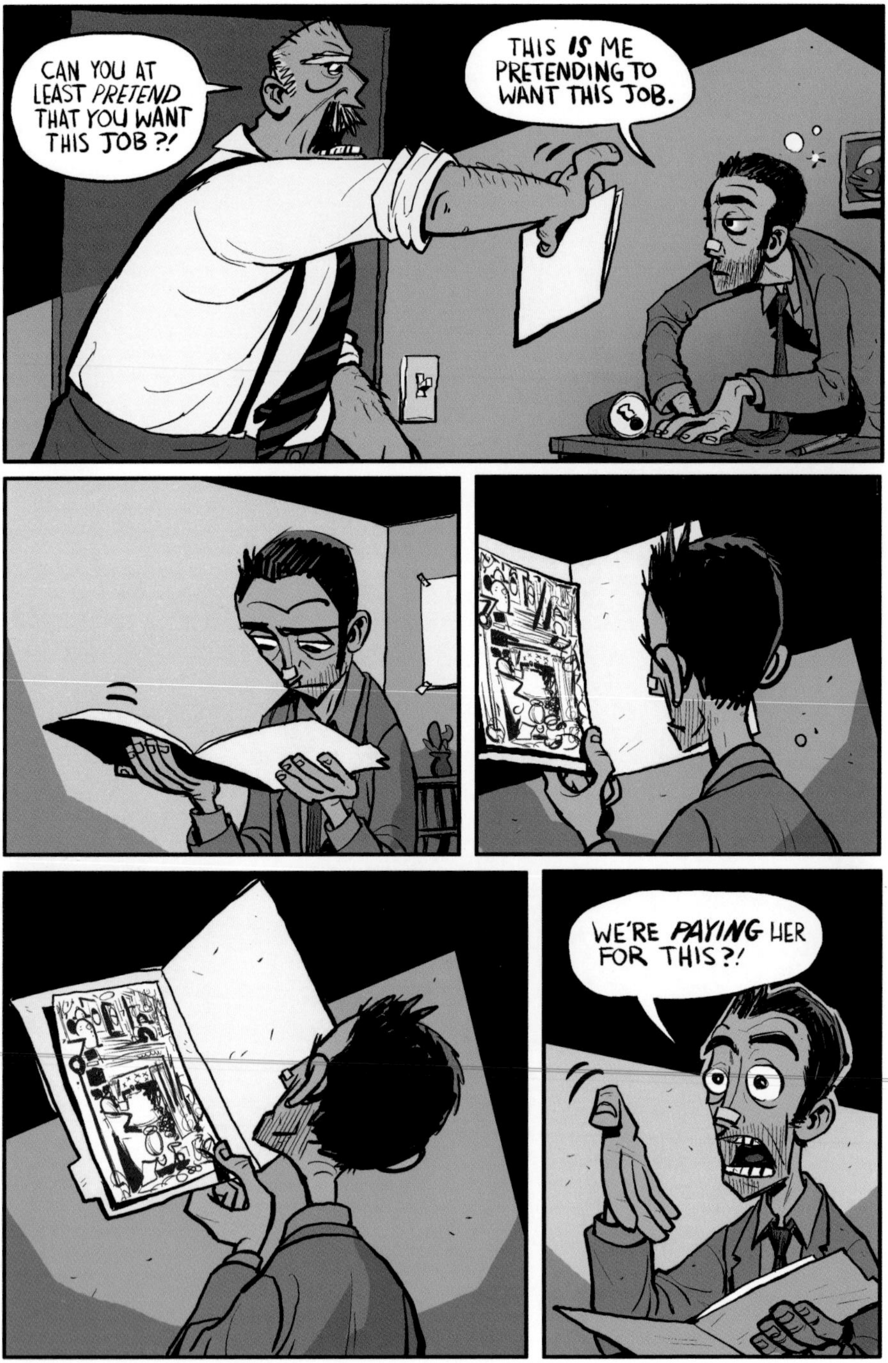
CAN YOU AT LEAST PRETEND THAT YOU WANT THIS JOB?!
THIS IS ME PRETENDING TO WANT THIS JOB.
WE'RE PAYING HER FOR THIS?!

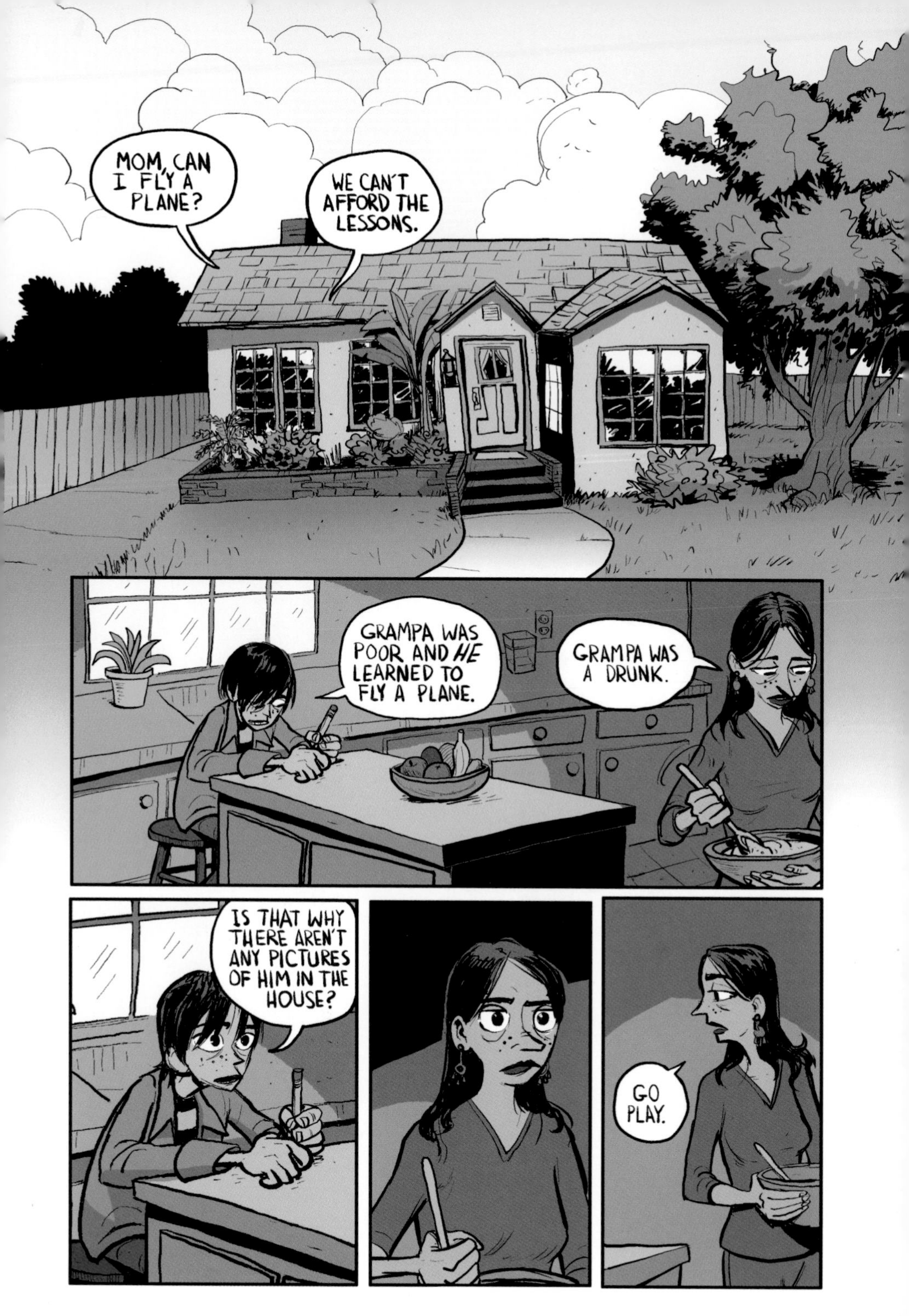
MOM, CAN I FLY A PLANE?
WE CAN'T AFFORD THE LESSONS.
GRAMPA WAS POOR AND *HE* LEARNED TO FLY A PLANE.
GRAMPA WAS A DRUNK.
IS THAT WHY THERE AREN'T ANY PICTURES OF HIM IN THE HOUSE?
GO PLAY.

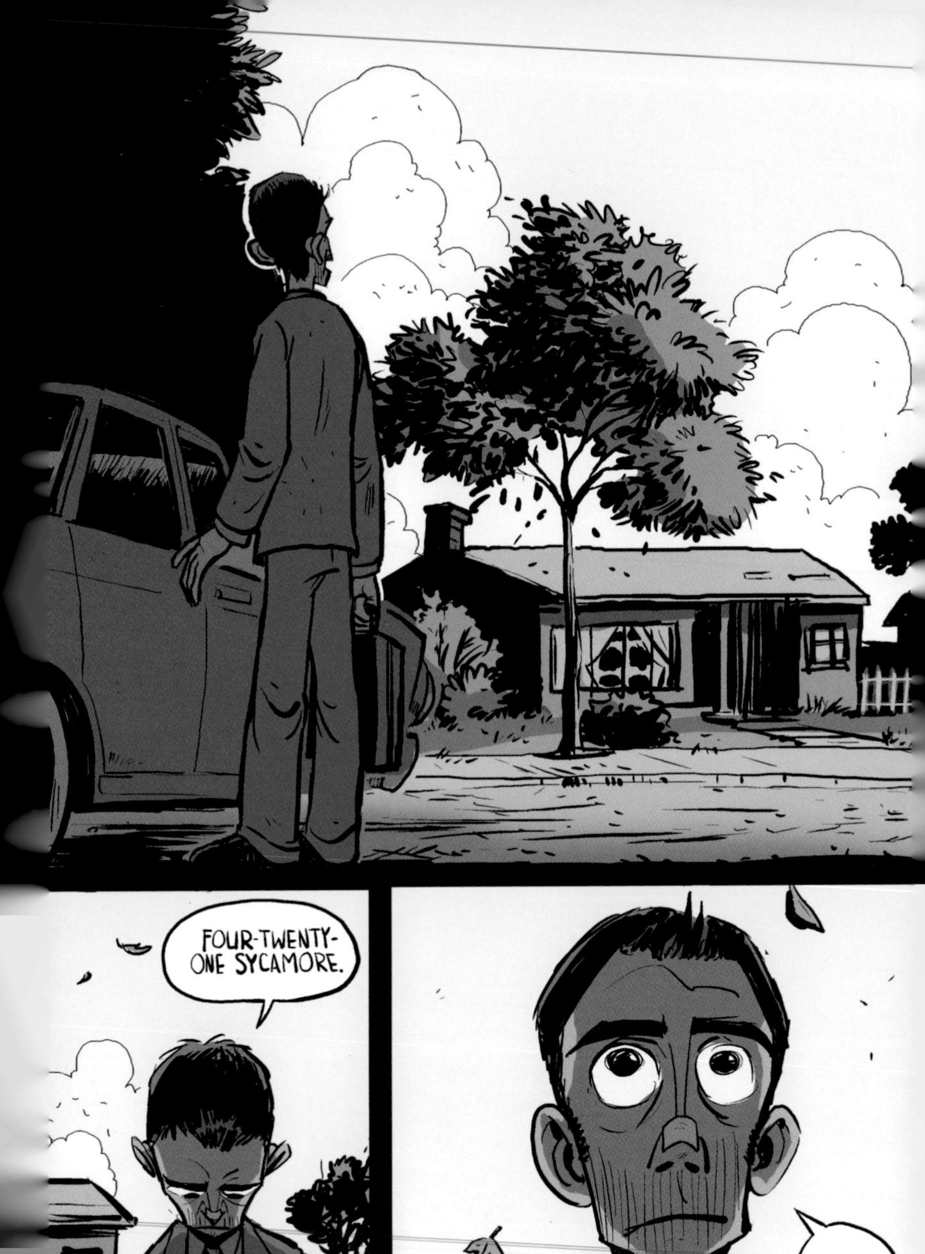
FOUR-TWENTY-ONE SYCAMORE.
YUP.

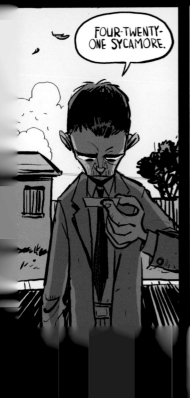

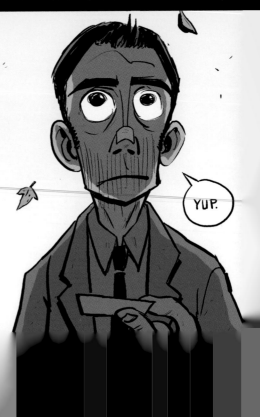

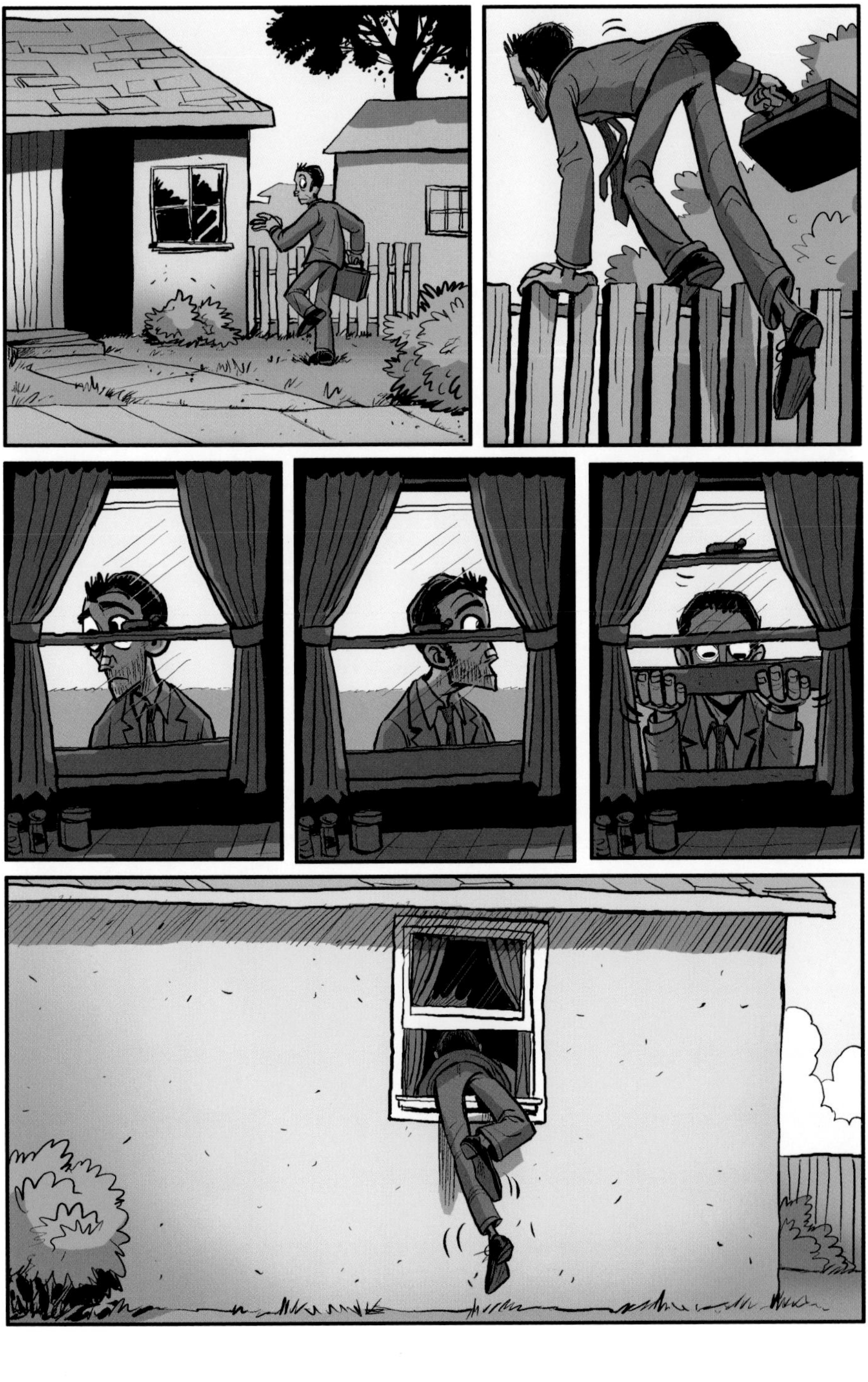

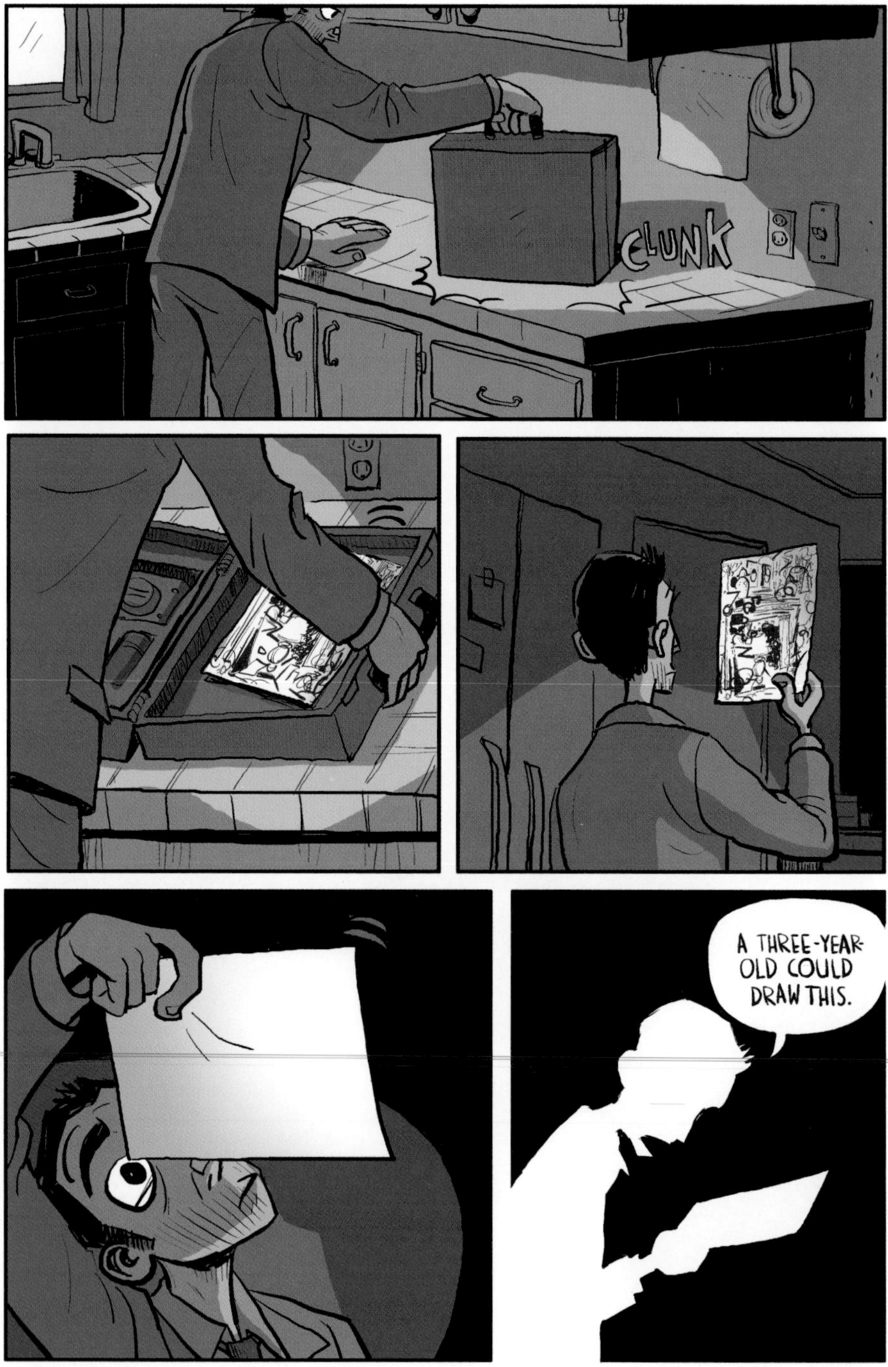
CLUNK
A THREE-YEAR-OLD COULD DRAW THIS.

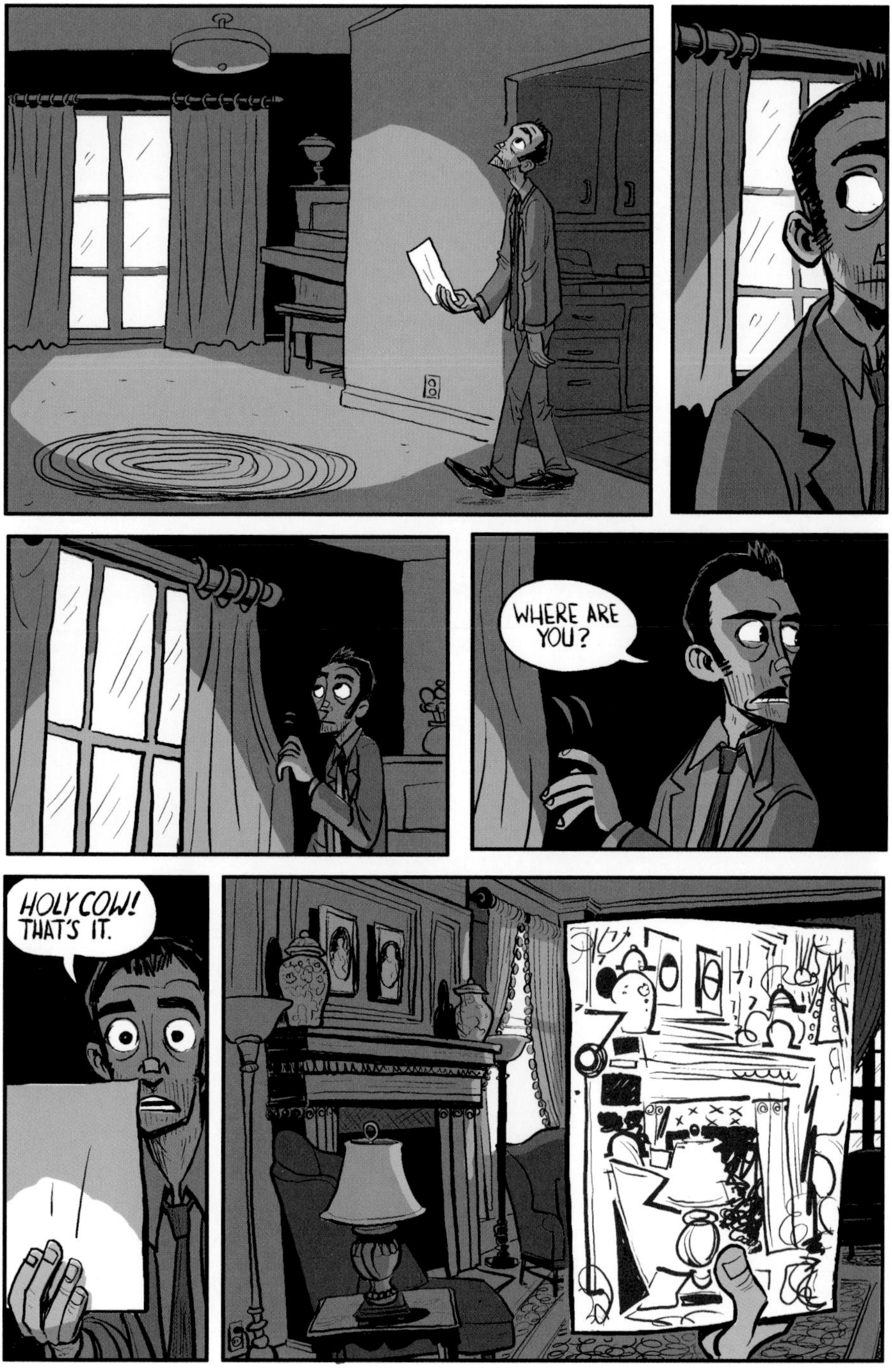
WHERE ARE YOU?
HOLY COW! THAT'S IT.

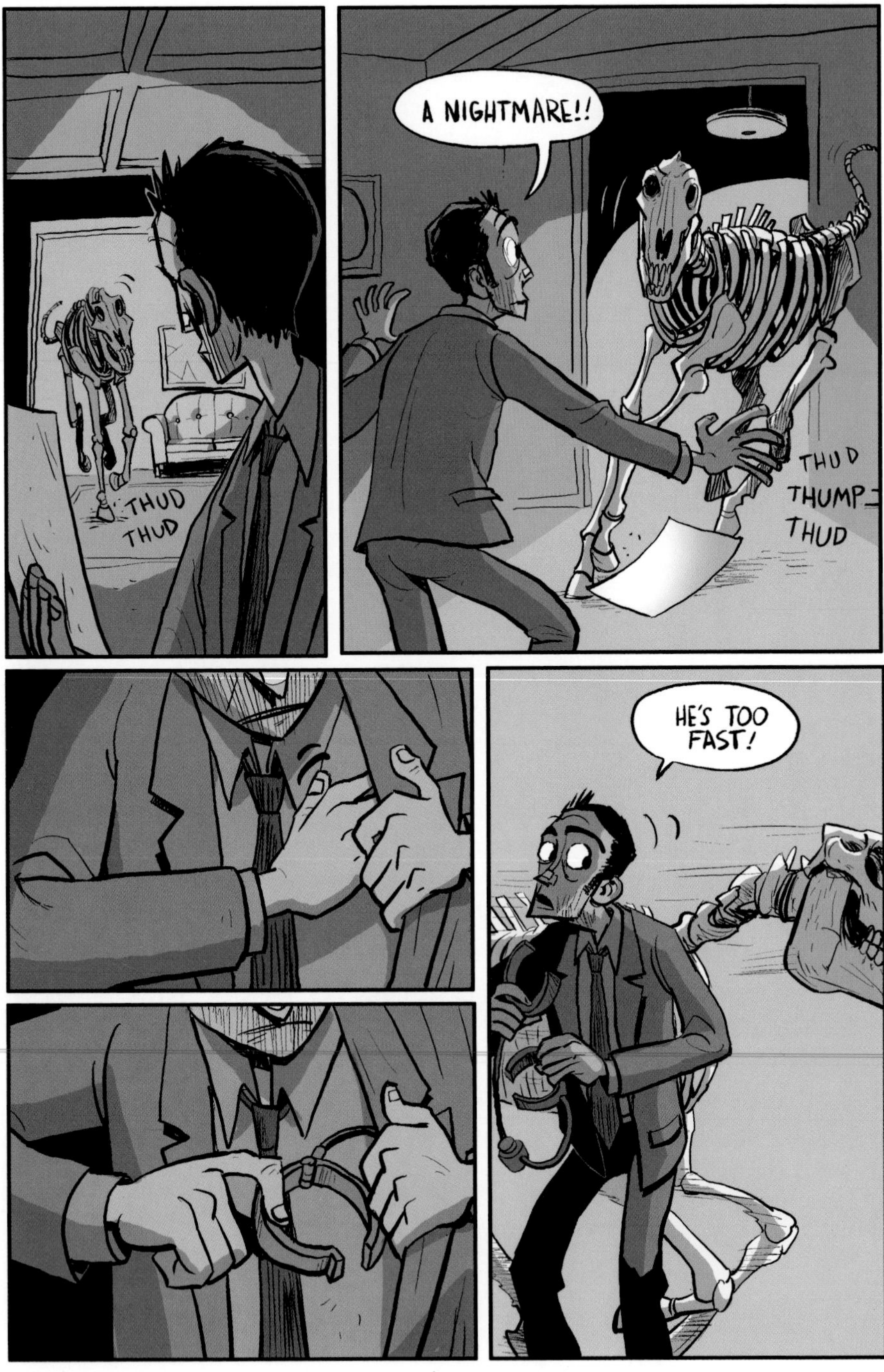
THUD
THUD
A NIGHTMARE!!
THUD
THUMP
THUD
HE'S TOO FAST!

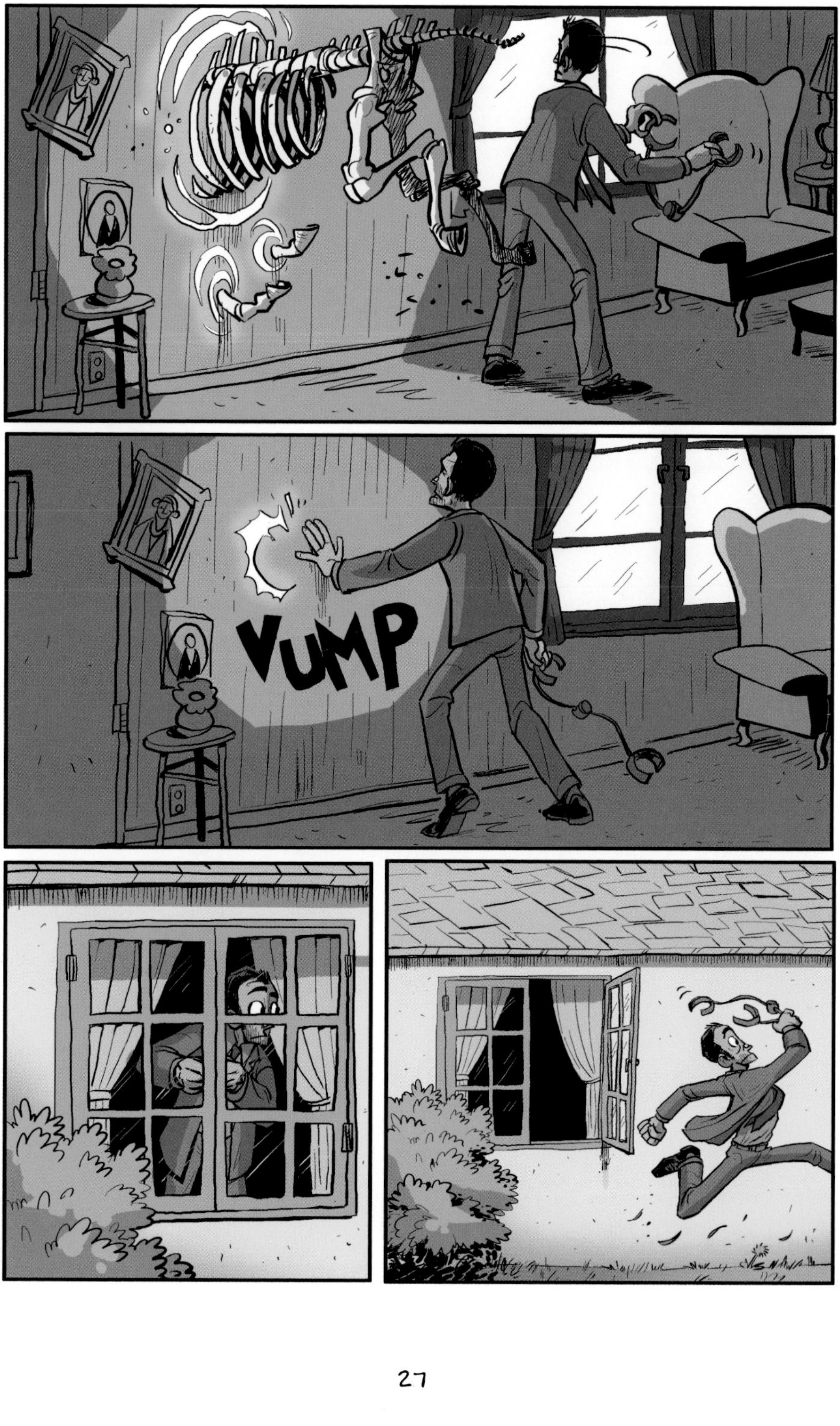
VUMP

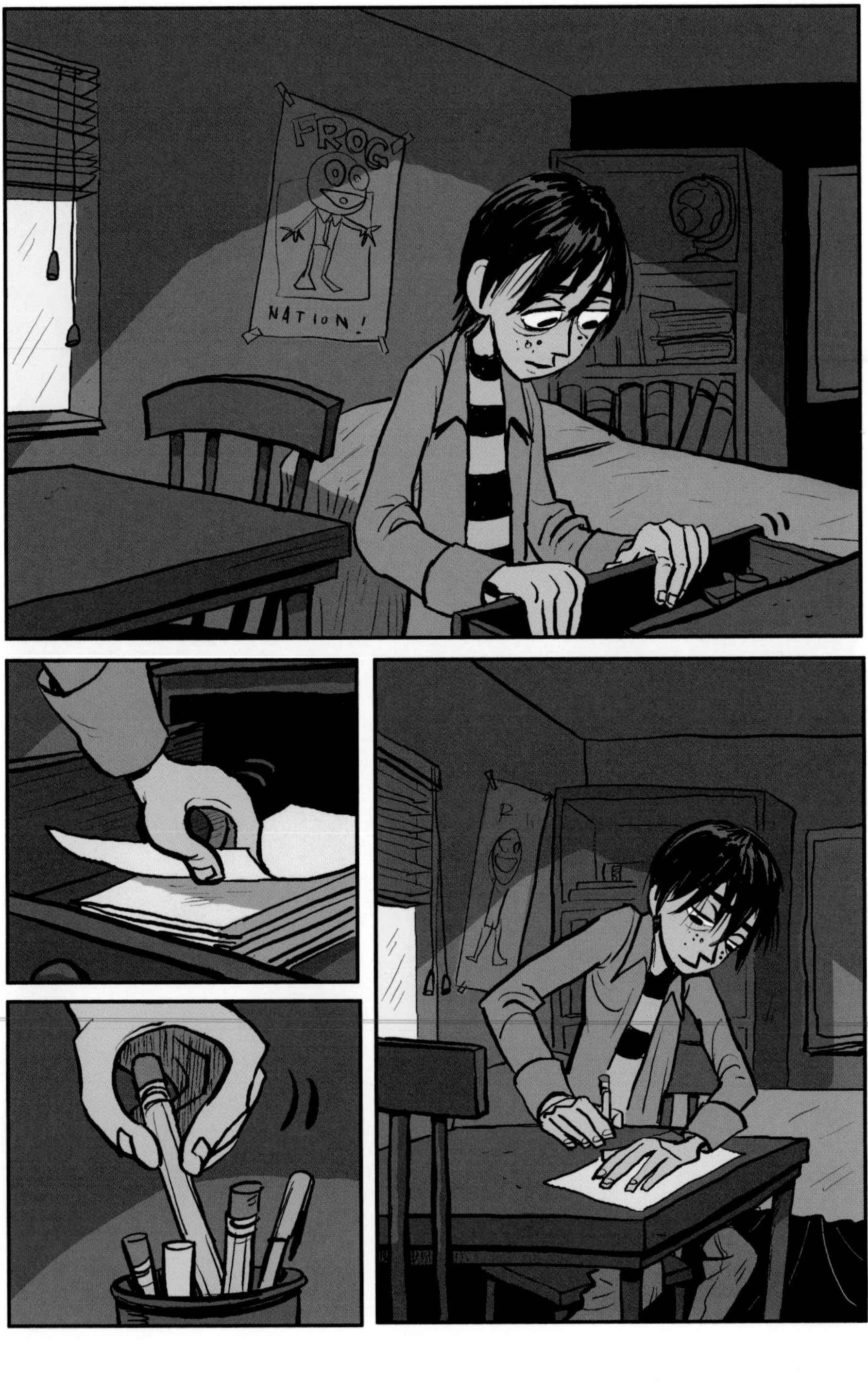
FROG
NATION!

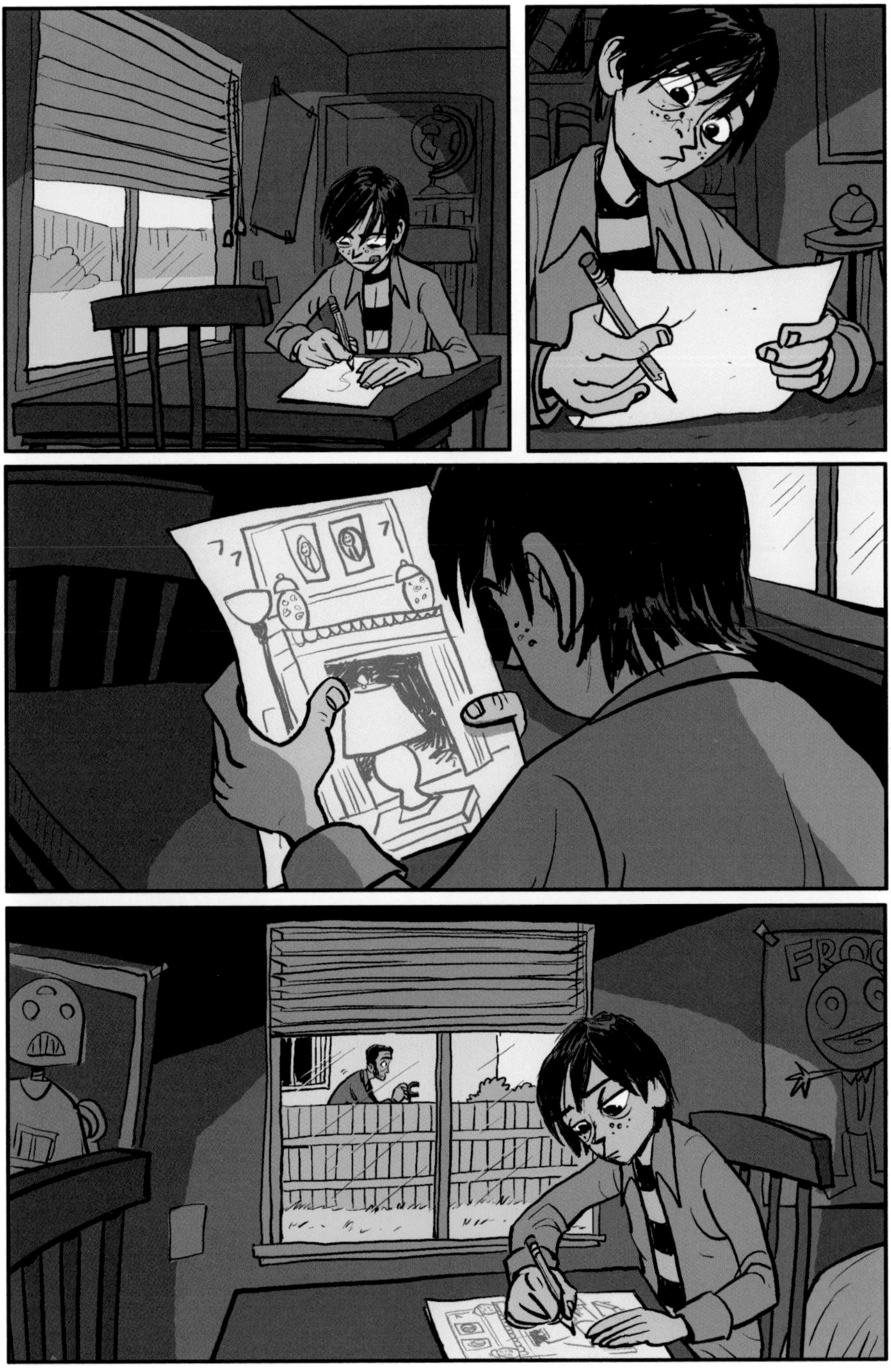

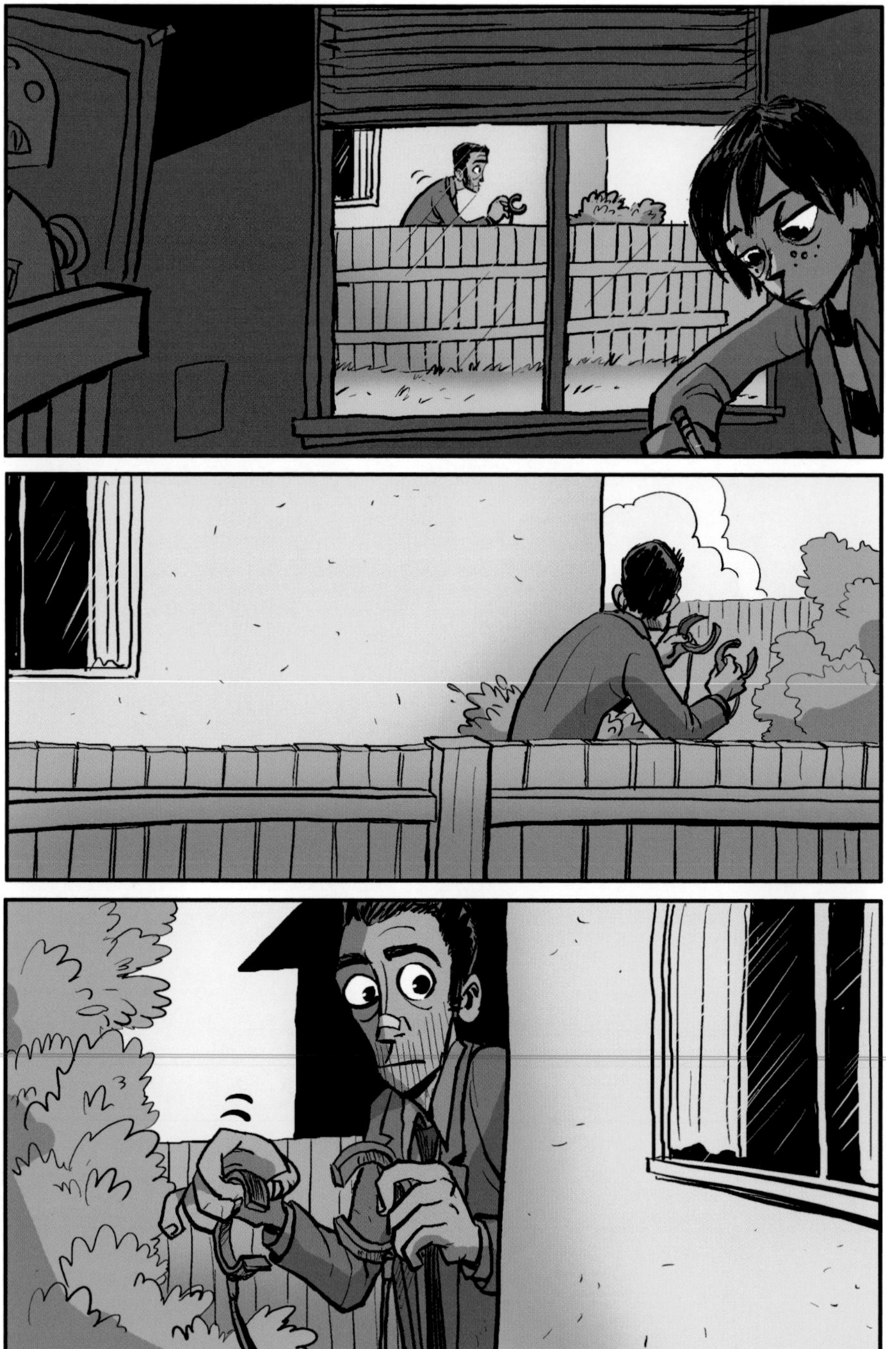

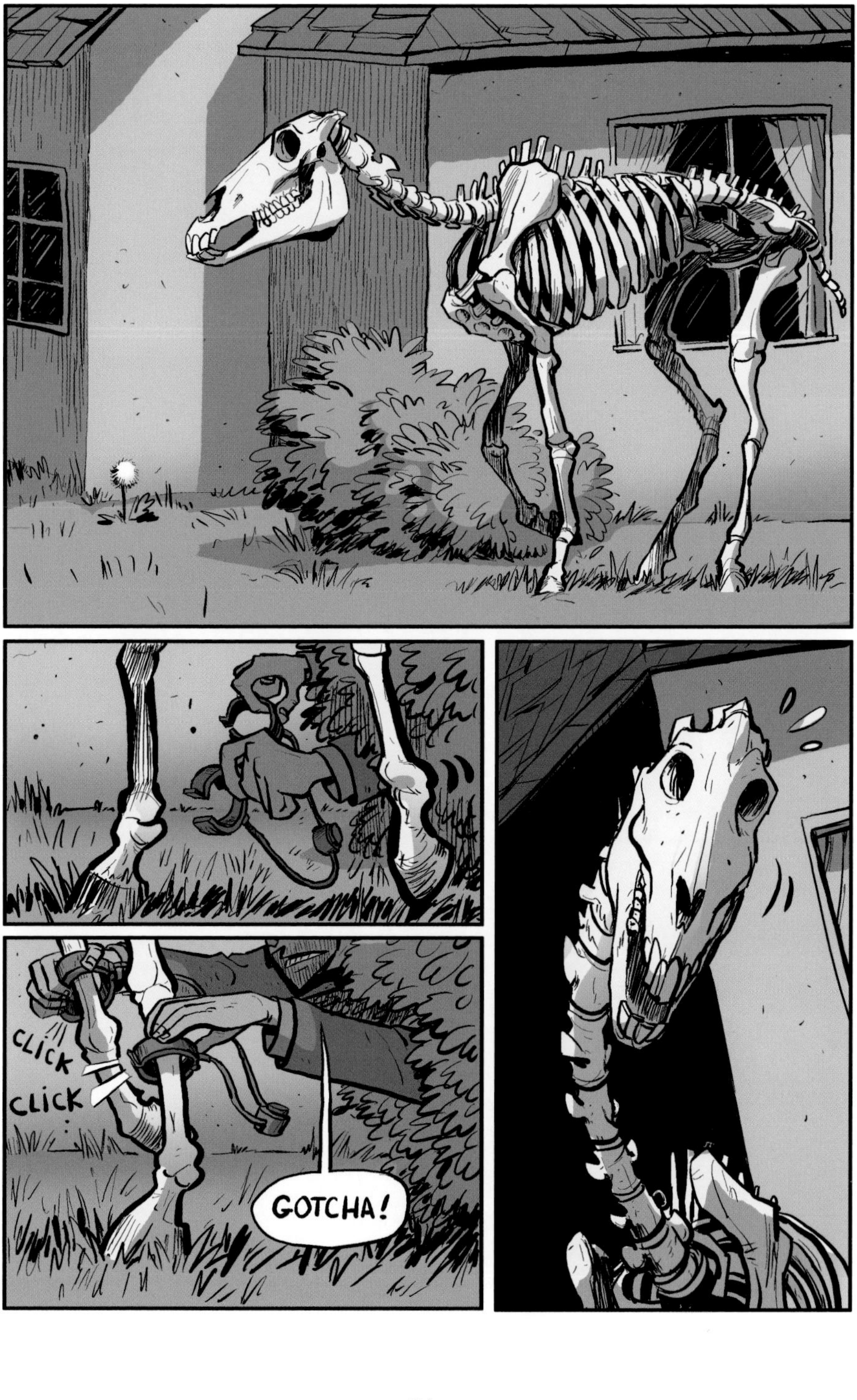
CLICK
CLICK
GOTCHA!

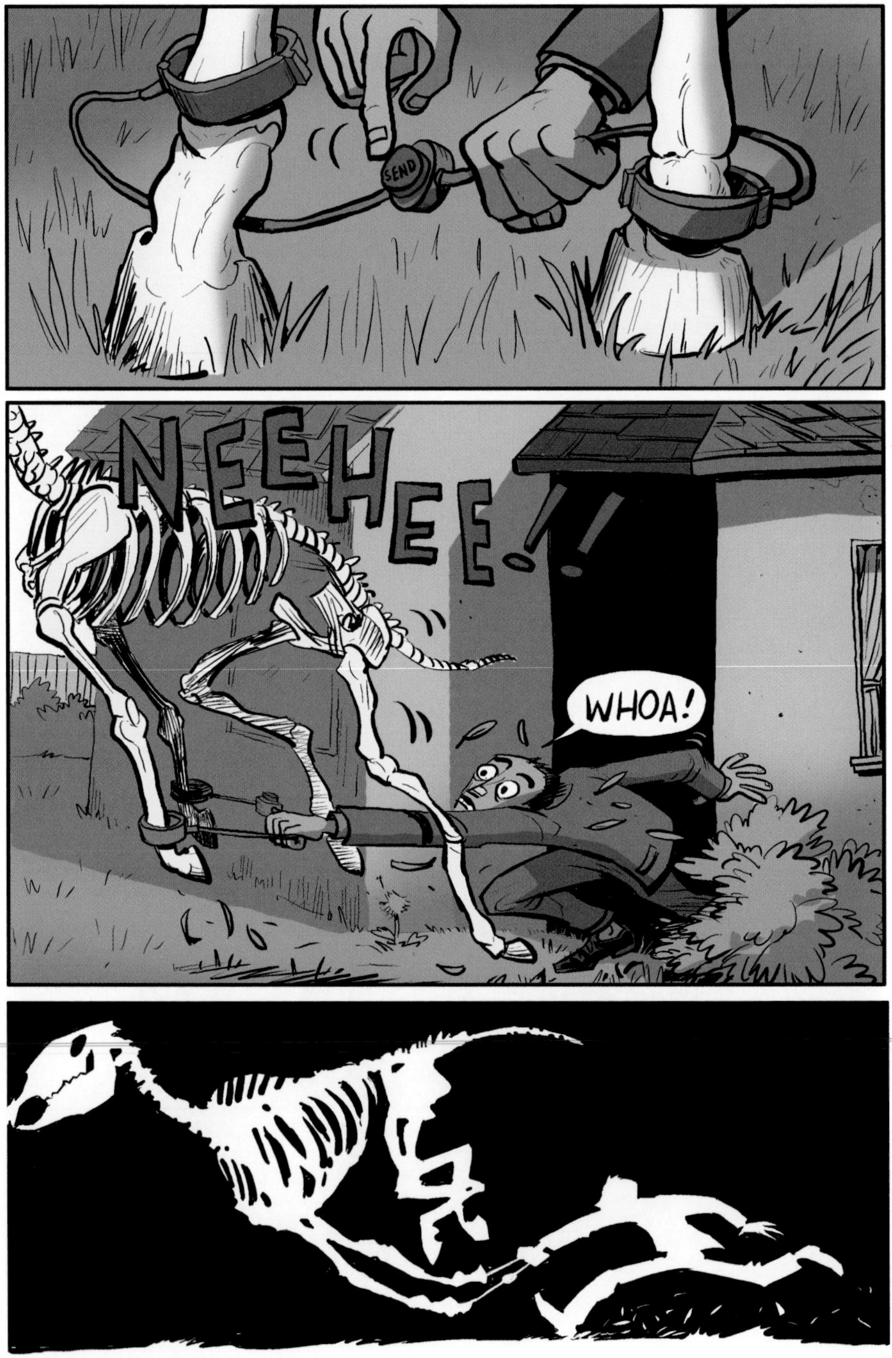
SEND
NEEHEEE!!
WHOA!

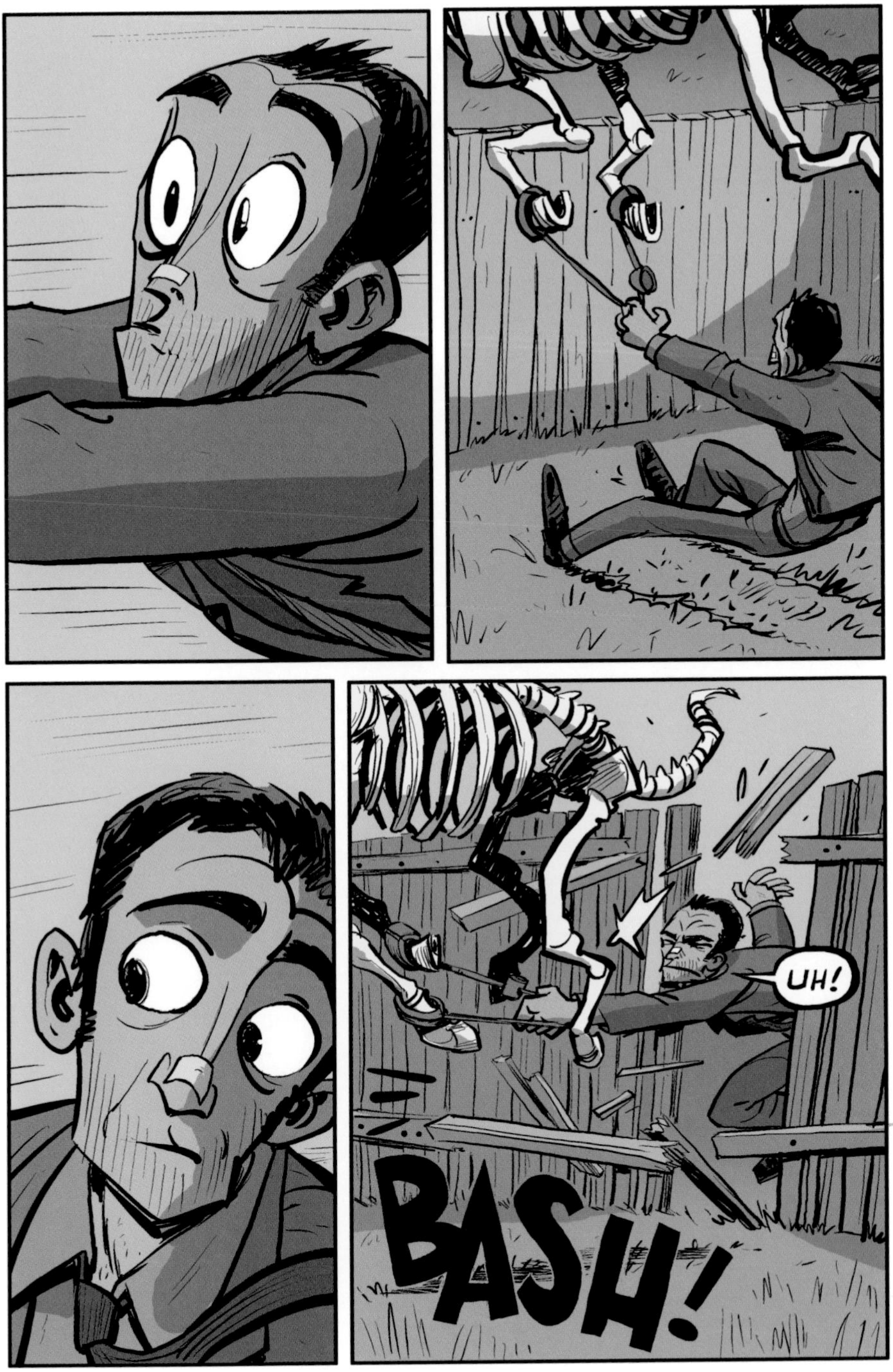
UH!
BASH!

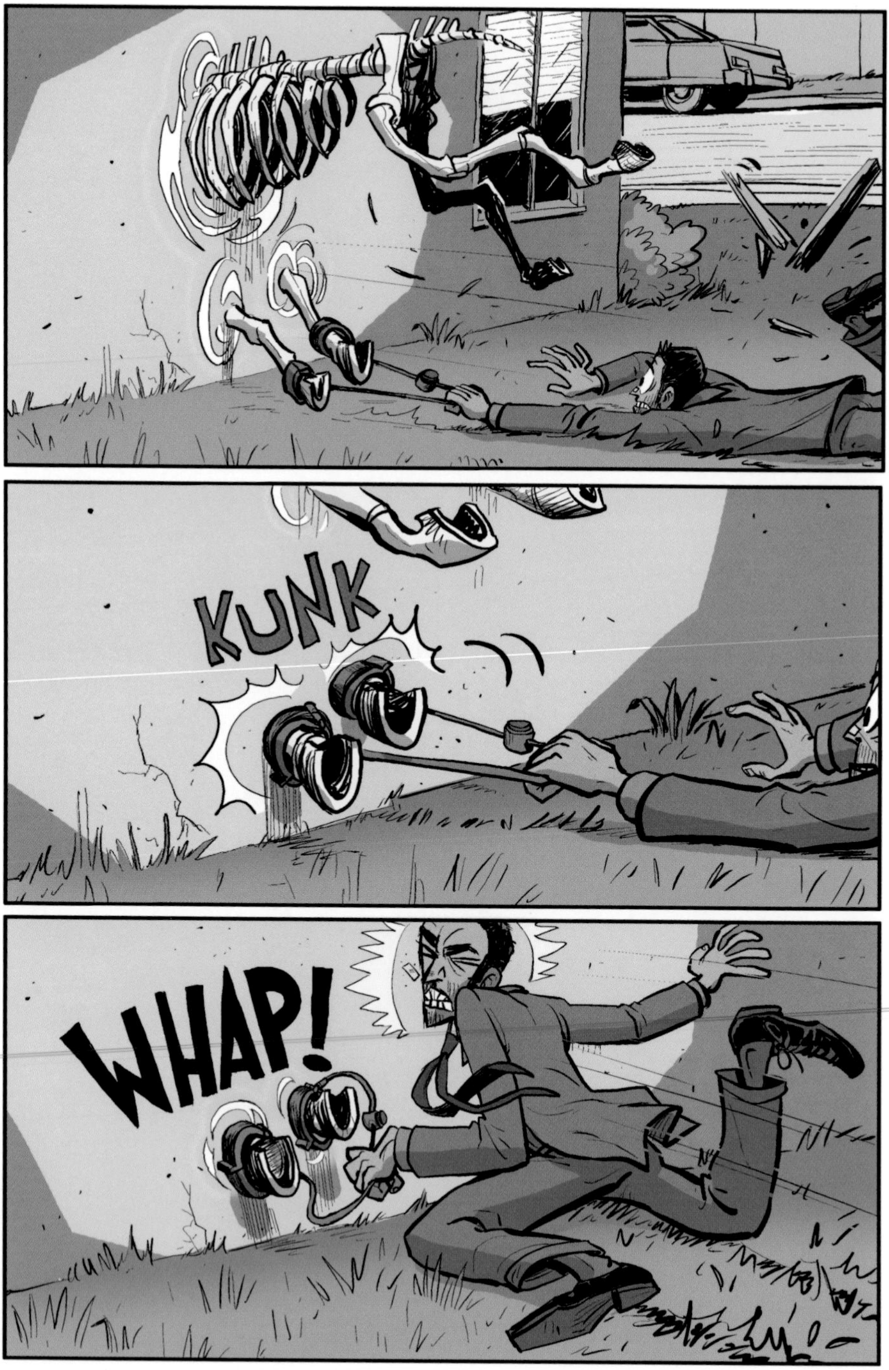
KUNK
WHAP!

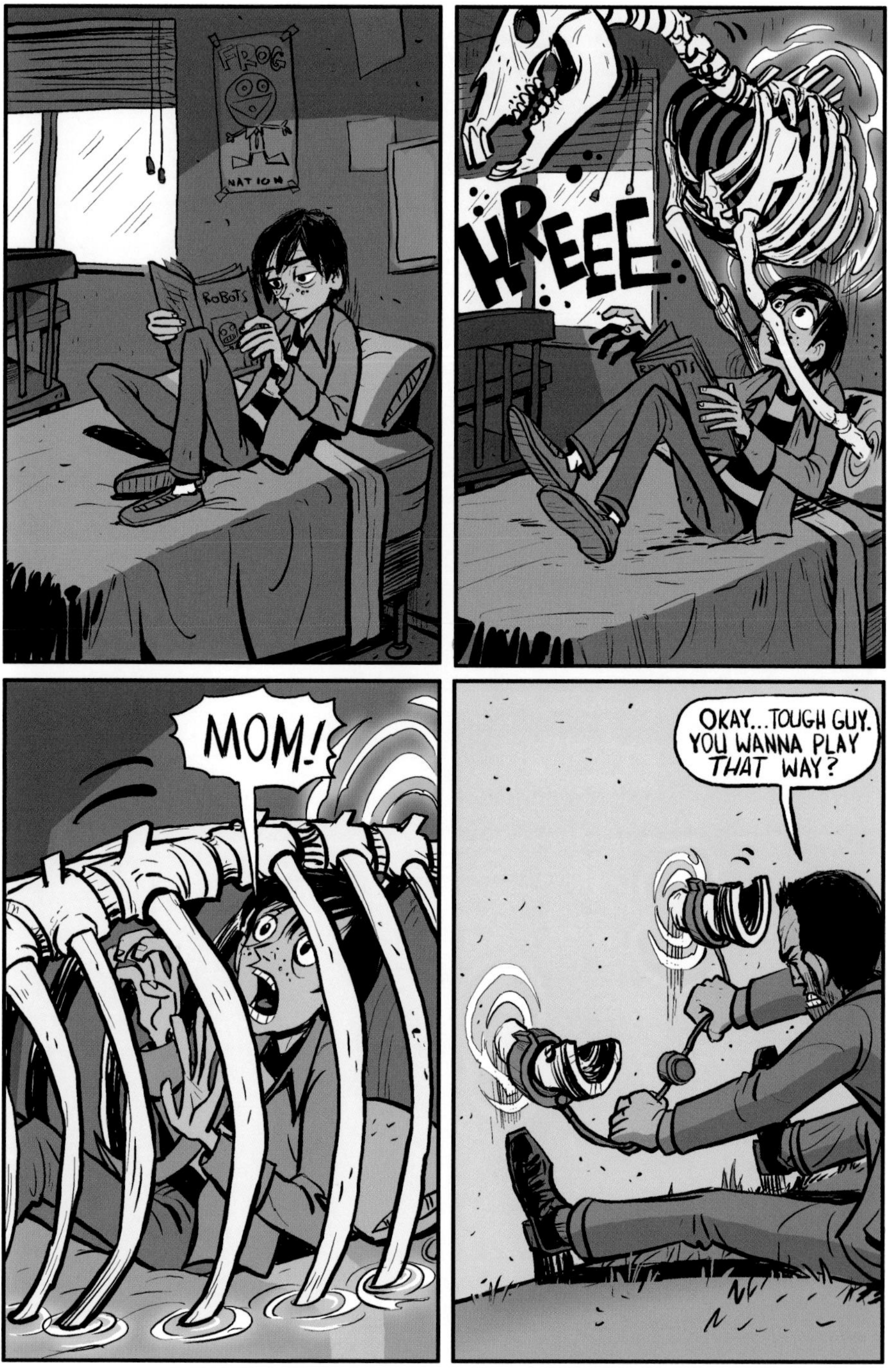
FROG
NATION
ROBOTS
HREEE
MOM!
OKAY...TOUGH GUY. YOU WANNA PLAY *THAT* WAY?

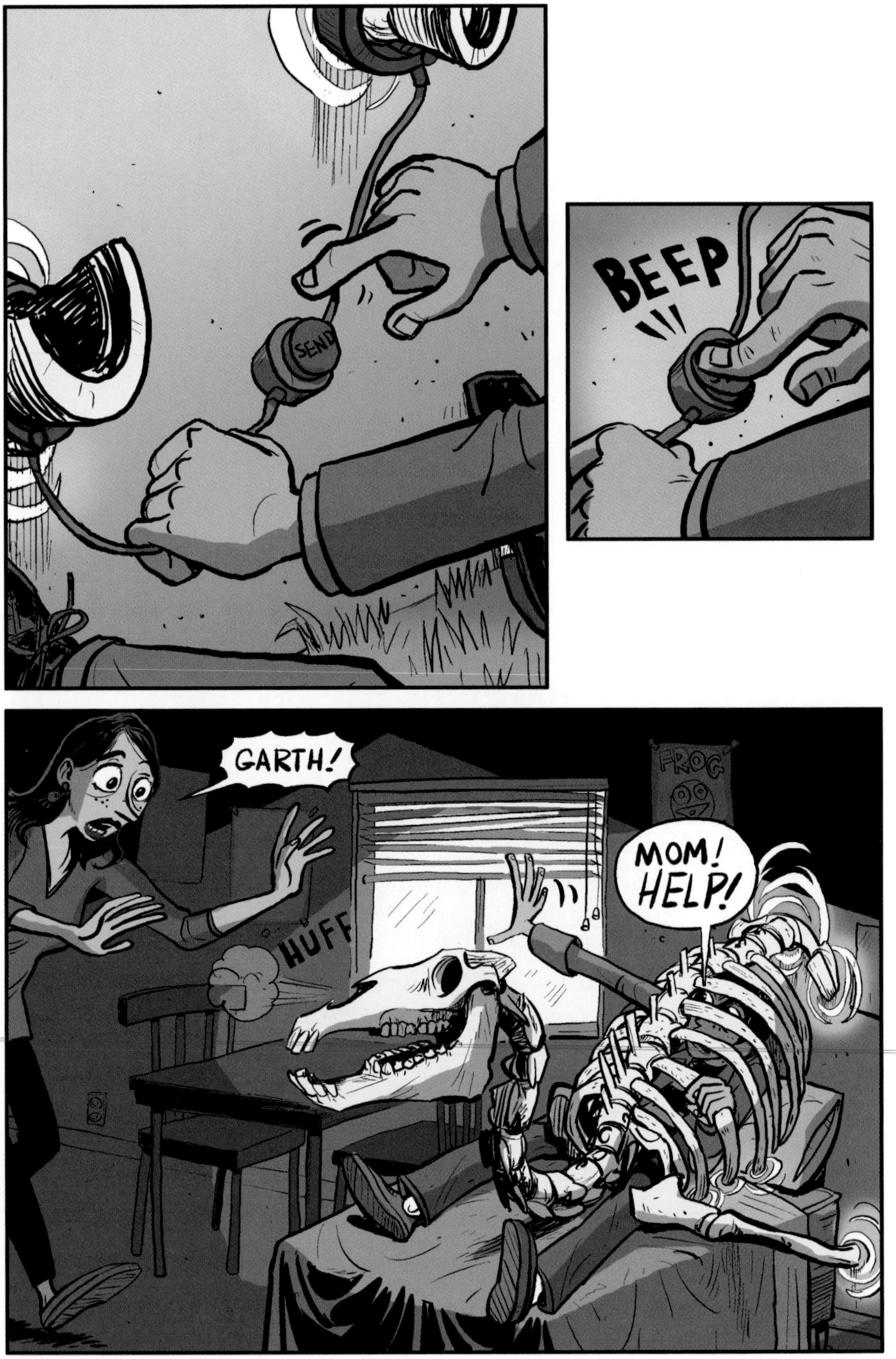
SEND
BEEP
GARTH!
FROG
HUFF
MOM! HELP!

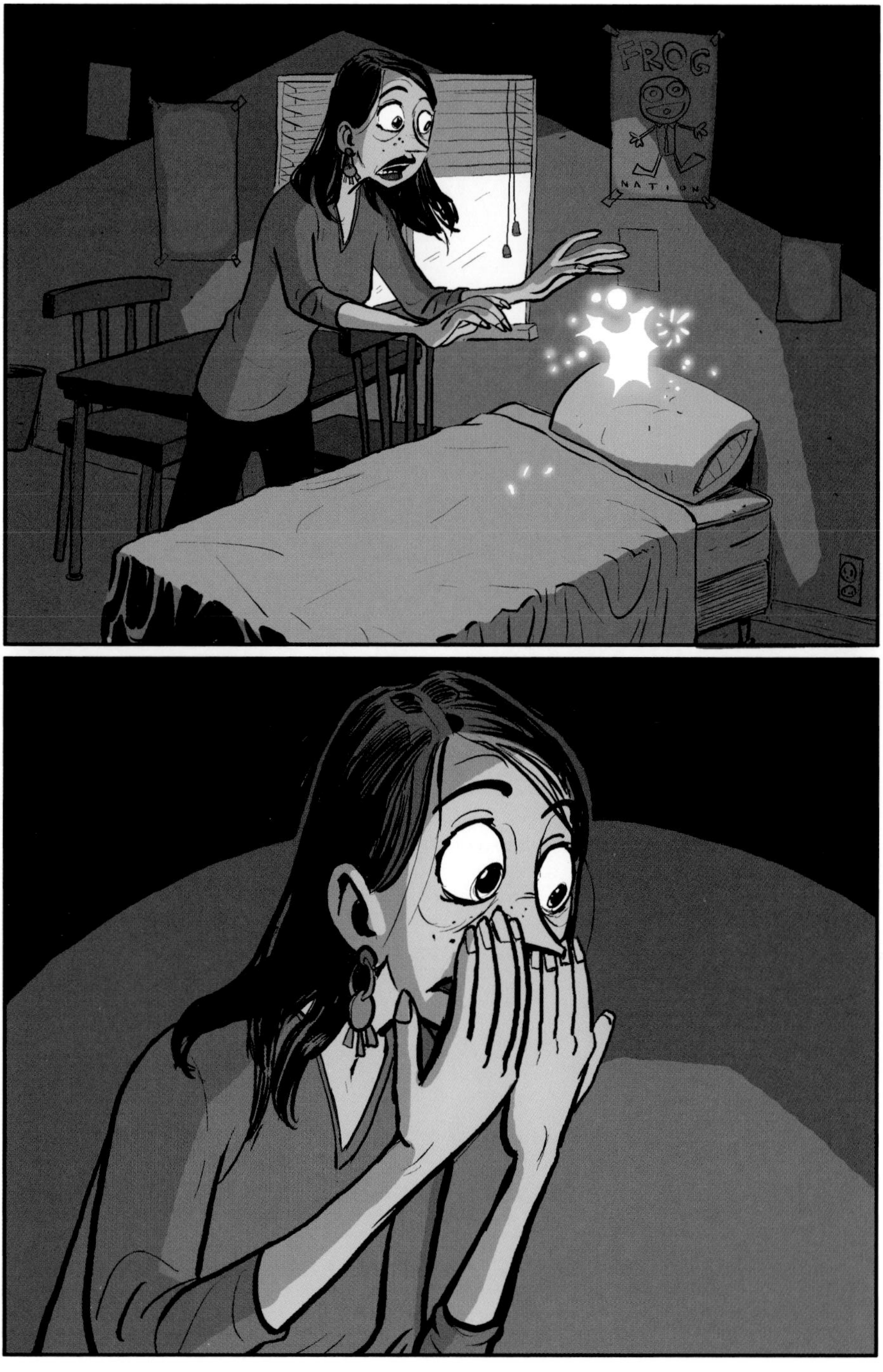
FROG
NATION

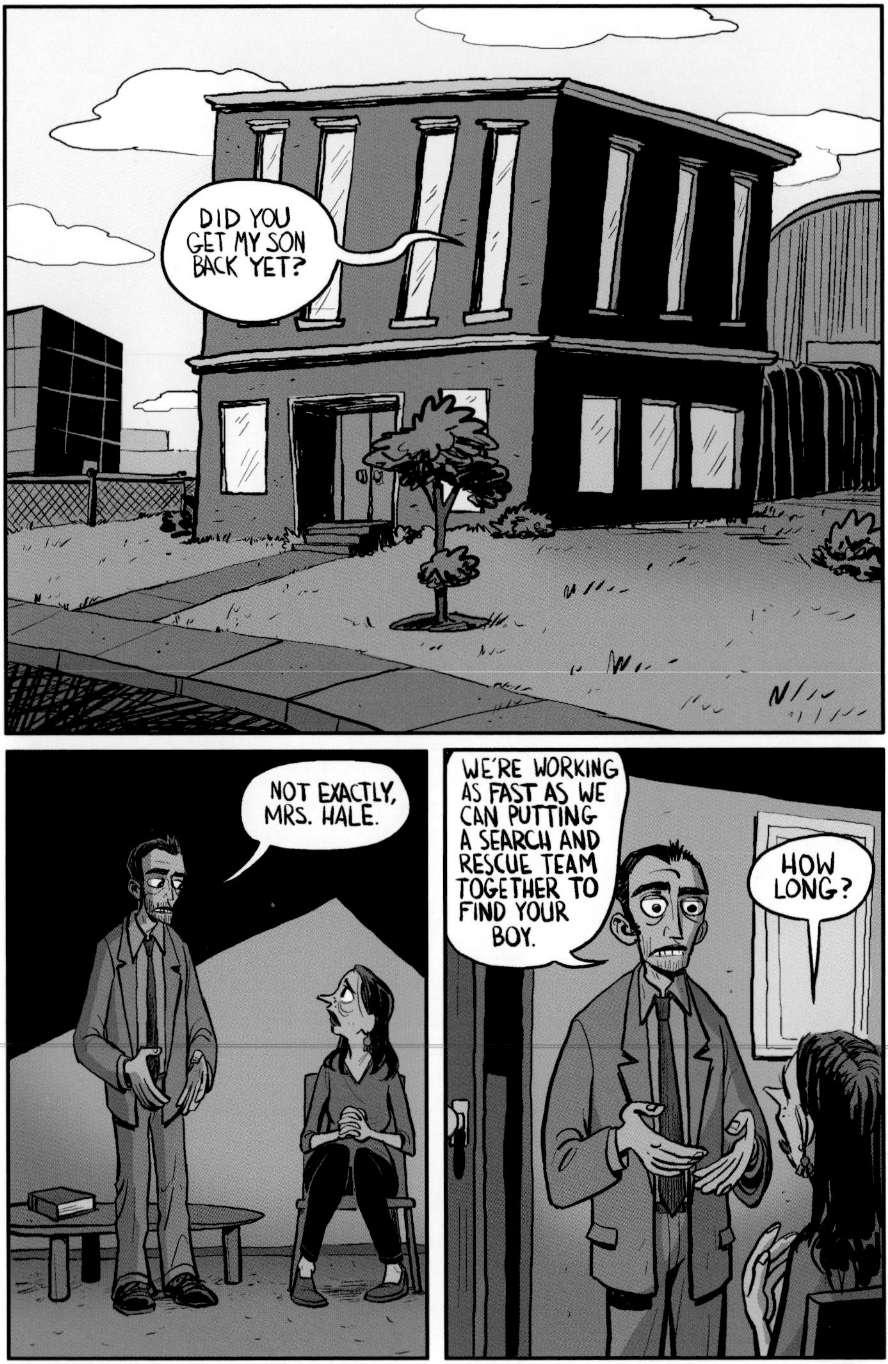
DID YOU GET MY SON BACK YET?
NOT EXACTLY, MRS. HALE.
WE'RE WORKING AS FAST AS WE CAN PUTTING A SEARCH AND RESCUE TEAM TOGETHER TO FIND YOUR BOY.
HOW LONG?

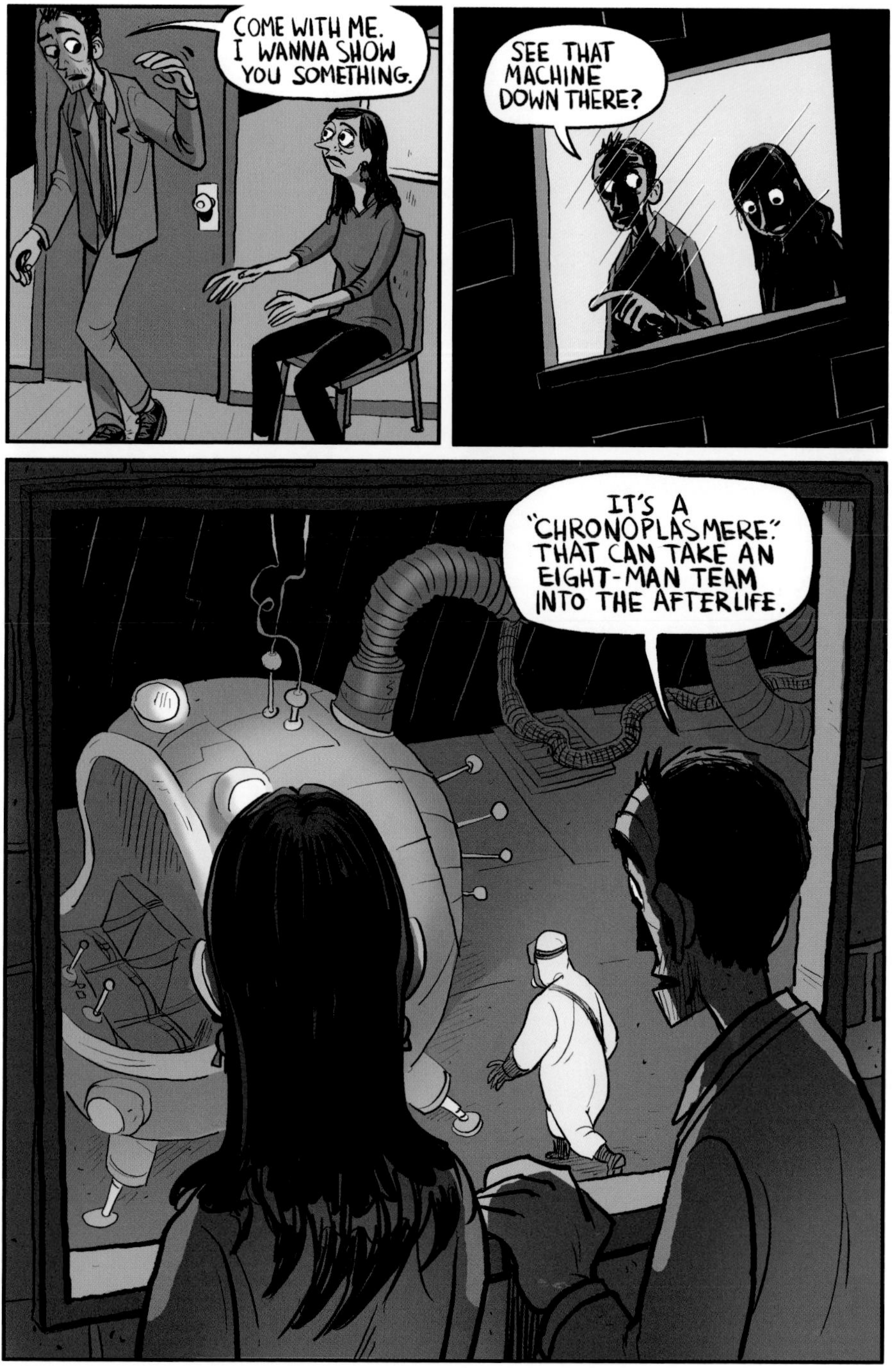
COME WITH ME. I WANNA SHOW YOU SOMETHING.
SEE THAT MACHINE DOWN THERE?
IT'S A "CHRONOPLASMERE." THAT CAN TAKE AN EIGHT-MAN TEAM INTO THE AFTERLIFE.

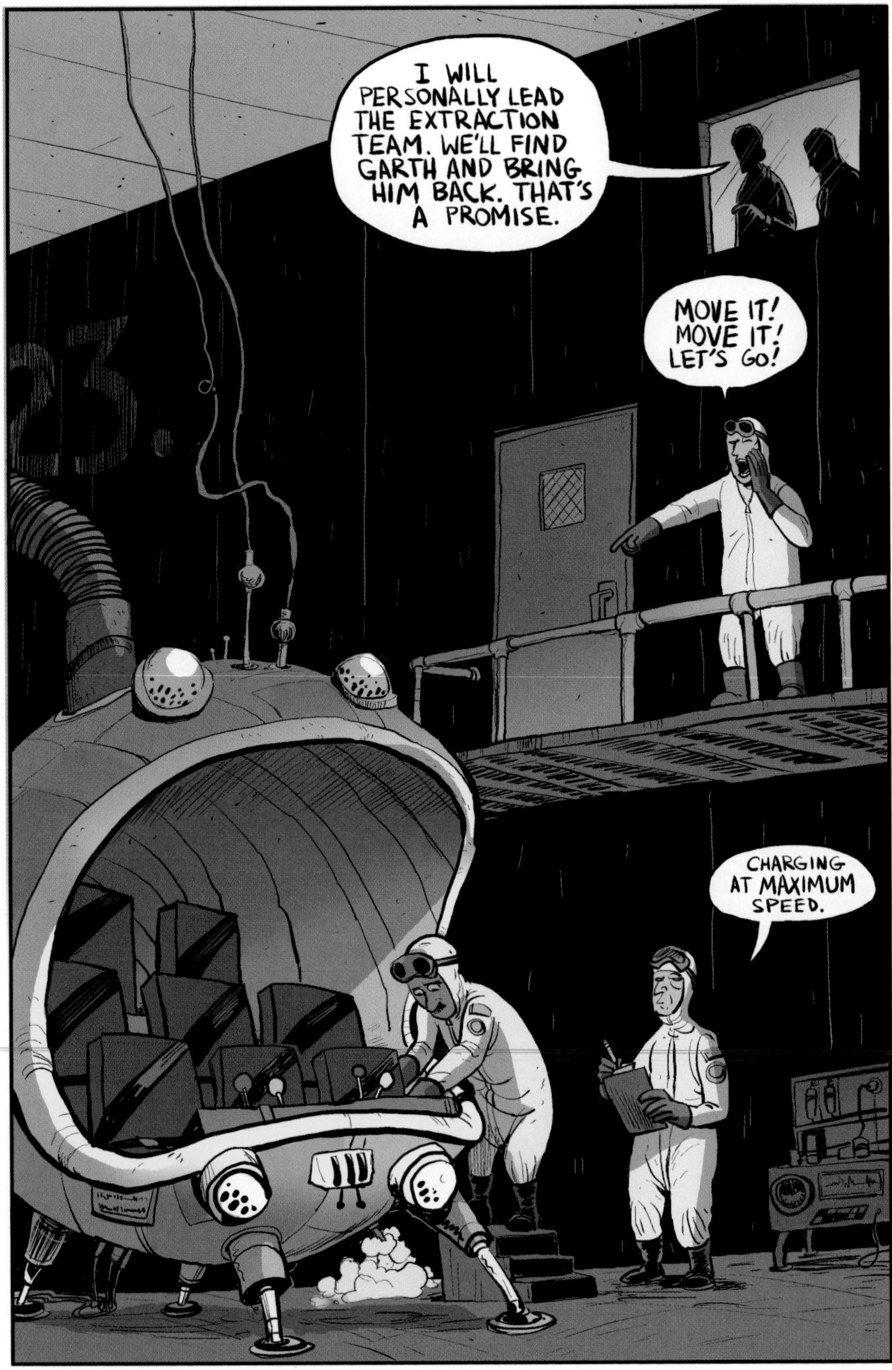
I WILL PERSONALLY LEAD THE EXTRACTION TEAM. WE'LL FIND GARTH AND BRING HIM BACK. THAT'S A PROMISE.
MOVE IT! MOVE IT! LET'S GO!
CHARGING AT MAXIMUM SPEED.

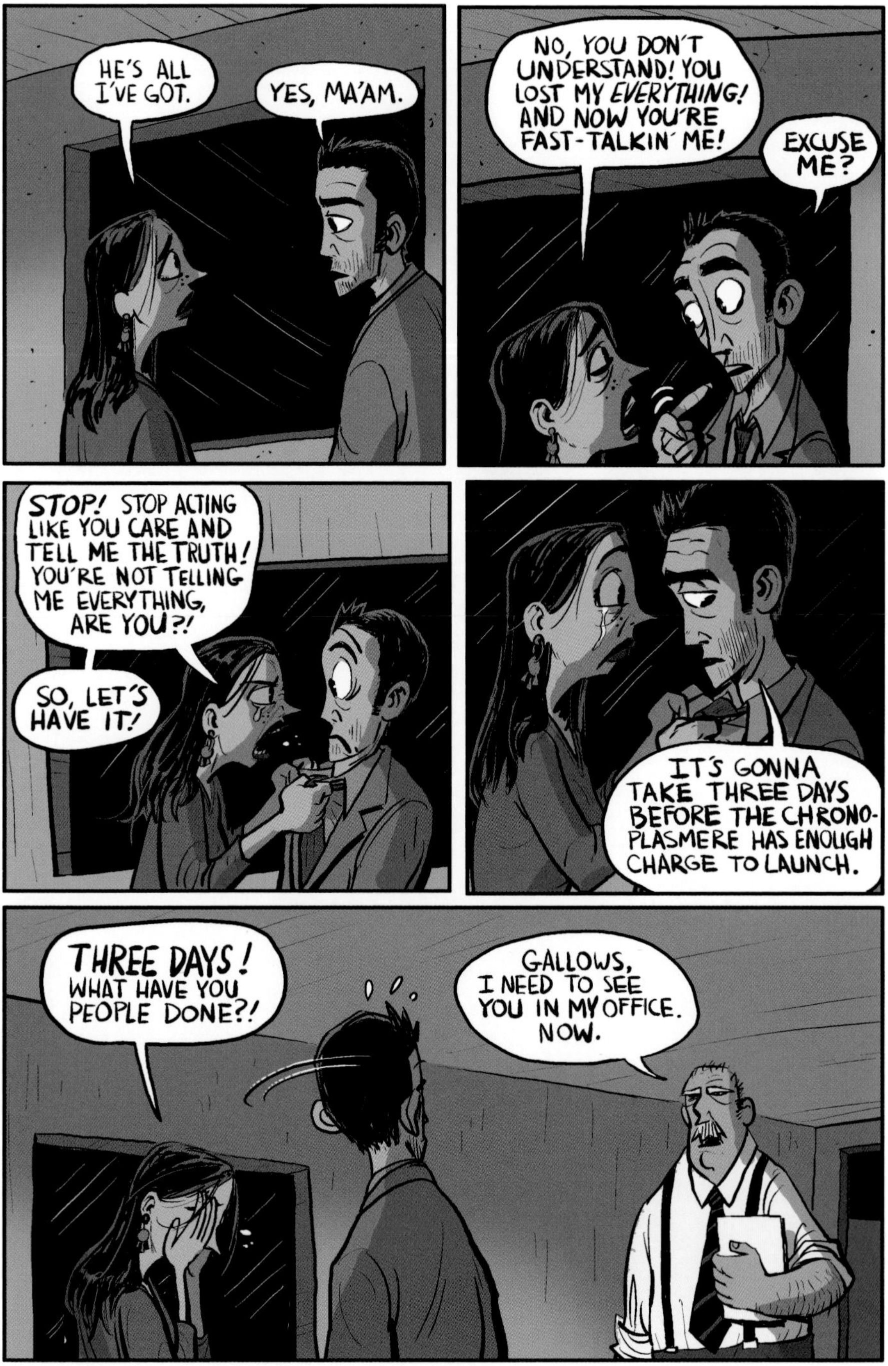
HE'S ALL I'VE GOT.
YES, MA'AM.
NO, YOU DON'T UNDERSTAND! YOU LOST MY *EVERYTHING!* AND NOW YOU'RE FAST-TALKIN' ME!
EXCUSE ME?
STOP! STOP ACTING LIKE YOU CARE AND TELL ME THE TRUTH! YOU'RE NOT TELLING ME EVERYTHING, ARE YOU?!
SO, LET'S HAVE IT!
IT'S GONNA TAKE THREE DAYS BEFORE THE CHRONO-PLASMERE HAS ENOUGH CHARGE TO LAUNCH.
THREE DAYS! WHAT HAVE YOU PEOPLE DONE?!
GALLOWS, I NEED TO SEE YOU IN MY OFFICE. NOW.

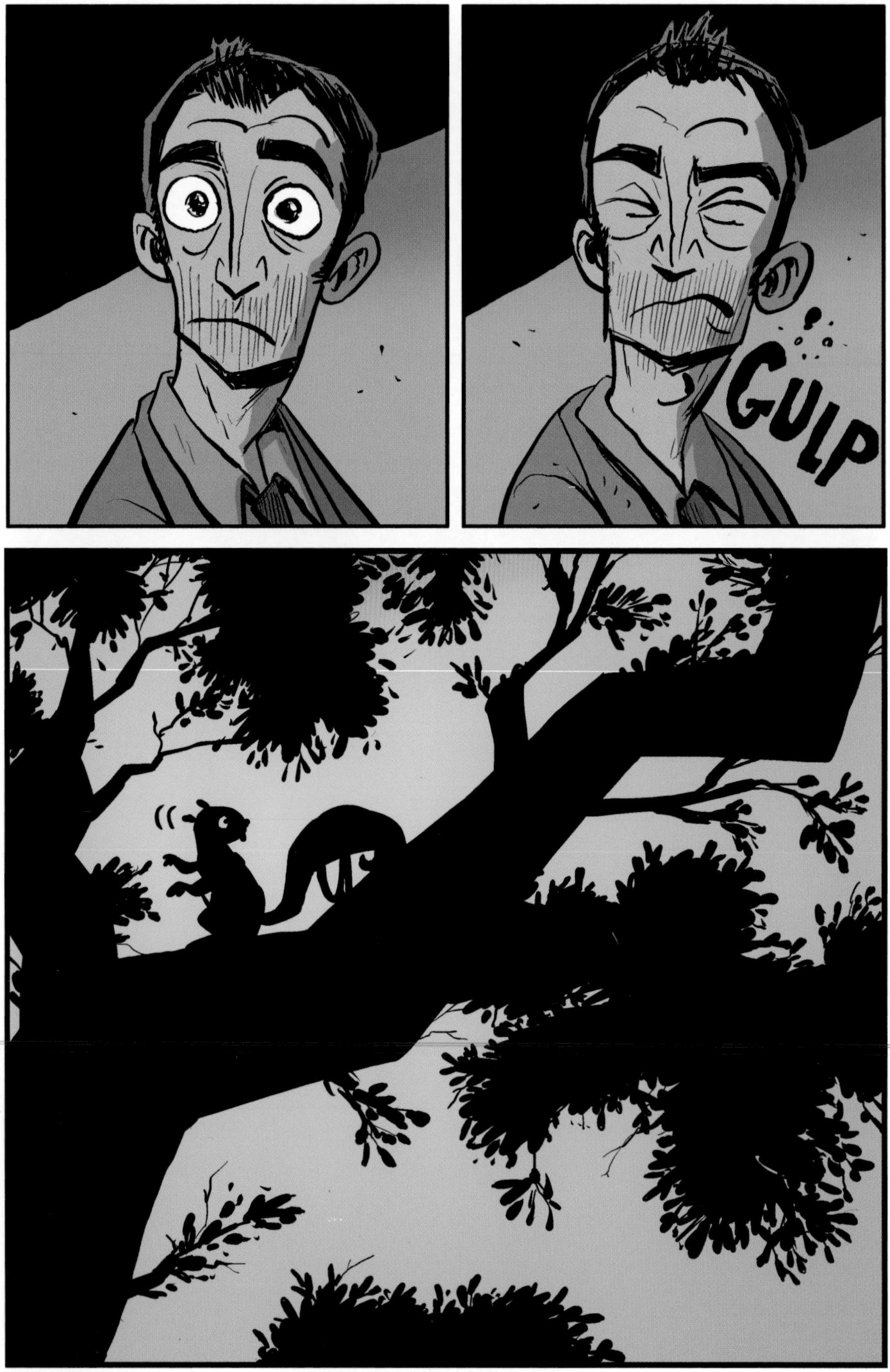
GULP

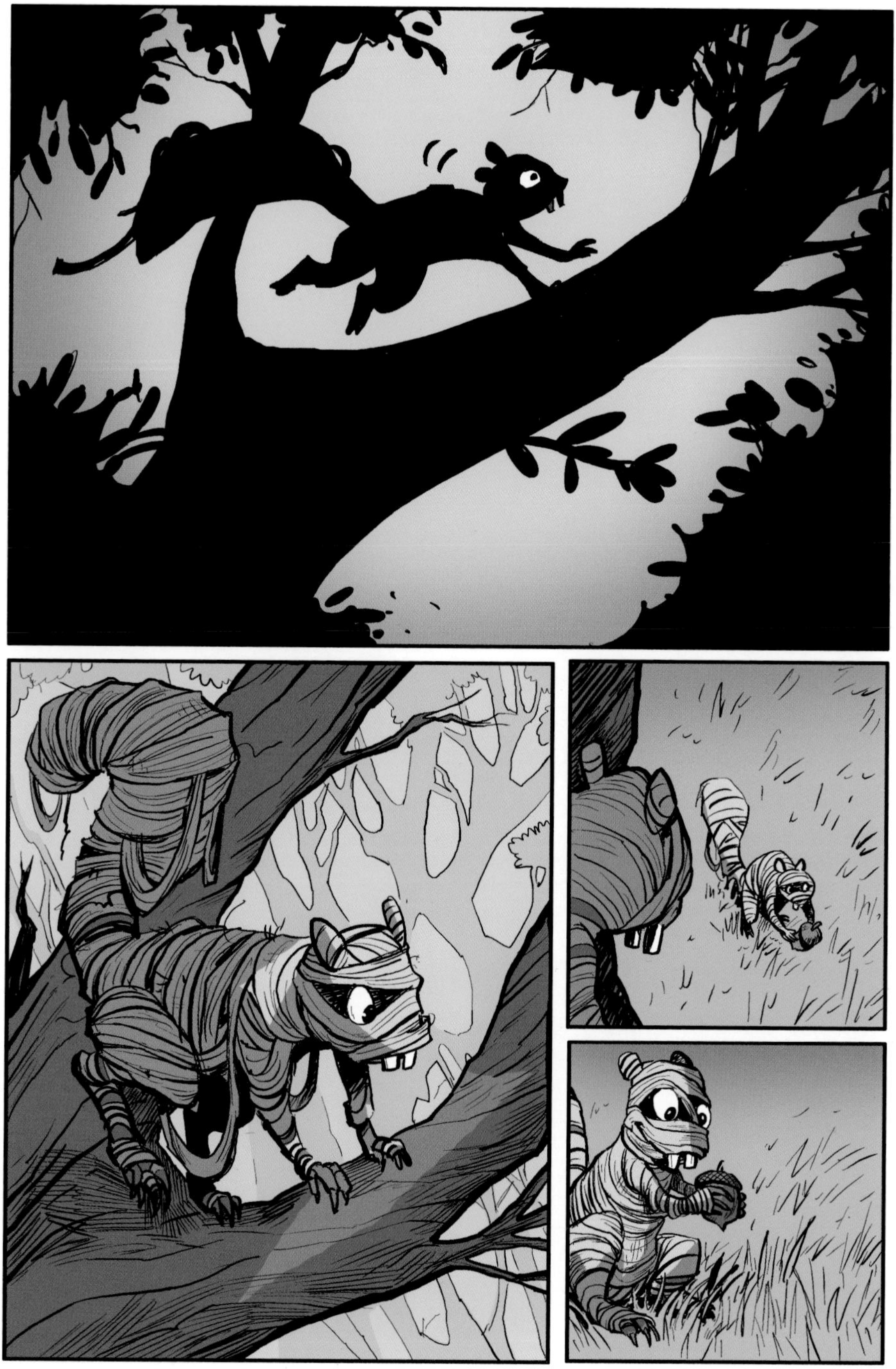

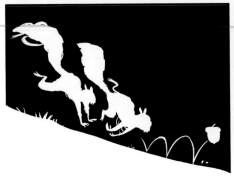

CRACK

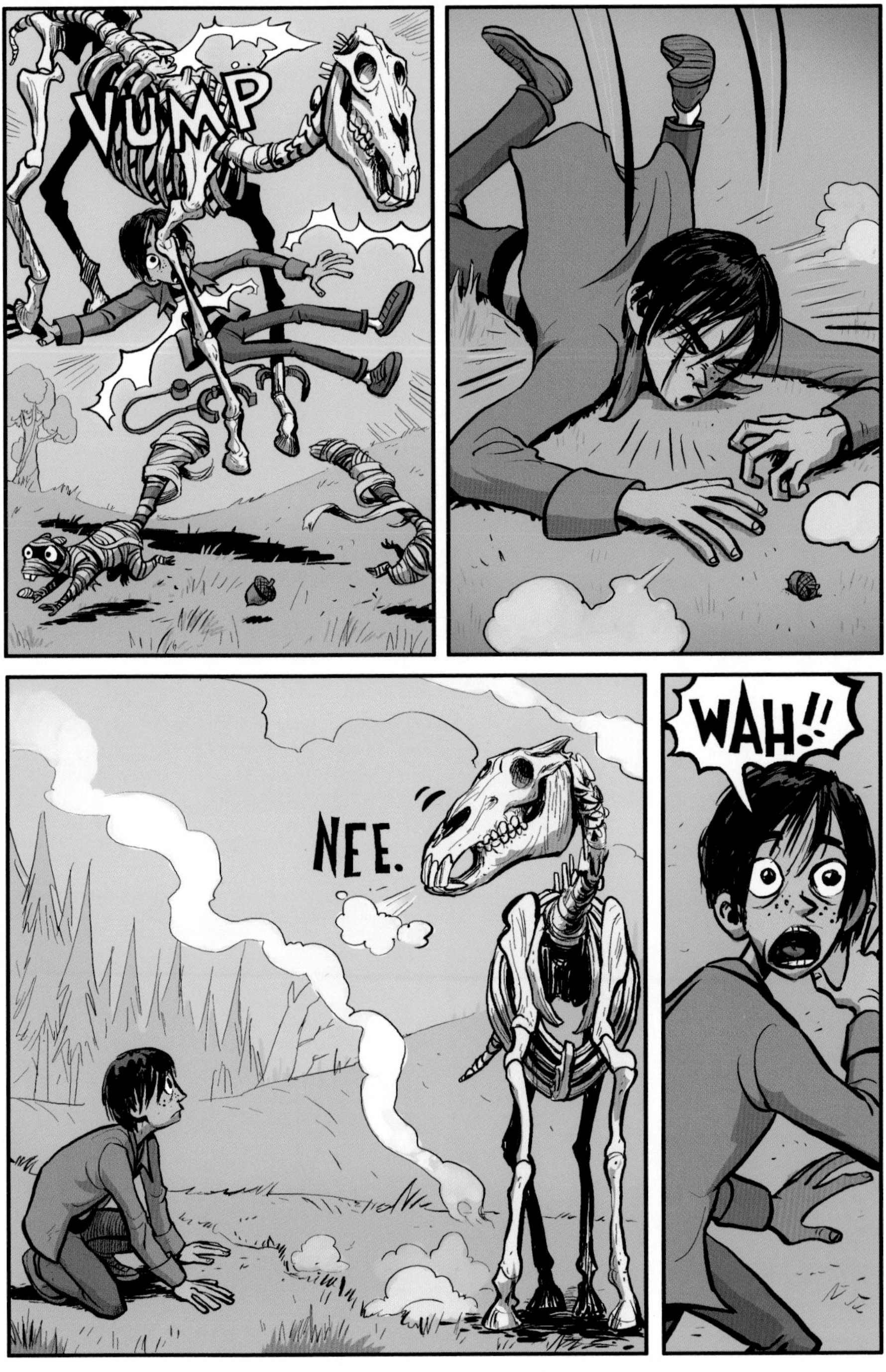
VUMP
NEE.
WAH!!

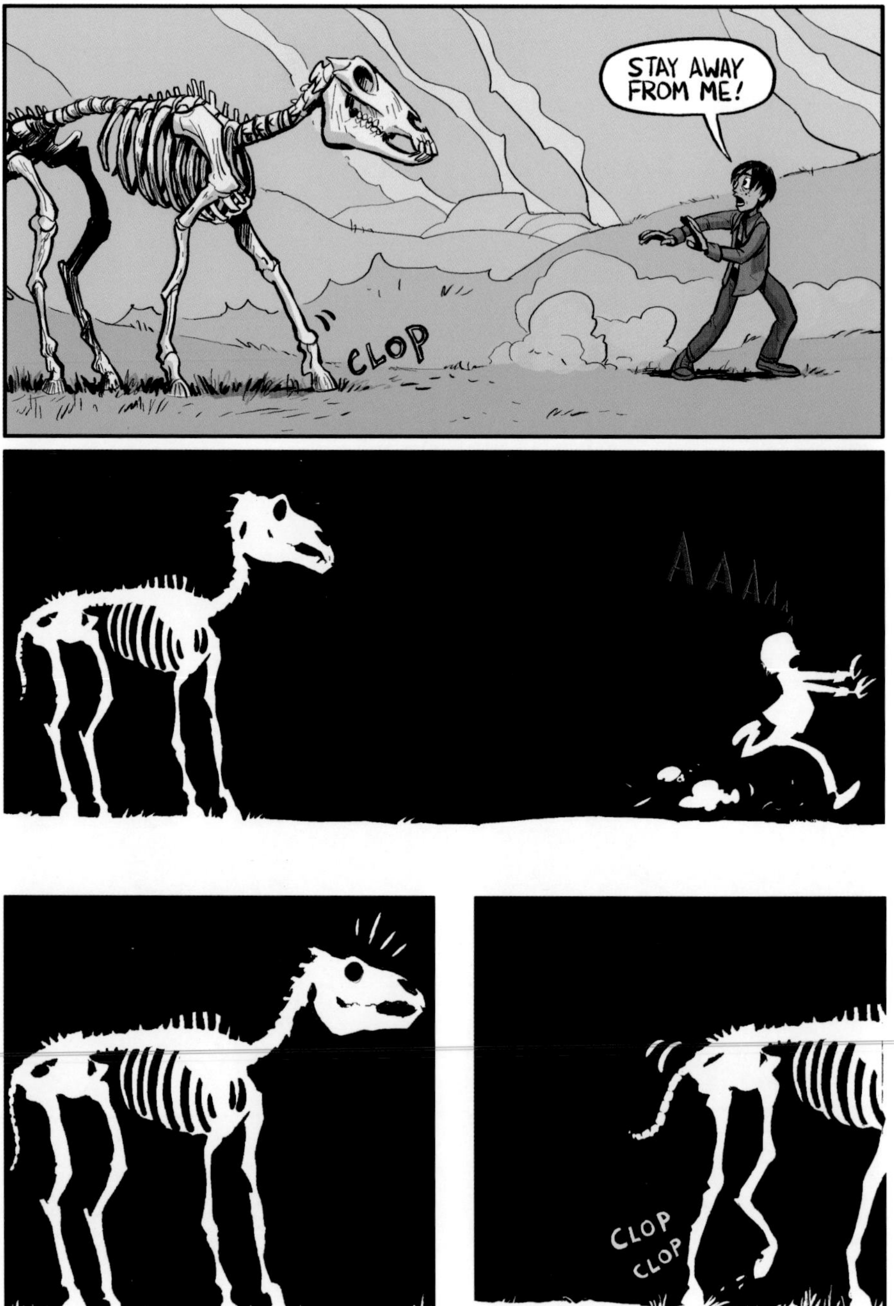
STAY AWAY FROM ME!
CLOP
AAAA
CLOP
CLOP

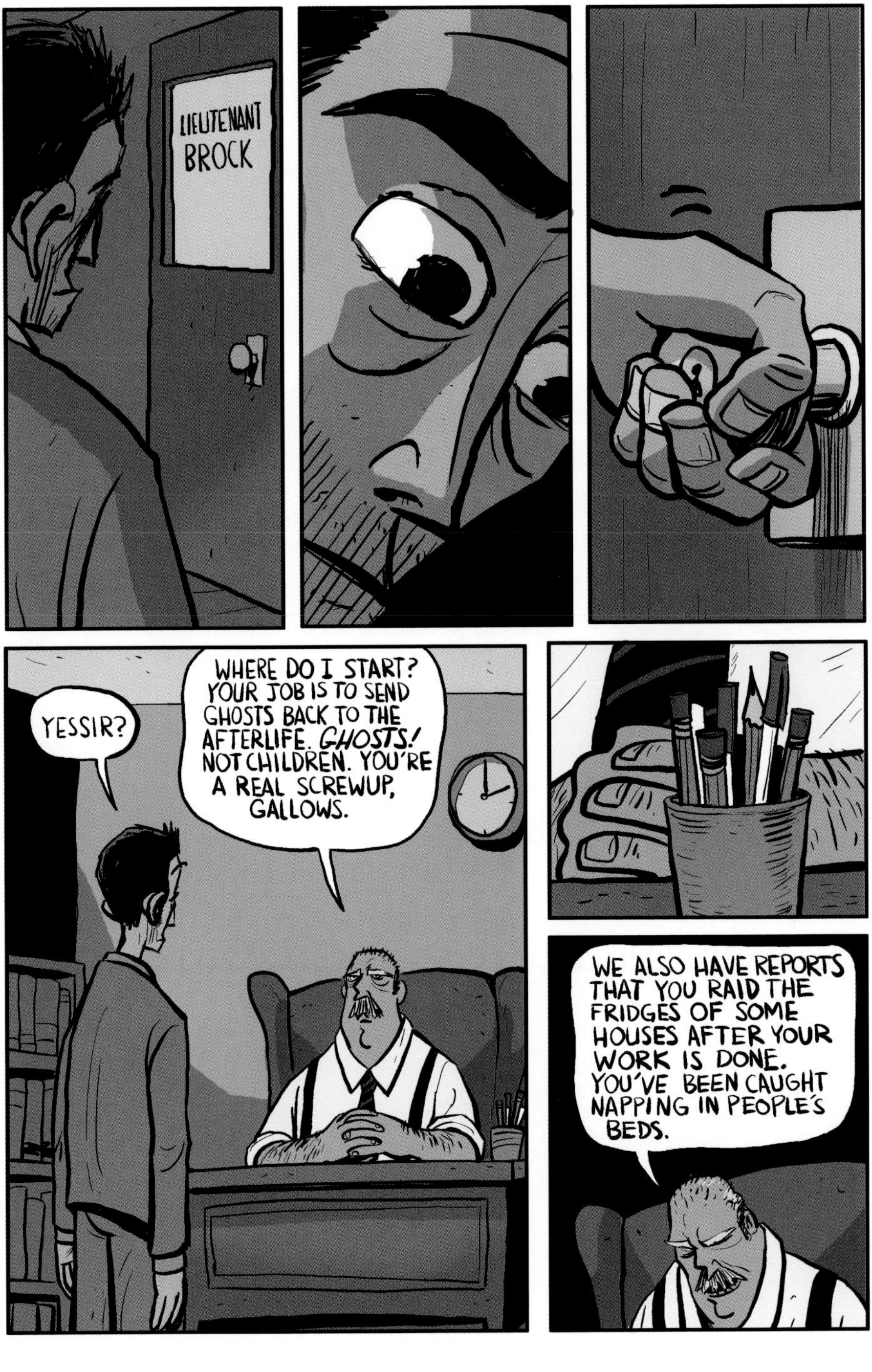
LIEUTENANT
BROCK
YESSIR?
WHERE DO I START? YOUR JOB IS TO SEND GHOSTS BACK TO THE AFTERLIFE. *GHOSTS!* NOT CHILDREN. YOU'RE A REAL SCREWUP, GALLOWS.
WE ALSO HAVE REPORTS THAT YOU RAID THE FRIDGES OF SOME HOUSES AFTER YOUR WORK IS DONE. YOU'VE BEEN CAUGHT NAPPING IN PEOPLE'S BEDS.

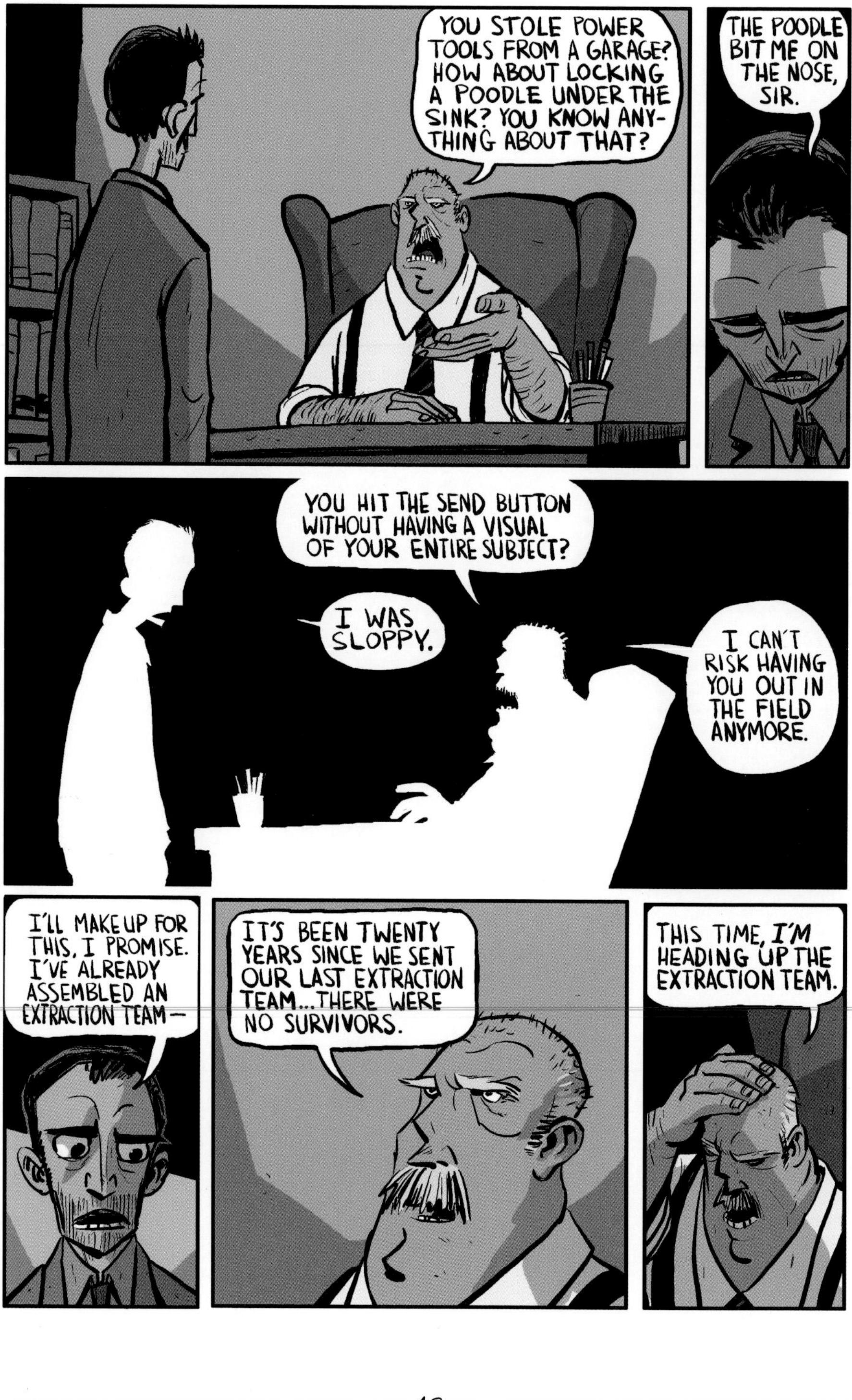
YOU STOLE POWER TOOLS FROM A GARAGE? HOW ABOUT LOCKING A POODLE UNDER THE SINK? YOU KNOW ANYTHING ABOUT THAT?
THE POODLE BIT ME ON THE NOSE, SIR.
YOU HIT THE SEND BUTTON WITHOUT HAVING A VISUAL OF YOUR ENTIRE SUBJECT?
I WAS SLOPPY.
I CAN'T RISK HAVING YOU OUT IN THE FIELD ANYMORE.
I'LL MAKE UP FOR THIS, I PROMISE. I'VE ALREADY ASSEMBLED AN EXTRACTION TEAM—
IT'S BEEN TWENTY YEARS SINCE WE SENT OUR LAST EXTRACTION TEAM...THERE WERE NO SURVIVORS.
THIS TIME, *I'M* HEADING UP THE EXTRACTION TEAM.

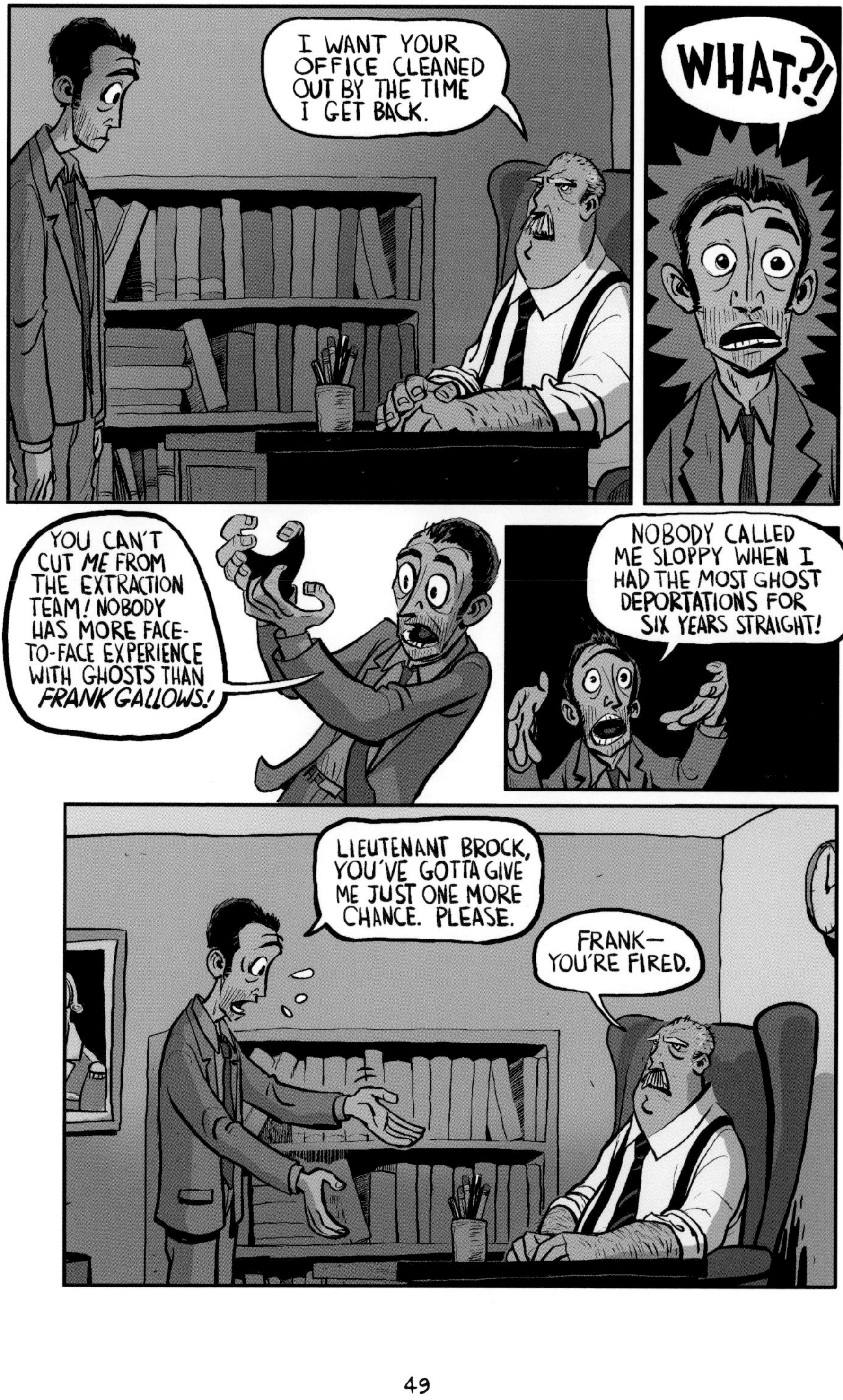
I WANT YOUR OFFICE CLEANED OUT BY THE TIME I GET BACK.
WHAT?!
YOU CAN'T CUT *ME* FROM THE EXTRACTION TEAM! NOBODY HAS MORE FACE-TO-FACE EXPERIENCE WITH GHOSTS THAN *FRANK GALLOWS!*
NOBODY CALLED ME SLOPPY WHEN I HAD THE MOST GHOST DEPORTATIONS FOR SIX YEARS STRAIGHT!
LIEUTENANT BROCK, YOU'VE GOTTA GIVE ME JUST ONE MORE CHANCE. PLEASE.
FRANK— YOU'RE FIRED.

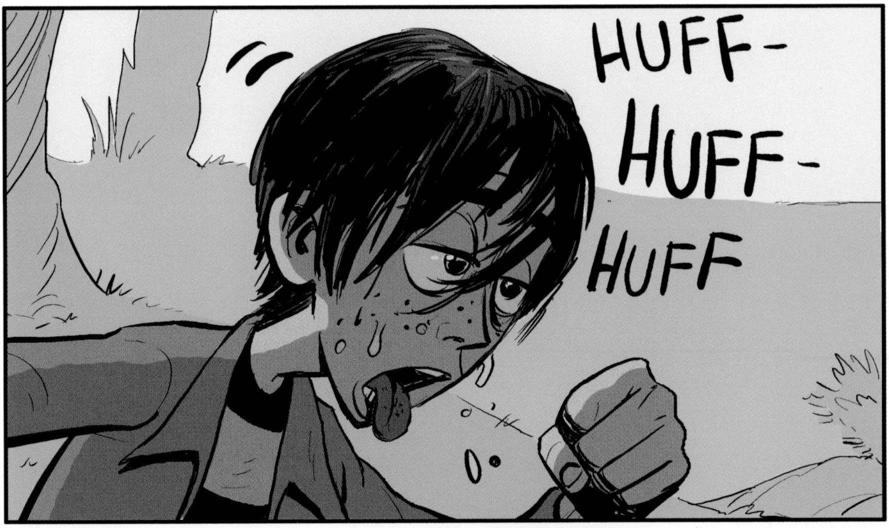
HUFF-
HUFF-
HUFF

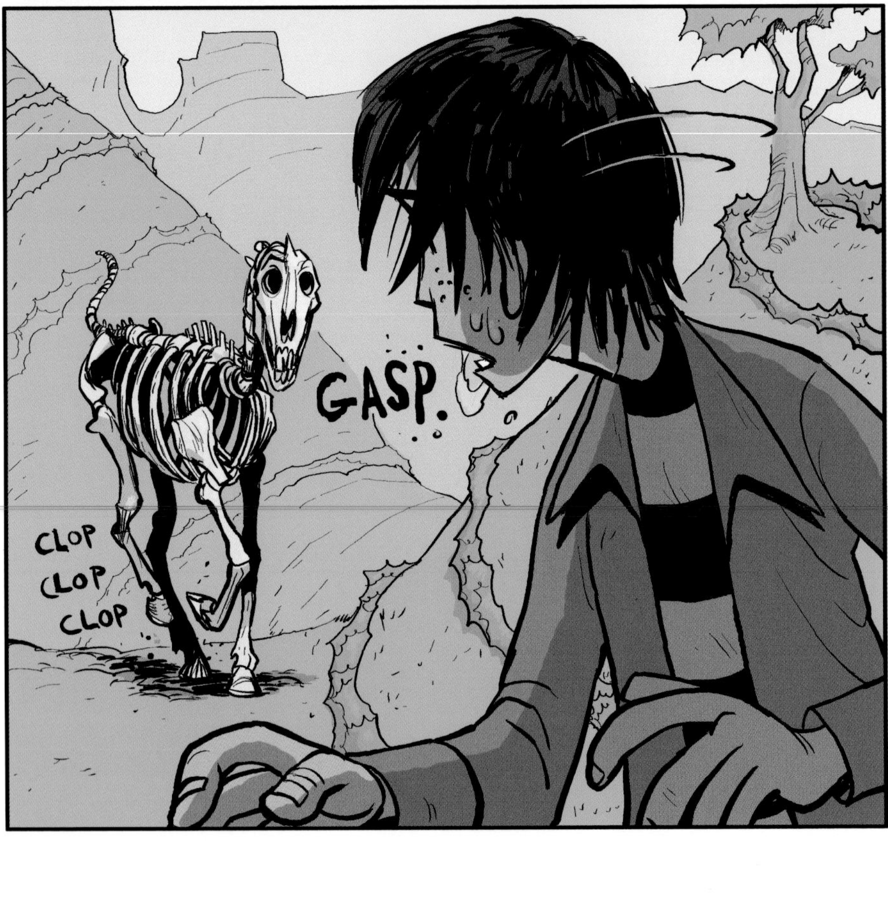
GASP.
CLOP
CLOP
CLOP

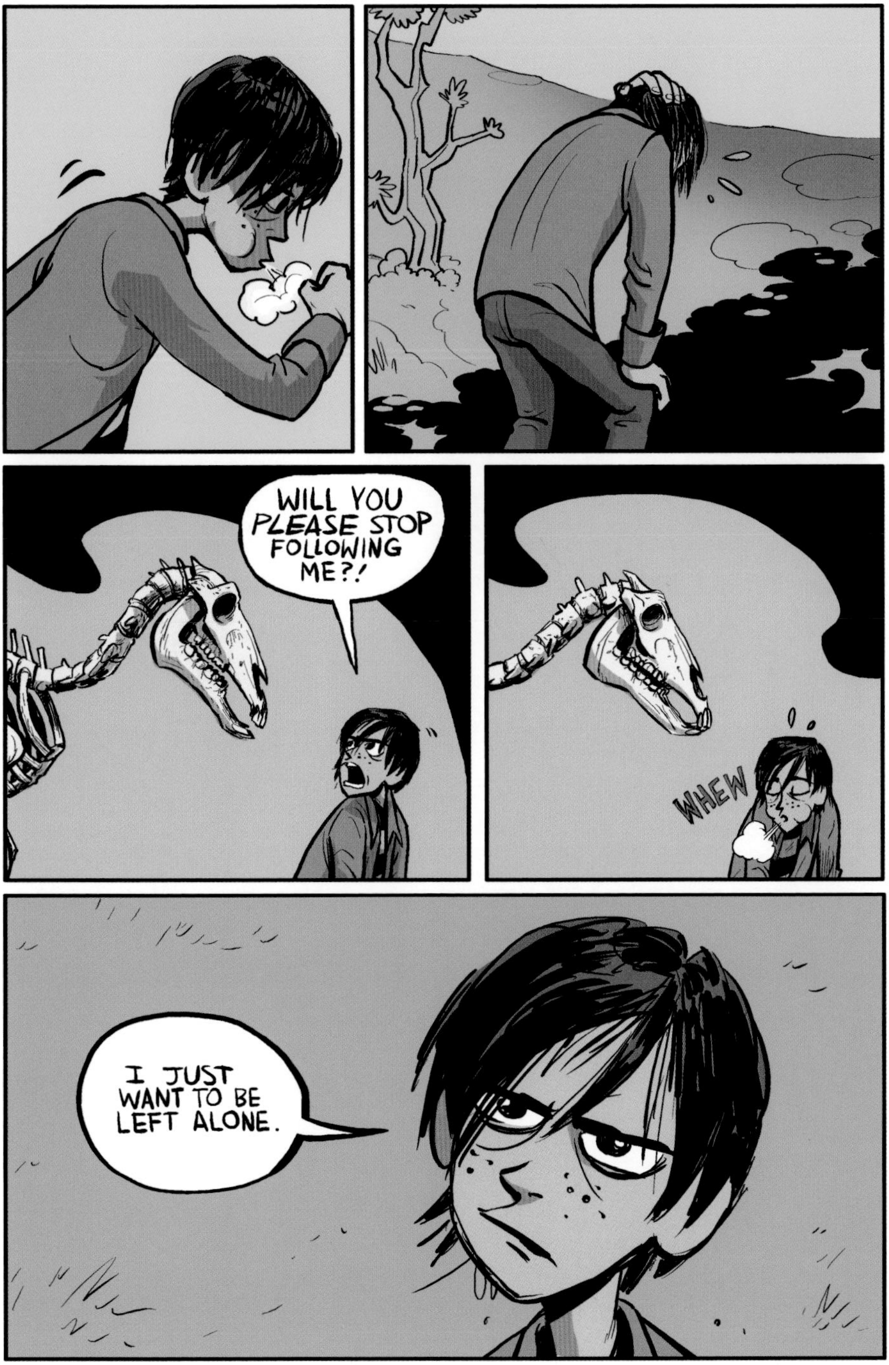
WILL YOU PLEASE STOP FOLLOWING ME?!
WHEW
I JUST WANT TO BE LEFT ALONE.

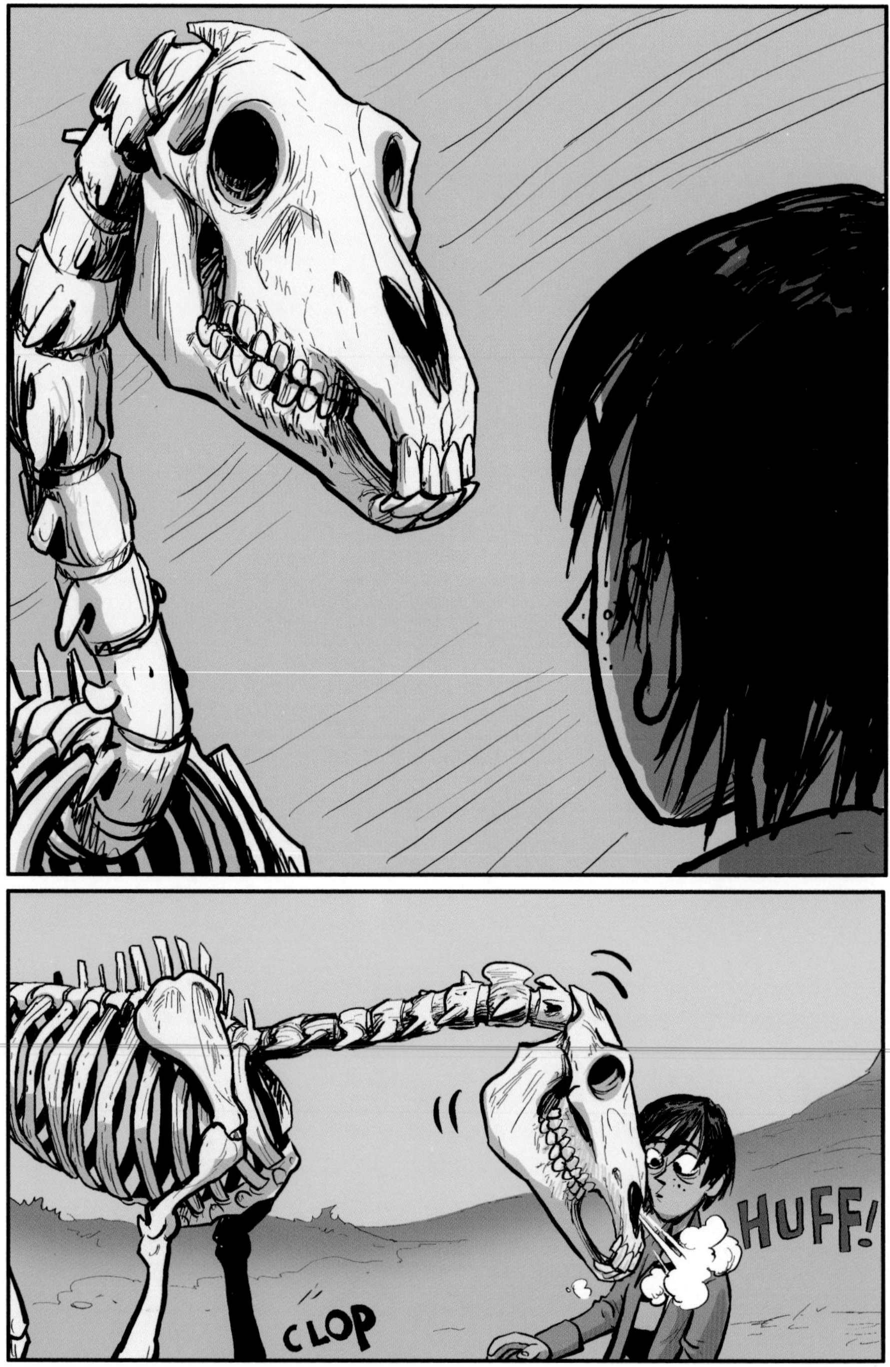
HUFF!
CLOP

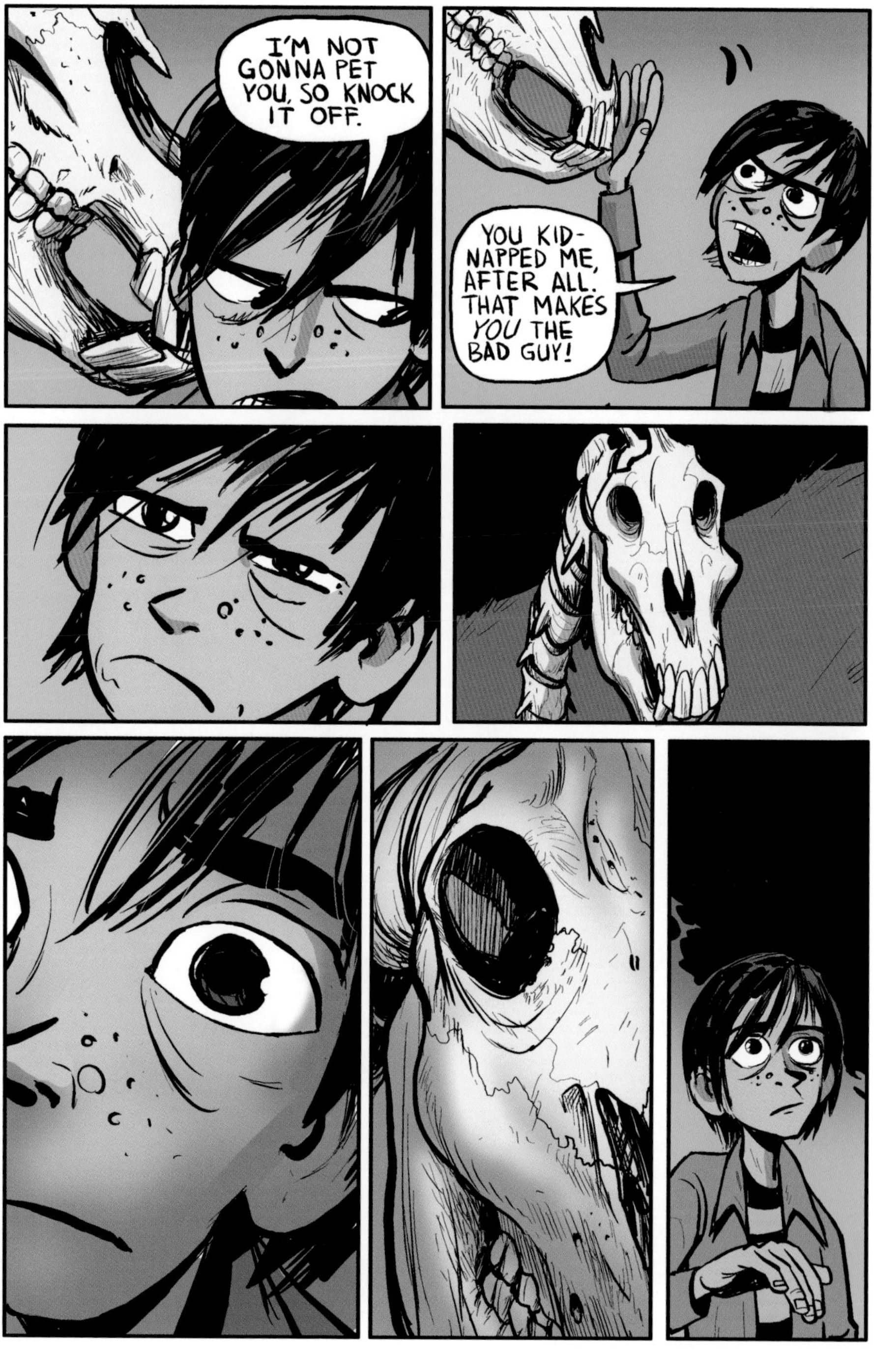
I'M NOT GONNA PET YOU, SO KNOCK IT OFF.
YOU KID-NAPPED ME, AFTER ALL. THAT MAKES *YOU* THE BAD GUY!

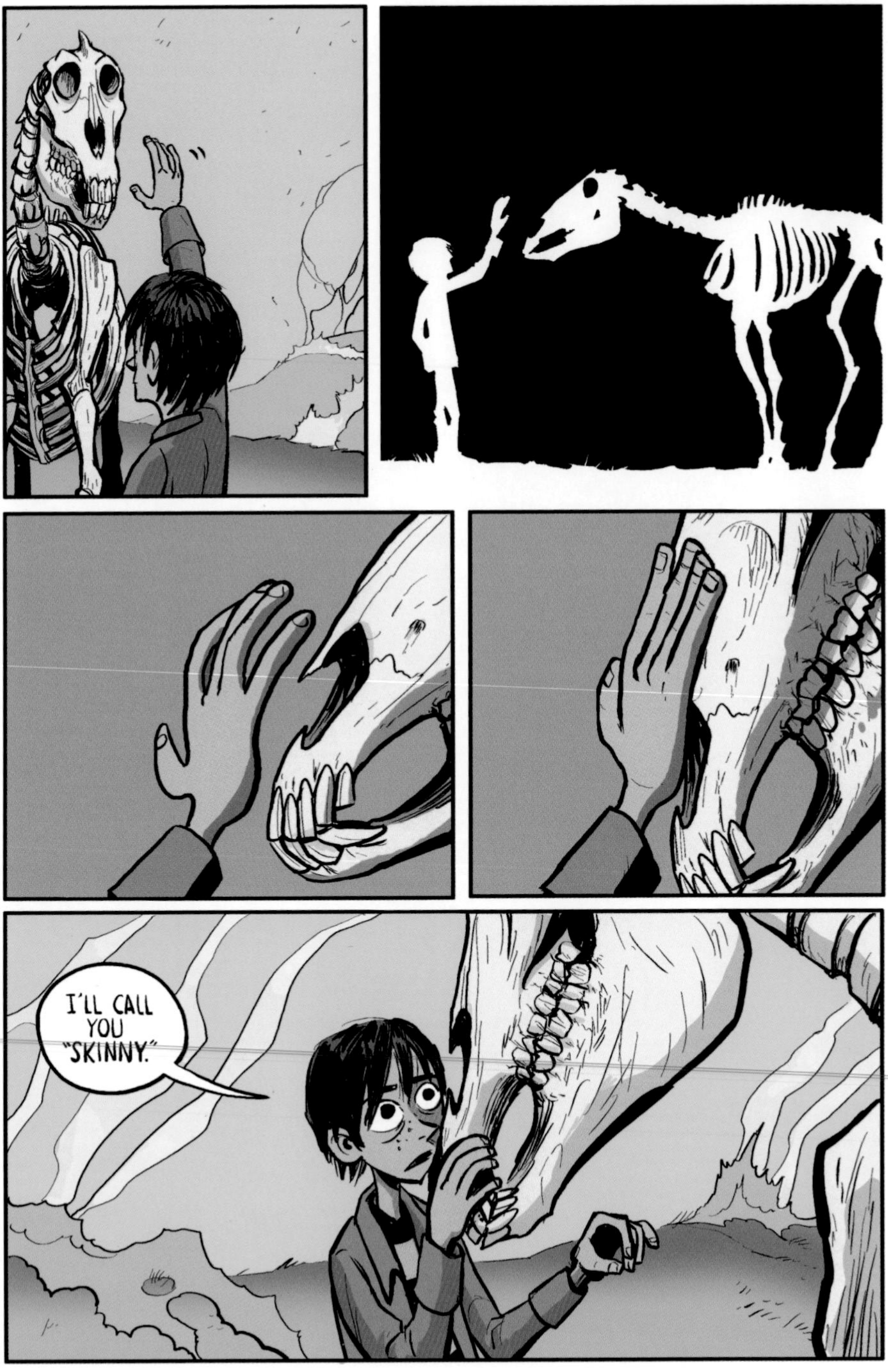
I'LL CALL YOU "SKINNY."

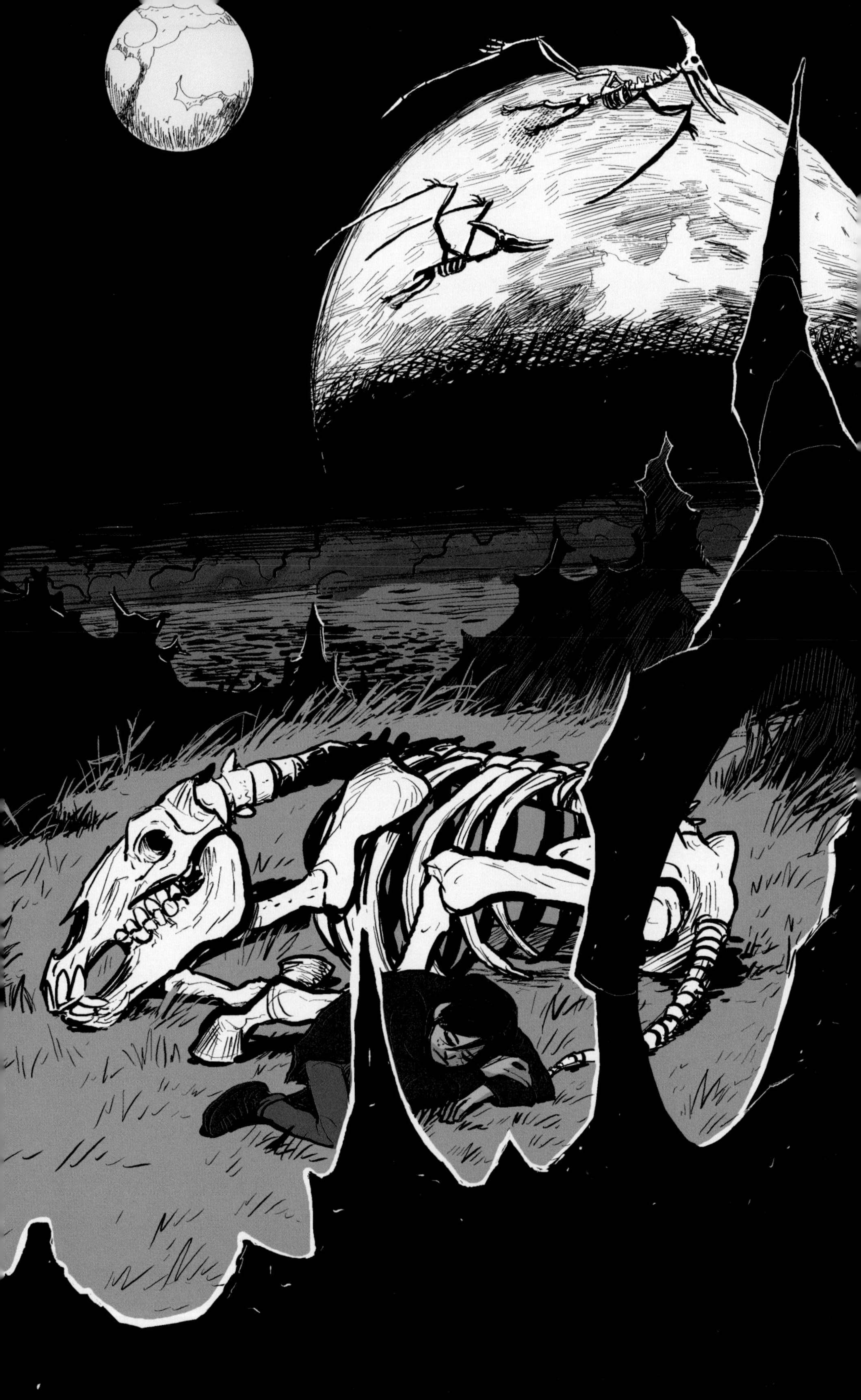

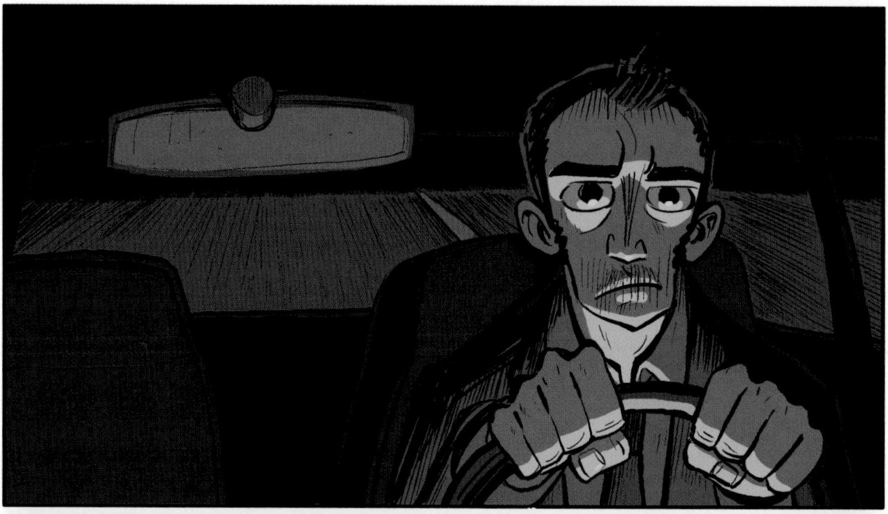

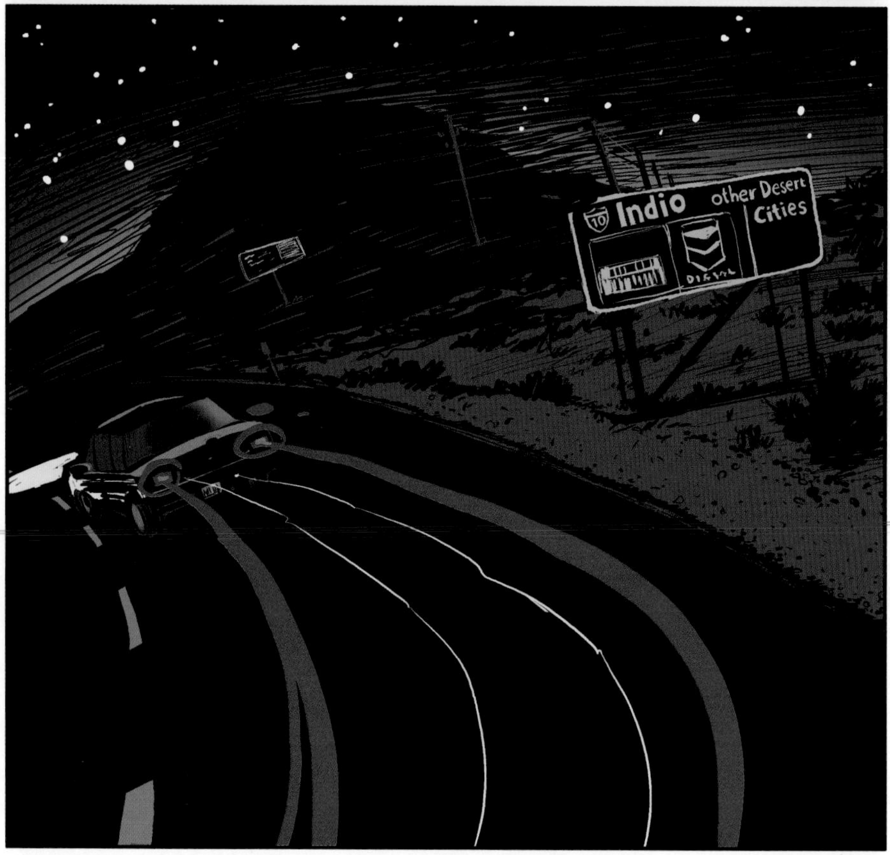
10
Indio
other Desert Cities

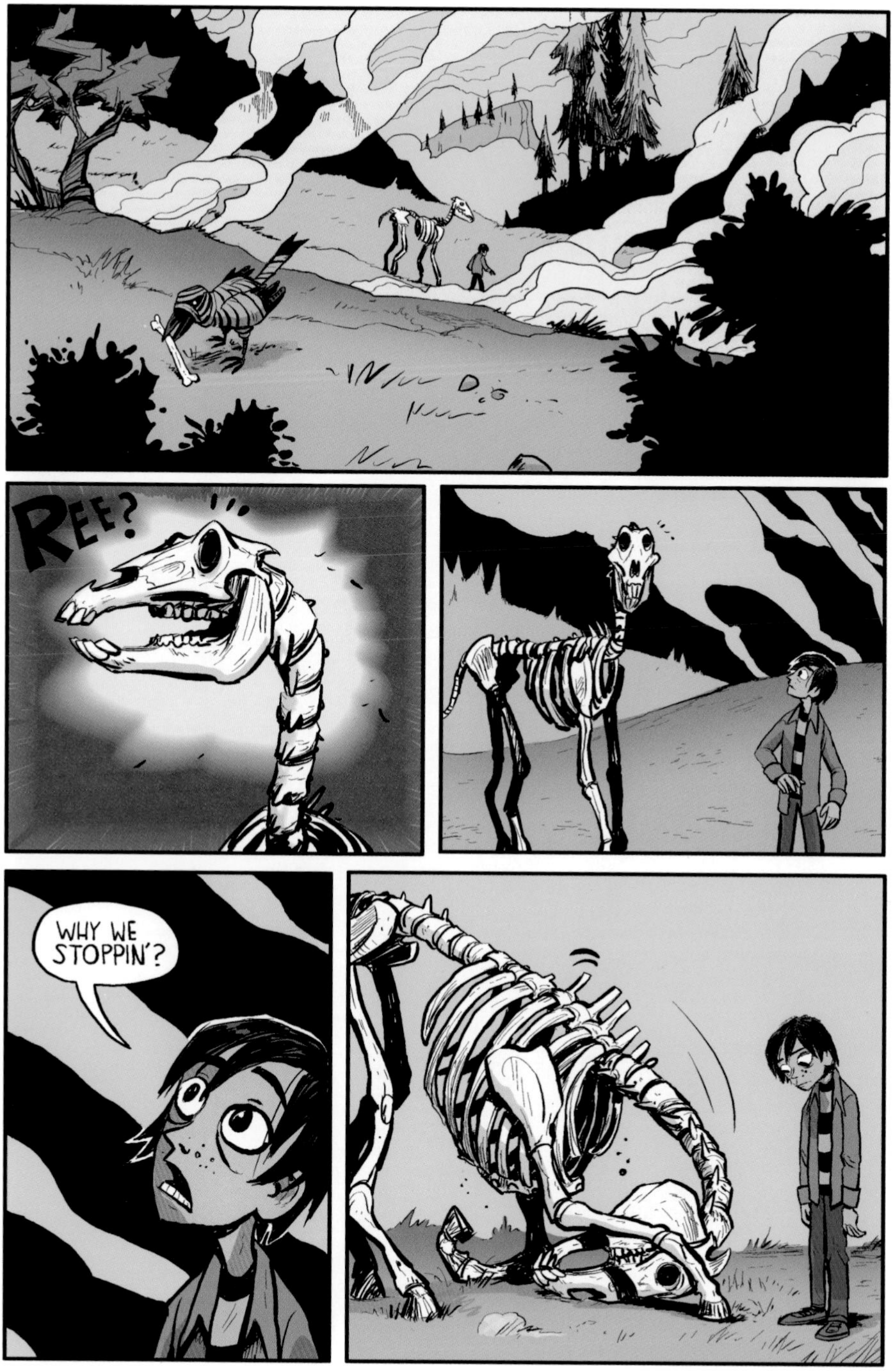
REE?
WHY WE STOPPIN'?

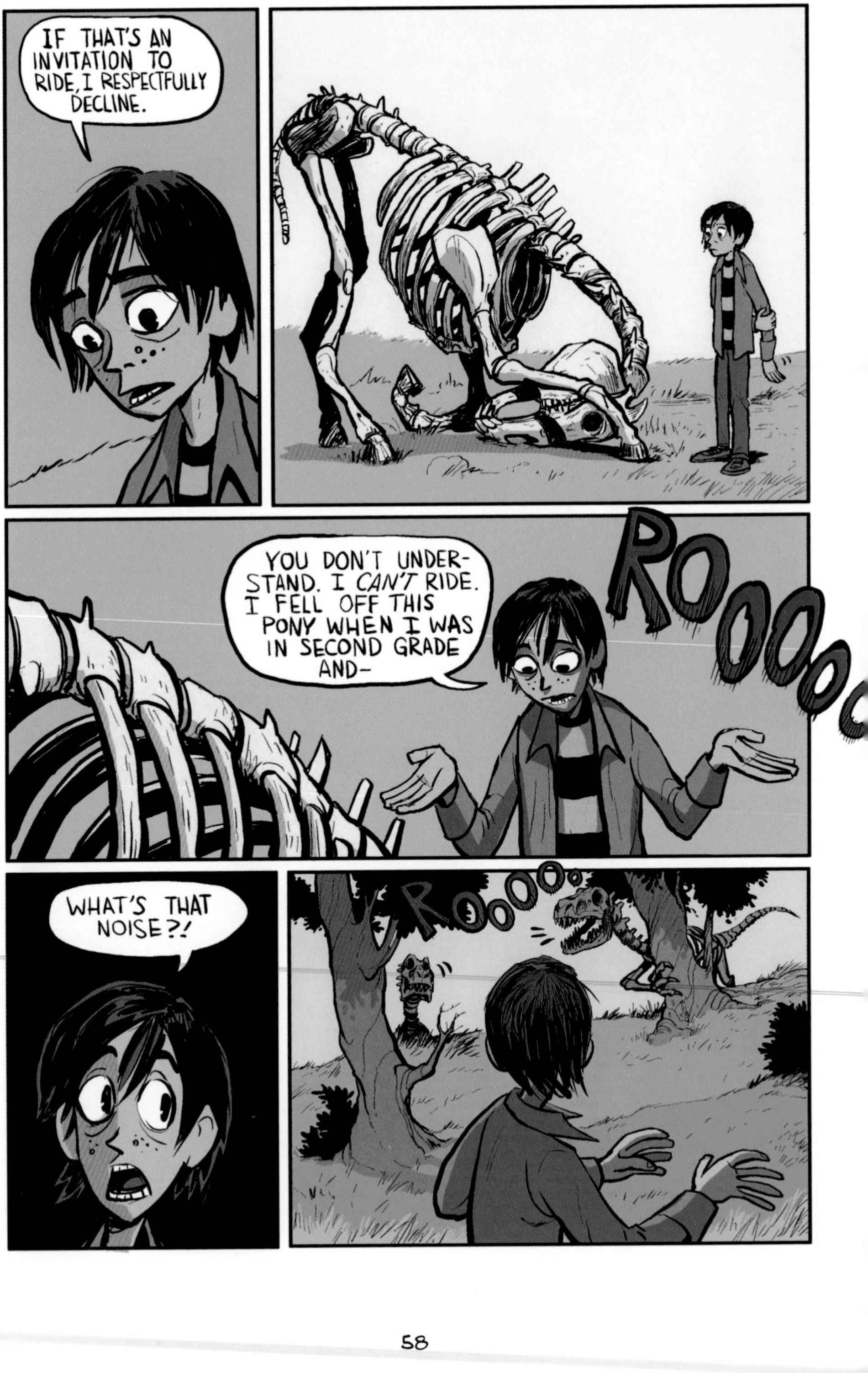
IF THAT'S AN INVITATION TO RIDE, I RESPECTFULLY DECLINE.
YOU DON'T UNDERSTAND. I CAN'T RIDE. I FELL OFF THIS PONY WHEN I WAS IN SECOND GRADE AND–
ROOOOO
WHAT'S THAT NOISE?!
ROOOOo

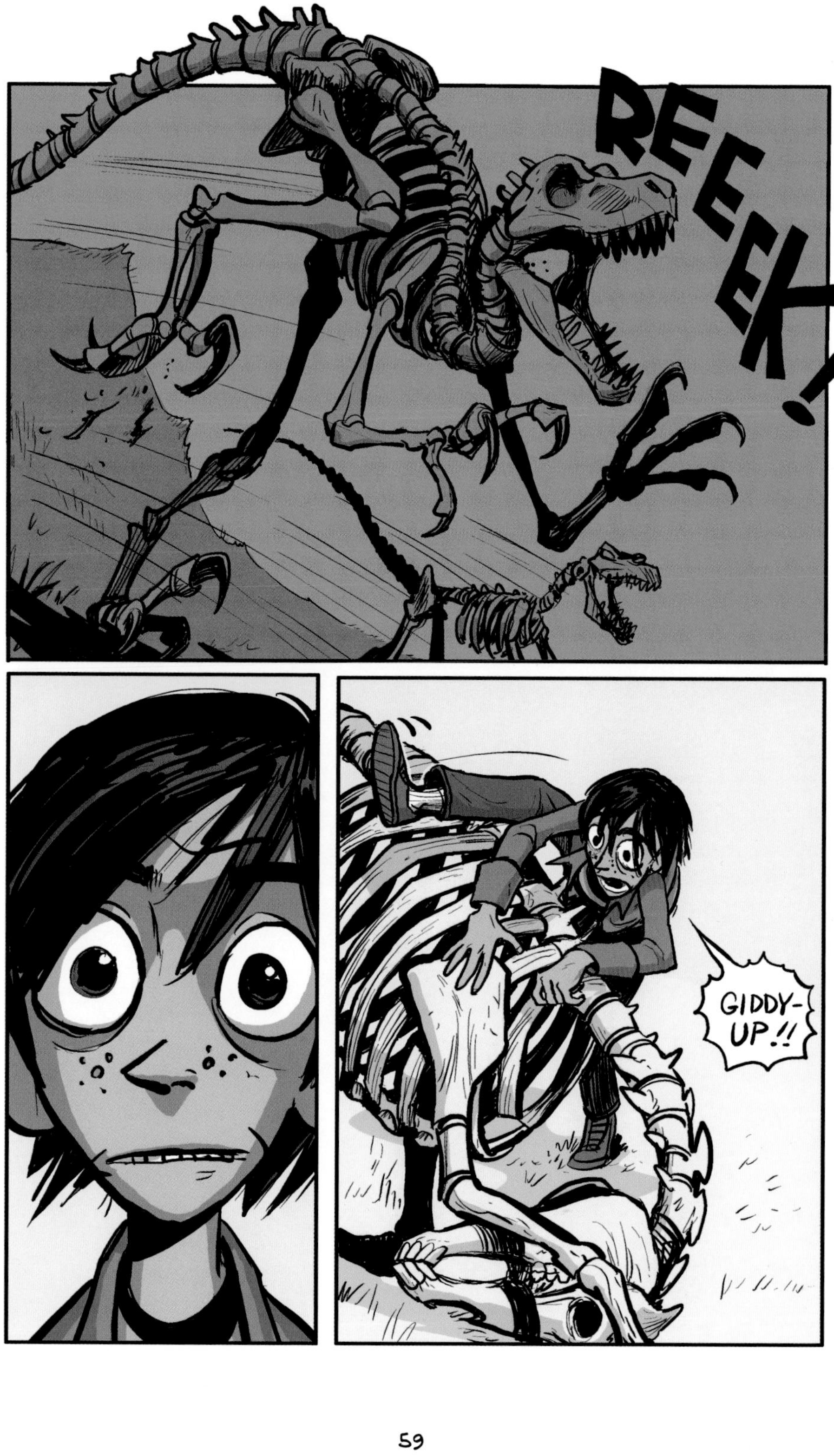
REEEK!
GIDDY-UP!!

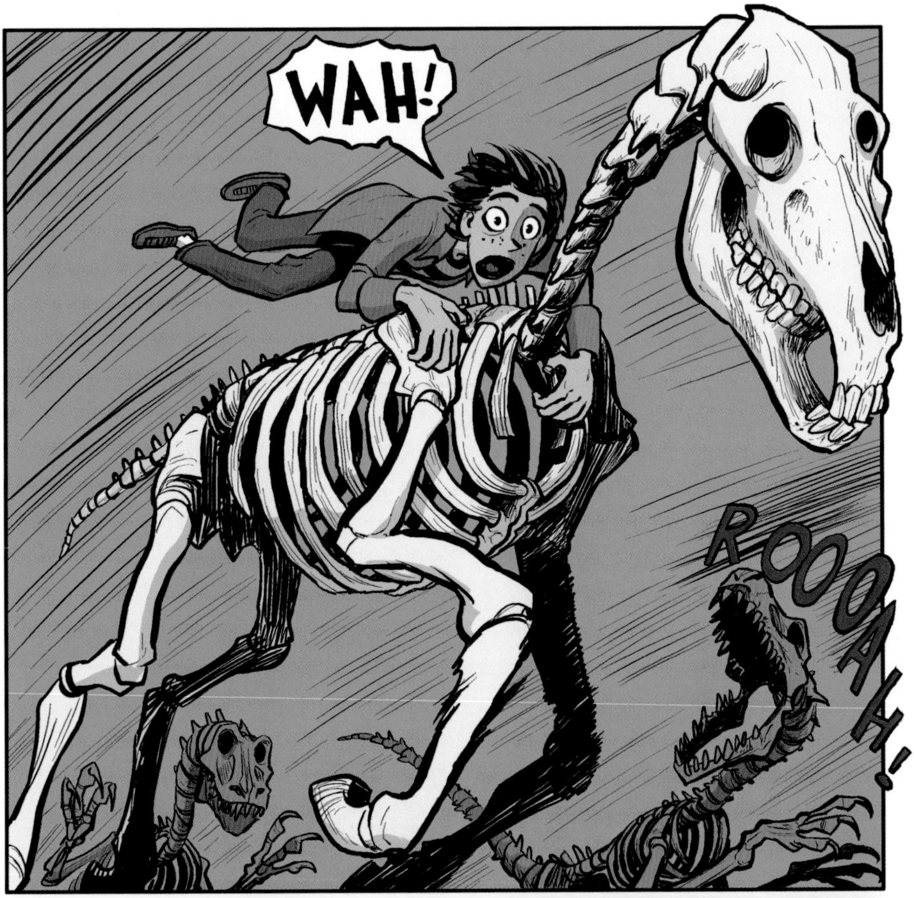
WAH!
ROOOAAH!!

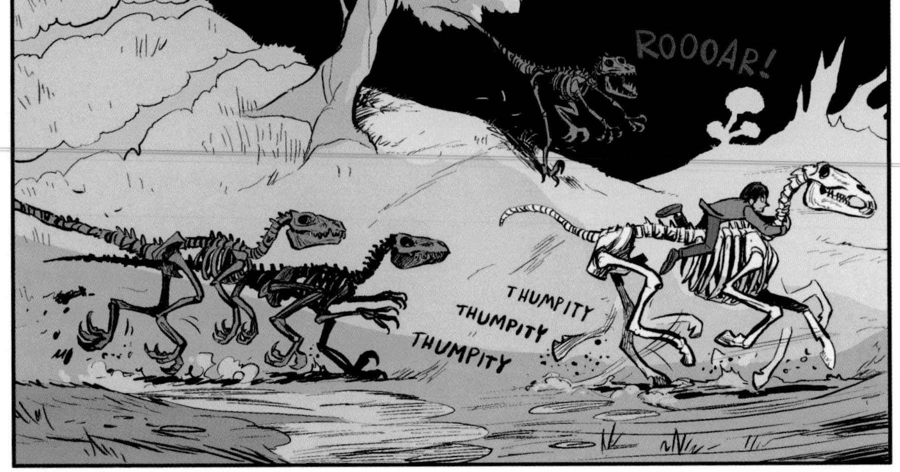
ROOOAR!
THUMPITY
THUMPITY
THUMPITY

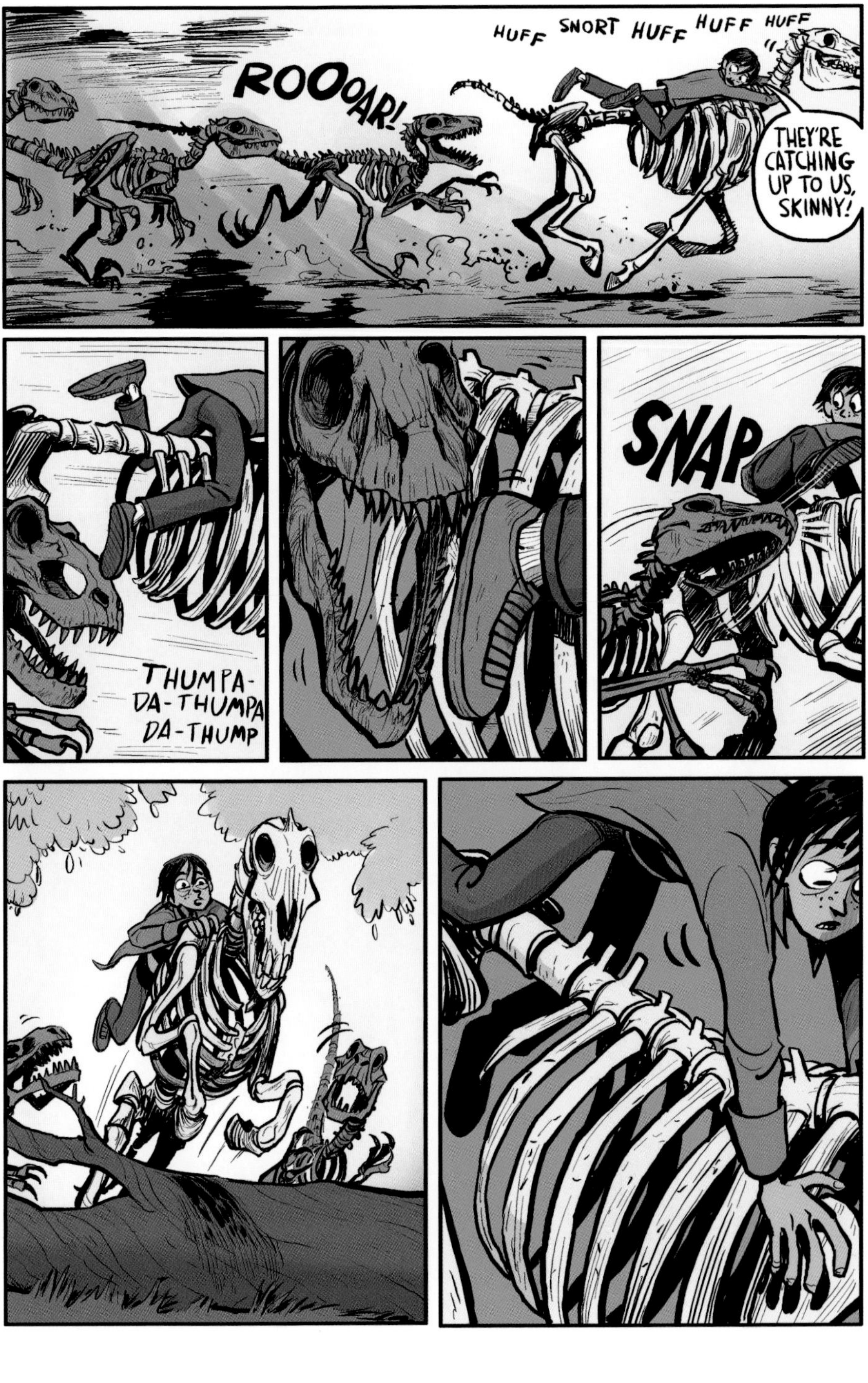
ROOOAR!
HUFF SNORT HUFF HUFF HUFF
THEY'RE CATCHING UP TO US, SKINNY!
THUMPA-DA-THUMPA DA-THUMP
SNAP

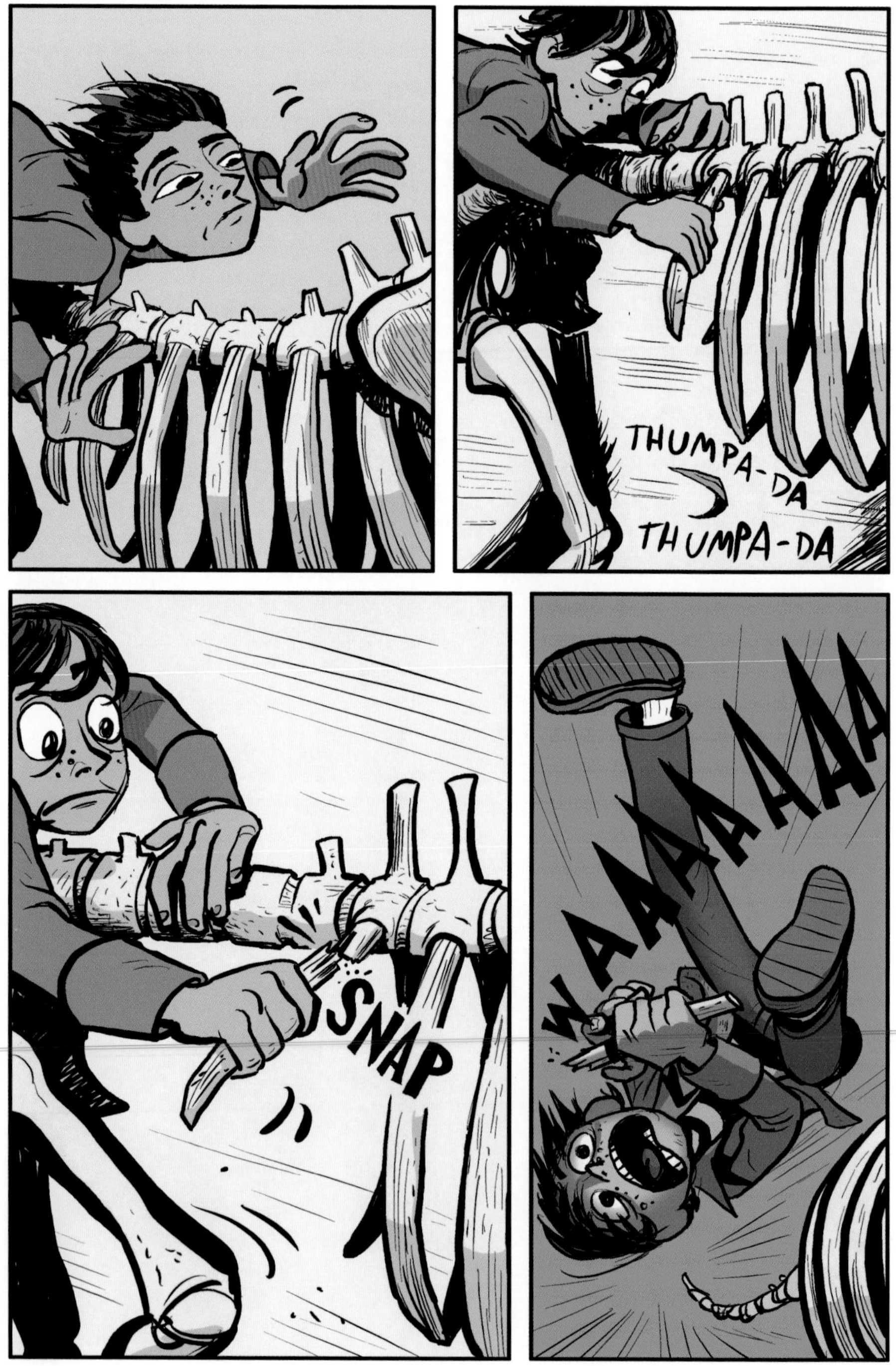
THUMPA-DA
THUMPA-DA
SNAP
WAAAAAAAA

UH!
ROOO!

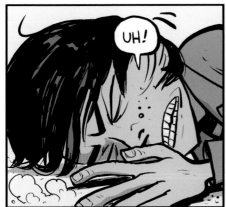

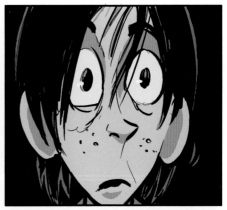

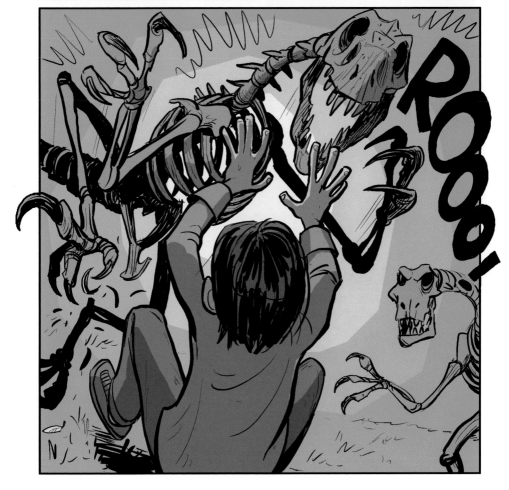

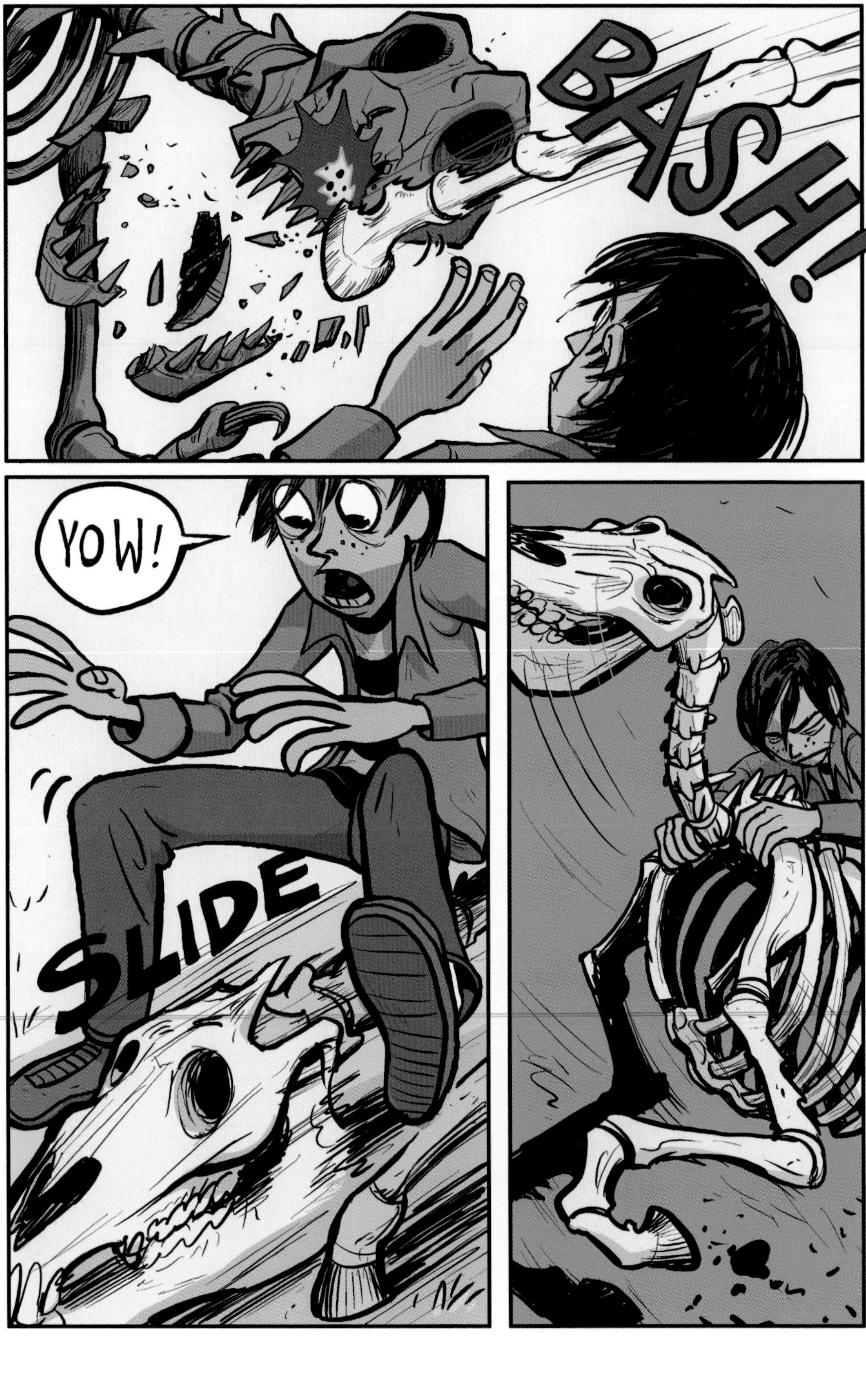
BASH!
YOW!
SLIDE

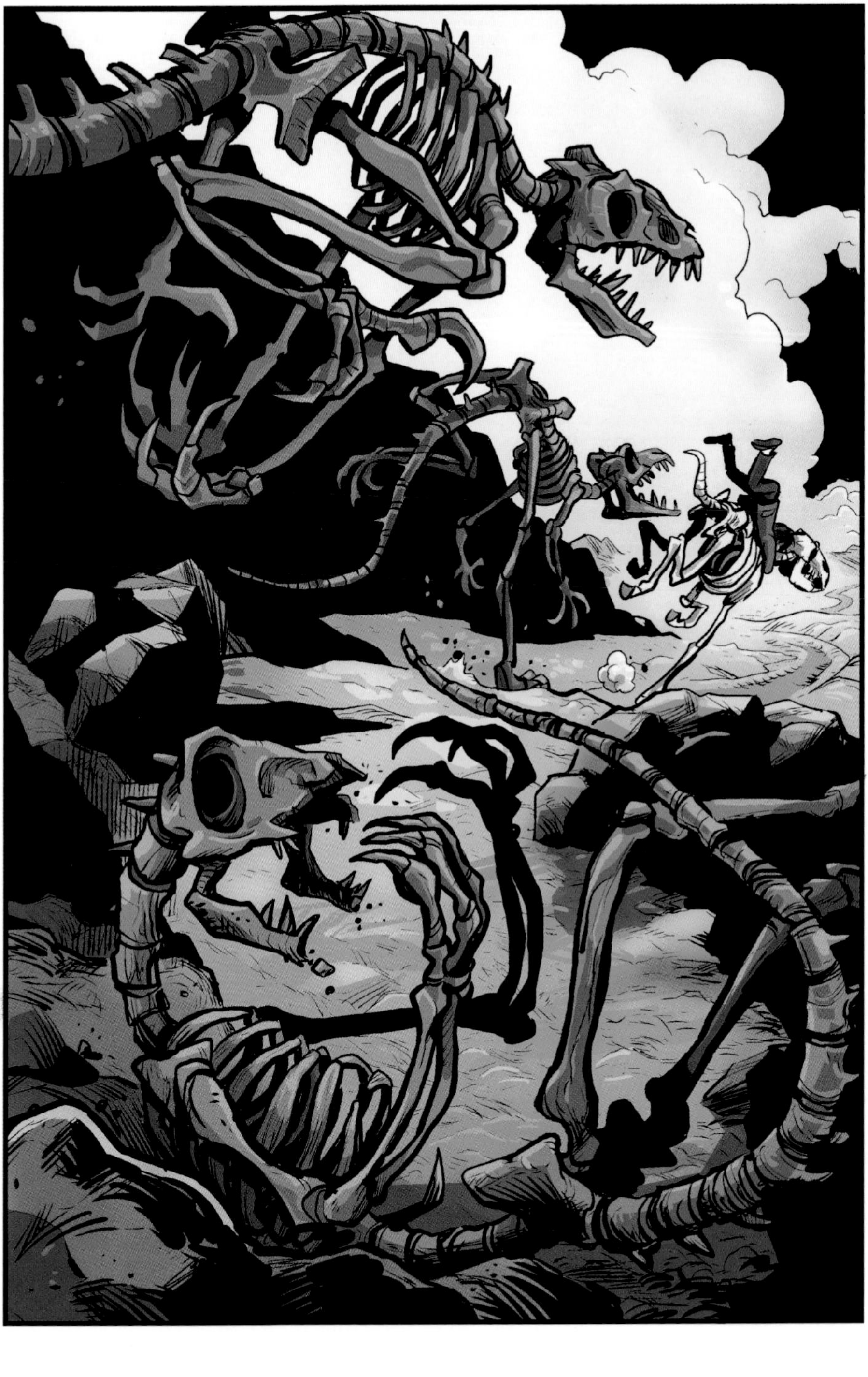

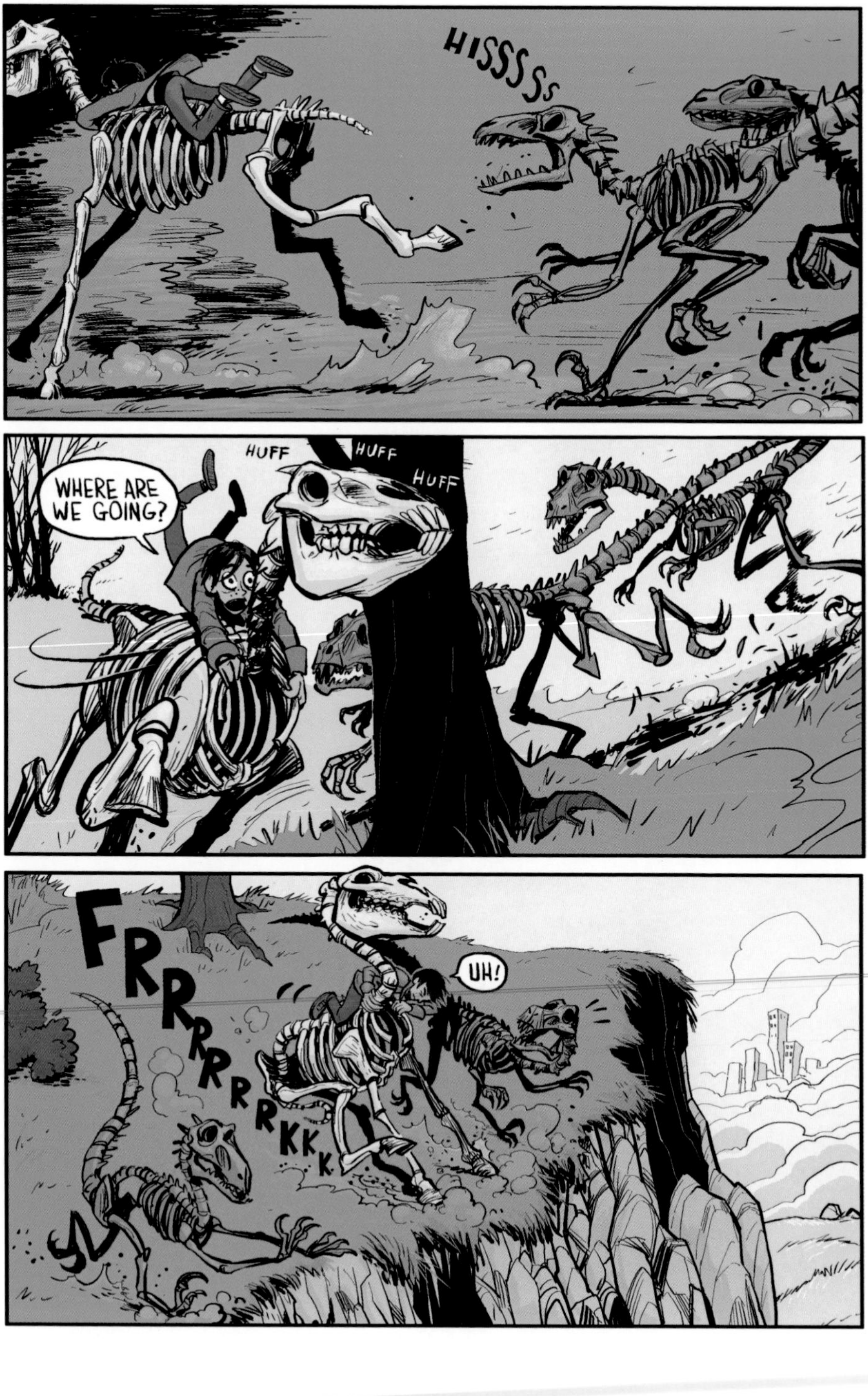
HISSSSSs
HUFF
HUFF
HUFF
WHERE ARE WE GOING?
FRRRRRRRKKK
UH!

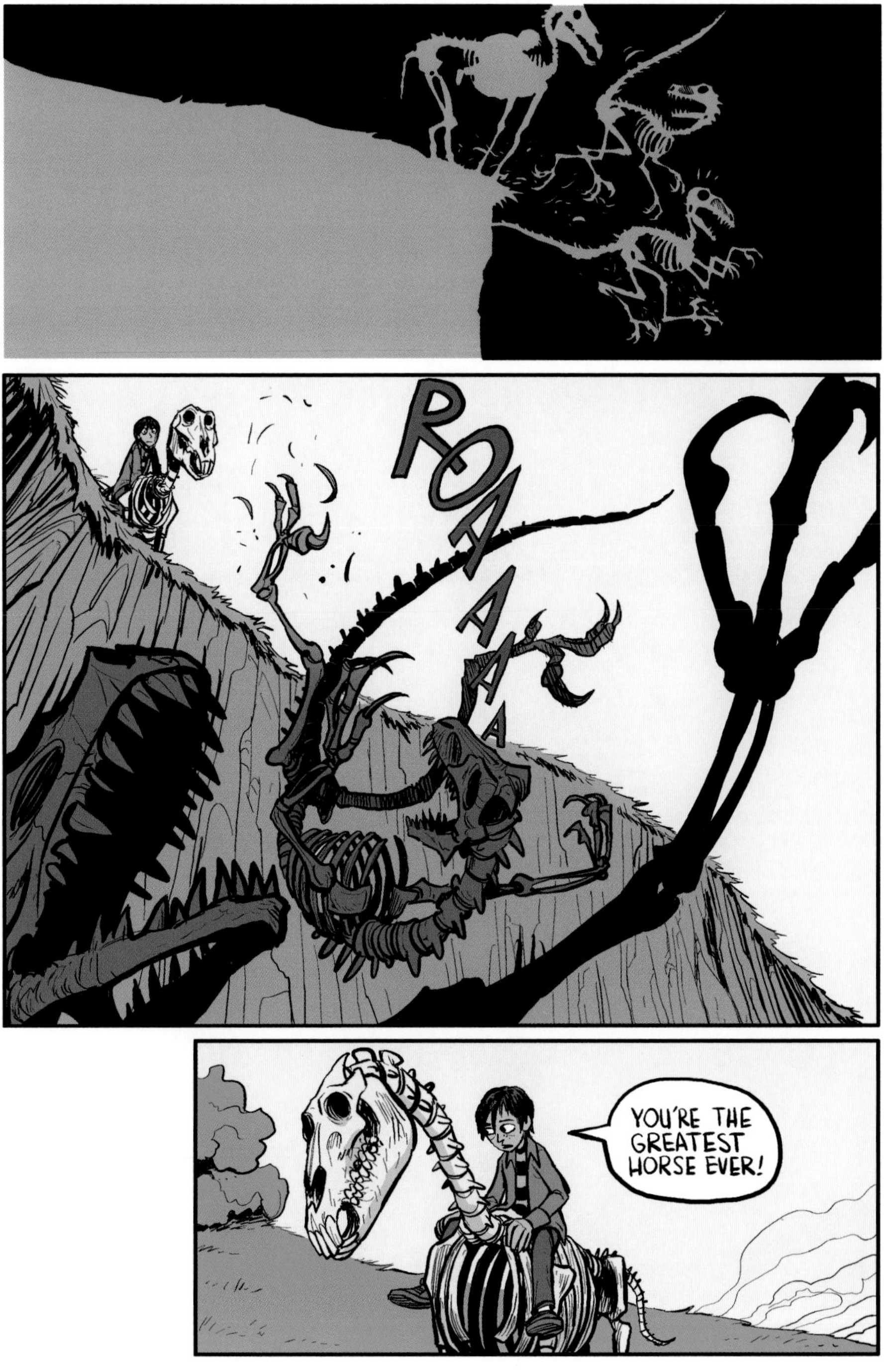
ROAAAAA
YOU'RE THE GREATEST HORSE EVER!

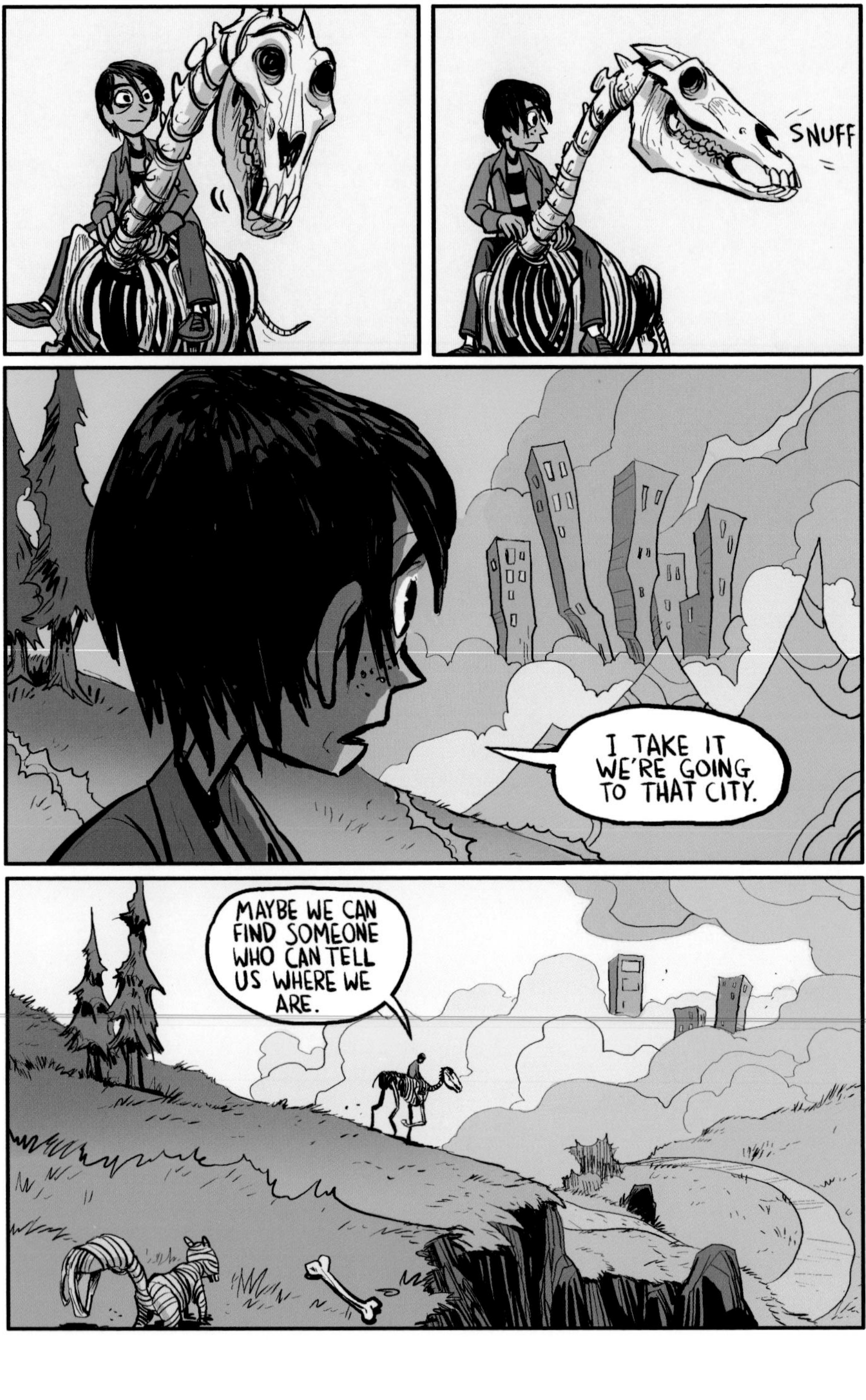
SNUFF
I TAKE IT WE'RE GOING TO THAT CITY.
MAYBE WE CAN FIND SOMEONE WHO CAN TELL US WHERE WE ARE.

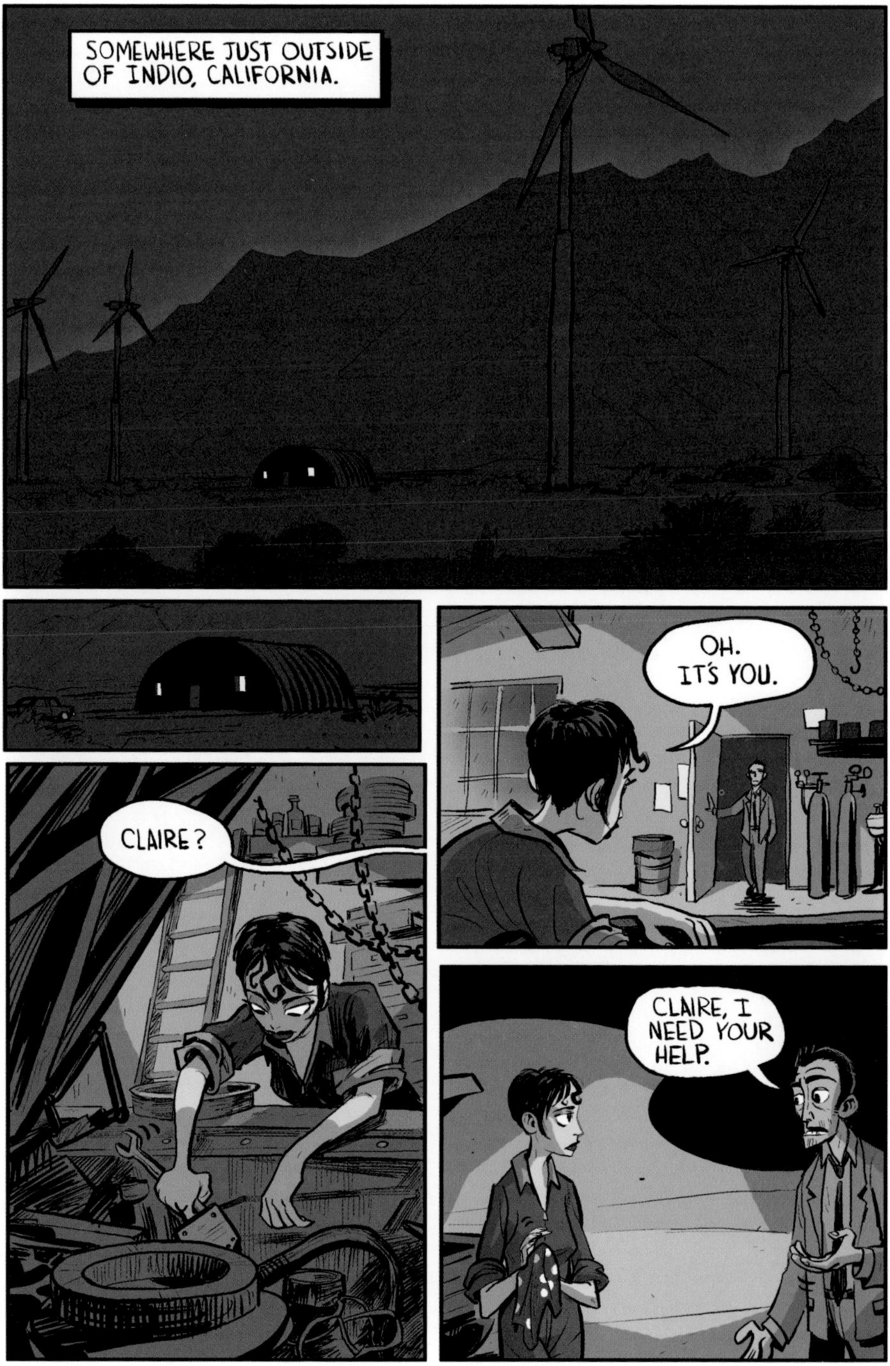
SOMEWHERE JUST OUTSIDE OF INDIO, CALIFORNIA.
OH. IT'S YOU.
CLAIRE?
CLAIRE, I NEED YOUR HELP.

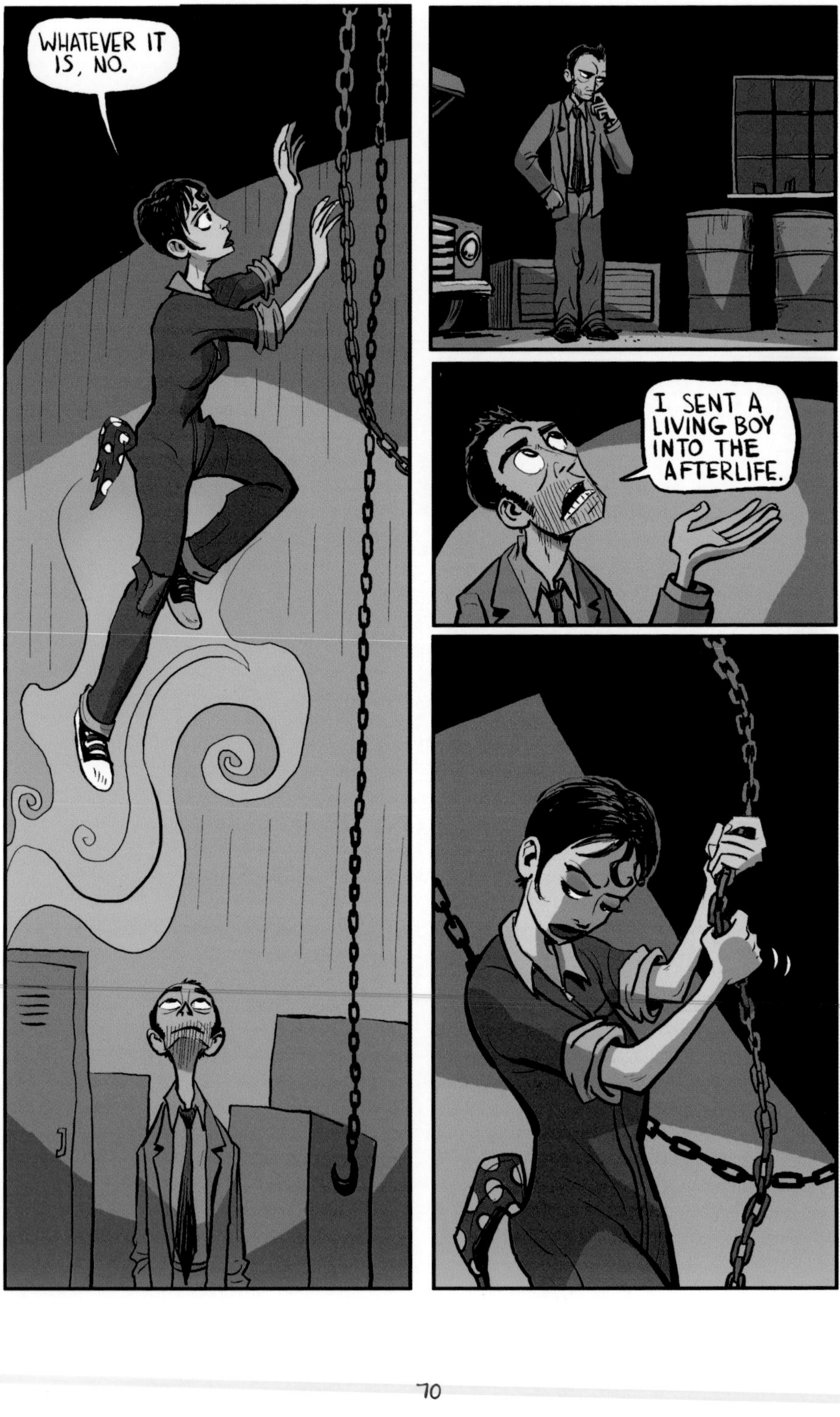
WHATEVER IT IS, NO.
I SENT A LIVING BOY INTO THE AFTERLIFE.

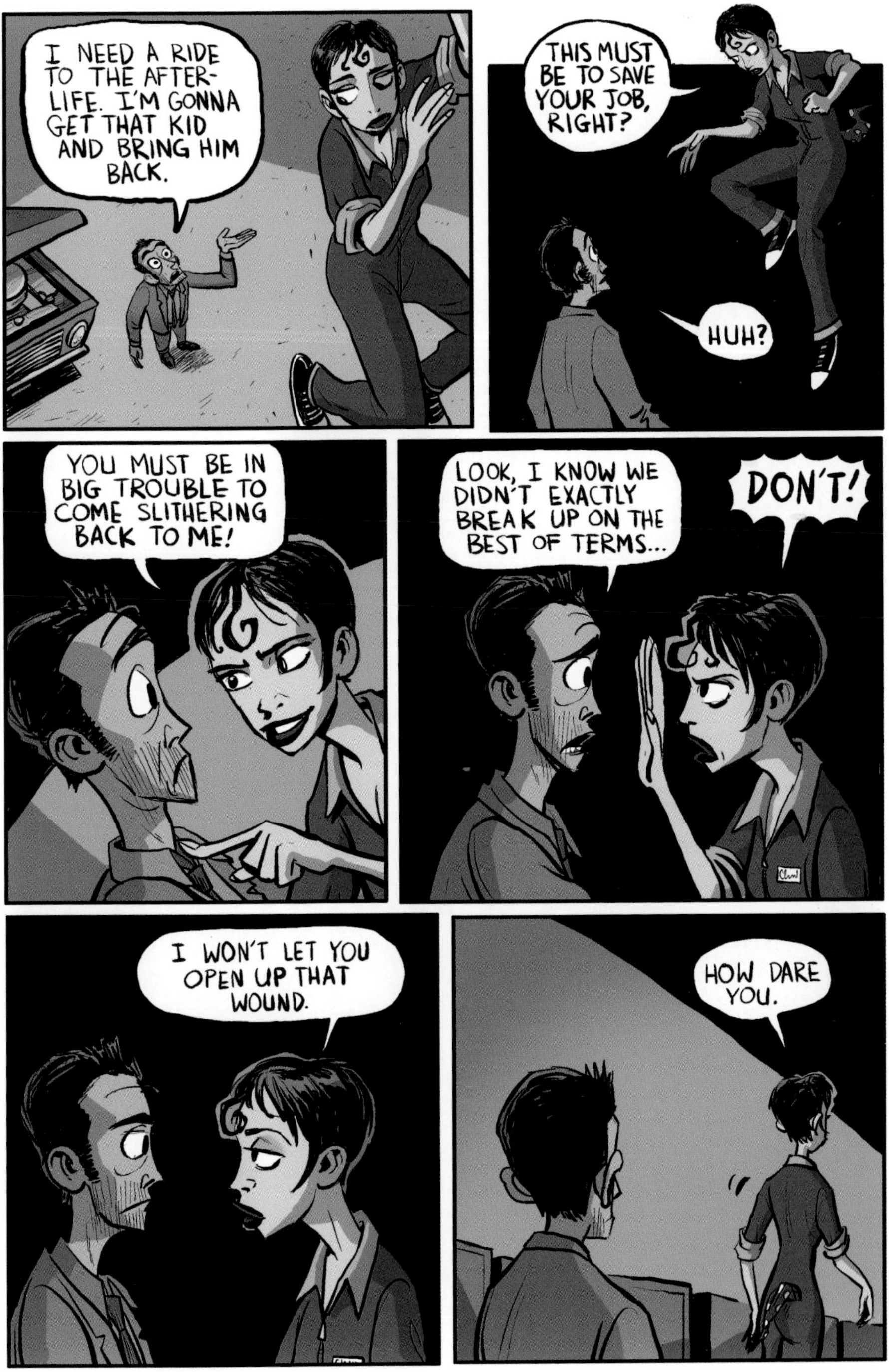
I NEED A RIDE TO THE AFTER-LIFE. I'M GONNA GET THAT KID AND BRING HIM BACK.
THIS MUST BE TO SAVE YOUR JOB, RIGHT?
HUH?
YOU MUST BE IN BIG TROUBLE TO COME SLITHERING BACK TO ME!
LOOK, I KNOW WE DIDN'T EXACTLY BREAK UP ON THE BEST OF TERMS...
DON'T!
I WON'T LET YOU OPEN UP THAT WOUND.
HOW DARE YOU.

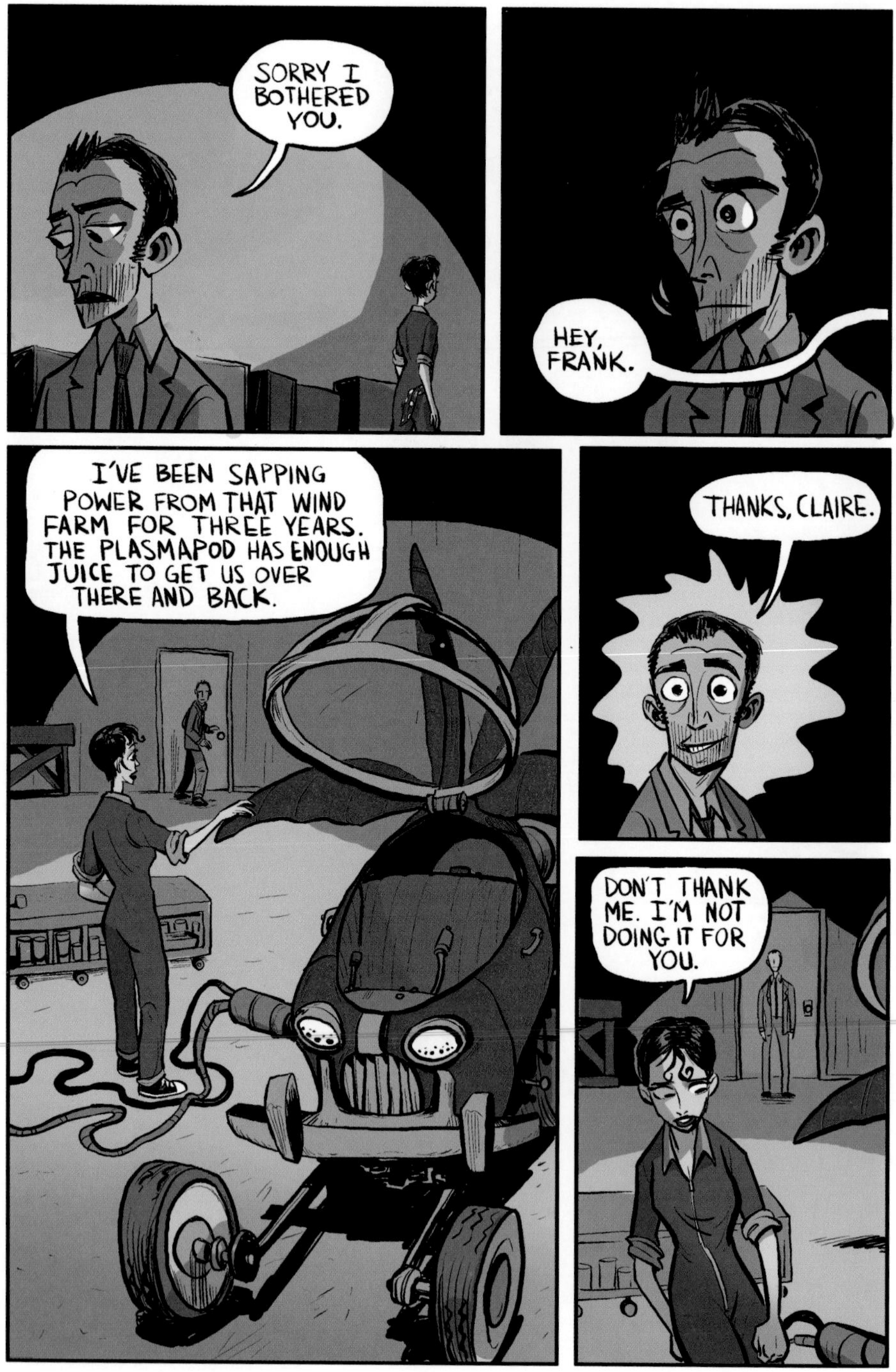
SORRY I BOTHERED YOU.
HEY, FRANK.
I'VE BEEN SAPPING POWER FROM THAT WIND FARM FOR THREE YEARS. THE PLASMAPOD HAS ENOUGH JUICE TO GET US OVER THERE AND BACK.
THANKS, CLAIRE.
DON'T THANK ME. I'M NOT DOING IT FOR YOU.

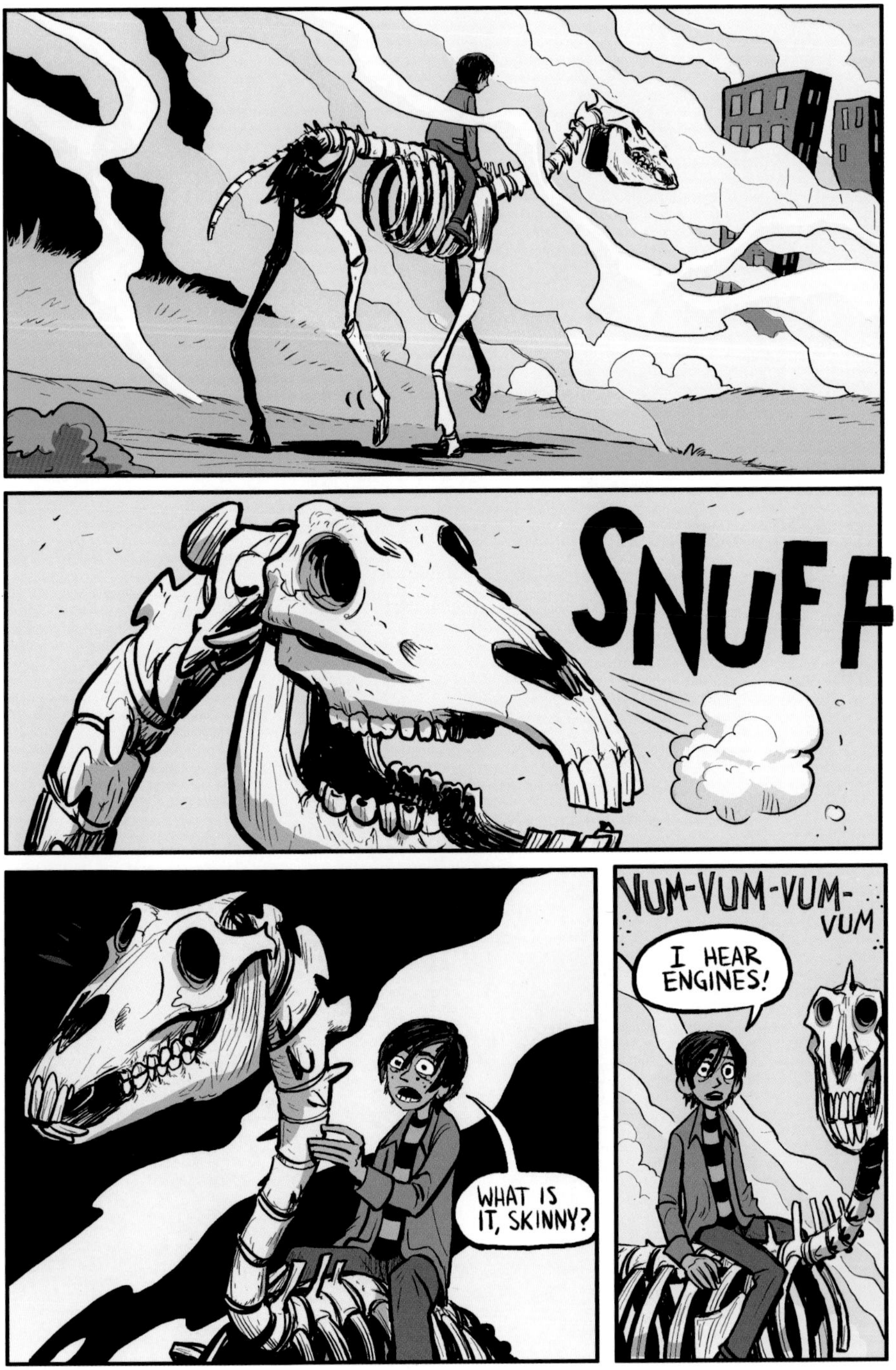
SNUFF
WHAT IS IT, SKINNY?
VUM-VUM-VUM-VUM
I HEAR ENGINES!

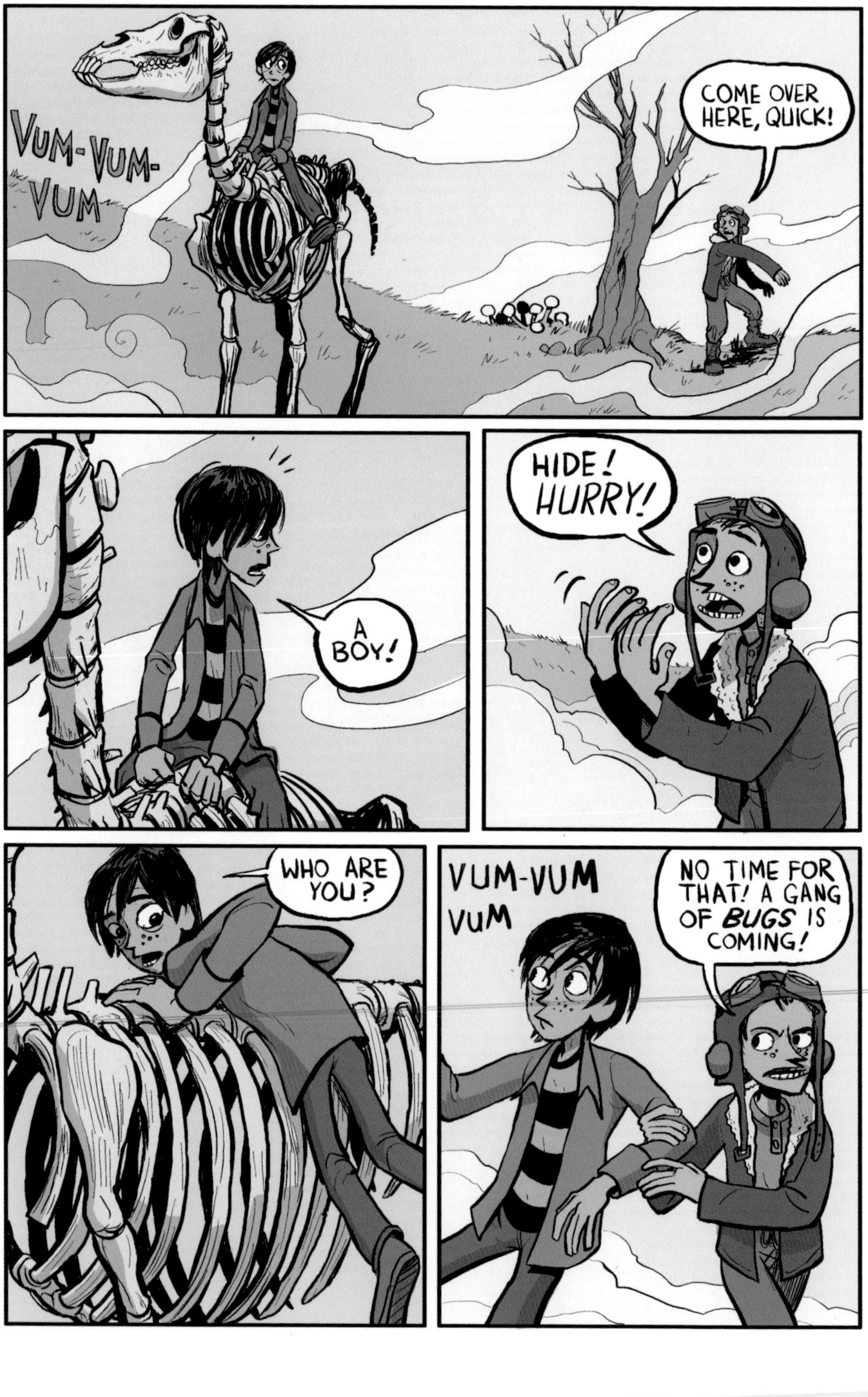
VUM-VUM-VUM
COME OVER HERE, QUICK!
A BOY!
HIDE! HURRY!
WHO ARE YOU?
VUM-VUM VUM
NO TIME FOR THAT! A GANG OF **BUGS** IS COMING!

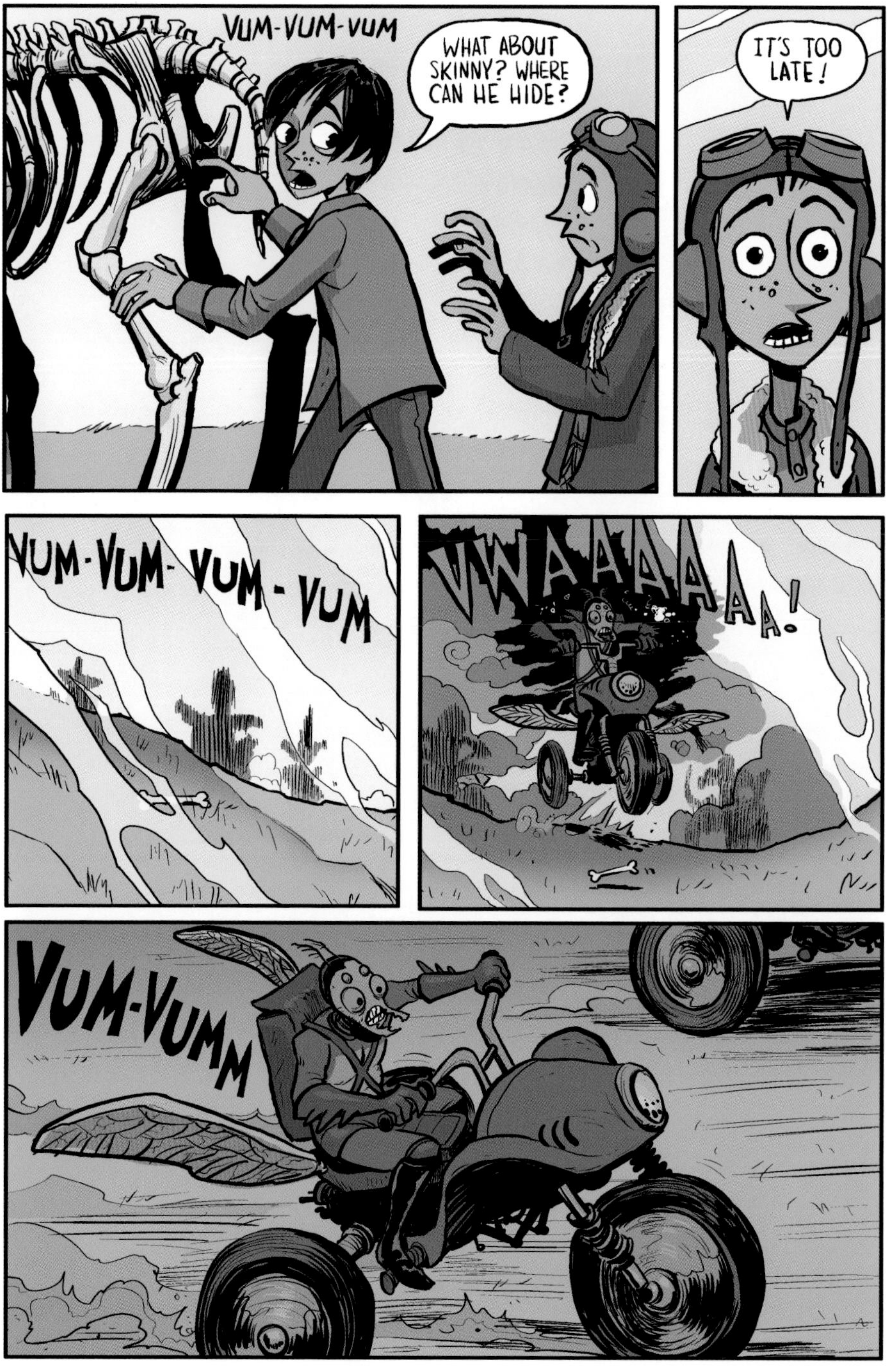

VUM-VUM-VUM
WHAT ABOUT SKINNY? WHERE CAN HE HIDE?
IT'S TOO LATE!
VUM-VUM-VUM-VUM
VWAAAAAA!
VUM-VUMM

FRRRRKK!!

PUTT
PUTT
PUTT

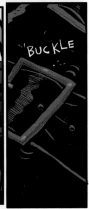

BUCKLE

SNUFF

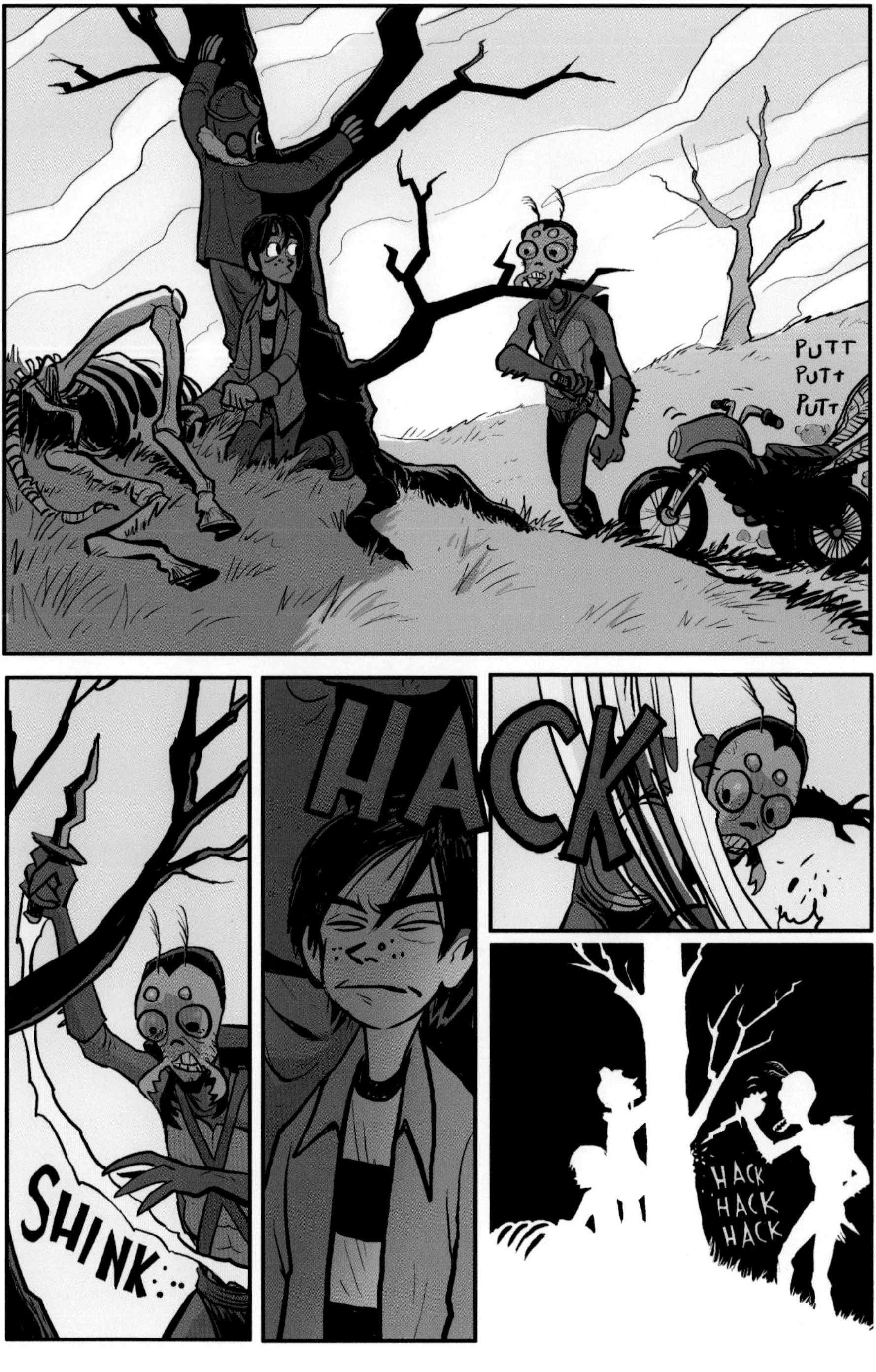
PUTT
PUTT
PUTT
SHINK
HACK
HACK
HACK
HACK

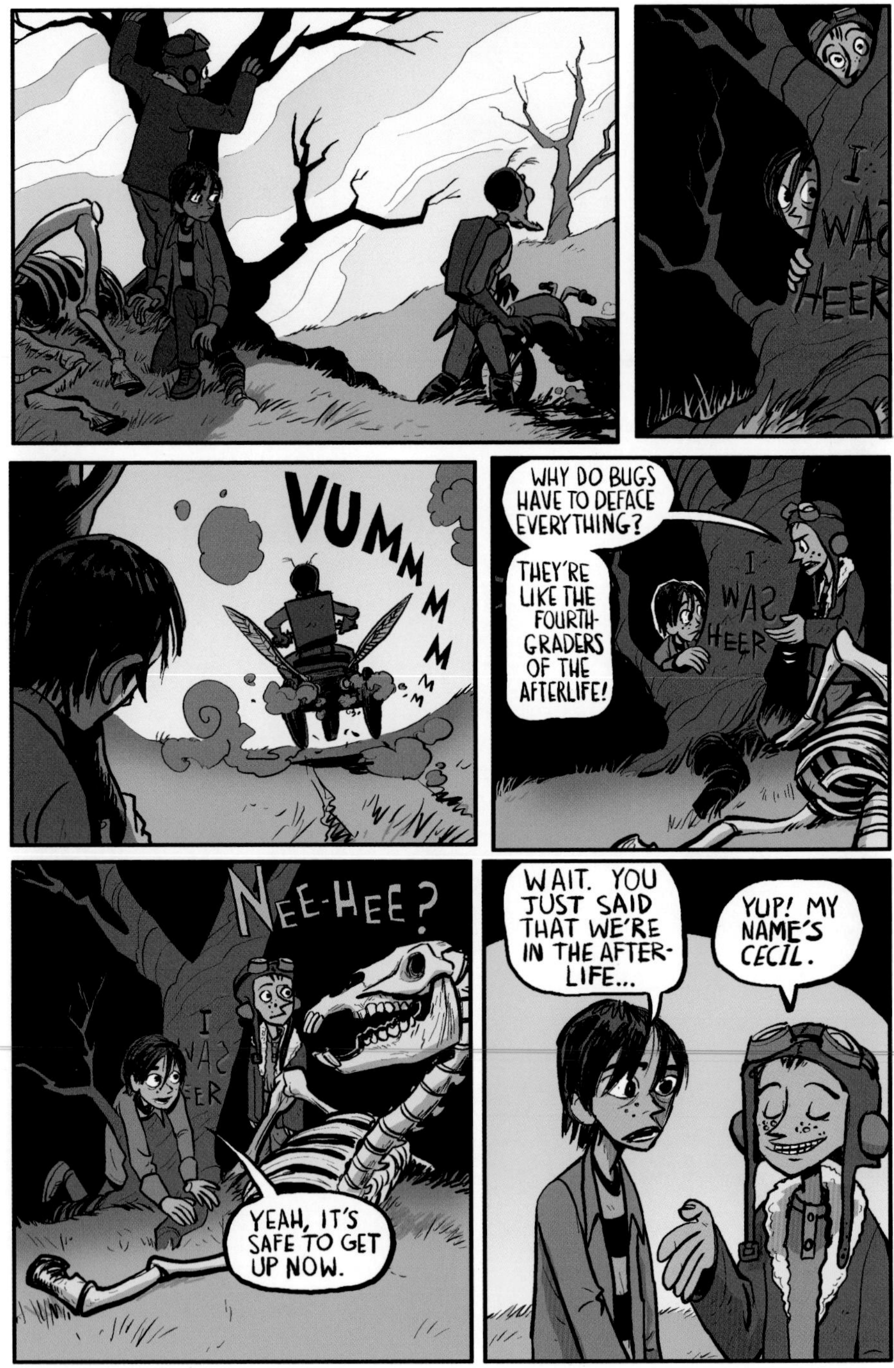
I WAS HEER
VUMMMMMMM
WHY DO BUGS HAVE TO DEFACE EVERYTHING?
THEY'RE LIKE THE FOURTH-GRADERS OF THE AFTERLIFE!
NEE-HEE?
YEAH, IT'S SAFE TO GET UP NOW.
WAIT. YOU JUST SAID THAT WE'RE IN THE AFTER-LIFE...
YUP! MY NAME'S CECIL.

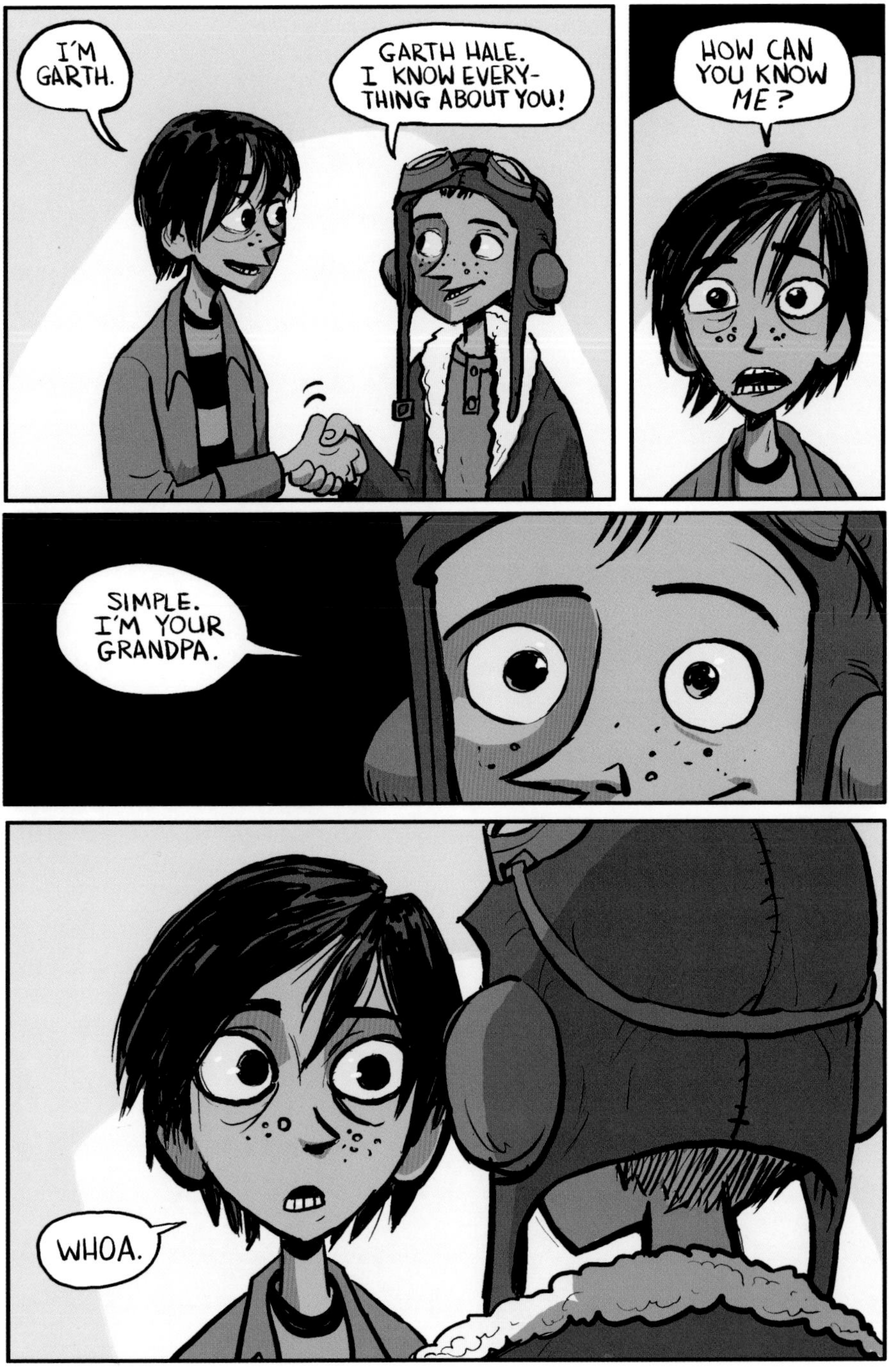
I'M GARTH.
GARTH HALE. I KNOW EVERYTHING ABOUT YOU!
HOW CAN YOU KNOW ME?
SIMPLE. I'M YOUR GRANDPA.
WHOA.

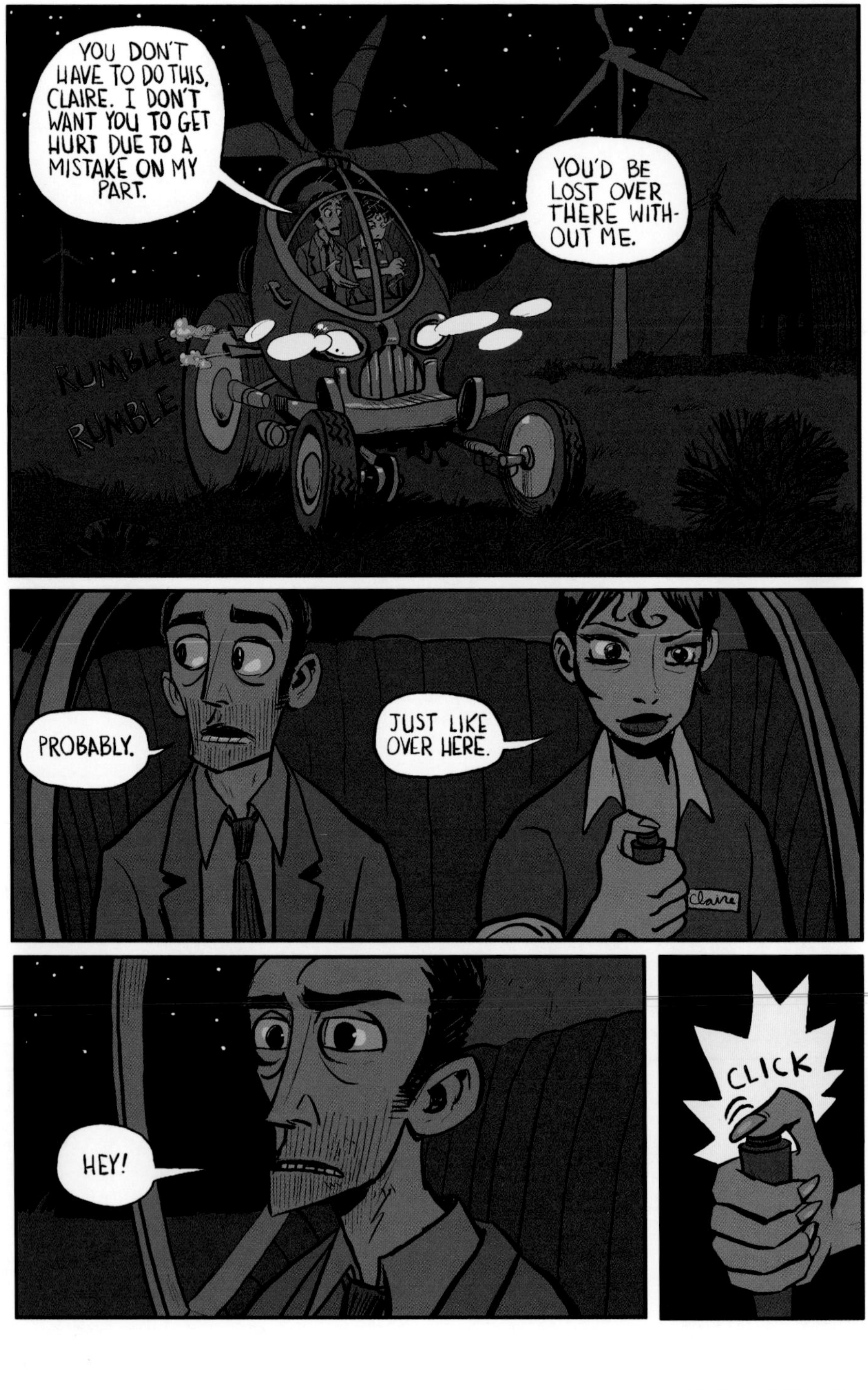
YOU DON'T HAVE TO DO THIS, CLAIRE. I DON'T WANT YOU TO GET HURT DUE TO A MISTAKE ON MY PART.
YOU'D BE LOST OVER THERE WITH-OUT ME.
RUMBLE RUMBLE
PROBABLY.
JUST LIKE OVER HERE.
Claire
HEY!
CLICK

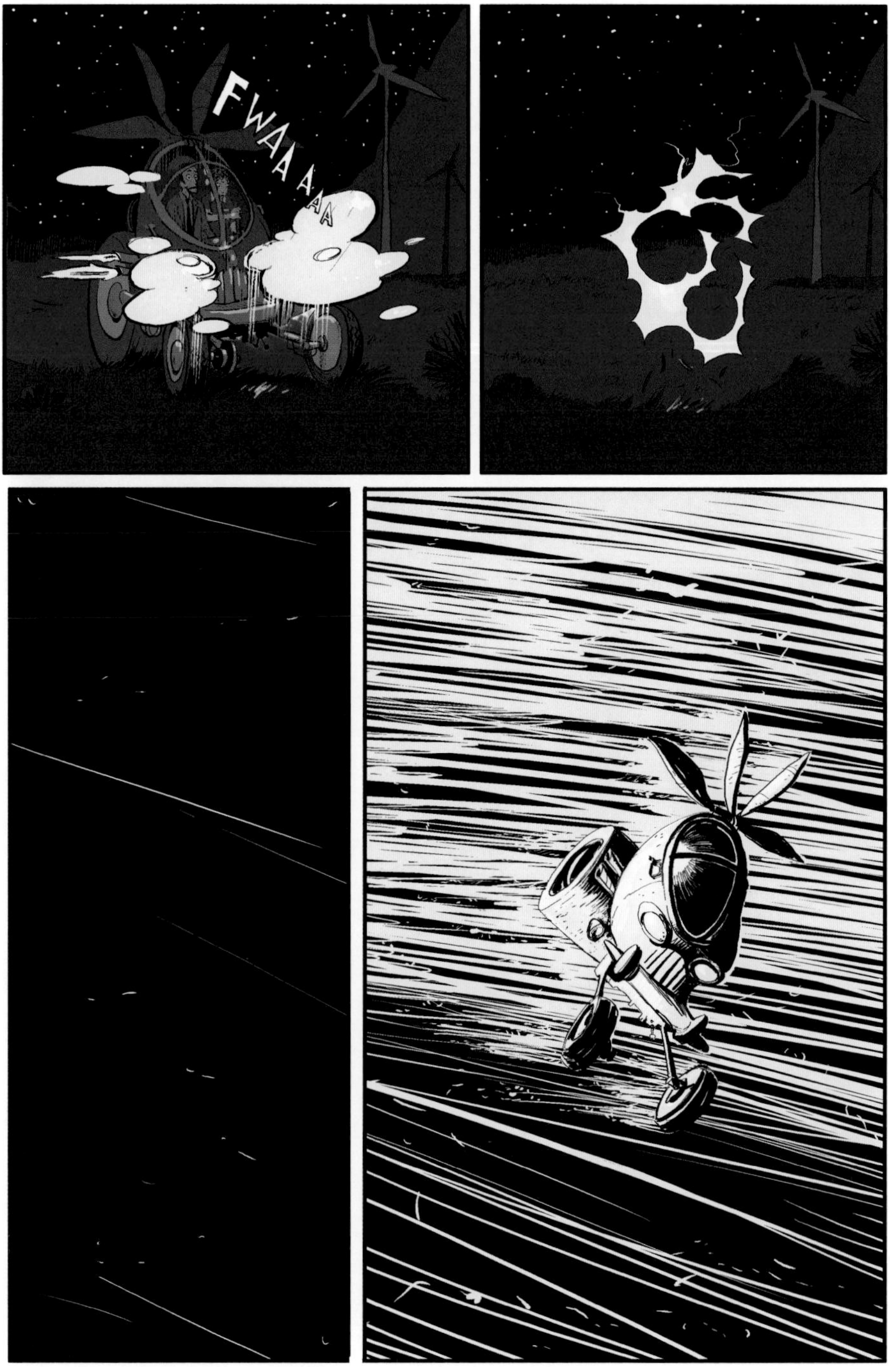
FWAAAAAA

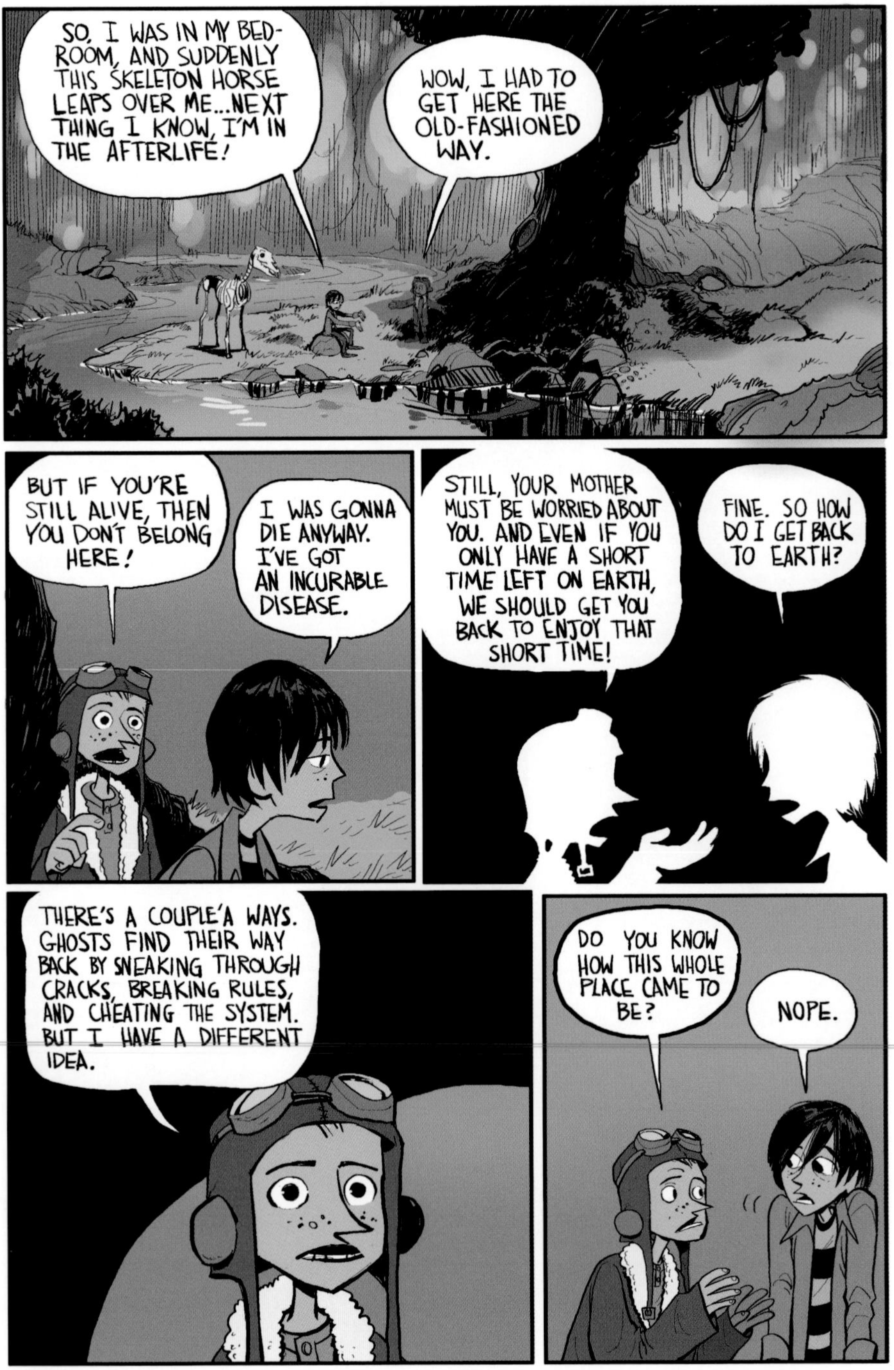
SO, I WAS IN MY BEDROOM, AND SUDDENLY THIS SKELETON HORSE LEAPS OVER ME...NEXT THING I KNOW, I'M IN THE AFTERLIFE!
WOW, I HAD TO GET HERE THE OLD-FASHIONED WAY.
BUT IF YOU'RE STILL ALIVE, THEN YOU DON'T BELONG HERE!
I WAS GONNA DIE ANYWAY. I'VE GOT AN INCURABLE DISEASE.
STILL, YOUR MOTHER MUST BE WORRIED ABOUT YOU. AND EVEN IF YOU ONLY HAVE A SHORT TIME LEFT ON EARTH, WE SHOULD GET YOU BACK TO ENJOY THAT SHORT TIME!
FINE. SO HOW DO I GET BACK TO EARTH?
THERE'S A COUPLE'A WAYS. GHOSTS FIND THEIR WAY BACK BY SNEAKING THROUGH CRACKS, BREAKING RULES, AND CHEATING THE SYSTEM. BUT I HAVE A DIFFERENT IDEA.
DO YOU KNOW HOW THIS WHOLE PLACE CAME TO BE?
NOPE.

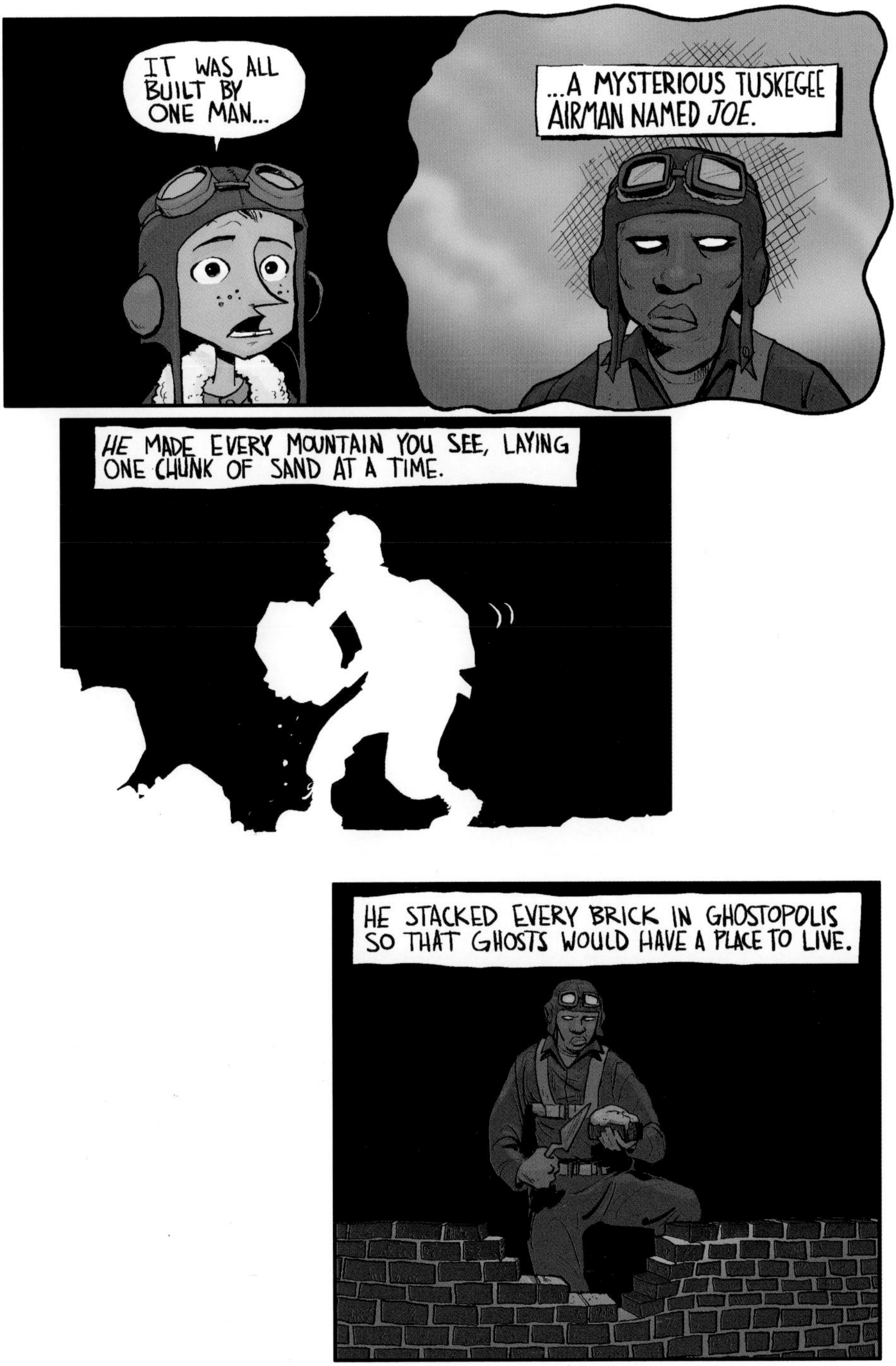
IT WAS ALL BUILT BY ONE MAN...
...A MYSTERIOUS TUSKEGEE AIRMAN NAMED JOE.
HE MADE EVERY MOUNTAIN YOU SEE, LAYING ONE CHUNK OF SAND AT A TIME.
HE STACKED EVERY BRICK IN GHOSTOPOLIS SO THAT GHOSTS WOULD HAVE A PLACE TO LIVE.

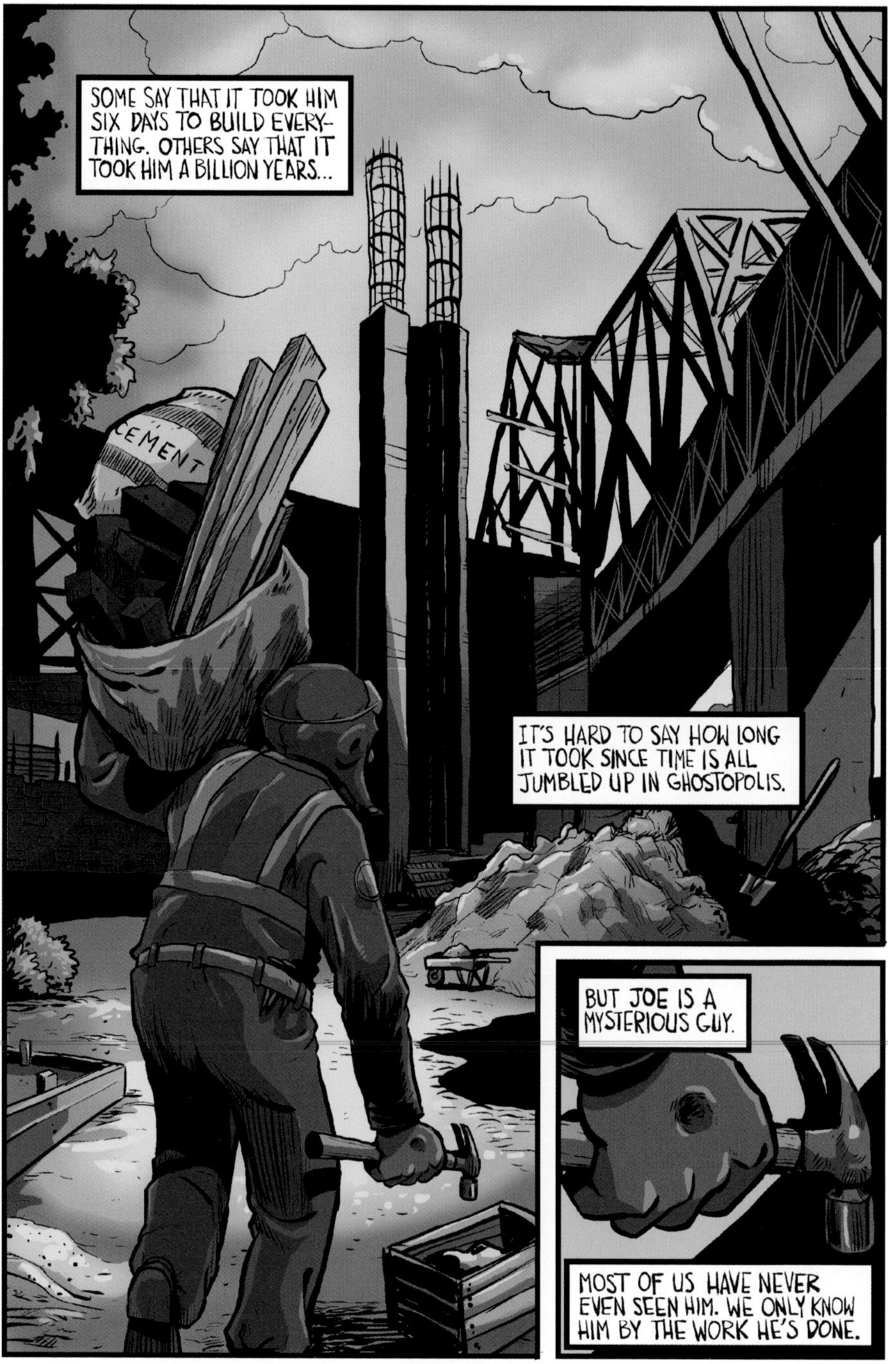
SOME SAY THAT IT TOOK HIM SIX DAYS TO BUILD EVERYTHING. OTHERS SAY THAT IT TOOK HIM A BILLION YEARS...
CEMENT
IT'S HARD TO SAY HOW LONG IT TOOK SINCE TIME IS ALL JUMBLED UP IN GHOSTOPOLIS.
BUT JOE IS A MYSTERIOUS GUY.
MOST OF US HAVE NEVER EVEN SEEN HIM. WE ONLY KNOW HIM BY THE WORK HE'S DONE.

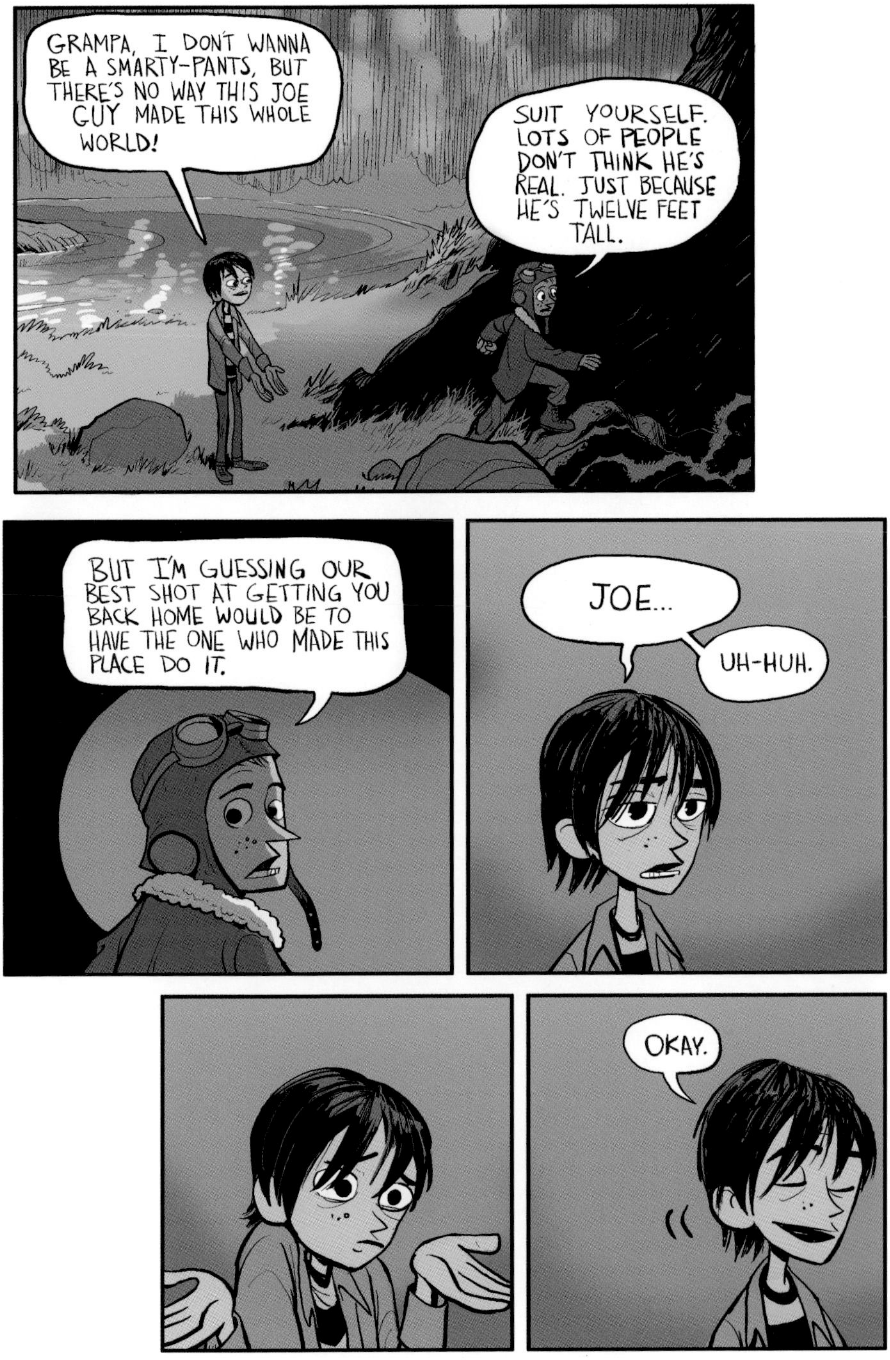
GRAMPA, I DON'T WANNA BE A SMARTY-PANTS, BUT THERE'S NO WAY THIS JOE GUY MADE THIS WHOLE WORLD!
SUIT YOURSELF. LOTS OF PEOPLE DON'T THINK HE'S REAL. JUST BECAUSE HE'S TWELVE FEET TALL.
BUT I'M GUESSING OUR BEST SHOT AT GETTING YOU BACK HOME WOULD BE TO HAVE THE ONE WHO MADE THIS PLACE DO IT.
JOE...
UH-HUH.
OKAY.

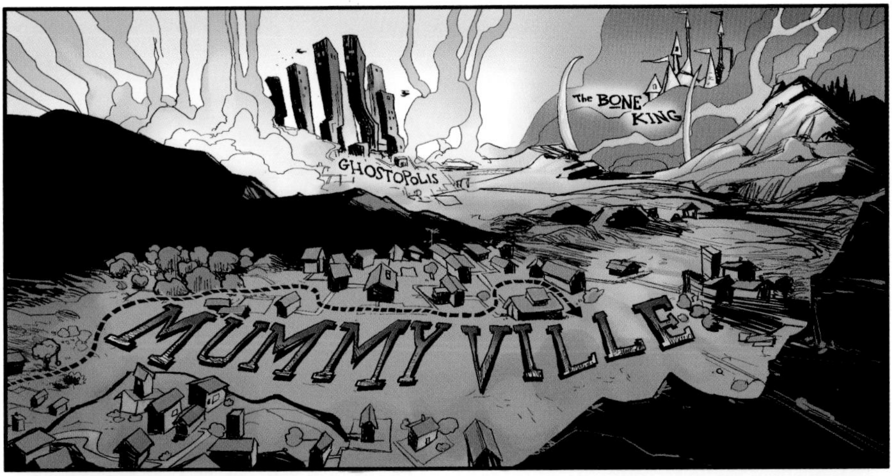
GHOSTOPOLIS
The BONE KING
MUMMY VILLE

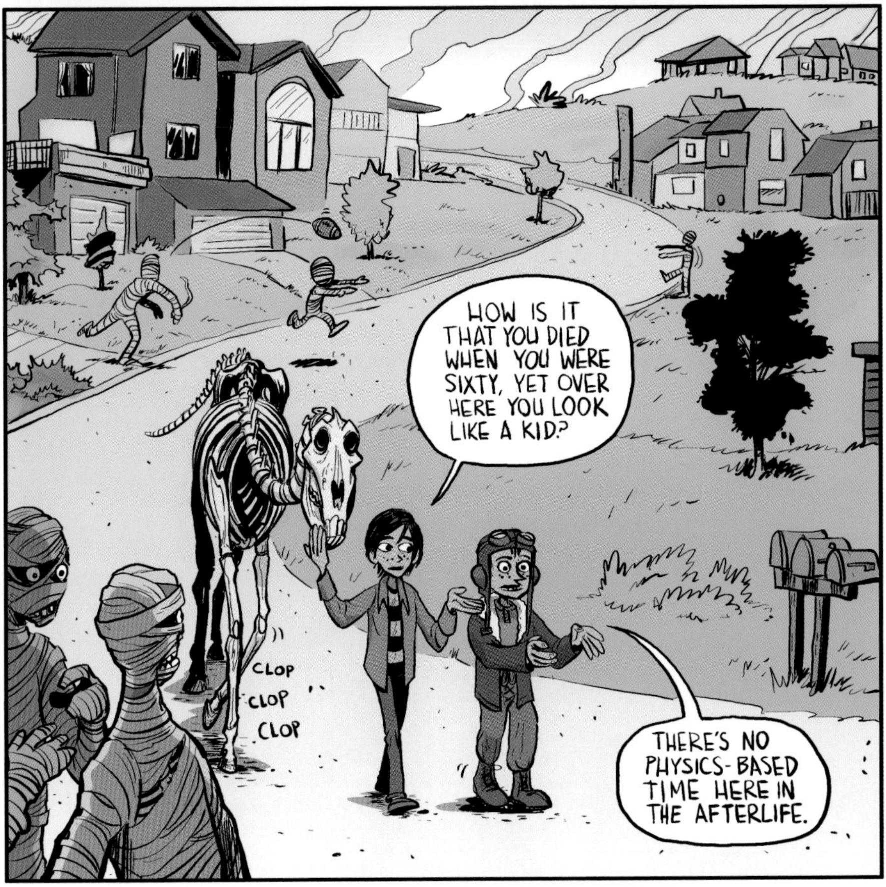
HOW IS IT THAT YOU DIED WHEN YOU WERE SIXTY, YET OVER HERE YOU LOOK LIKE A KID?
CLOP
CLOP
CLOP
THERE'S NO PHYSICS-BASED TIME HERE IN THE AFTERLIFE.

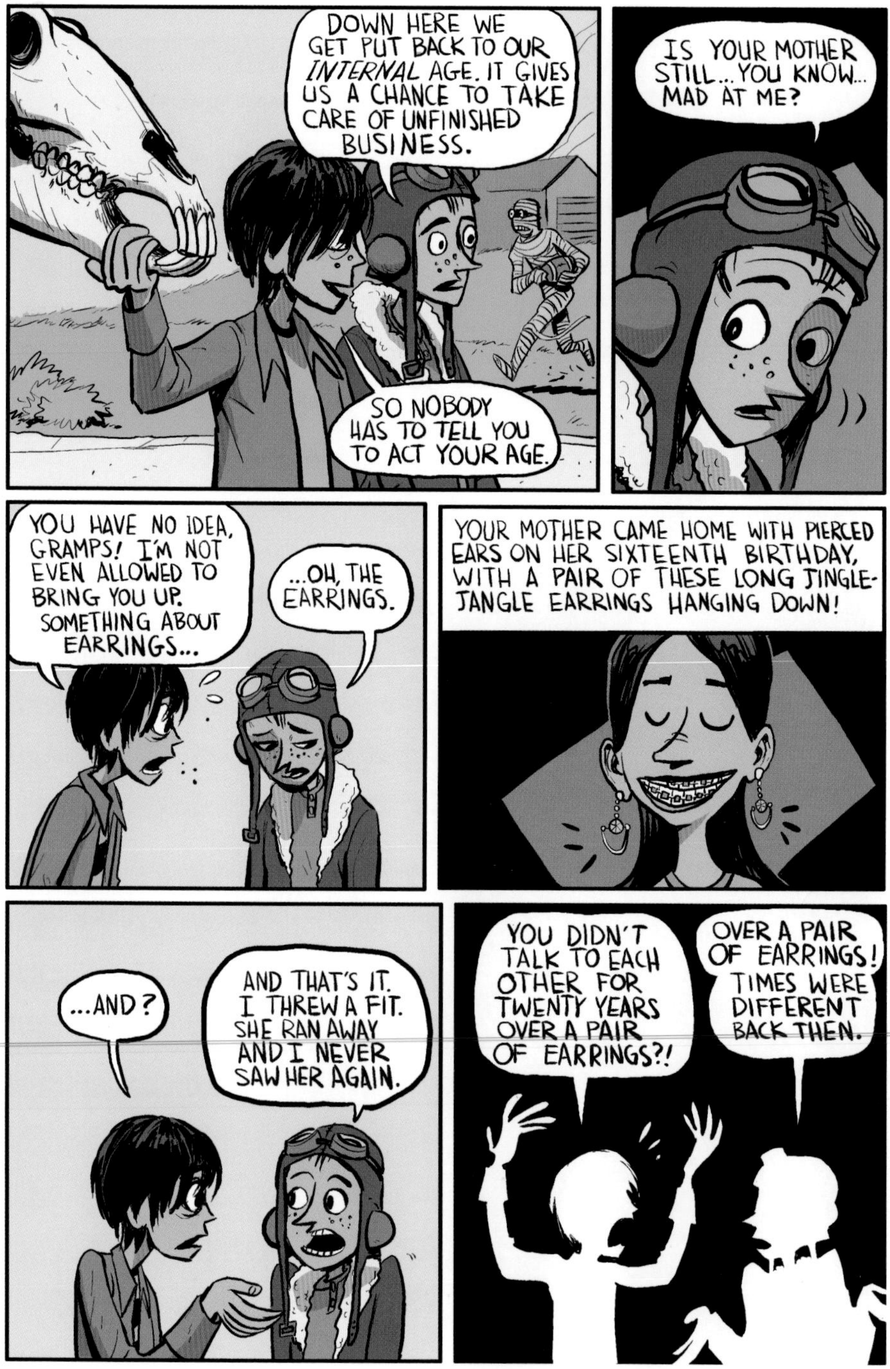
DOWN HERE WE GET PUT BACK TO OUR *INTERNAL* AGE. IT GIVES US A CHANCE TO TAKE CARE OF UNFINISHED BUSINESS.
SO NOBODY HAS TO TELL YOU TO ACT YOUR AGE.
IS YOUR MOTHER STILL... YOU KNOW... MAD AT ME?
YOU HAVE NO IDEA, GRAMPS! I'M NOT EVEN ALLOWED TO BRING YOU UP. SOMETHING ABOUT EARRINGS...
...OH, THE EARRINGS.
YOUR MOTHER CAME HOME WITH PIERCED EARS ON HER SIXTEENTH BIRTHDAY, WITH A PAIR OF THESE LONG JINGLE-JANGLE EARRINGS HANGING DOWN!
...AND?
AND THAT'S IT. I THREW A FIT. SHE RAN AWAY AND I NEVER SAW HER AGAIN.
YOU DIDN'T TALK TO EACH OTHER FOR TWENTY YEARS OVER A PAIR OF EARRINGS?!
OVER A PAIR OF EARRINGS! TIMES WERE DIFFERENT BACK THEN.

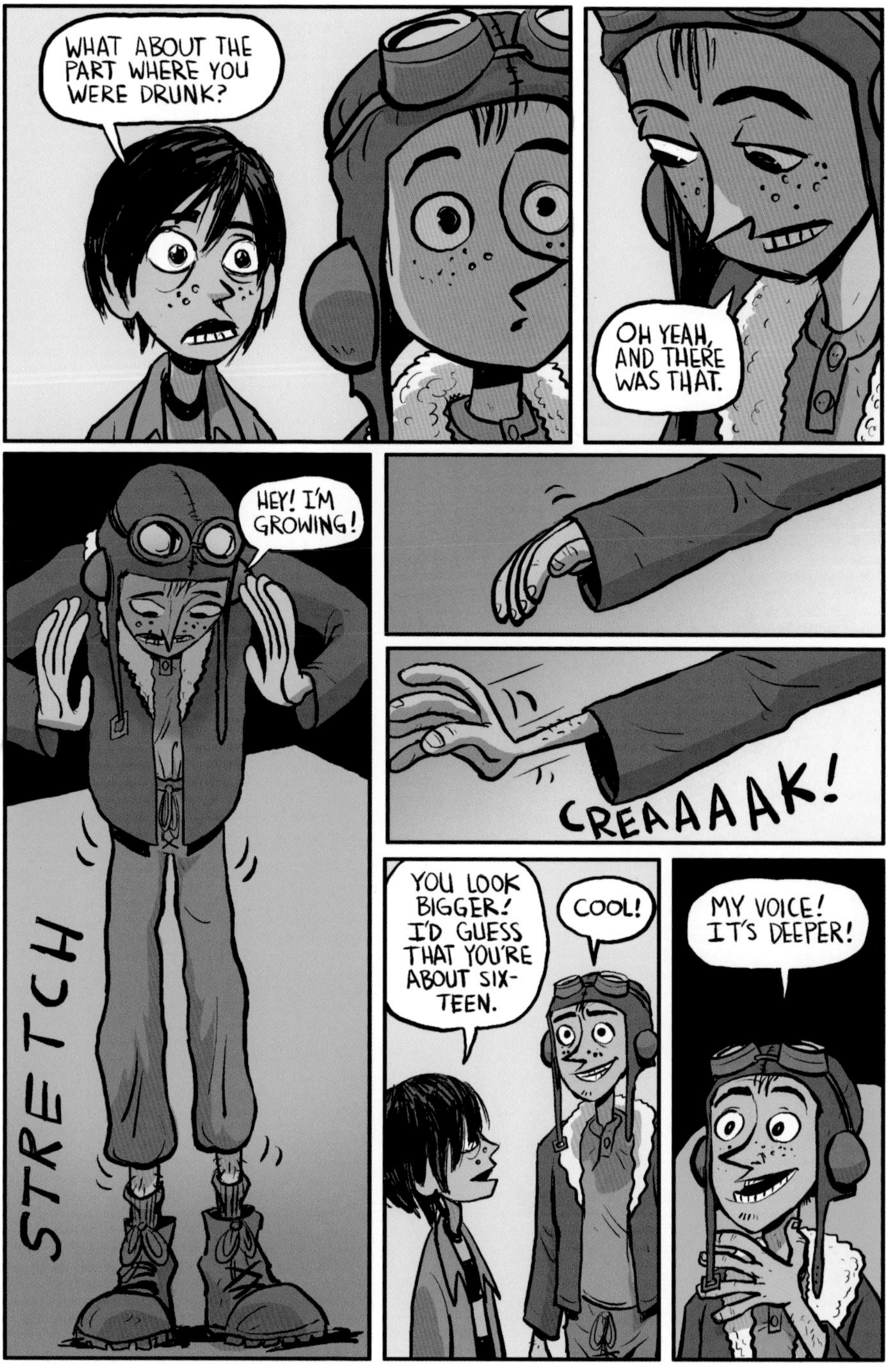
WHAT ABOUT THE PART WHERE YOU WERE DRUNK?
OH YEAH, AND THERE WAS THAT.
HEY! I'M GROWING!
STRETCH
CREAAAAK!
YOU LOOK BIGGER! I'D GUESS THAT YOU'RE ABOUT SIX-TEEN.
COOL!
MY VOICE! IT'S DEEPER!

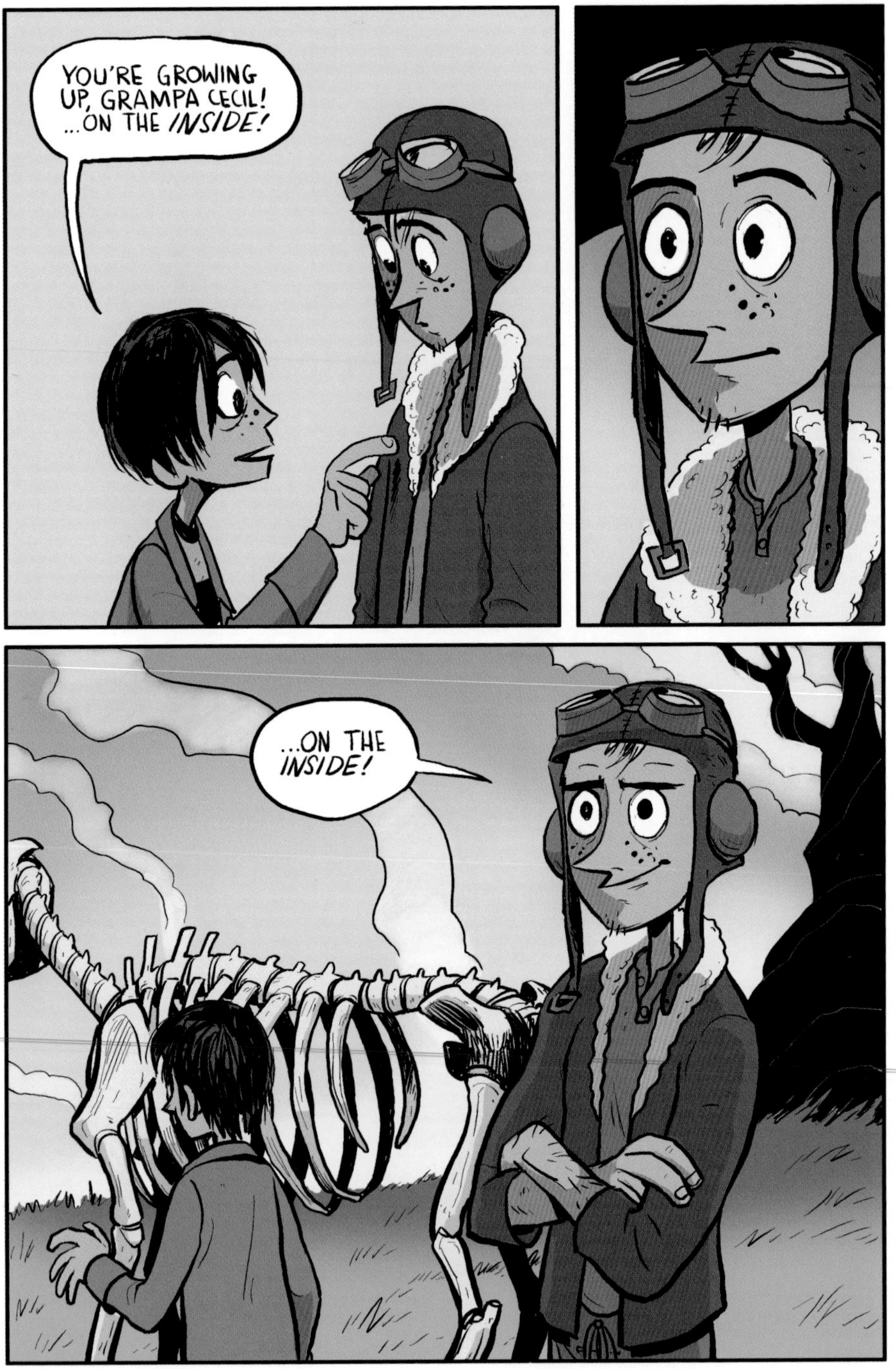
YOU'RE GROWING UP, GRAMPA CECIL! ...ON THE INSIDE!
...ON THE INSIDE!

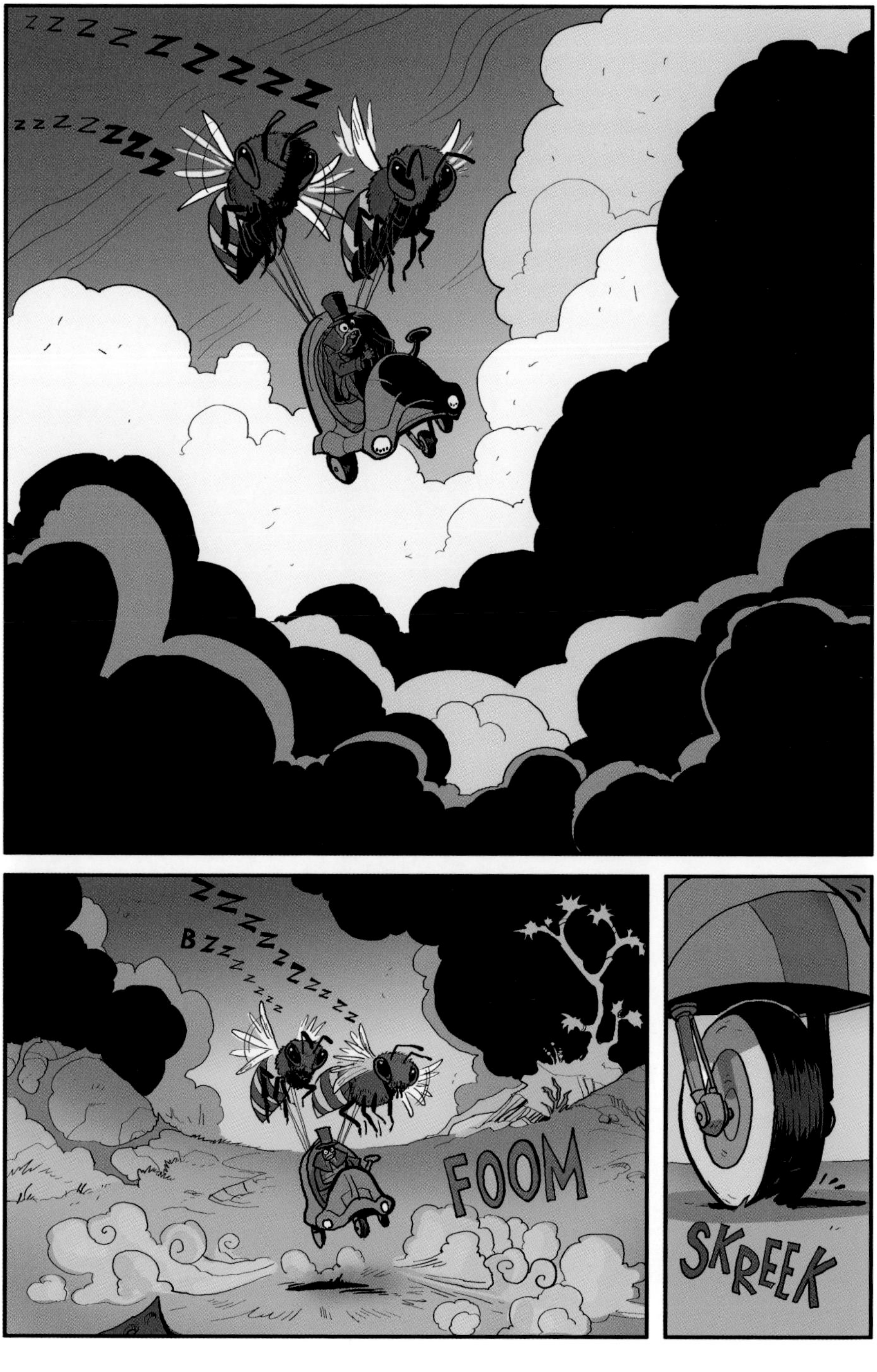
zzzzZZZZZZ
zzZZZZZZ
ZZZZ
BZZZZZZZZZZZZ
FOOM
SKREEK

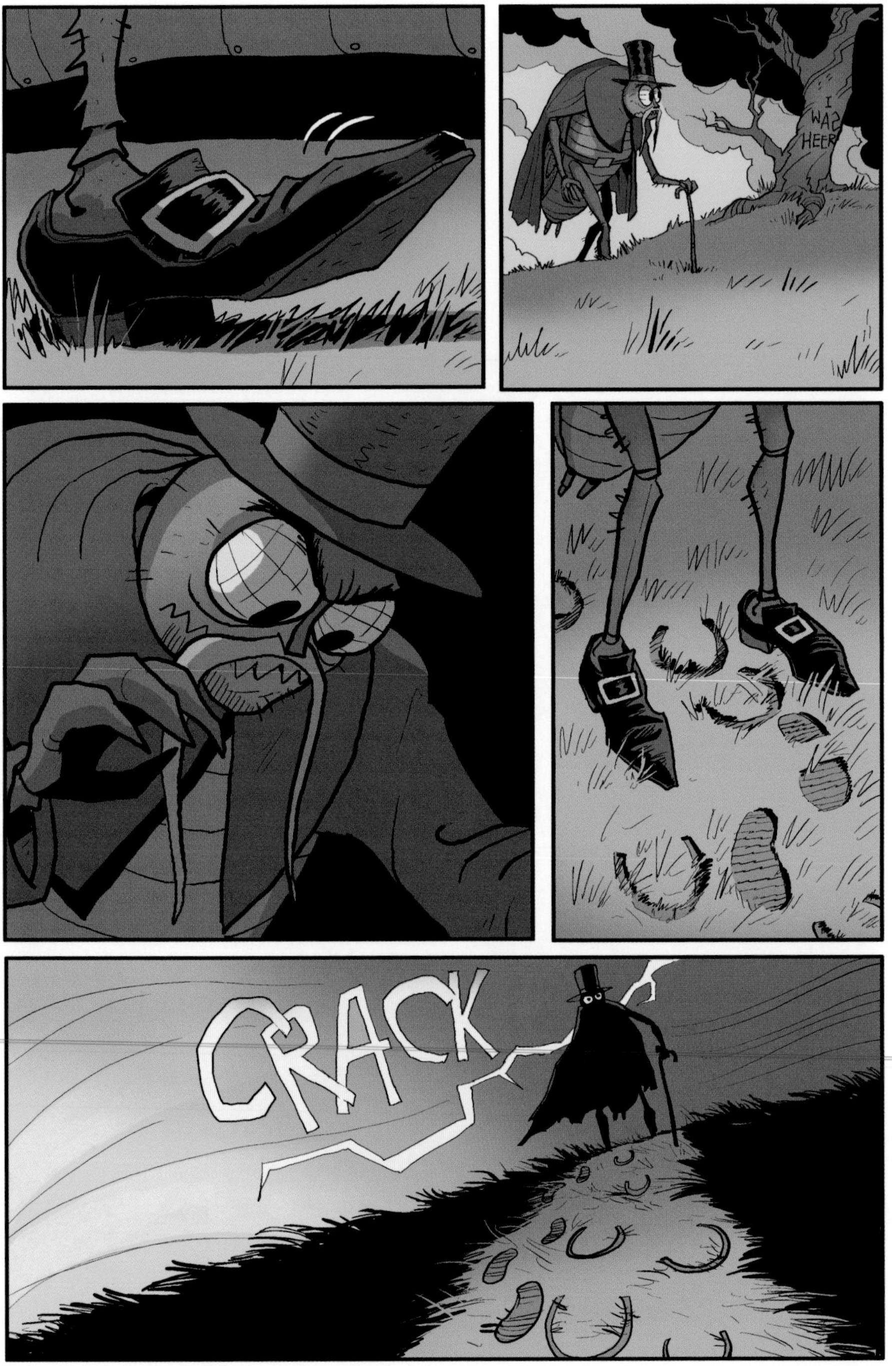
I WAS HEER
CRACK

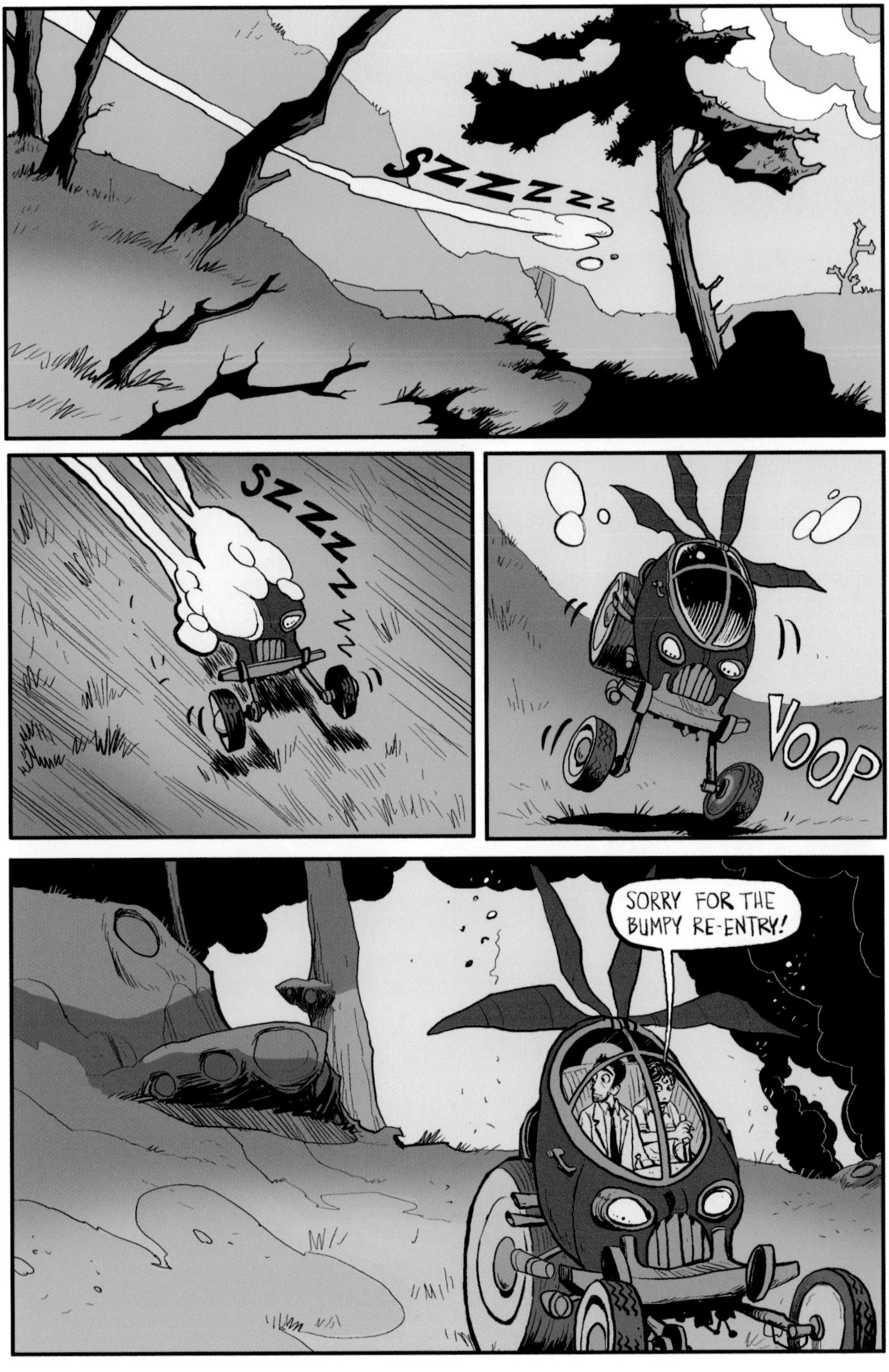
SZZZZzz
SZZZZZZZ
VOOP
SORRY FOR THE BUMPY RE-ENTRY!

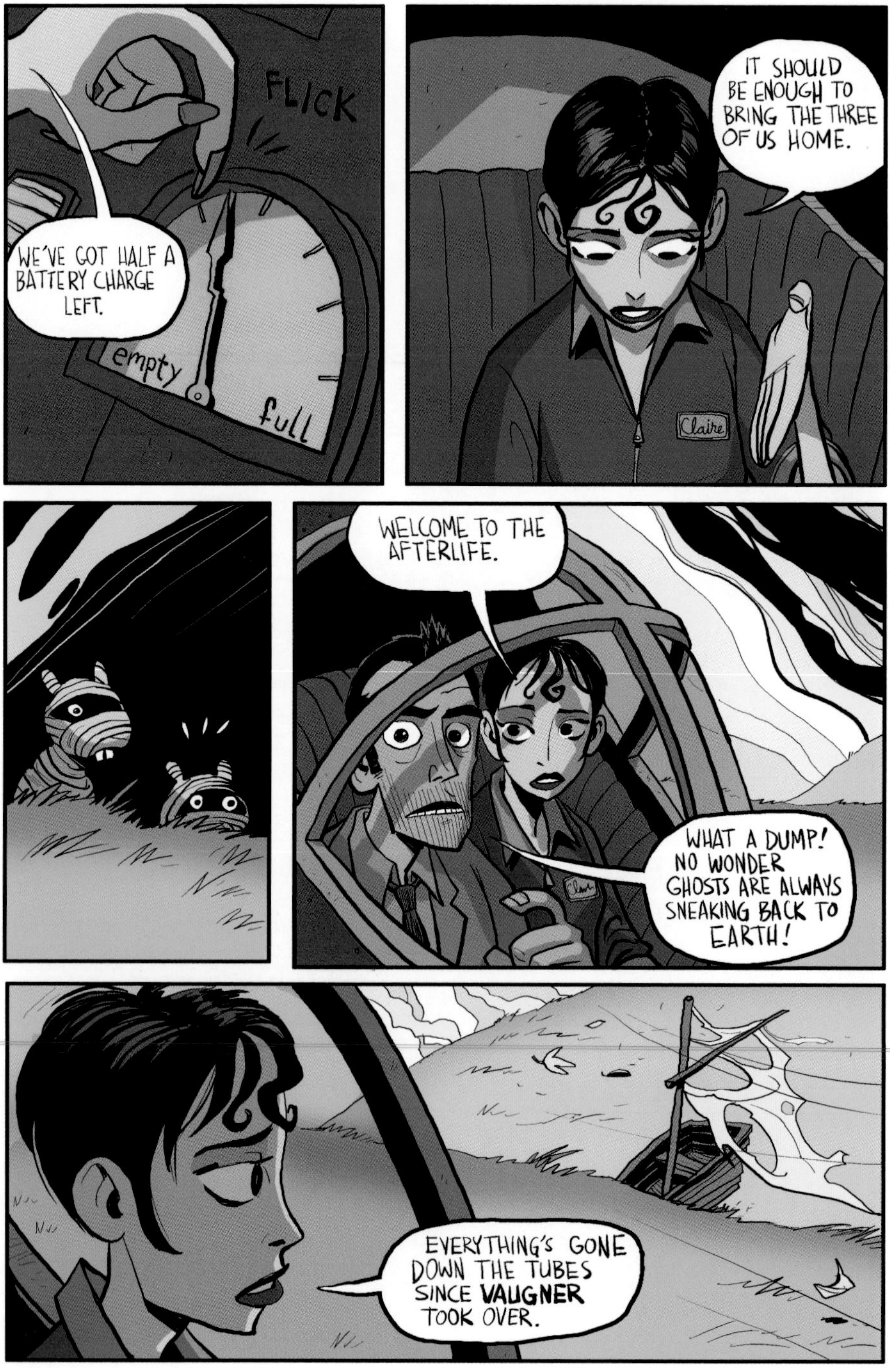
FLICK
WE'VE GOT HALF A BATTERY CHARGE LEFT.
empty
full
IT SHOULD BE ENOUGH TO BRING THE THREE OF US HOME.
Claire
WELCOME TO THE AFTERLIFE.
WHAT A DUMP! NO WONDER GHOSTS ARE ALWAYS SNEAKING BACK TO EARTH!
EVERYTHING'S GONE DOWN THE TUBES SINCE VAUGNER TOOK OVER.

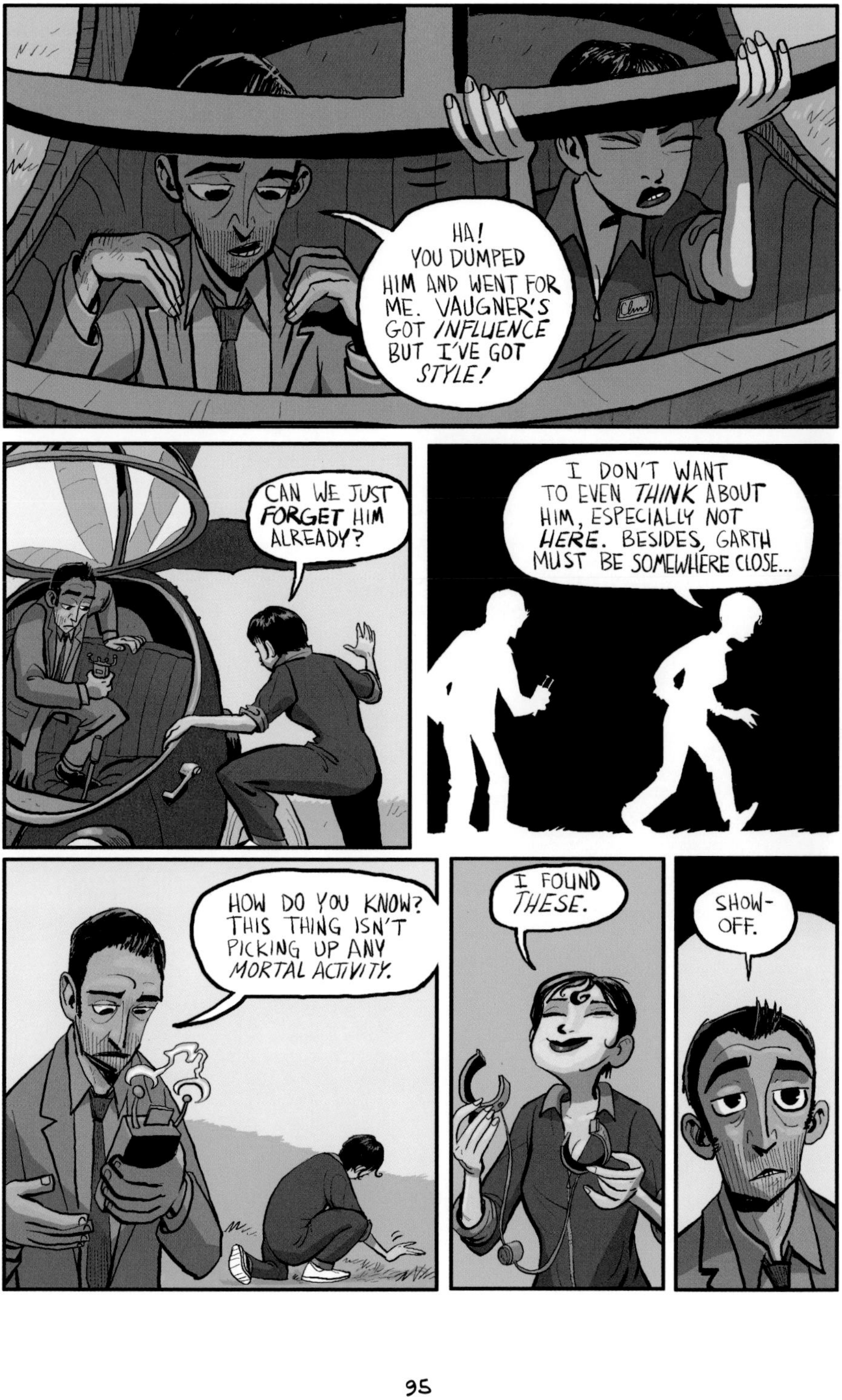
HA! YOU DUMPED HIM AND WENT FOR ME. VAUGNER'S GOT *INFLUENCE* BUT I'VE GOT *STYLE!*
CAN WE JUST **FORGET** HIM ALREADY?
I DON'T WANT TO EVEN *THINK* ABOUT HIM, ESPECIALLY NOT *HERE*. BESIDES, GARTH MUST BE SOMEWHERE CLOSE...
HOW DO YOU KNOW? THIS THING ISN'T PICKING UP ANY *MORTAL ACTIVITY*.
I FOUND *THESE*.
SHOW-OFF.

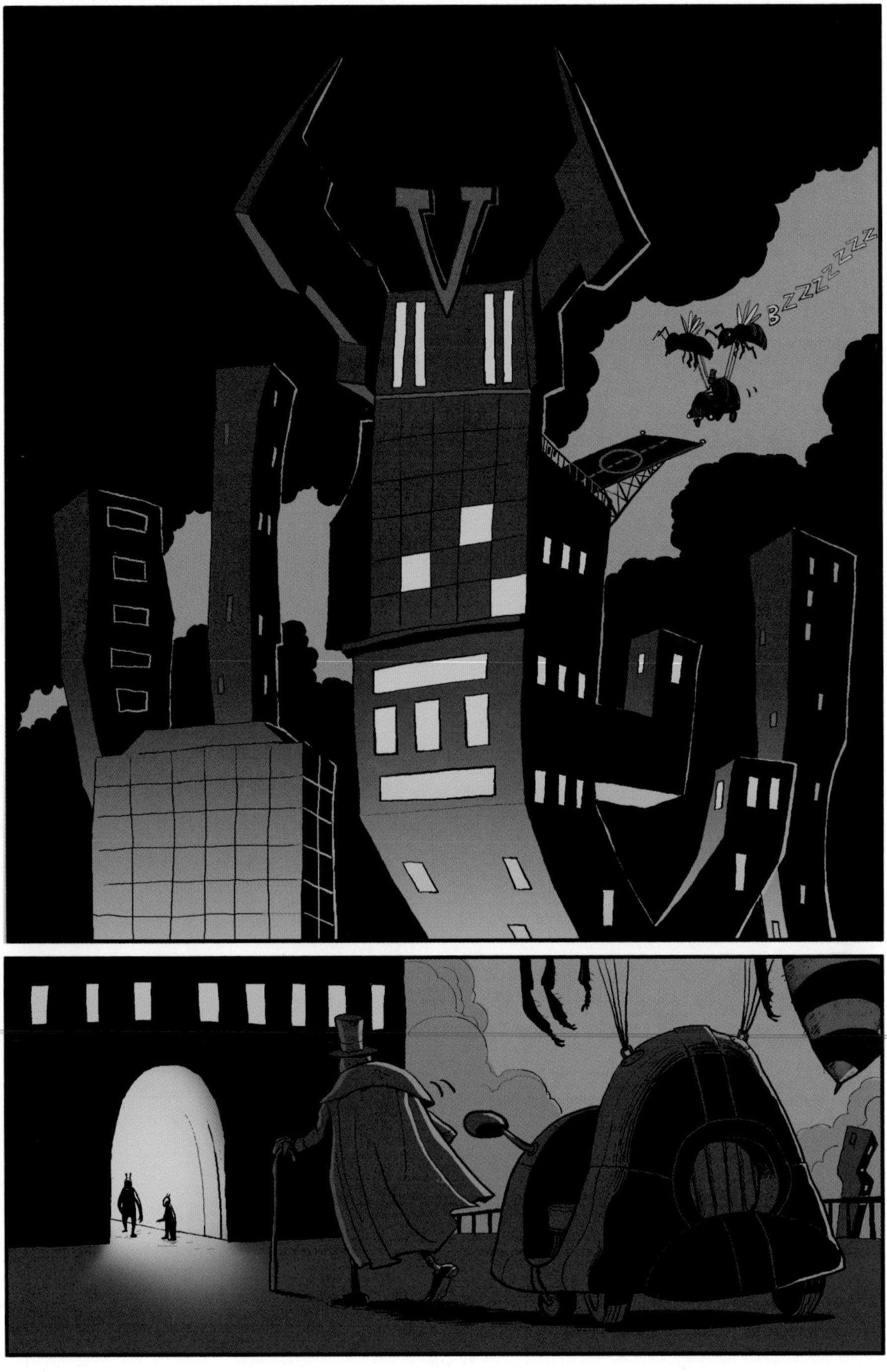
V
BZZZZZZZ

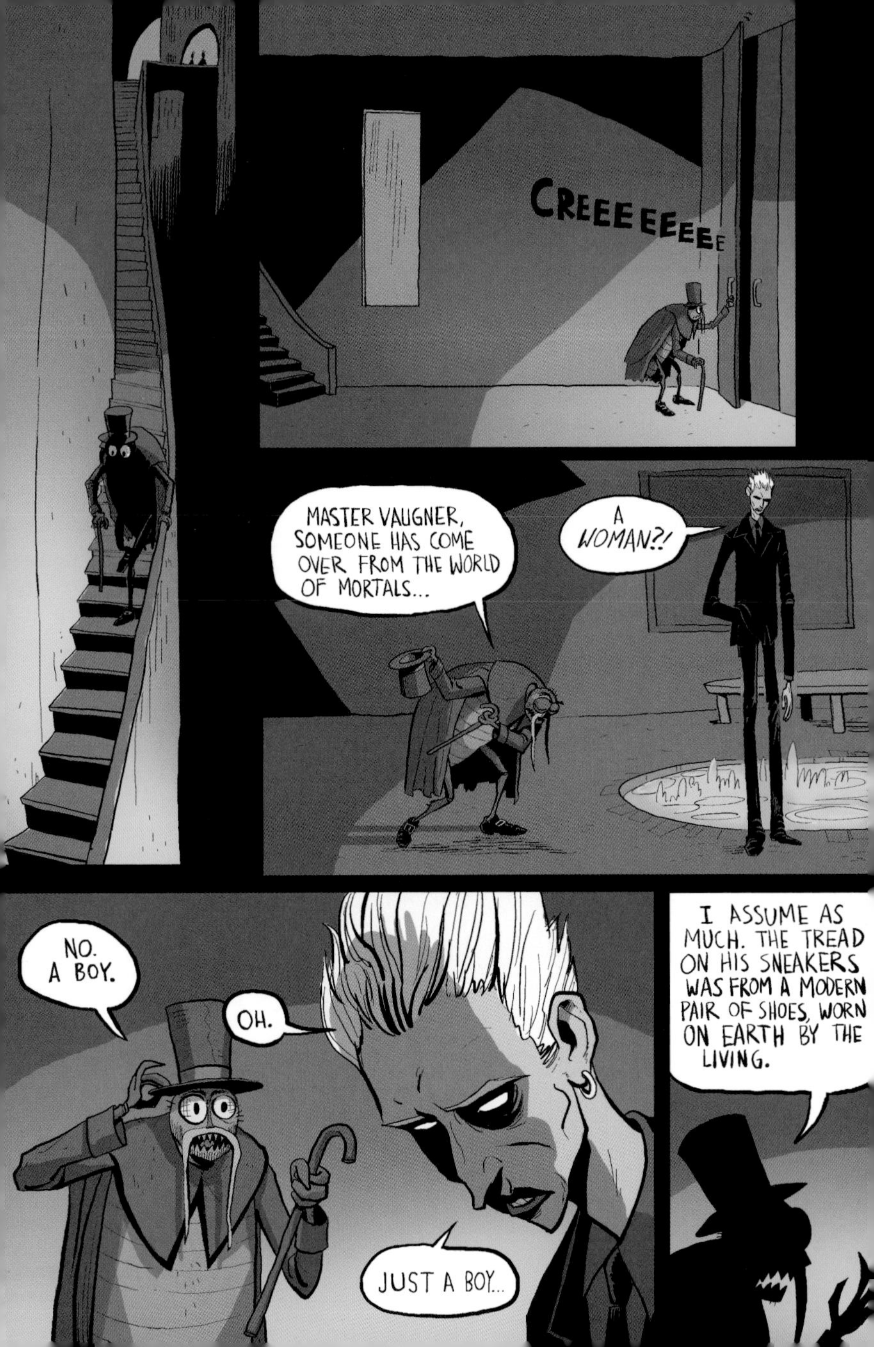
CREEEEEEEE
MASTER VAUGNER, SOMEONE HAS COME OVER FROM THE WORLD OF MORTALS...
A WOMAN?!
NO. A BOY.
OH.
JUST A BOY...
I ASSUME AS MUCH. THE TREAD ON HIS SNEAKERS WAS FROM A MODERN PAIR OF SHOES, WORN ON EARTH BY THE LIVING.

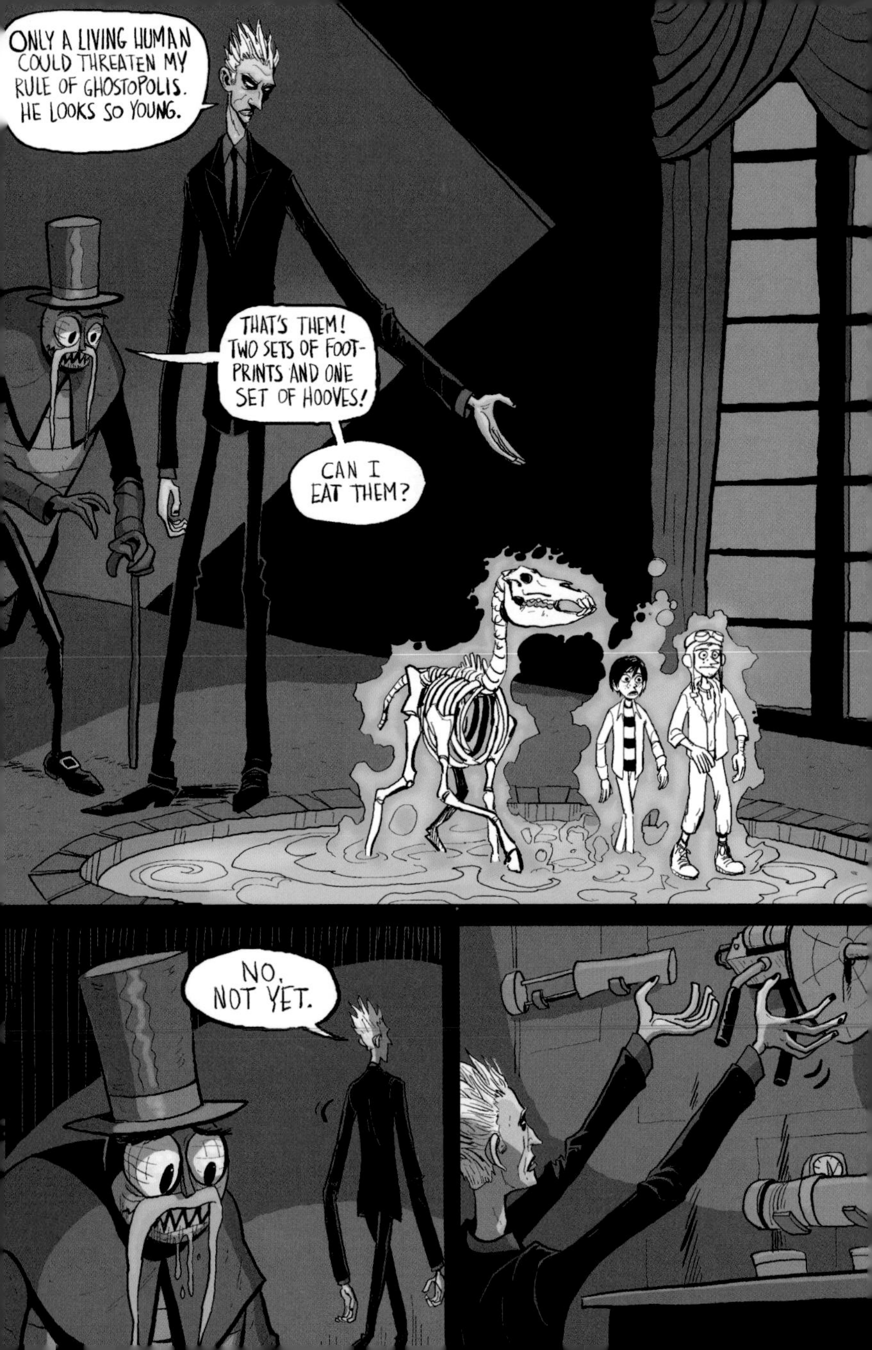
ONLY A LIVING HUMAN COULD THREATEN MY RULE OF GHOSTOPOLIS. HE LOOKS SO YOUNG.
THAT'S THEM! TWO SETS OF FOOT-PRINTS AND ONE SET OF HOOVES!
CAN I EAT THEM?
NO, NOT YET.

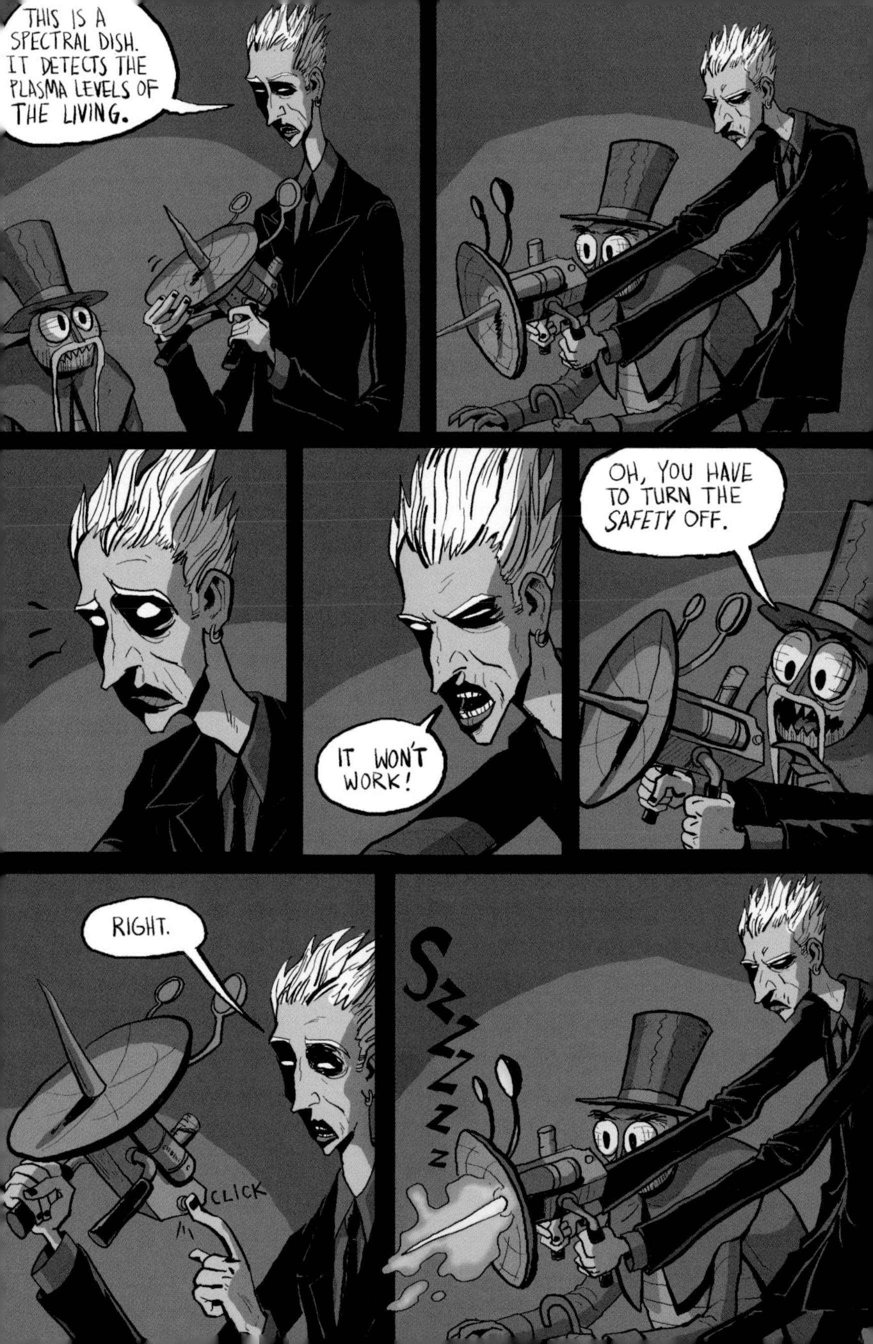
THIS IS A SPECTRAL DISH. IT DETECTS THE PLASMA LEVELS OF THE LIVING.
IT WON'T WORK!
OH, YOU HAVE TO TURN THE SAFETY OFF.
RIGHT.
CLICK
SZZZZZZ

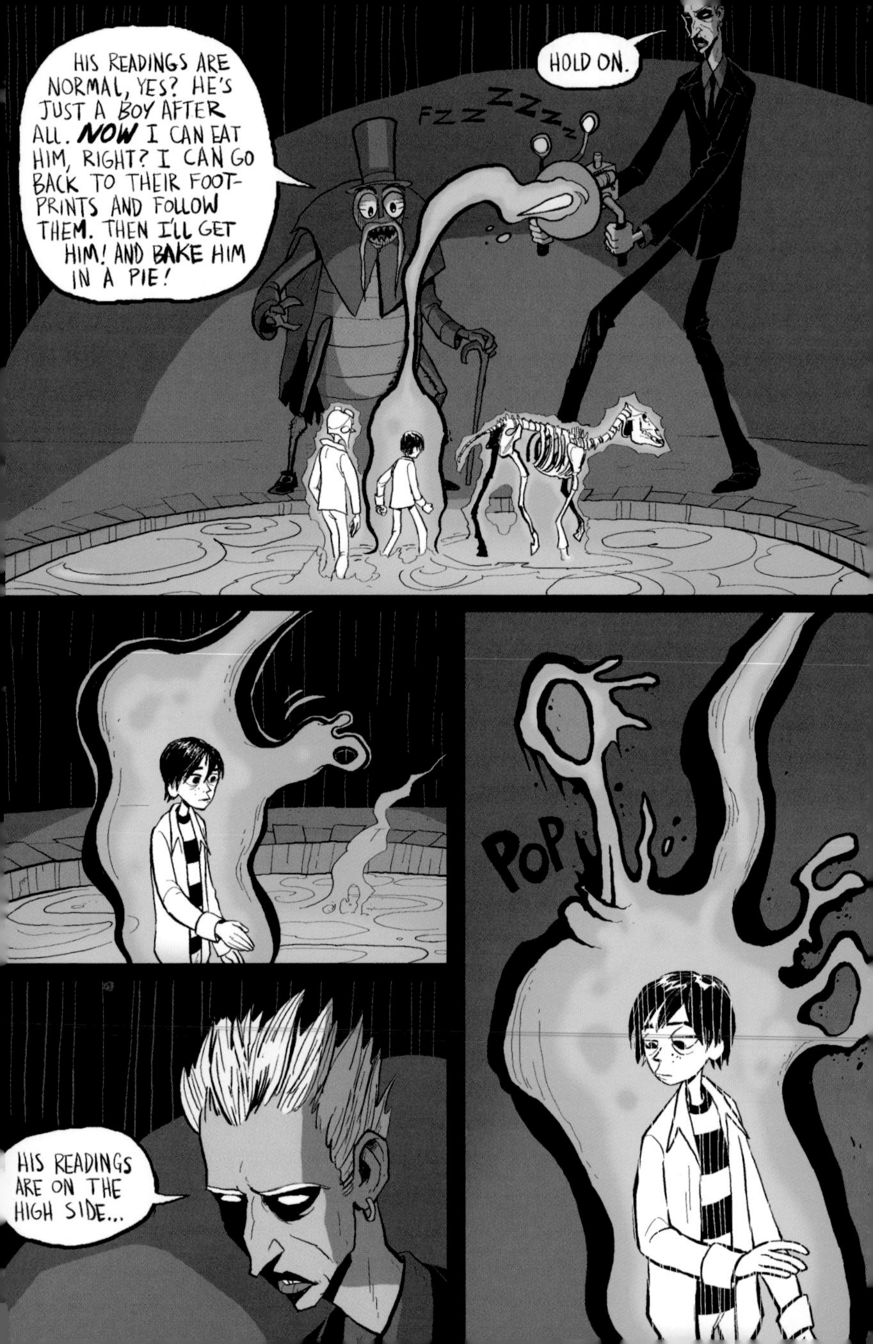
HIS READINGS ARE NORMAL, YES? HE'S JUST A BOY AFTER ALL. NOW I CAN EAT HIM, RIGHT? I CAN GO BACK TO THEIR FOOT-PRINTS AND FOLLOW THEM. THEN I'LL GET HIM! AND BAKE HIM IN A PIE!
HOLD ON.
FZZ ZZZzz
POP
HIS READINGS ARE ON THE HIGH SIDE...

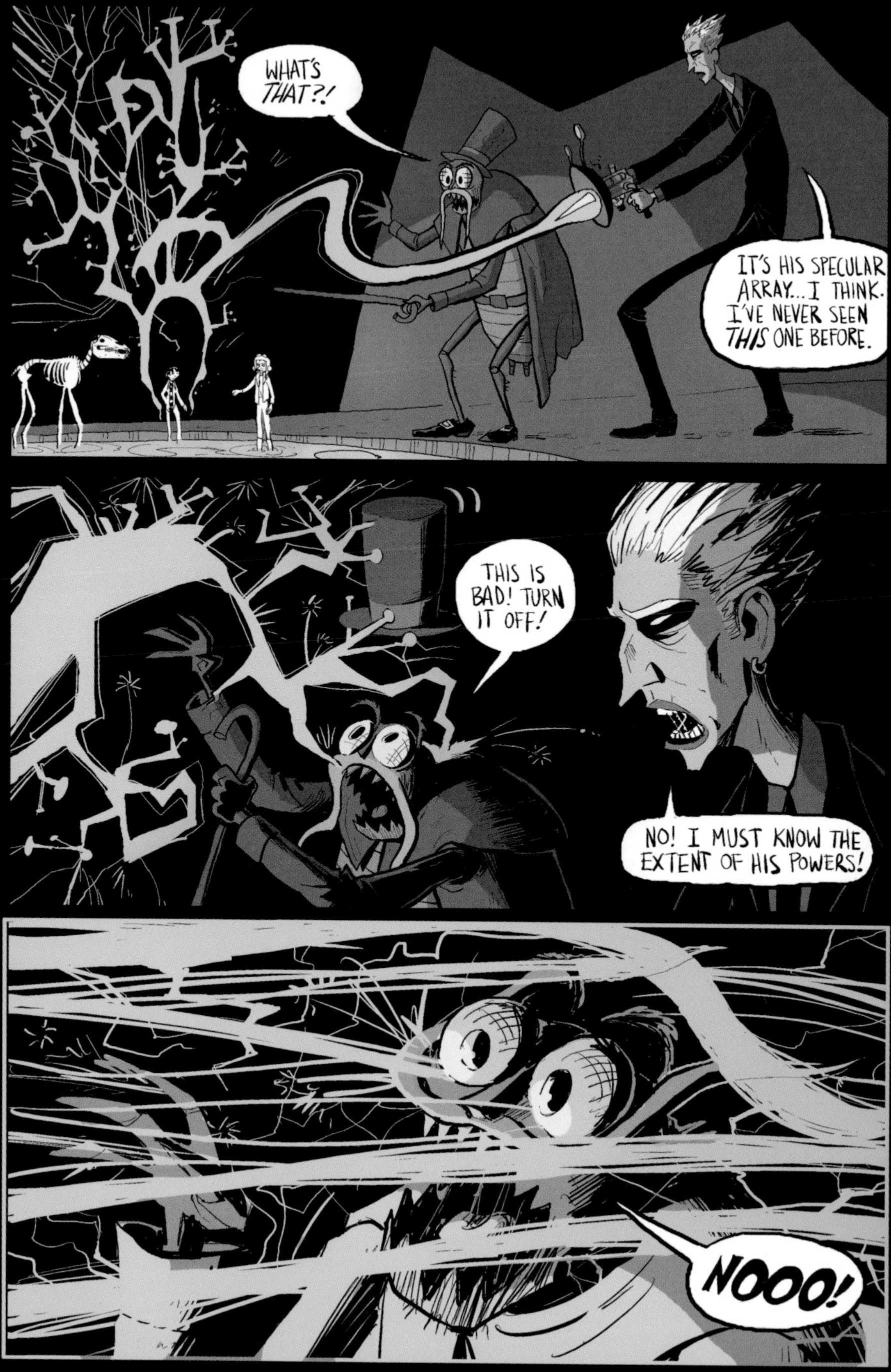
WHAT'S THAT?!
IT'S HIS SPECULAR ARRAY... I THINK. I'VE NEVER SEEN THIS ONE BEFORE.
THIS IS BAD! TURN IT OFF!
NO! I MUST KNOW THE EXTENT OF HIS POWERS!
NOOO!

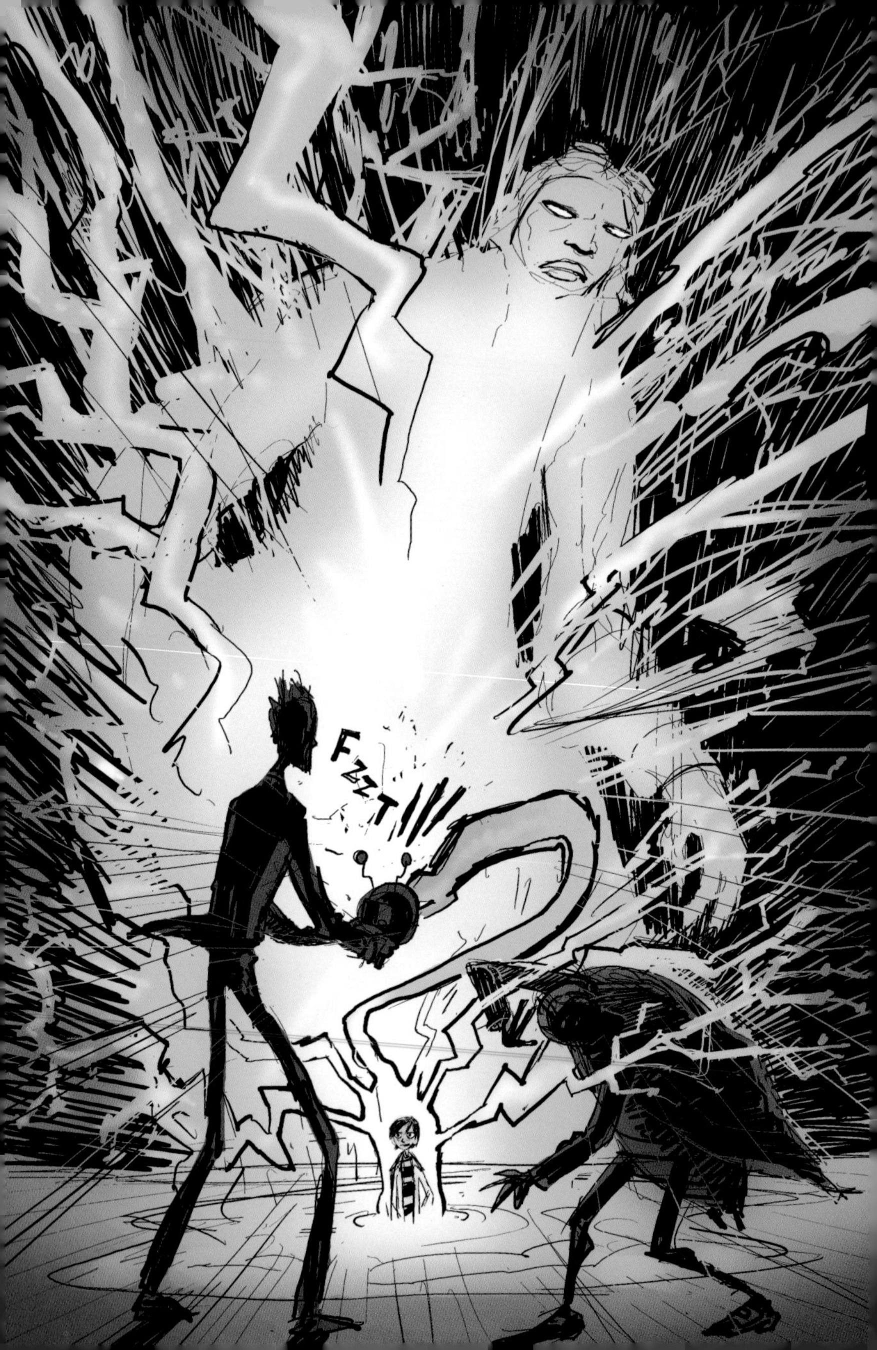
FZZT!!!!

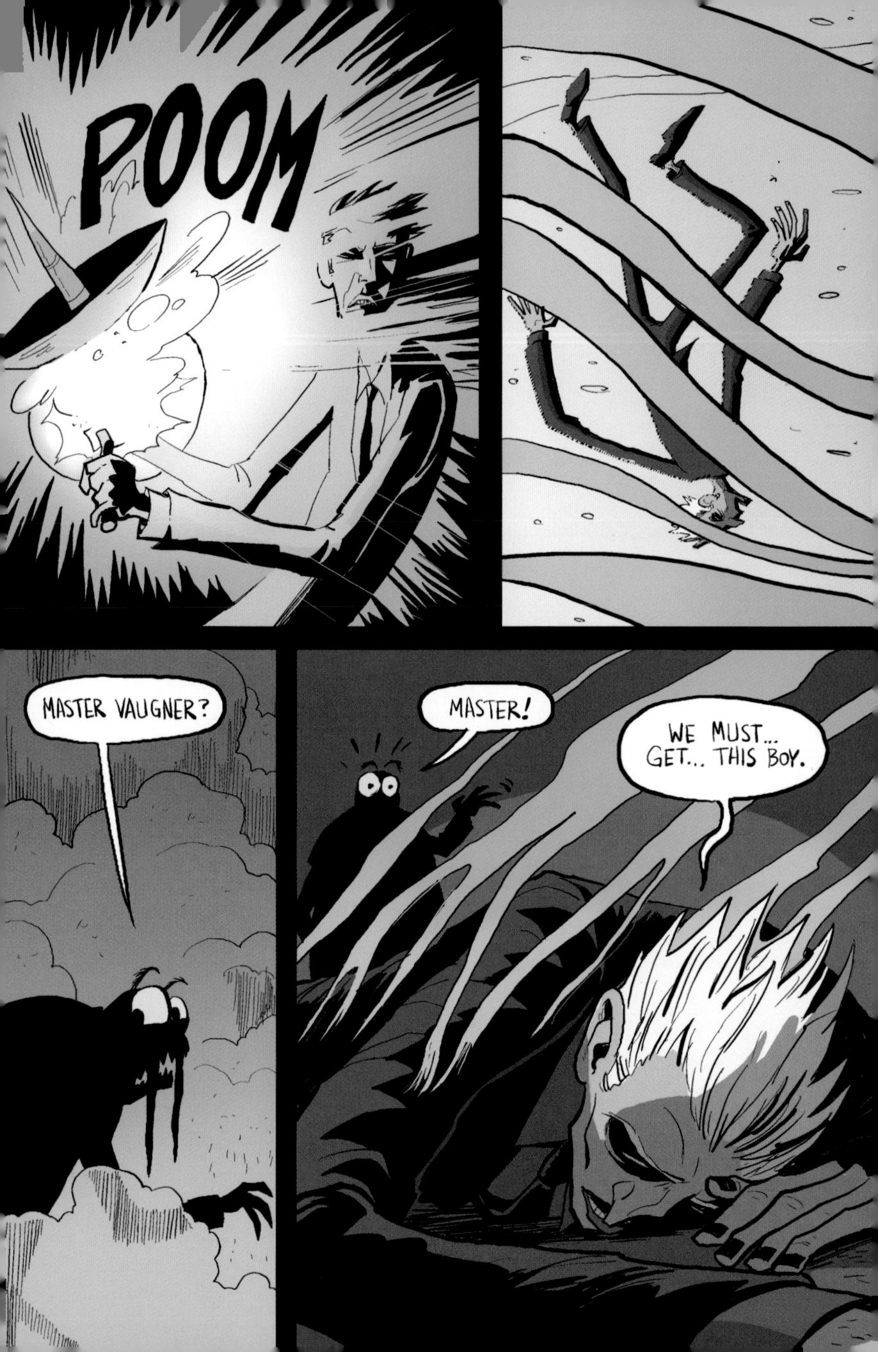
POOM
MASTER VAUGNER?
MASTER!
WE MUST... GET... THIS BOY.

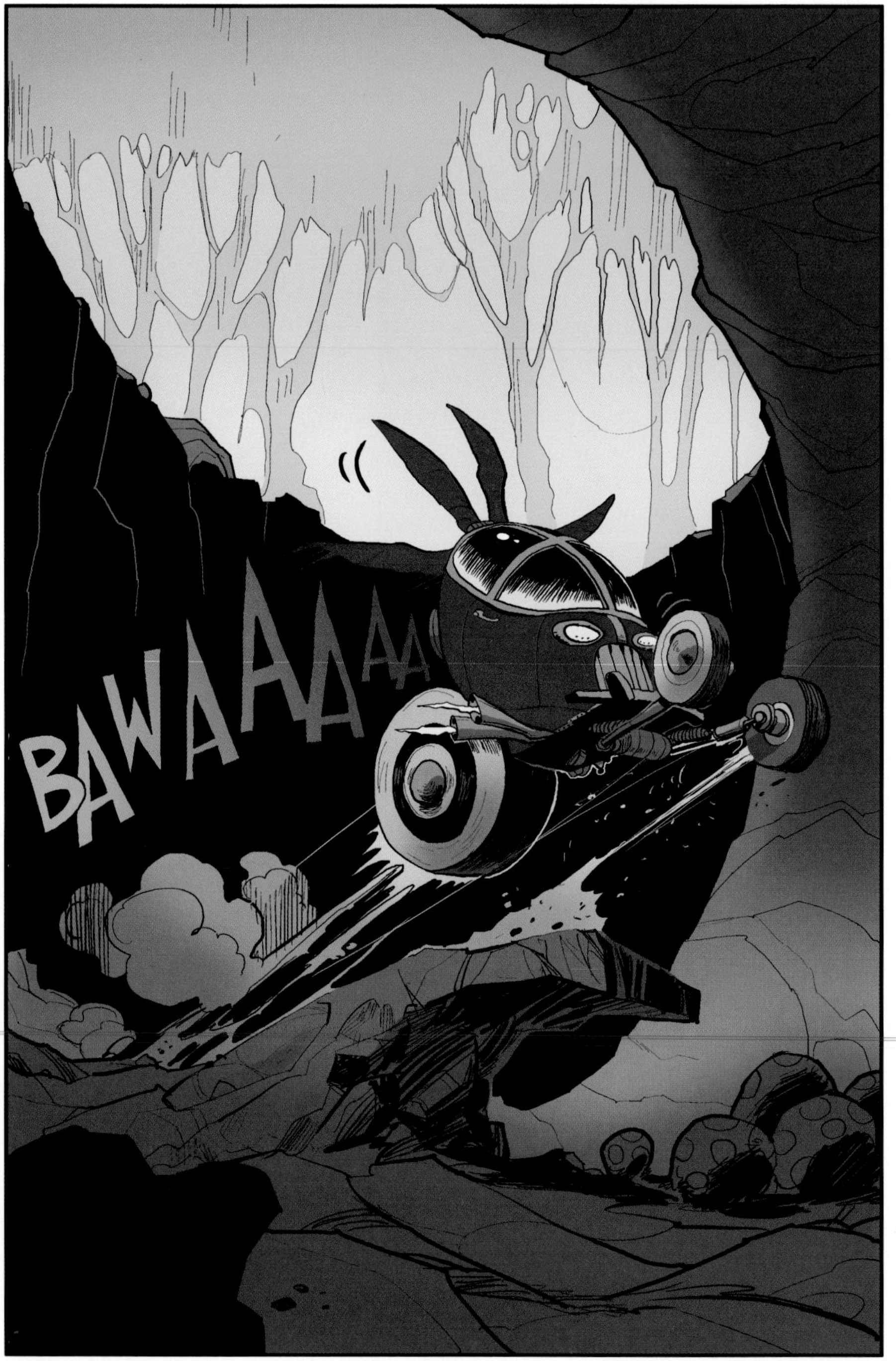
BAWAAAAAA

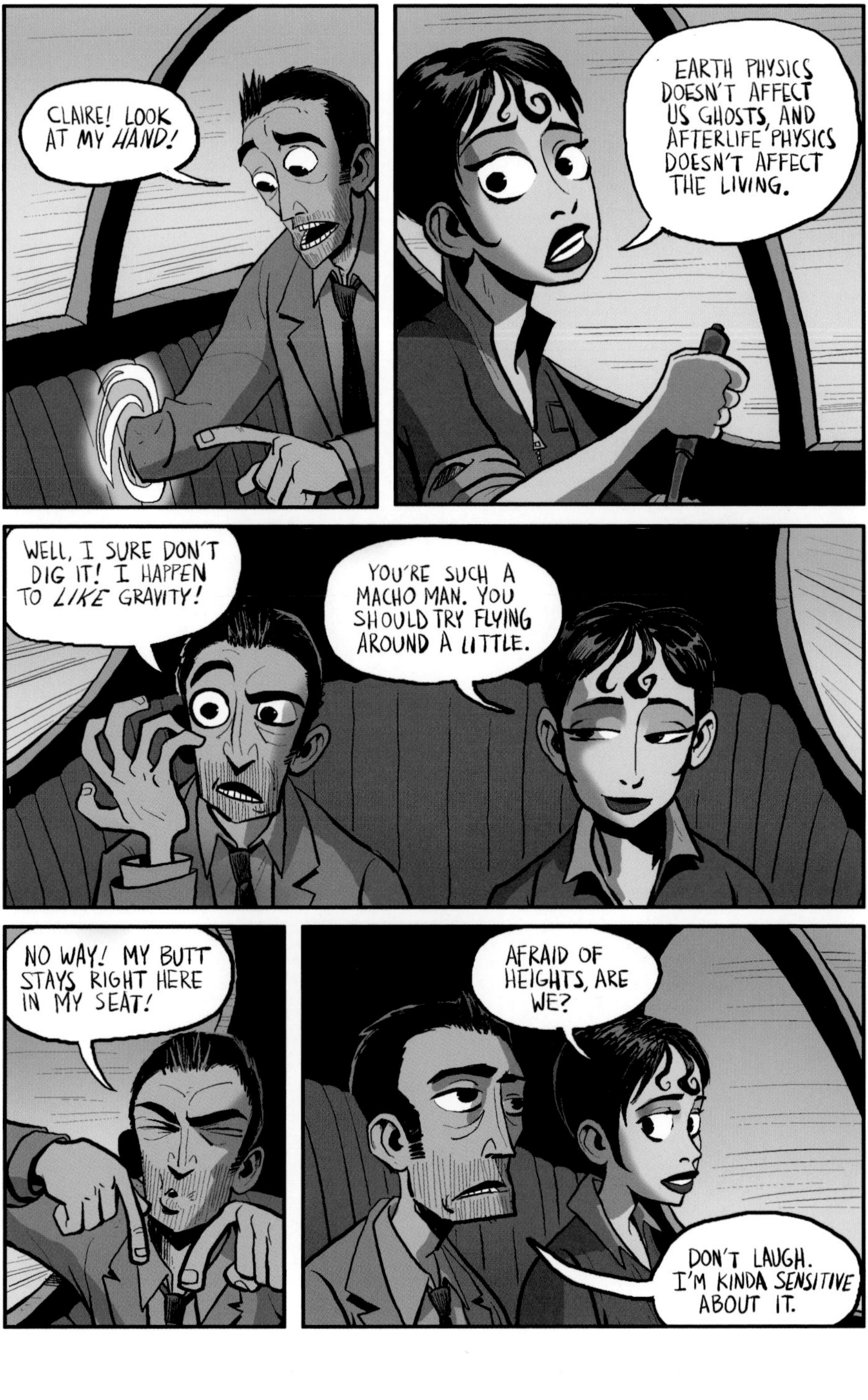
CLAIRE! LOOK AT MY *HAND!*
EARTH PHYSICS DOESN'T AFFECT US GHOSTS, AND AFTERLIFE PHYSICS DOESN'T AFFECT THE LIVING.
WELL, I SURE DON'T DIG IT! I HAPPEN TO *LIKE* GRAVITY!
YOU'RE SUCH A MACHO MAN. YOU SHOULD TRY FLYING AROUND A LITTLE.
NO WAY! MY BUTT STAYS RIGHT HERE IN MY SEAT!
AFRAID OF HEIGHTS, ARE WE?
DON'T LAUGH. I'M KINDA *SENSITIVE* ABOUT IT.

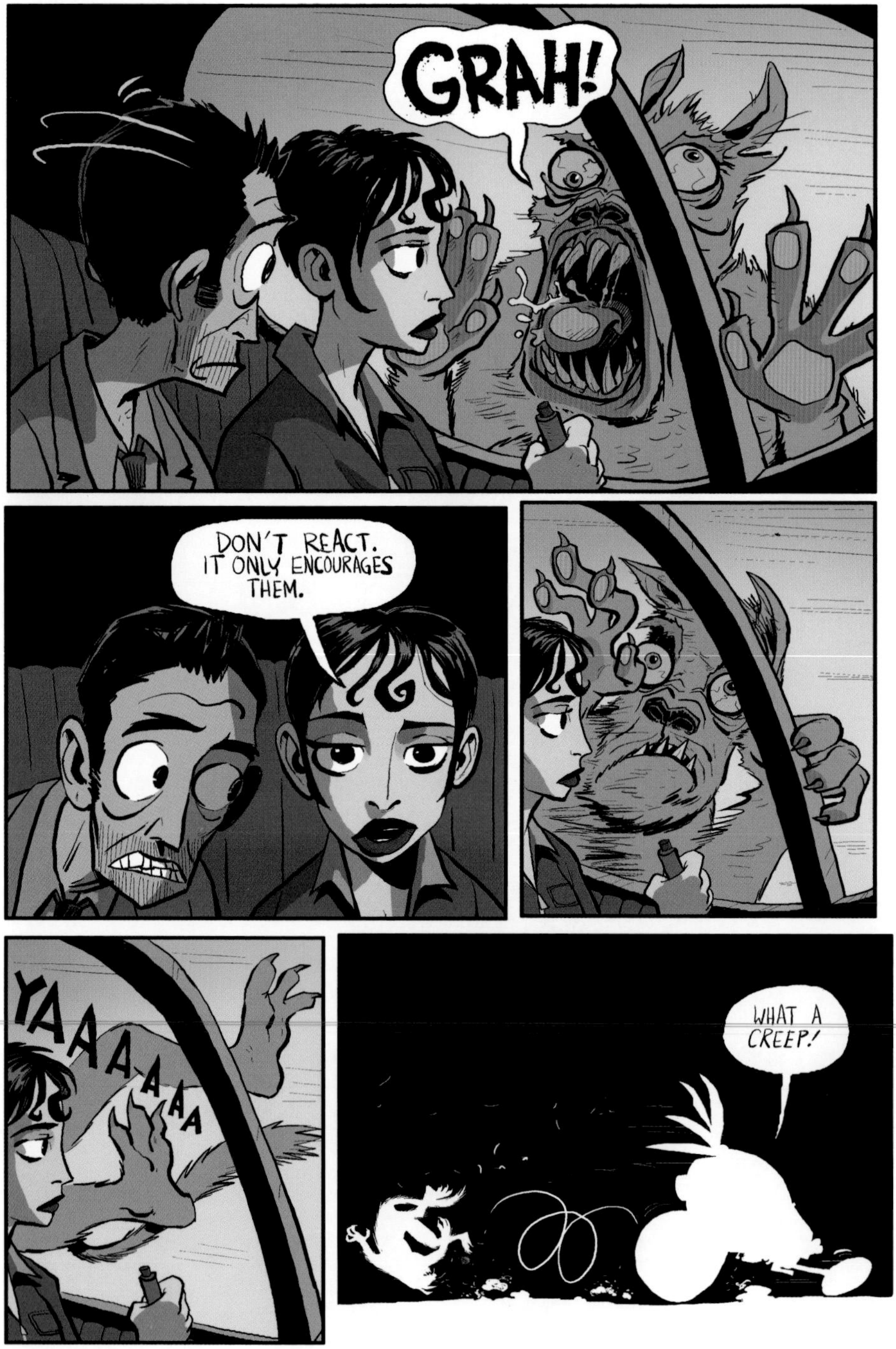
GRAH!
DON'T REACT. IT ONLY ENCOURAGES THEM.
YAAAAAAA
WHAT A CREEP!

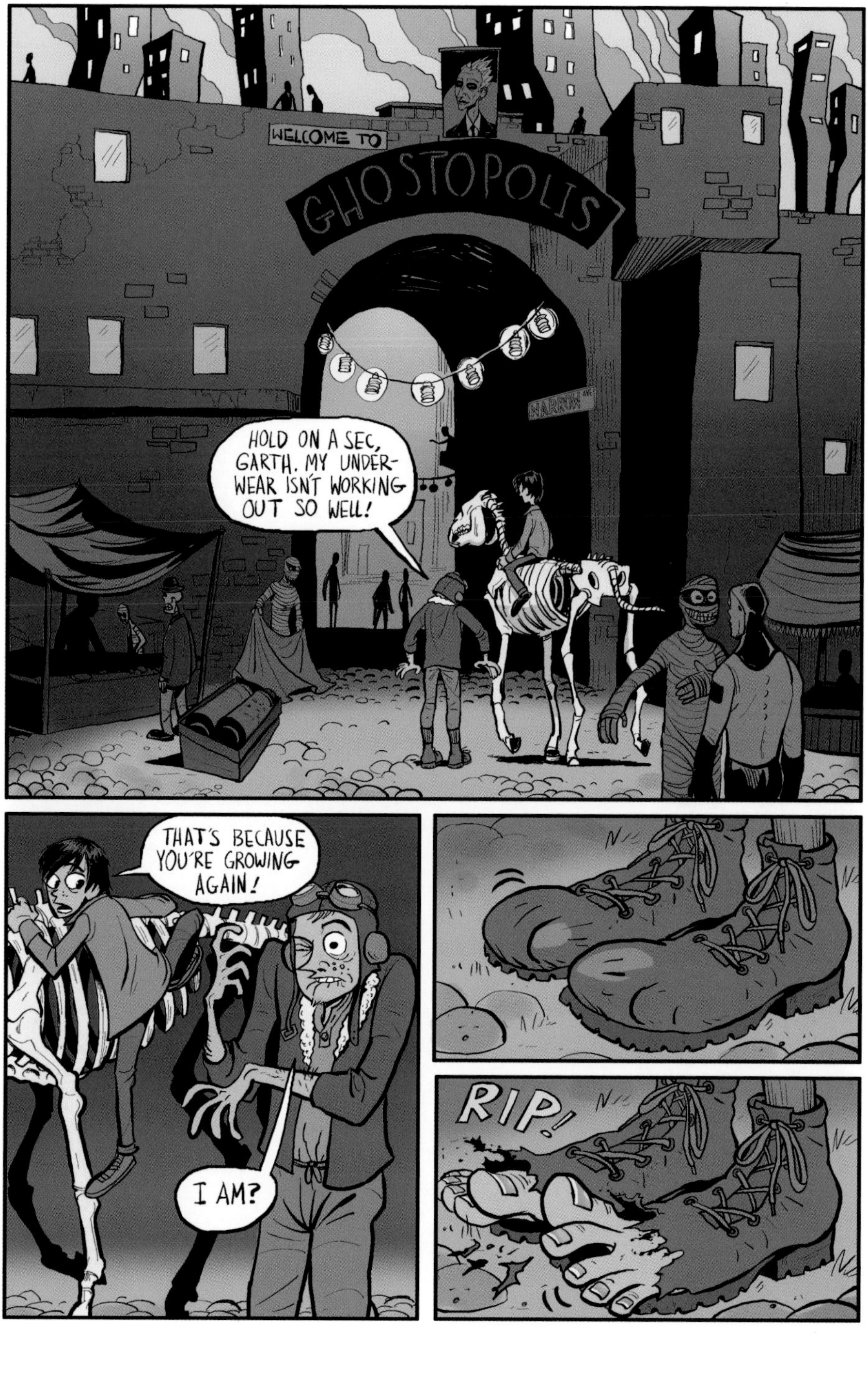
WELCOME TO
GHOSTOPOLIS
NARROW AVE
HOLD ON A SEC, GARTH. MY UNDERWEAR ISN'T WORKING OUT SO WELL!
THAT'S BECAUSE YOU'RE GROWING AGAIN!
I AM?
RIP!

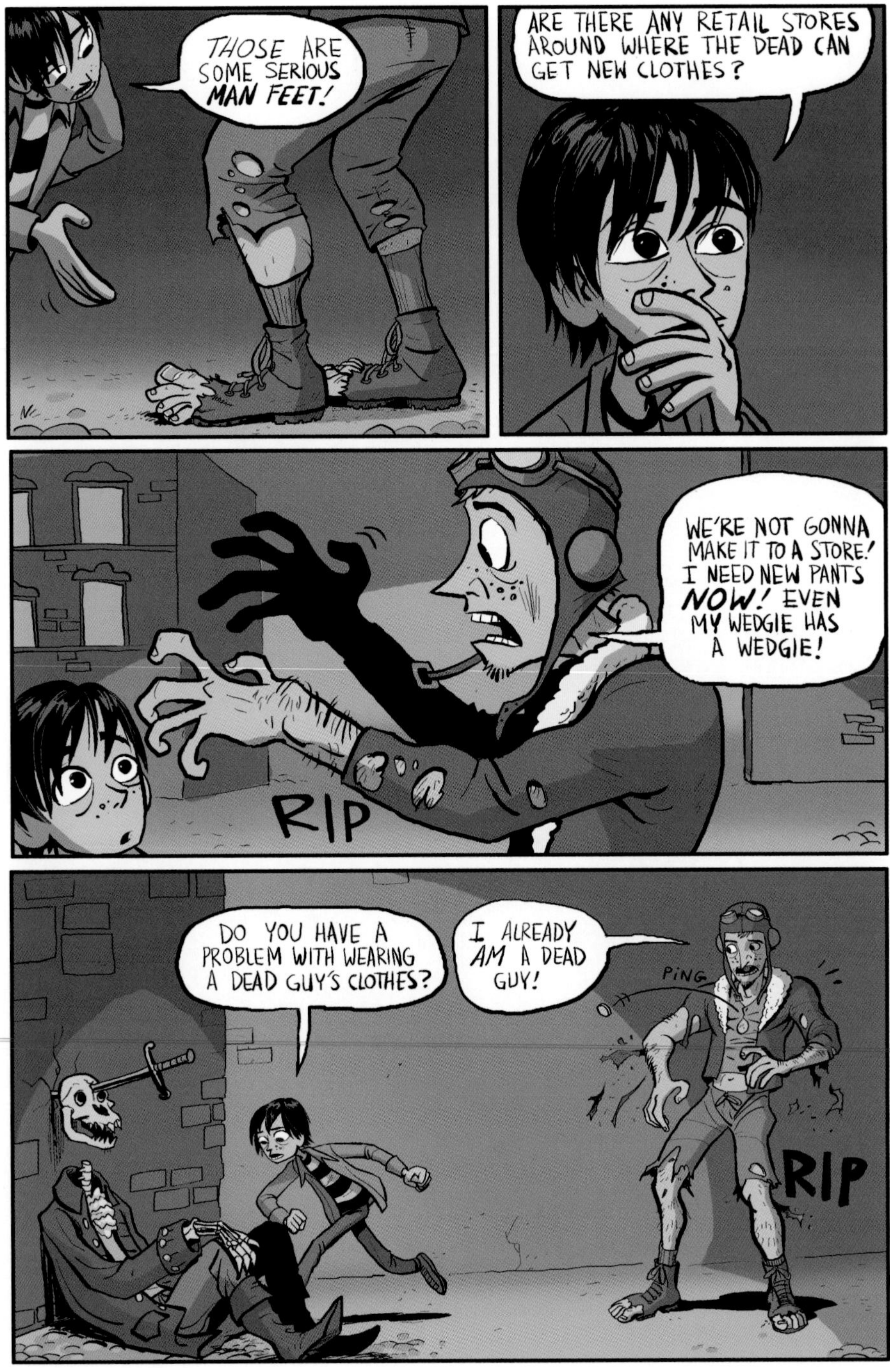
THOSE ARE SOME SERIOUS MAN FEET!
ARE THERE ANY RETAIL STORES AROUND WHERE THE DEAD CAN GET NEW CLOTHES?
WE'RE NOT GONNA MAKE IT TO A STORE! I NEED NEW PANTS NOW! EVEN MY WEDGIE HAS A WEDGIE!
RIP
DO YOU HAVE A PROBLEM WITH WEARING A DEAD GUY'S CLOTHES?
I ALREADY AM A DEAD GUY!
PING
RIP

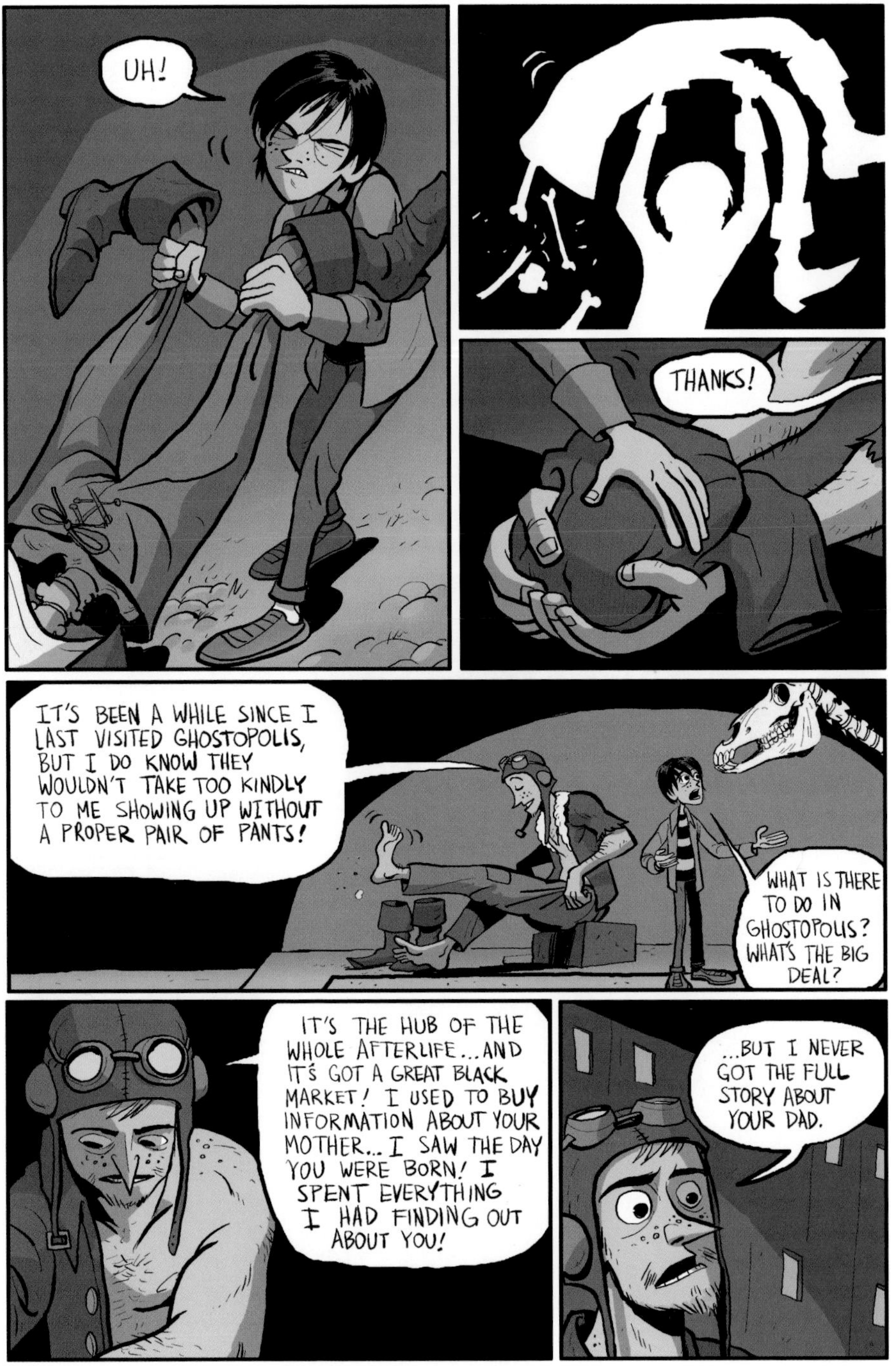
UH!
THANKS!
IT'S BEEN A WHILE SINCE I LAST VISITED GHOSTOPOLIS, BUT I DO KNOW THEY WOULDN'T TAKE TOO KINDLY TO ME SHOWING UP WITHOUT A PROPER PAIR OF PANTS!
WHAT IS THERE TO DO IN GHOSTOPOLIS? WHAT'S THE BIG DEAL?
IT'S THE HUB OF THE WHOLE AFTERLIFE... AND IT'S GOT A GREAT BLACK MARKET! I USED TO BUY INFORMATION ABOUT YOUR MOTHER... I SAW THE DAY YOU WERE BORN! I SPENT EVERYTHING I HAD FINDING OUT ABOUT YOU!
...BUT I NEVER GOT THE FULL STORY ABOUT YOUR DAD.

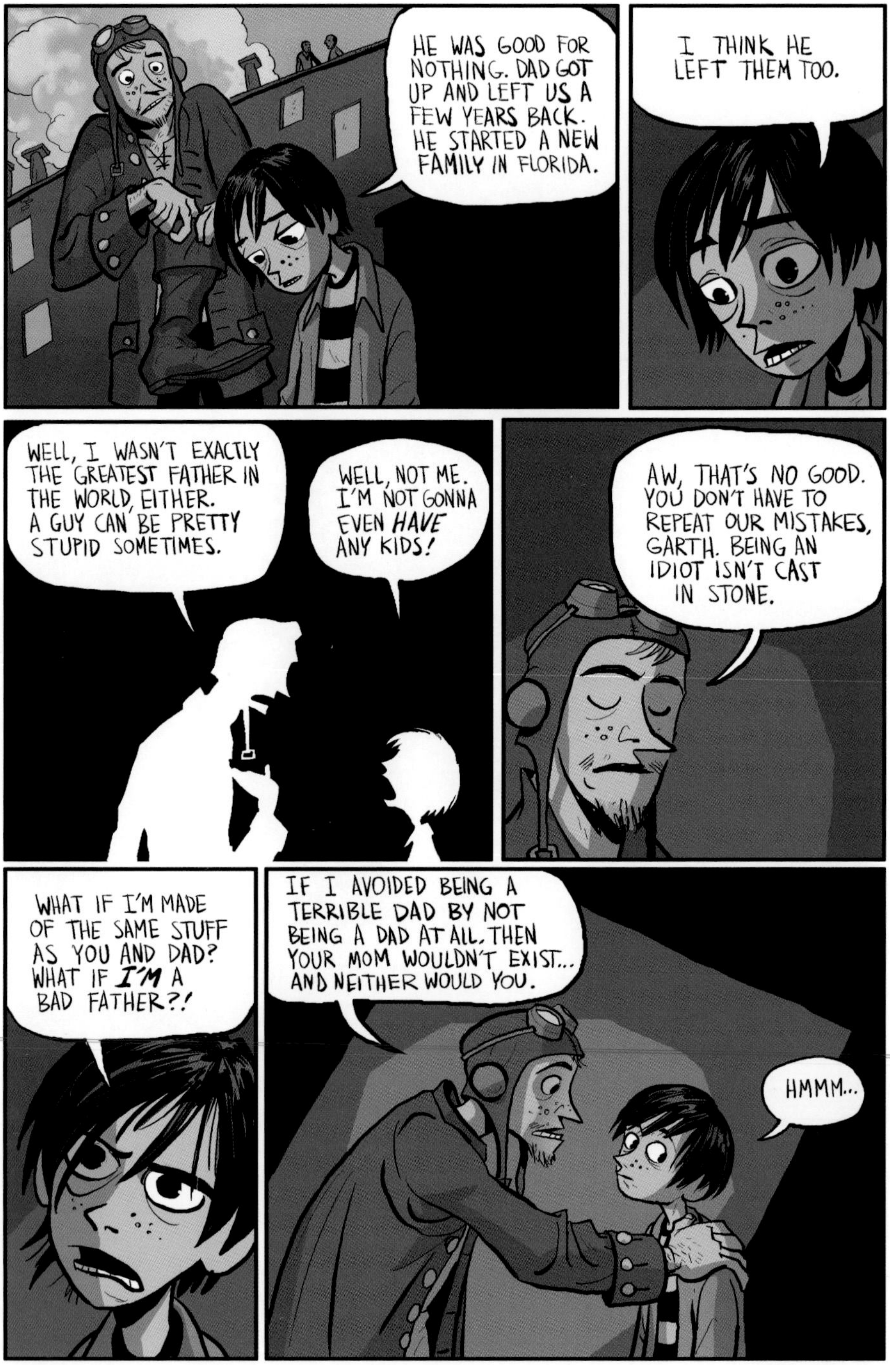
HE WAS GOOD FOR NOTHING. DAD GOT UP AND LEFT US A FEW YEARS BACK. HE STARTED A NEW FAMILY IN FLORIDA.
I THINK HE LEFT THEM TOO.
WELL, I WASN'T EXACTLY THE GREATEST FATHER IN THE WORLD, EITHER. A GUY CAN BE PRETTY STUPID SOMETIMES.
WELL, NOT ME. I'M NOT GONNA EVEN *HAVE* ANY KIDS!
AW, THAT'S NO GOOD. YOU DON'T HAVE TO REPEAT OUR MISTAKES, GARTH. BEING AN IDIOT ISN'T CAST IN STONE.
WHAT IF I'M MADE OF THE SAME STUFF AS YOU AND DAD? WHAT IF *I'M* A BAD FATHER?!
IF I AVOIDED BEING A TERRIBLE DAD BY NOT BEING A DAD AT ALL, THEN YOUR MOM WOULDN'T EXIST... AND NEITHER WOULD YOU.
HMMM...

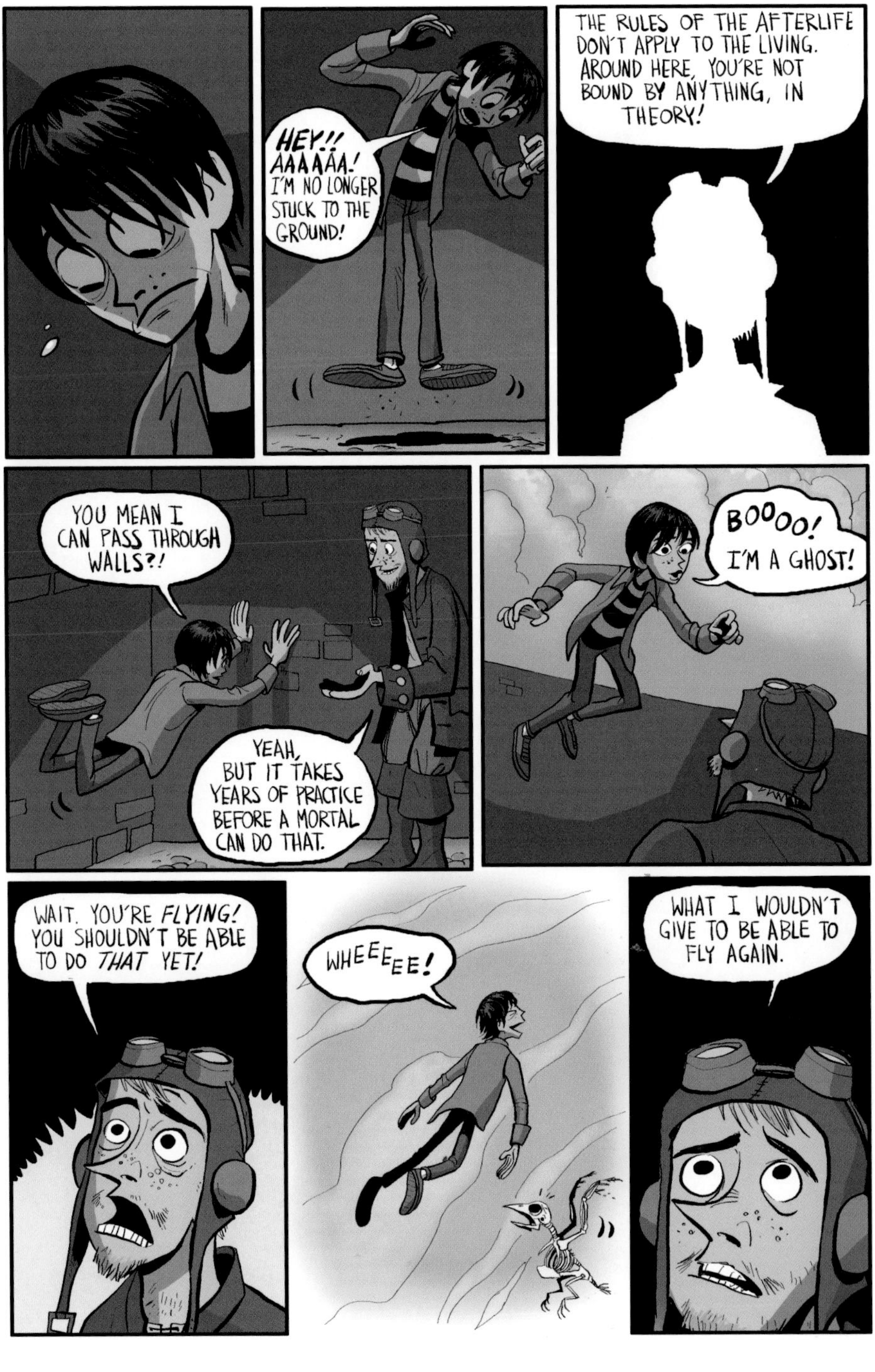
HEY!! AAAAAA! I'M NO LONGER STUCK TO THE GROUND!
THE RULES OF THE AFTERLIFE DON'T APPLY TO THE LIVING. AROUND HERE, YOU'RE NOT BOUND BY ANYTHING, IN THEORY!
YOU MEAN I CAN PASS THROUGH WALLS?!
YEAH, BUT IT TAKES YEARS OF PRACTICE BEFORE A MORTAL CAN DO THAT.
BOOOO! I'M A GHOST!
WAIT. YOU'RE *FLYING!* YOU SHOULDN'T BE ABLE TO DO *THAT* YET!
WHEEEEEE!
WHAT I WOULDN'T GIVE TO BE ABLE TO FLY AGAIN.

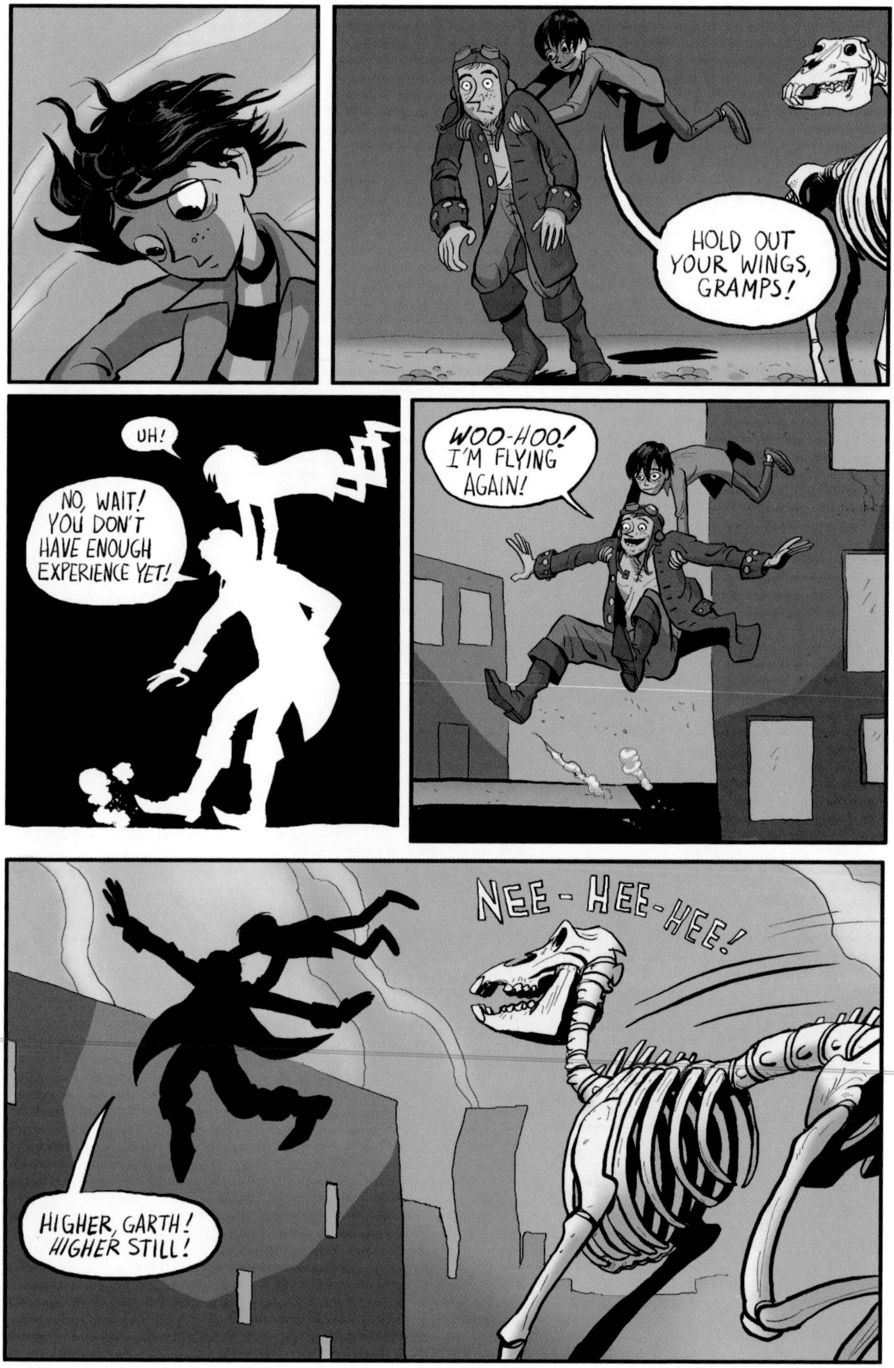
HOLD OUT YOUR WINGS, GRAMPS!
UH!
NO, WAIT! YOU DON'T HAVE ENOUGH EXPERIENCE YET!
WOO-HOO! I'M FLYING AGAIN!
NEE-HEE-HEE!
HIGHER, GARTH! HIGHER STILL!

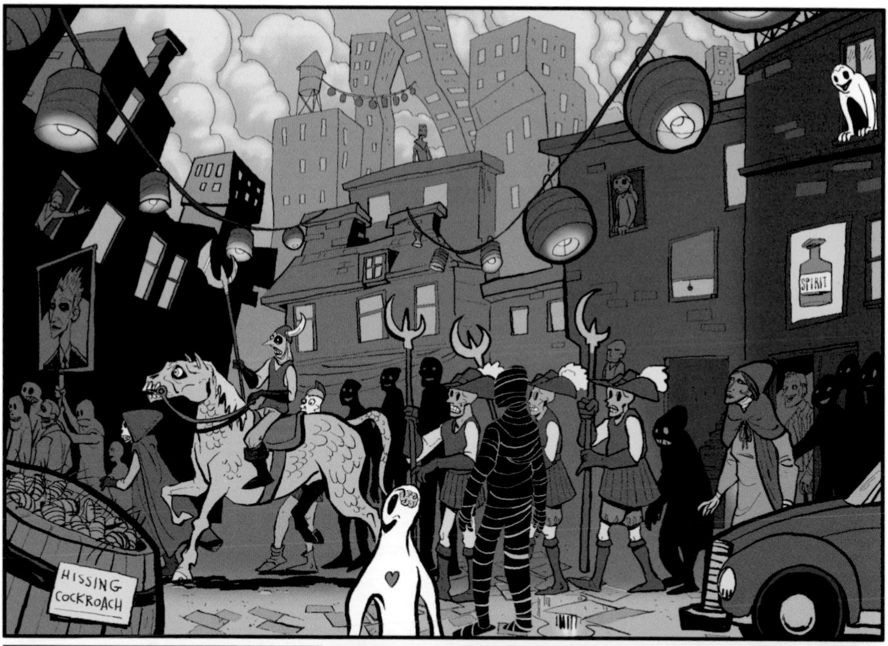
SPIRIT
HISSING COCKROACH

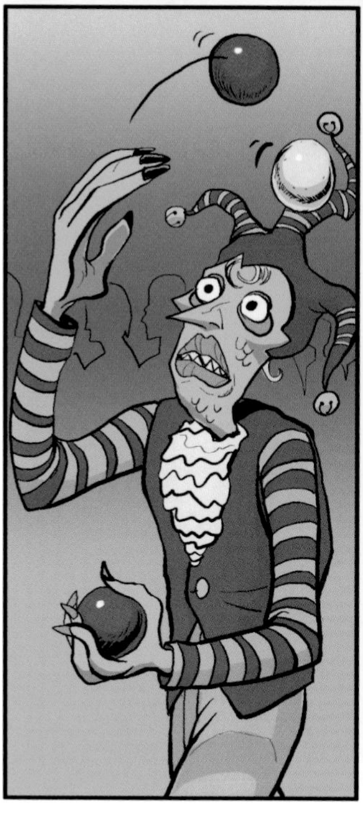

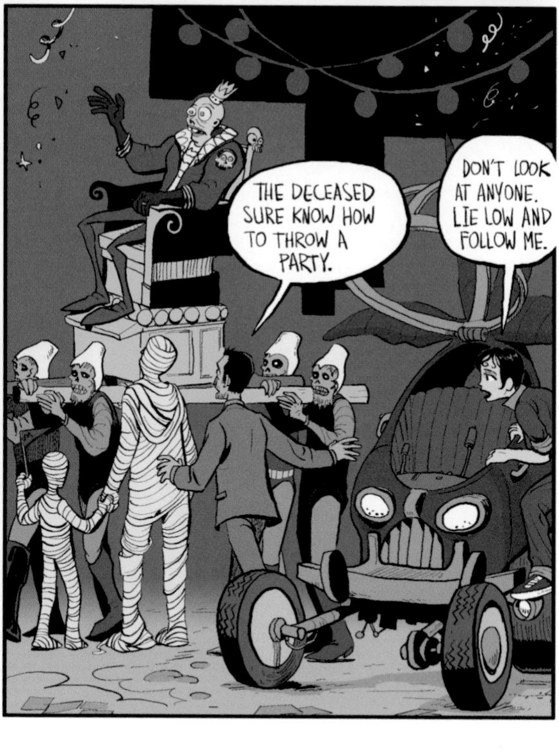
THE DECEASED SURE KNOW HOW TO THROW A PARTY.
DON'T LOOK AT ANYONE. LIE LOW AND FOLLOW ME.

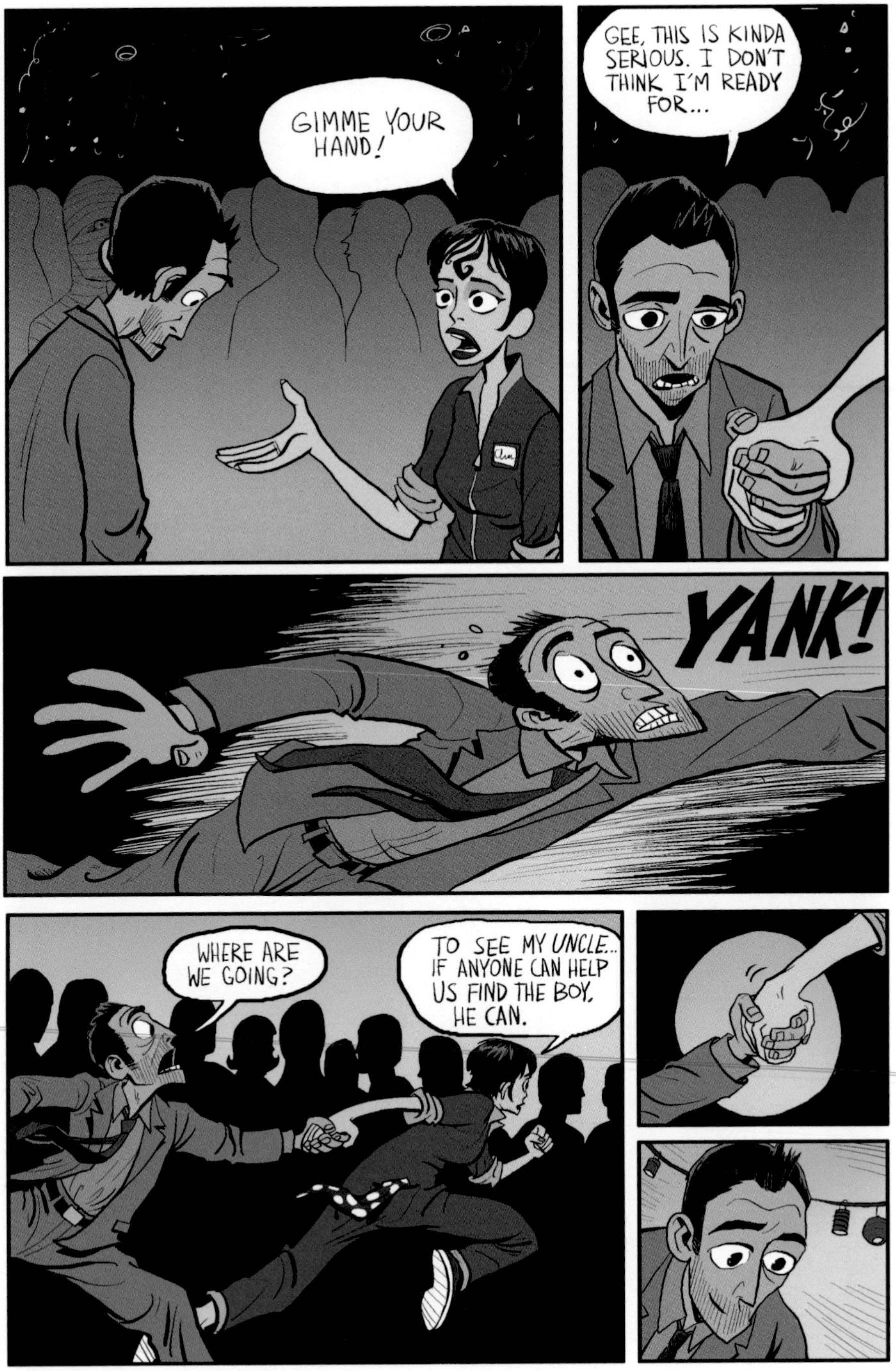
GIMME YOUR HAND!
GEE, THIS IS KINDA SERIOUS. I DON'T THINK I'M READY FOR...
YANK!
WHERE ARE WE GOING?
TO SEE MY UNCLE... IF ANYONE CAN HELP US FIND THE BOY, HE CAN.

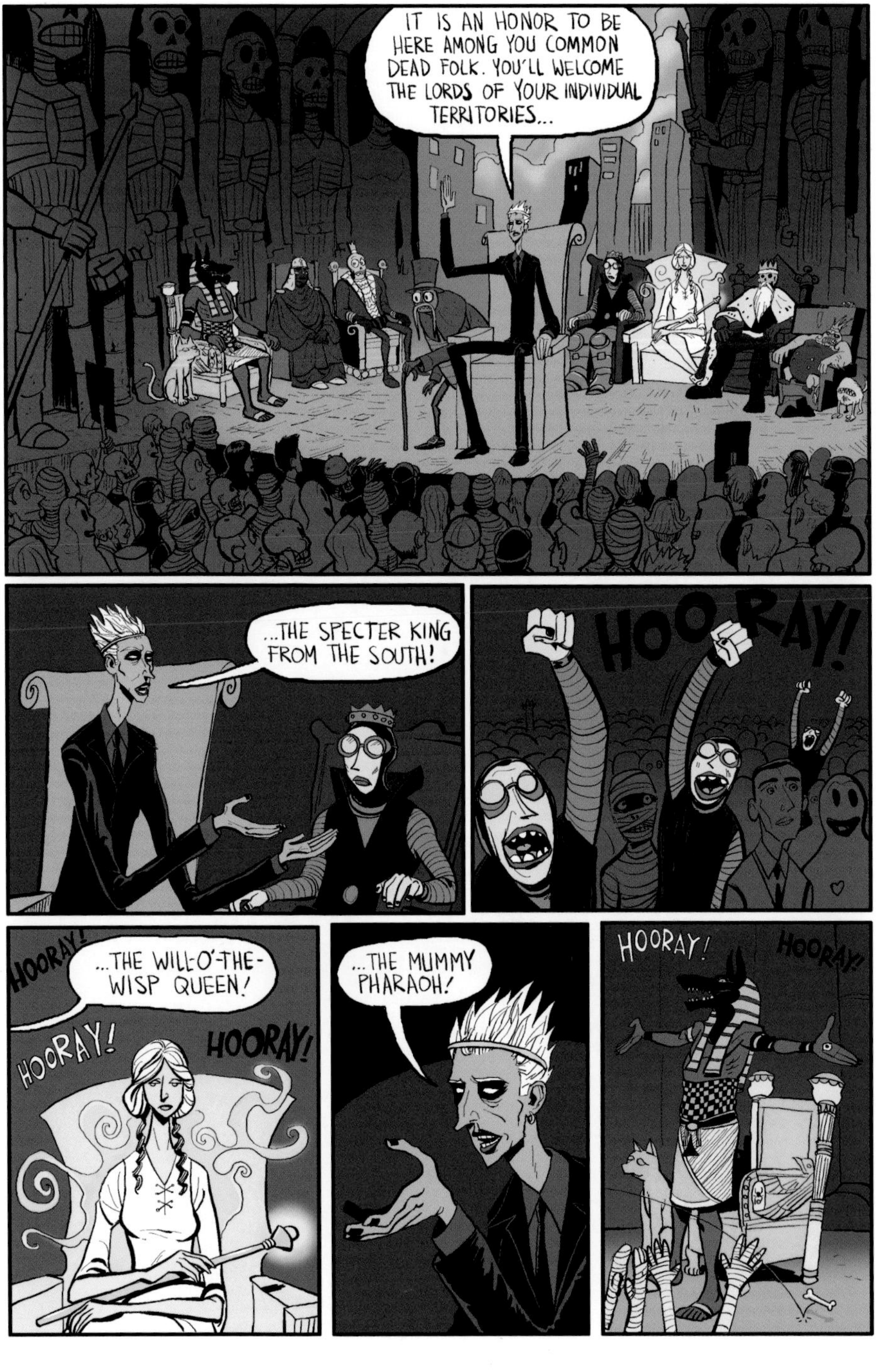

IT IS AN HONOR TO BE HERE AMONG YOU COMMON DEAD FOLK. YOU'LL WELCOME THE LORDS OF YOUR INDIVIDUAL TERRITORIES...
...THE SPECTER KING FROM THE SOUTH!
HOORAY!
HOORAY!
...THE WILL-O'-THE-WISP QUEEN!
HOORAY!
HOORAY!
...THE MUMMY PHARAOH!
HOORAY!
HOORAY!

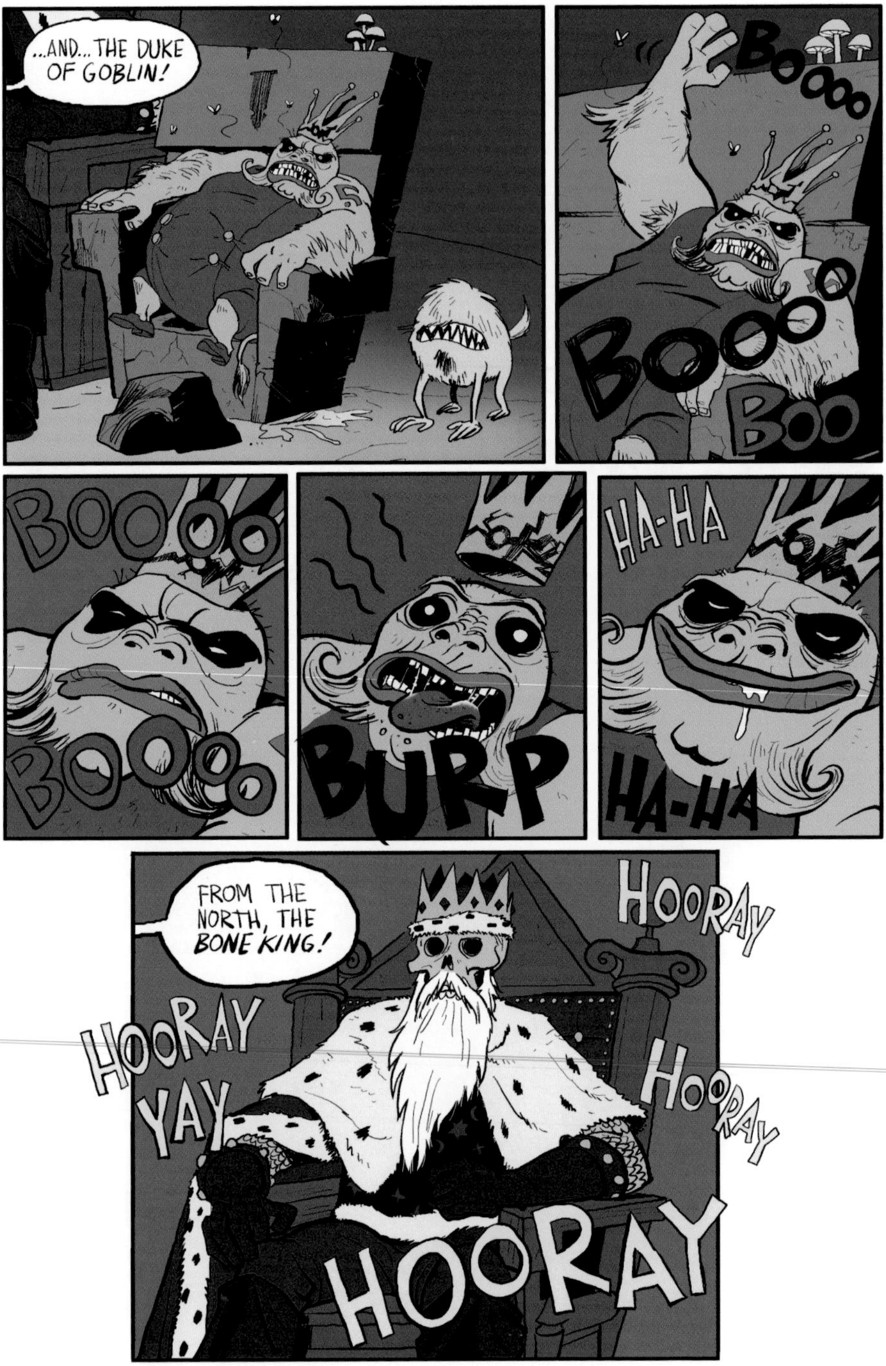

...AND... THE DUKE OF GOBLIN!
BOOOOO
BOOOOO
BOO
BOOOOO
BOOOOO
BURP
HA-HA
HA-HA
FROM THE NORTH, THE BONE KING!
HOORAY
HOORAY
YAY
HOORAY
HOORAY

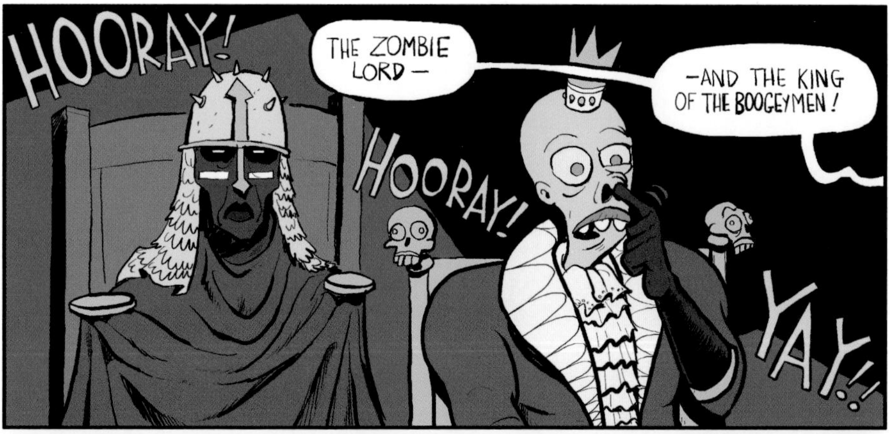
HOORAY!
THE ZOMBIE LORD —
—AND THE KING OF THE BOOGEYMEN!
HOORAY!
YAY!!

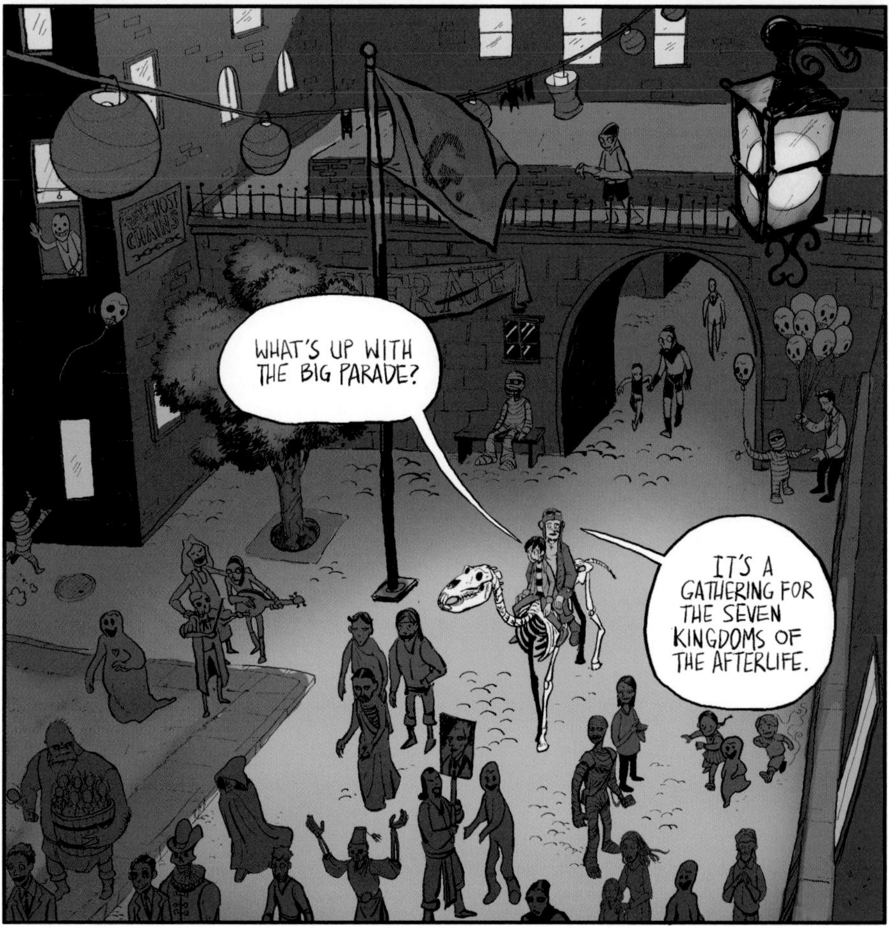
WHAT'S UP WITH THE BIG PARADE?
IT'S A GATHERING FOR THE SEVEN KINGDOMS OF THE AFTERLIFE.

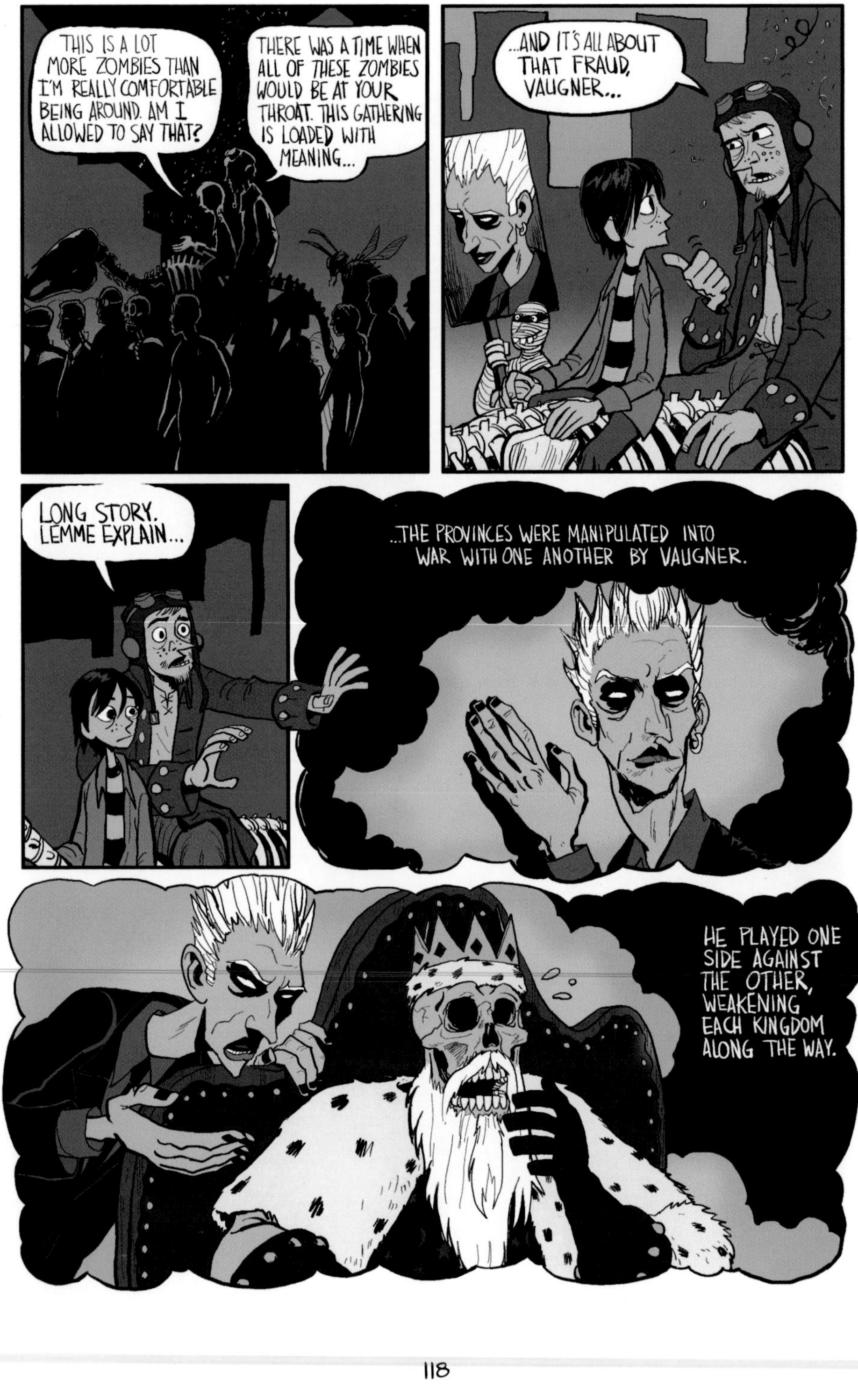
THIS IS A LOT MORE ZOMBIES THAN I'M REALLY COMFORTABLE BEING AROUND. AM I ALLOWED TO SAY THAT?
THERE WAS A TIME WHEN ALL OF THESE ZOMBIES WOULD BE AT YOUR THROAT. THIS GATHERING IS LOADED WITH MEANING...
...AND IT'S ALL ABOUT THAT FRAUD, VAUGNER...
LONG STORY. LEMME EXPLAIN...
...THE PROVINCES WERE MANIPULATED INTO WAR WITH ONE ANOTHER BY VAUGNER.
HE PLAYED ONE SIDE AGAINST THE OTHER, WEAKENING EACH KINGDOM ALONG THE WAY.

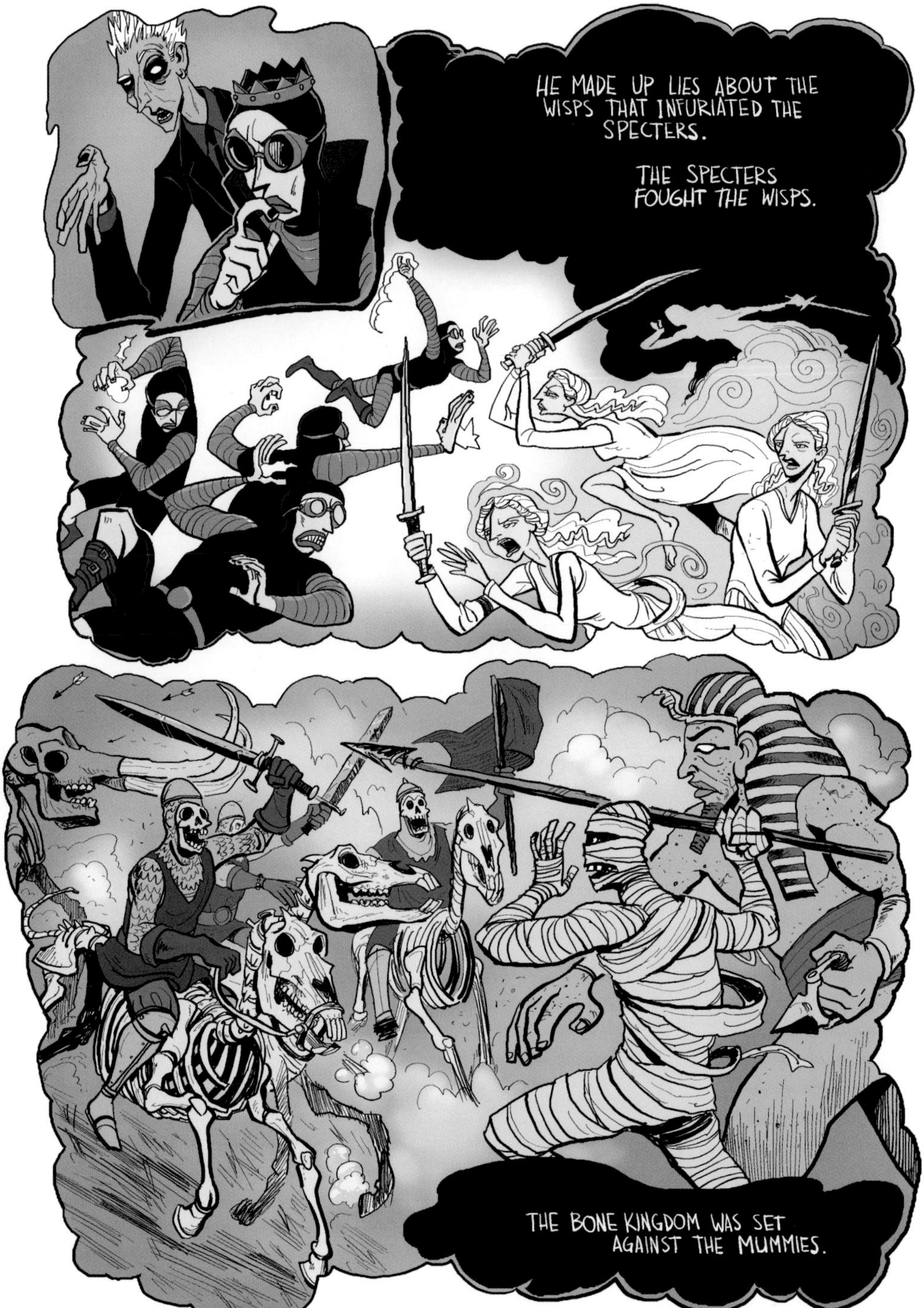
HE MADE UP LIES ABOUT THE WISPS THAT INFURIATED THE SPECTERS.
THE SPECTERS FOUGHT THE WISPS.
THE BONE KINGDOM WAS SET AGAINST THE MUMMIES.

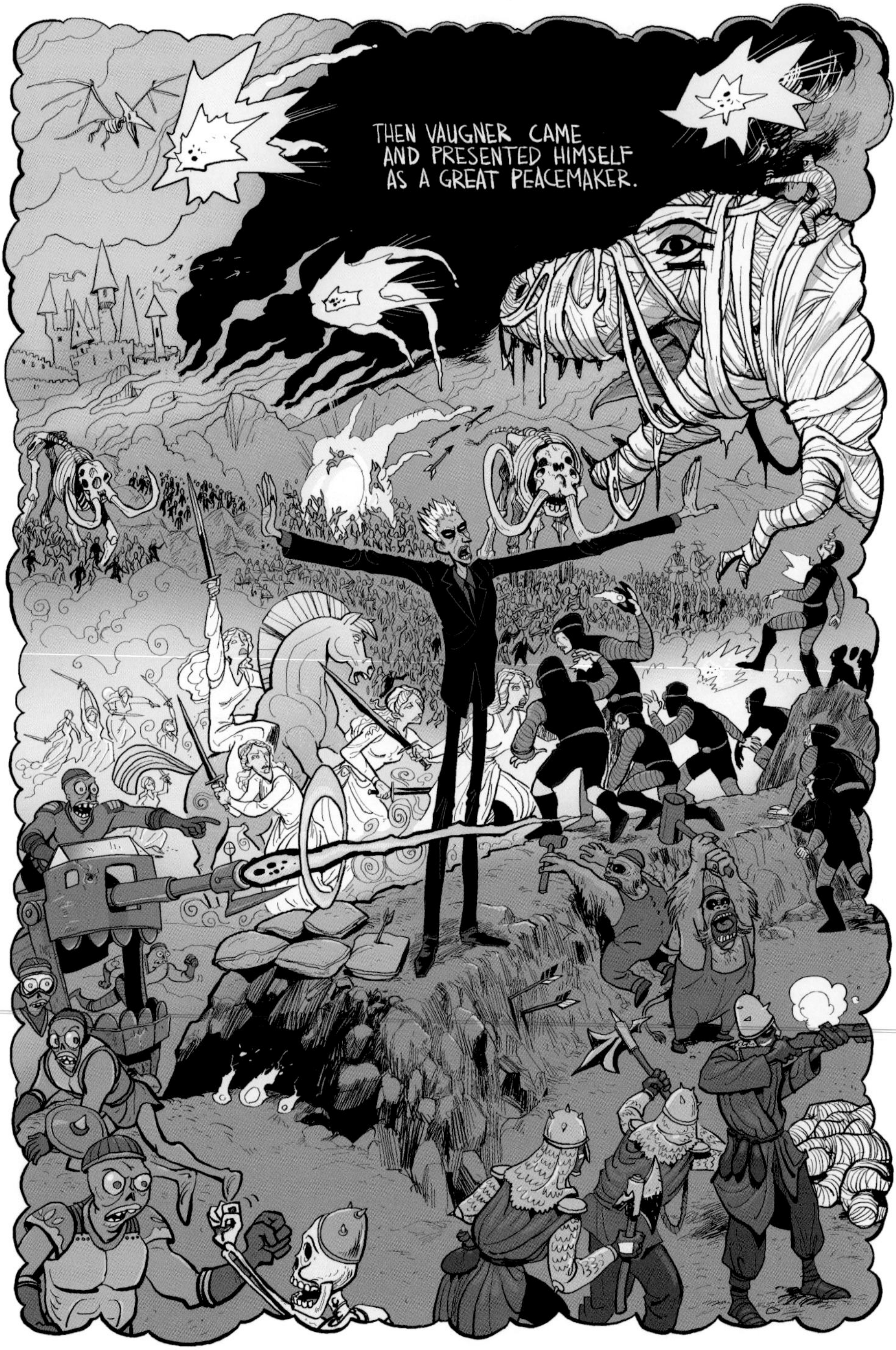
THEN VAUGNER CAME AND PRESENTED HIMSELF AS A GREAT PEACEMAKER.

HE PROMISED THEM UNITY. UNDER VAUGNER'S ONE STATE OF GHOSTOPOLIS, OF COURSE. EVERYTHING WAS FINE...

...UNTIL HE STARTED CONJURING UP INSECTS FROM THE UNDERWORLD TO DO HIS BIDDING.

NOW GHOSTOPOLIS IS A DUMP FULL OF CRIME AND BUGS. ALL GOOD GHOSTS DREAM OF ESCAPING TO EARTH.

I HATE BUGS!

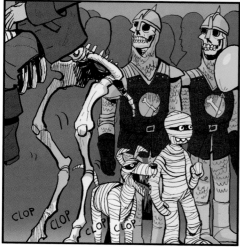

CLOP CLOP CLOP CLOP

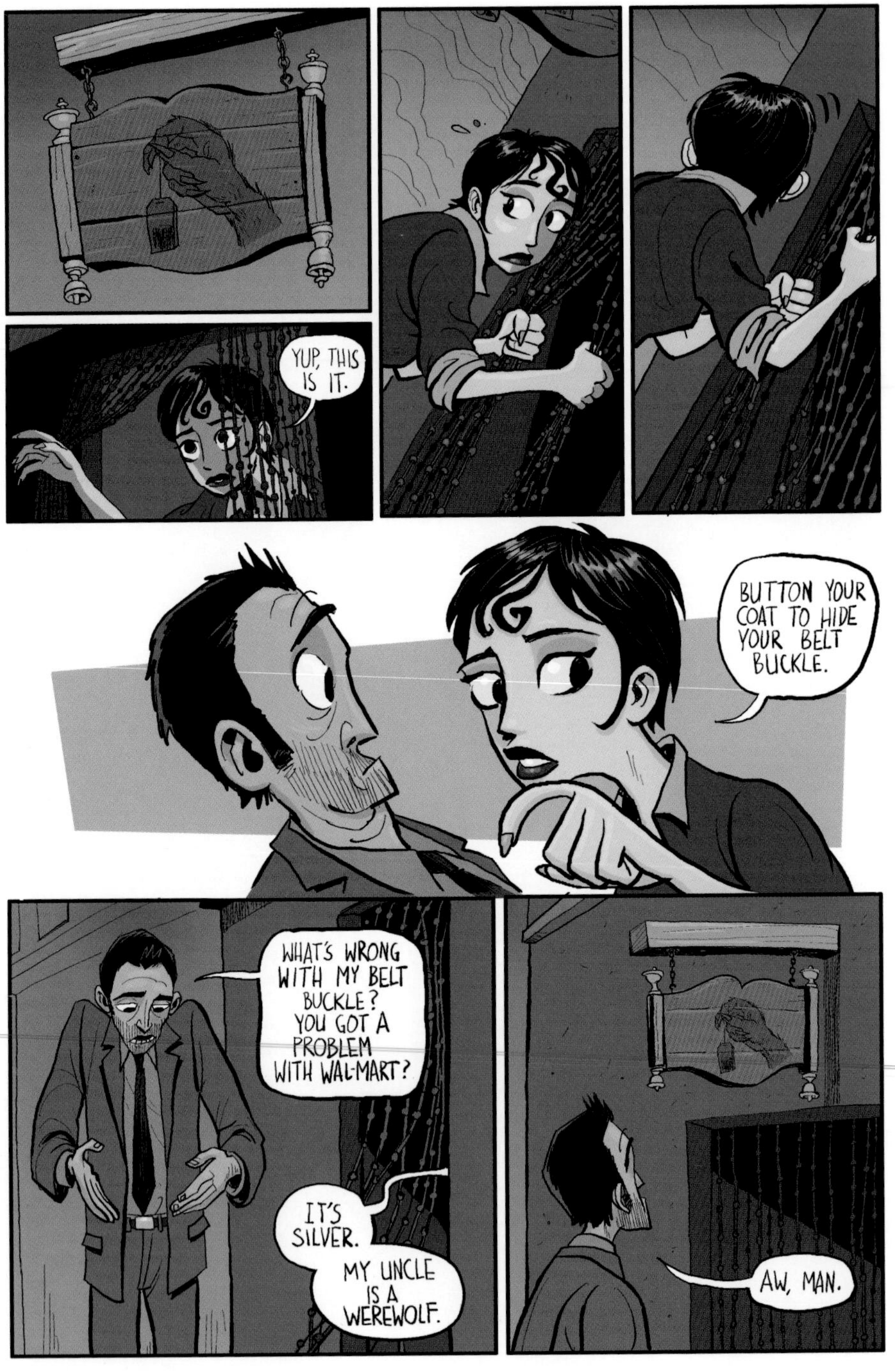
YUP, THIS IS IT.
BUTTON YOUR COAT TO HIDE YOUR BELT BUCKLE.
WHAT'S WRONG WITH MY BELT BUCKLE? YOU GOT A PROBLEM WITH WAL-MART?
IT'S SILVER.
MY UNCLE IS A WEREWOLF.
AW, MAN.

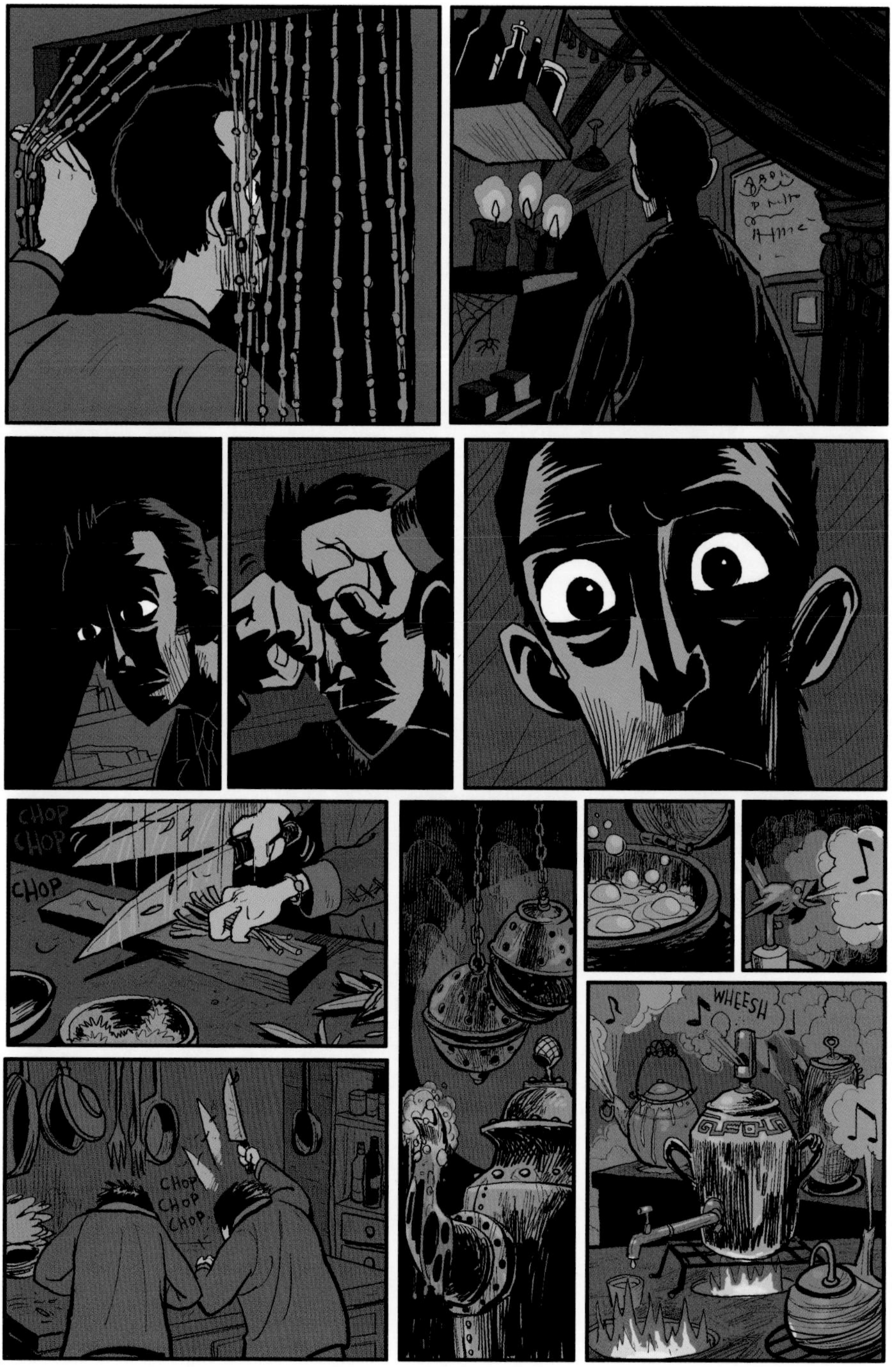
CHOP
CHOP
CHOP
WHEESH
CHOP
CHOP
CHOP

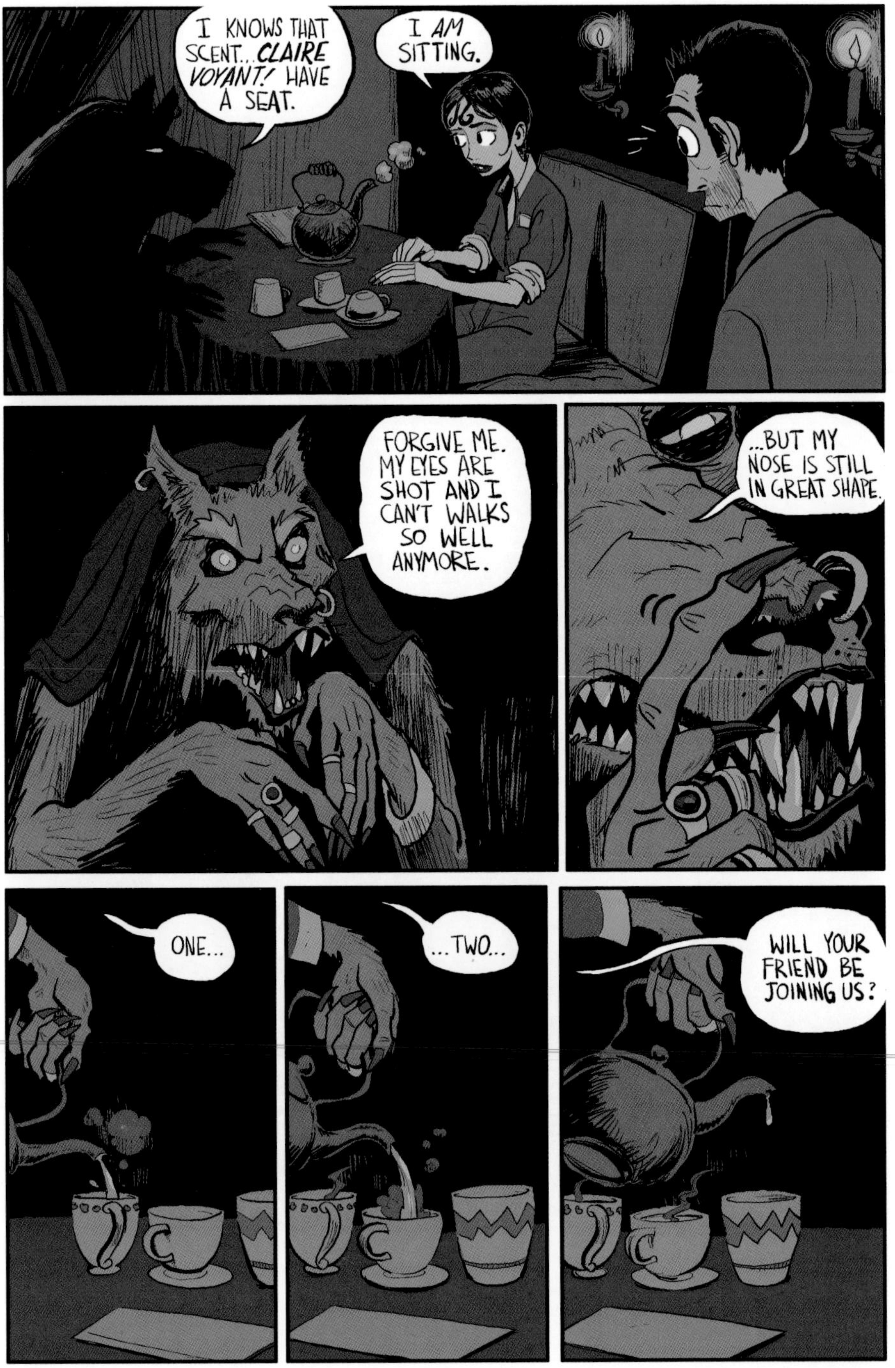
I KNOWS THAT SCENT... CLAIRE VOYANT! HAVE A SEAT.
I AM SITTING.
FORGIVE ME. MY EYES ARE SHOT AND I CAN'T WALKS SO WELL ANYMORE.
...BUT MY NOSE IS STILL IN GREAT SHAPE.
ONE...
...TWO...
WILL YOUR FRIEND BE JOINING US?

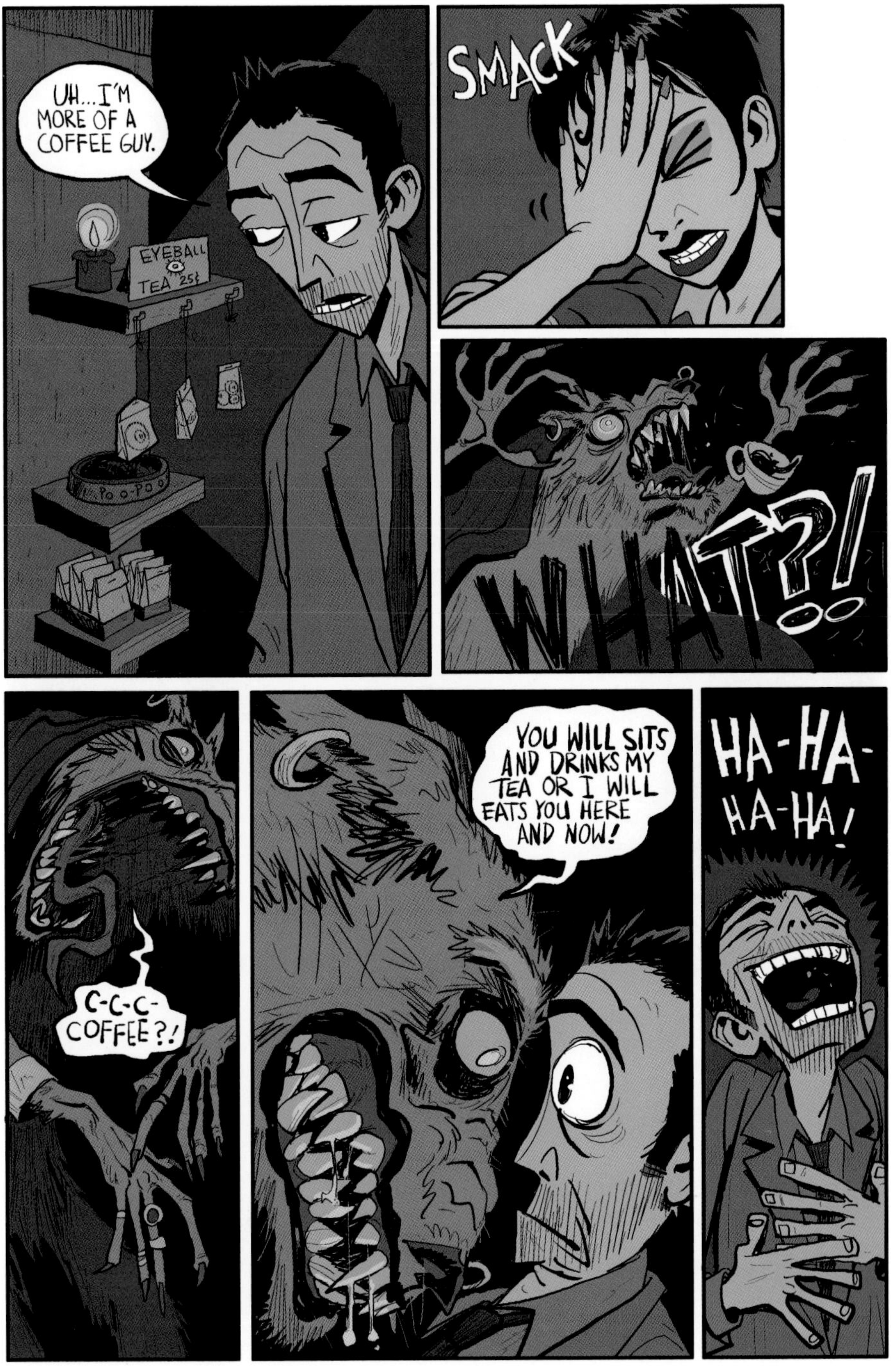
UH... I'M MORE OF A COFFEE GUY.
EYEBALL TEA 25¢
PO-PO
SMACK
WHAT?!
C-C-C-COFFEE?!
YOU WILL SITS AND DRINKS MY TEA OR I WILL EATS YOU HERE AND NOW!
HA-HA-HA-HA!

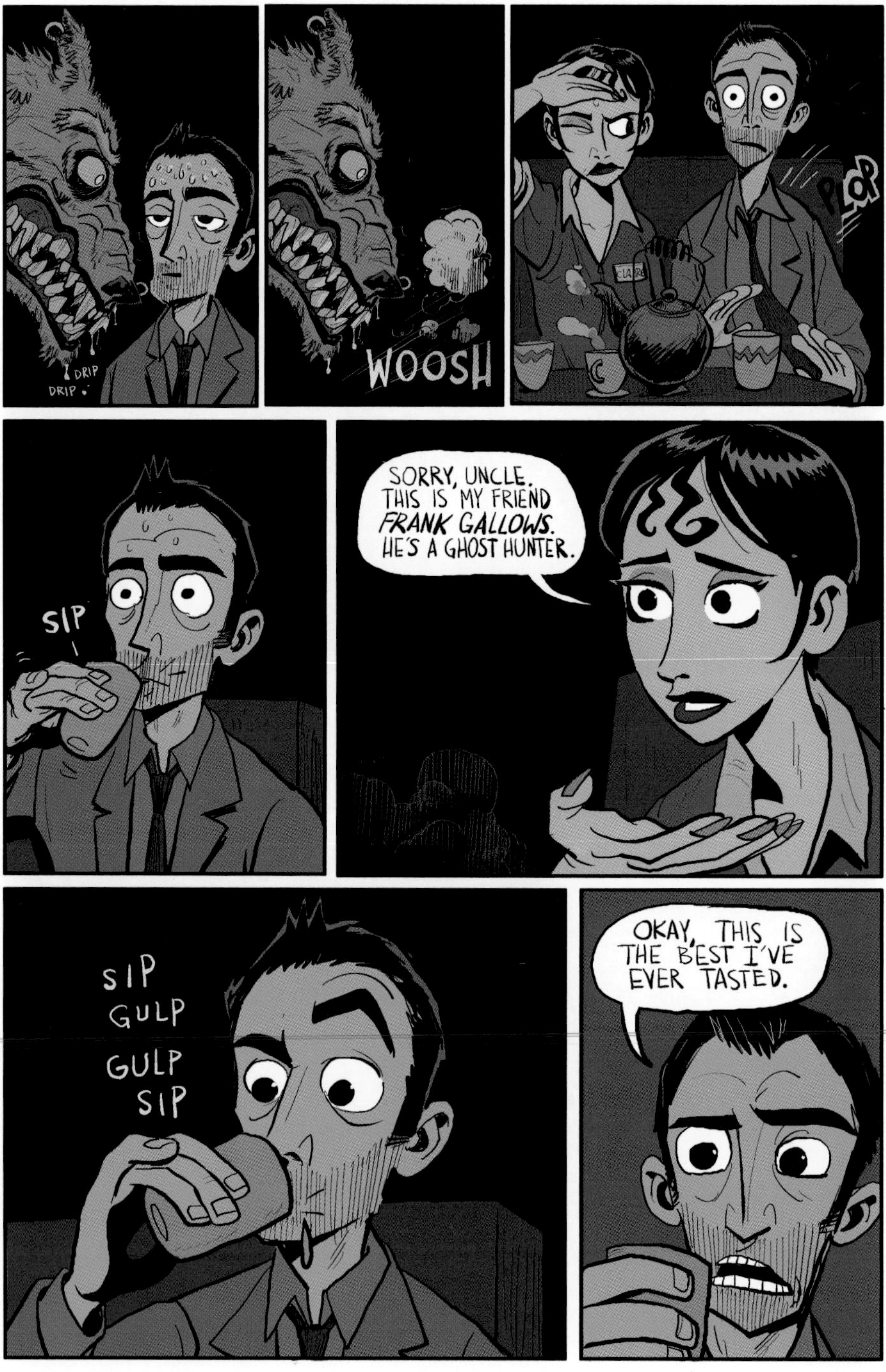
DRIP
DRIP
WOOSH
PLOP
SIP
SORRY, UNCLE. THIS IS MY FRIEND *FRANK GALLOWS.* HE'S A GHOST HUNTER.
SIP
GULP
GULP
SIP
OKAY, THIS IS THE BEST I'VE EVER TASTED.

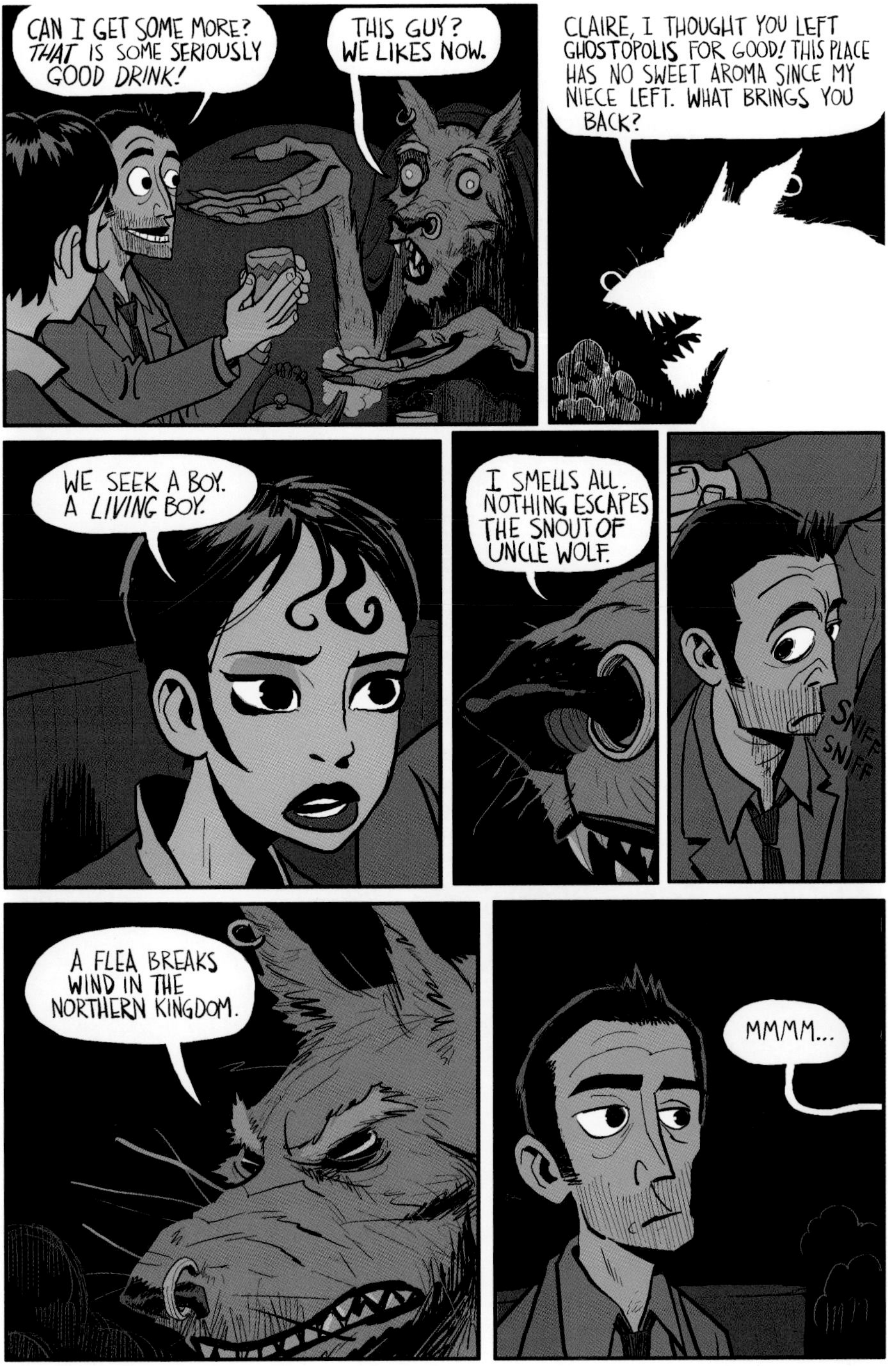

CAN I GET SOME MORE? THAT IS SOME SERIOUSLY GOOD DRINK!
THIS GUY? WE LIKES NOW.
CLAIRE, I THOUGHT YOU LEFT GHOSTOPOLIS FOR GOOD! THIS PLACE HAS NO SWEET AROMA SINCE MY NIECE LEFT. WHAT BRINGS YOU BACK?
WE SEEK A BOY. A LIVING BOY.
I SMELLS ALL. NOTHING ESCAPES THE SNOUT OF UNCLE WOLF.
SNIFF SNIFF
A FLEA BREAKS WIND IN THE NORTHERN KINGDOM.
MMMM...

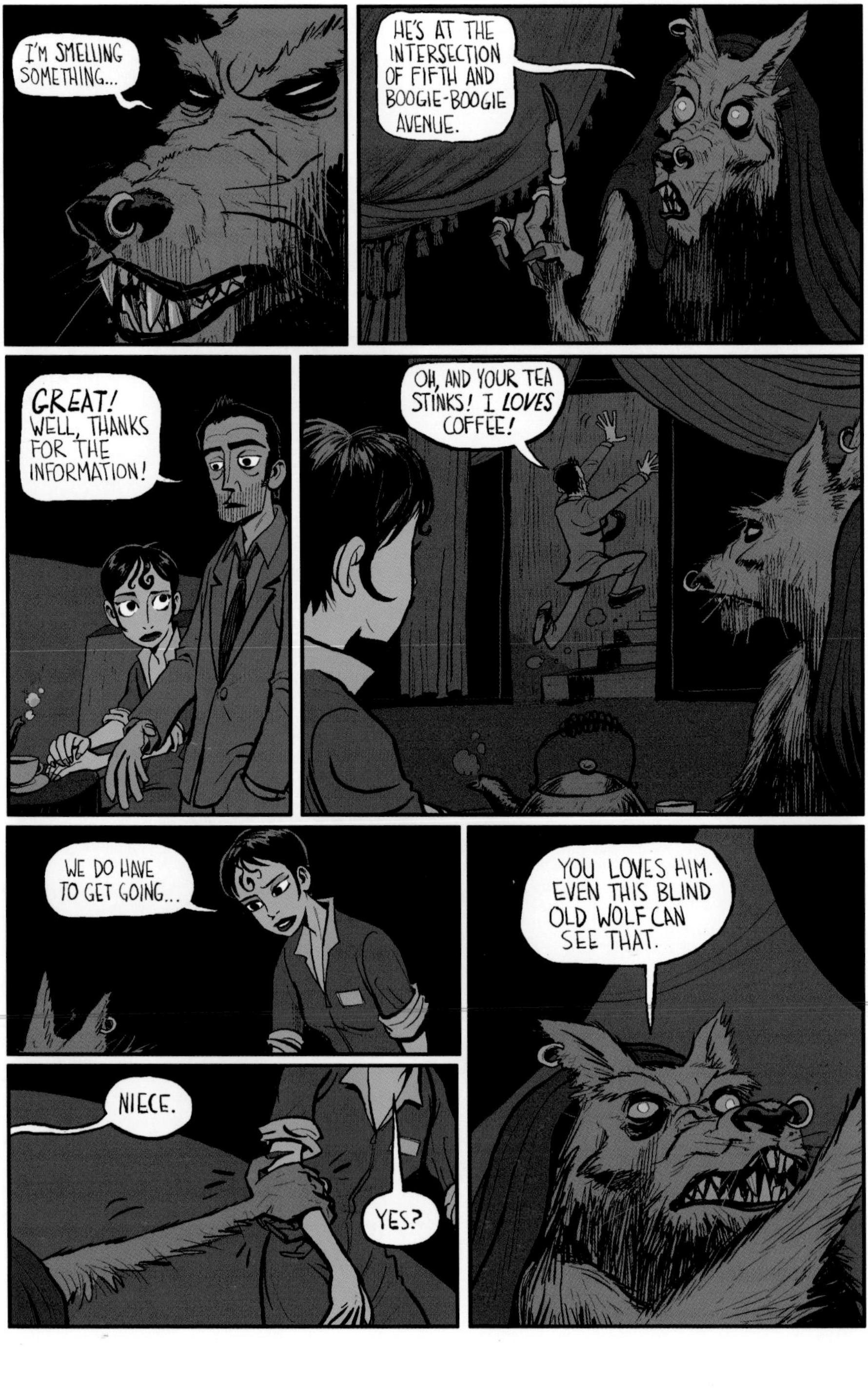
I'M SMELLING SOMETHING...
HE'S AT THE INTERSECTION OF FIFTH AND BOOGIE-BOOGIE AVENUE.
GREAT! WELL, THANKS FOR THE INFORMATION!
OH, AND YOUR TEA STINKS! I LOVES COFFEE!
WE DO HAVE TO GET GOING...
NIECE.
YES?
YOU LOVES HIM. EVEN THIS BLIND OLD WOLF CAN SEE THAT.

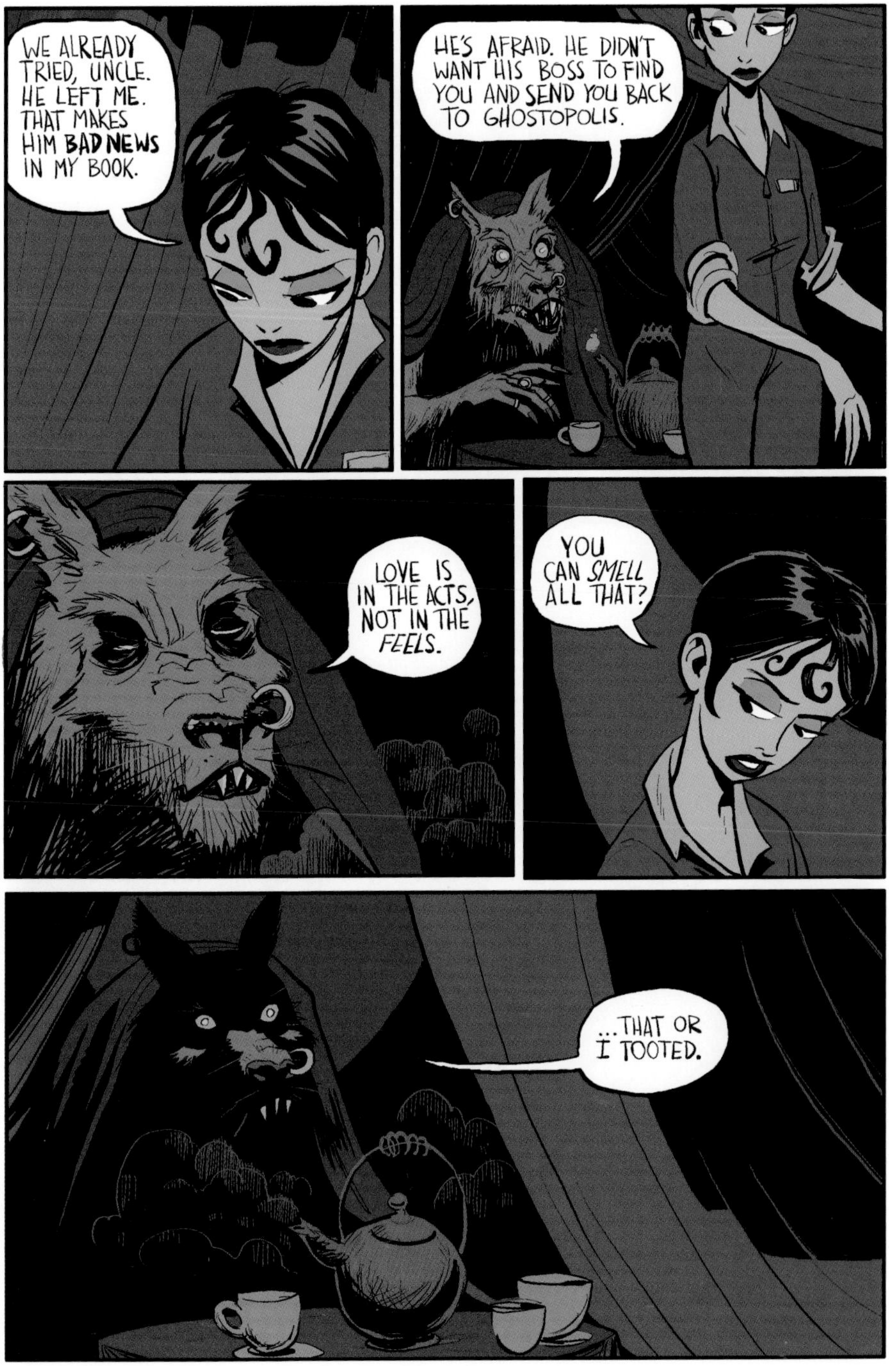
WE ALREADY TRIED, UNCLE. HE LEFT ME. THAT MAKES HIM **BAD NEWS** IN MY BOOK.
HE'S AFRAID. HE DIDN'T WANT HIS BOSS TO FIND YOU AND **SEND** YOU BACK TO GHOSTOPOLIS.
LOVE IS IN THE ACTS, NOT IN THE *FEELS*.
YOU CAN *SMELL* ALL THAT?
...THAT OR I TOOTED.

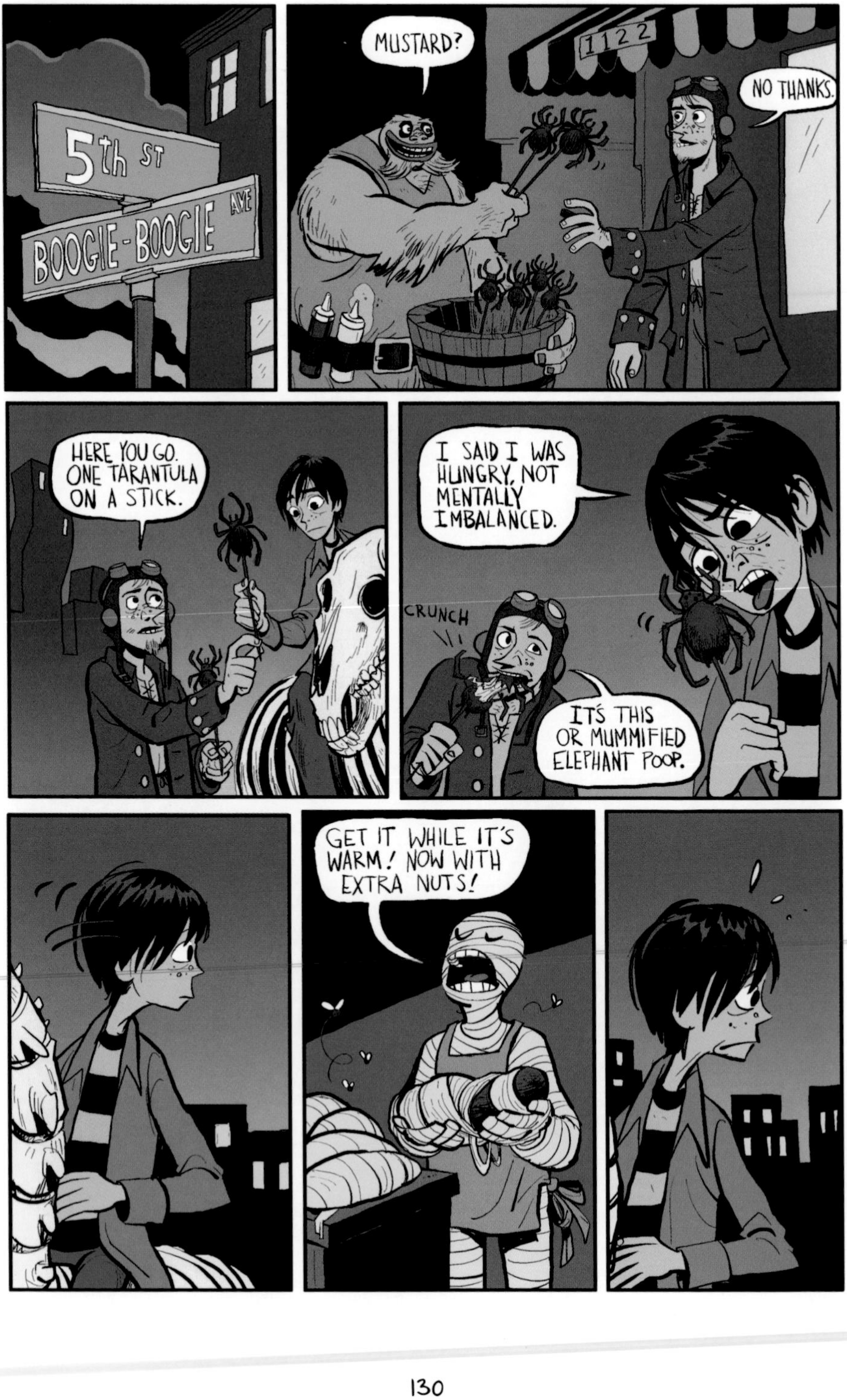
5th ST
BOOGIE-BOOGIE AVE
MUSTARD?
1122
NO THANKS.
HERE YOU GO. ONE TARANTULA ON A STICK.
I SAID I WAS HUNGRY, NOT MENTALLY IMBALANCED.
CRUNCH
IT'S THIS OR MUMMIFIED ELEPHANT POOP.
GET IT WHILE IT'S WARM! NOW WITH EXTRA NUTS!

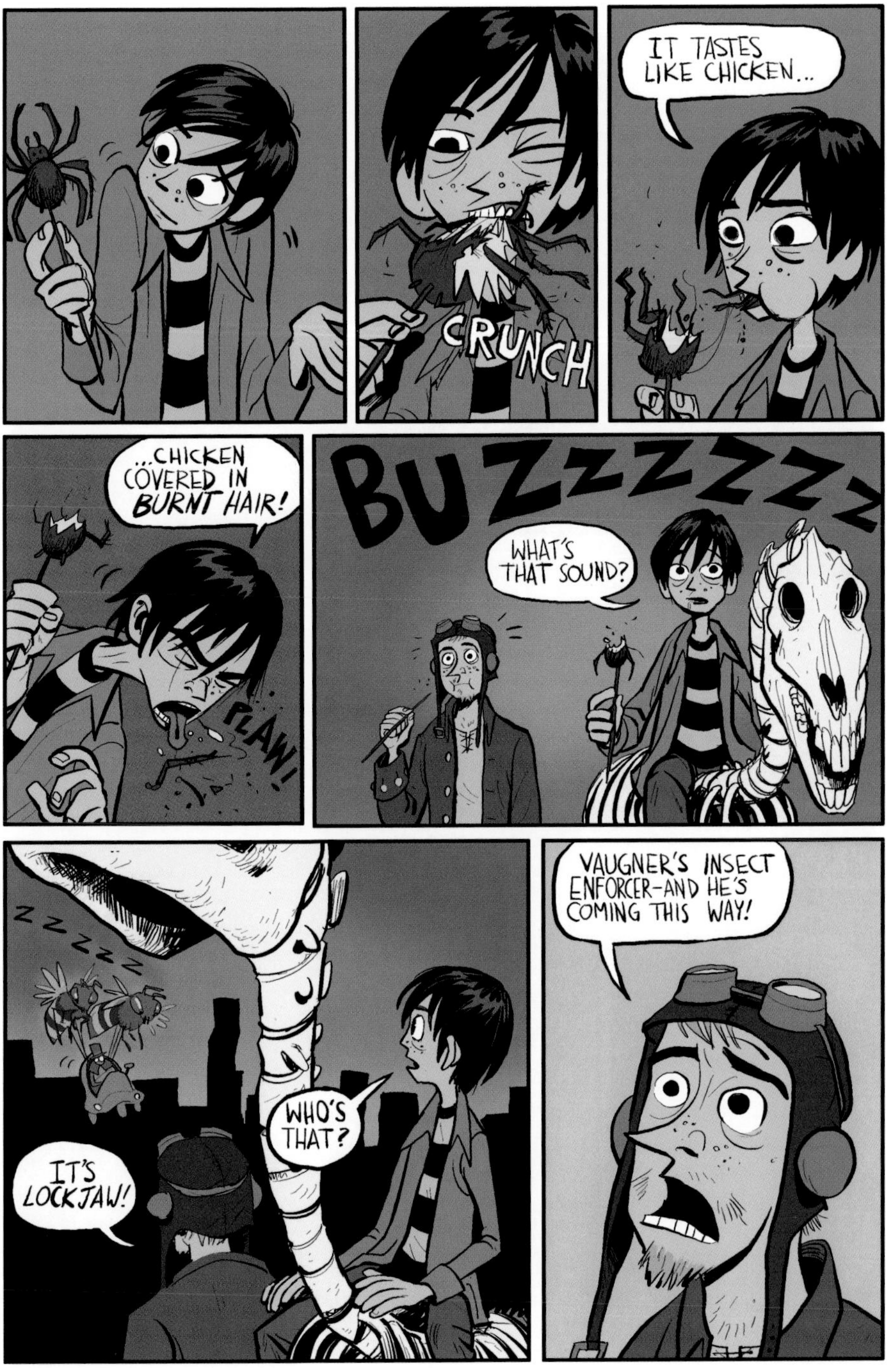
CRUNCH
IT TASTES LIKE CHICKEN...
...CHICKEN COVERED IN BURNT HAIR!
PLAW!
BUZZZZZZZ
WHAT'S THAT SOUND?
ZZZZZZ
WHO'S THAT?
IT'S LOCKJAW!
VAUGNER'S INSECT ENFORCER-AND HE'S COMING THIS WAY!

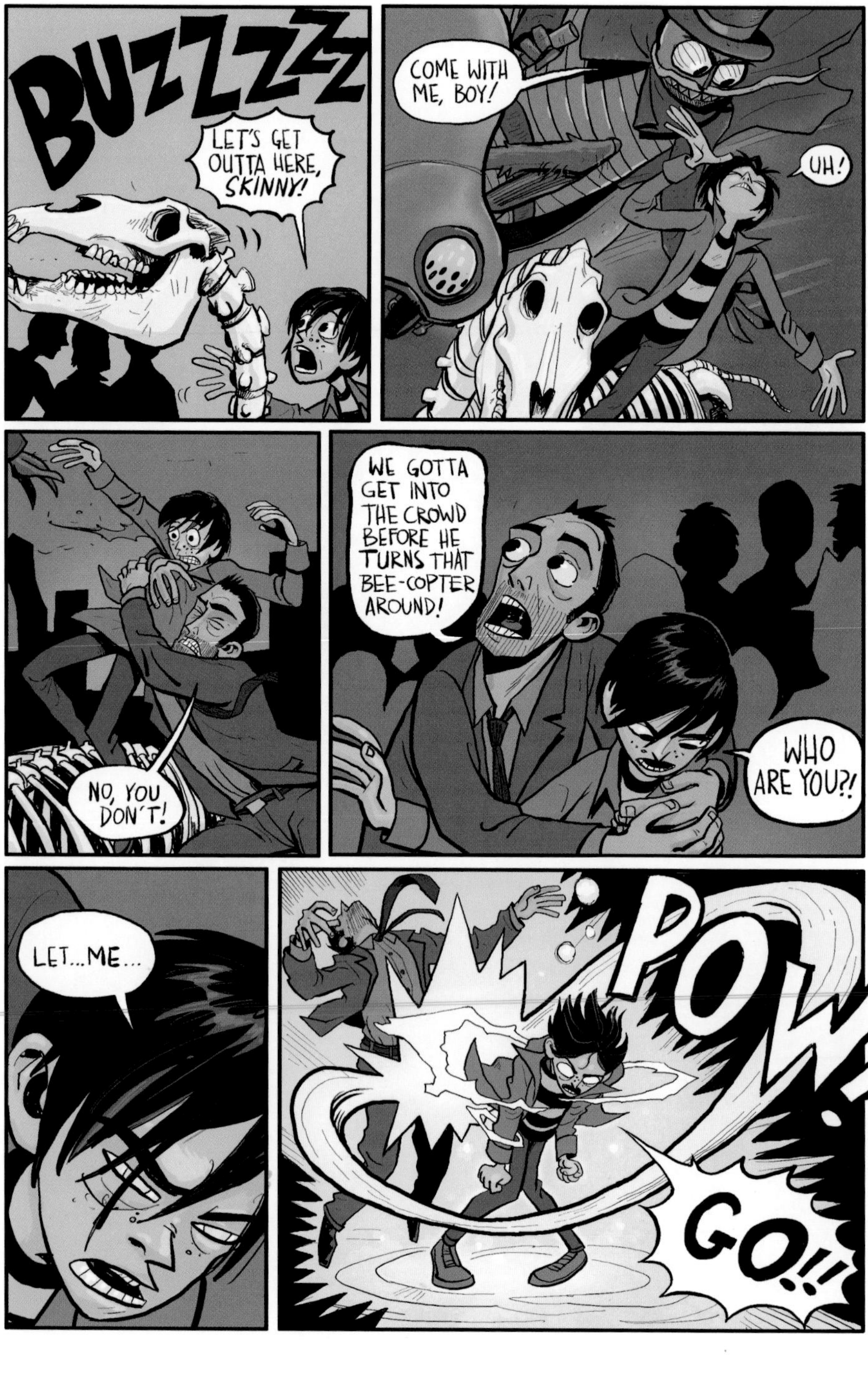
BUZZZZZ
LET'S GET OUTTA HERE, SKINNY!
COME WITH ME, BOY!
UH!
NO, YOU DON'T!
WE GOTTA GET INTO THE CROWD BEFORE HE TURNS THAT BEE-COPTER AROUND!
WHO ARE YOU?!
LET...ME...
POW!
GO!!

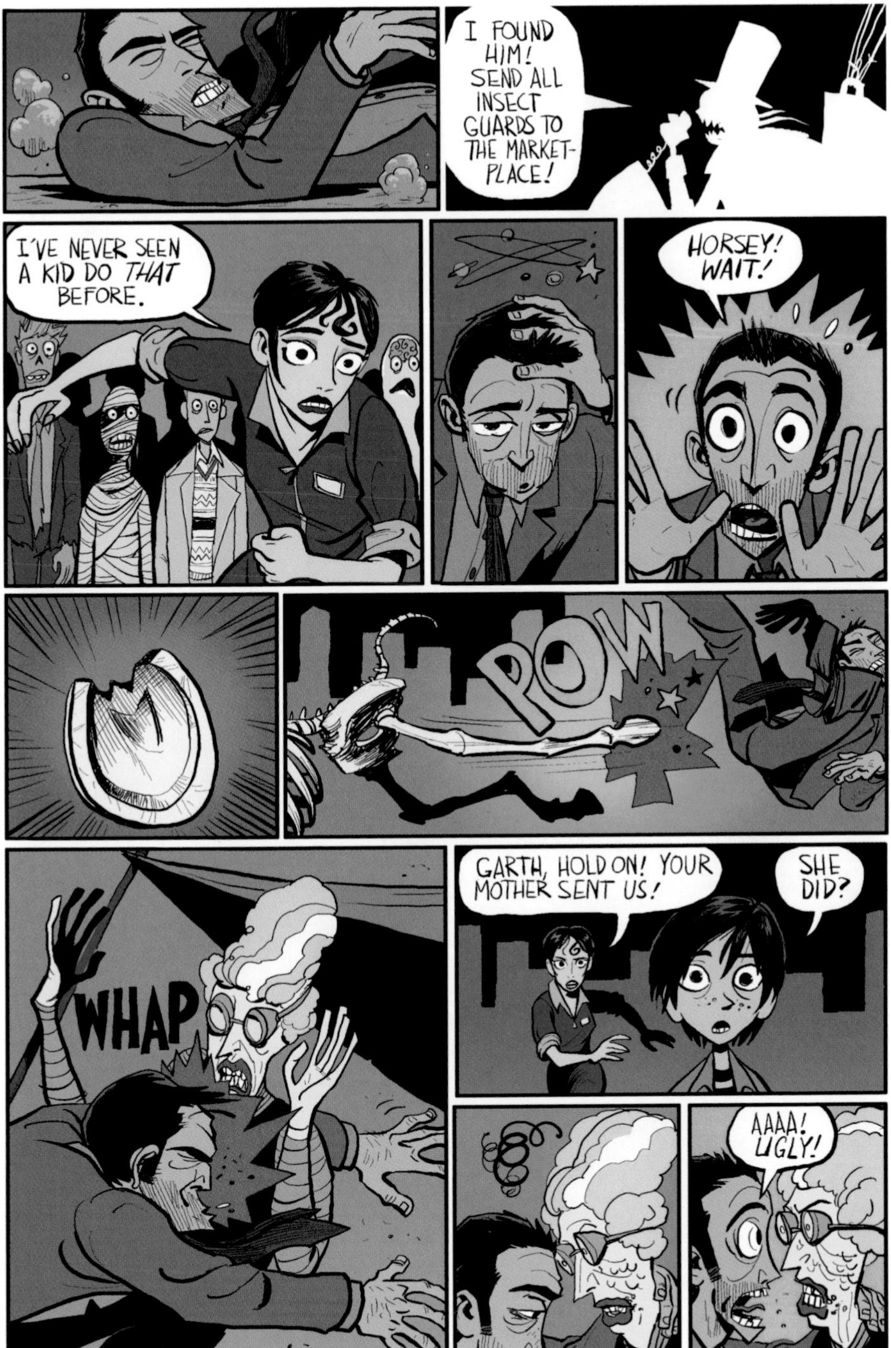
I FOUND HIM! SEND ALL INSECT GUARDS TO THE MARKET-PLACE!
I'VE NEVER SEEN A KID DO *THAT* BEFORE.
HORSEY! WAIT!
POW
WHAP
GARTH, HOLD ON! YOUR MOTHER SENT US!
SHE DID?
AAAA! UGLY!

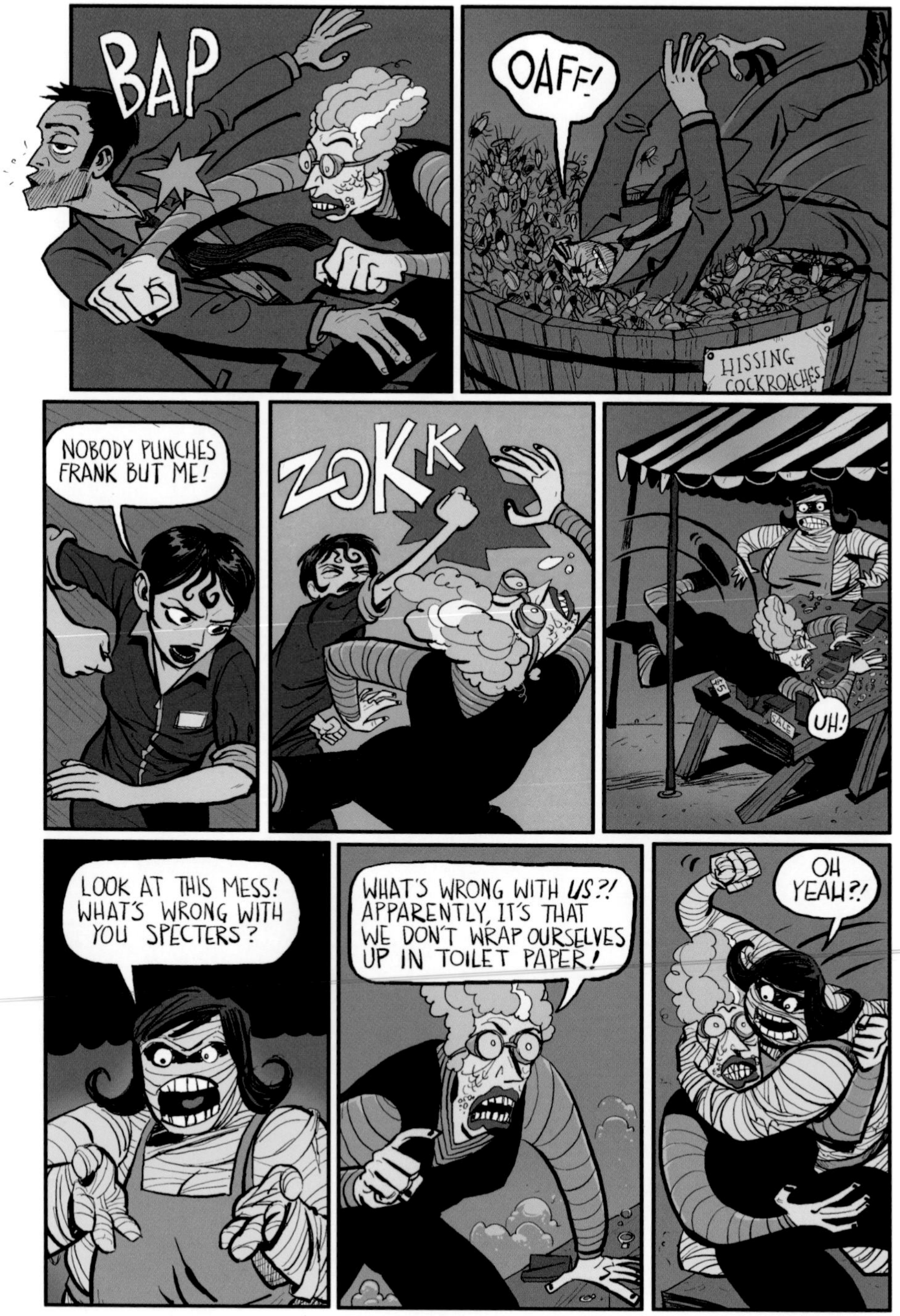
BAP
OAFF!
HISSING COCKROACHES
NOBODY PUNCHES FRANK BUT ME!
ZOKK
UH!
SALE
LOOK AT THIS MESS! WHAT'S WRONG WITH YOU SPECTERS?
WHAT'S WRONG WITH *US*?! APPARENTLY, IT'S THAT WE DON'T WRAP OURSELVES UP IN TOILET PAPER!
OH YEAH?!

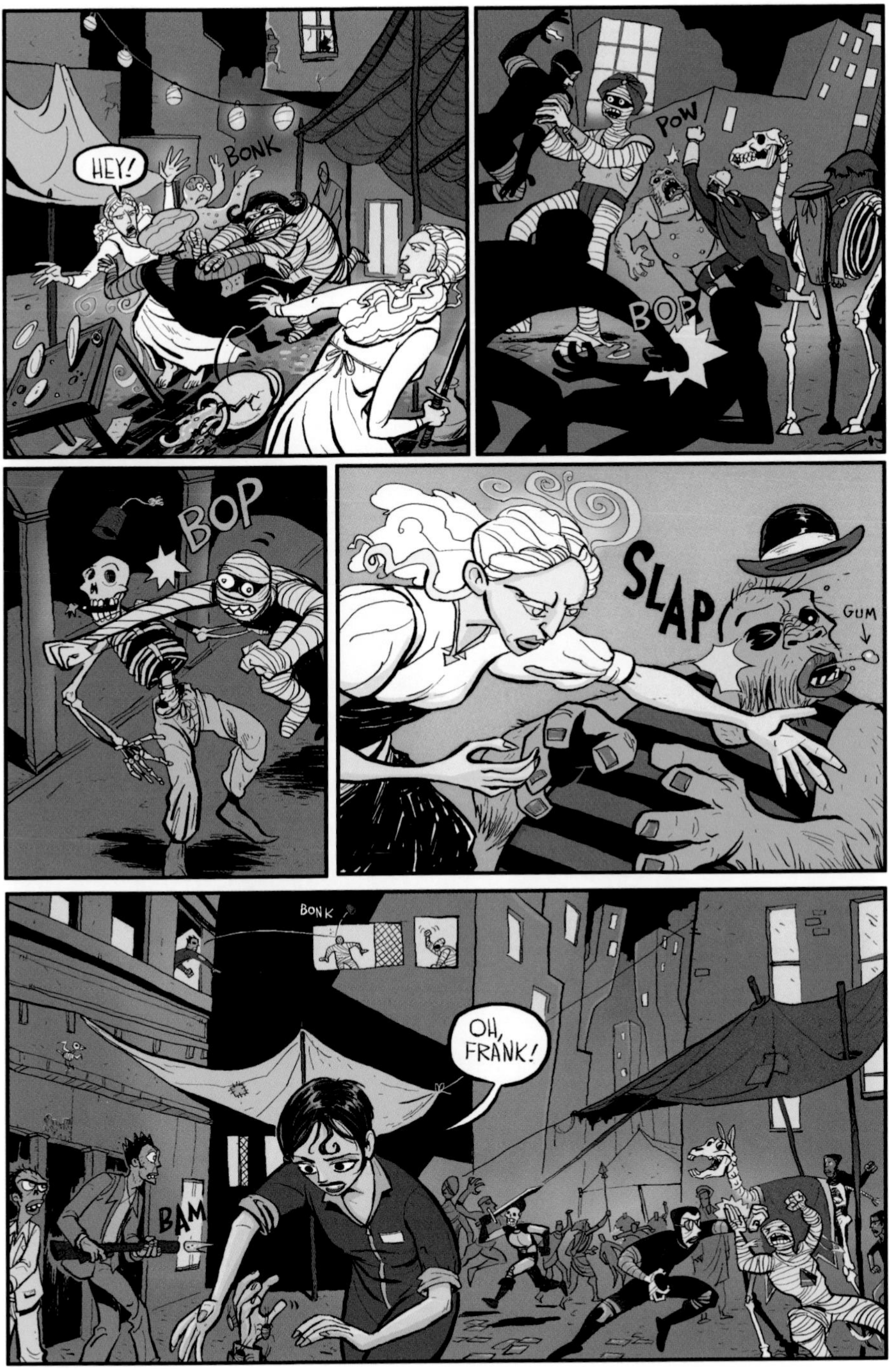
HEY!
BONK
POW
BOP
BOP
SLAP
GUM
BONK
OH, FRANK!
BAM

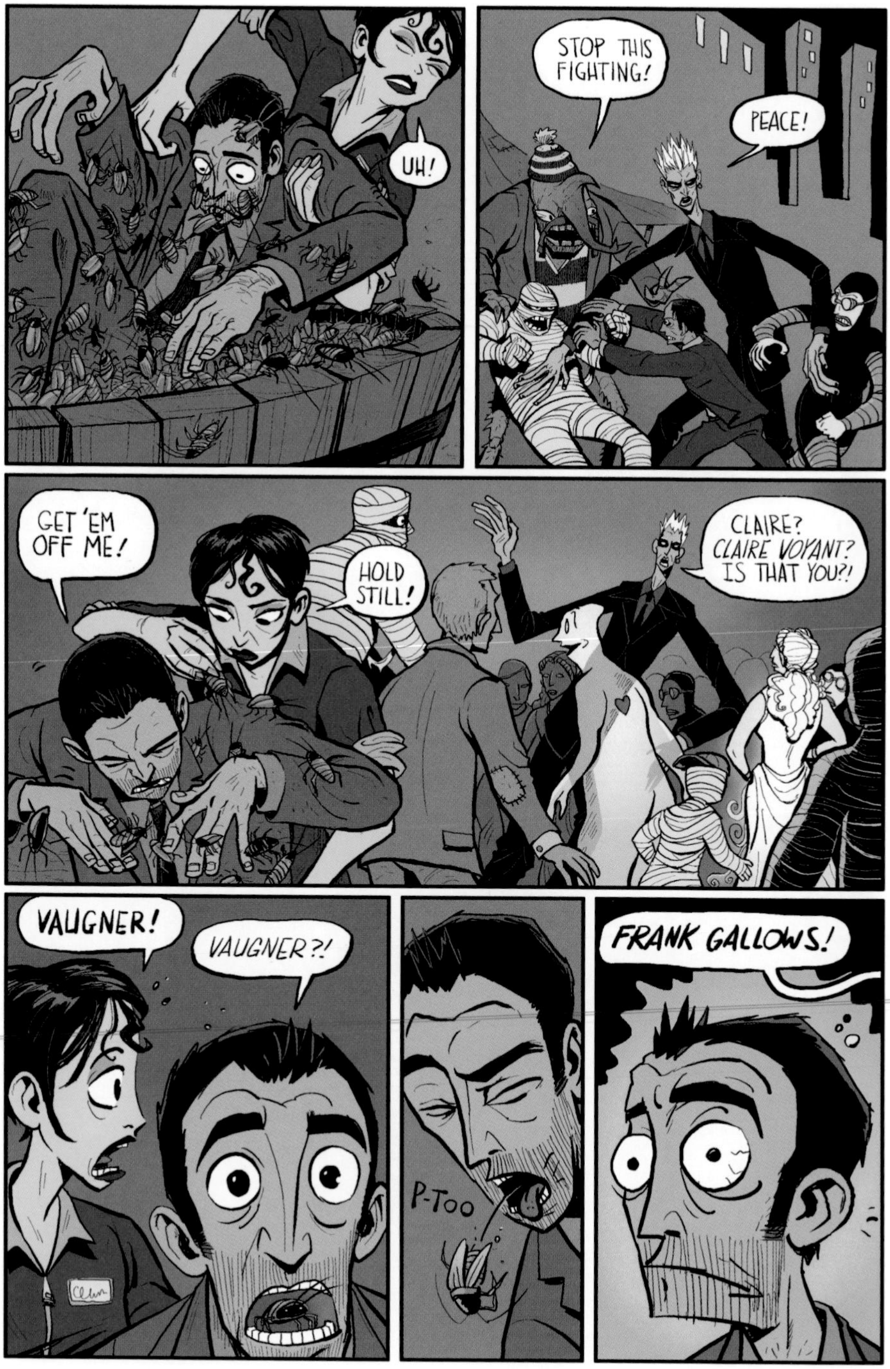
UH!
STOP THIS FIGHTING!
PEACE!
GET 'EM OFF ME!
HOLD STILL!
CLAIRE? CLAIRE VOYANT? IS THAT YOU?!
VAUGNER!
VAUGNER?!
P-TOO
FRANK GALLOWS!

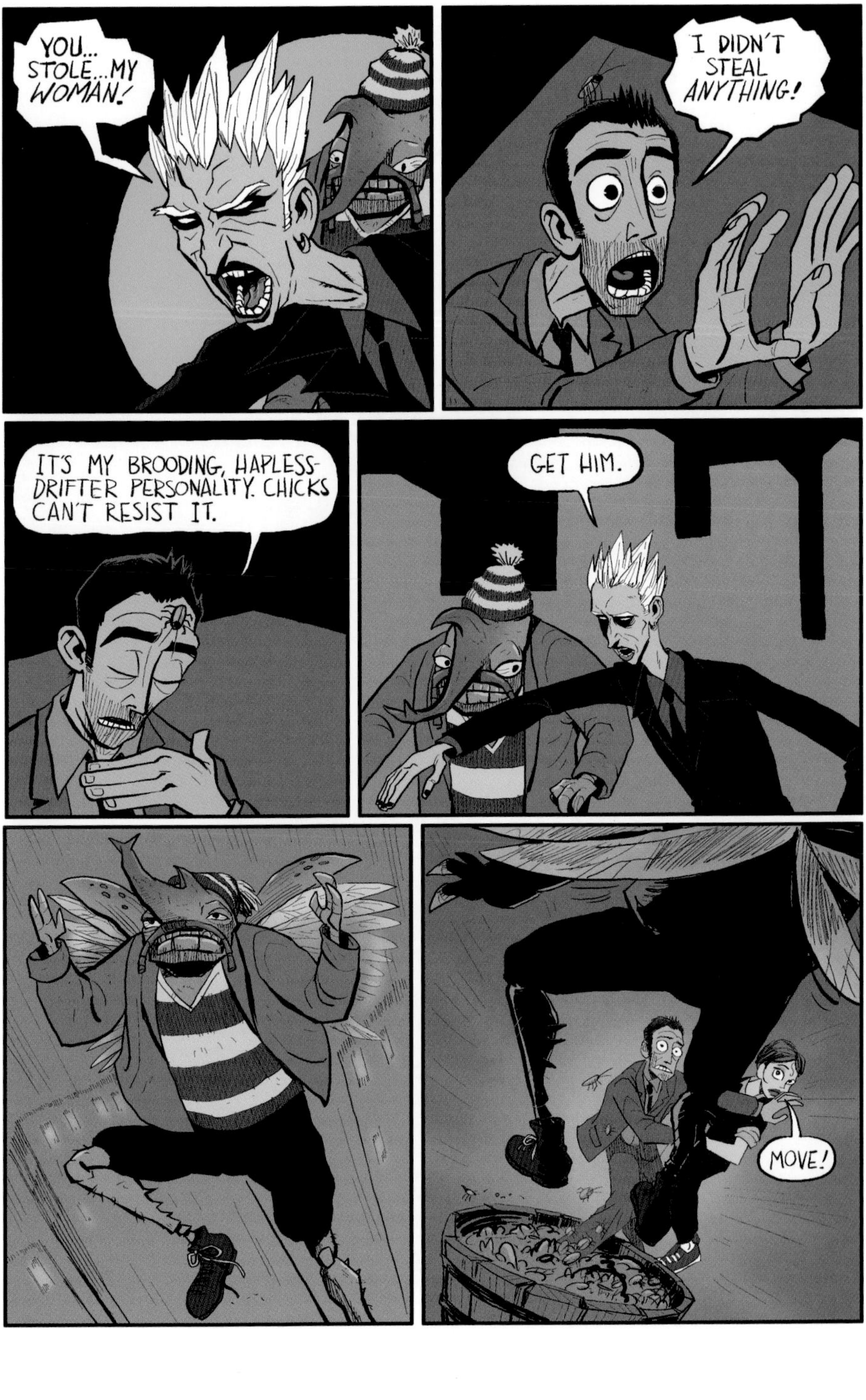
YOU... STOLE...MY WOMAN!
I DIDN'T STEAL ANYTHING!
IT'S MY BROODING, HAPLESS-DRIFTER PERSONALITY. CHICKS CAN'T RESIST IT.
GET HIM.
MOVE!

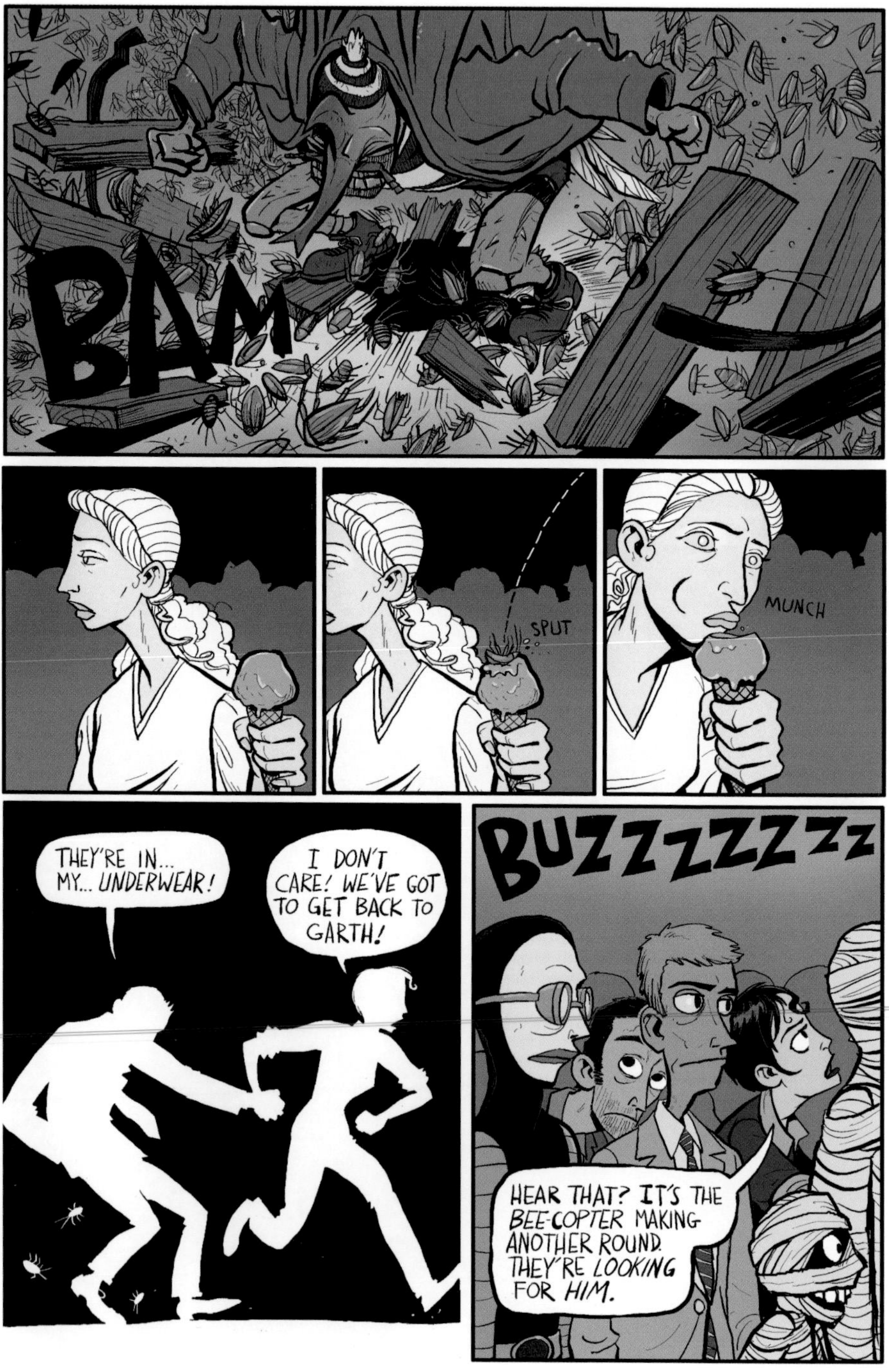
BAM
SPUT
MUNCH
THEY'RE IN... MY... UNDERWEAR!
I DON'T CARE! WE'VE GOT TO GET BACK TO GARTH!
BUZZZZZZzz
HEAR THAT? IT'S THE BEE-COPTER MAKING ANOTHER ROUND. THEY'RE LOOKING FOR HIM.

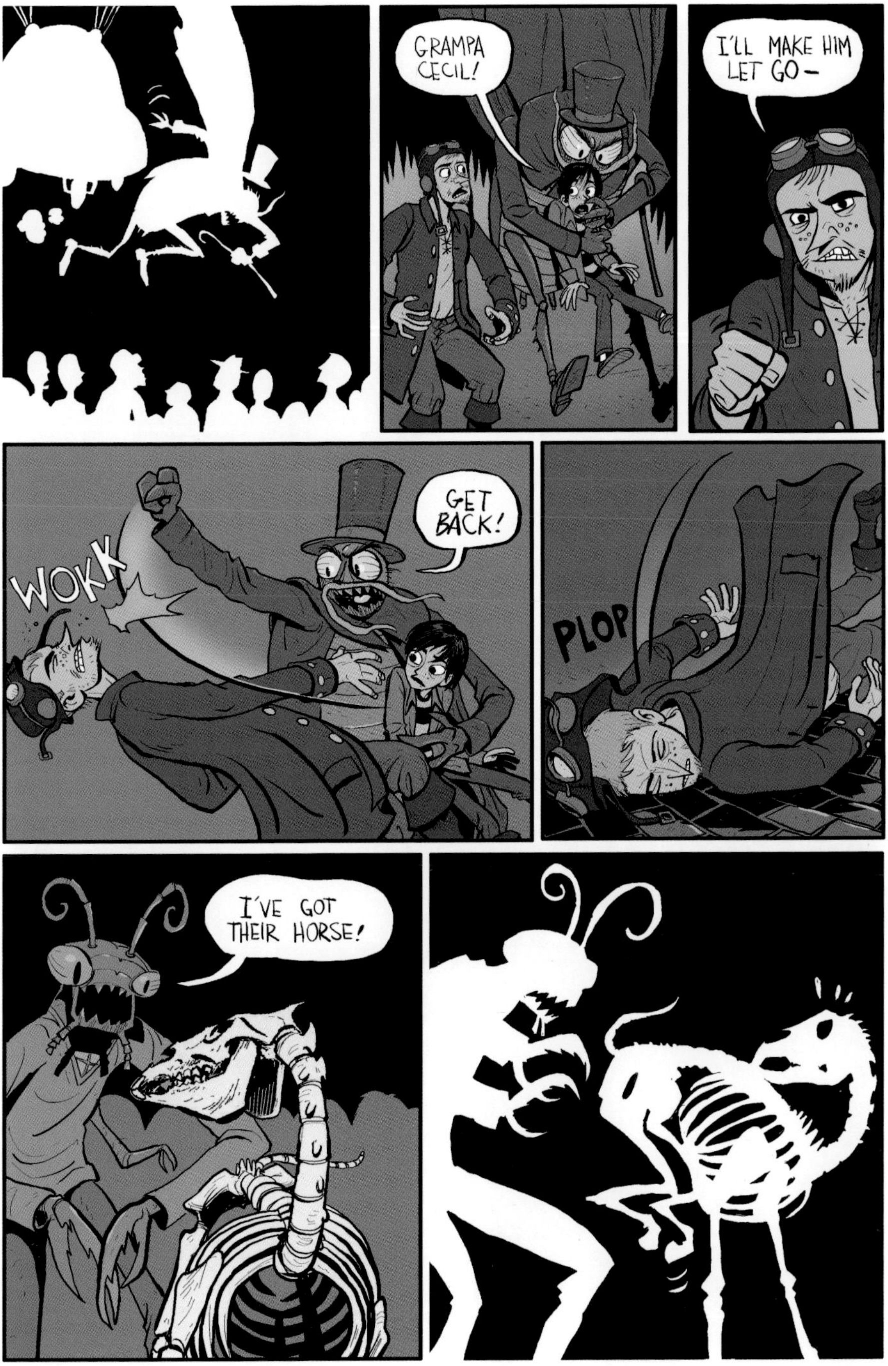
GRAMPA CECIL!
I'LL MAKE HIM LET GO—
WOKK
GET BACK!
PLOP
I'VE GOT THEIR HORSE!

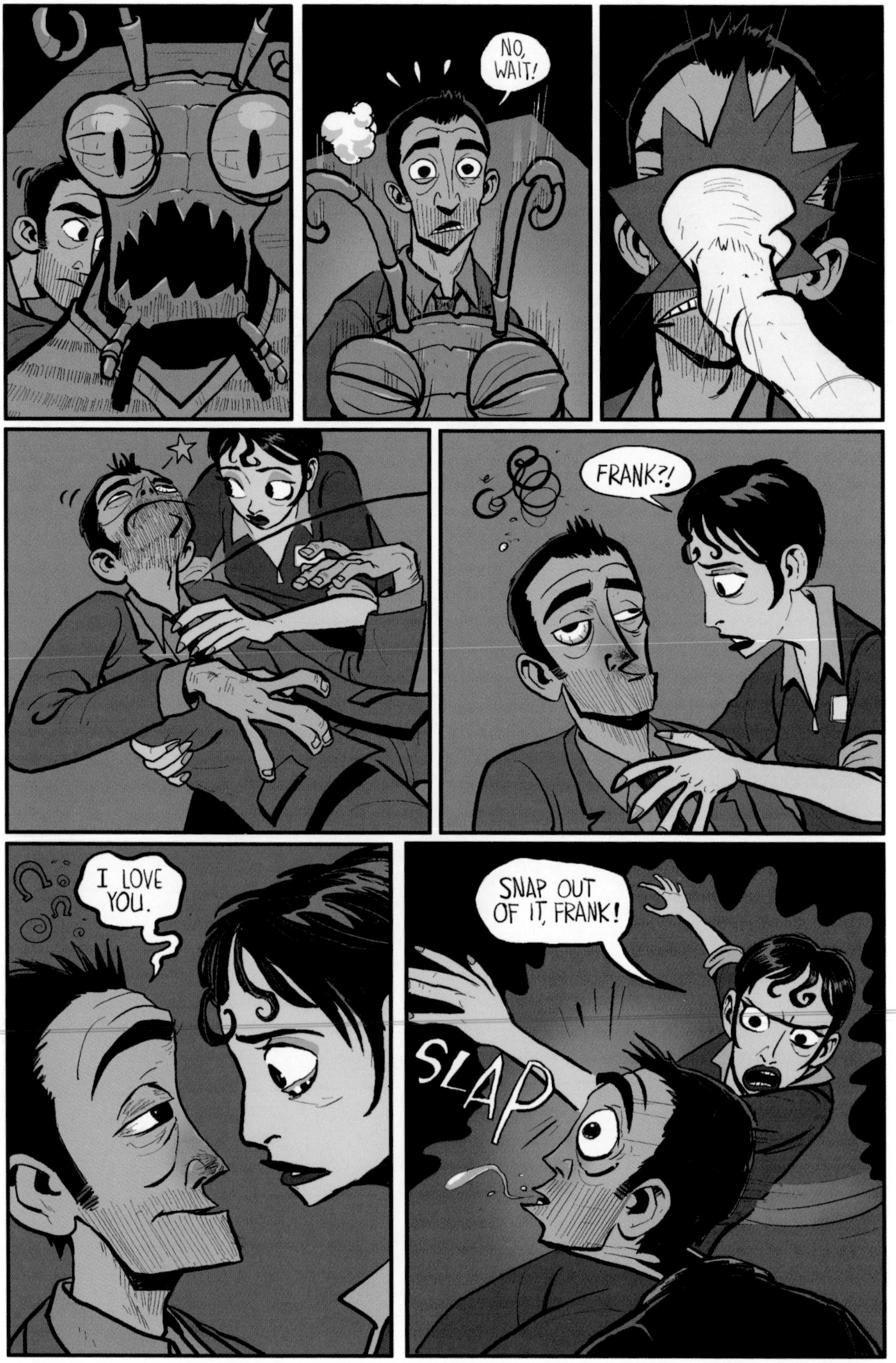
NO, WAIT!
FRANK?!
I LOVE YOU.
SNAP OUT OF IT, FRANK!
SLAP

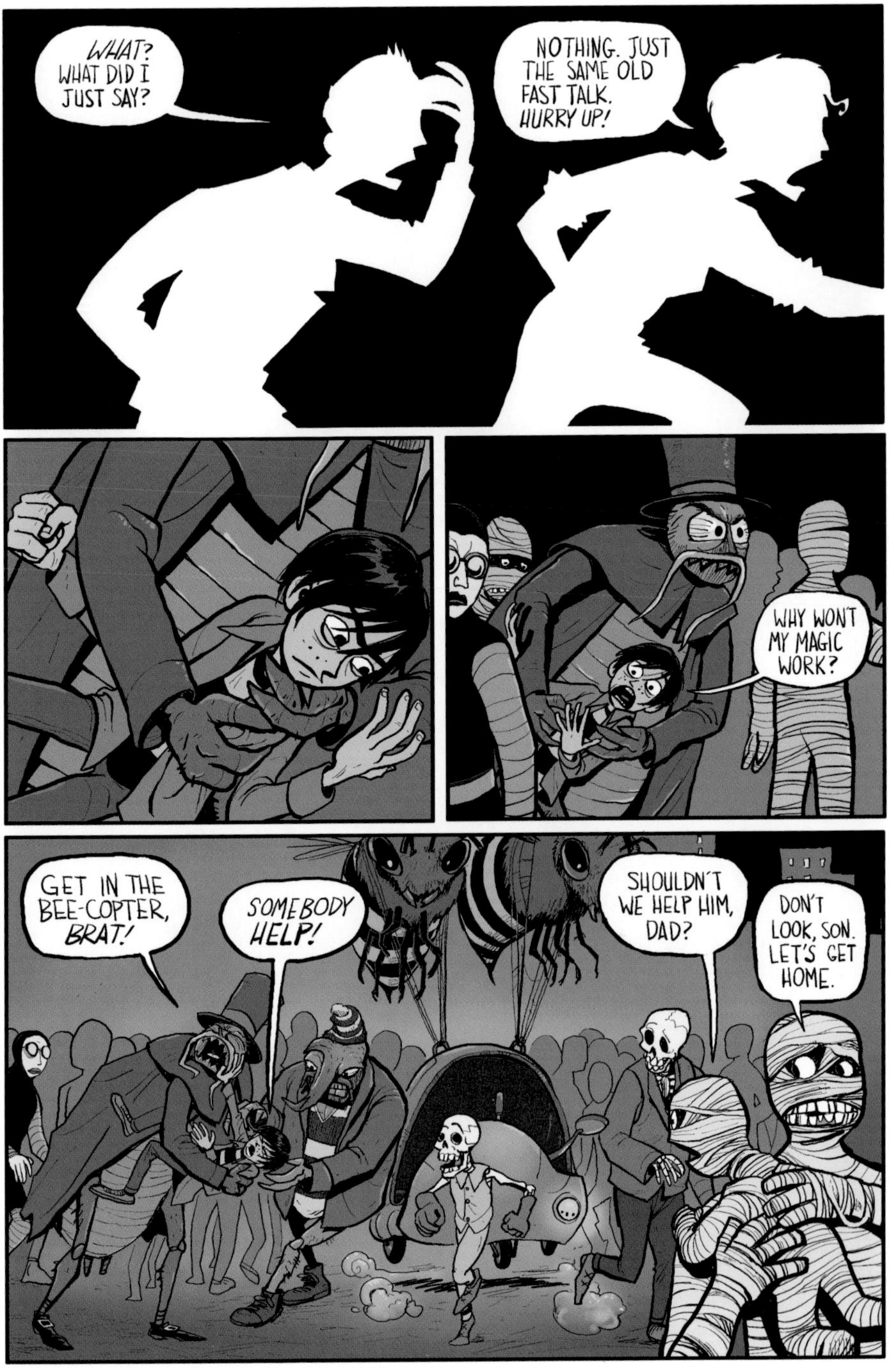
WHAT? WHAT DID I JUST SAY?
NOTHING. JUST THE SAME OLD FAST TALK. HURRY UP!
WHY WON'T MY MAGIC WORK?
GET IN THE BEE-COPTER, BRAT!
SOMEBODY HELP!
SHOULDN'T WE HELP HIM, DAD?
DON'T LOOK, SON. LET'S GET HOME.

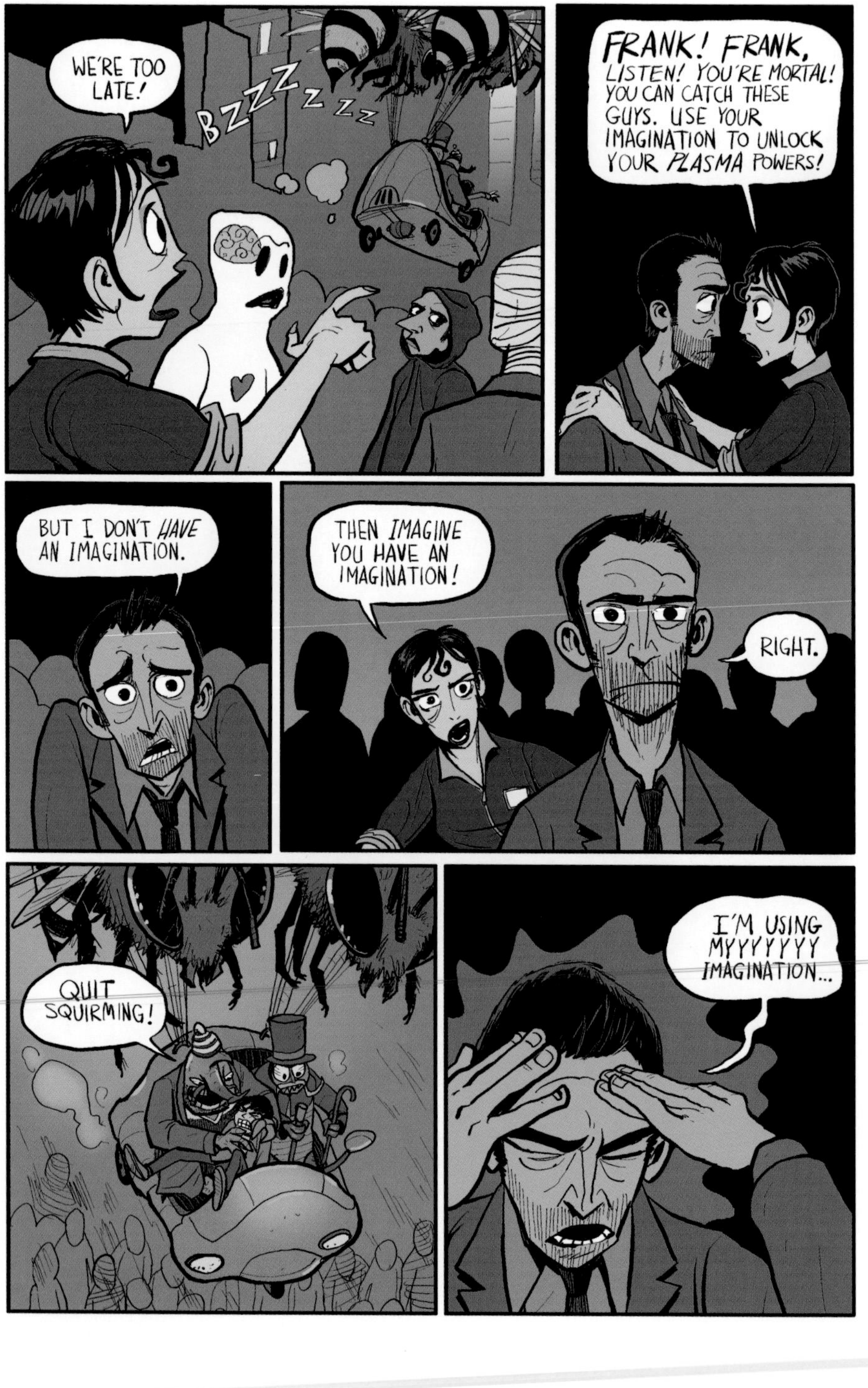
WE'RE TOO LATE!
BZZZZ Z Z Z
FRANK! FRANK, LISTEN! YOU'RE MORTAL! YOU CAN CATCH THESE GUYS. USE YOUR IMAGINATION TO UNLOCK YOUR PLASMA POWERS!
BUT I DON'T HAVE AN IMAGINATION.
THEN IMAGINE YOU HAVE AN IMAGINATION!
RIGHT.
QUIT SQUIRMING!
I'M USING MYYYYYYY IMAGINATION...

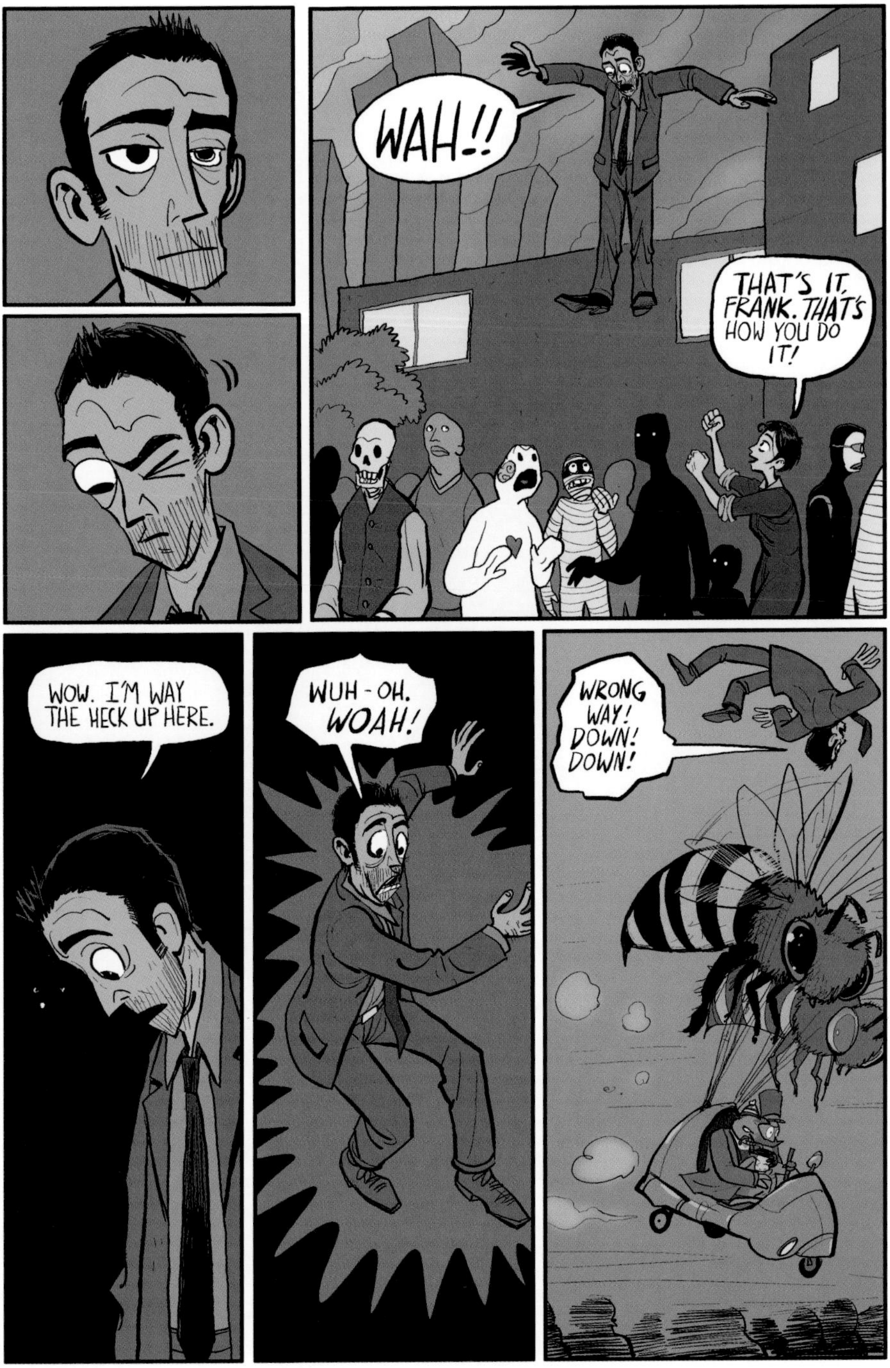
WAH!!
THAT'S IT, FRANK. THAT'S HOW YOU DO IT!
WOW. I'M WAY THE HECK UP HERE.
WUH - OH. WOAH!
WRONG WAY! DOWN! DOWN!

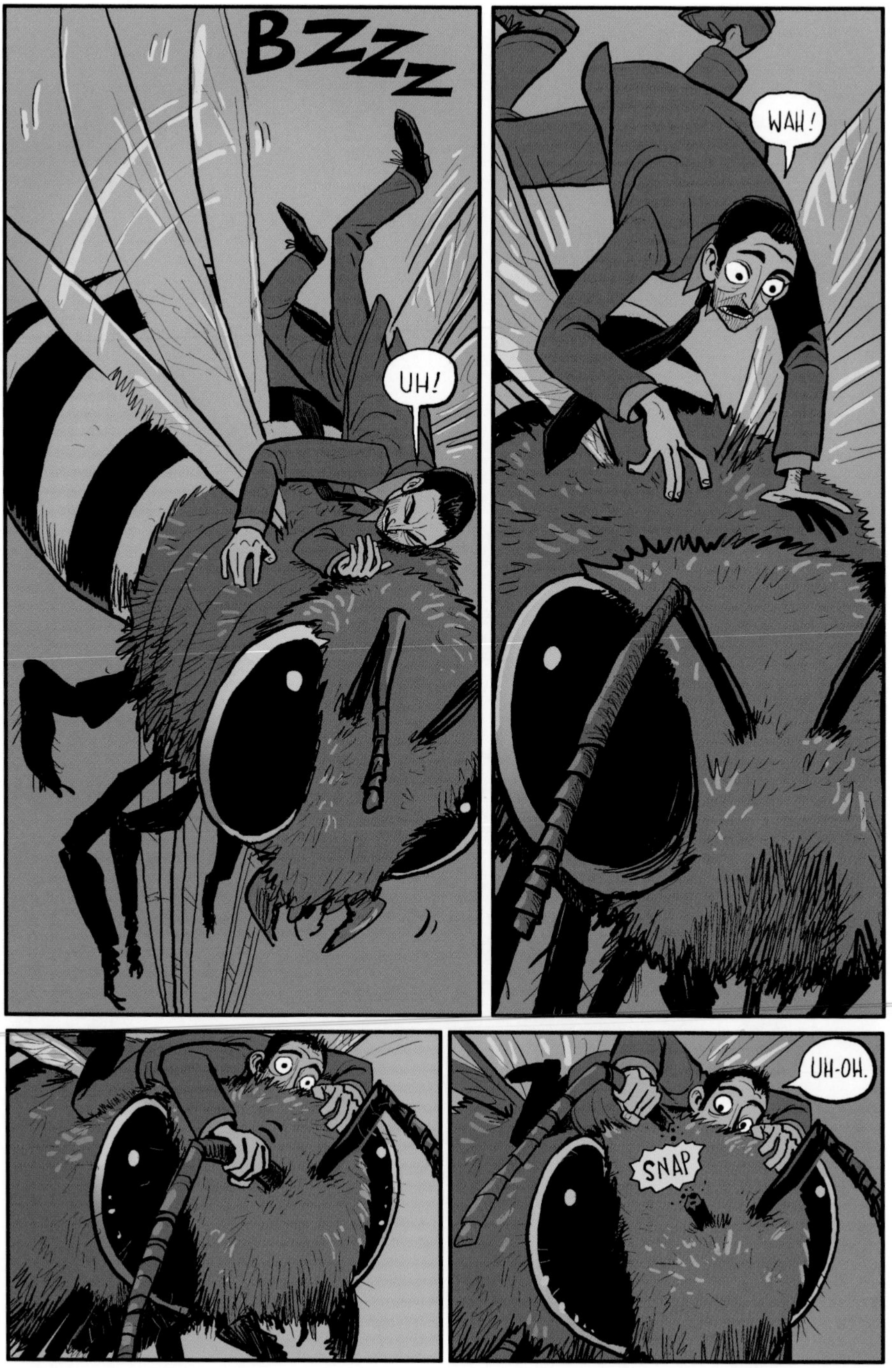
BZZZZ
UH!
WAH!
UH-OH.
SNAP

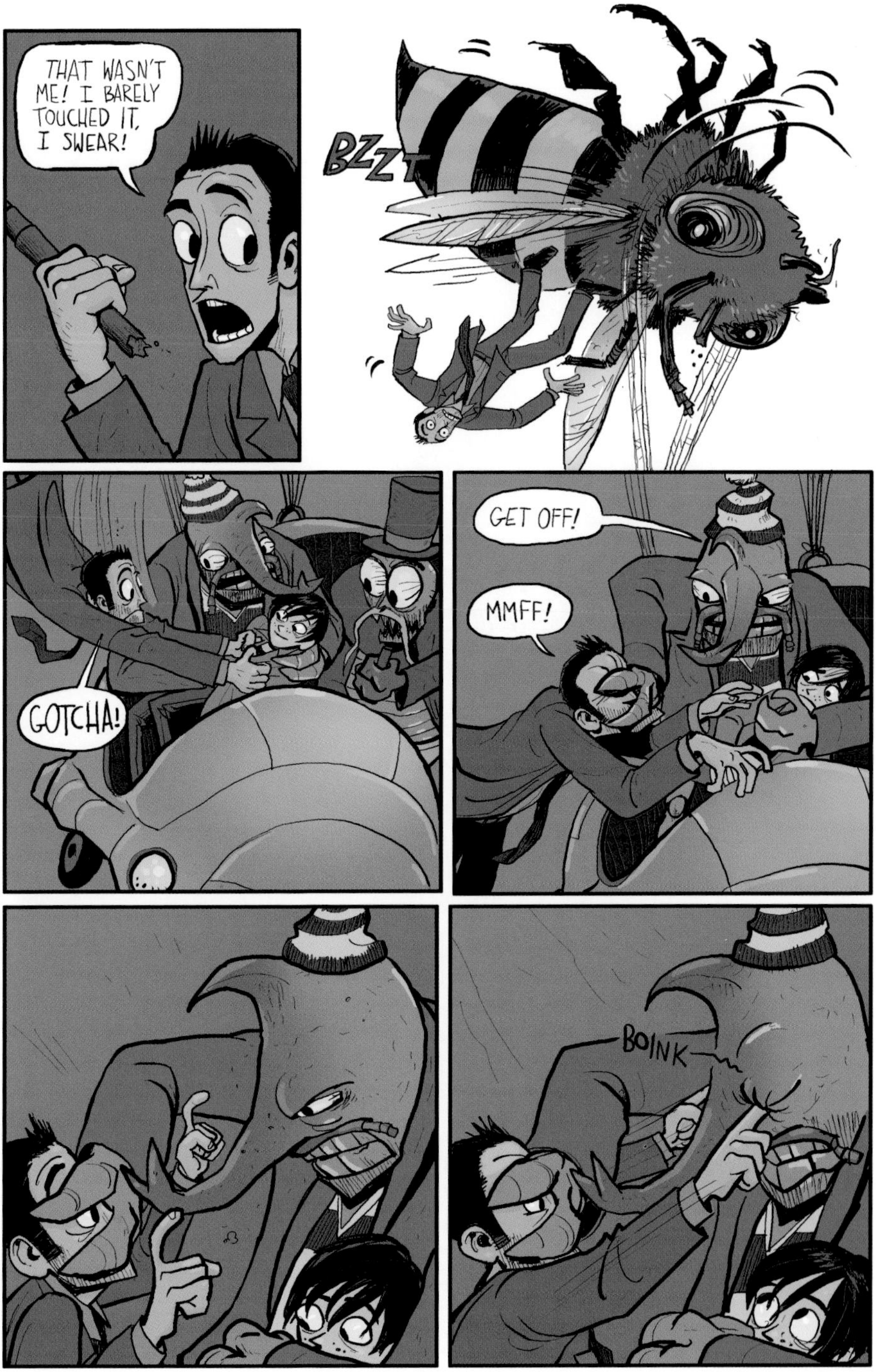
THAT WASN'T ME! I BARELY TOUCHED IT, I SWEAR!
BZZT
GOTCHA!
GET OFF!
MMFF!
BOINK

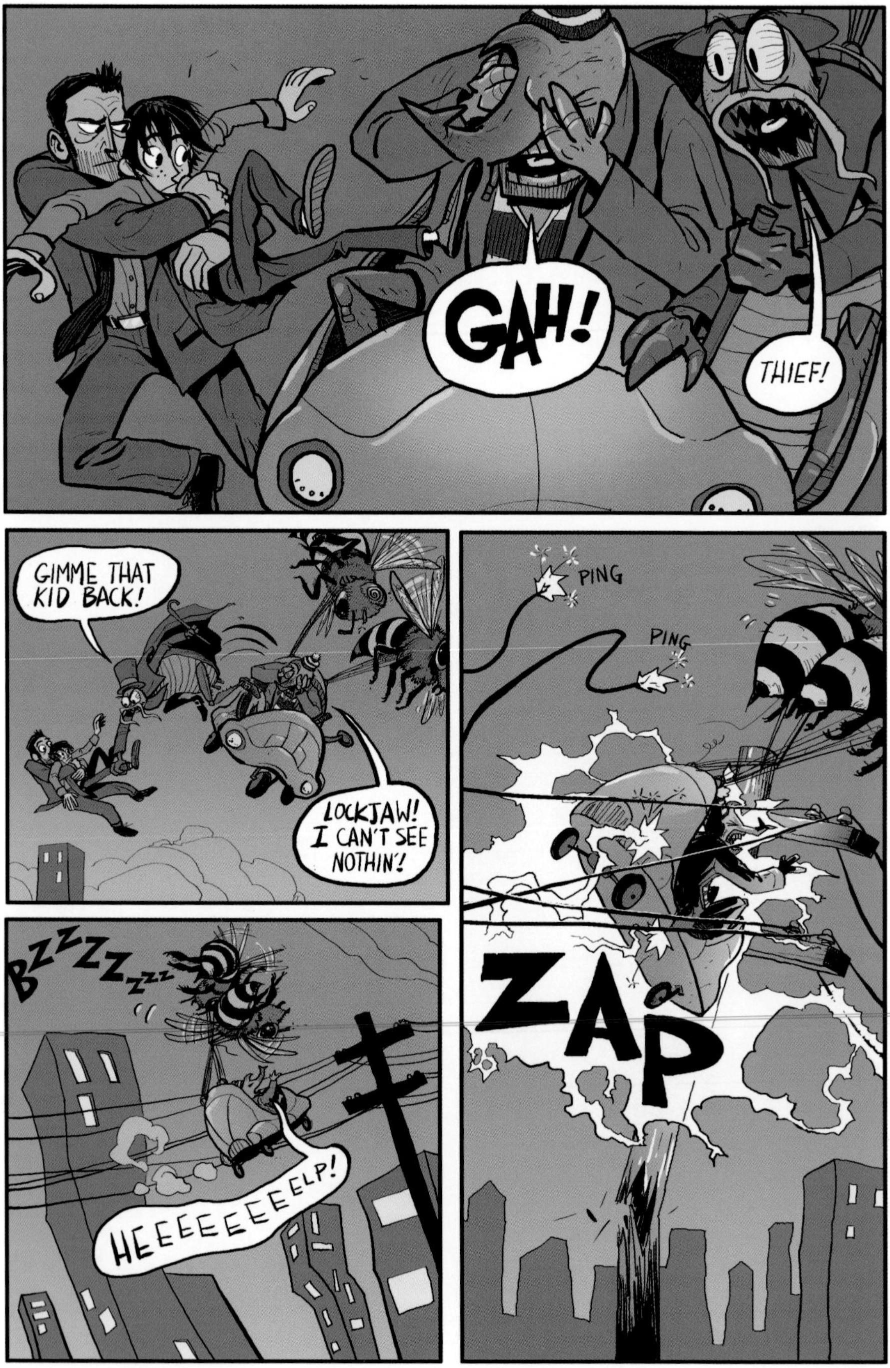
GAH!
THIEF!
GIMME THAT KID BACK!
LOCKJAW! I CAN'T SEE NOTHIN'!
PING
PING
ZAP
BZZZZZzzz
HEEEEEEEEELP!

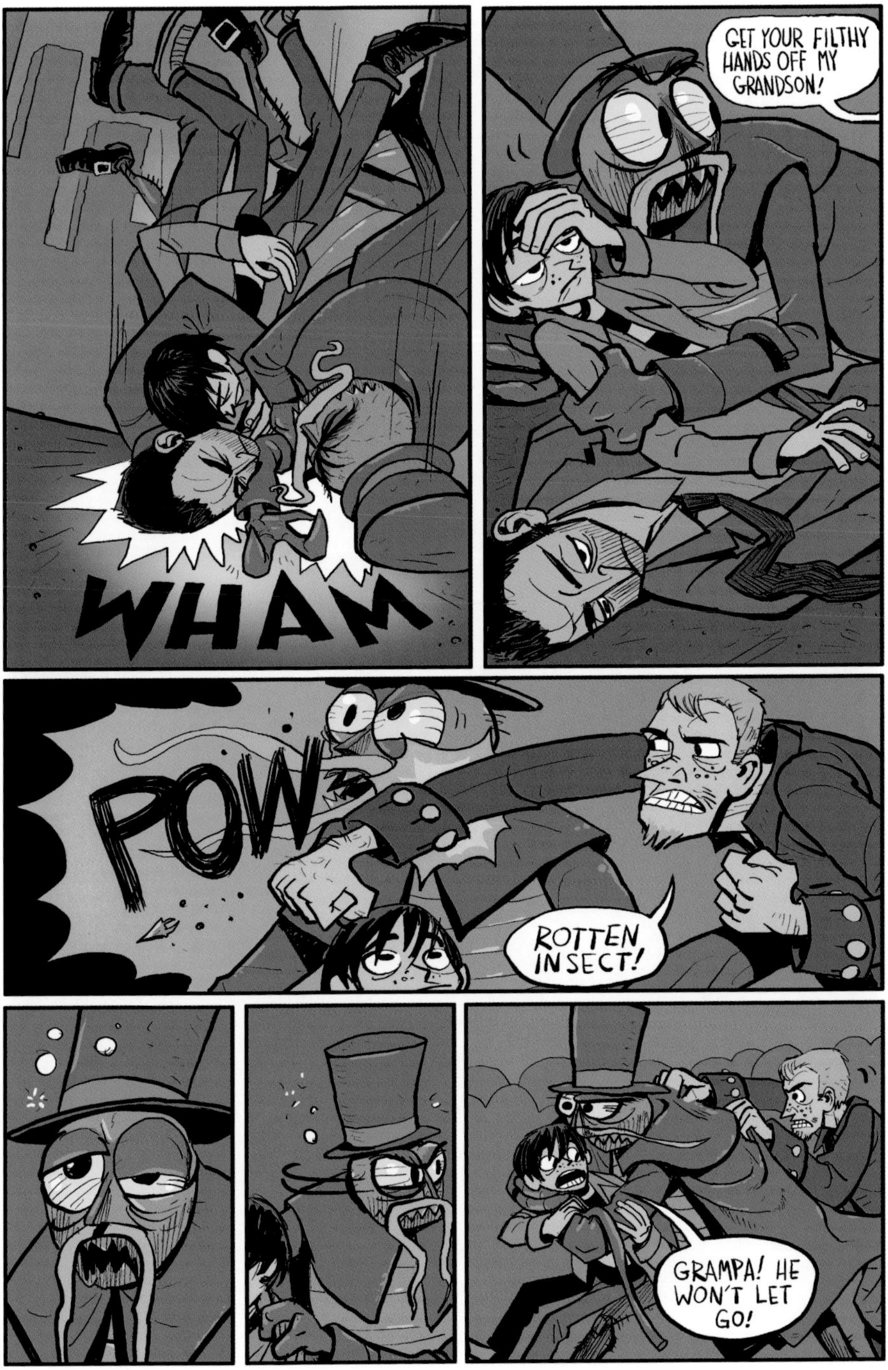
WHAM
GET YOUR FILTHY HANDS OFF MY GRANDSON!
POW
ROTTEN INSECT!
GRAMPA! HE WON'T LET GO!

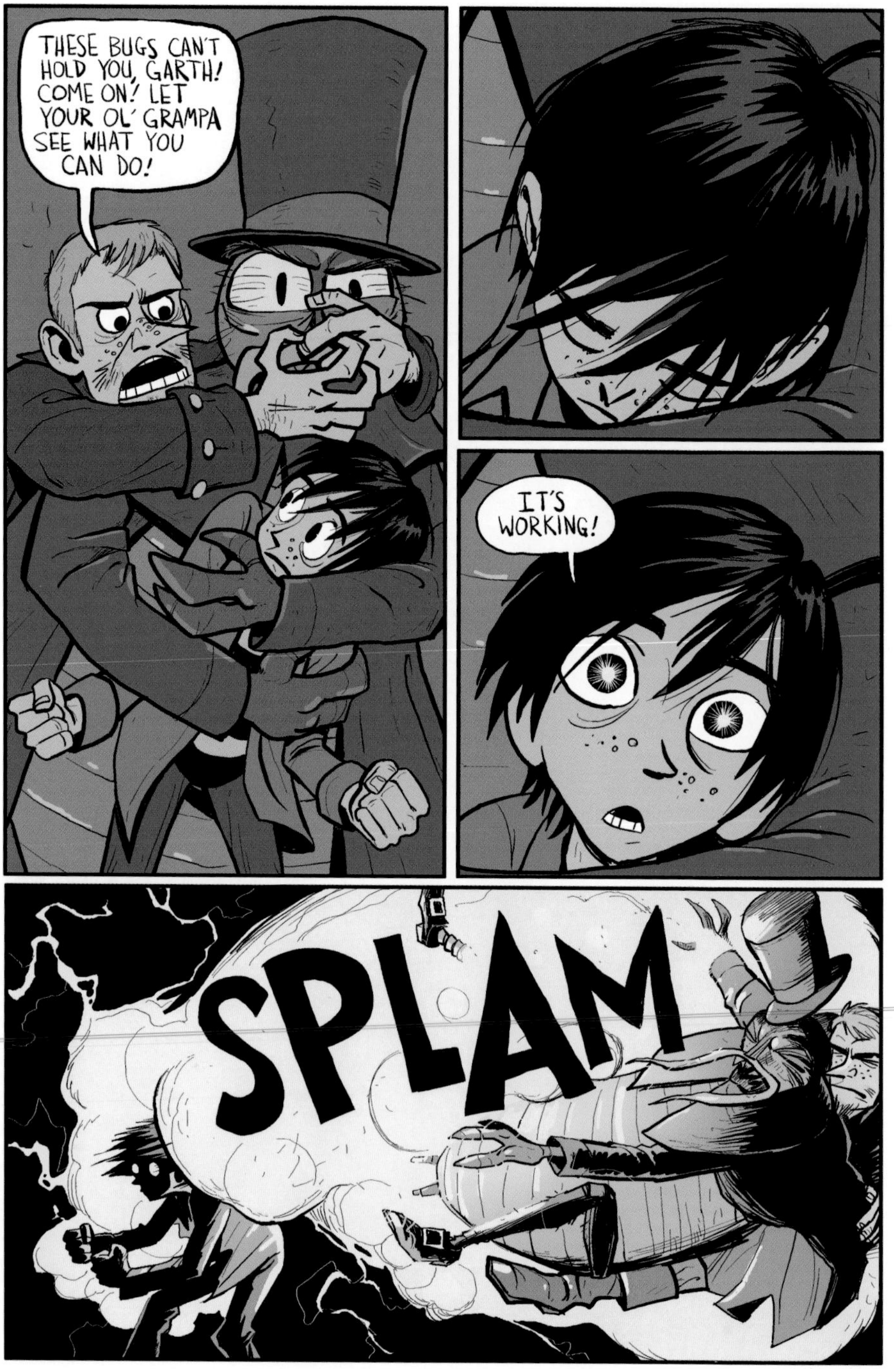

THESE BUGS CAN'T HOLD YOU, GARTH! COME ON! LET YOUR OL' GRAMPA SEE WHAT YOU CAN DO!
IT'S WORKING!
SPLAM

WHAP

NICE WORK, GARTH. OUCH!

CLICK

IT'S A TRANSPORT!

FZZZ

FWAAA

I DON'T KNOW WHERE I'M GOING, BUT YOU'RE COMING WITH ME!

LEMME GO!

GRAMPA!

WAIT! THAT'S OUR ONLY WAY HOME!

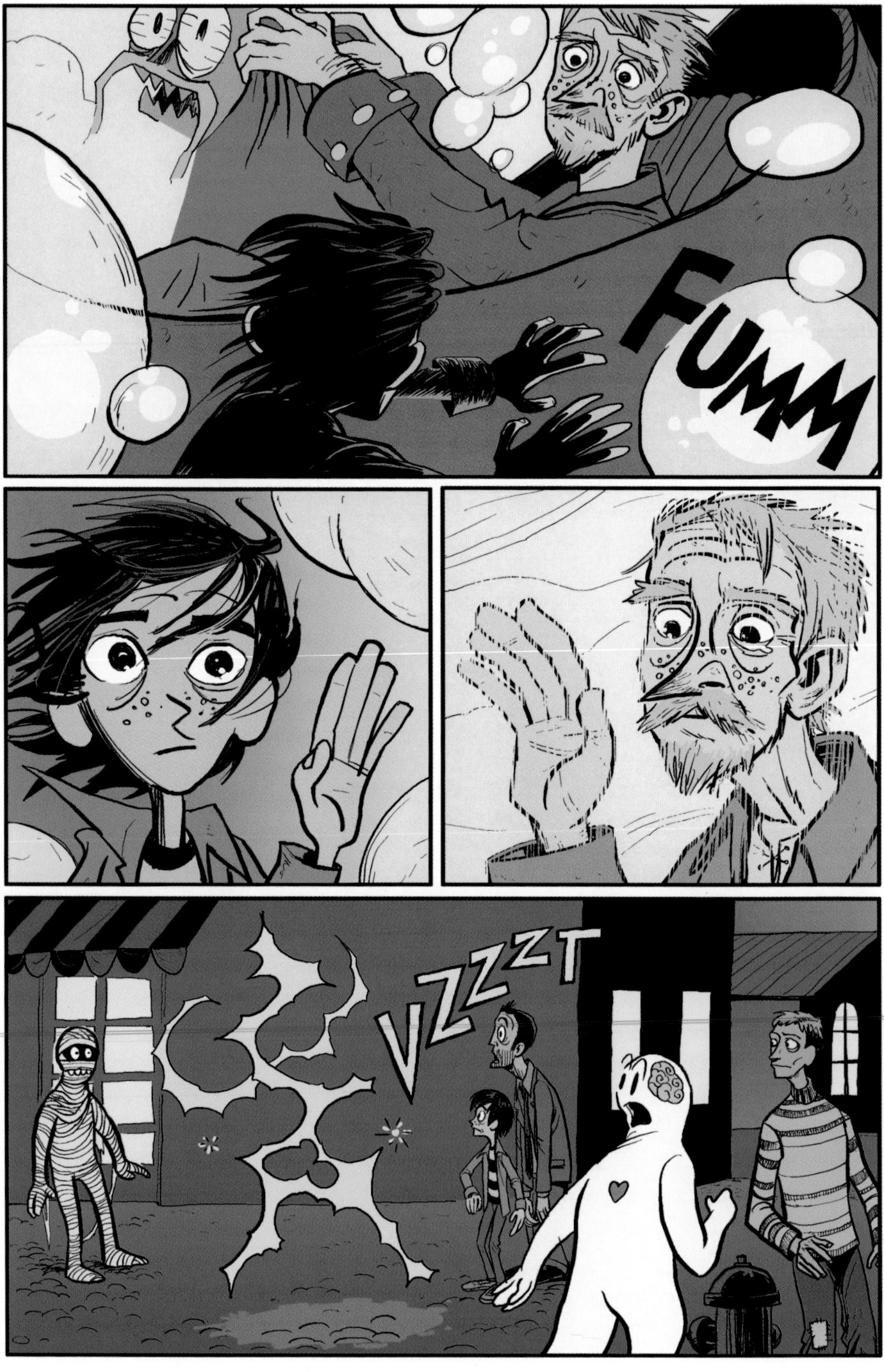
FUMM
VZZZZT

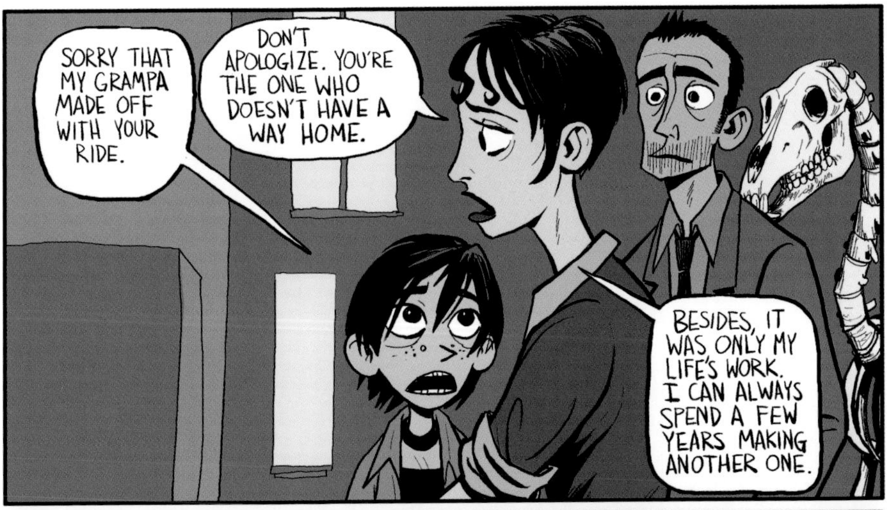
SORRY THAT MY GRAMPA MADE OFF WITH YOUR RIDE.
DON'T APOLOGIZE. YOU'RE THE ONE WHO DOESN'T HAVE A WAY HOME.
BESIDES, IT WAS ONLY MY LIFE'S WORK. I CAN ALWAYS SPEND A FEW YEARS MAKING ANOTHER ONE.

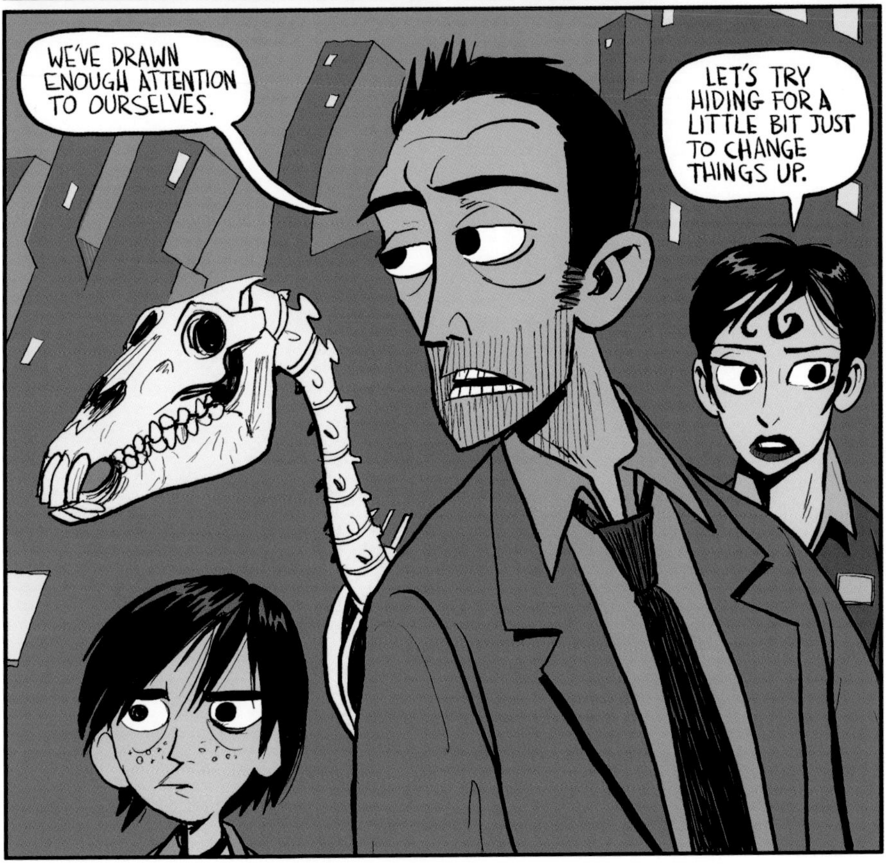
WE'VE DRAWN ENOUGH ATTENTION TO OURSELVES.
LET'S TRY HIDING FOR A LITTLE BIT JUST TO CHANGE THINGS UP.

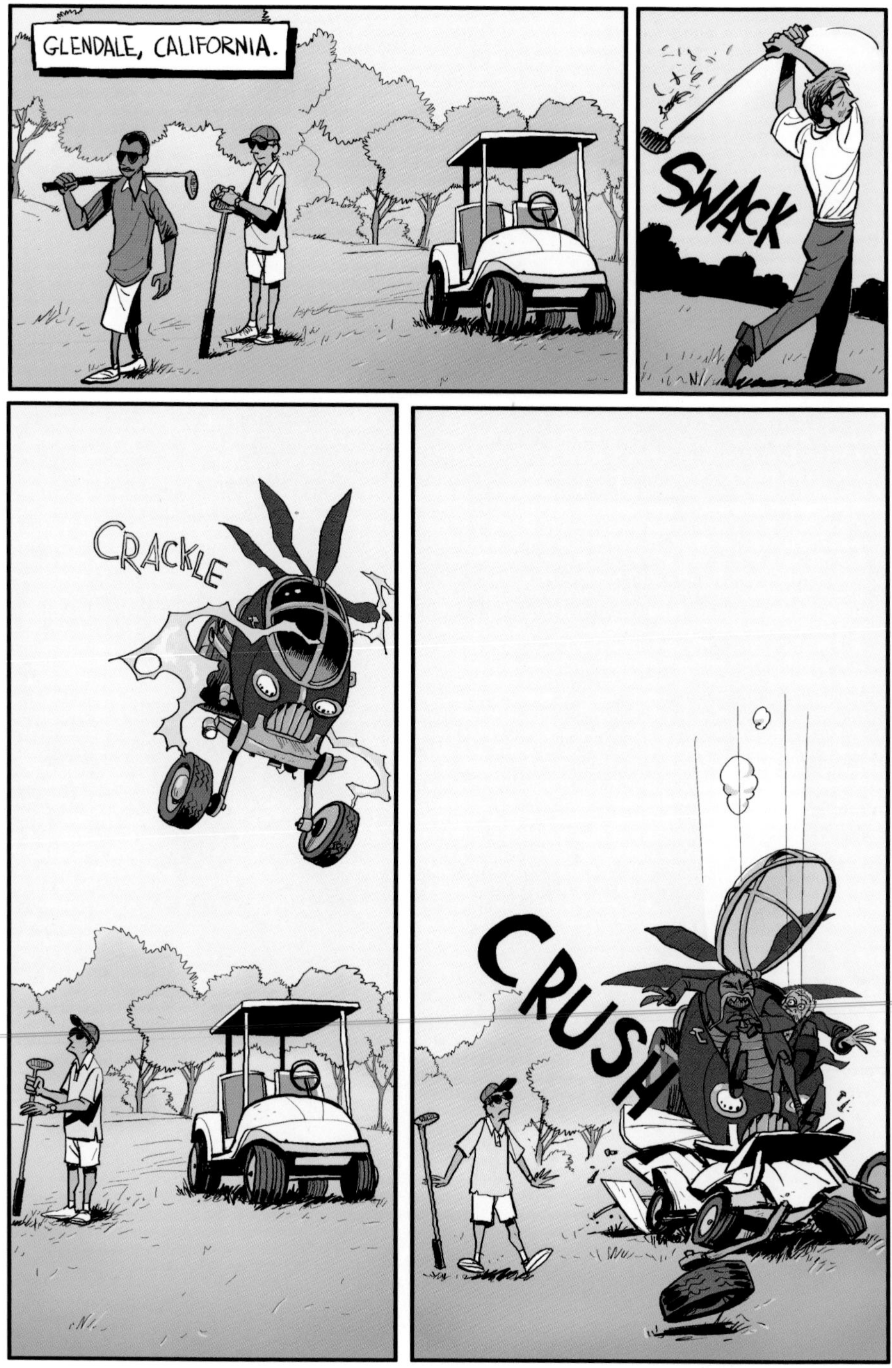
GLENDALE, CALIFORNIA.
SWACK
CRACKLE
CRUSH

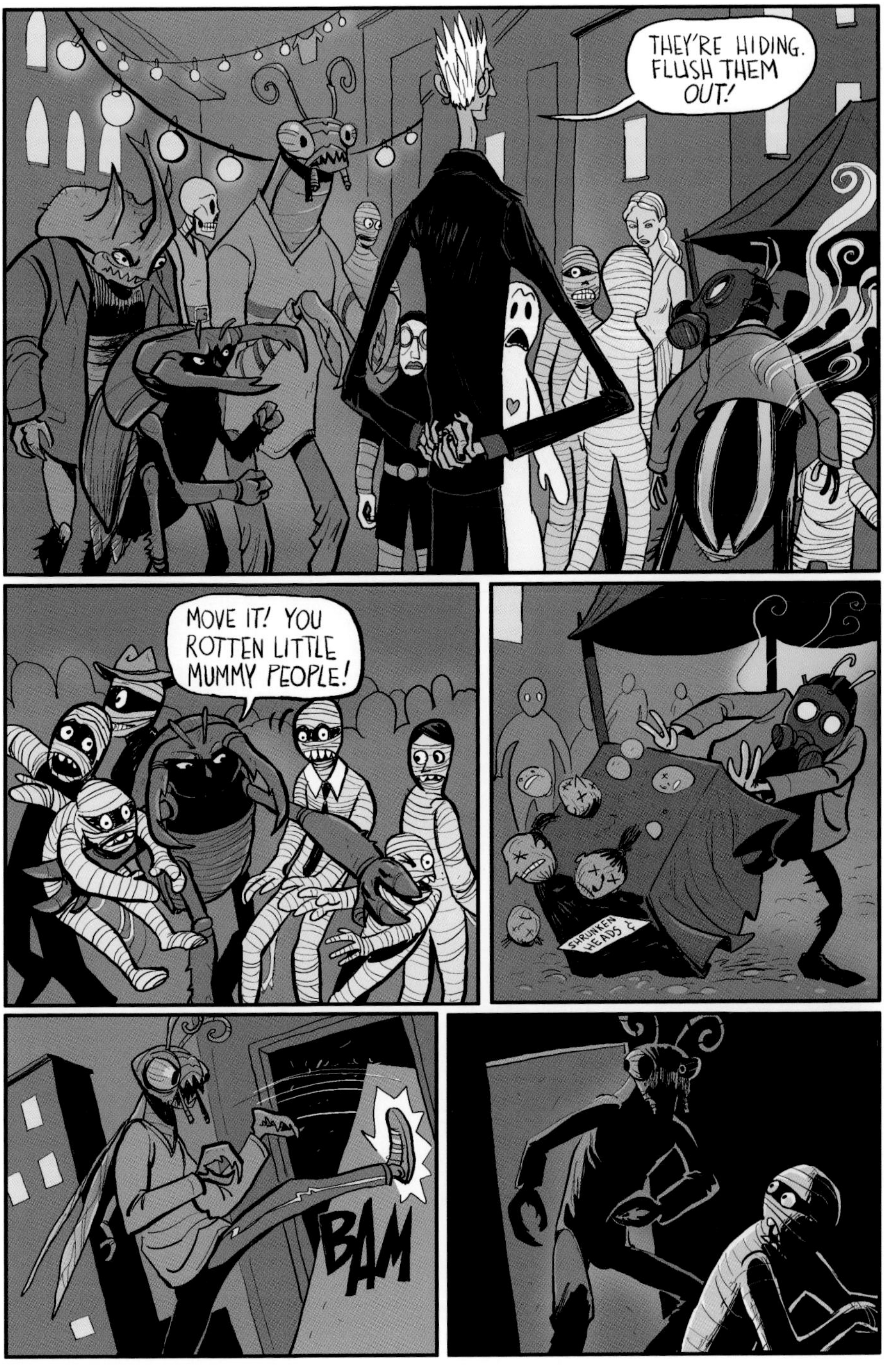
THEY'RE HIDING. FLUSH THEM OUT!
MOVE IT! YOU ROTTEN LITTLE MUMMY PEOPLE!
SHRUNKEN HEADS
BAM

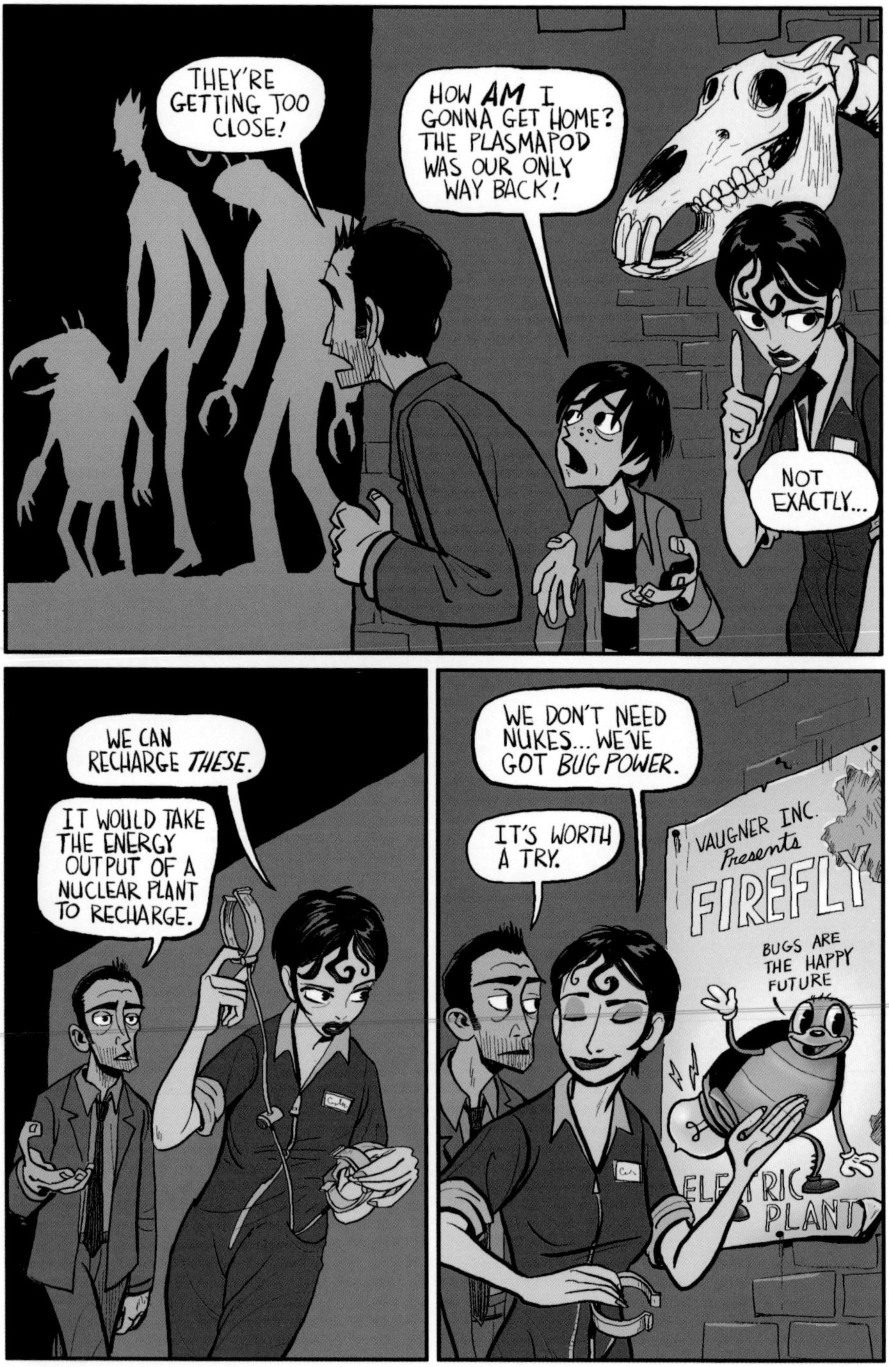
THEY'RE GETTING TOO CLOSE!
HOW **AM** I GONNA GET HOME? THE PLASMAPOD WAS OUR ONLY WAY BACK!
NOT EXACTLY...
WE CAN RECHARGE *THESE*.
IT WOULD TAKE THE ENERGY OUTPUT OF A NUCLEAR PLANT TO RECHARGE.
WE DON'T NEED NUKES... WE'VE GOT *BUG POWER*.
IT'S WORTH A TRY.
VAUGNER INC.
Presents
FIREFLY
BUGS ARE THE HAPPY FUTURE
ELECTRIC PLANT

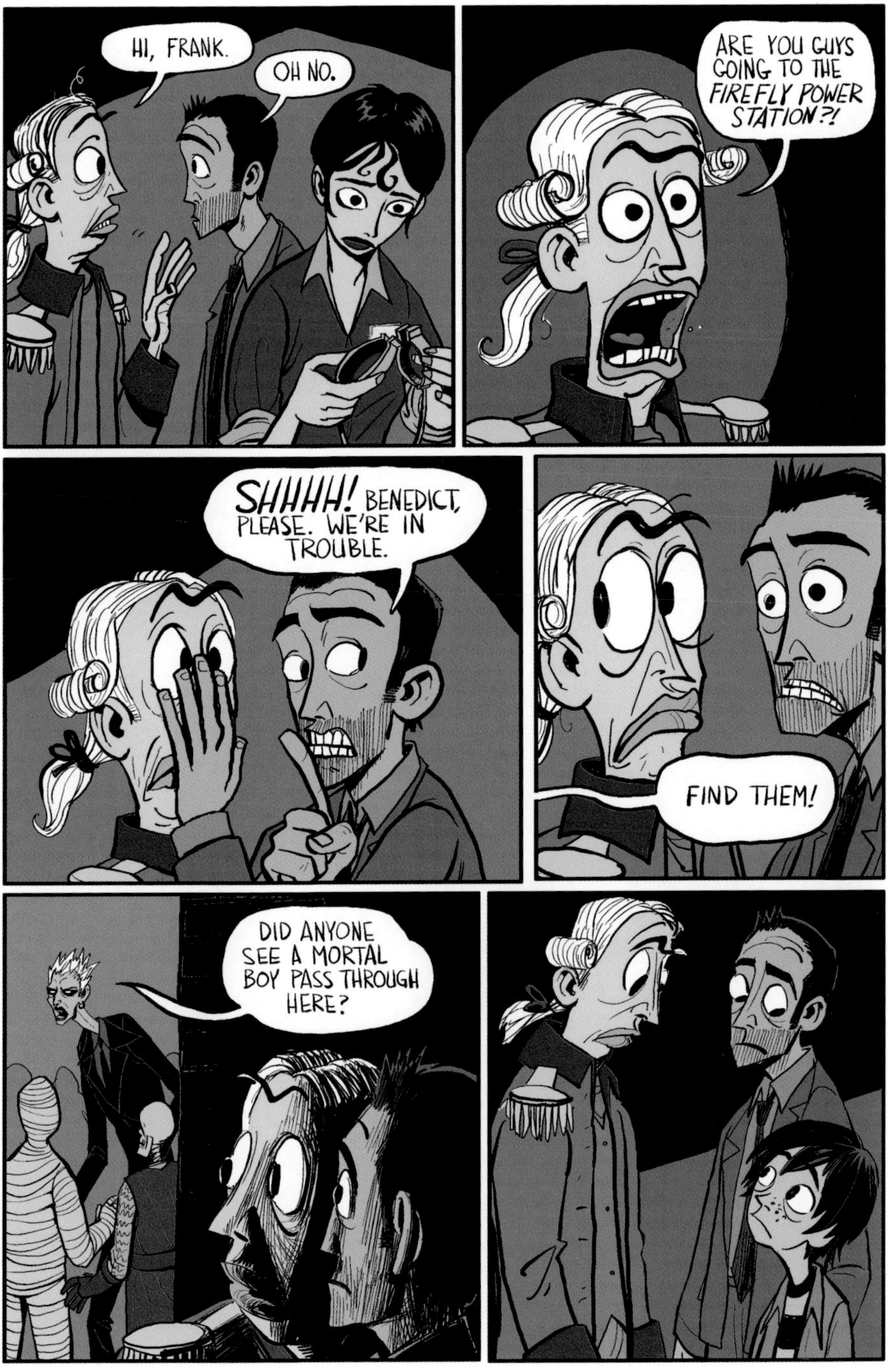
HI, FRANK.
OH NO.
ARE YOU GUYS GOING TO THE FIREFLY POWER STATION?!
SHHHH! BENEDICT, PLEASE. WE'RE IN TROUBLE.
FIND THEM!
DID ANYONE SEE A MORTAL BOY PASS THROUGH HERE?

BENEDICT, PLEASE. YOU GOTTA HELP ME OUT, BRO.
OVER HERE!
HERE! HERE!
AW, CRUD.
THIS WAY! THEY'RE OVER HERE!

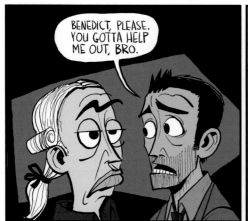

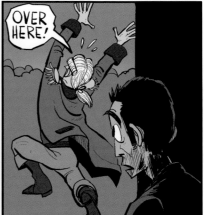

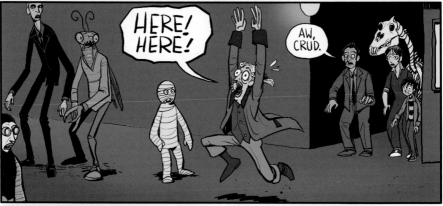

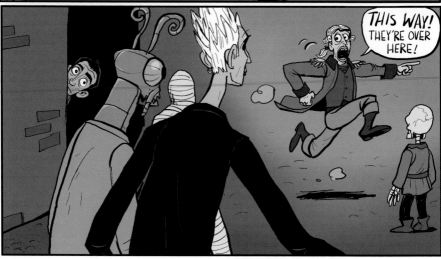

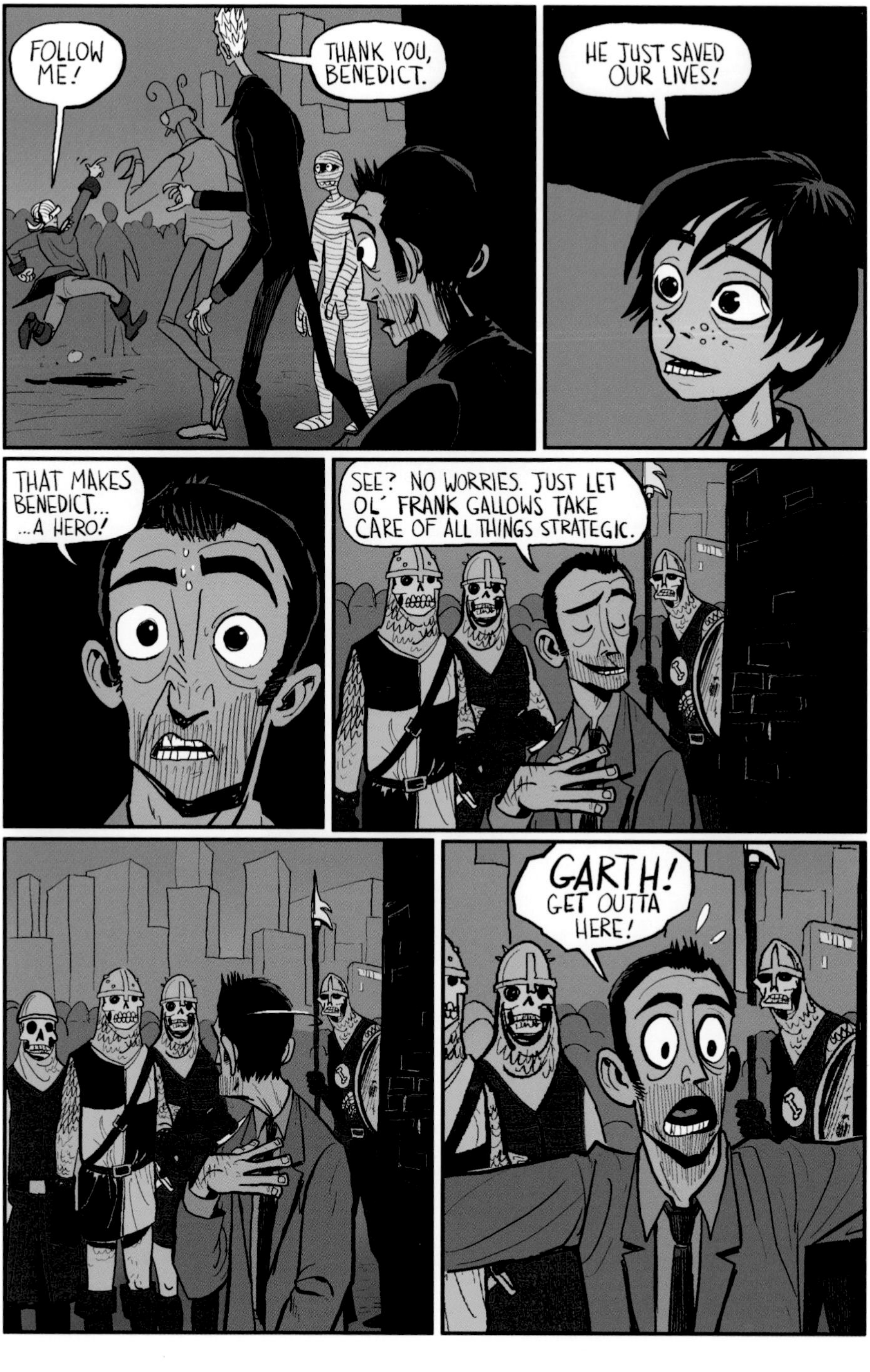
FOLLOW ME!
THANK YOU, BENEDICT.
HE JUST SAVED OUR LIVES!
THAT MAKES BENEDICT... ...A HERO!
SEE? NO WORRIES. JUST LET OL' FRANK GALLOWS TAKE CARE OF ALL THINGS STRATEGIC.
GARTH! GET OUTTA HERE!

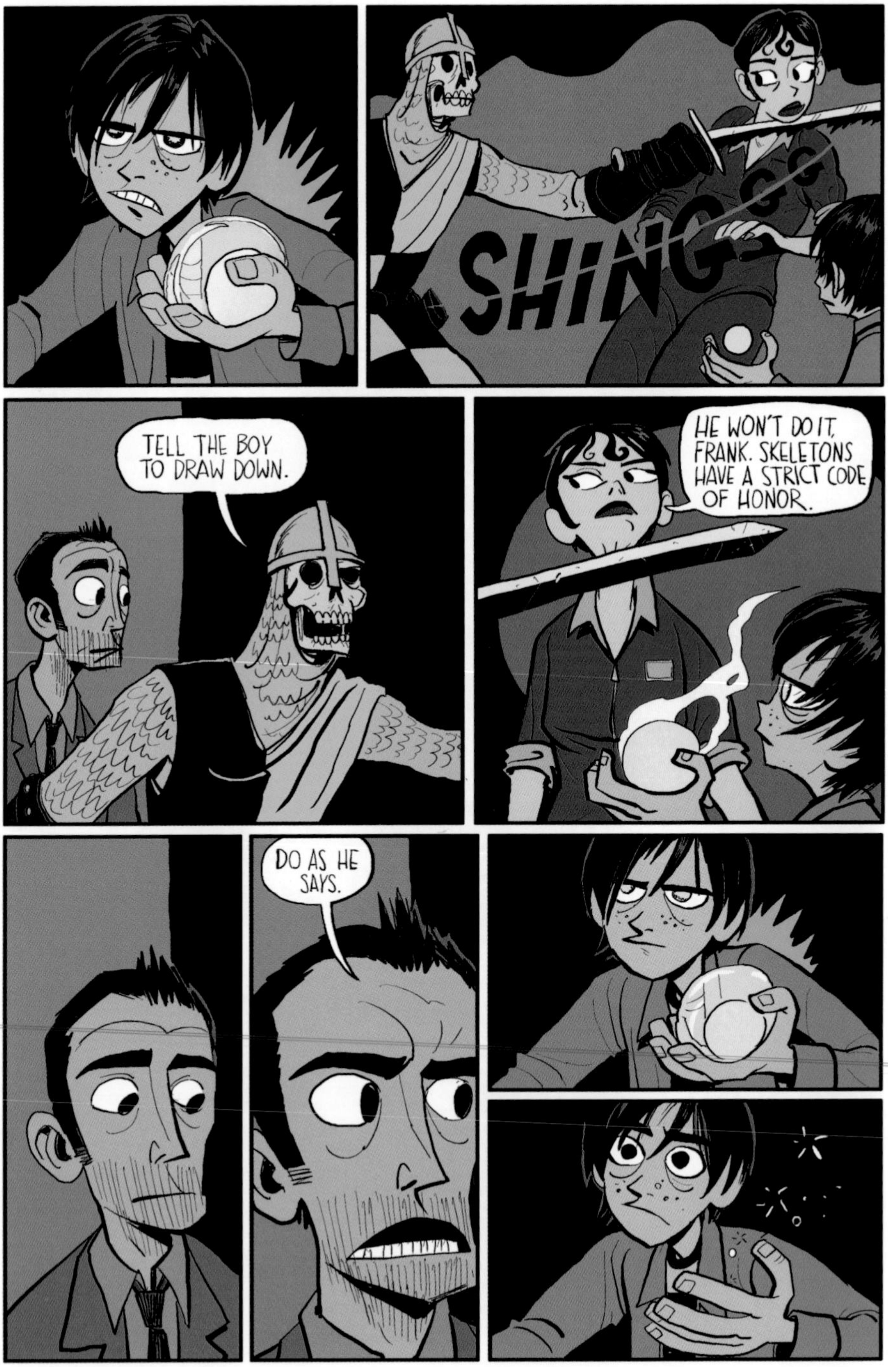
SHING
TELL THE BOY TO DRAW DOWN.
HE WON'T DO IT, FRANK. SKELETONS HAVE A STRICT CODE OF HONOR.
DO AS HE SAYS.

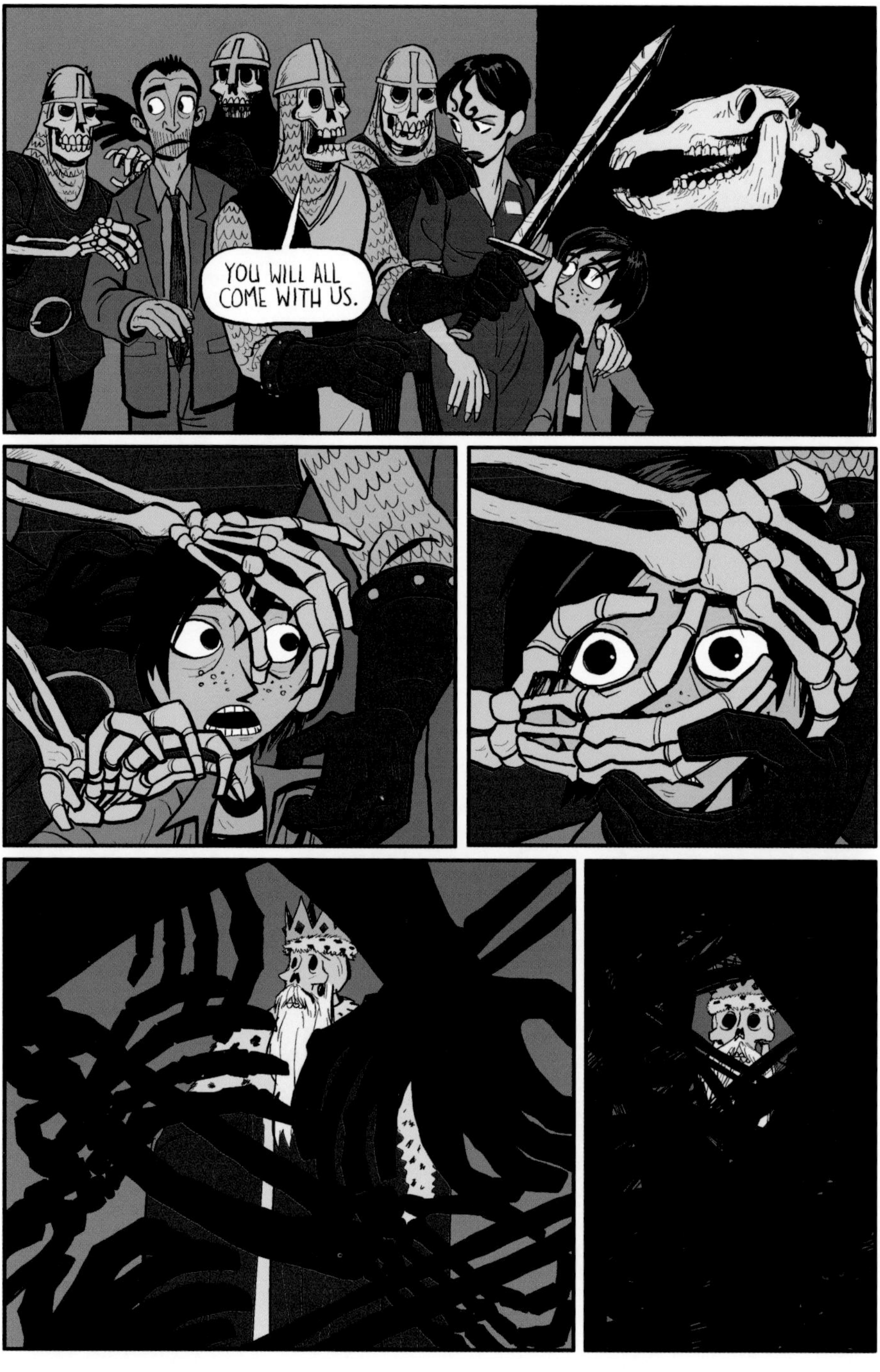
YOU WILL ALL
COME WITH US.

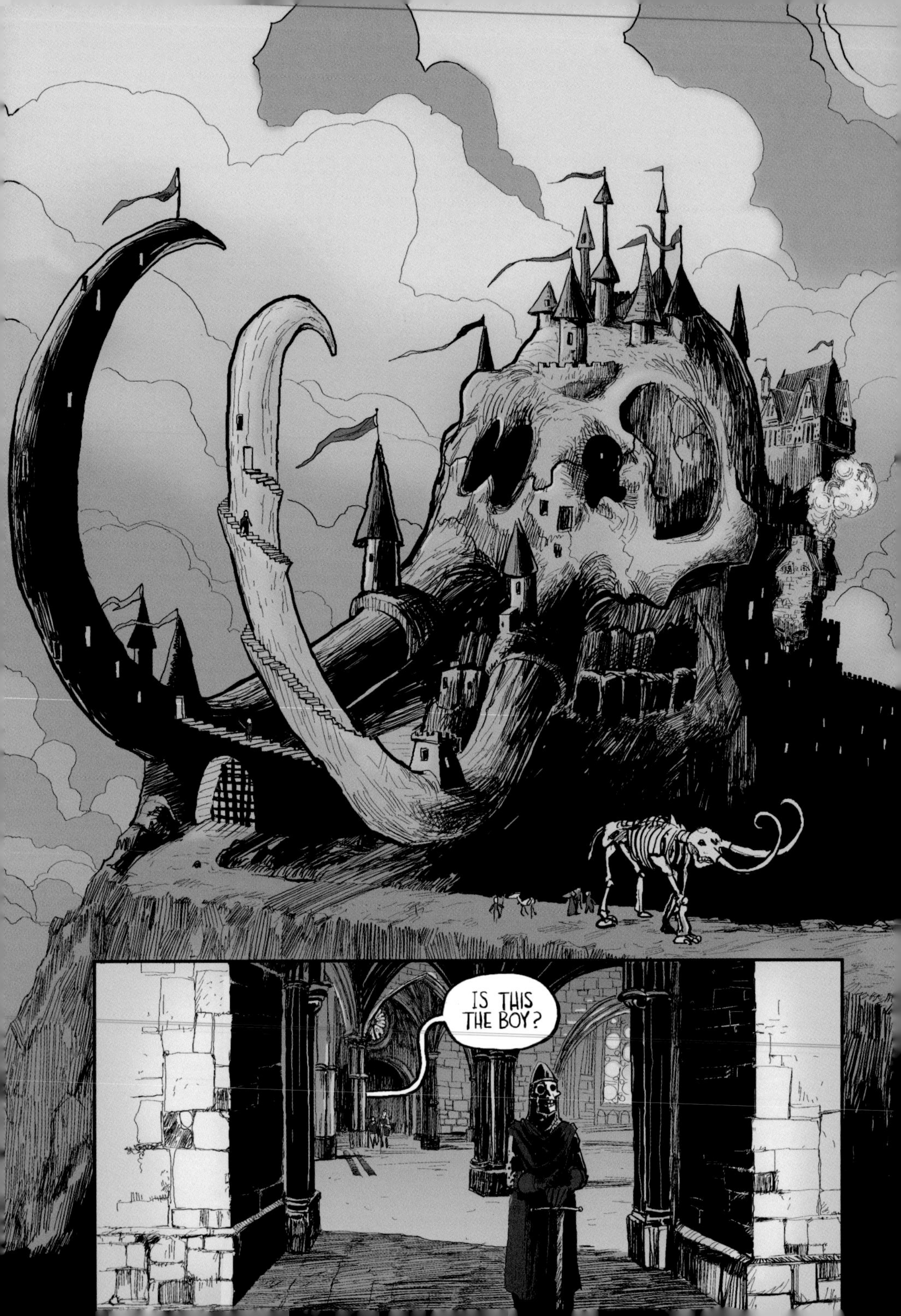
IS THIS THE BOY?

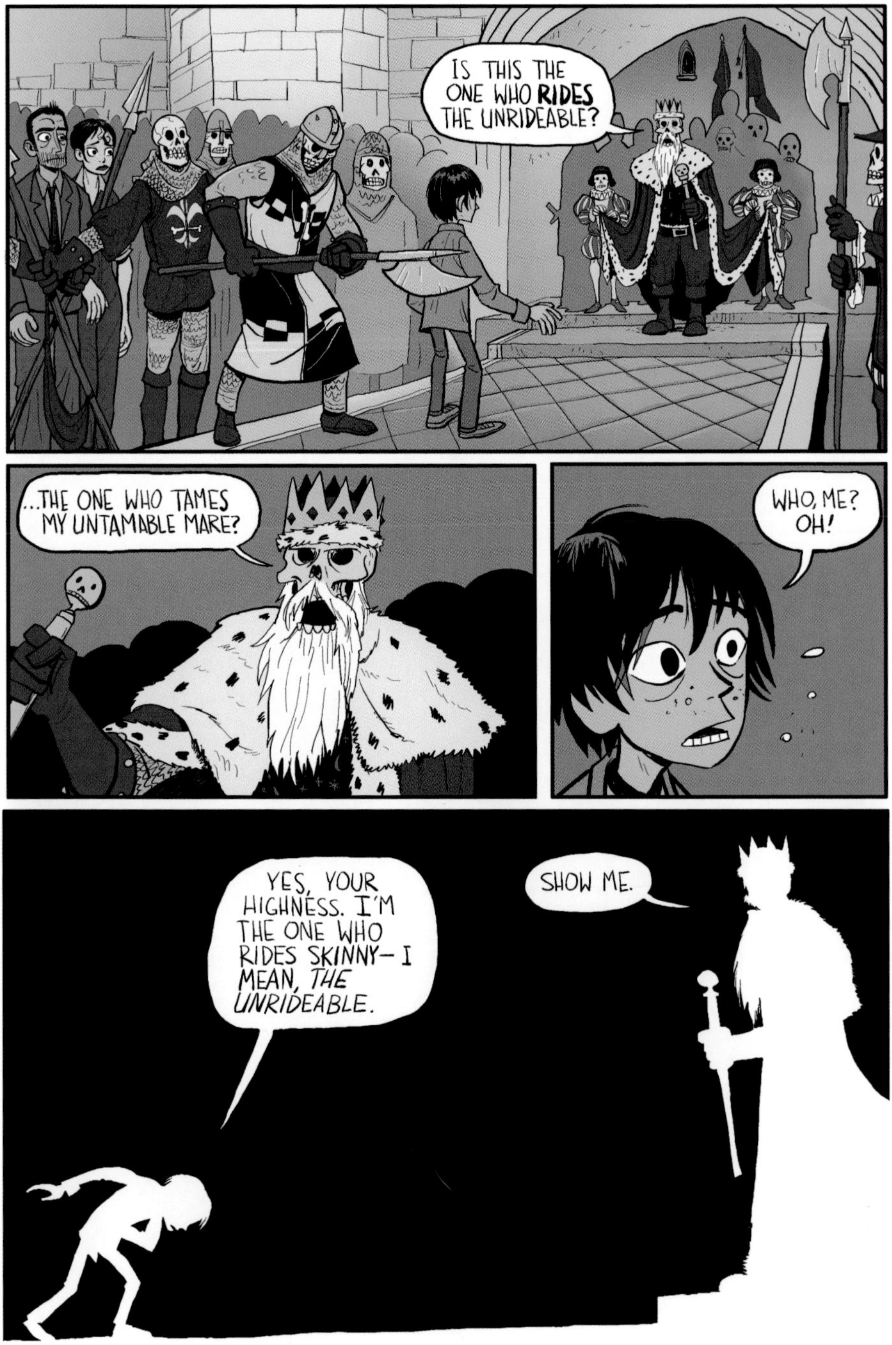

IS THIS THE ONE WHO **RIDES** THE UNRIDEABLE?
...THE ONE WHO TAMES MY UNTAMABLE MARE?
WHO, ME? OH!
YES, YOUR HIGHNESS. I'M THE ONE WHO RIDES SKINNY— I MEAN, *THE UNRIDEABLE*.
SHOW ME.

SNAP
SKINNY, COME!
CLOP
CLOP
CLOP
CLOP
CLOP
CLOP
GOOD BOY.
I HAVE TRIED TO GET THAT NAG TO HEEL FOR TWO HUNDRED YEARS, TO NO AVAIL!
DOWN.

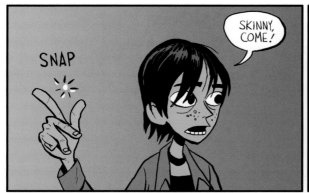

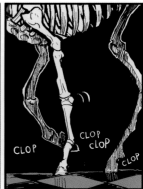

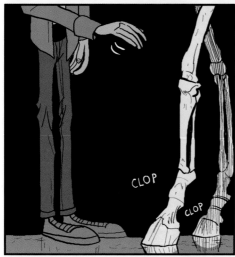

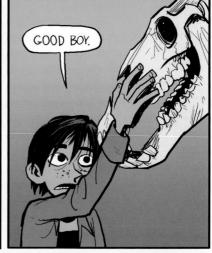

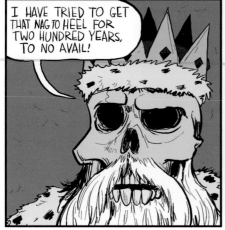

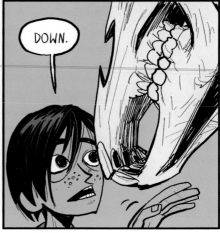

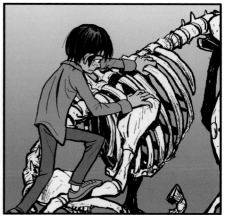

THIS IS IMPOSSIBLE! WHAT MAGIC DOES THIS BOY POSSESS?

GO!

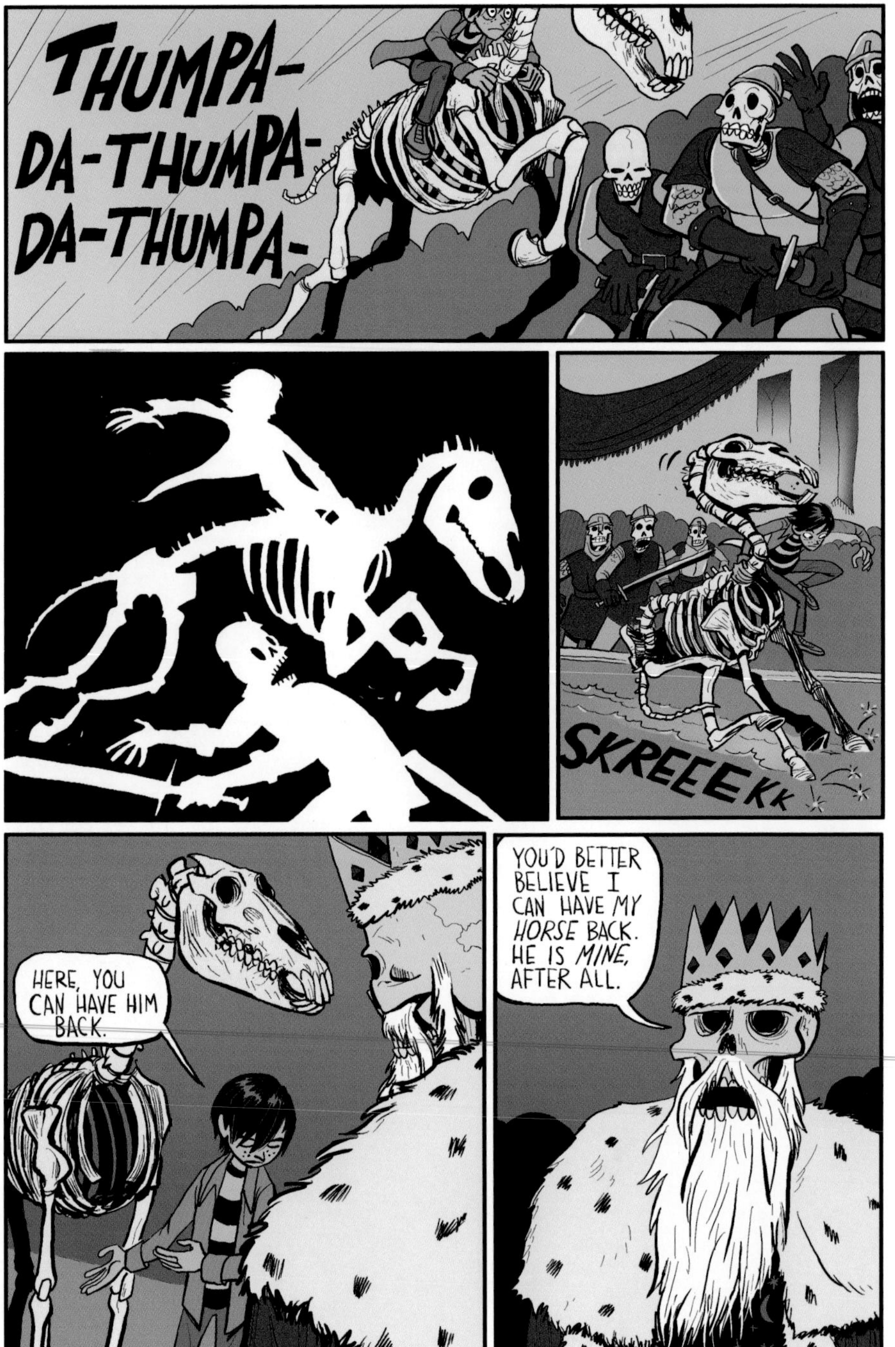
THUMPA-
DA-THUMPA-
DA-THUMPA-
SKREEEKK
HERE, YOU CAN HAVE HIM BACK.
YOU'D BETTER BELIEVE I CAN HAVE MY HORSE BACK. HE IS MINE, AFTER ALL.

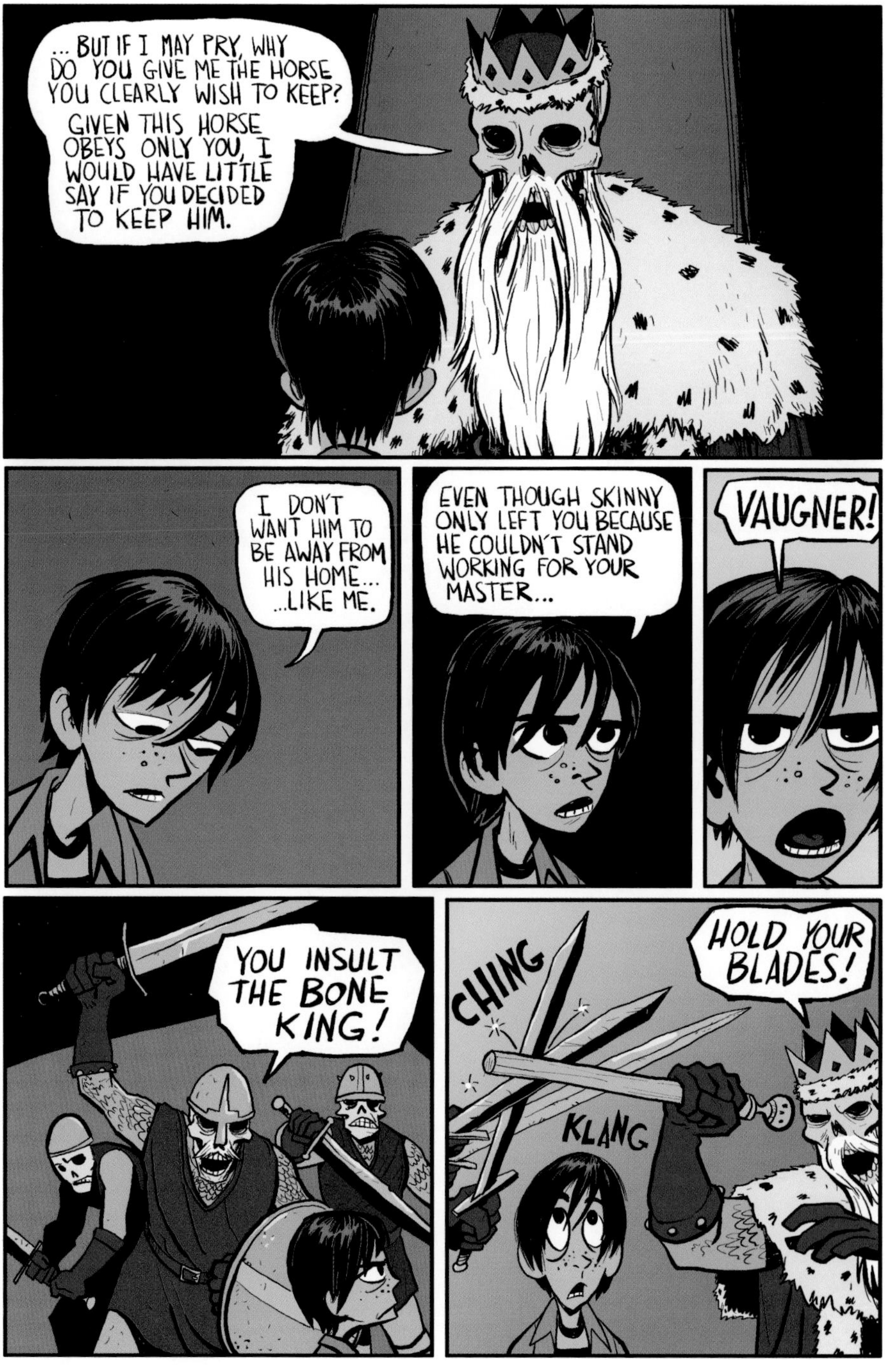

... BUT IF I MAY PRY, WHY DO YOU GIVE ME THE HORSE YOU CLEARLY WISH TO KEEP?
GIVEN THIS HORSE OBEYS ONLY YOU, I WOULD HAVE LITTLE SAY IF YOU DECIDED TO KEEP HIM.
I DON'T WANT HIM TO BE AWAY FROM HIS HOME... ...LIKE ME.
EVEN THOUGH SKINNY ONLY LEFT YOU BECAUSE HE COULDN'T STAND WORKING FOR YOUR MASTER...
VAUGNER!
YOU INSULT THE BONE KING!
CHING
KLANG
HOLD YOUR BLADES!

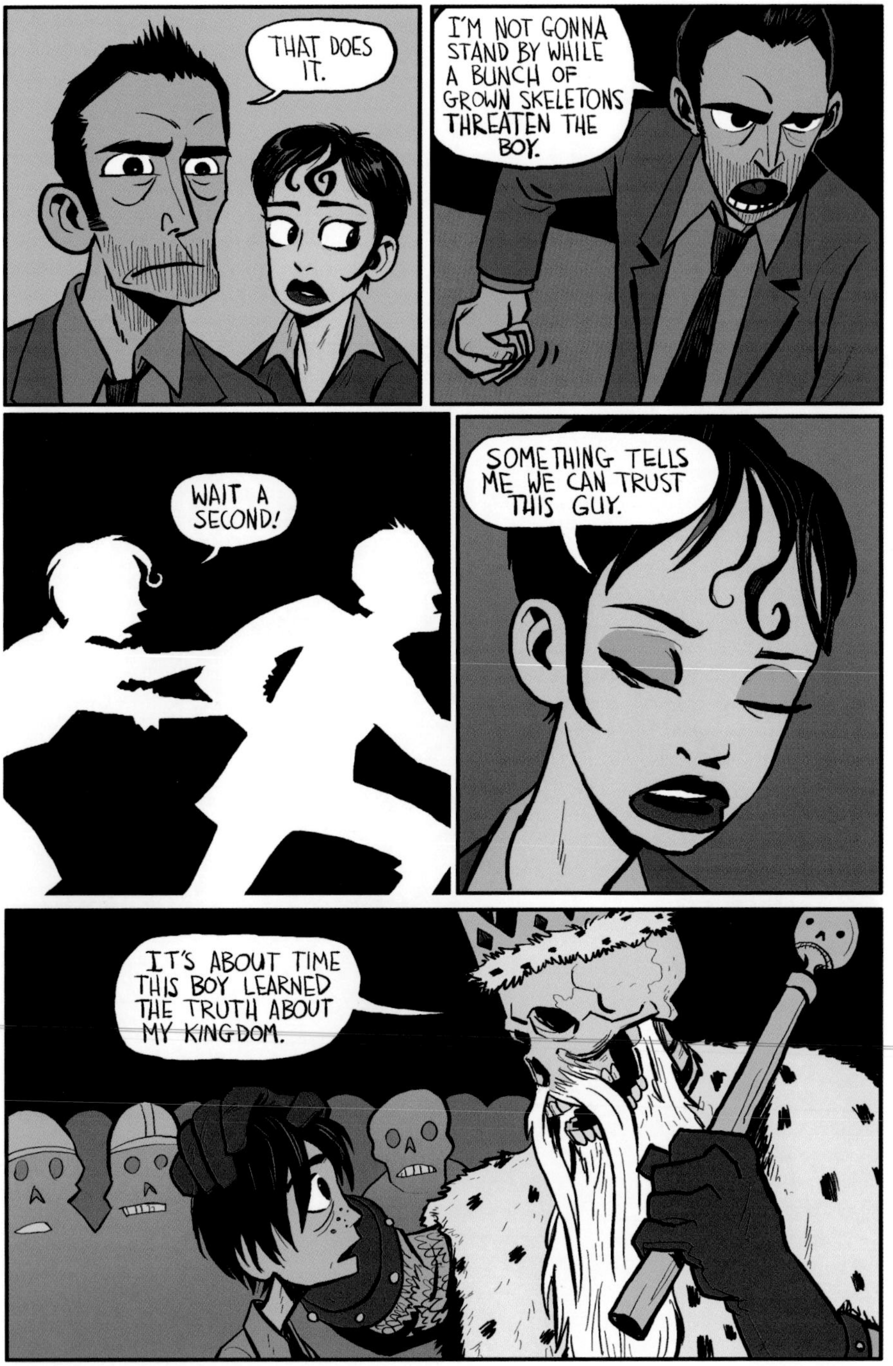
THAT DOES IT.
I'M NOT GONNA STAND BY WHILE A BUNCH OF GROWN SKELETONS THREATEN THE BOY.
WAIT A SECOND!
SOMETHING TELLS ME WE CAN TRUST THIS GUY.
IT'S ABOUT TIME THIS BOY LEARNED THE TRUTH ABOUT MY KINGDOM.

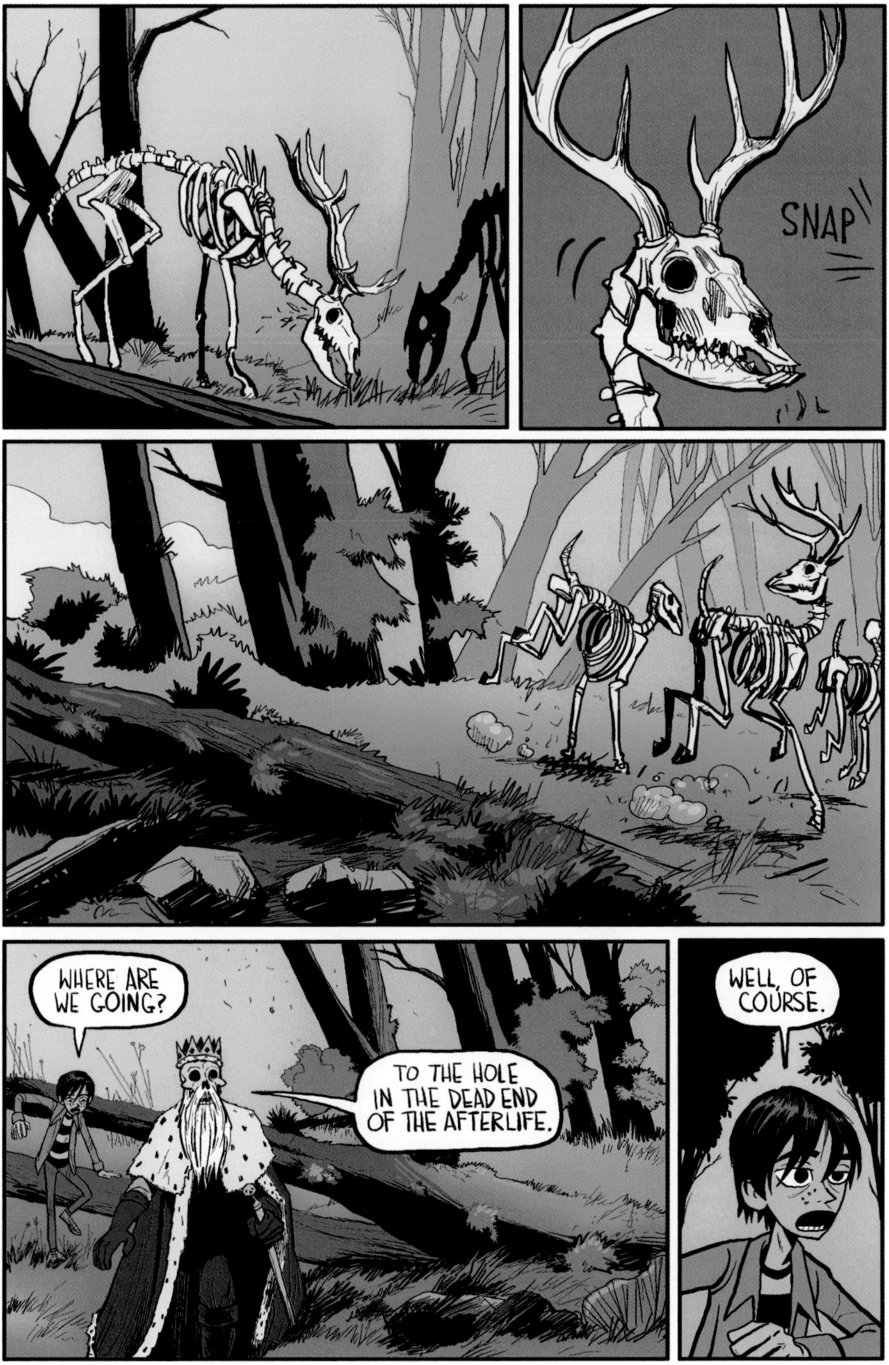
SNAP
WHERE ARE WE GOING?
TO THE HOLE IN THE DEAD END OF THE AFTERLIFE.
WELL, OF COURSE.

BLOOP
BLOOP
BLOOP
BLOOP
MOOOK

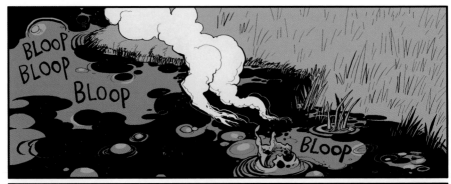

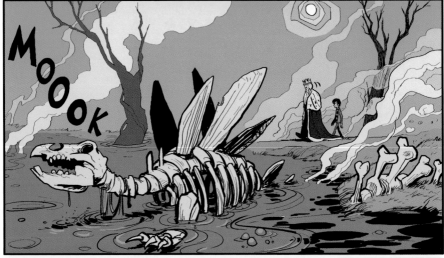

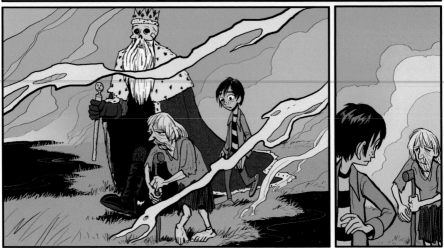

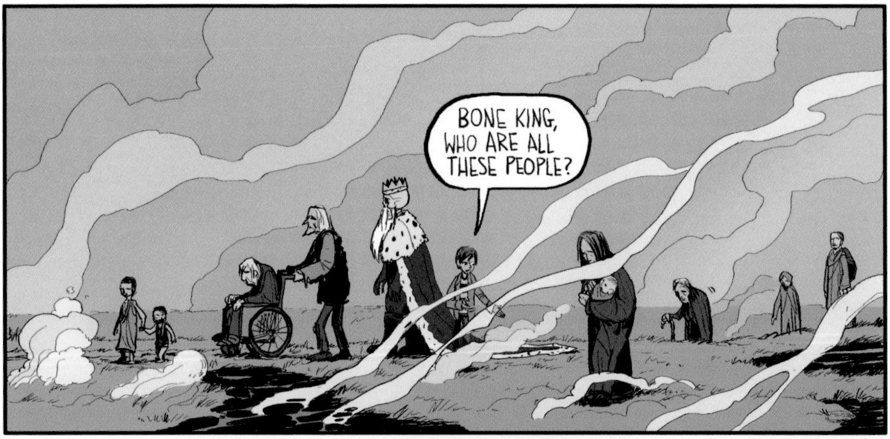
BONE KING, WHO ARE ALL THESE PEOPLE?

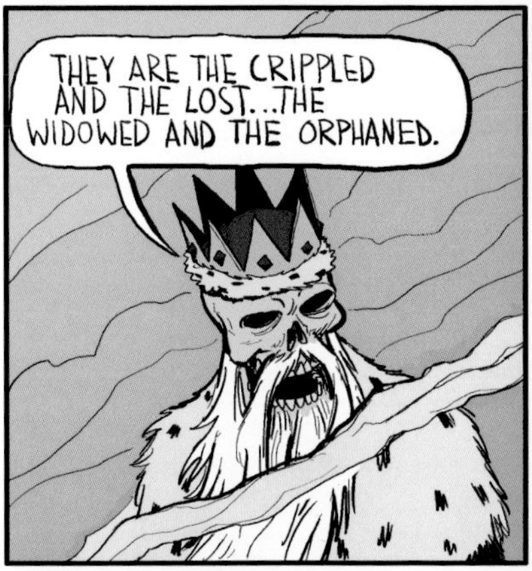
THEY ARE THE CRIPPLED AND THE LOST...THE WIDOWED AND THE ORPHANED.

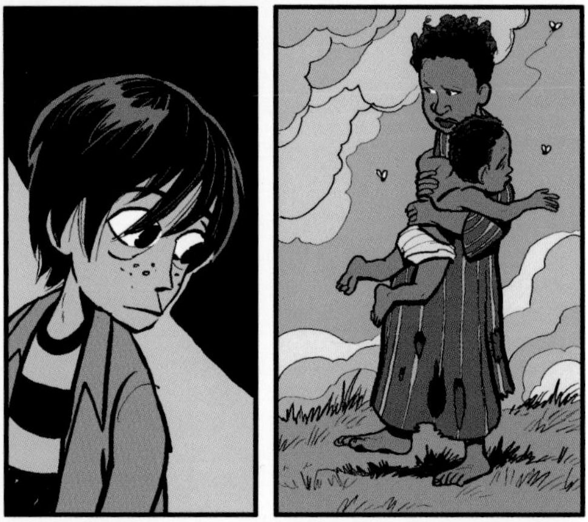

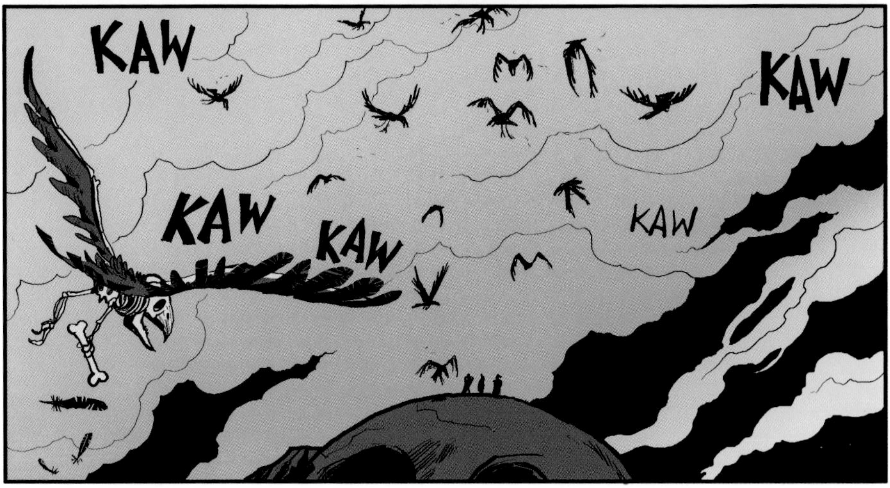
KAW
KAW
KAW
KAW
KAW

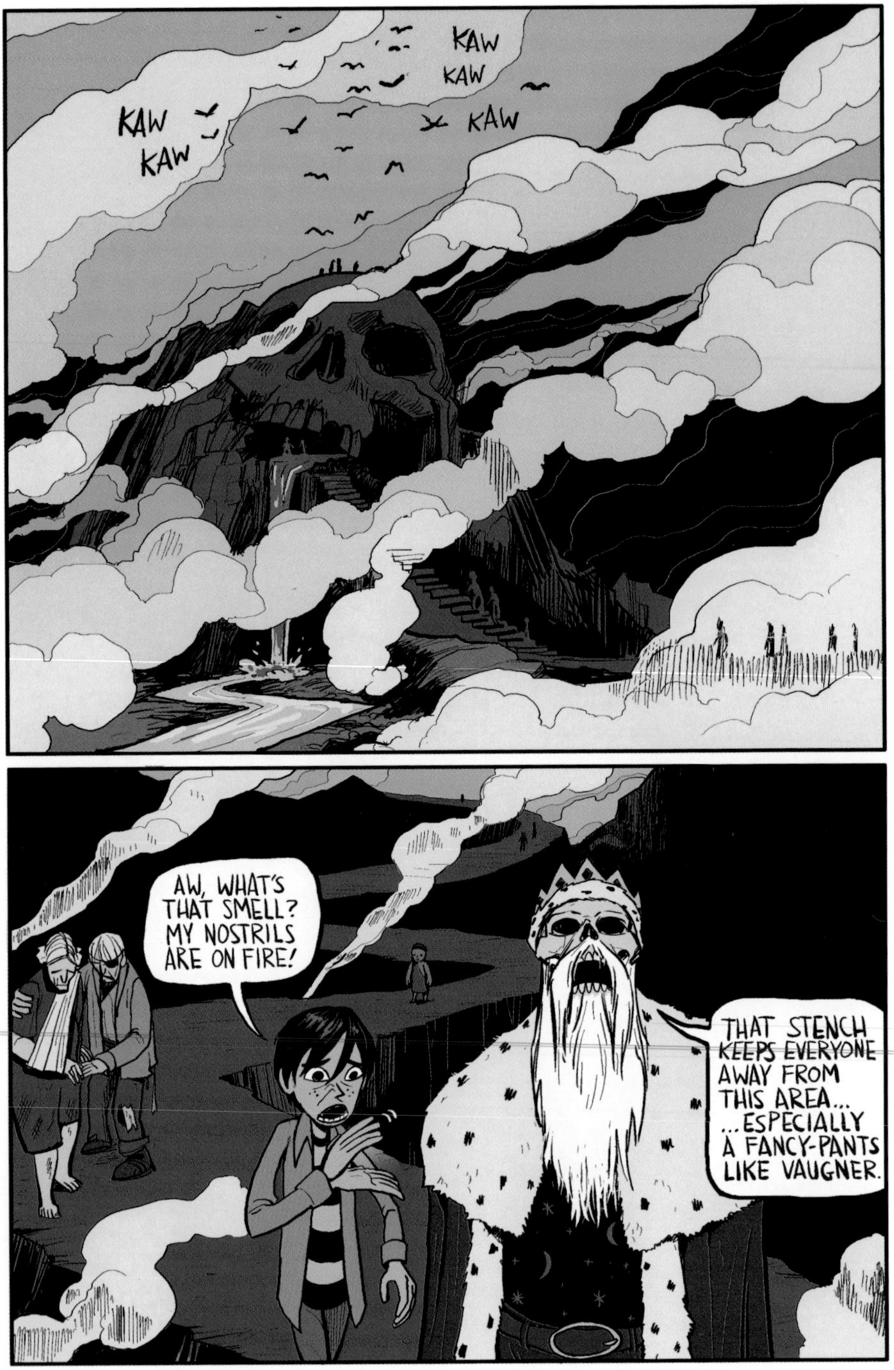
KAW
KAW
KAW
KAW
KAW
KAW
AW, WHAT'S THAT SMELL? MY NOSTRILS ARE ON FIRE!
THAT STENCH KEEPS EVERYONE AWAY FROM THIS AREA... ...ESPECIALLY A FANCY-PANTS LIKE VAUGNER.

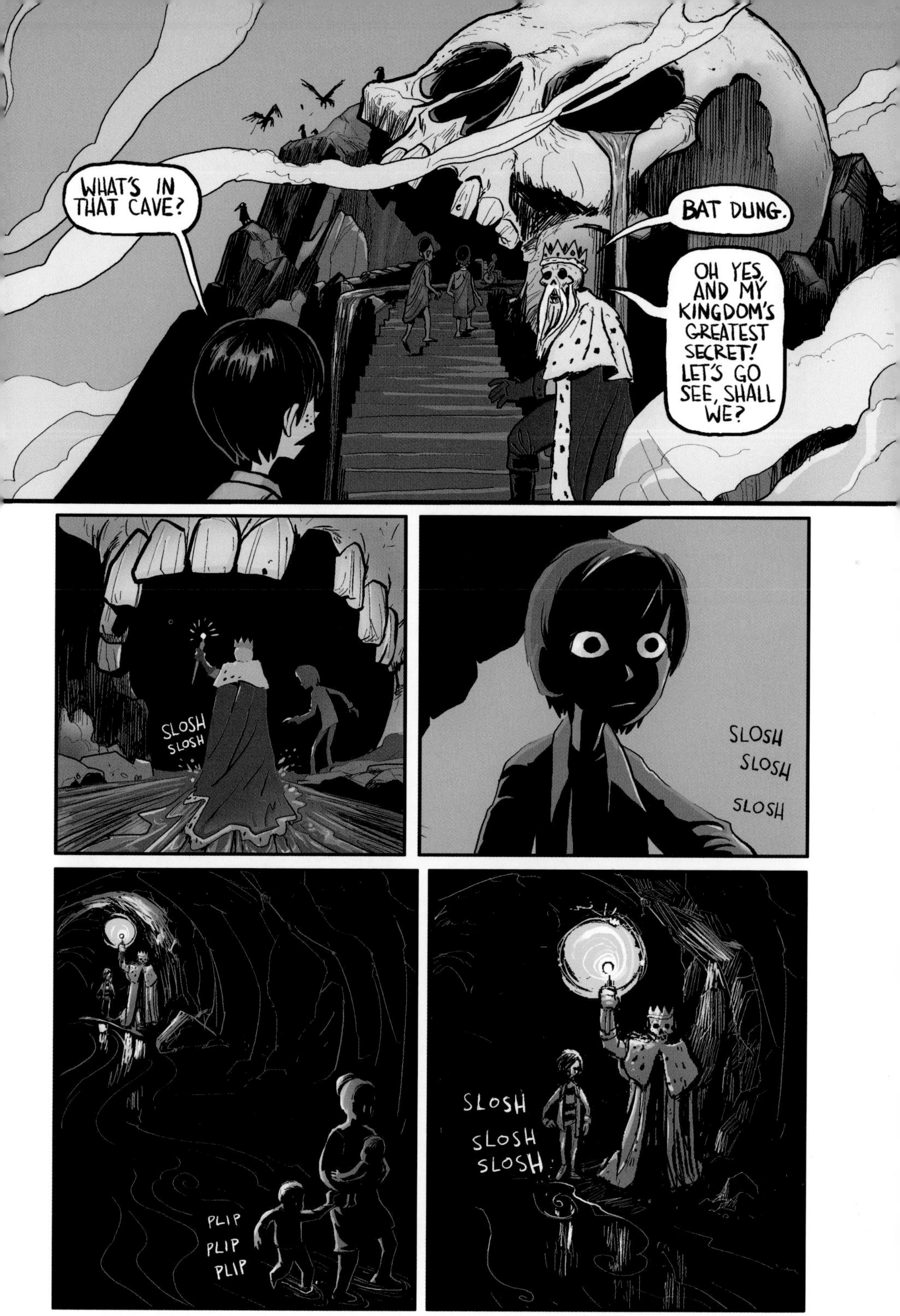
WHAT'S IN THAT CAVE?
BAT DUNG.
OH YES, AND MY KINGDOM'S GREATEST SECRET! LET'S GO SEE, SHALL WE?
SLOSH SLOSH
SLOSH SLOSH SLOSH
PLIP PLIP PLIP
SLOSH SLOSH SLOSH

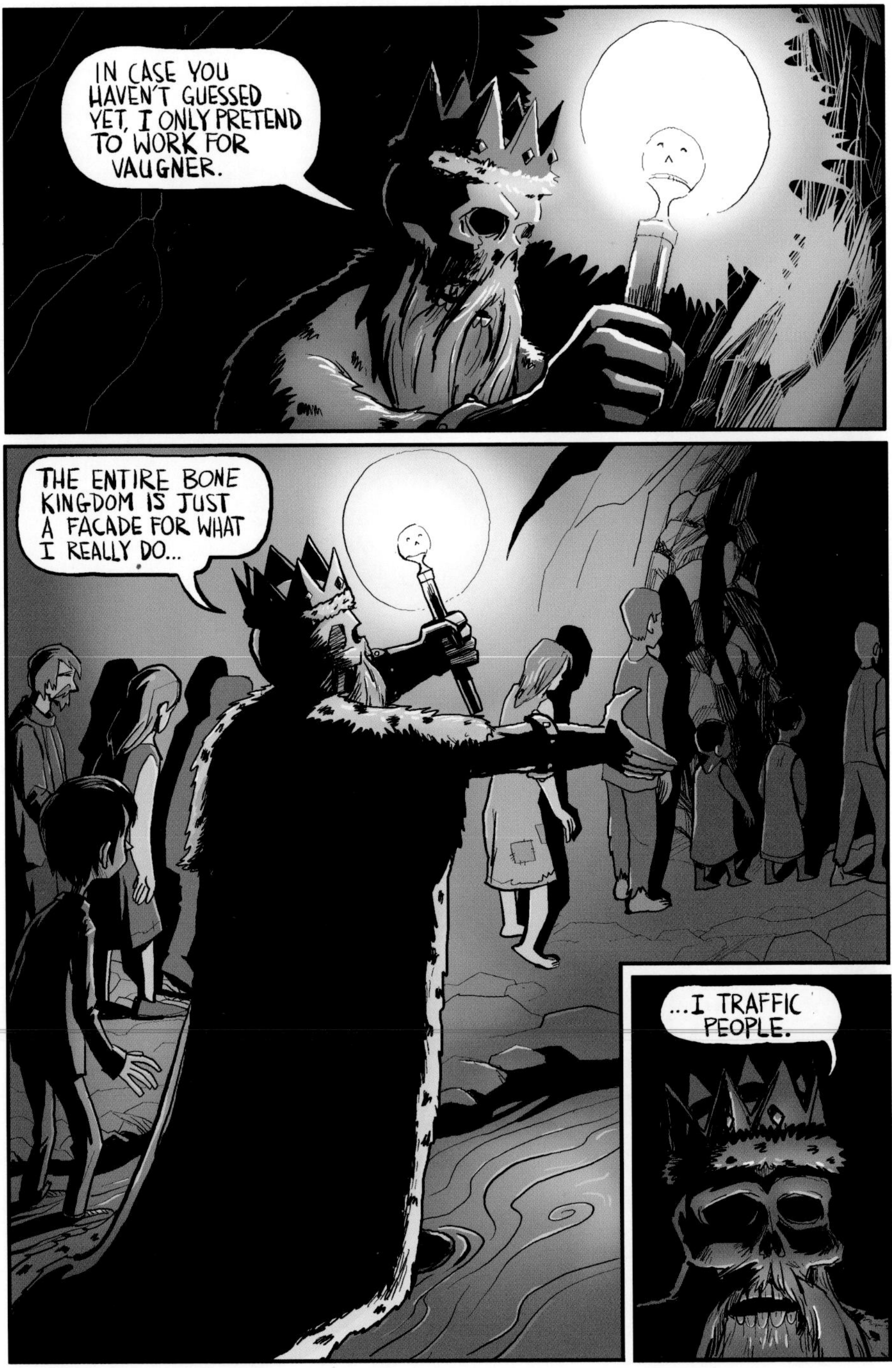
IN CASE YOU HAVEN'T GUESSED YET, I ONLY PRETEND TO WORK FOR VAUGNER.
THE ENTIRE BONE KINGDOM IS JUST A FACADE FOR WHAT I REALLY DO...
...I TRAFFIC PEOPLE.

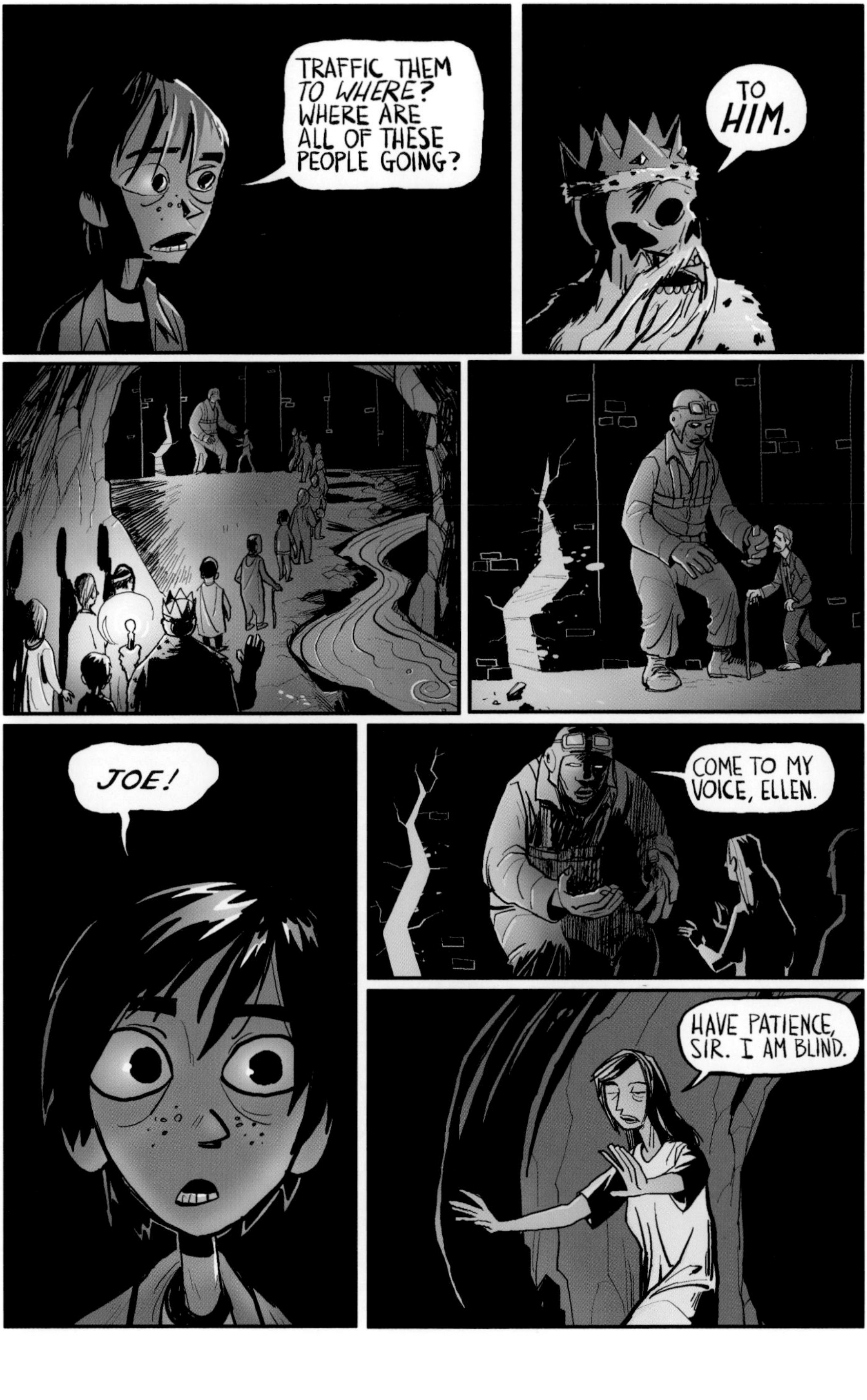
TRAFFIC THEM TO *WHERE?* WHERE ARE ALL OF THESE PEOPLE GOING?
TO *HIM.*
JOE!
COME TO MY VOICE, ELLEN.
HAVE PATIENCE, SIR. I AM BLIND.

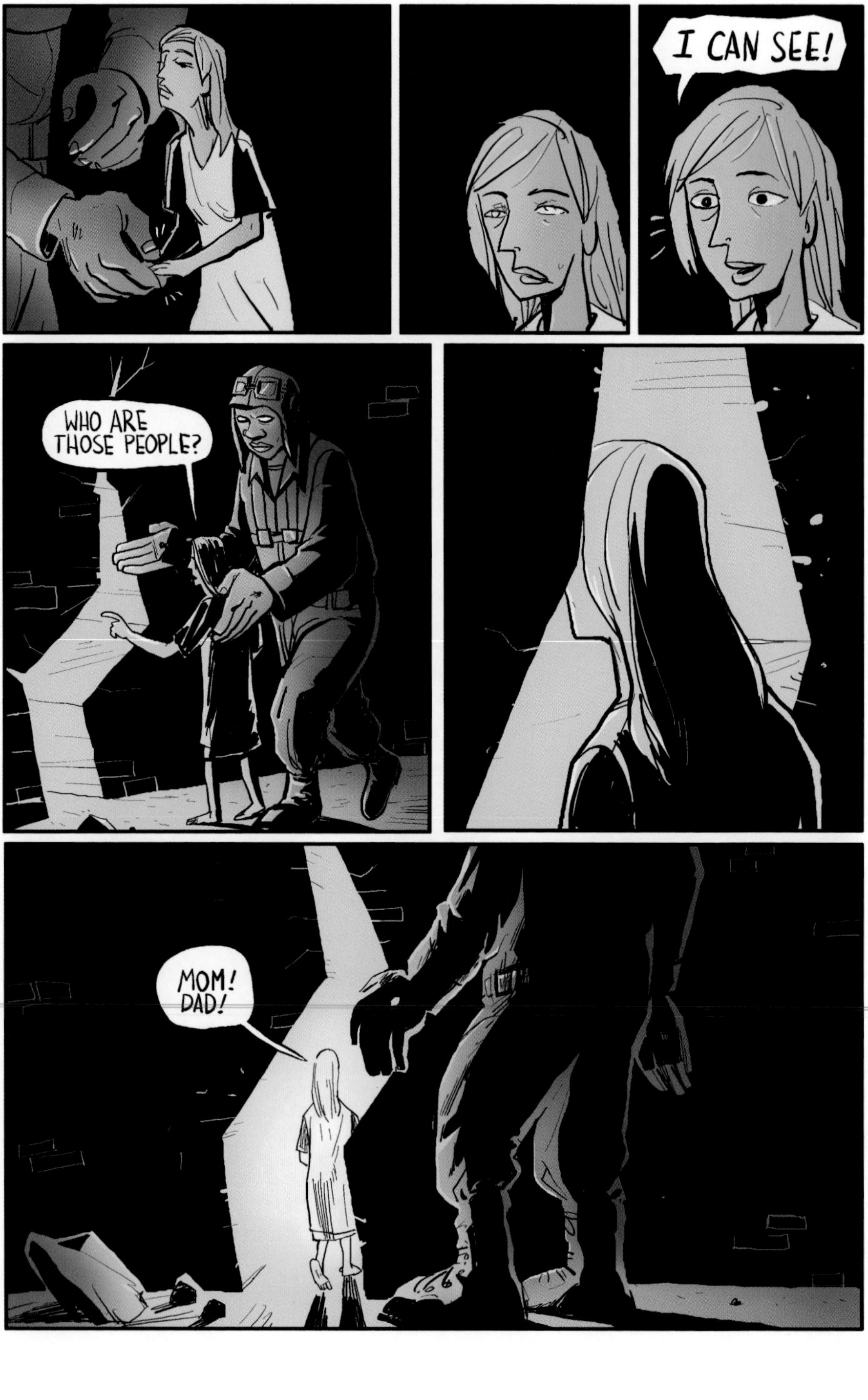

I CAN SEE!
WHO ARE THOSE PEOPLE?
MOM! DAD!

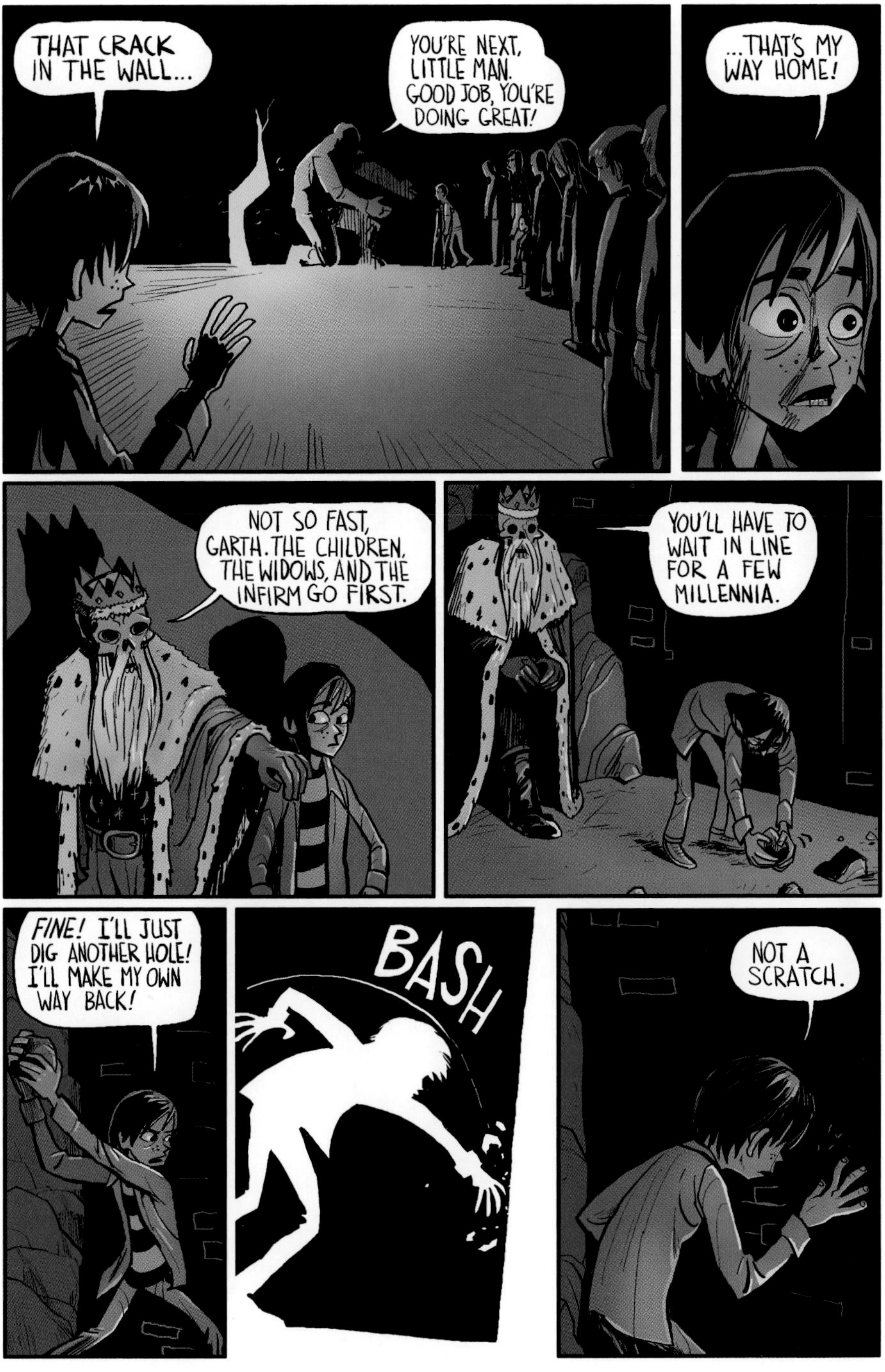
THAT CRACK IN THE WALL...
YOU'RE NEXT, LITTLE MAN. GOOD JOB, YOU'RE DOING GREAT!
...THAT'S MY WAY HOME!
NOT SO FAST, GARTH. THE CHILDREN, THE WIDOWS, AND THE INFIRM GO FIRST.
YOU'LL HAVE TO WAIT IN LINE FOR A FEW MILLENNIA.
FINE! I'LL JUST DIG ANOTHER HOLE! I'LL MAKE MY OWN WAY BACK!
BASH
NOT A SCRATCH.

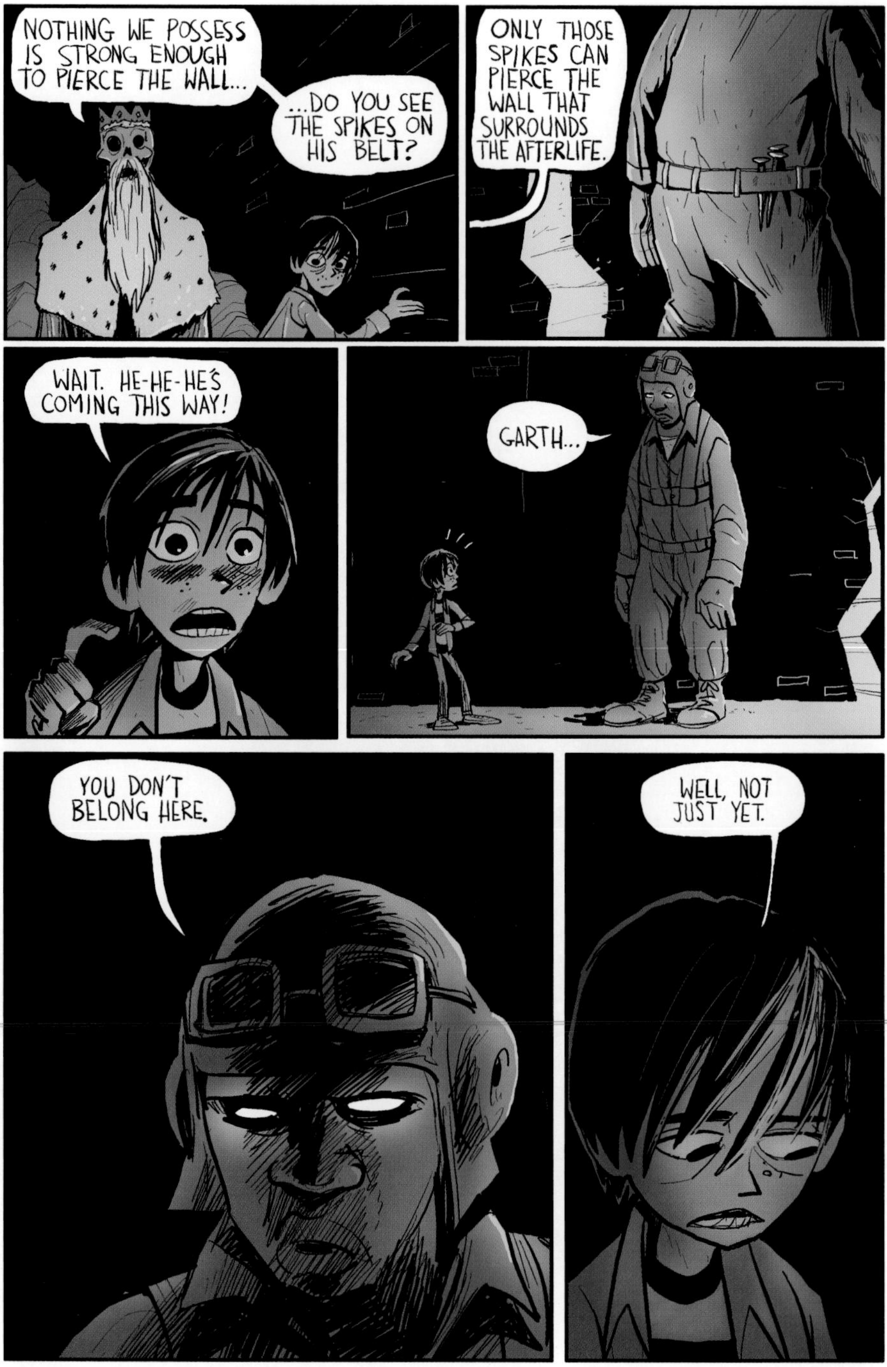
NOTHING WE POSSESS IS STRONG ENOUGH TO PIERCE THE WALL...
...DO YOU SEE THE SPIKES ON HIS BELT?
ONLY THOSE SPIKES CAN PIERCE THE WALL THAT SURROUNDS THE AFTERLIFE.
WAIT. HE-HE-HE'S COMING THIS WAY!
GARTH...
YOU DON'T BELONG HERE.
WELL, NOT JUST YET.

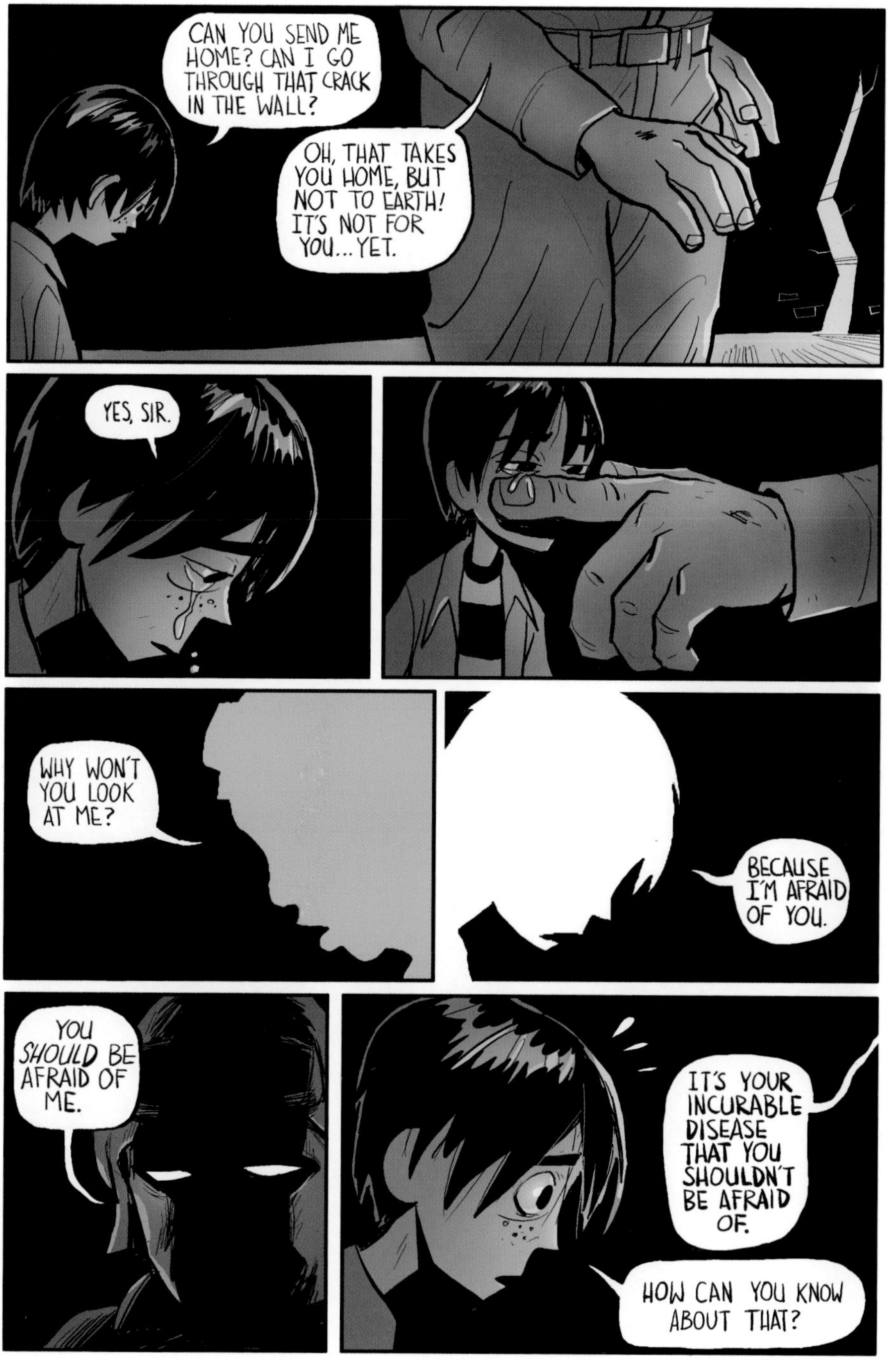
CAN YOU SEND ME HOME? CAN I GO THROUGH THAT CRACK IN THE WALL?
OH, THAT TAKES YOU HOME, BUT NOT TO EARTH! IT'S NOT FOR YOU... YET.
YES, SIR.
WHY WON'T YOU LOOK AT ME?
BECAUSE I'M AFRAID OF YOU.
YOU *SHOULD* BE AFRAID OF ME.
IT'S YOUR INCURABLE DISEASE THAT YOU SHOULDN'T BE AFRAID OF.
HOW CAN YOU KNOW ABOUT THAT?

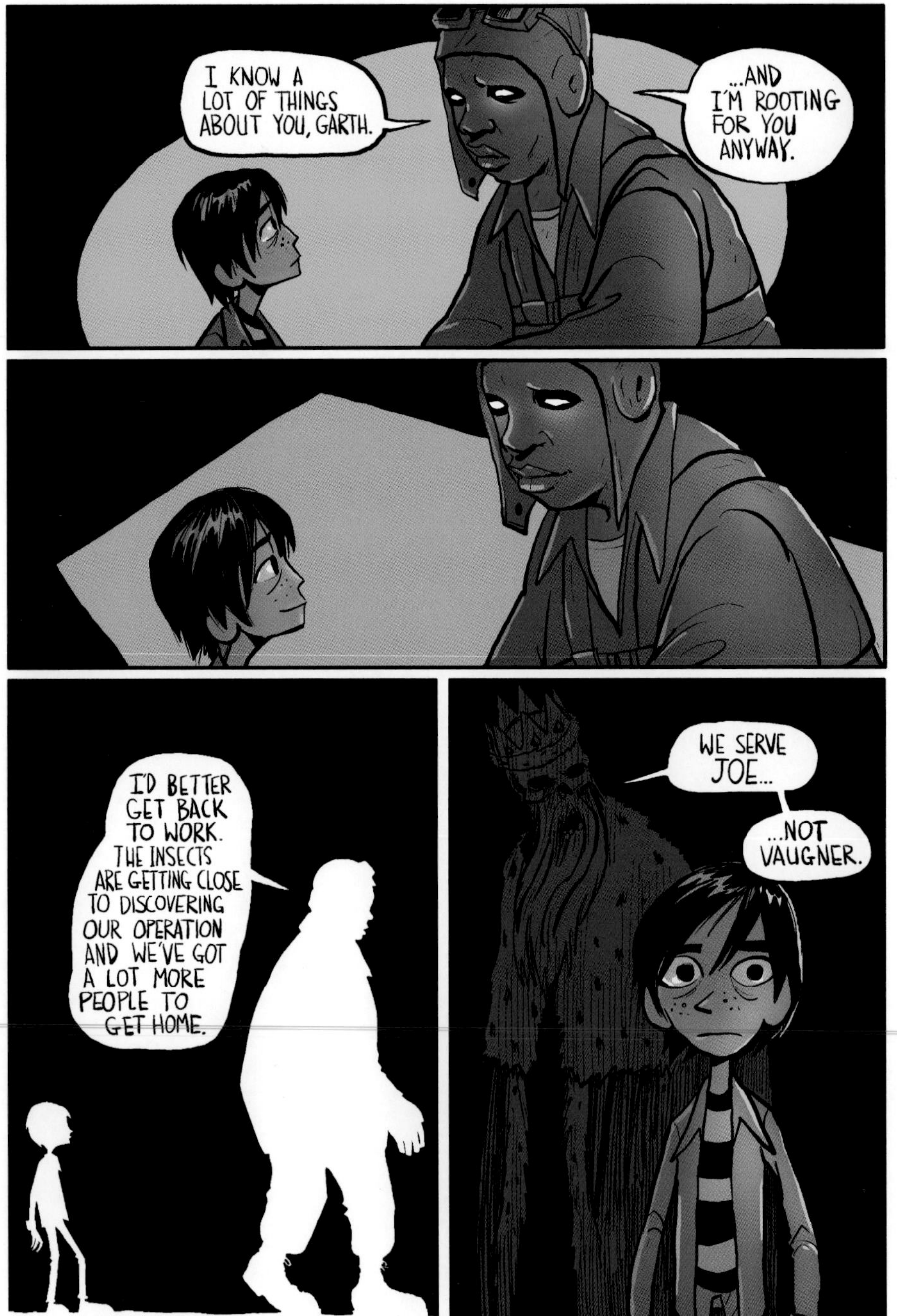
I KNOW A LOT OF THINGS ABOUT YOU, GARTH.
...AND I'M ROOTING FOR YOU ANYWAY.
I'D BETTER GET BACK TO WORK. THE INSECTS ARE GETTING CLOSE TO DISCOVERING OUR OPERATION AND WE'VE GOT A LOT MORE PEOPLE TO GET HOME.
WE SERVE JOE...
...NOT VAUGNER.

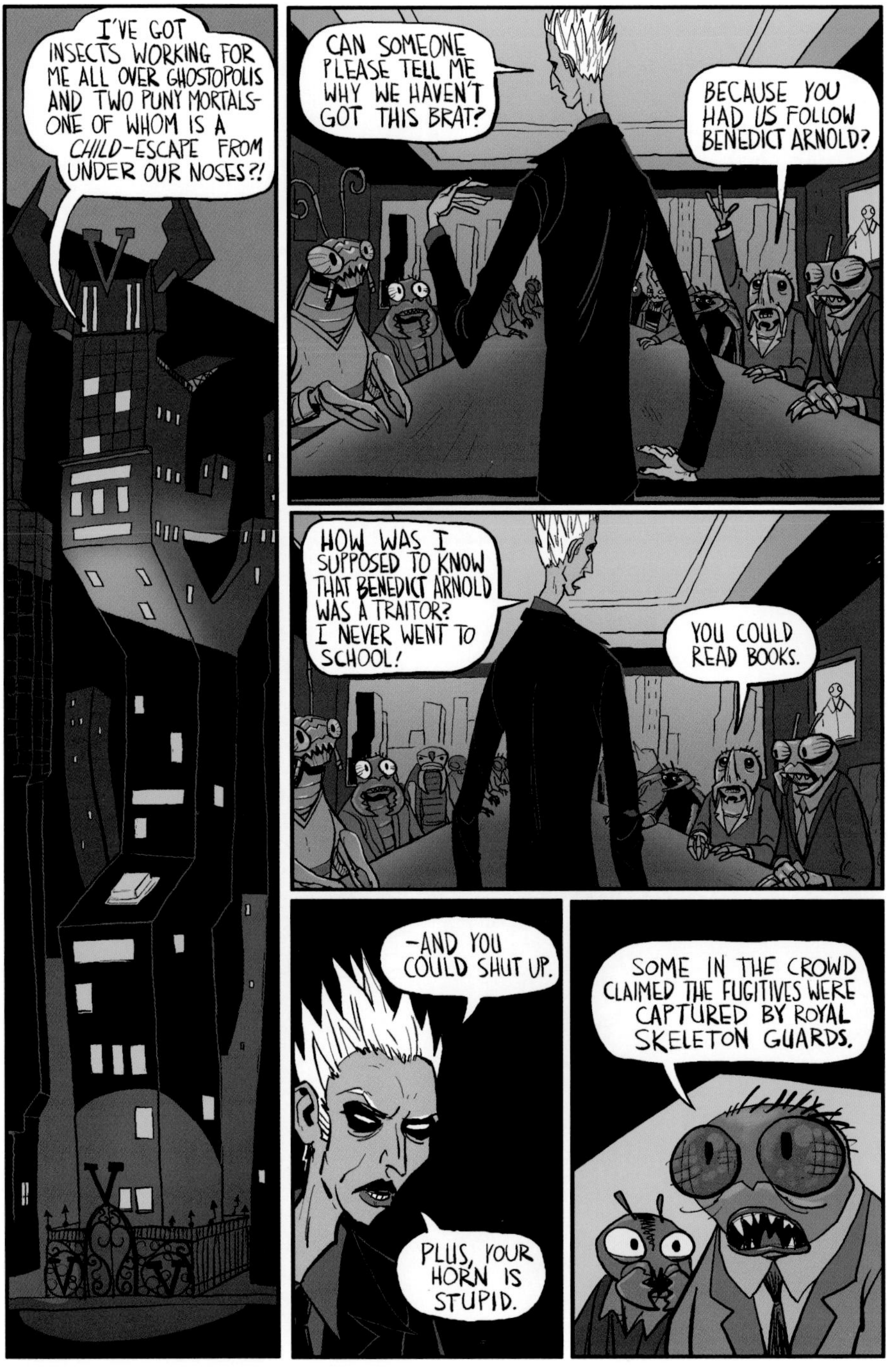
I'VE GOT INSECTS WORKING FOR ME ALL OVER GHOSTOPOLIS AND TWO PUNY MORTALS- ONE OF WHOM IS A *CHILD*-ESCAPE FROM UNDER OUR NOSES?!
CAN SOMEONE PLEASE TELL ME WHY WE HAVEN'T GOT THIS BRAT?
BECAUSE *YOU* HAD US FOLLOW BENEDICT ARNOLD?
HOW WAS I SUPPOSED TO KNOW THAT BENEDICT ARNOLD WAS A TRAITOR? I NEVER WENT TO SCHOOL!
YOU COULD READ BOOKS.
-AND YOU COULD SHUT UP.
PLUS, YOUR HORN IS STUPID.
SOME IN THE CROWD CLAIMED THE FUGITIVES WERE CAPTURED BY ROYAL SKELETON GUARDS.

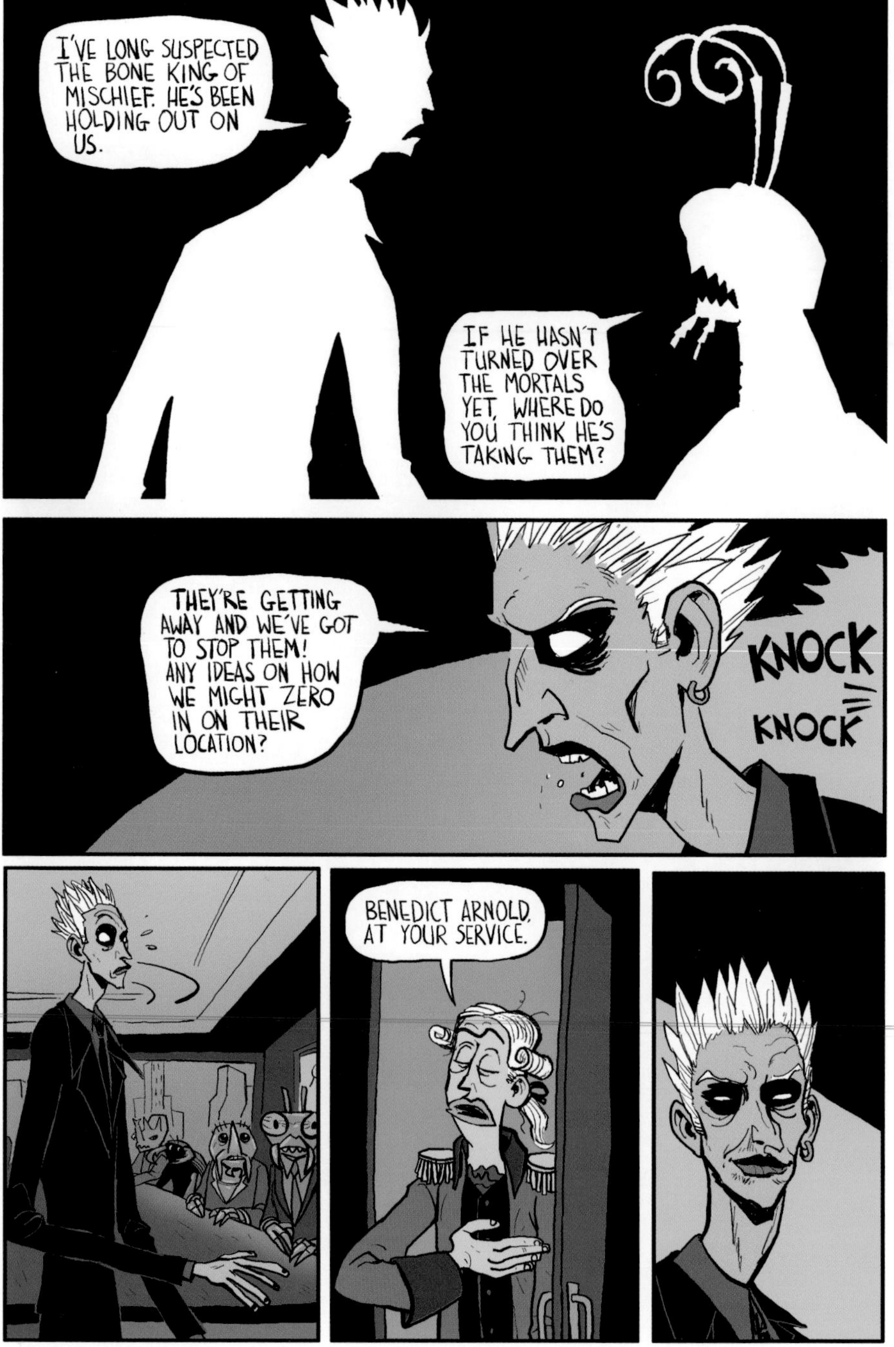
I'VE LONG SUSPECTED THE BONE KING OF MISCHIEF. HE'S BEEN HOLDING OUT ON US.
IF HE HASN'T TURNED OVER THE MORTALS YET, WHERE DO YOU THINK HE'S TAKING THEM?
THEY'RE GETTING AWAY AND WE'VE GOT TO STOP THEM! ANY IDEAS ON HOW WE MIGHT ZERO IN ON THEIR LOCATION?
KNOCK
KNOCK
BENEDICT ARNOLD, AT YOUR SERVICE.

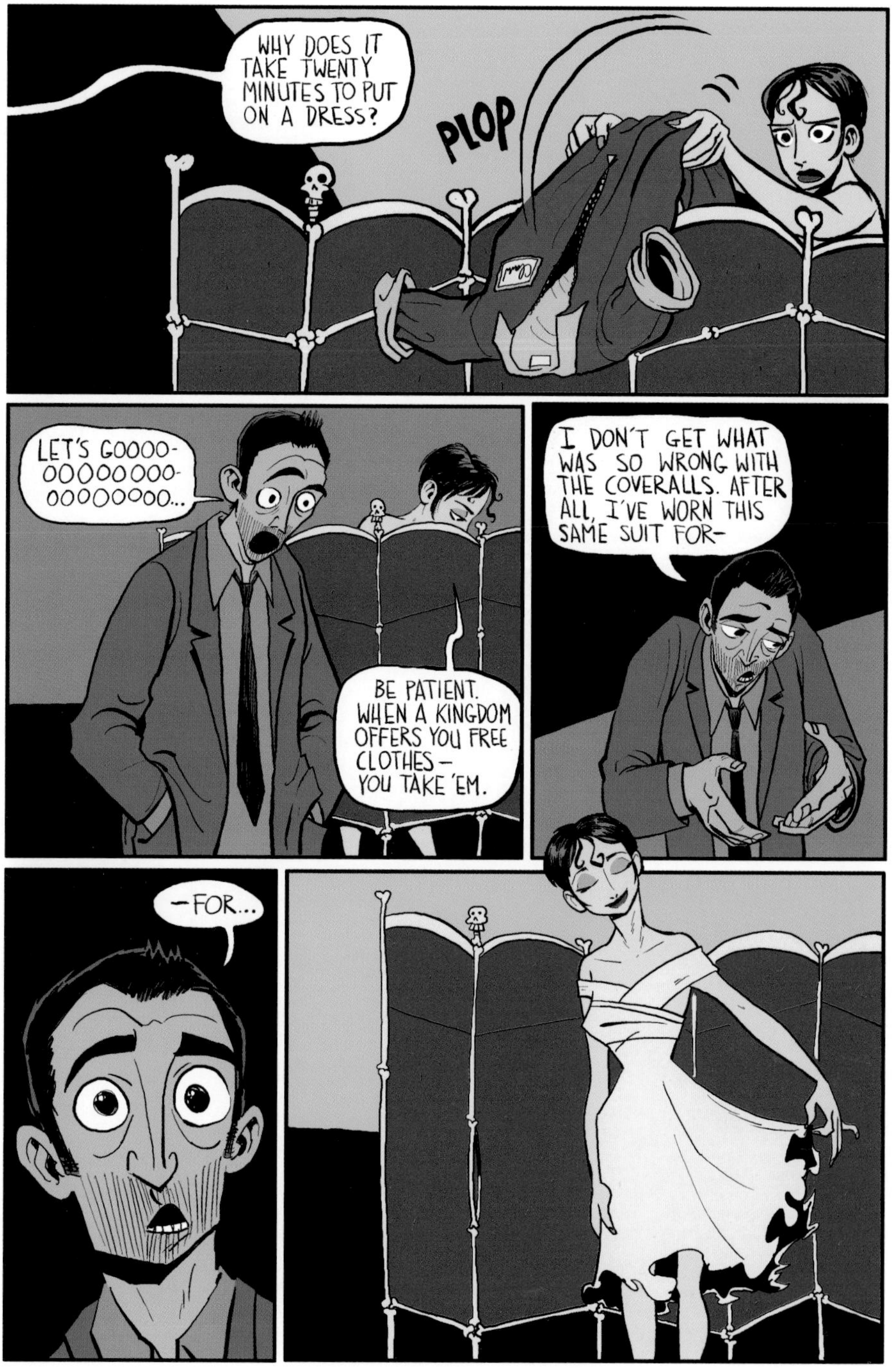
WHY DOES IT TAKE TWENTY MINUTES TO PUT ON A DRESS?
PLOP
LET'S GOOOO-OOOOOOOO-OOOOOOOO...
BE PATIENT. WHEN A KINGDOM OFFERS YOU FREE CLOTHES — YOU TAKE 'EM.
I DON'T GET WHAT WAS SO WRONG WITH THE COVERALLS. AFTER ALL, I'VE WORN THIS SAME SUIT FOR–
–FOR...

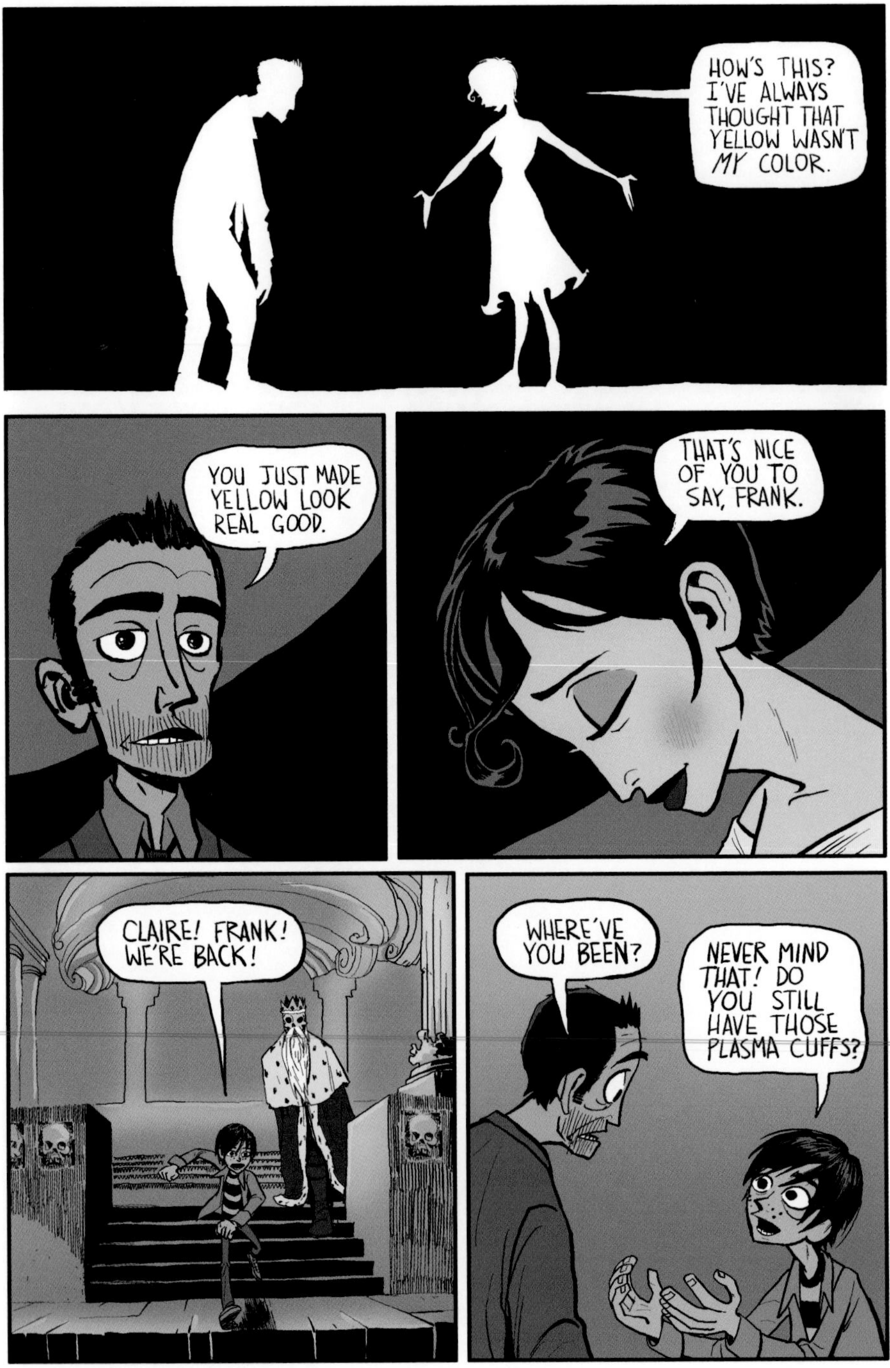
HOW'S THIS? I'VE ALWAYS THOUGHT THAT YELLOW WASN'T MY COLOR.
YOU JUST MADE YELLOW LOOK REAL GOOD.
THAT'S NICE OF YOU TO SAY, FRANK.
CLAIRE! FRANK! WE'RE BACK!
WHERE'VE YOU BEEN?
NEVER MIND THAT! DO YOU STILL HAVE THOSE PLASMA CUFFS?

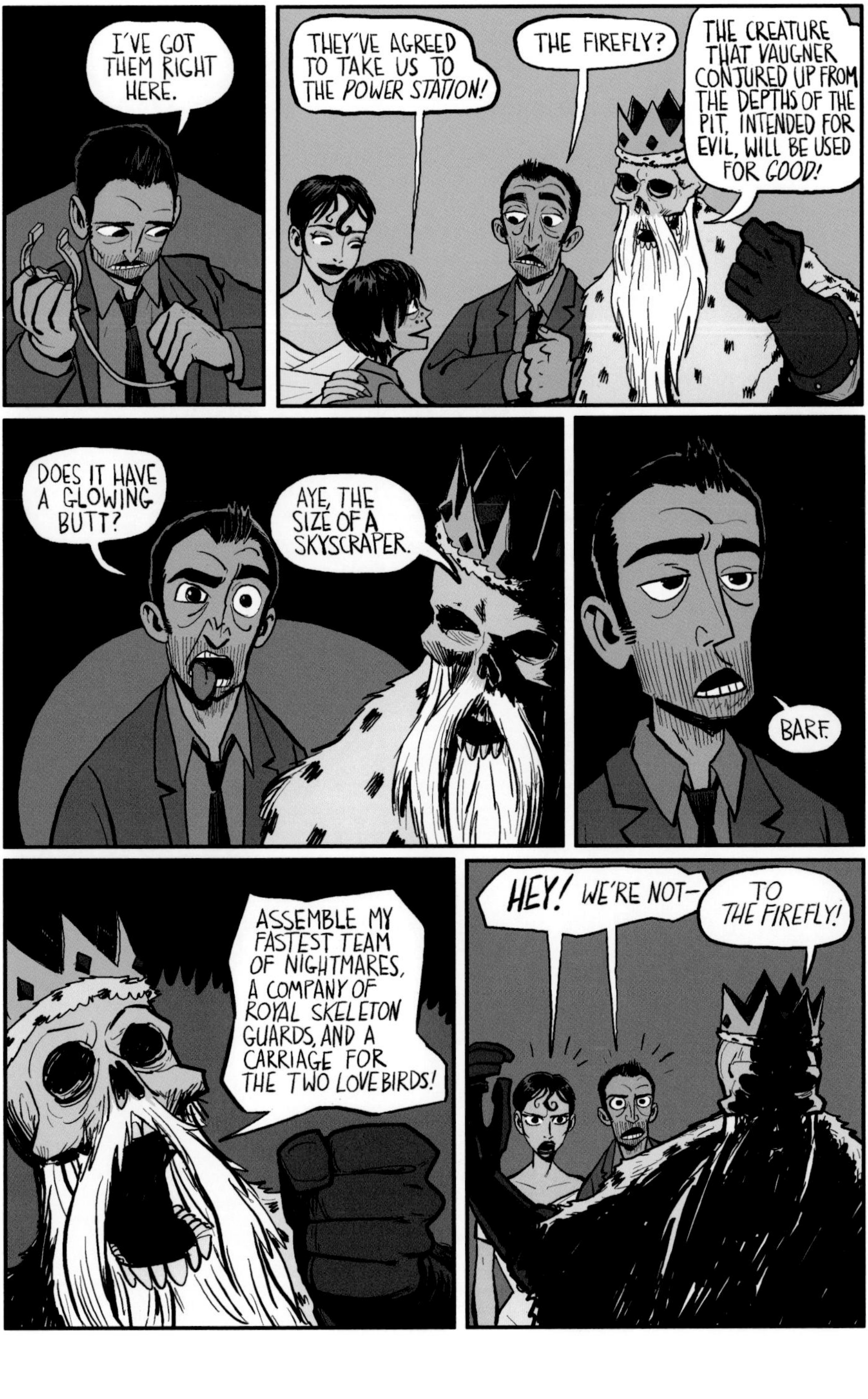
I'VE GOT THEM RIGHT HERE.
THEY'VE AGREED TO TAKE US TO THE *POWER STATION!*
THE FIREFLY?
THE CREATURE THAT VAUGNER CONJURED UP FROM THE DEPTHS OF THE PIT, INTENDED FOR EVIL, WILL BE USED FOR *GOOD!*
DOES IT HAVE A GLOWING BUTT?
AYE, THE SIZE OF A SKYSCRAPER.
BARF.
ASSEMBLE MY FASTEST TEAM OF NIGHTMARES, A COMPANY OF ROYAL SKELETON GUARDS, AND A CARRIAGE FOR THE TWO LOVEBIRDS!
HEY! WE'RE NOT–
TO *THE FIREFLY!*

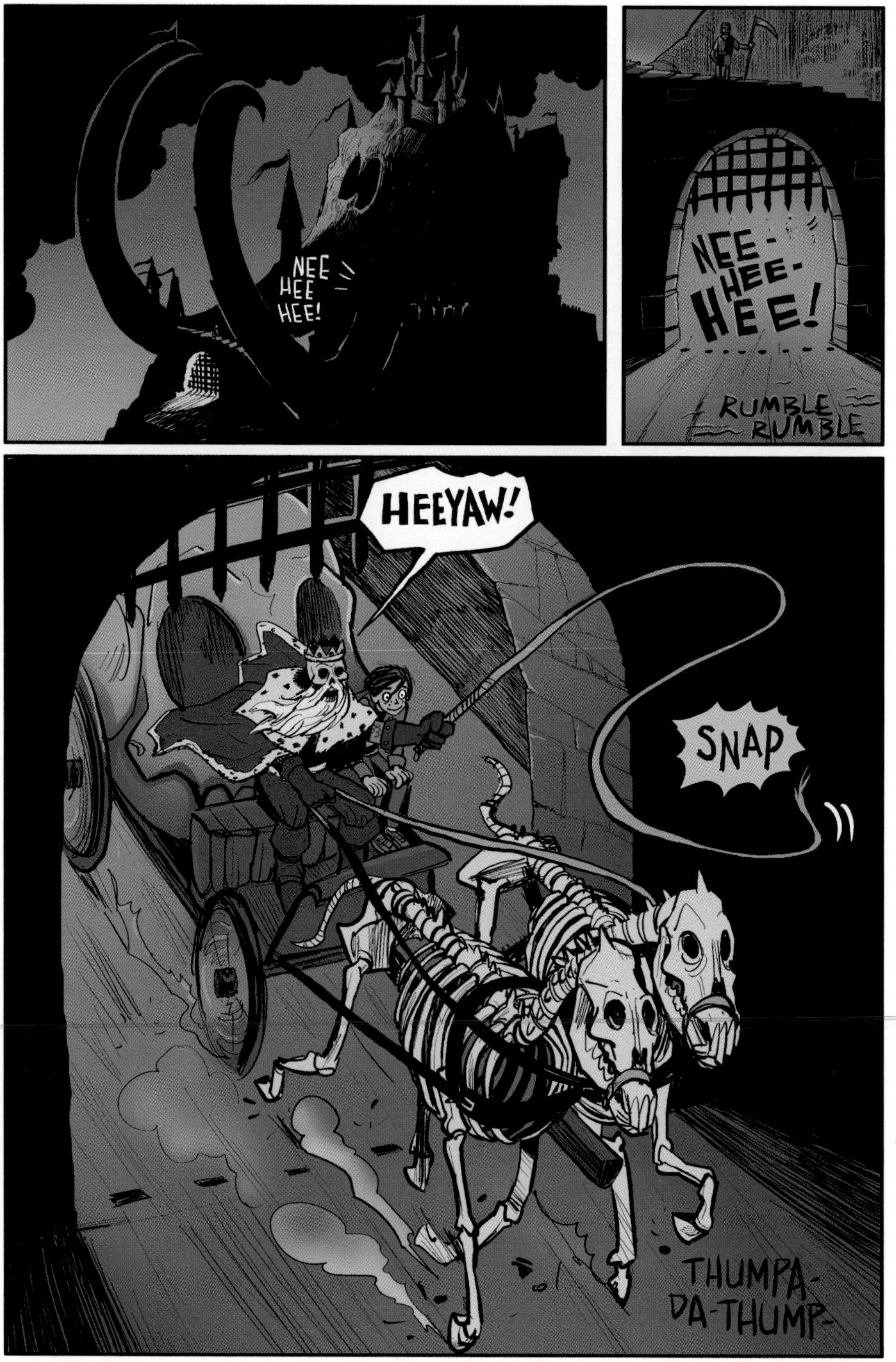
NEE
HEE
HEE!
NEE-
HEE-
HEE!
RUMBLE
RUMBLE
HEEYAW!
SNAP
THUMPA-
DA-THUMP-

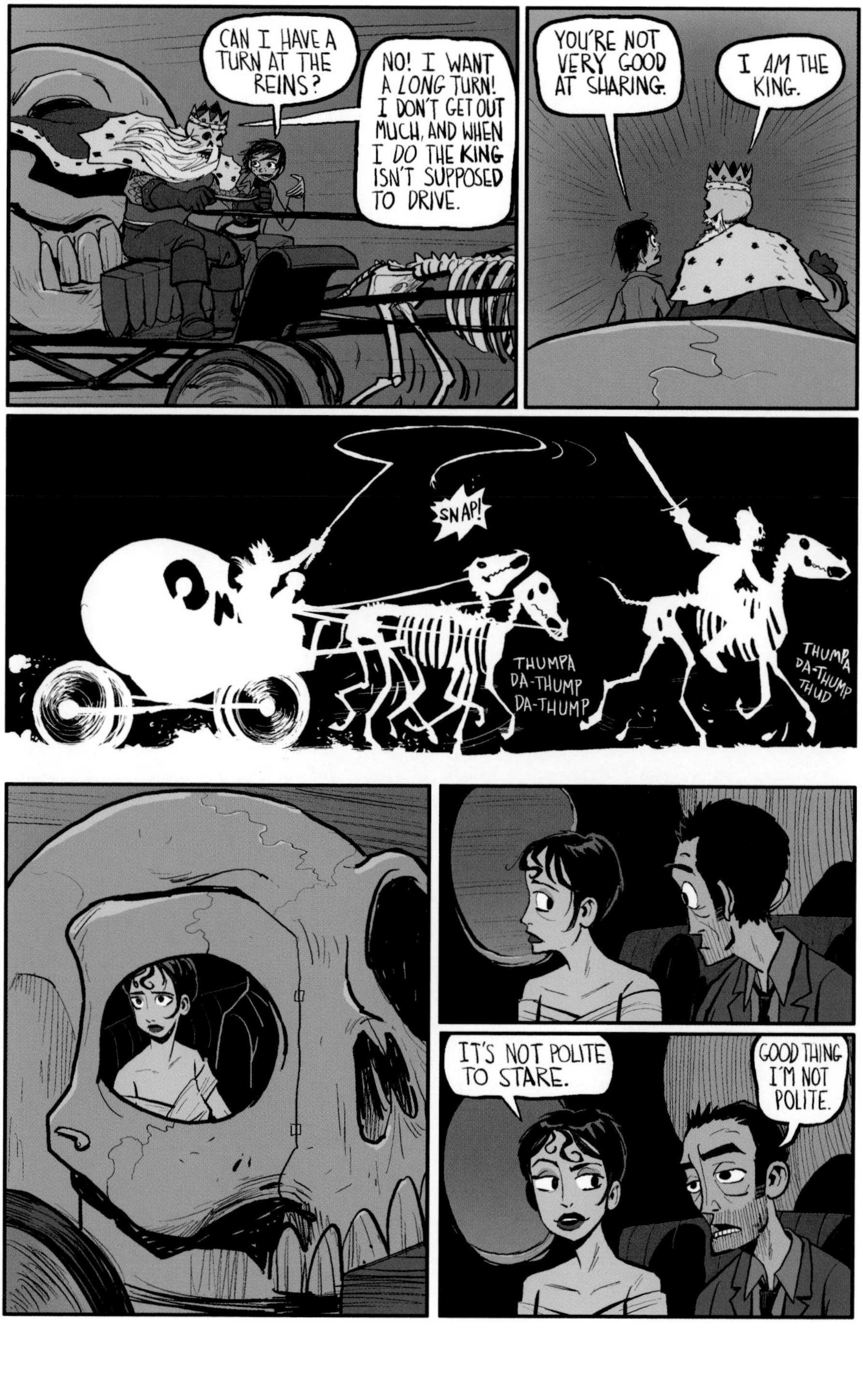
CAN I HAVE A TURN AT THE REINS?
NO! I WANT A *LONG* TURN! I DON'T GET OUT MUCH, AND WHEN I *DO* THE **KING** ISN'T SUPPOSED TO DRIVE.
YOU'RE NOT VERY GOOD AT SHARING.
I *AM* THE KING.
SNAP!
THUMPA DA-THUMP DA-THUMP
THUMPA DA-THUMP THUD
IT'S NOT POLITE TO STARE.
GOOD THING I'M NOT POLITE.

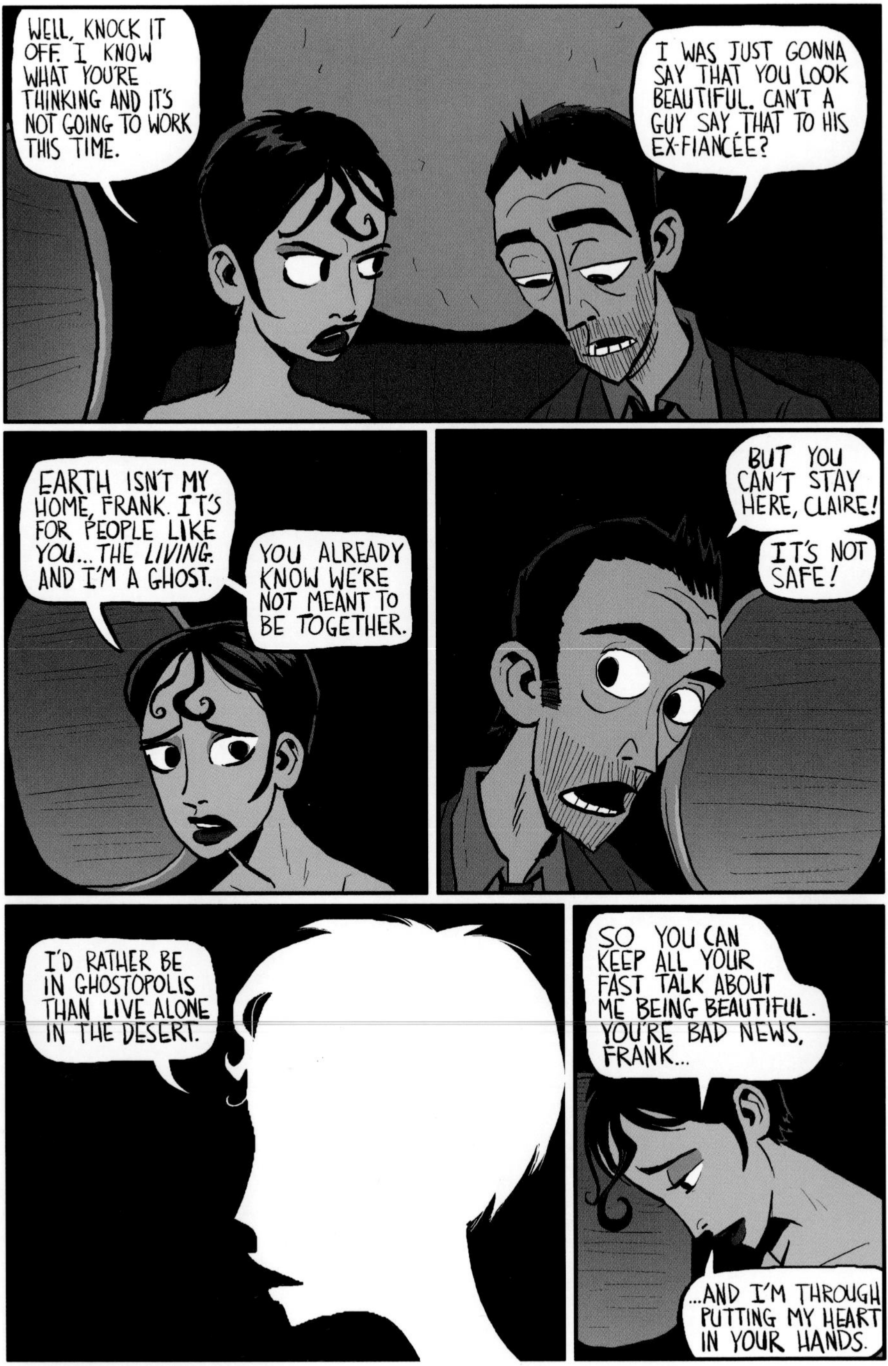
WELL, KNOCK IT OFF. I KNOW WHAT YOU'RE THINKING AND IT'S NOT GOING TO WORK THIS TIME.
I WAS JUST GONNA SAY THAT YOU LOOK BEAUTIFUL. CAN'T A GUY SAY THAT TO HIS EX-FIANCÉE?
EARTH ISN'T MY HOME, FRANK. IT'S FOR PEOPLE LIKE YOU... THE *LIVING*. AND I'M A GHOST.
YOU ALREADY KNOW WE'RE NOT MEANT TO BE TOGETHER.
BUT YOU CAN'T STAY HERE, CLAIRE!
IT'S NOT SAFE!
I'D RATHER BE IN GHOSTOPOLIS THAN LIVE ALONE IN THE DESERT.
SO YOU CAN KEEP ALL YOUR FAST TALK ABOUT ME BEING BEAUTIFUL. YOU'RE BAD NEWS, FRANK...
...AND I'M THROUGH PUTTING MY HEART IN YOUR HANDS.

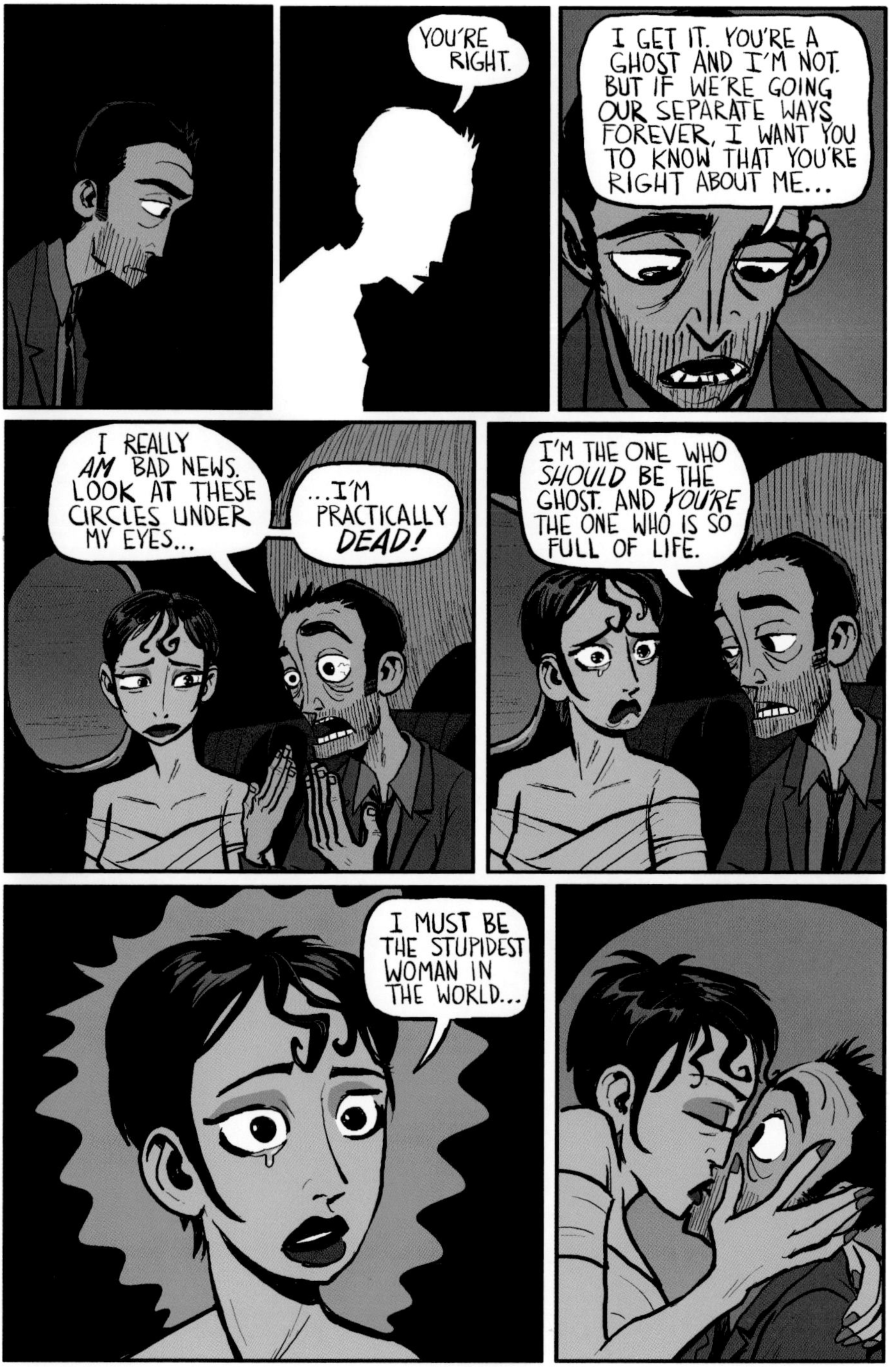
YOU'RE RIGHT.
I GET IT. YOU'RE A GHOST AND I'M NOT. BUT IF WE'RE GOING OUR SEPARATE WAYS FOREVER, I WANT YOU TO KNOW THAT YOU'RE RIGHT ABOUT ME...
I REALLY *AM* BAD NEWS. LOOK AT THESE CIRCLES UNDER MY EYES...
...I'M PRACTICALLY *DEAD!*
I'M THE ONE WHO *SHOULD* BE THE GHOST. AND *YOU'RE* THE ONE WHO IS SO FULL OF LIFE.
I MUST BE THE STUPIDEST WOMAN IN THE WORLD...

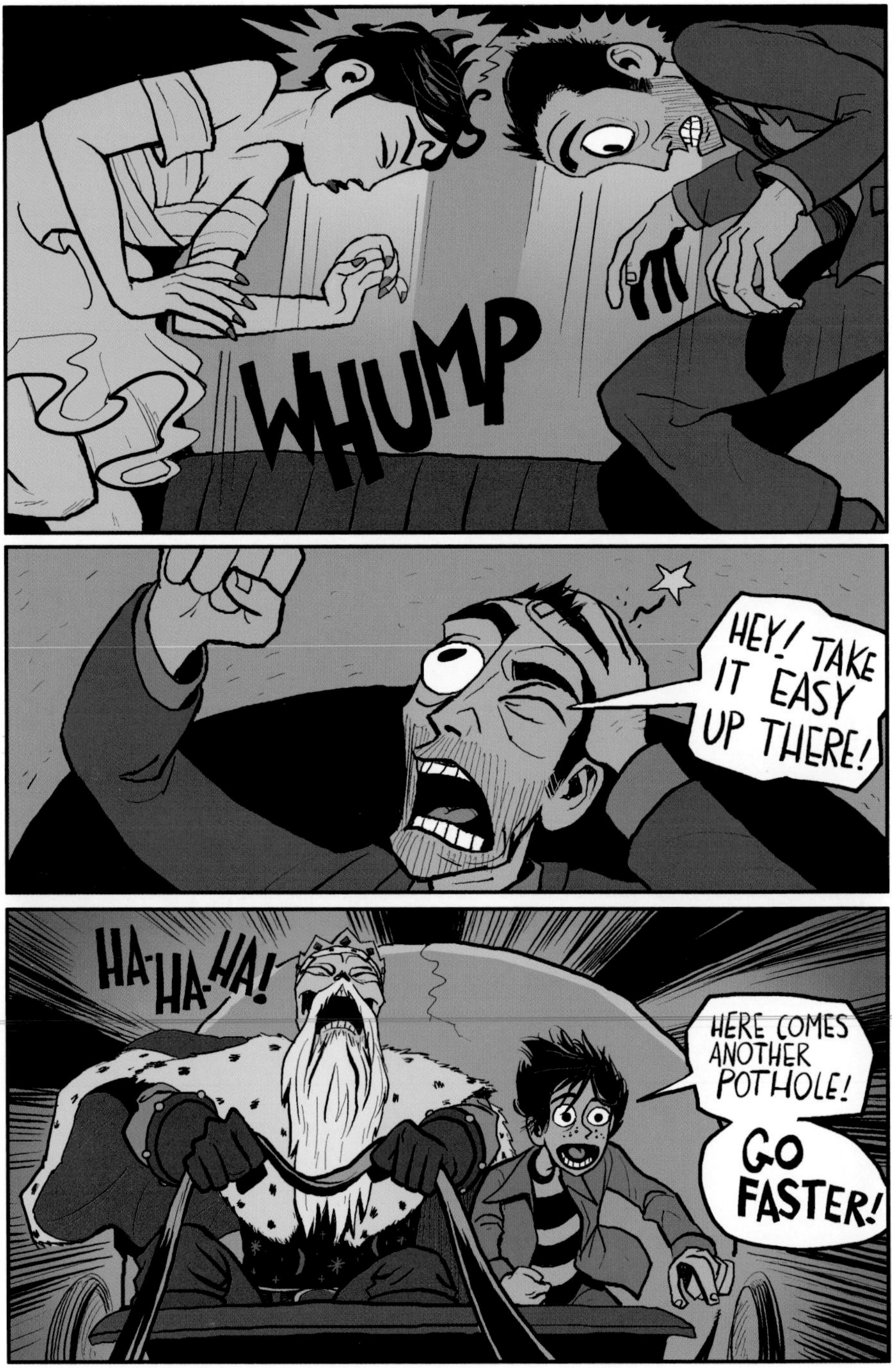
WHUMP
HEY! TAKE IT EASY UP THERE!
HA-HA-HA!
HERE COMES ANOTHER POTHOLE!
GO FASTER!

GHOSTOPOLIS
POWER DISTRICT
HALT!
CLOP
CLOP
CLOP
GOOD EVENING, OFFICER.
BONE KING!
IN THE NON-FLESH!
WHAT'S YOUR BUSINESS TONIGHT, YOUR HIGHNESS?
I'M JUST TAKING A FEW FRIENDS ON A TOUR OF THE POWER STATION.

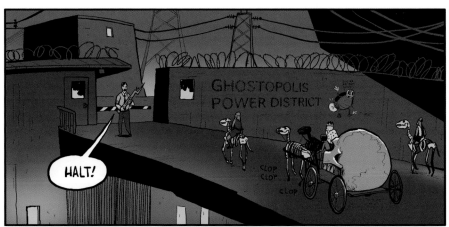

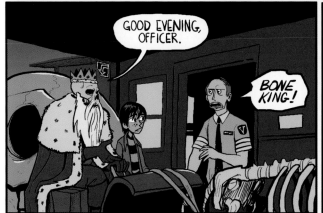

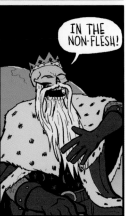

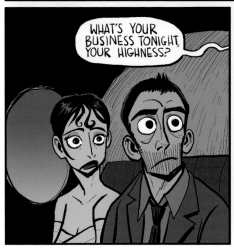

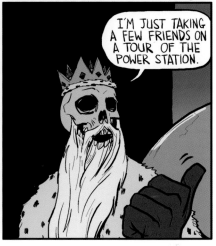

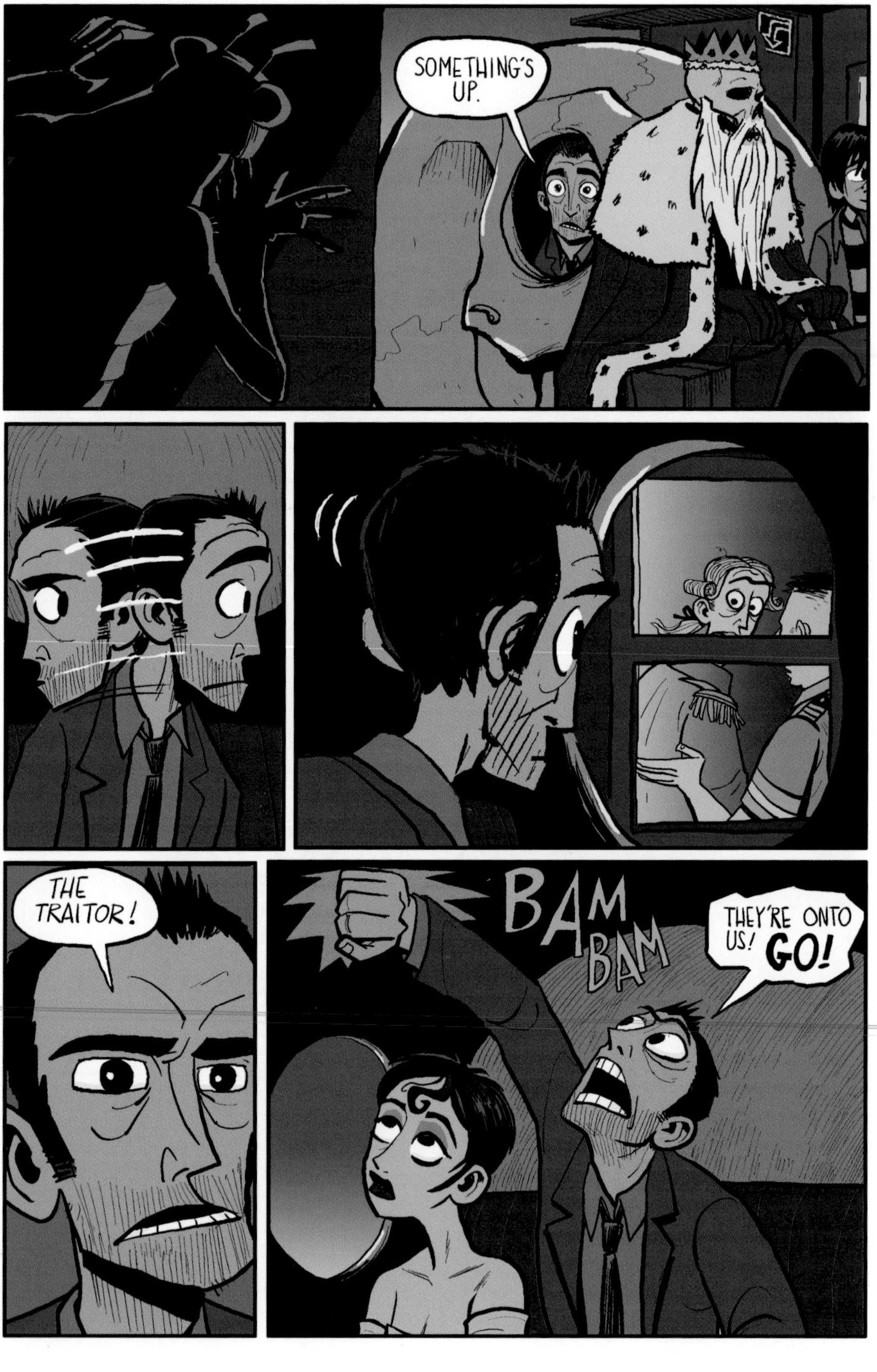
SOMETHING'S UP.
THE TRAITOR!
BAM
BAM
THEY'RE ONTO US! GO!

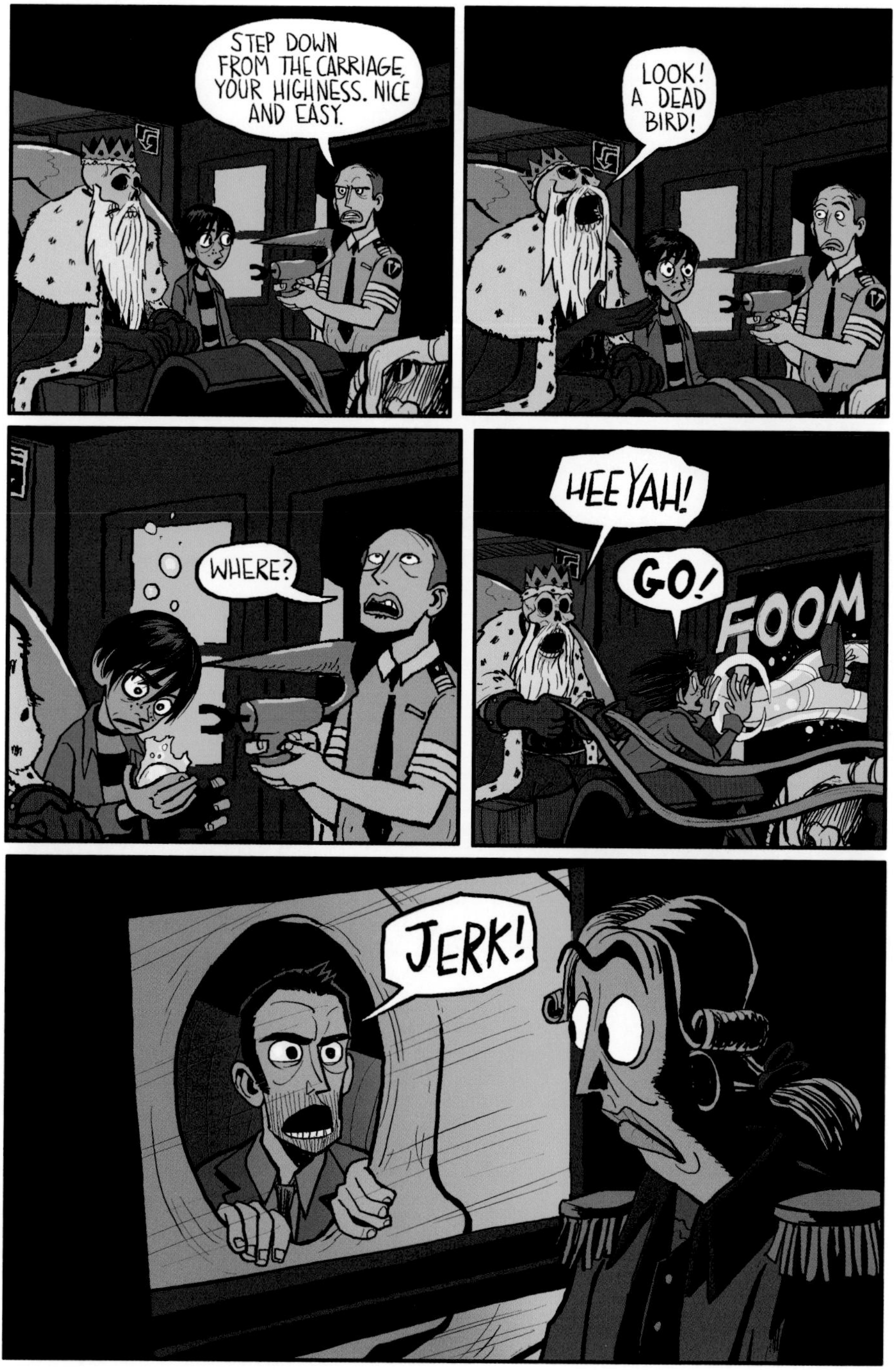
STEP DOWN FROM THE CARRIAGE, YOUR HIGHNESS. NICE AND EASY.
LOOK! A DEAD BIRD!
WHERE?
HEEYAH!
GO!
FOOM
JERK!

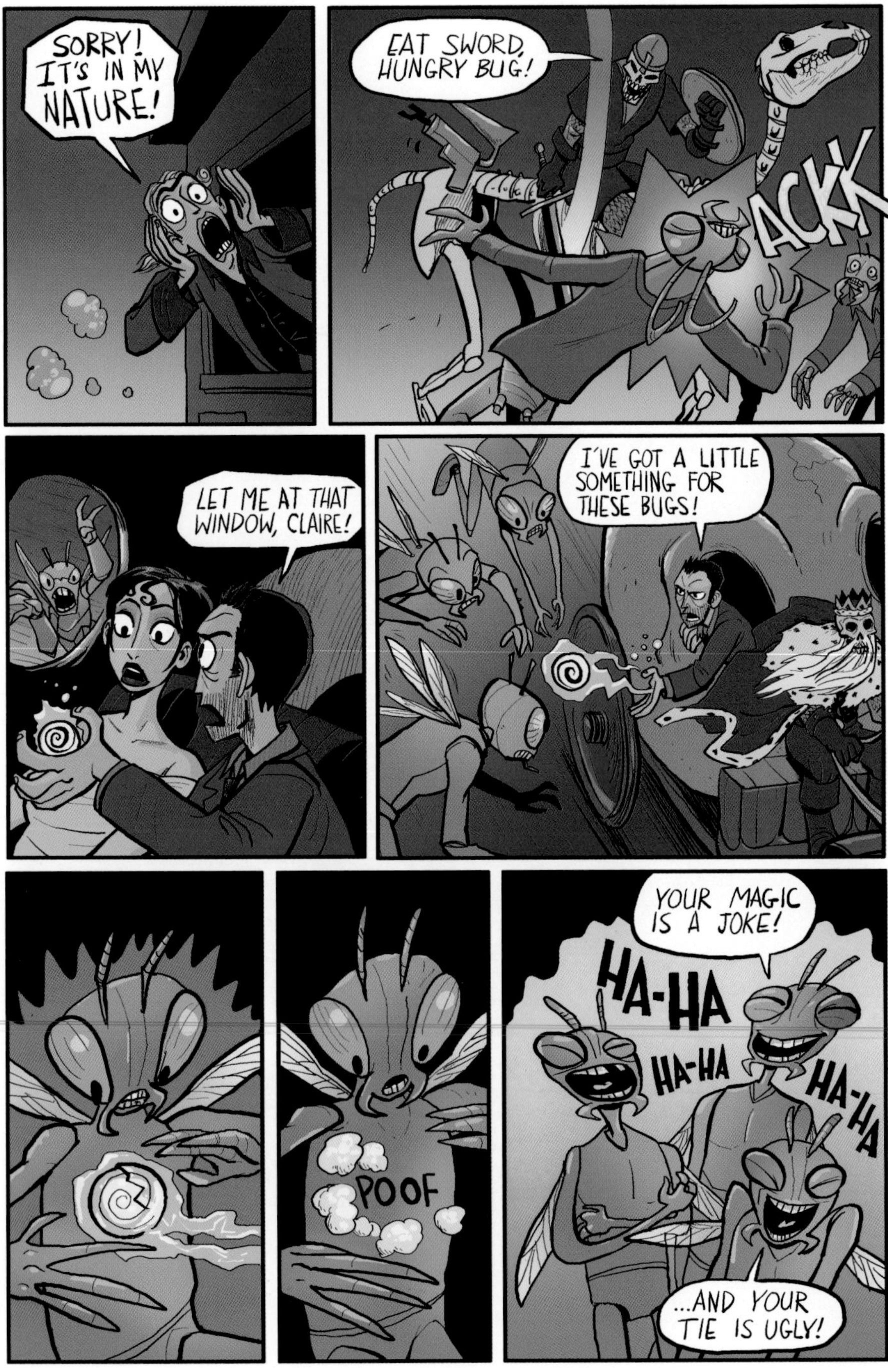
SORRY! IT'S IN MY NATURE!
EAT SWORD, HUNGRY BUG!
ACKK
LET ME AT THAT WINDOW, CLAIRE!
I'VE GOT A LITTLE SOMETHING FOR THESE BUGS!
POOF
YOUR MAGIC IS A JOKE!
HA-HA
HA-HA
HA-HA
...AND YOUR TIE IS UGLY!

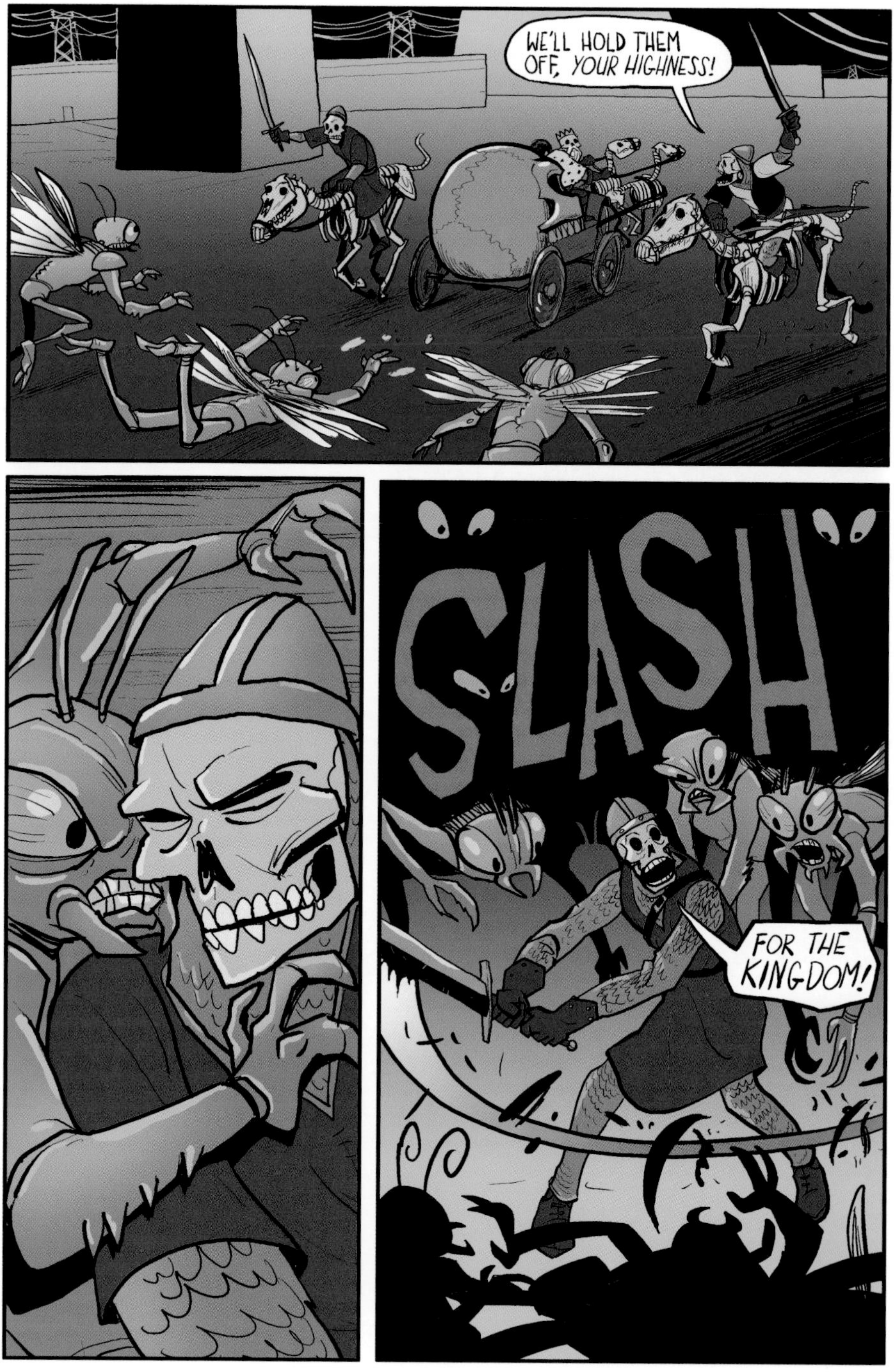
WE'LL HOLD THEM OFF, YOUR HIGHNESS!
SLASH
FOR THE KINGDOM!

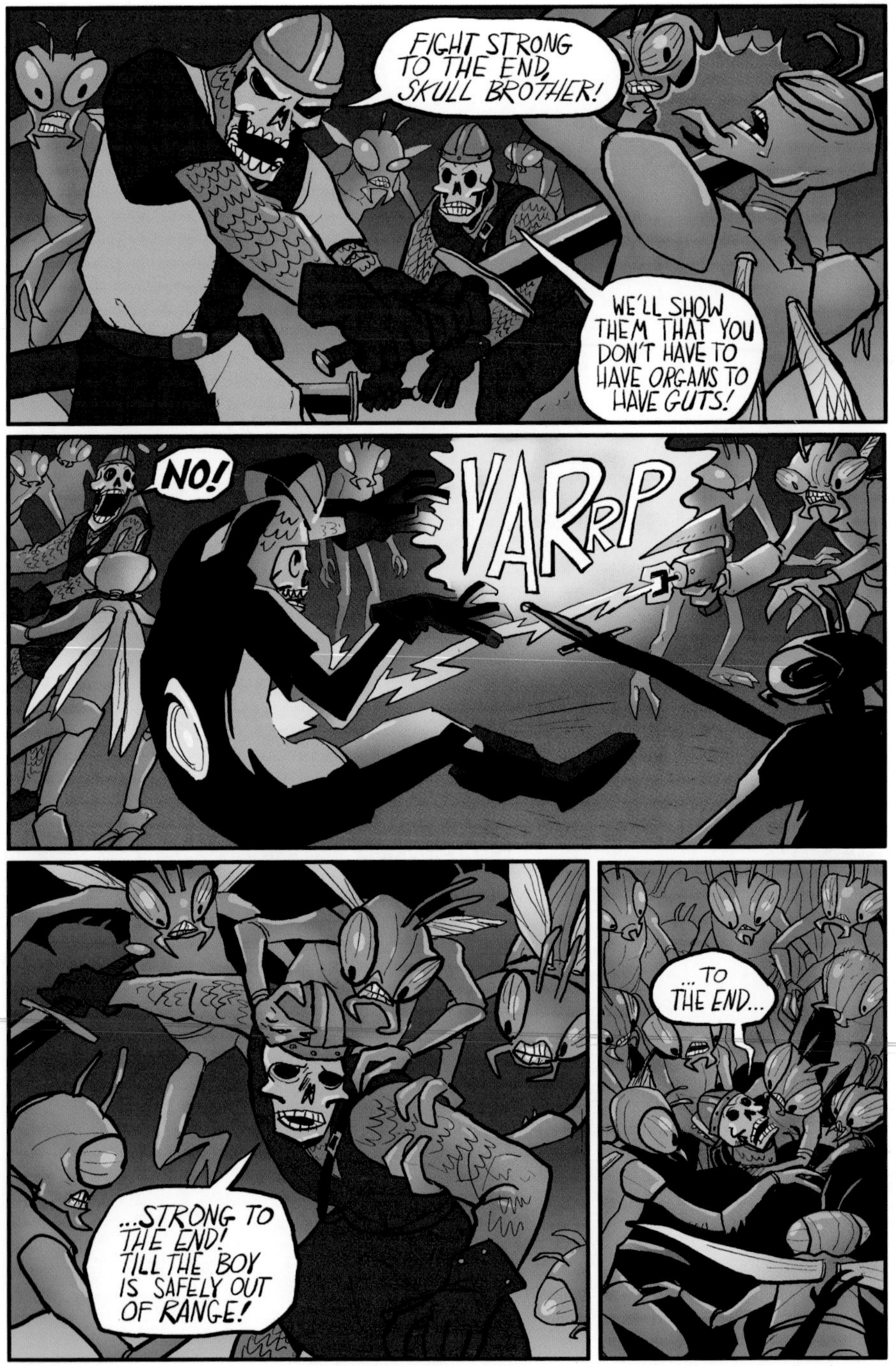
FIGHT STRONG TO THE END, SKULL BROTHER!
WE'LL SHOW THEM THAT YOU DON'T HAVE TO HAVE ORGANS TO HAVE GUTS!
NO!
VARRRP
...STRONG TO THE END! TILL THE BOY IS SAFELY OUT OF RANGE!
...TO THE END...

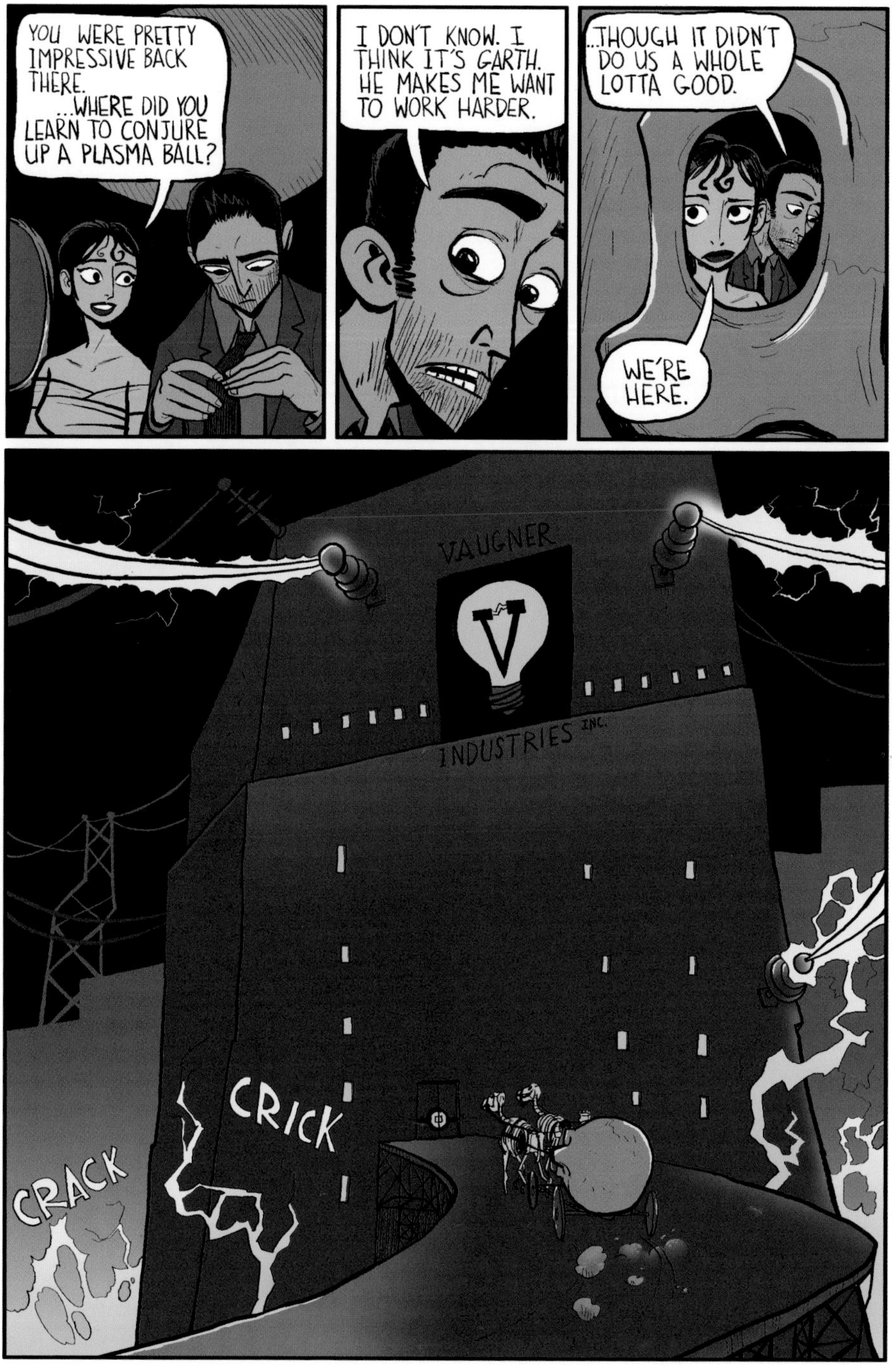
YOU WERE PRETTY IMPRESSIVE BACK THERE.
...WHERE DID YOU LEARN TO CONJURE UP A PLASMA BALL?
I DON'T KNOW. I THINK IT'S GARTH. HE MAKES ME WANT TO WORK HARDER.
...THOUGH IT DIDN'T DO US A WHOLE LOTTA GOOD.
WE'RE HERE.
VAUGNER
V
INDUSTRIES INC.
CRICK
CRACK

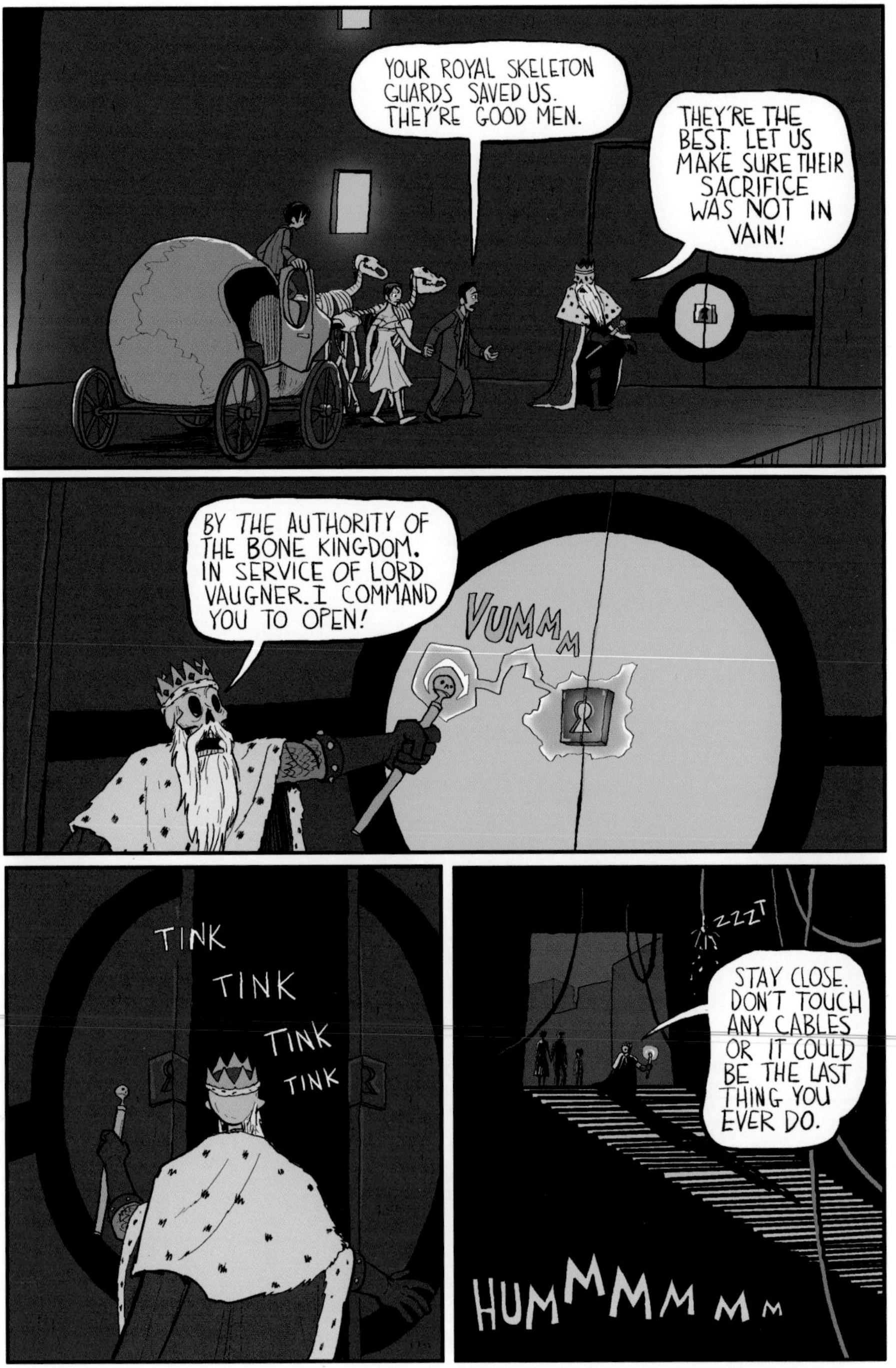
YOUR ROYAL SKELETON GUARDS SAVED US. THEY'RE GOOD MEN.
THEY'RE THE BEST. LET US MAKE SURE THEIR SACRIFICE WAS NOT IN VAIN!
BY THE AUTHORITY OF THE BONE KINGDOM. IN SERVICE OF LORD VAUGNER. I COMMAND YOU TO OPEN!
VUMMMM
TINK
TINK
TINK
TINK
ZZZT
STAY CLOSE. DON'T TOUCH ANY CABLES OR IT COULD BE THE LAST THING YOU EVER DO.
HUMMMMMM

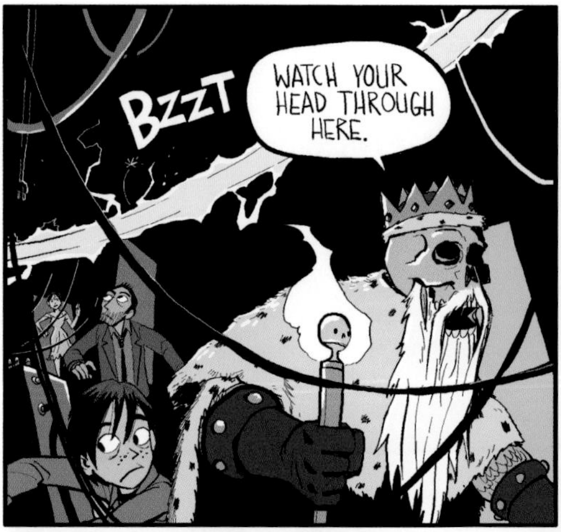
BZZT
WATCH YOUR HEAD THROUGH HERE.

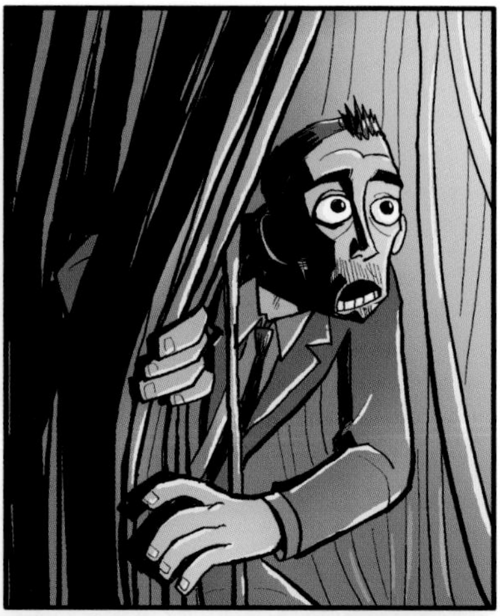

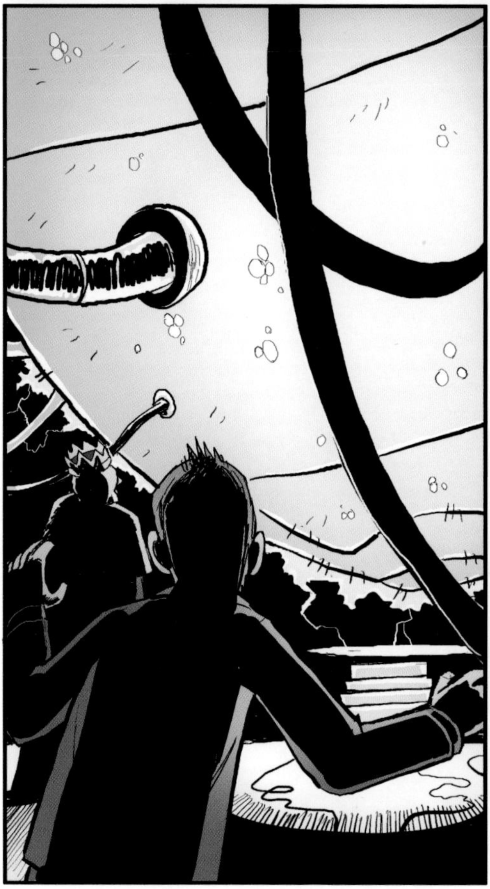

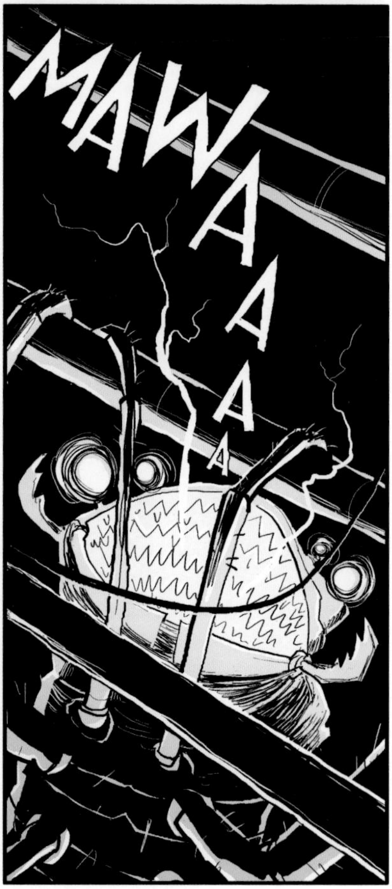
MAWAAAAA

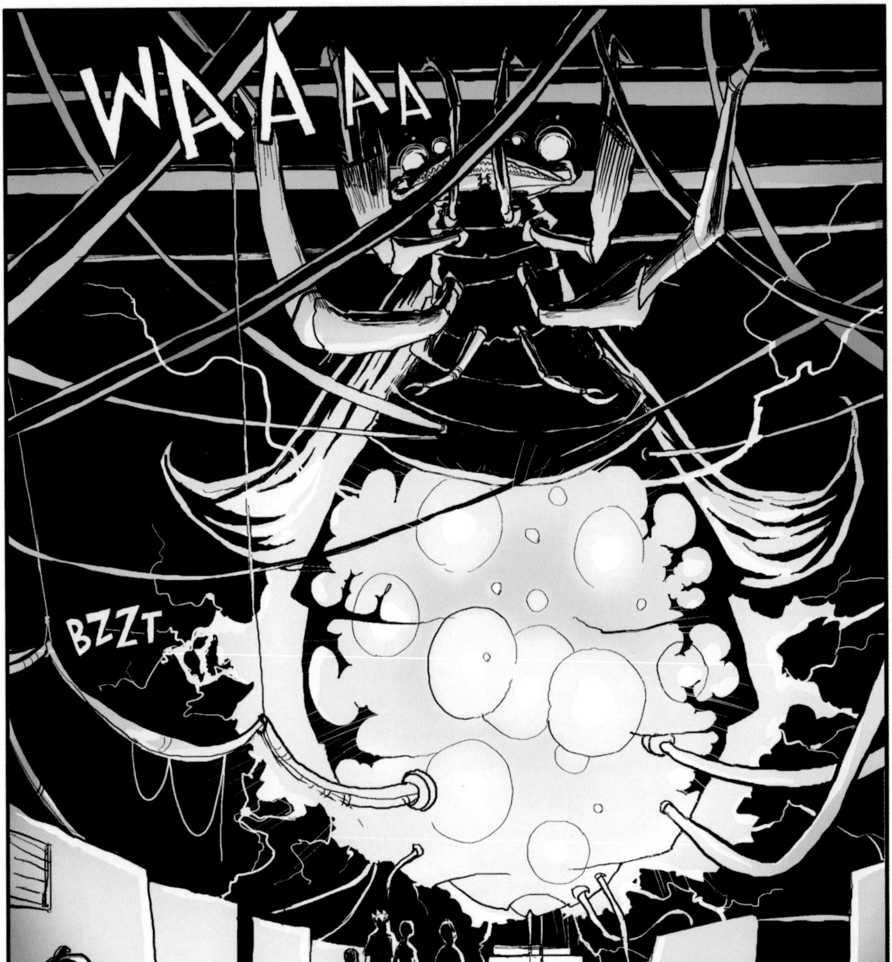
WAAAA
BZZT

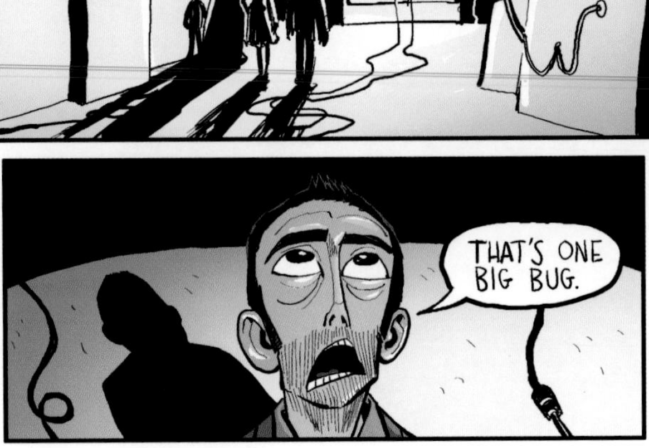
THAT'S ONE BIG BUG.

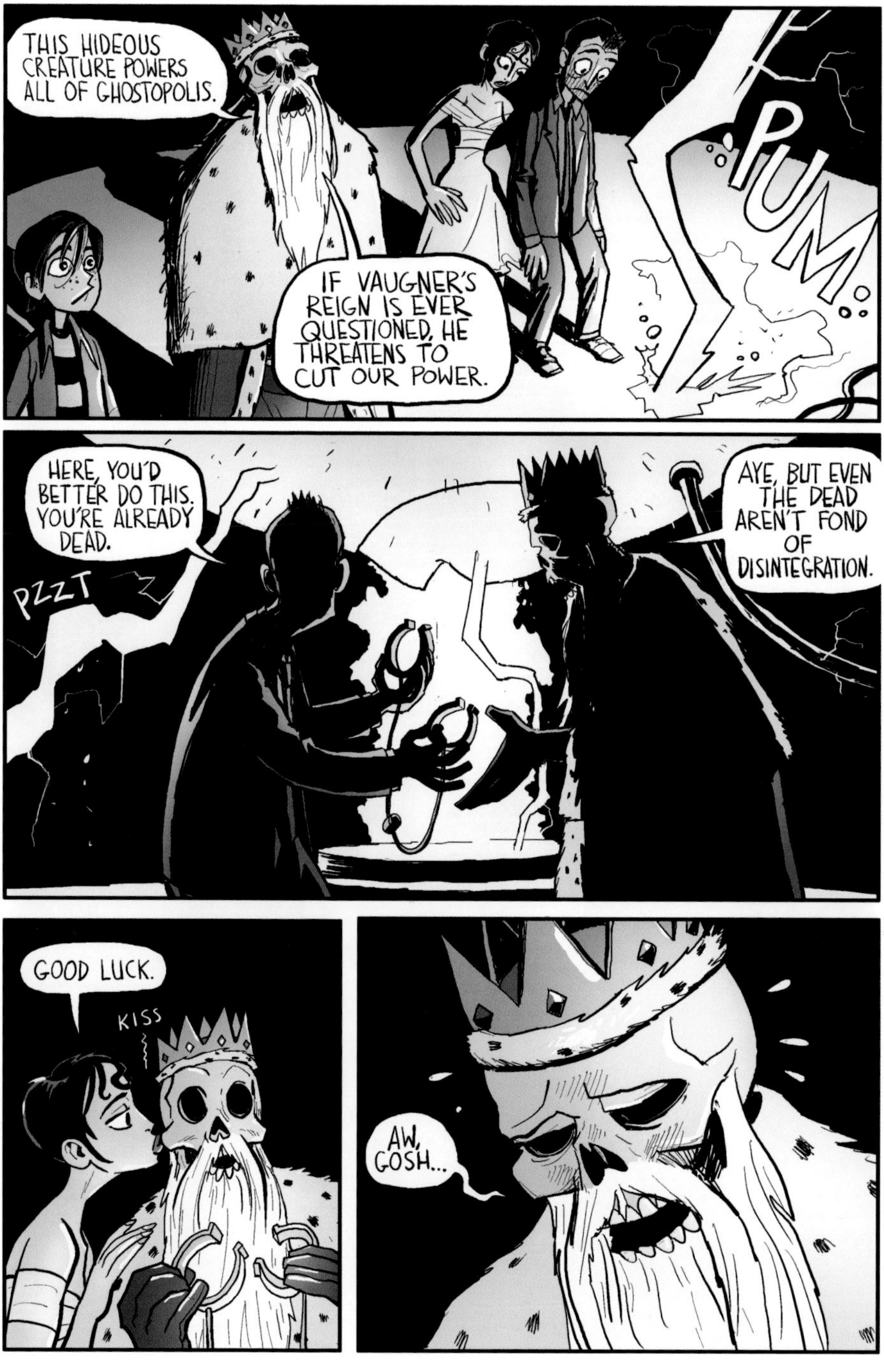
THIS HIDEOUS CREATURE POWERS ALL OF GHOSTOPOLIS.
PUM
IF VAUGNER'S REIGN IS EVER QUESTIONED, HE THREATENS TO CUT OUR POWER.
HERE, YOU'D BETTER DO THIS. YOU'RE ALREADY DEAD.
PZZT
AYE, BUT EVEN THE DEAD AREN'T FOND OF DISINTEGRATION.
GOOD LUCK.
KISS
AW, GOSH...

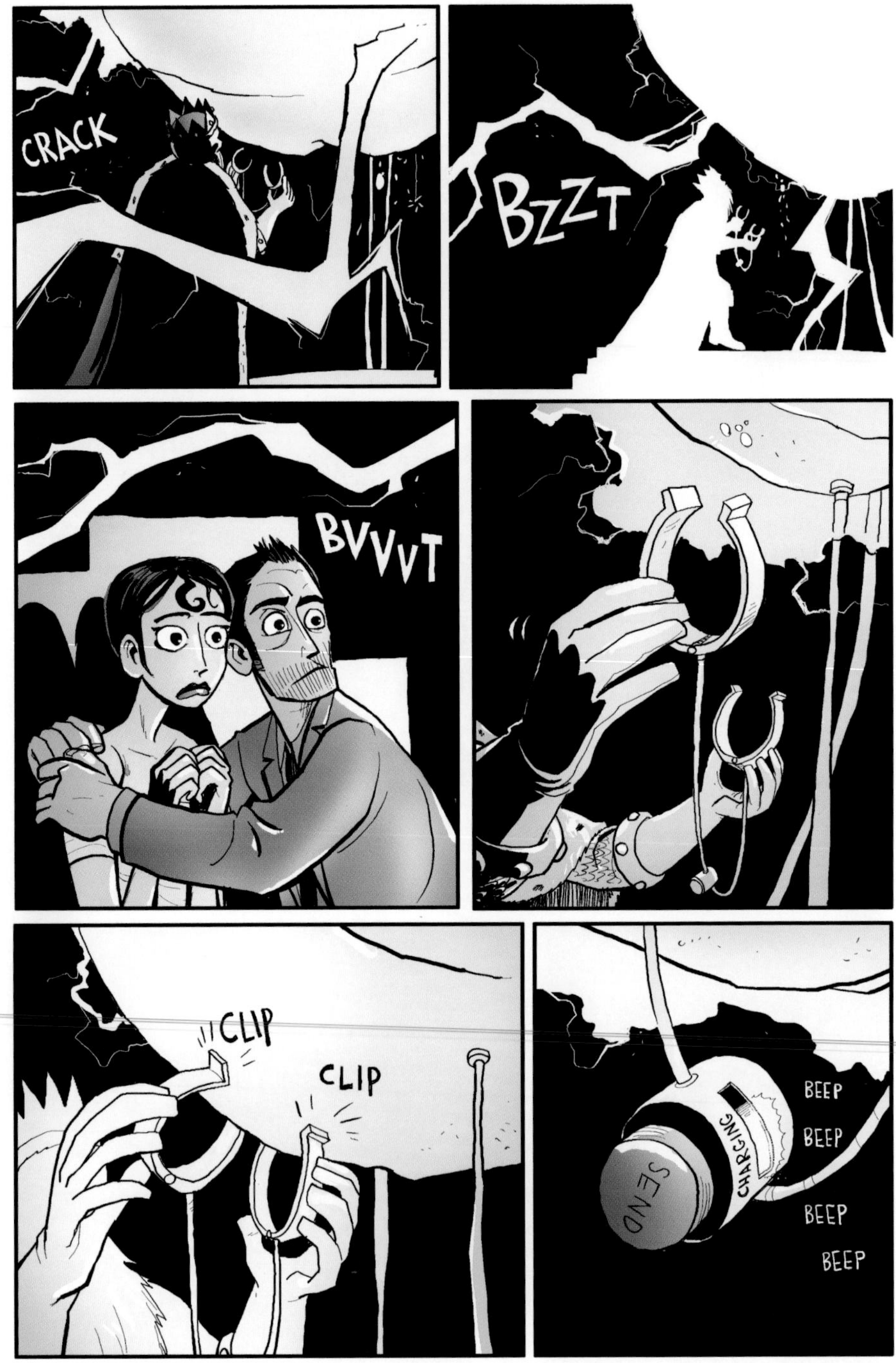
CRACK
BZZZT
BVVVT
CLIP
CLIP
CHARGING
SEND
BEEP
BEEP
BEEP
BEEP

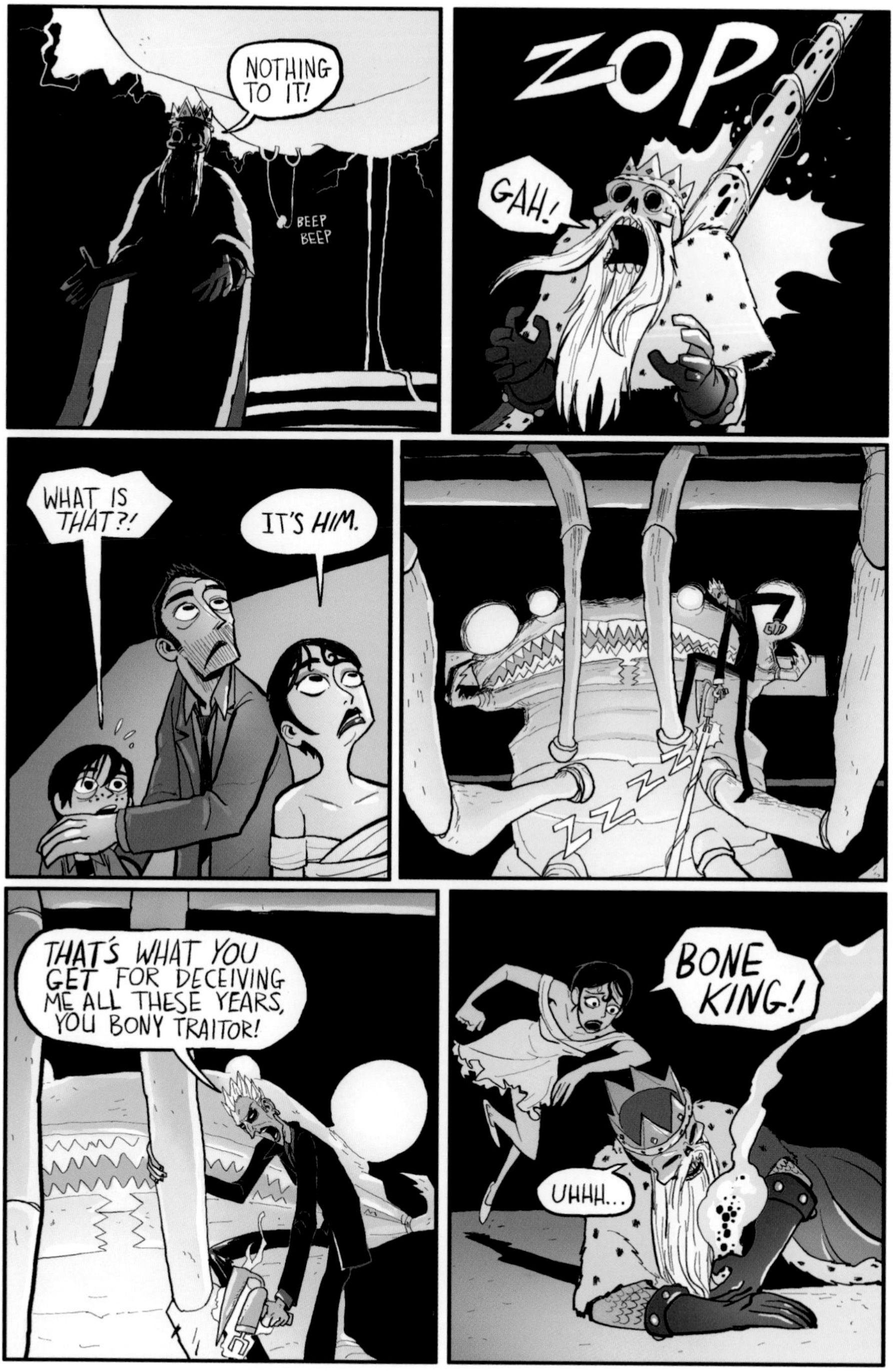
NOTHING TO IT!
BEEP BEEP
ZOP
GAH!
WHAT IS THAT?!
IT'S HIM.
THAT'S WHAT YOU GET FOR DECEIVING ME ALL THESE YEARS, YOU BONY TRAITOR!
BONE KING!
UHHH...

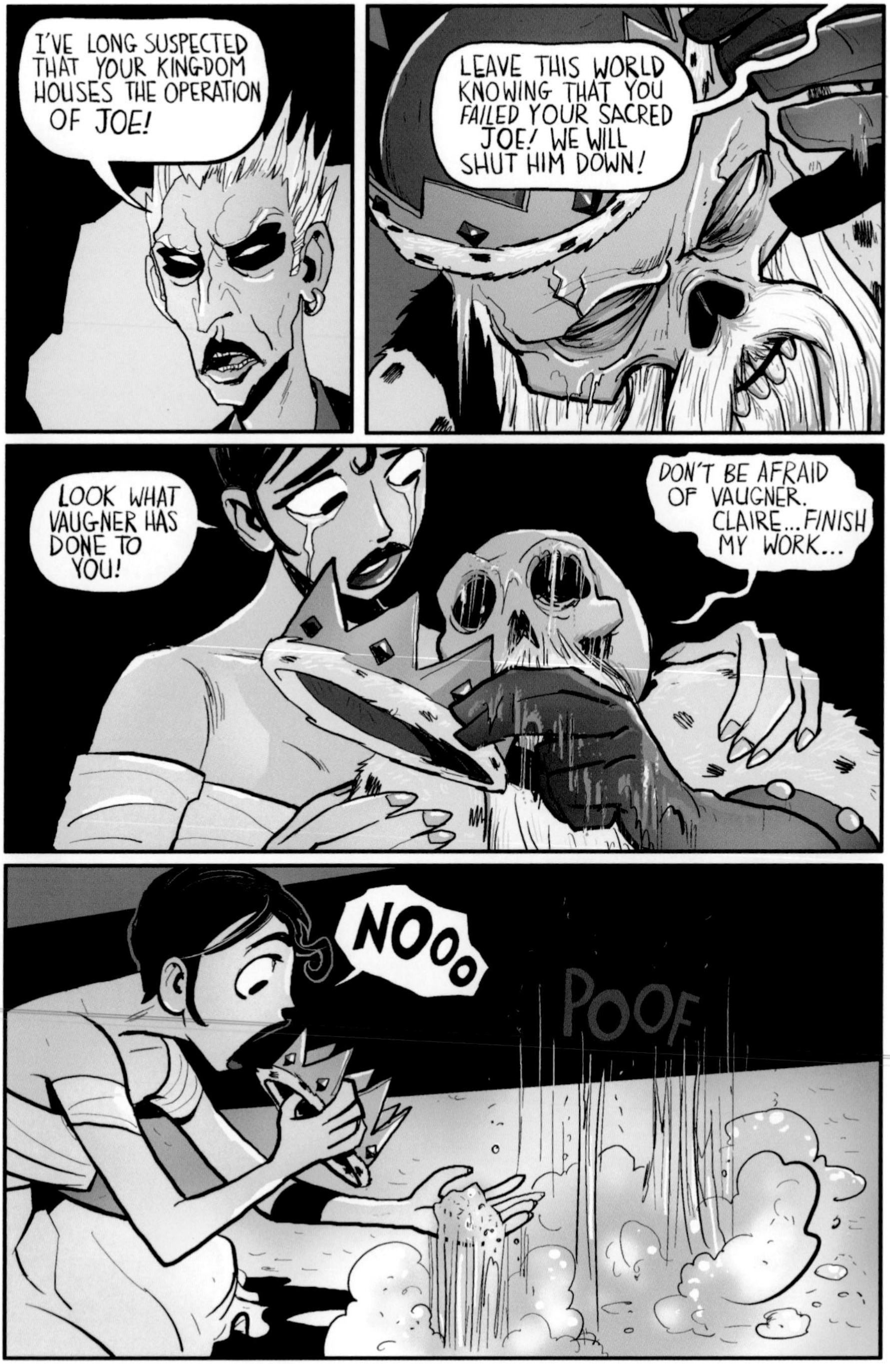
I'VE LONG SUSPECTED THAT YOUR KINGDOM HOUSES THE OPERATION OF JOE!
LEAVE THIS WORLD KNOWING THAT YOU FAILED YOUR SACRED JOE! WE WILL SHUT HIM DOWN!
LOOK WHAT VAUGNER HAS DONE TO YOU!
DON'T BE AFRAID OF VAUGNER. CLAIRE...FINISH MY WORK...
NOOO
POOF

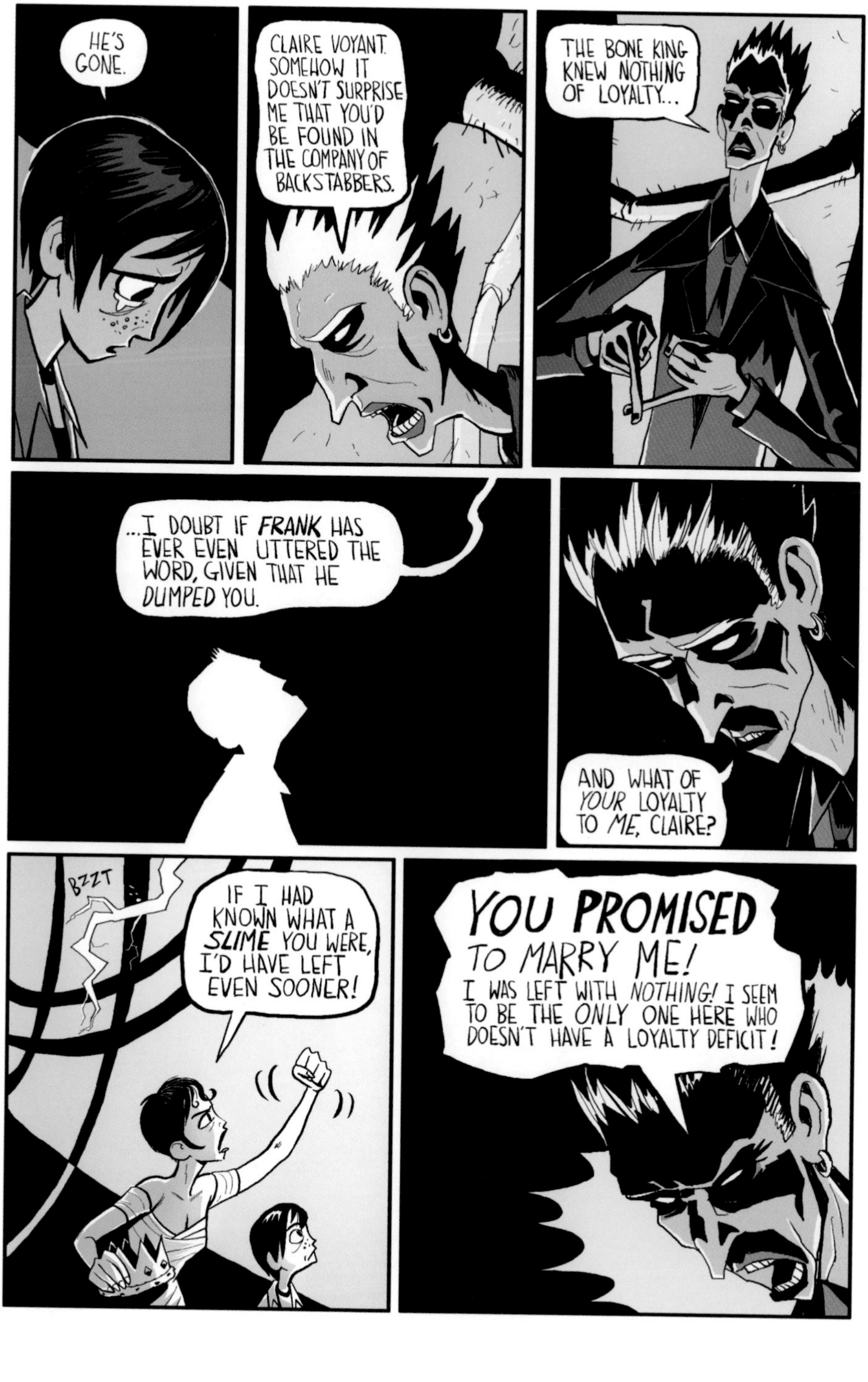
HE'S GONE.
CLAIRE VOYANT. SOMEHOW IT DOESN'T SURPRISE ME THAT YOU'D BE FOUND IN THE COMPANY OF BACKSTABBERS.
THE BONE KING KNEW NOTHING OF LOYALTY...
...I DOUBT IF FRANK HAS EVER EVEN UTTERED THE WORD, GIVEN THAT HE DUMPED YOU.
AND WHAT OF YOUR LOYALTY TO ME, CLAIRE?
BZZT
IF I HAD KNOWN WHAT A SLIME YOU WERE, I'D HAVE LEFT EVEN SOONER!
YOU PROMISED TO MARRY ME!
I WAS LEFT WITH NOTHING! I SEEM TO BE THE ONLY ONE HERE WHO DOESN'T HAVE A LOYALTY DEFICIT!

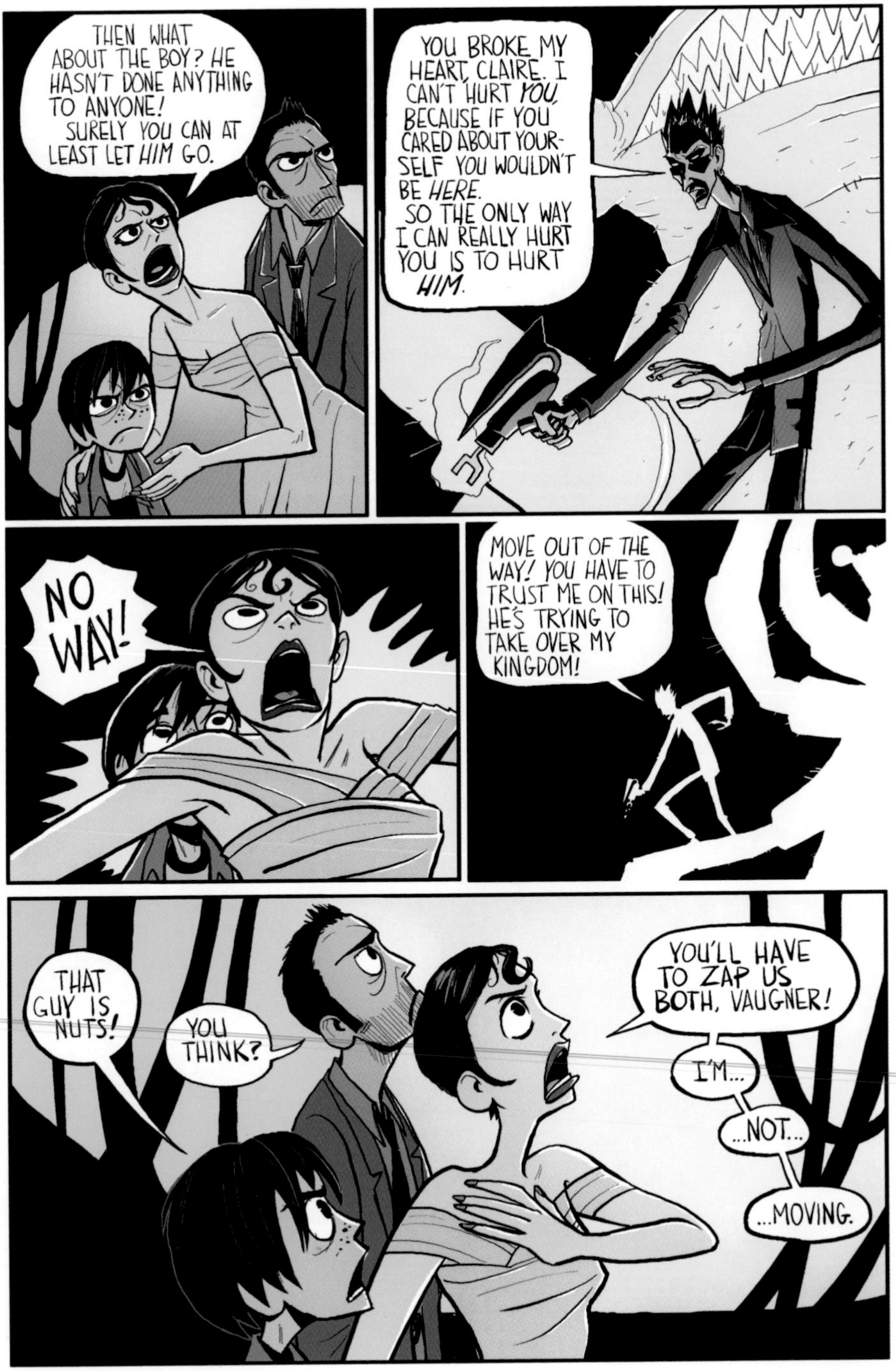
THEN WHAT ABOUT THE BOY? HE HASN'T DONE ANYTHING TO ANYONE! SURELY YOU CAN AT LEAST LET HIM GO.
YOU BROKE MY HEART, CLAIRE. I CAN'T HURT YOU, BECAUSE IF YOU CARED ABOUT YOURSELF YOU WOULDN'T BE HERE. SO THE ONLY WAY I CAN REALLY HURT YOU IS TO HURT HIM.
NO WAY!
MOVE OUT OF THE WAY! YOU HAVE TO TRUST ME ON THIS! HE'S TRYING TO TAKE OVER MY KINGDOM!
THAT GUY IS NUTS!
YOU THINK?
YOU'LL HAVE TO ZAP US BOTH, VAUGNER!
I'M...
...NOT...
...MOVING.

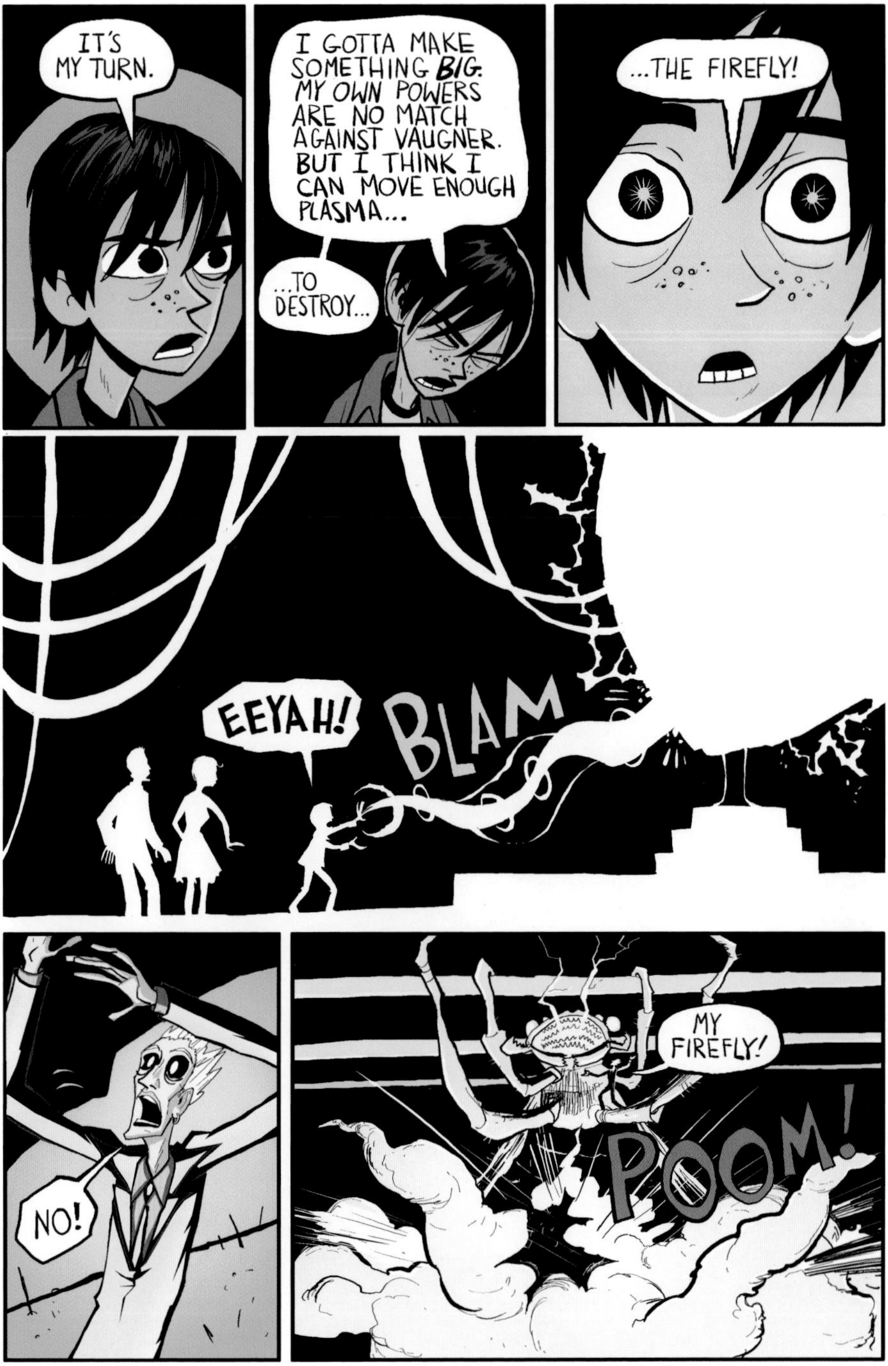
IT'S MY TURN.
I GOTTA MAKE SOMETHING BIG. MY OWN POWERS ARE NO MATCH AGAINST VAUGNER. BUT I THINK I CAN MOVE ENOUGH PLASMA...
...TO DESTROY...
...THE FIREFLY!
EEYAH!
BLAM
NO!
MY FIREFLY!
POOM!

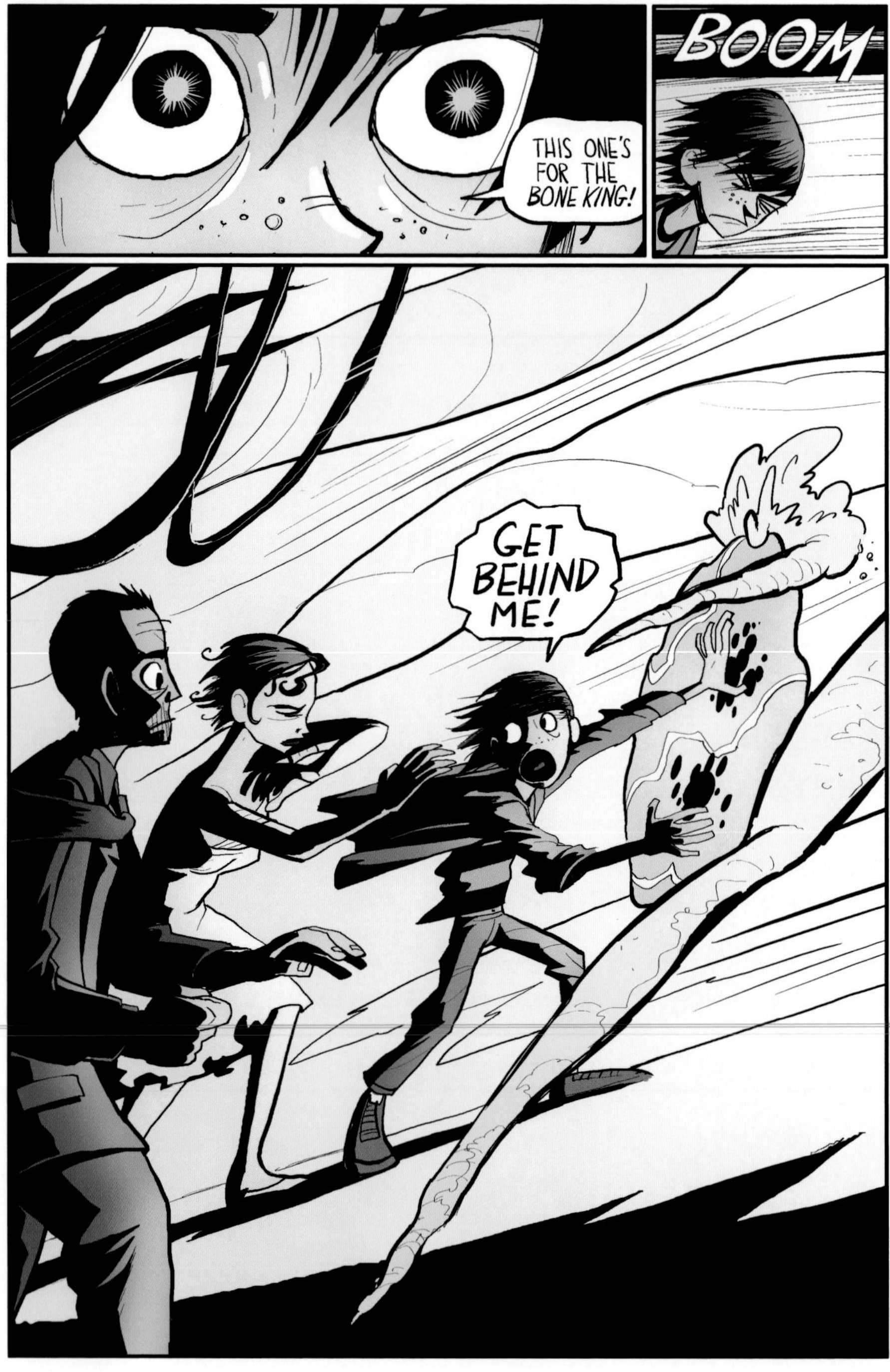
THIS ONE'S FOR THE BONE KING!
BOOM
GET BEHIND ME!

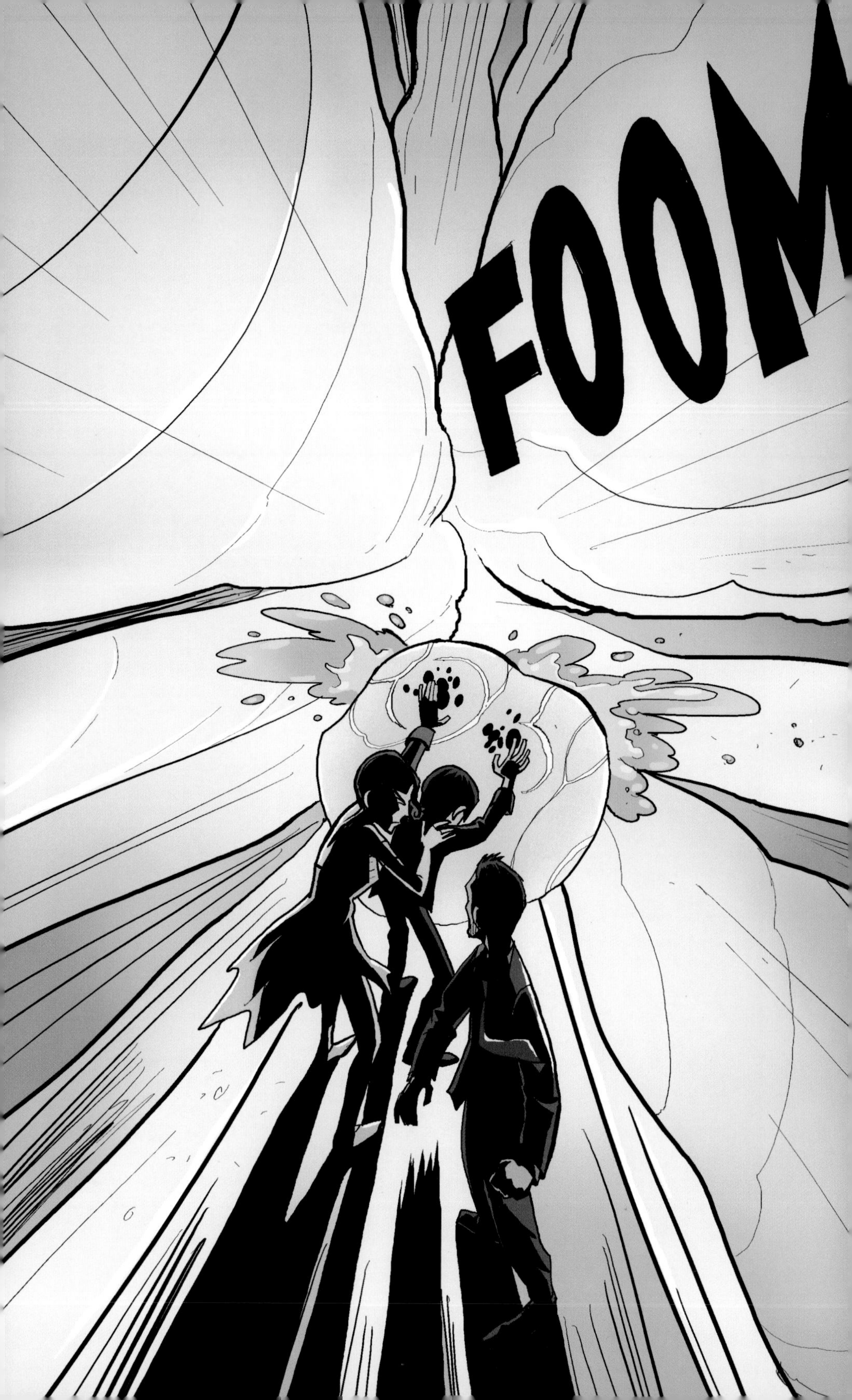
FOOM

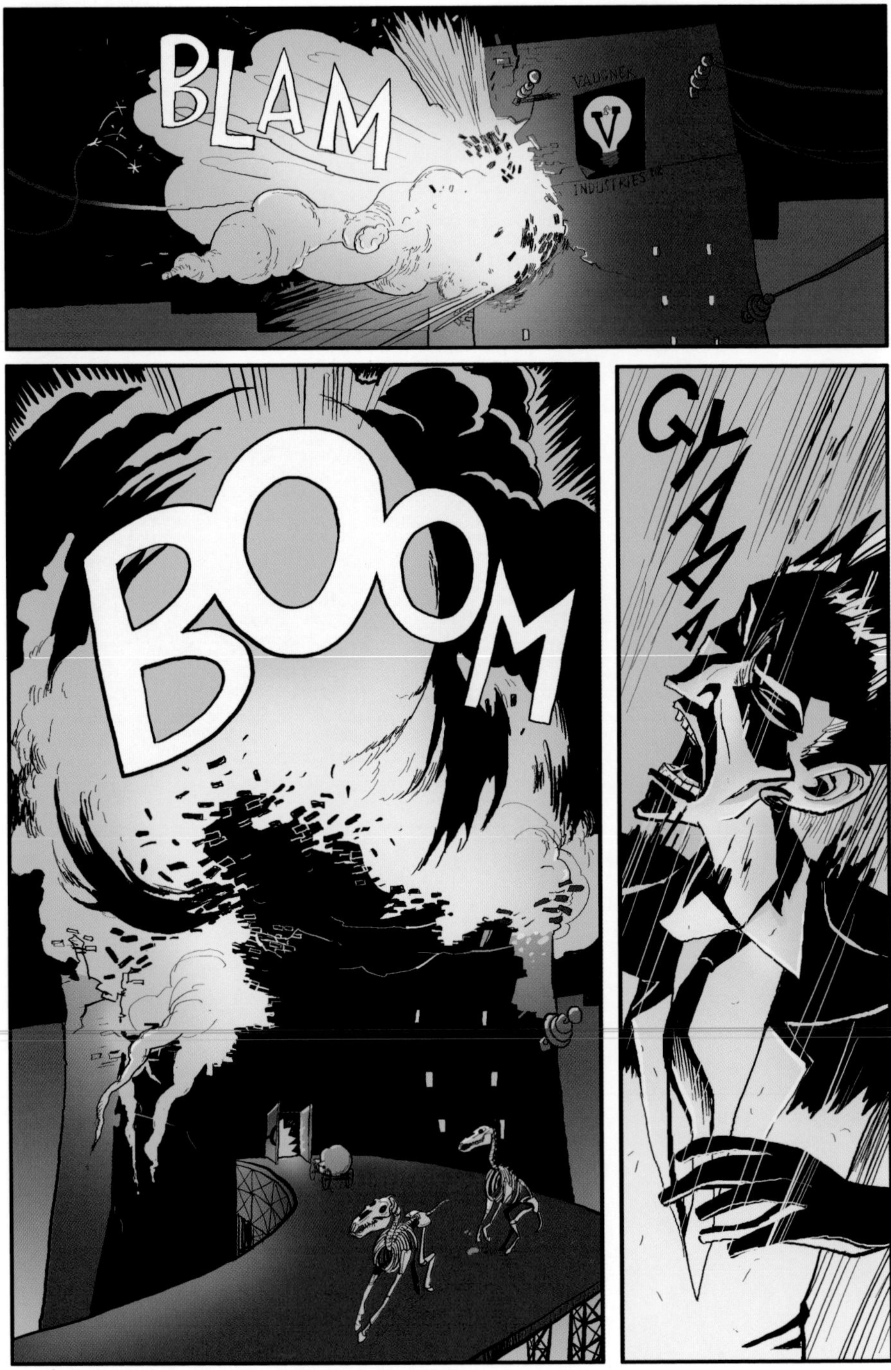
BLAM
INDUSTRIES
BOOM
GYAAAA

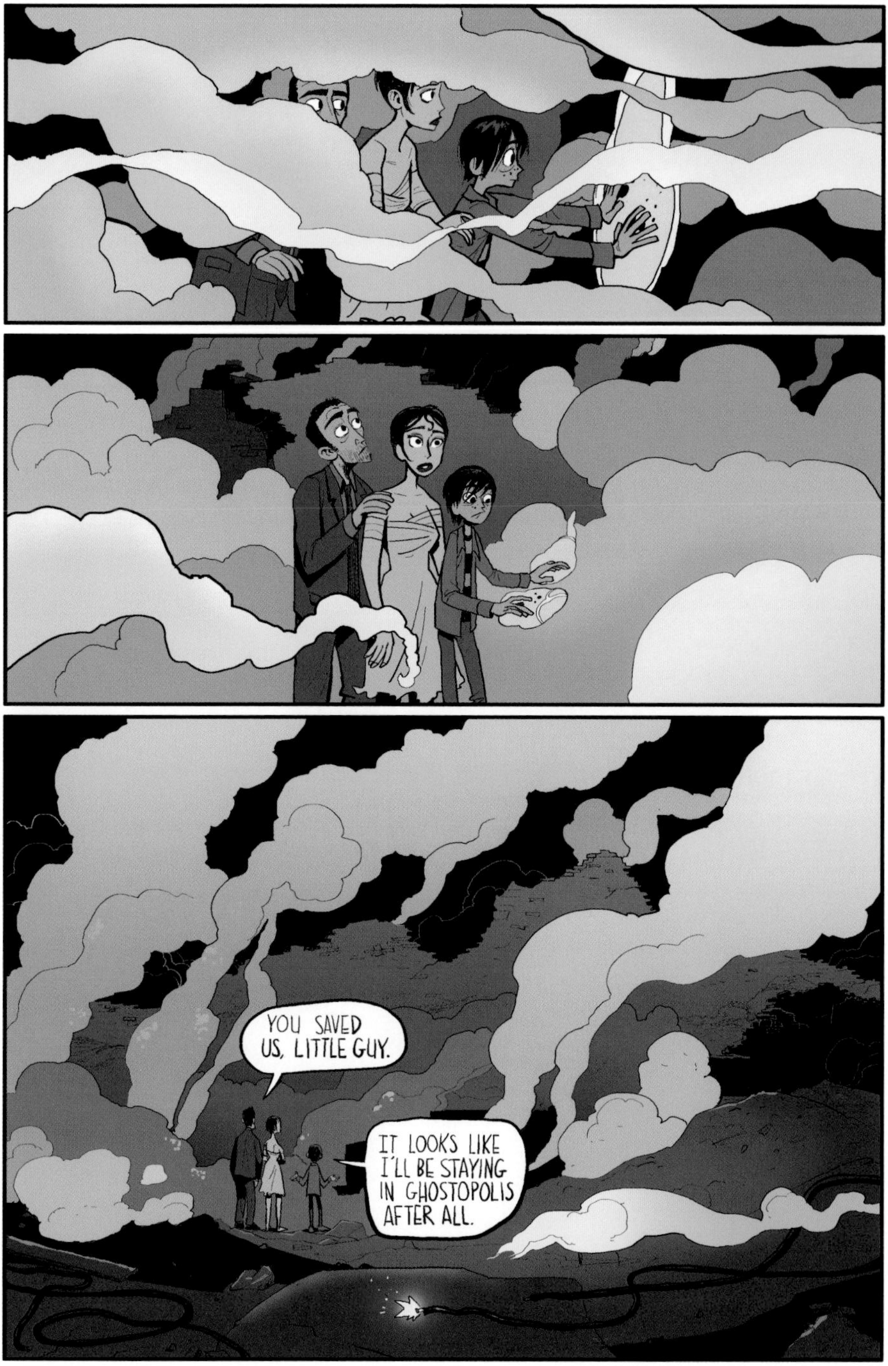
YOU SAVED US, LITTLE GUY.
IT LOOKS LIKE I'LL BE STAYING IN GHOSTOPOLIS AFTER ALL.

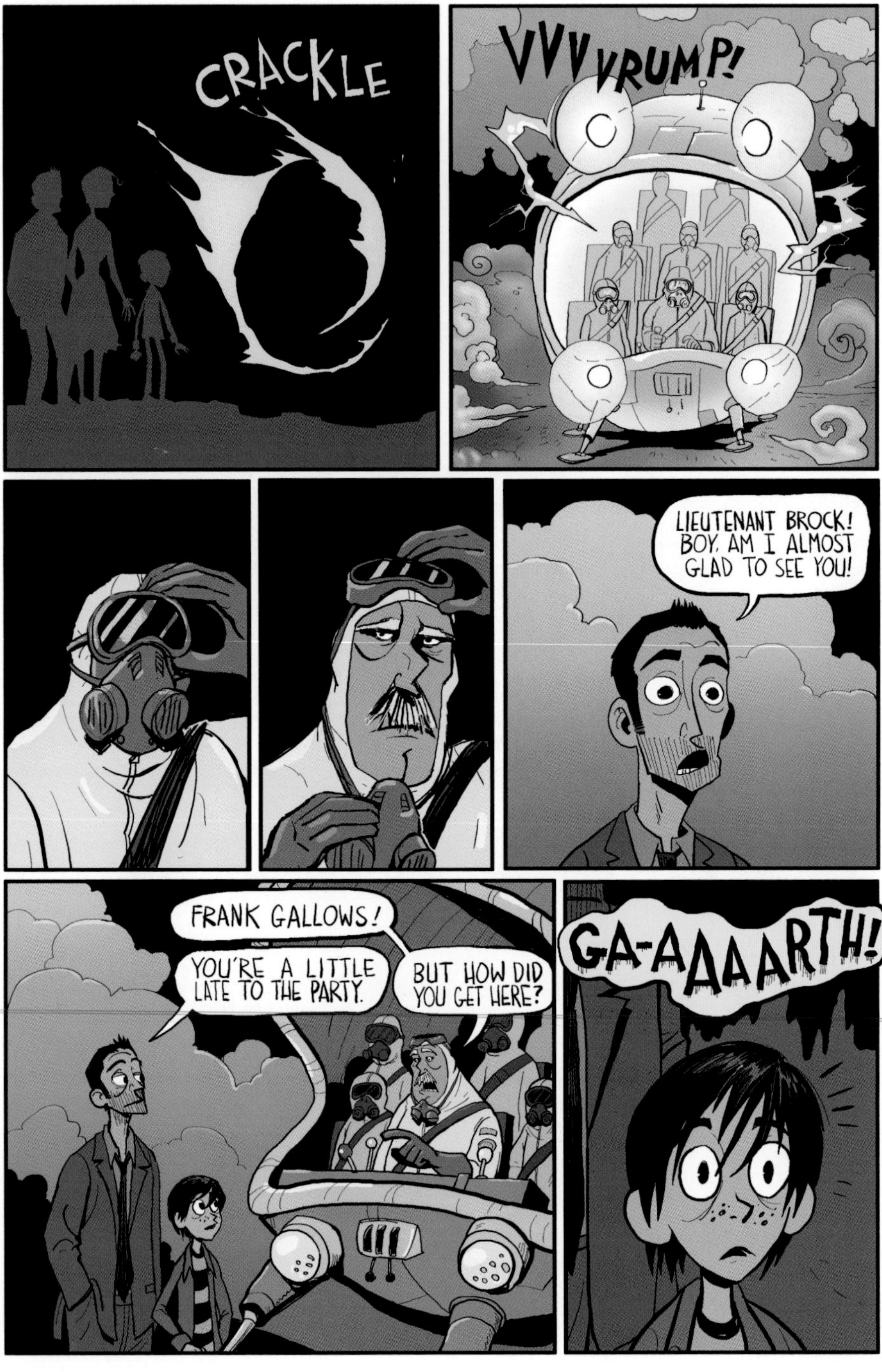
CRACKLE
VVVVRUMP!
LIEUTENANT BROCK! BOY, AM I ALMOST GLAD TO SEE YOU!
FRANK GALLOWS!
YOU'RE A LITTLE LATE TO THE PARTY.
BUT HOW DID YOU GET HERE?
GA-AAAARTH!

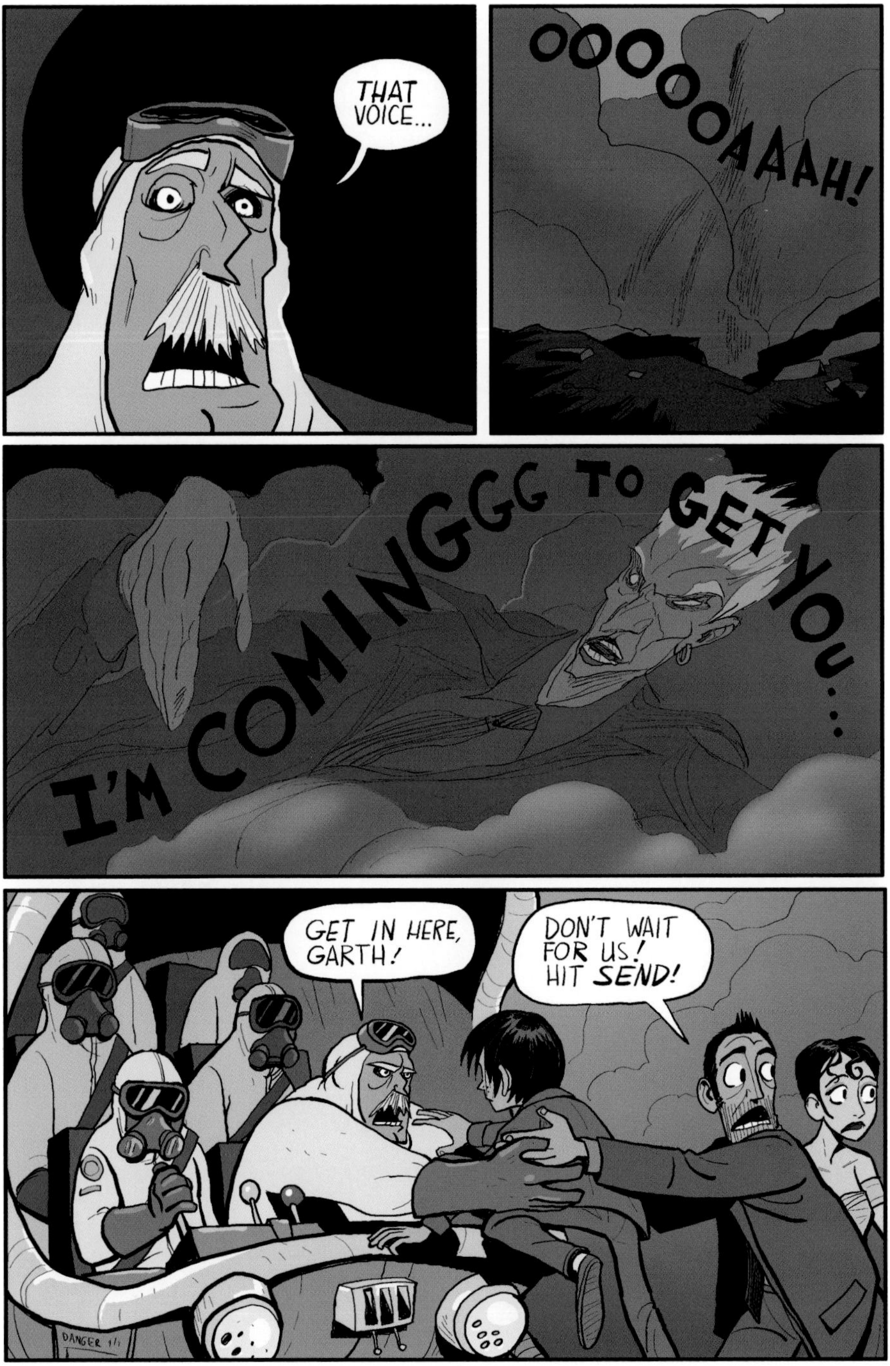
THAT VOICE...
OOOOOOAAAAH!
I'M COMINGGG TO GET YOU...
GET IN HERE, GARTH!
DON'T WAIT FOR US! HIT SEND!
DANGER

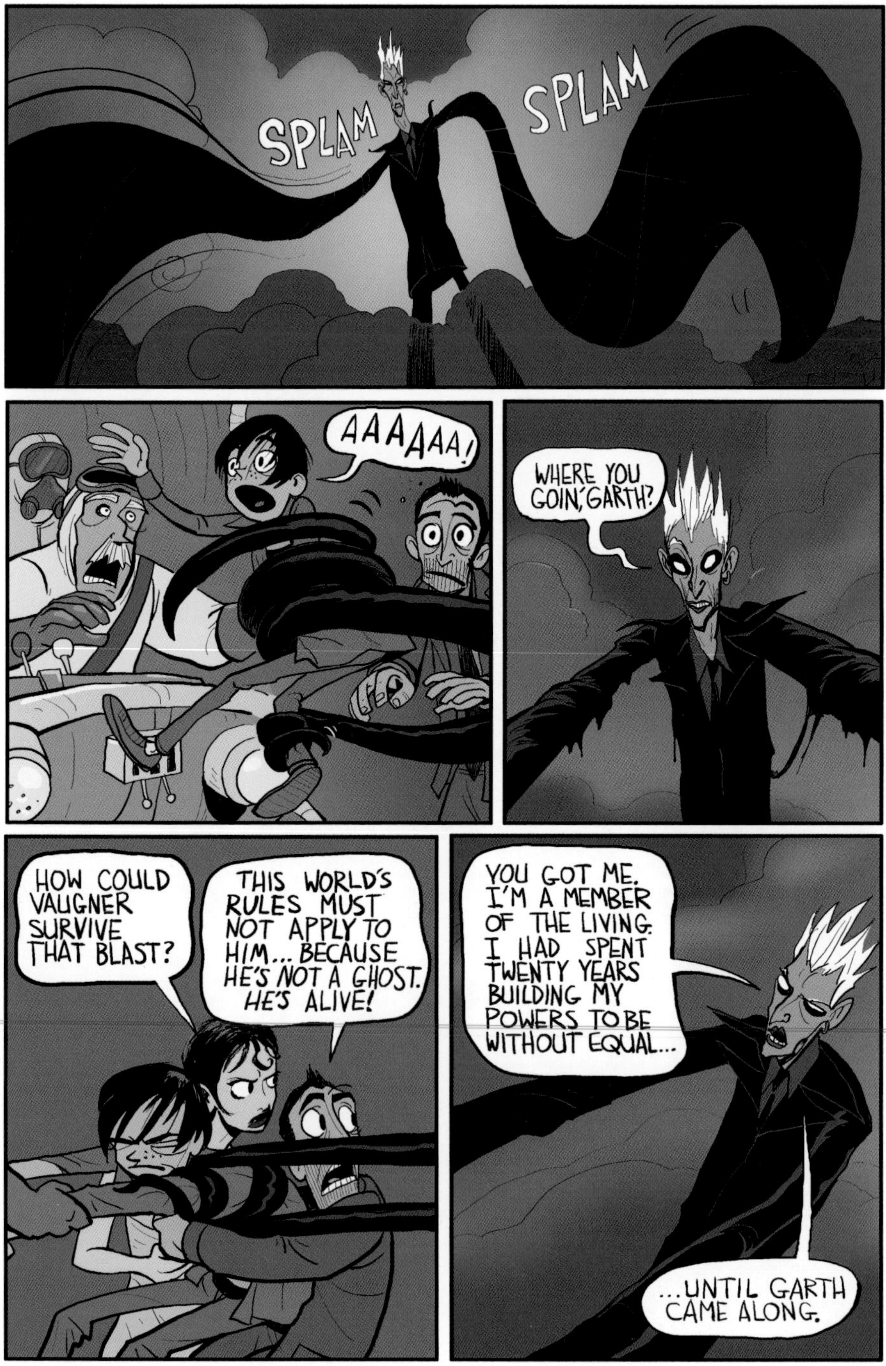
SPLAM
SPLAM
AAAAAA!
WHERE YOU GOIN', GARTH?
HOW COULD VAUGNER SURVIVE THAT BLAST?
THIS WORLD'S RULES MUST NOT APPLY TO HIM... BECAUSE HE'S NOT A GHOST. HE'S ALIVE!
YOU GOT ME. I'M A MEMBER OF THE LIVING. I HAD SPENT TWENTY YEARS BUILDING MY POWERS TO BE WITHOUT EQUAL...
...UNTIL GARTH CAME ALONG.

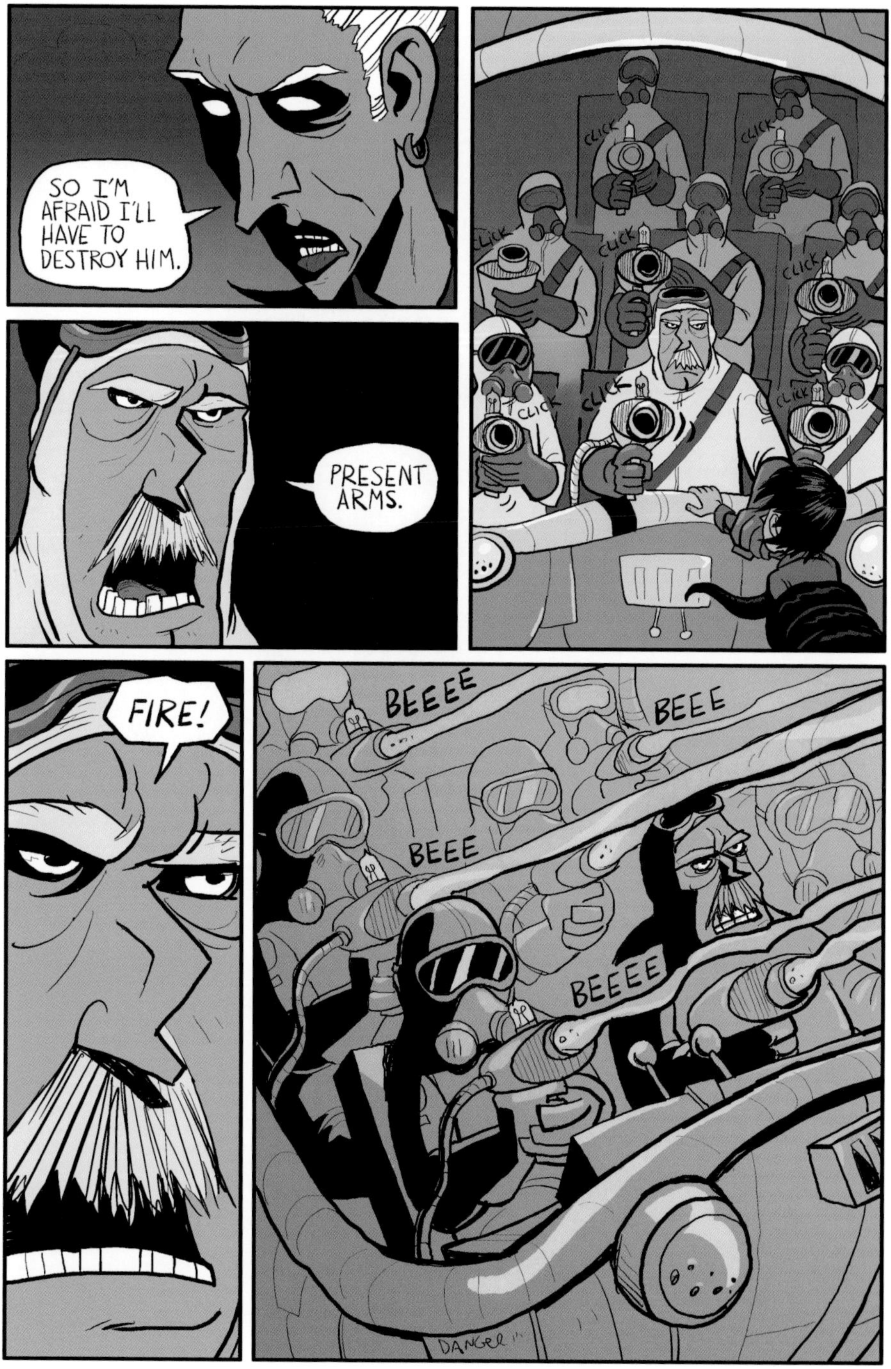
SO I'M AFRAID I'LL HAVE TO DESTROY HIM.
CLICK
CLICK
CLICK
CLICK
CLICK
CLICK
CLICK
CLICK
PRESENT ARMS.
FIRE!
BEEEE
BEEE
BEEE
BEEEE
DANGER '11

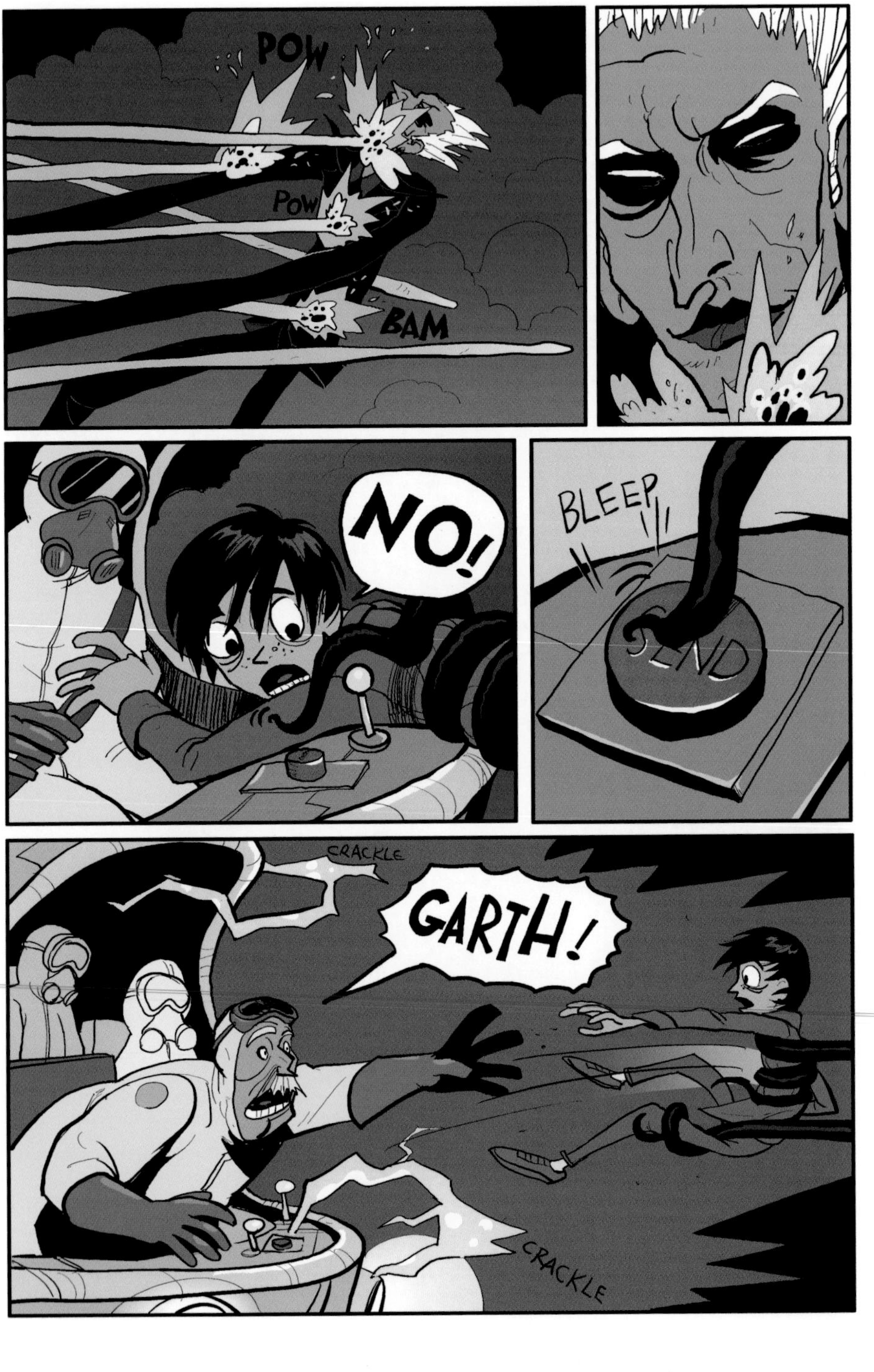
POW
POW
BAM
NO!
BLEEP
SEND
CRACKLE
GARTH!
CRACKLE

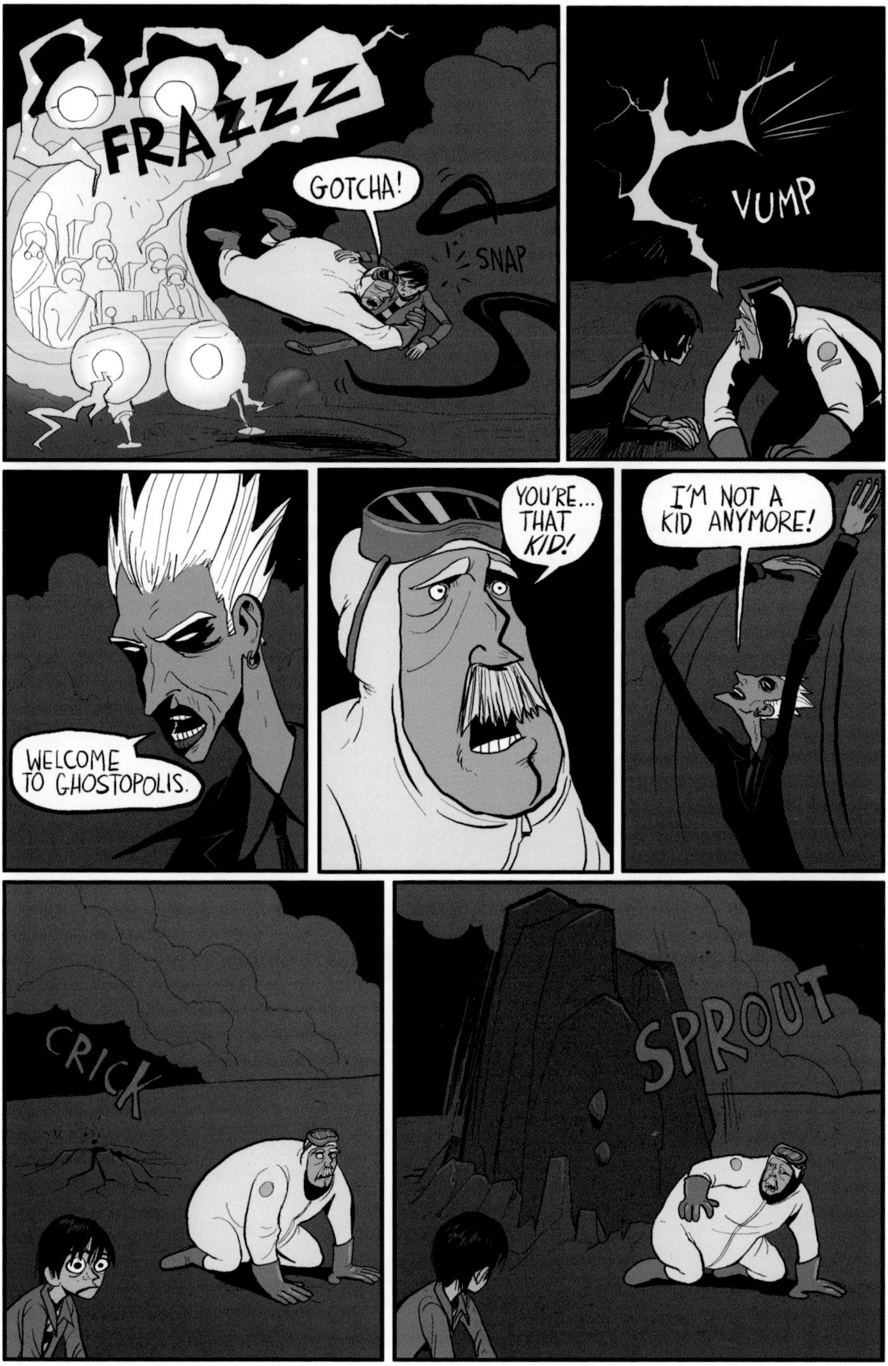
FRAZZZ
GOTCHA!
SNAP
VUMP
WELCOME TO GHOSTOPOLIS.
YOU'RE... THAT KID!
I'M NOT A KID ANYMORE!
CRICK
SPROUT

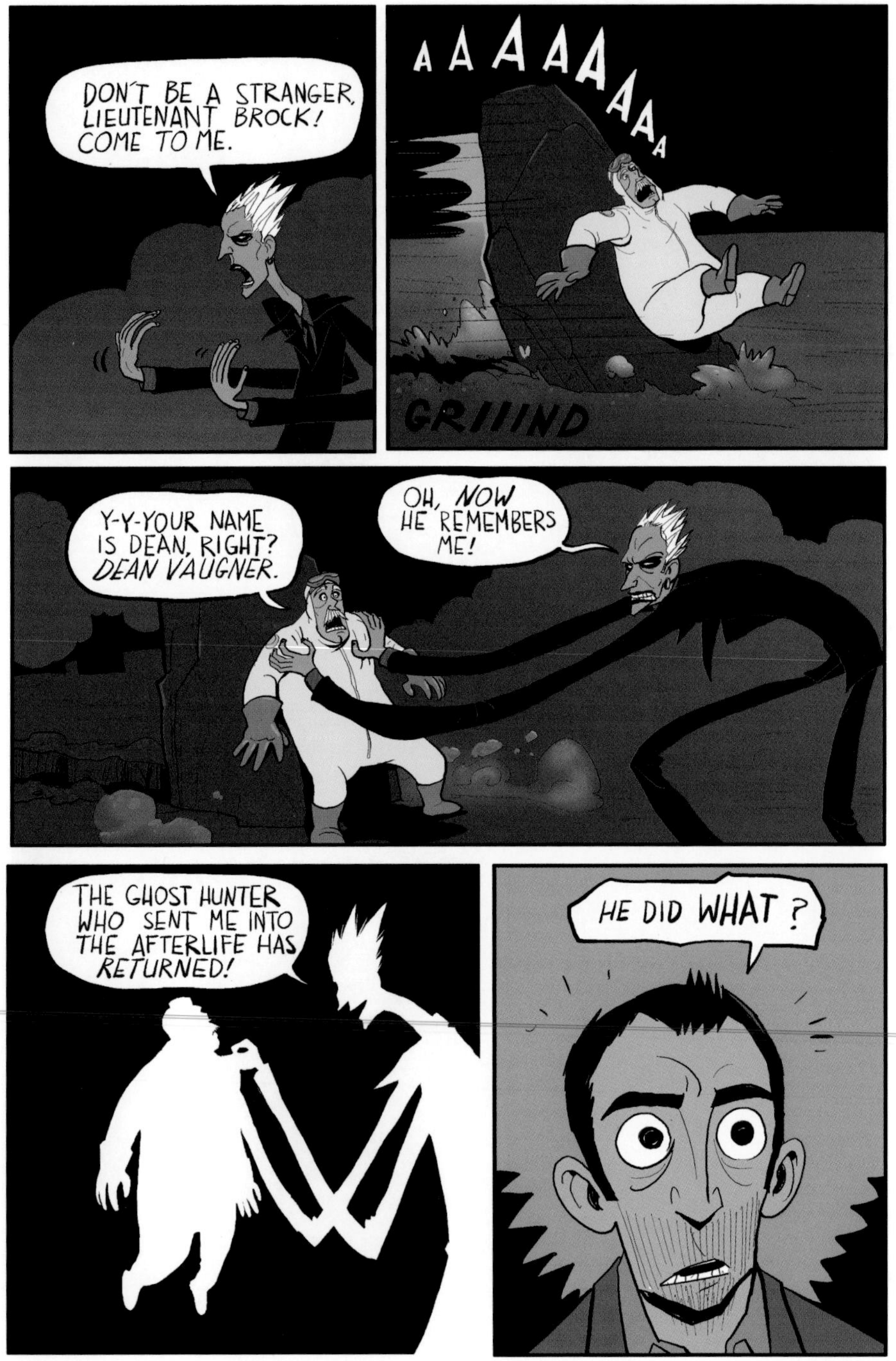
DON'T BE A STRANGER, LIEUTENANT BROCK! COME TO ME.
AAAAAAAAA
GRIIIND
Y-Y-YOUR NAME IS DEAN, RIGHT? DEAN VAUGNER.
OH, NOW HE REMEMBERS ME!
THE GHOST HUNTER WHO SENT ME INTO THE AFTERLIFE HAS RETURNED!
HE DID WHAT ?

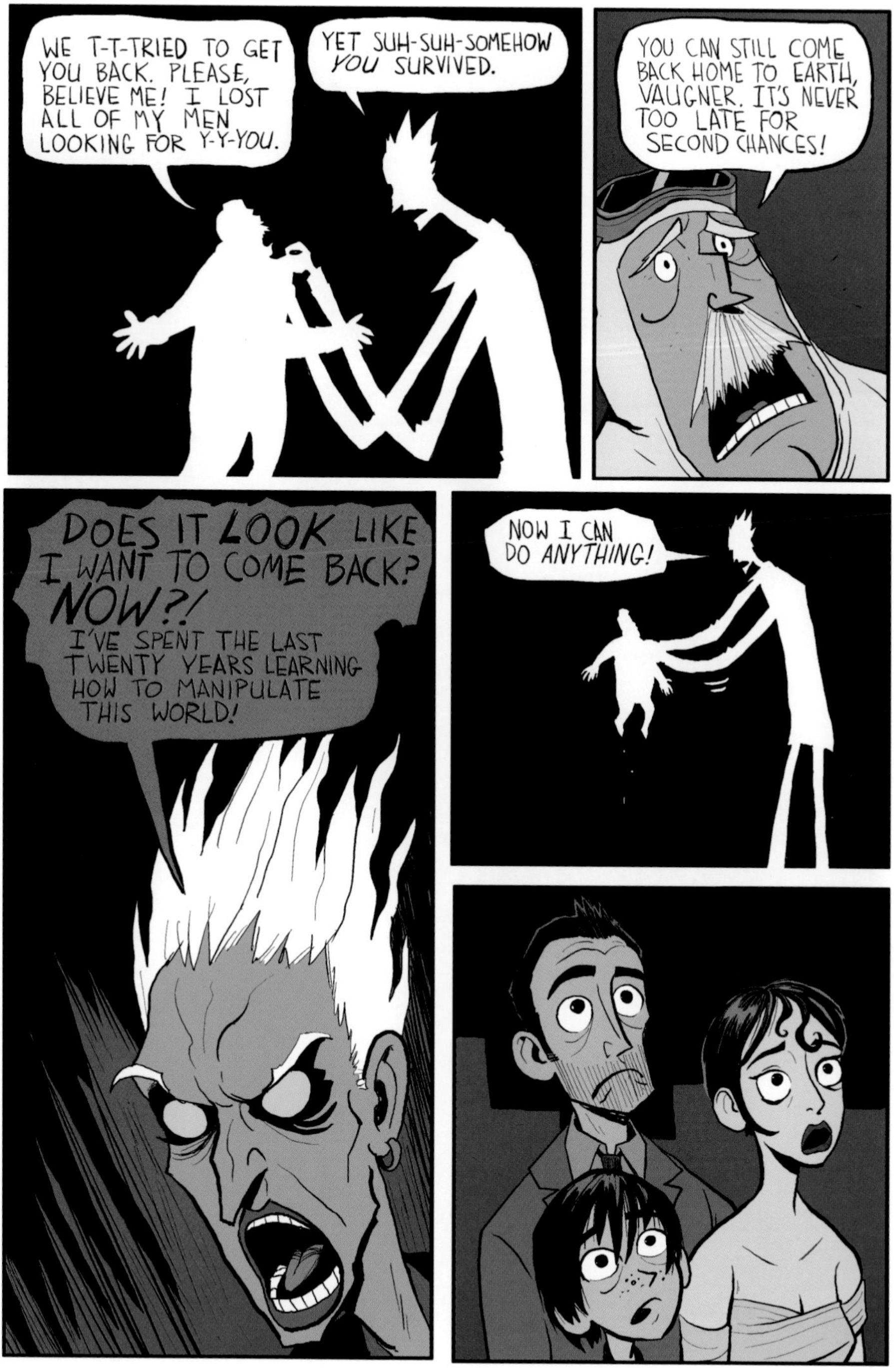
WE T-T-TRIED TO GET YOU BACK. PLEASE, BELIEVE ME! I LOST ALL OF MY MEN LOOKING FOR Y-Y-YOU.
YET SUH-SUH-SOMEHOW YOU SURVIVED.
YOU CAN STILL COME BACK HOME TO EARTH, VAUGNER. IT'S NEVER TOO LATE FOR SECOND CHANCES!
DOES IT LOOK LIKE I WANT TO COME BACK? NOW?! I'VE SPENT THE LAST TWENTY YEARS LEARNING HOW TO MANIPULATE THIS WORLD!
NOW I CAN DO ANYTHING!

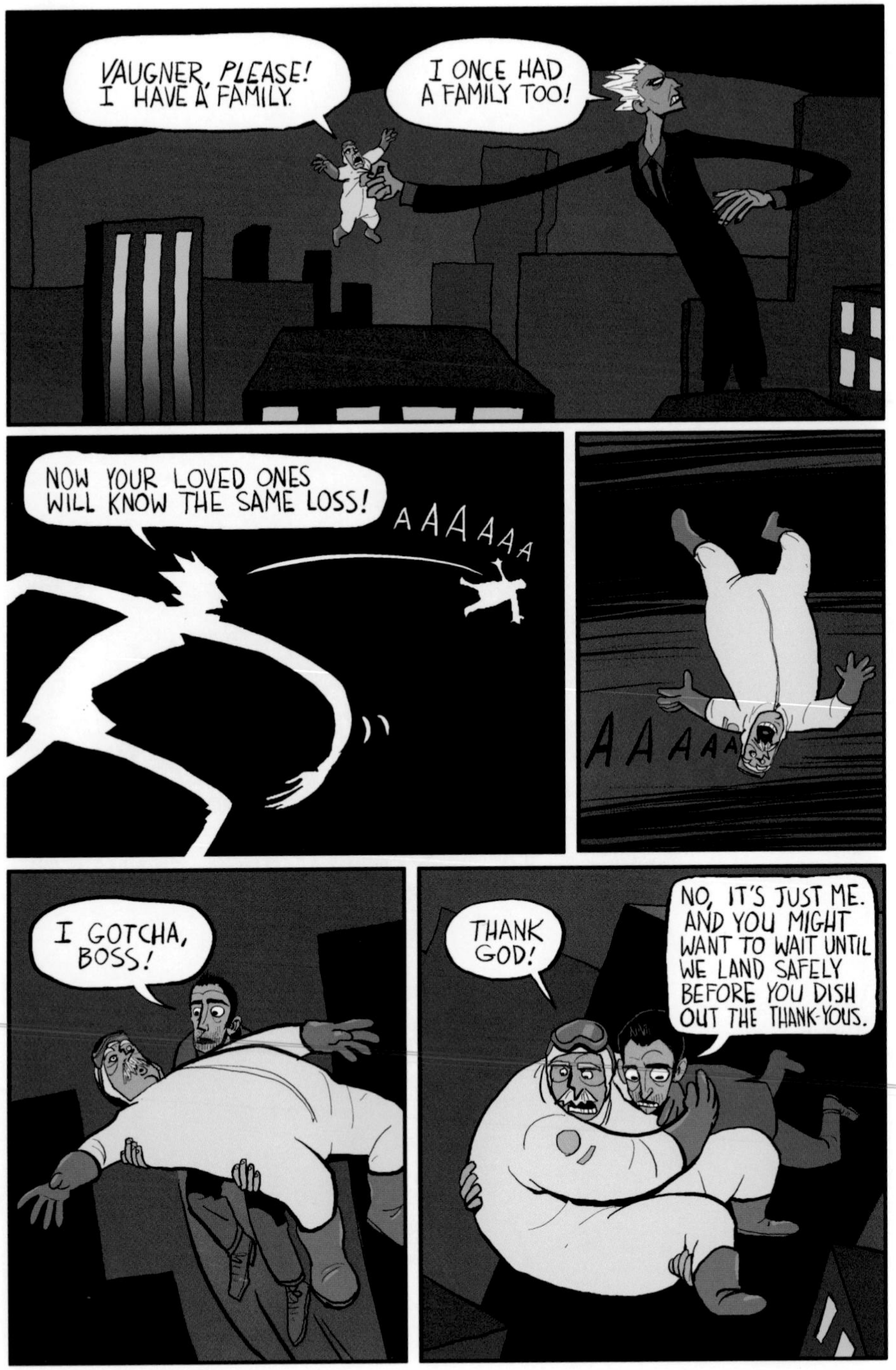
VAUGNER, PLEASE! I HAVE A FAMILY.
I ONCE HAD A FAMILY TOO!
NOW YOUR LOVED ONES WILL KNOW THE SAME LOSS!
AAAAAA
AAAAA
I GOTCHA, BOSS!
THANK GOD!
NO, IT'S JUST ME. AND YOU MIGHT WANT TO WAIT UNTIL WE LAND SAFELY BEFORE YOU DISH OUT THE THANK-YOUS.

WHAT'S THAT SUPPOSED TO MEAN? YOU CAN FLY, RIGHT?!
SORT OF.
AAAAAAAAA
AAAAAAAAAAAA
THERE YOU ARE!

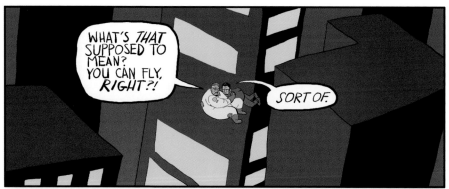

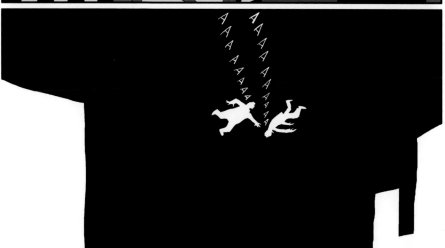

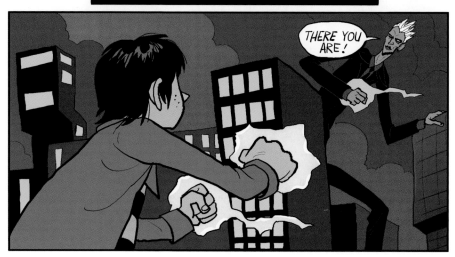

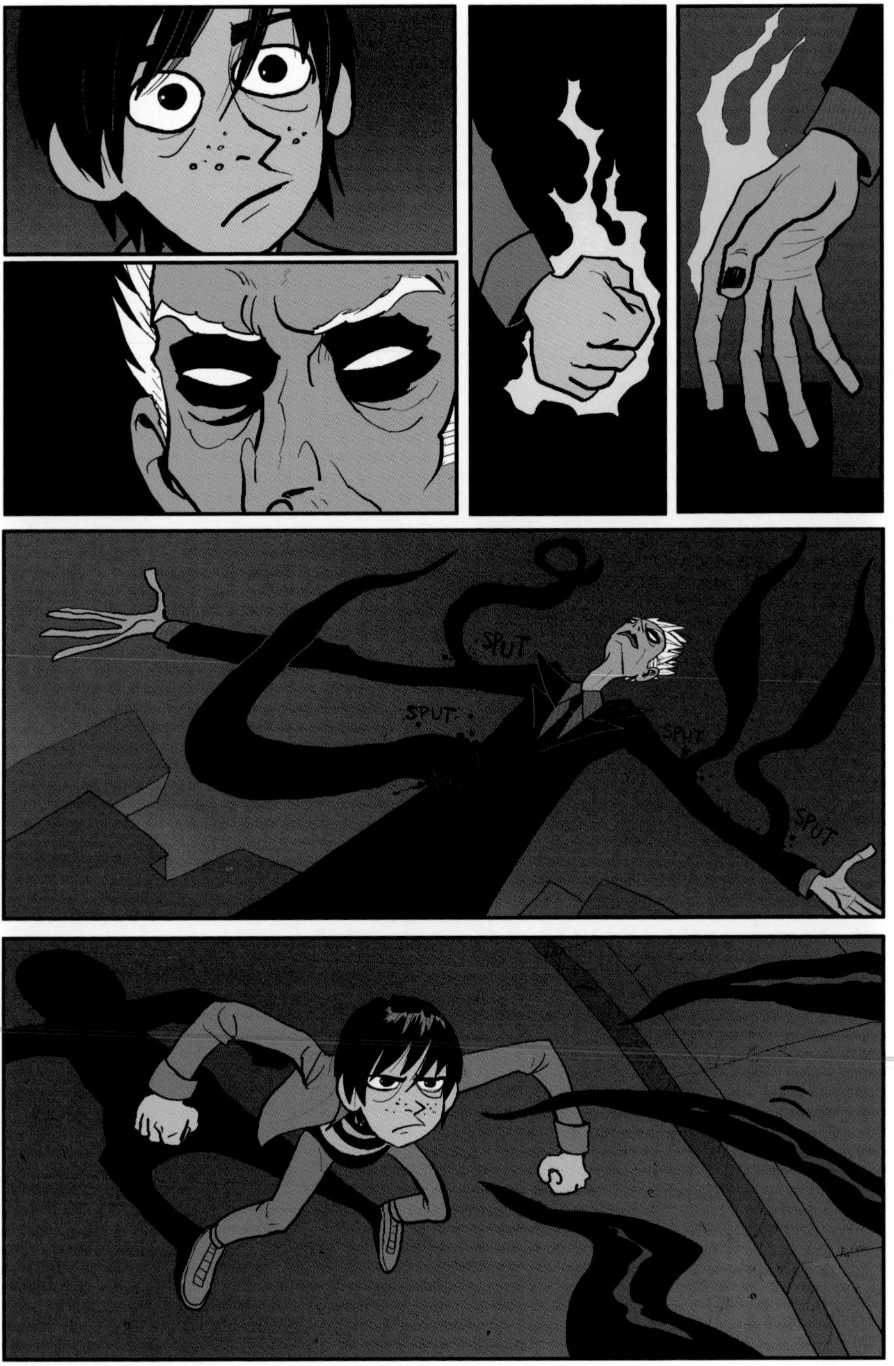
SPUT
SPUT
SPUT
SPUT

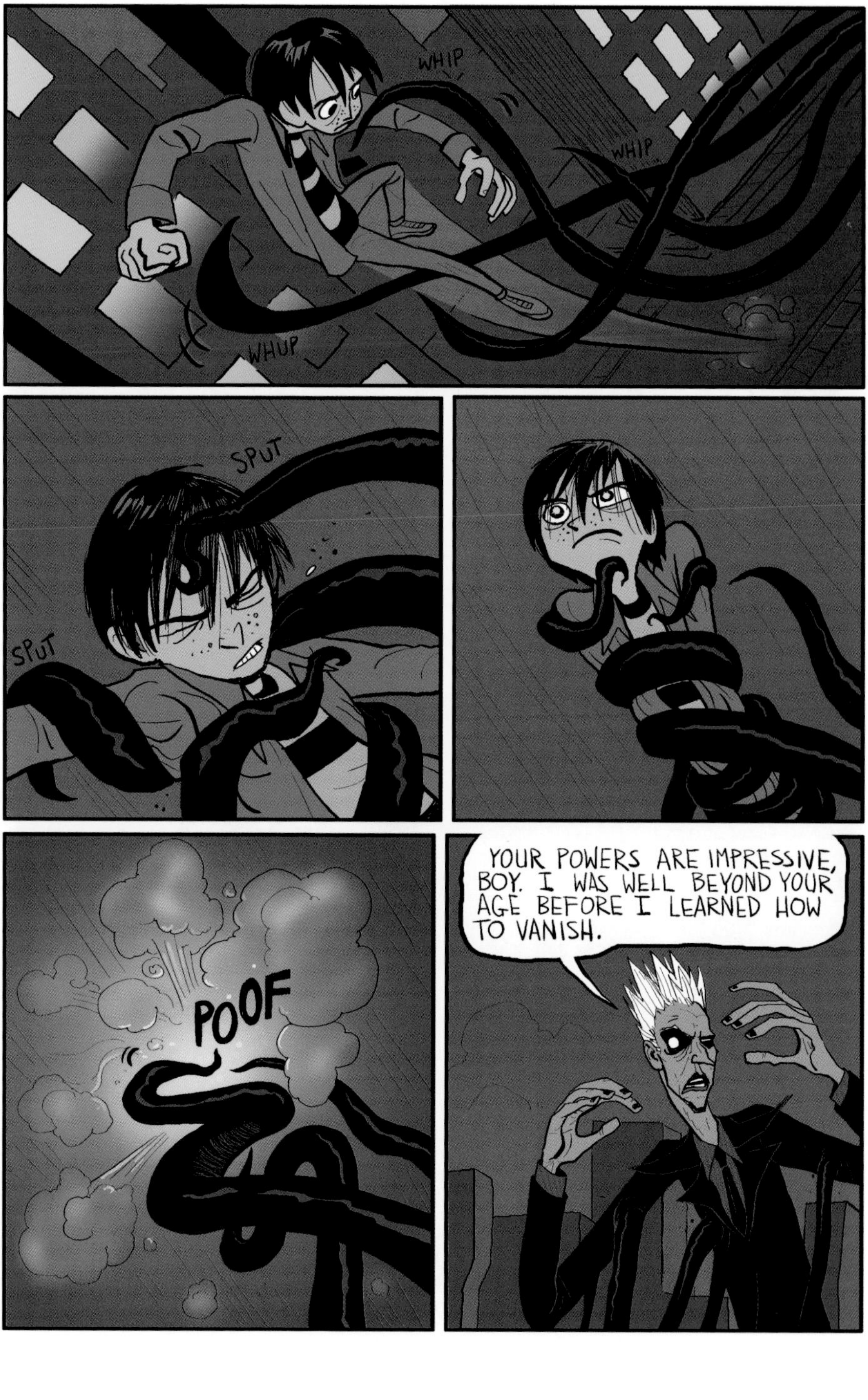
WHIP
WHIP
WHUP
SPUT
SPUT
POOF
YOUR POWERS ARE IMPRESSIVE, BOY. I WAS WELL BEYOND YOUR AGE BEFORE I LEARNED HOW TO VANISH.

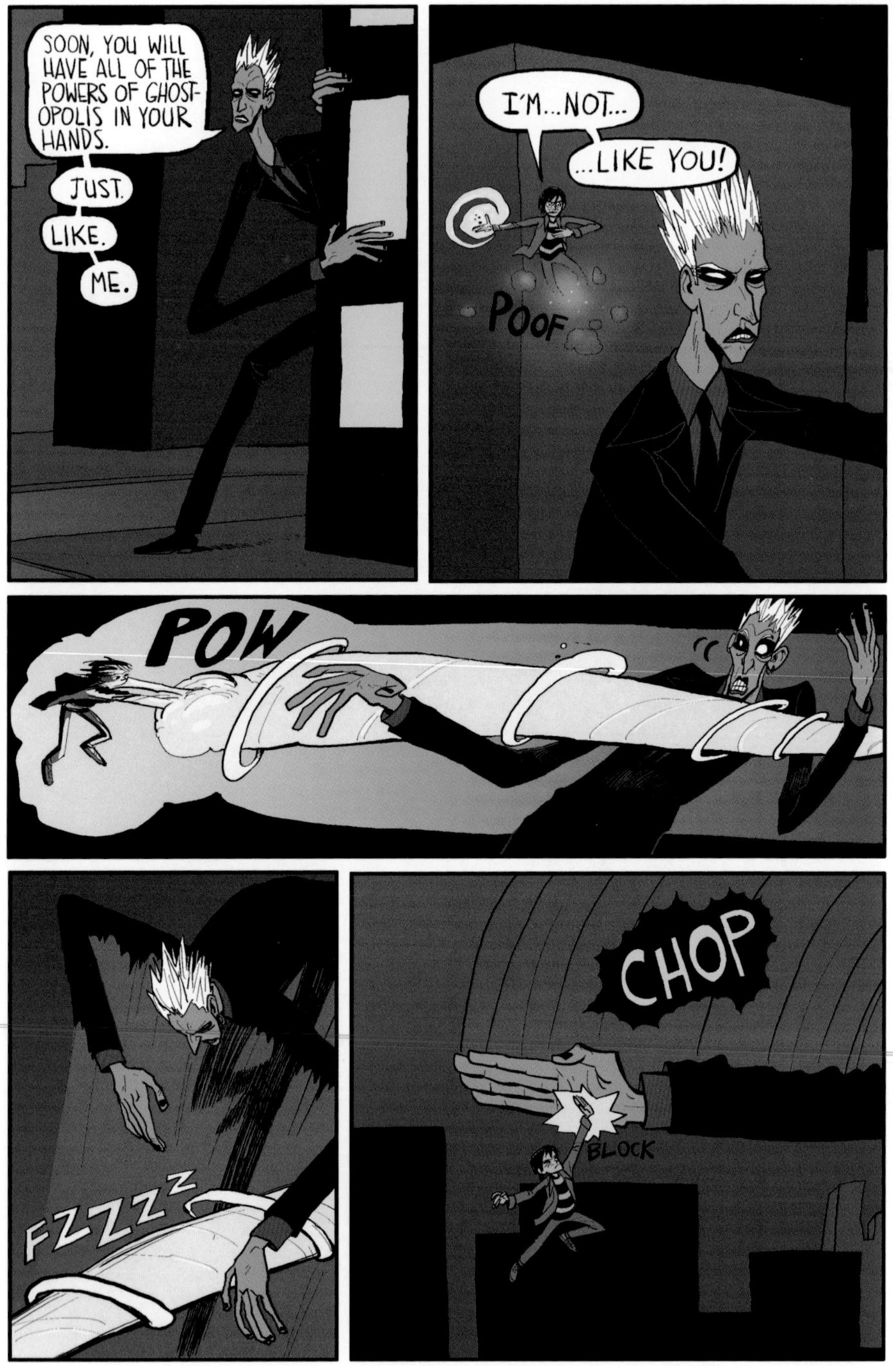
SOON, YOU WILL HAVE ALL OF THE POWERS OF GHOST-OPOLIS IN YOUR HANDS.
JUST.
LIKE.
ME.
I'M...NOT...
...LIKE YOU!
POOF
POW
FZZZZZ
CHOP
BLOCK

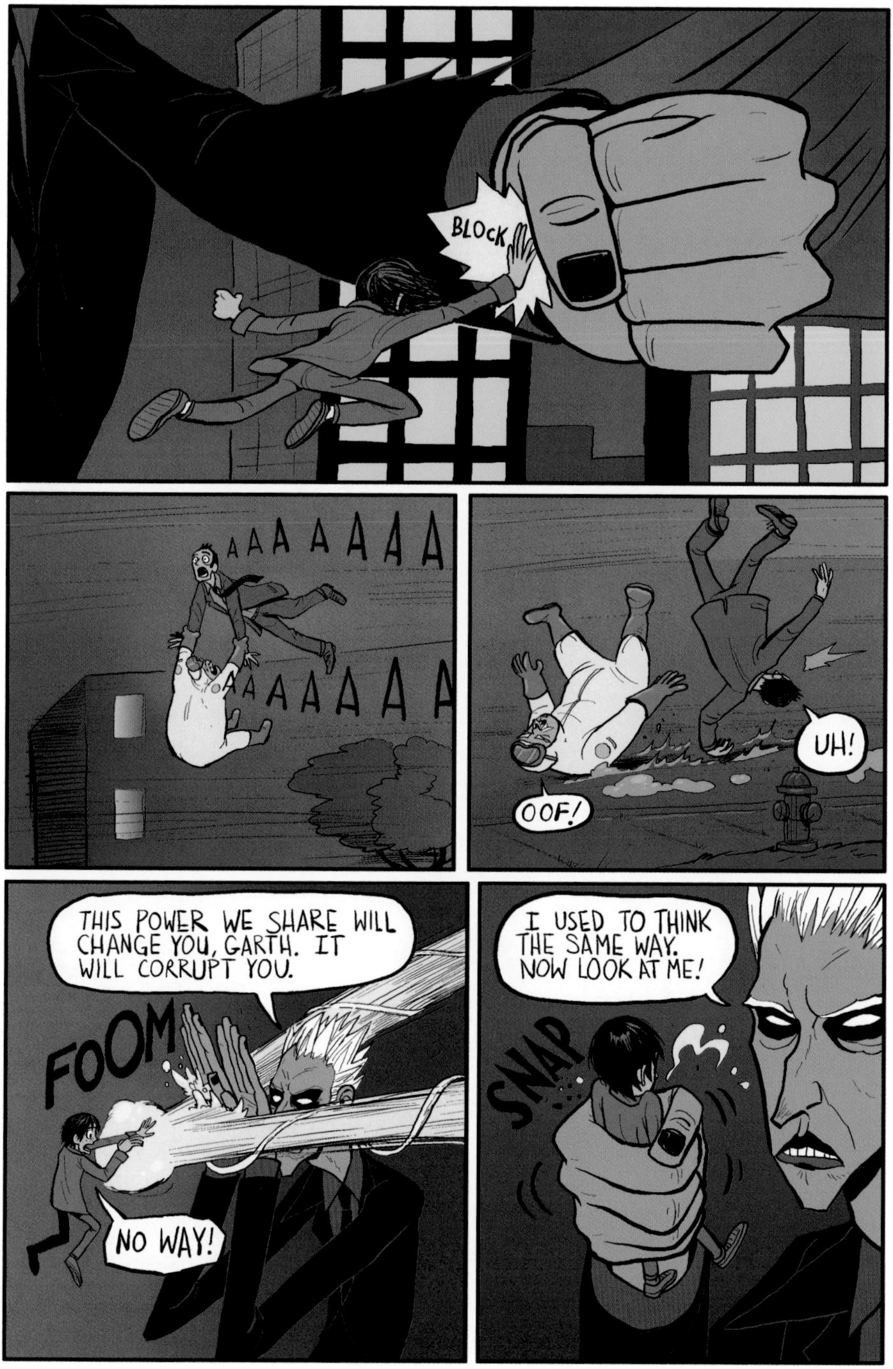
BLOCK
AAAAAAA
AAAAAAAA
UH!
OOF!
THIS POWER WE SHARE WILL CHANGE YOU, GARTH. IT WILL CORRUPT YOU.
FOOM
NO WAY!
I USED TO THINK THE SAME WAY. NOW LOOK AT ME!
SNAP

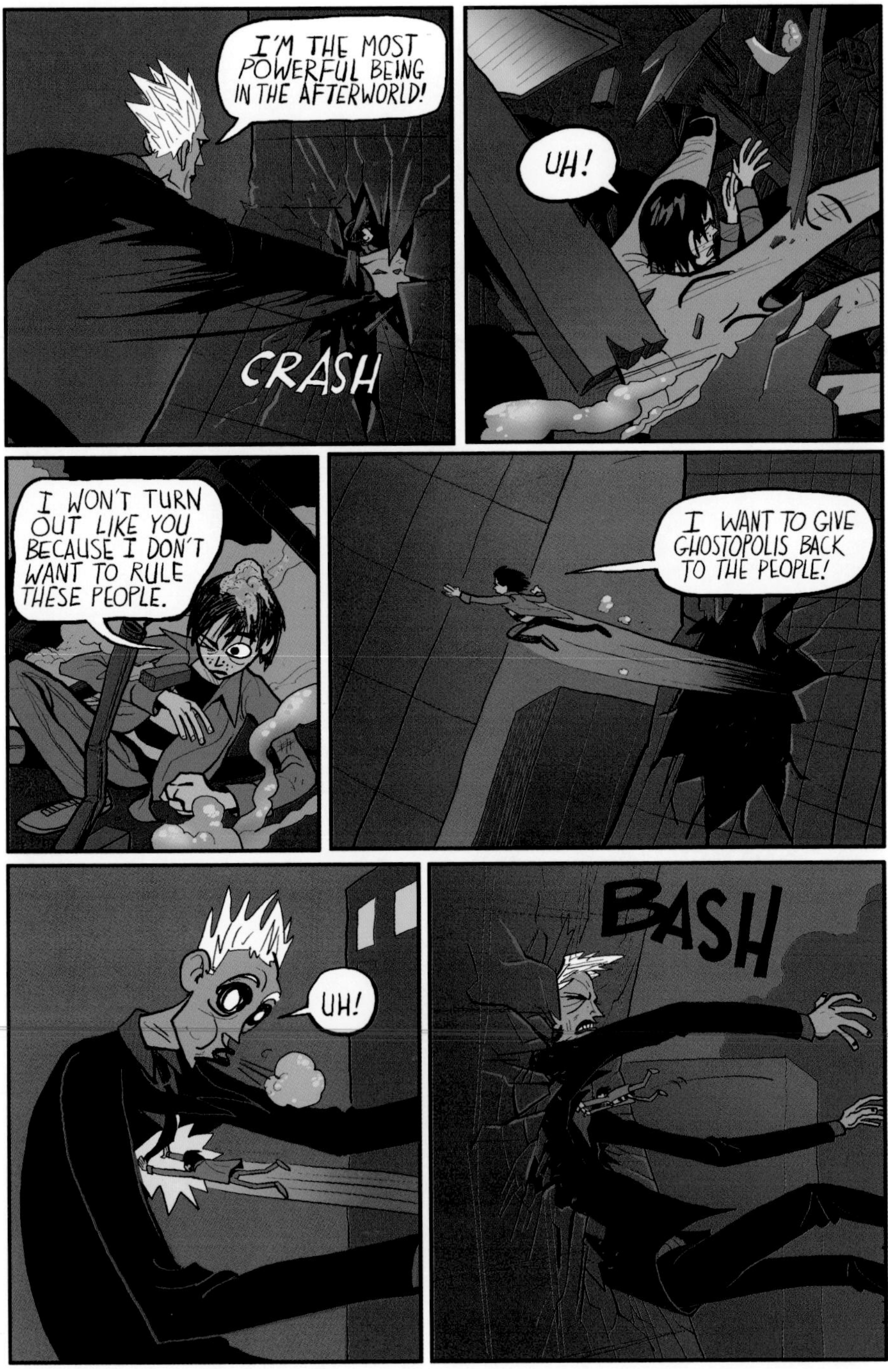
I'M THE MOST POWERFUL BEING IN THE AFTERWORLD!
CRASH
UH!
I WON'T TURN OUT LIKE YOU BECAUSE I DON'T WANT TO RULE THESE PEOPLE.
I WANT TO GIVE GHOSTOPOLIS BACK TO THE PEOPLE!
UH!
BASH

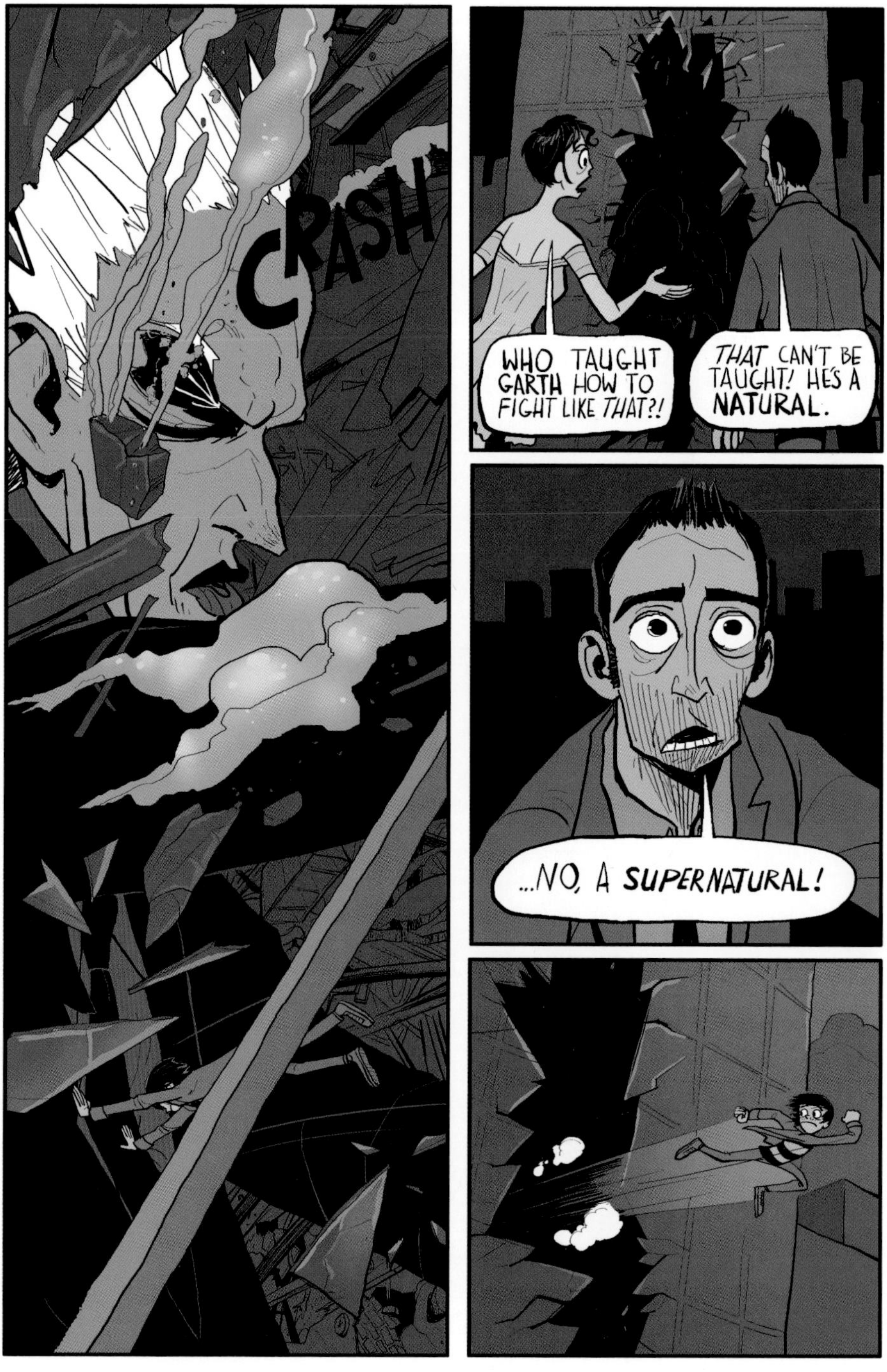
CRASH
WHO TAUGHT GARTH HOW TO FIGHT LIKE THAT?!
THAT CAN'T BE TAUGHT! HE'S A NATURAL.
...NO, A SUPERNATURAL!

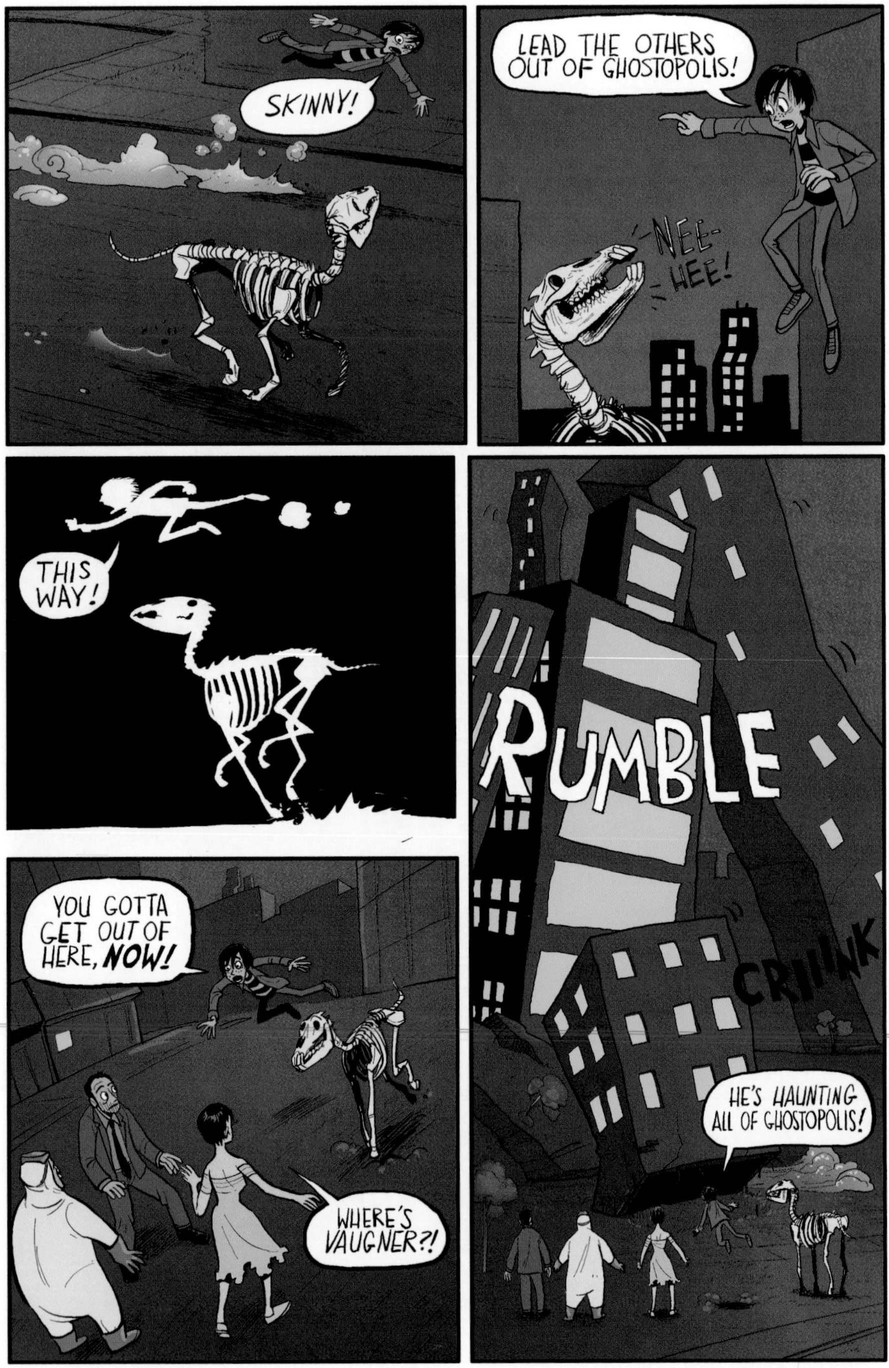
SKINNY!
LEAD THE OTHERS OUT OF GHOSTOPOLIS!
NEE-HEE!
THIS WAY!
RUMBLE
YOU GOTTA GET OUT OF HERE, NOW!
WHERE'S VAUGNER?!
CRIIINK
HE'S HAUNTING ALL OF GHOSTOPOLIS!

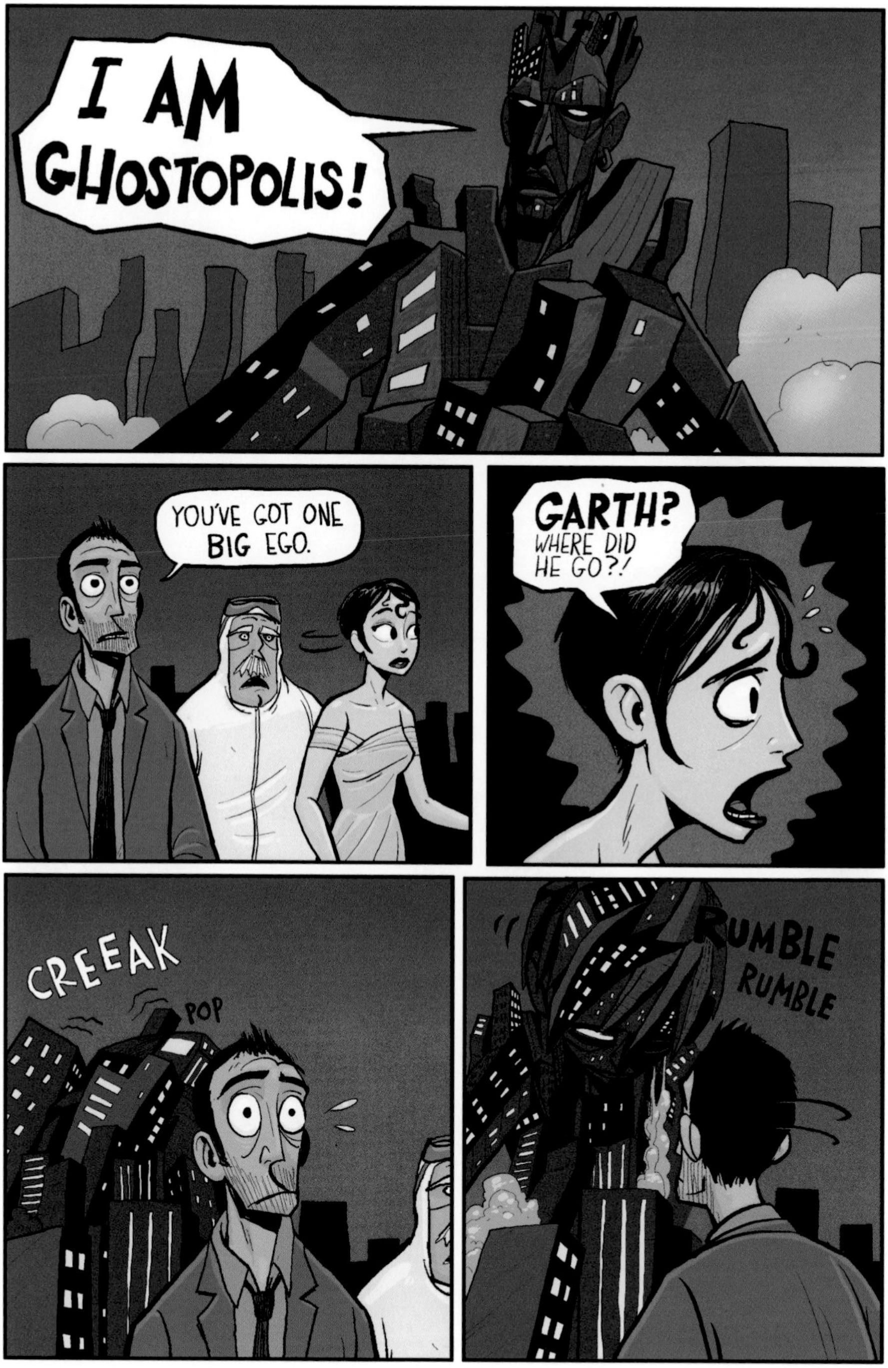
I AM GHOSTOPOLIS!
YOU'VE GOT ONE BIG EGO.
GARTH? WHERE DID HE GO?!
CREEAK
POP
RUMBLE
RUMBLE

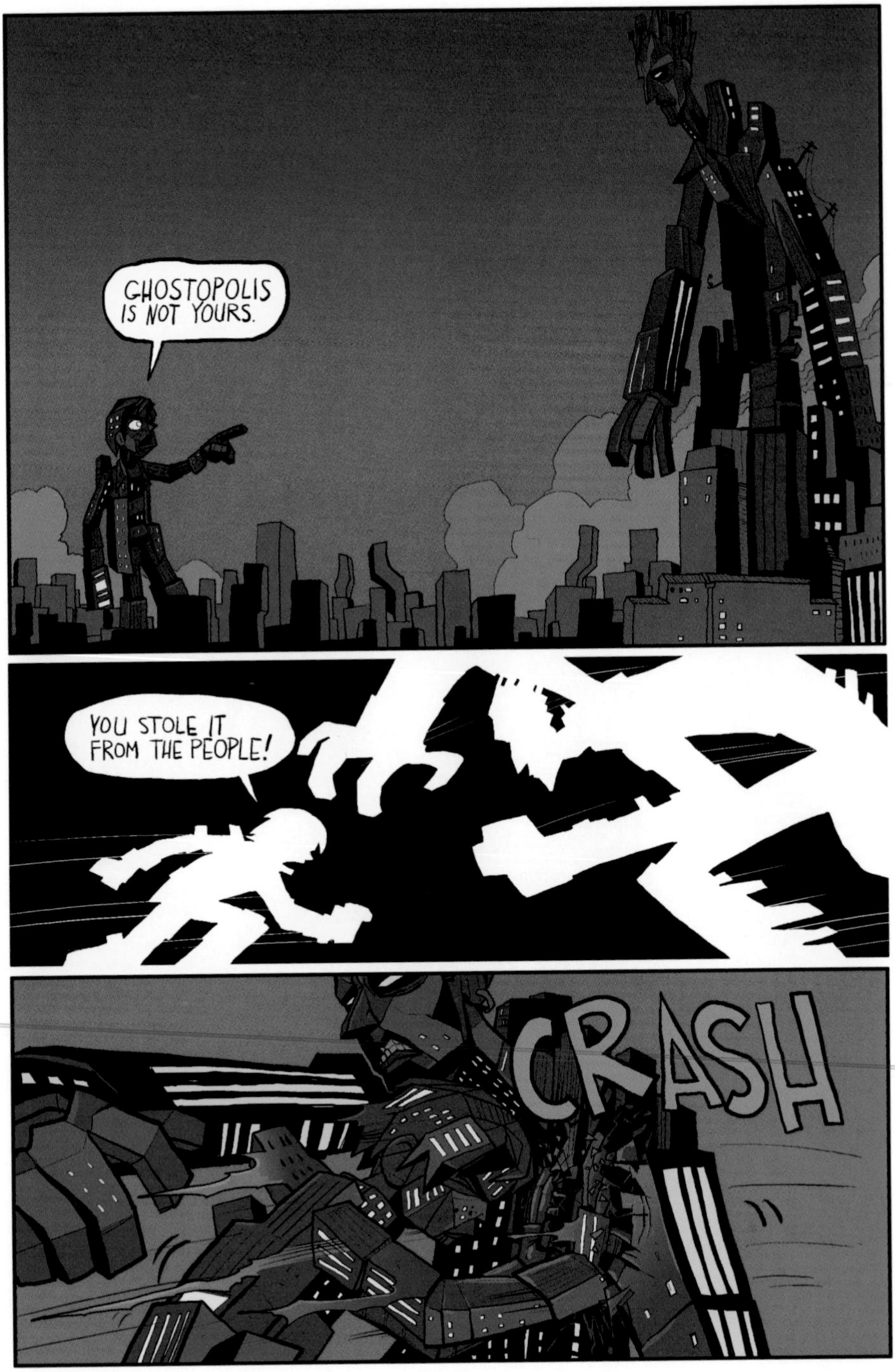
GHOSTOPOLIS IS NOT YOURS.
YOU STOLE IT FROM THE PEOPLE!
CRASH

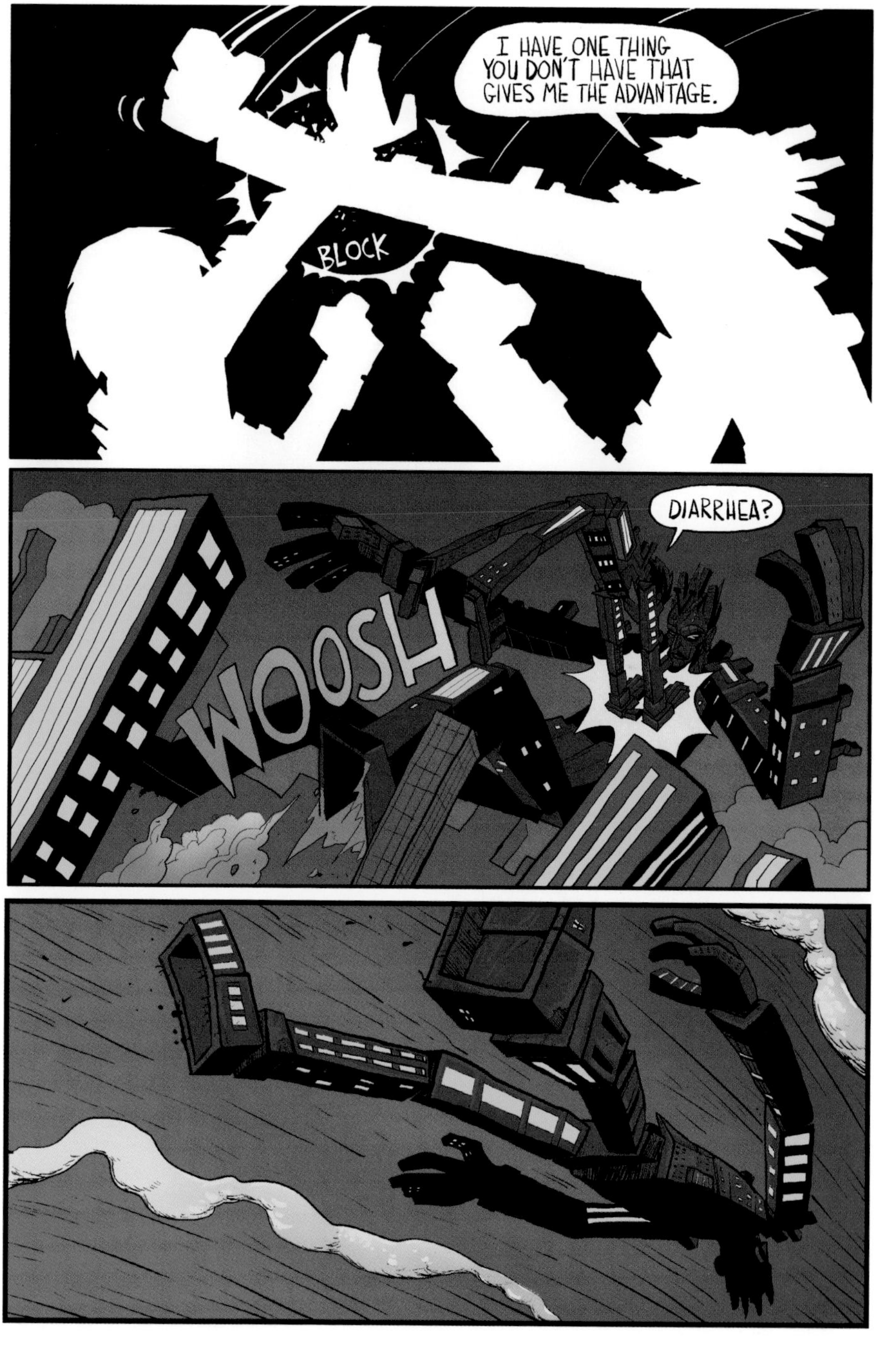
I HAVE ONE THING YOU DON'T HAVE THAT GIVES ME THE ADVANTAGE.
BLOCK
DIARRHEA?
WOOSH

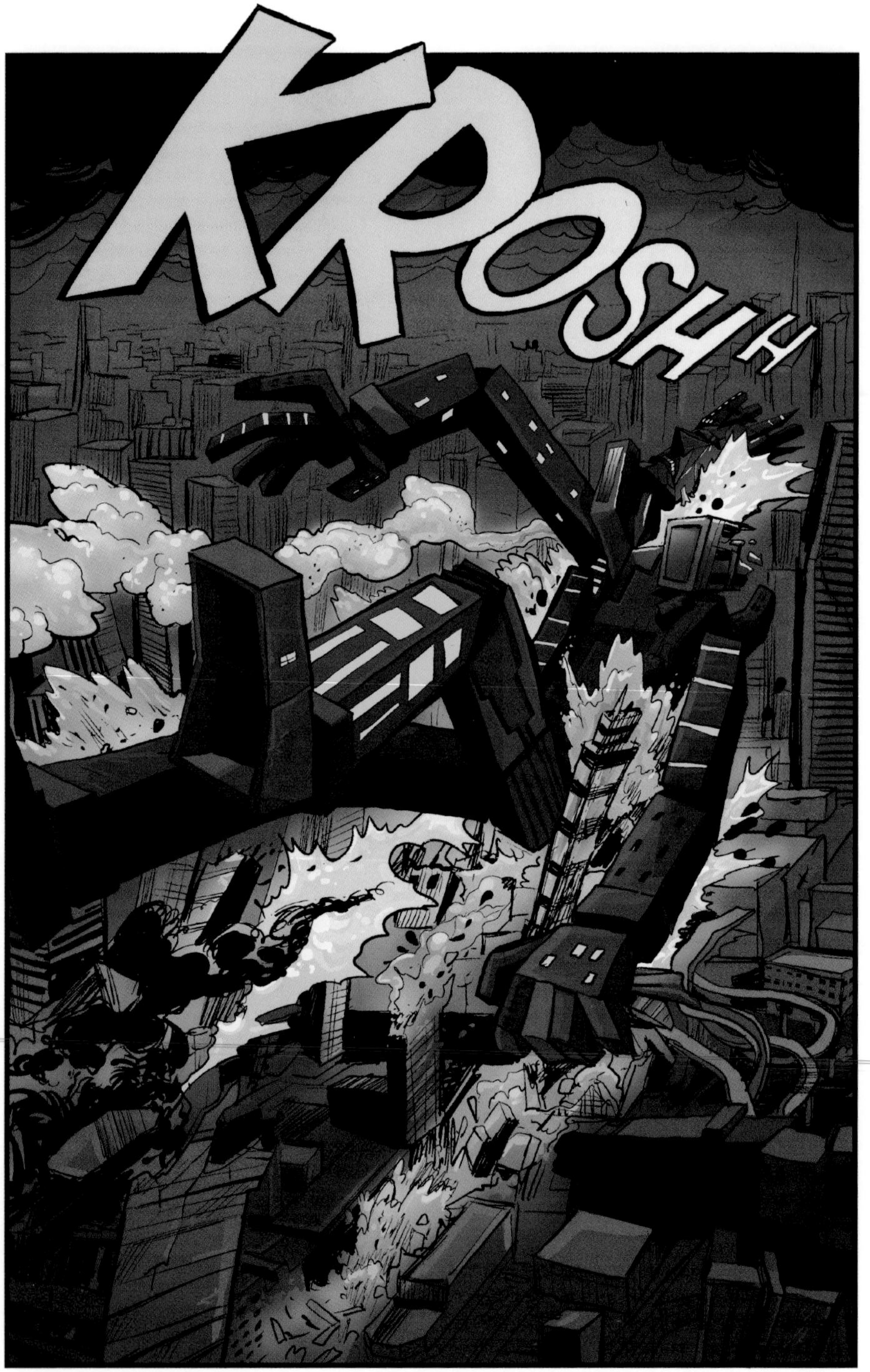
KROSHH

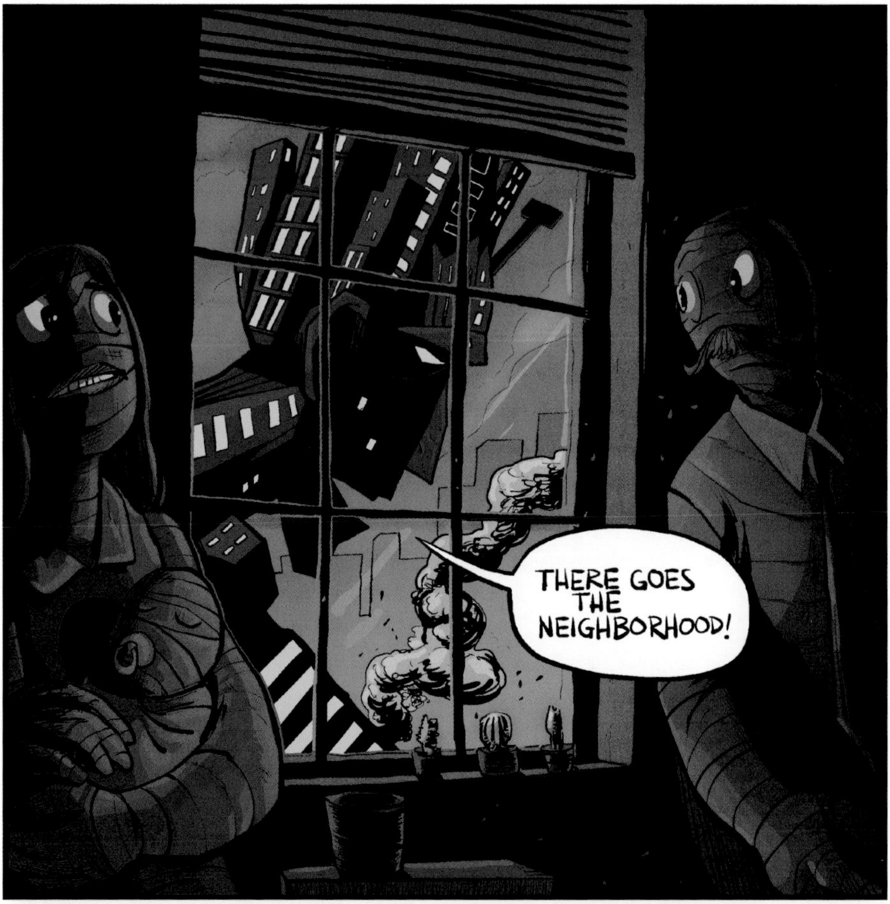
THERE GOES THE NEIGHBORHOOD!

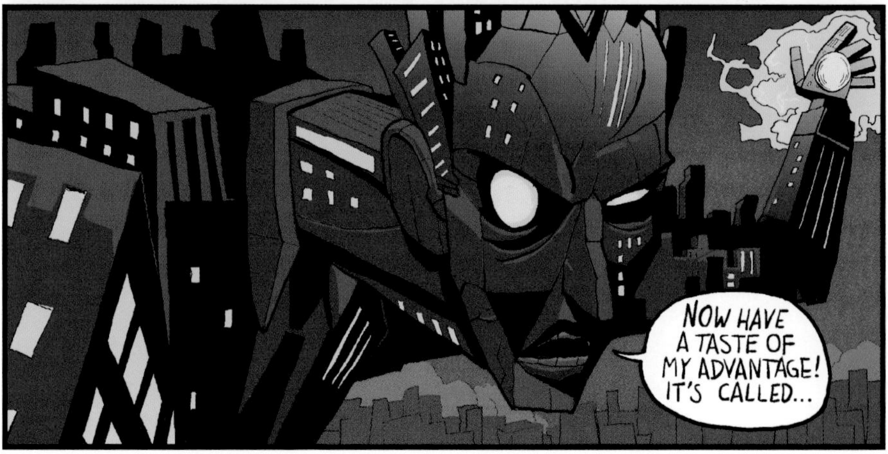
NOW HAVE A TASTE OF MY ADVANTAGE! IT'S CALLED...

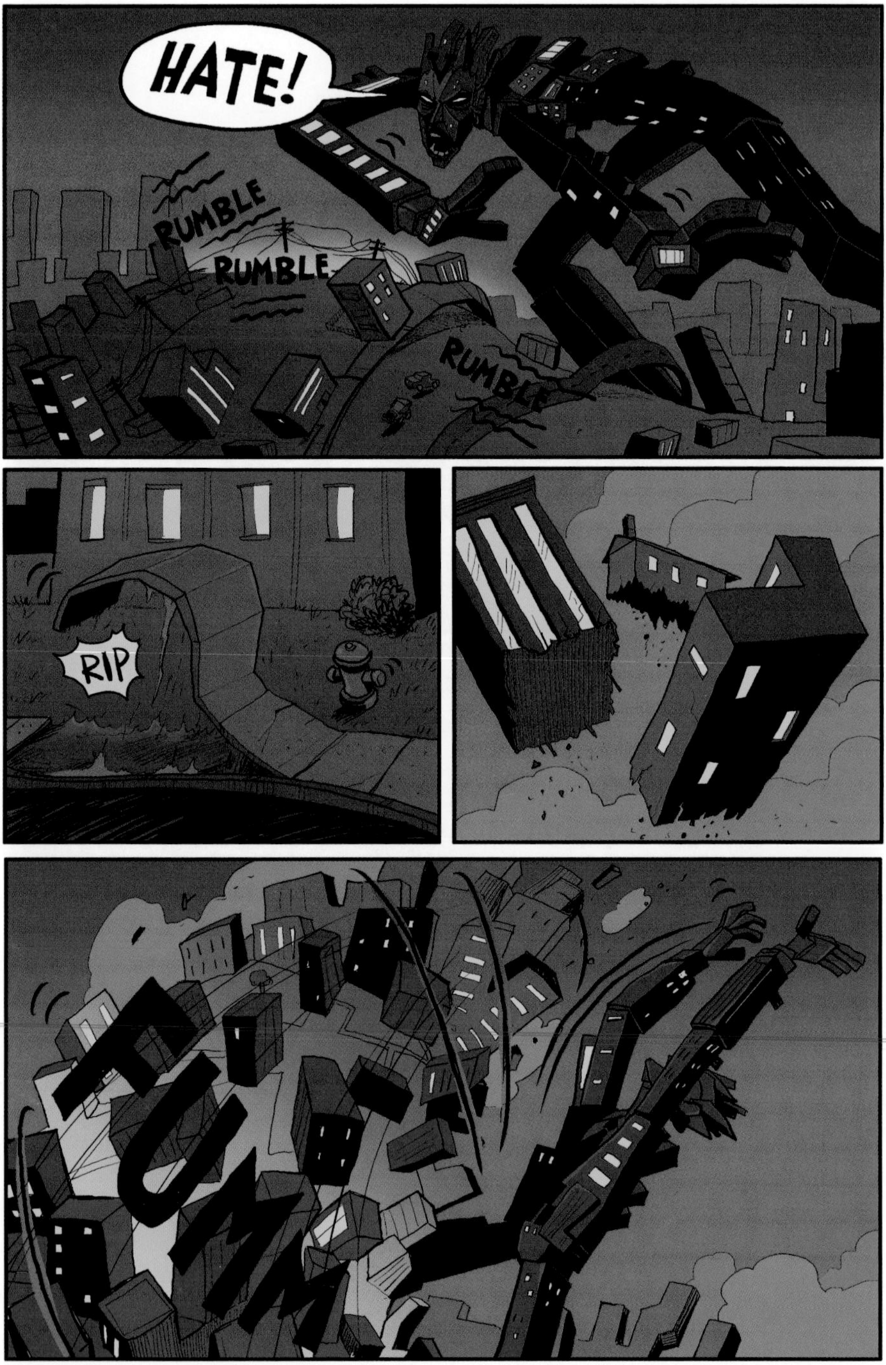
HATE!
RUMBLE
RUMBLE
RUMBLE
RIP
FUMM

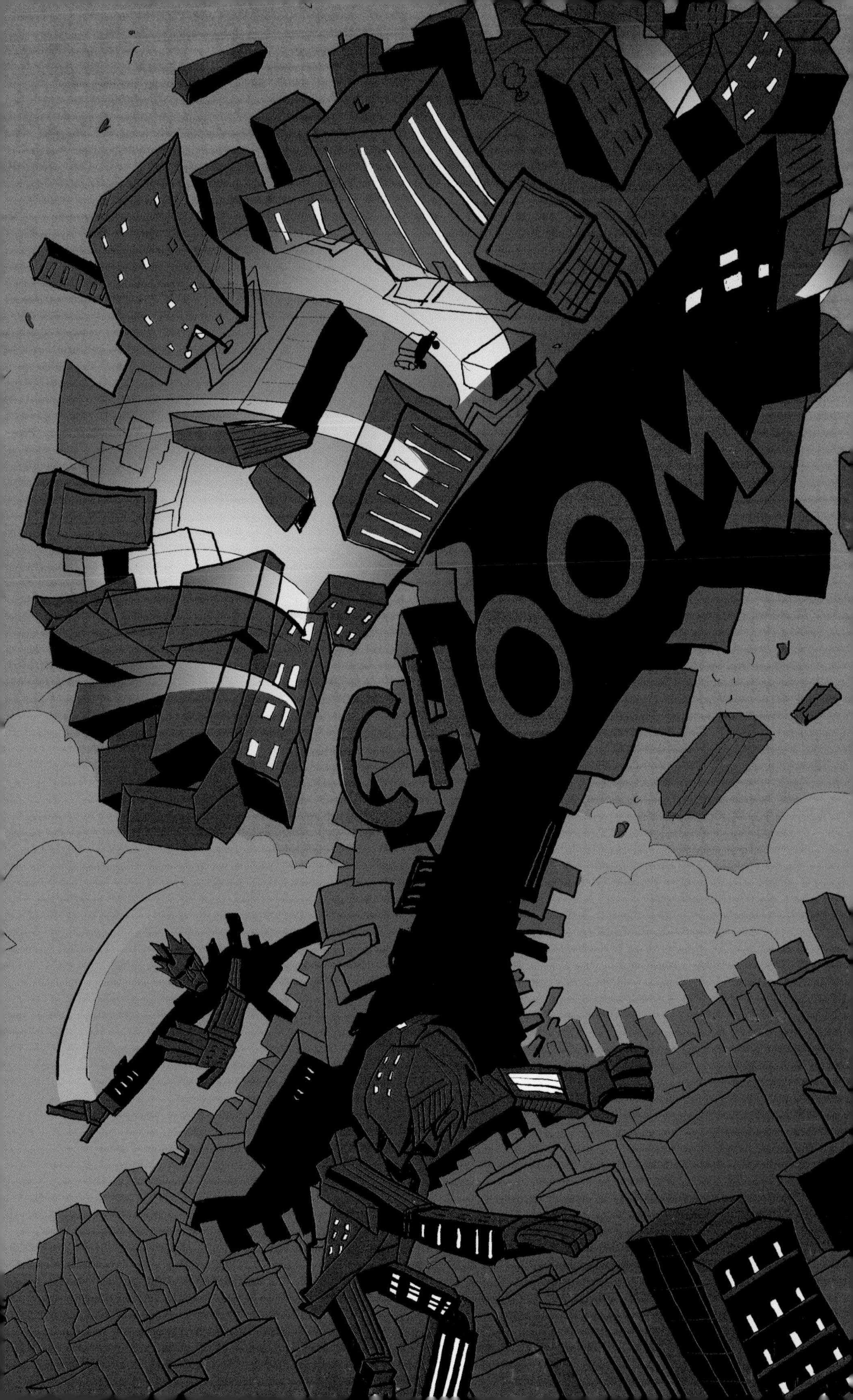
CHOOM

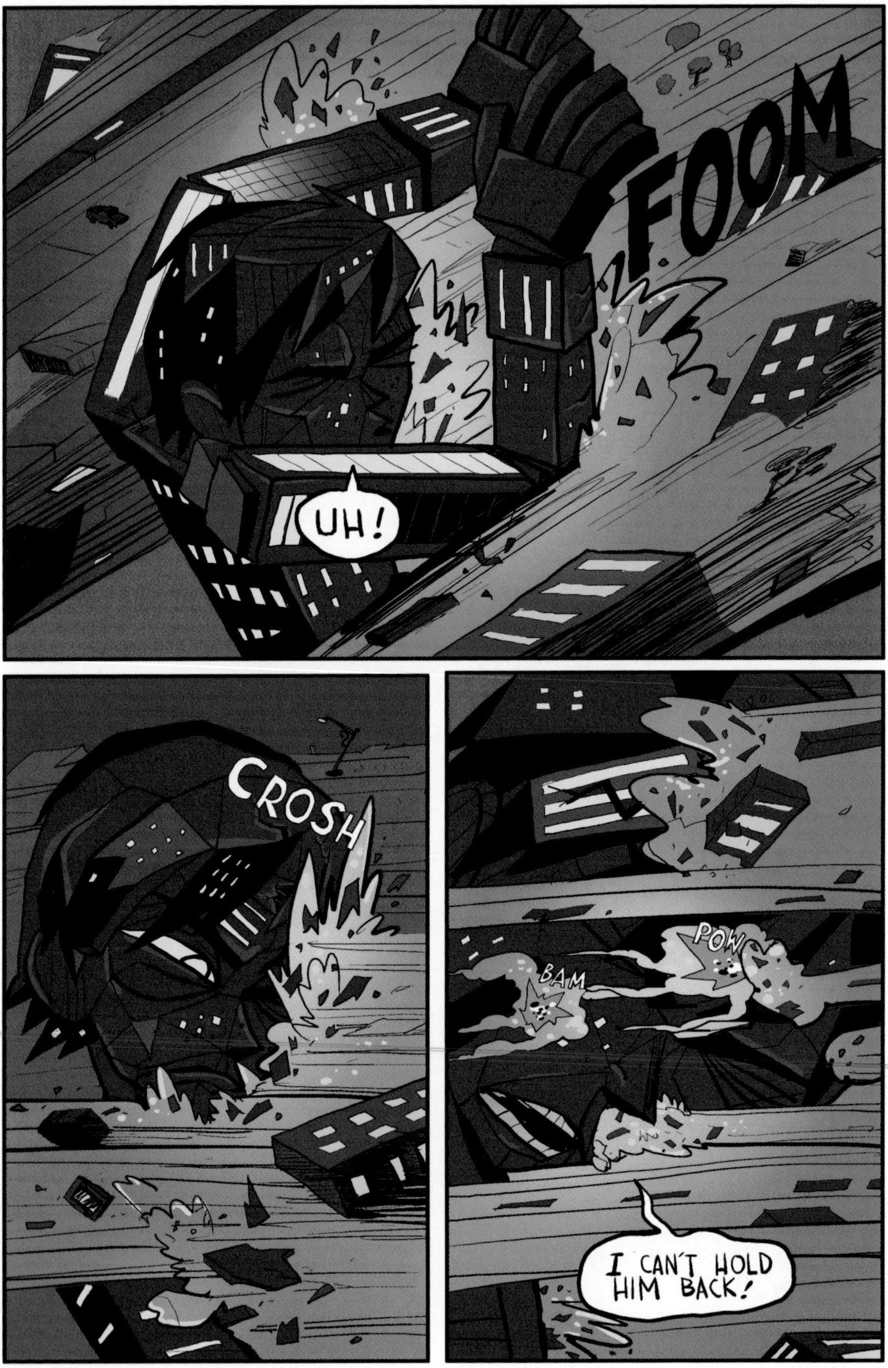
FOOM
UH!
CROSH
BAM
POW
I CAN'T HOLD HIM BACK!

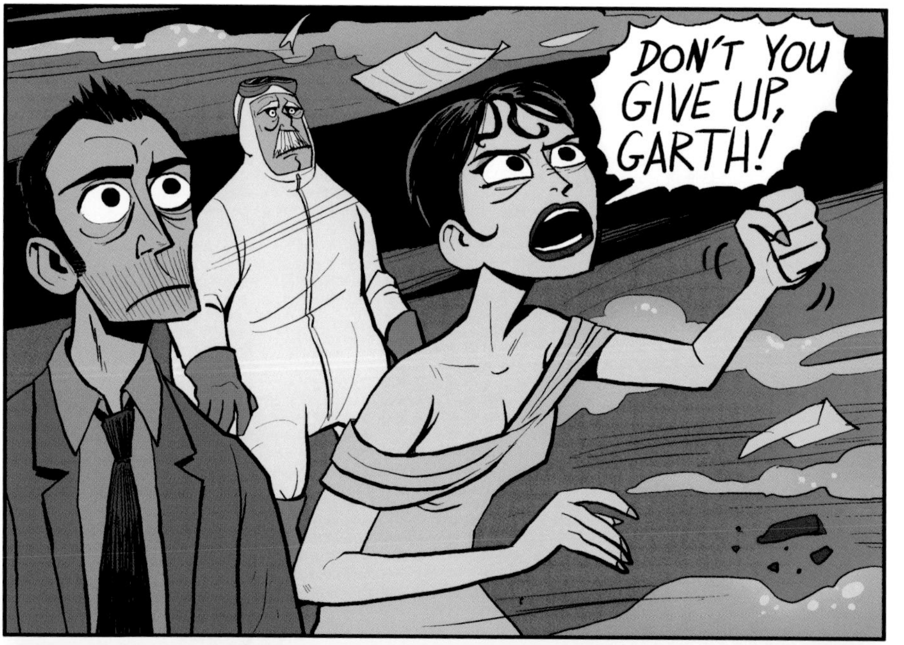
DON'T YOU GIVE UP, GARTH!

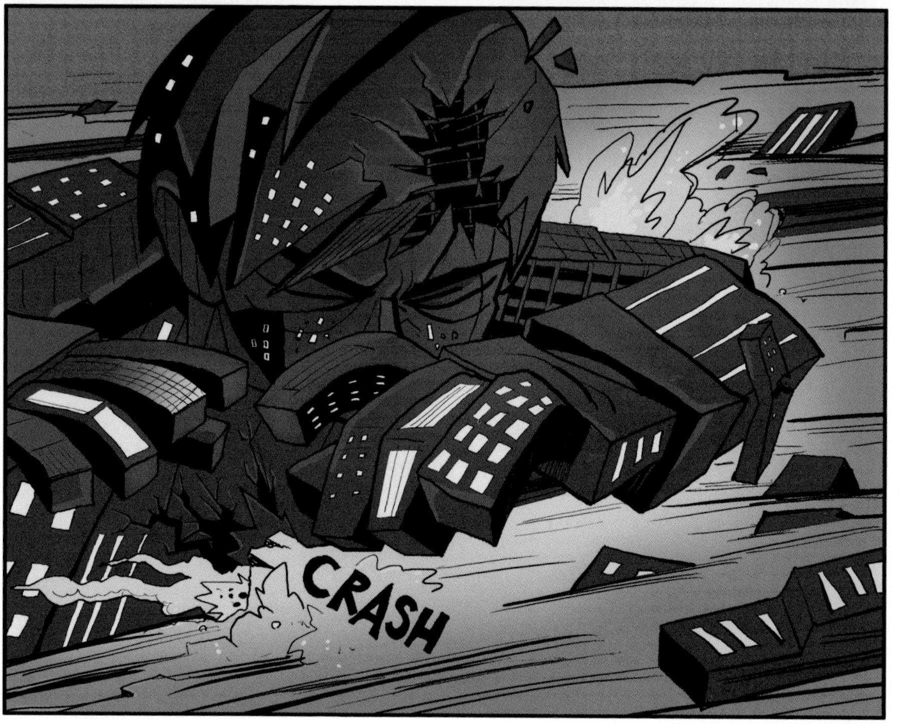
CRASH

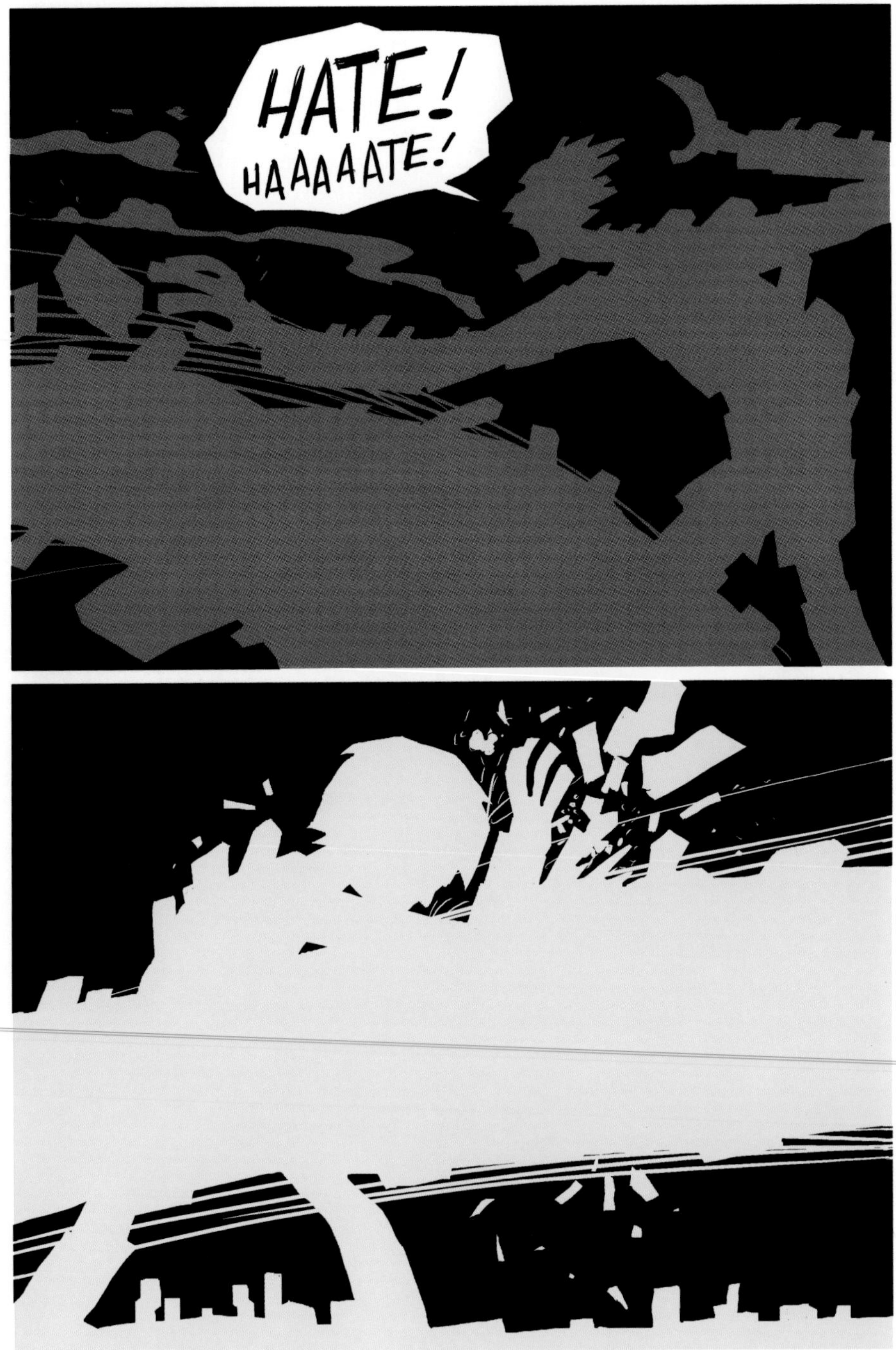
HATE! HAAAAATE!

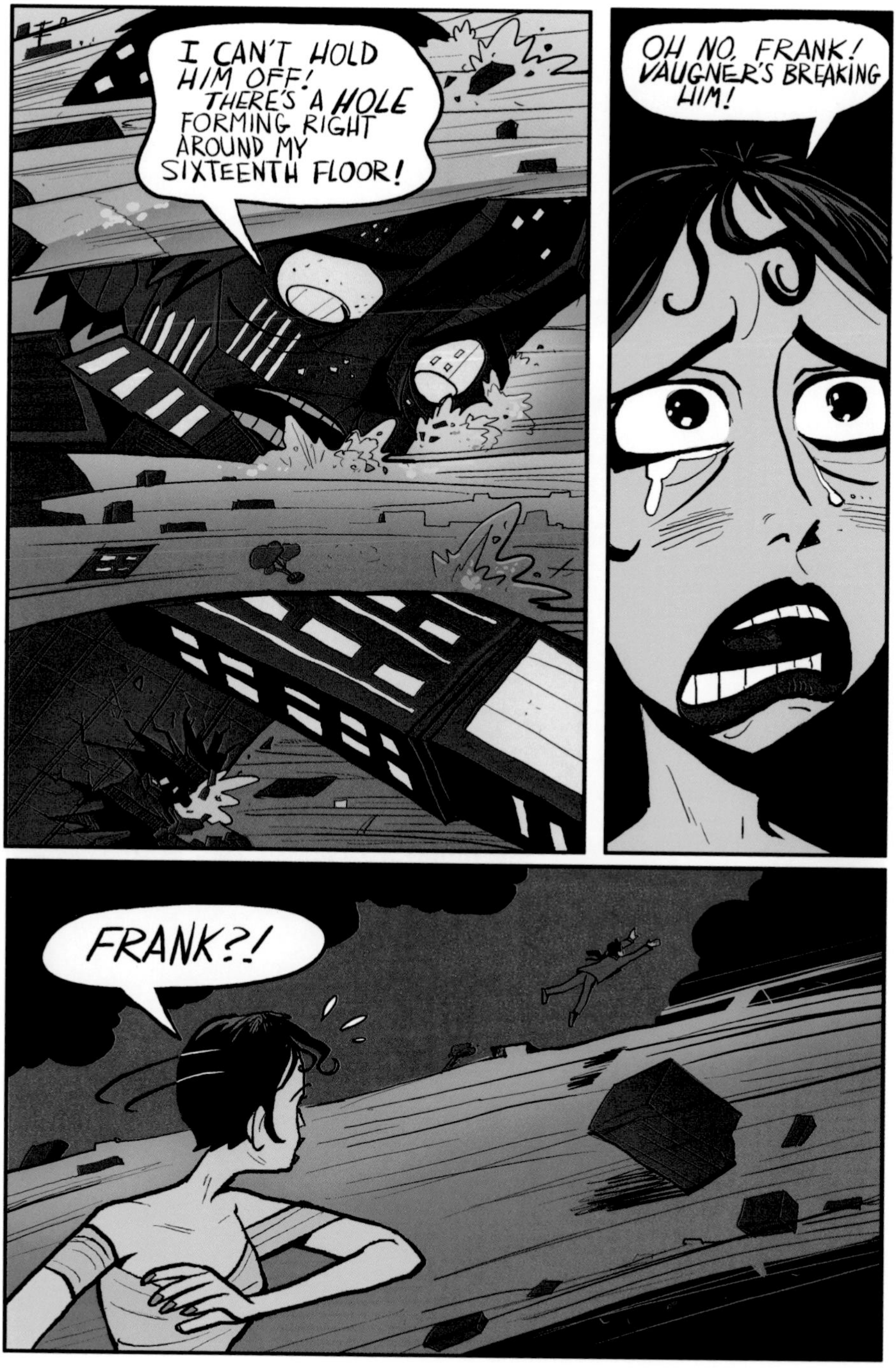
I CAN'T HOLD HIM OFF! THERE'S A HOLE FORMING RIGHT AROUND MY SIXTEENTH FLOOR!
OH NO, FRANK! VAUGNER'S BREAKING HIM!
FRANK?!

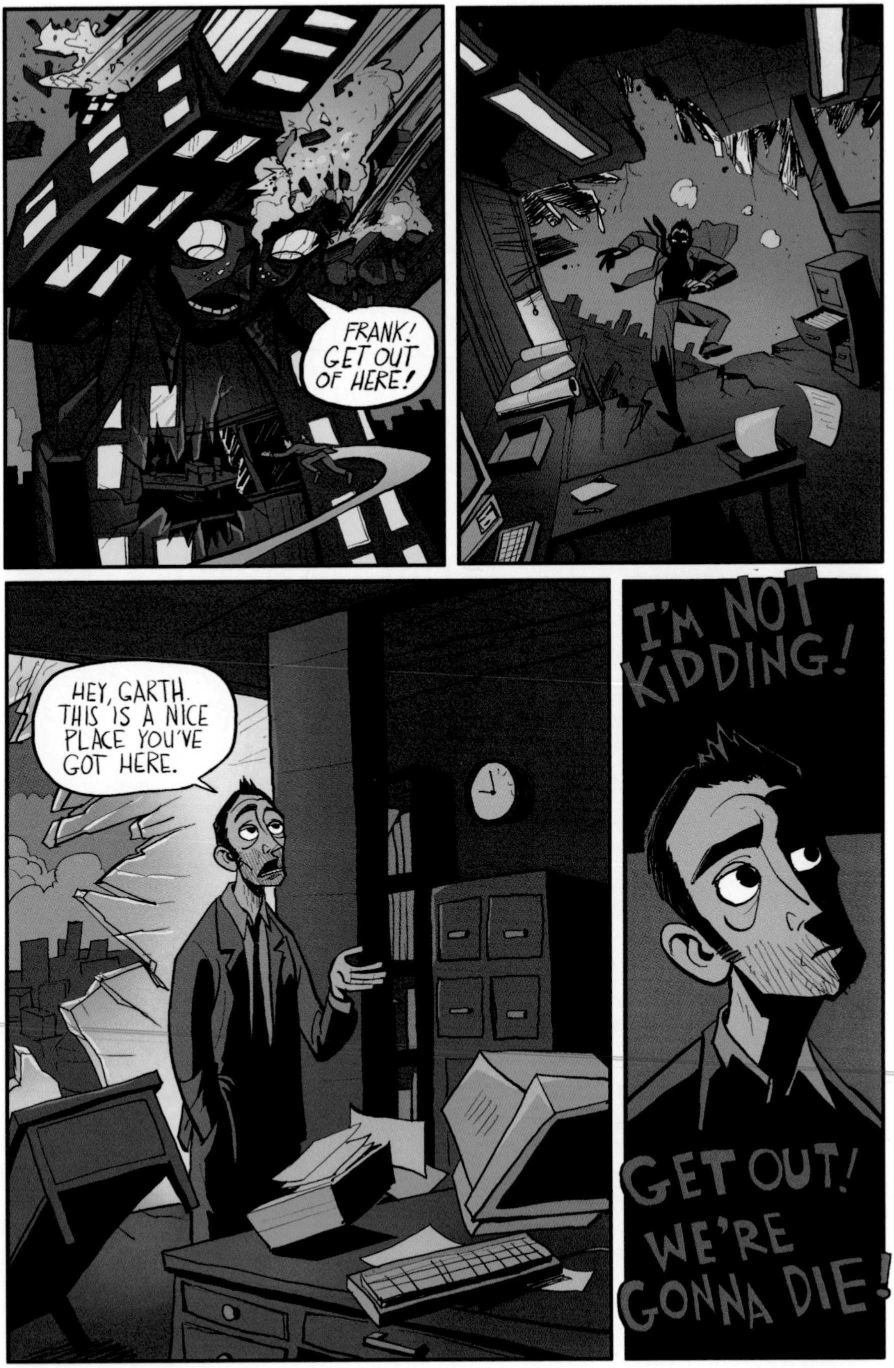
FRANK! GET OUT OF HERE!
HEY, GARTH. THIS IS A NICE PLACE YOU'VE GOT HERE.
I'M NOT KIDDING!
GET OUT! WE'RE GONNA DIE!

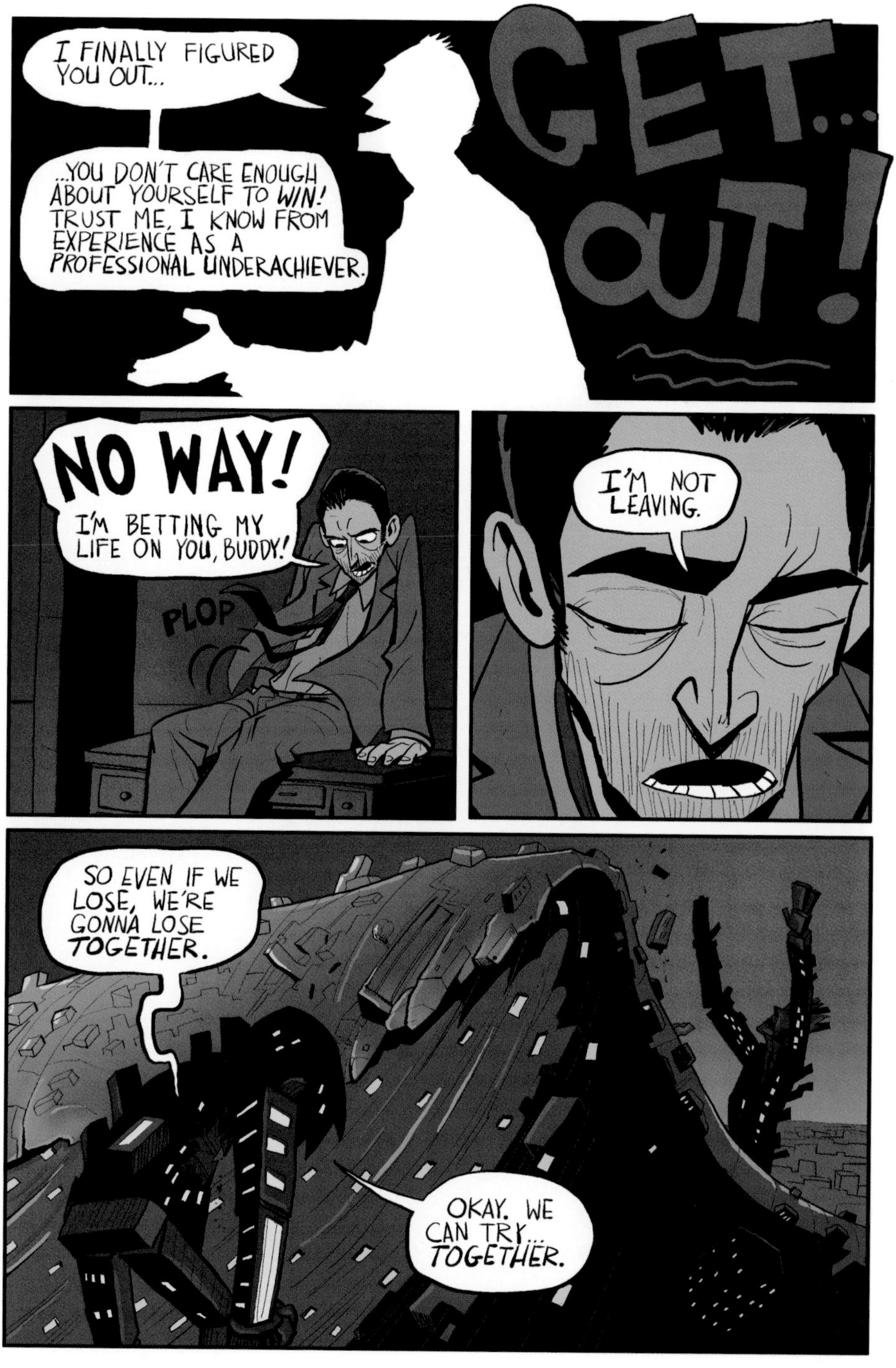
I FINALLY FIGURED YOU OUT...
...YOU DON'T CARE ENOUGH ABOUT YOURSELF TO WIN! TRUST ME, I KNOW FROM EXPERIENCE AS A PROFESSIONAL UNDERACHIEVER.
GET... OUT!
NO WAY!
I'M BETTING MY LIFE ON YOU, BUDDY!
PLOP
I'M NOT LEAVING.
SO EVEN IF WE LOSE, WE'RE GONNA LOSE TOGETHER.
OKAY. WE CAN TRY... TOGETHER.

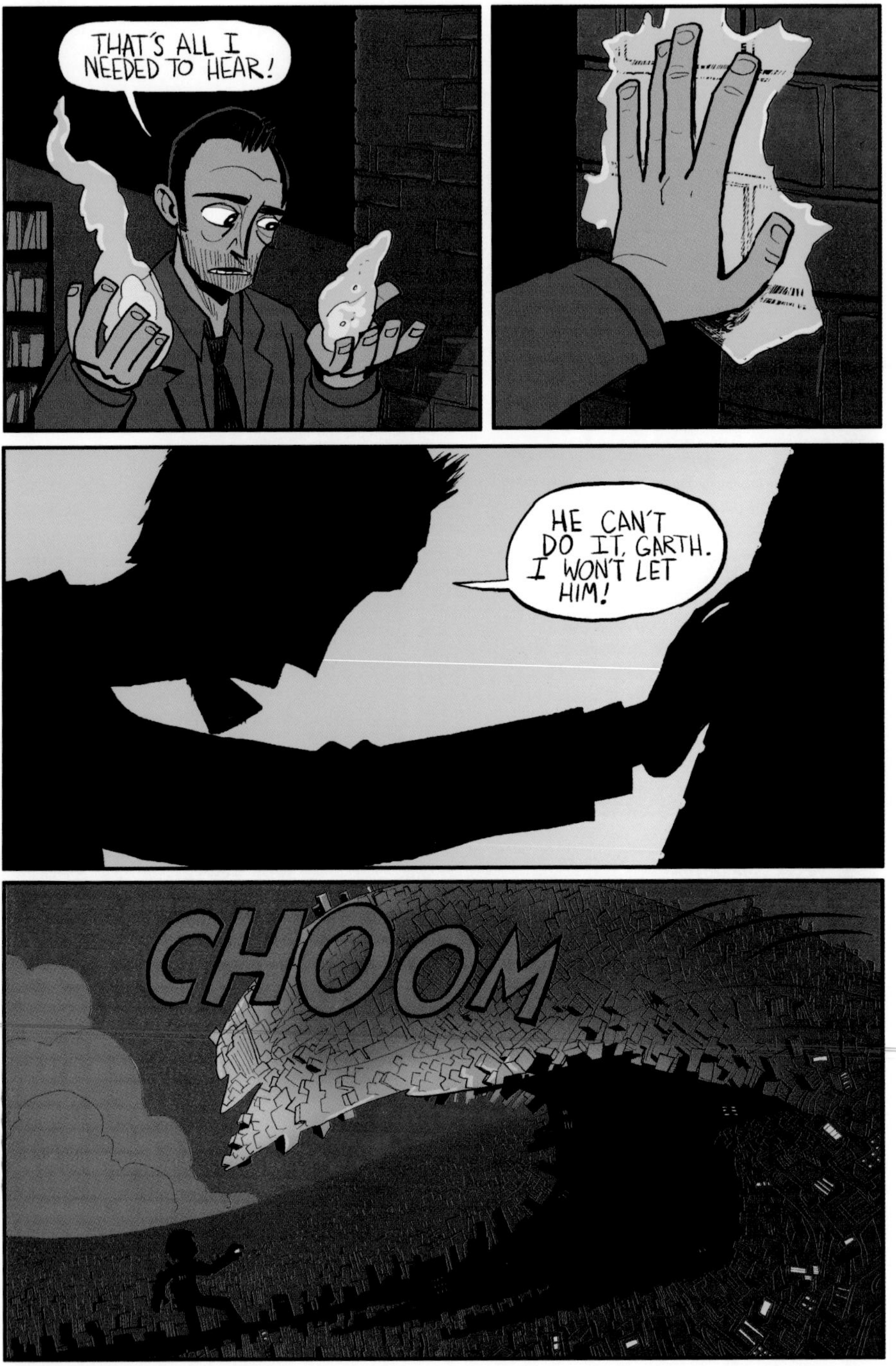
THAT'S ALL I NEEDED TO HEAR!
HE CAN'T DO IT, GARTH. I WON'T LET HIM!
CHOOM

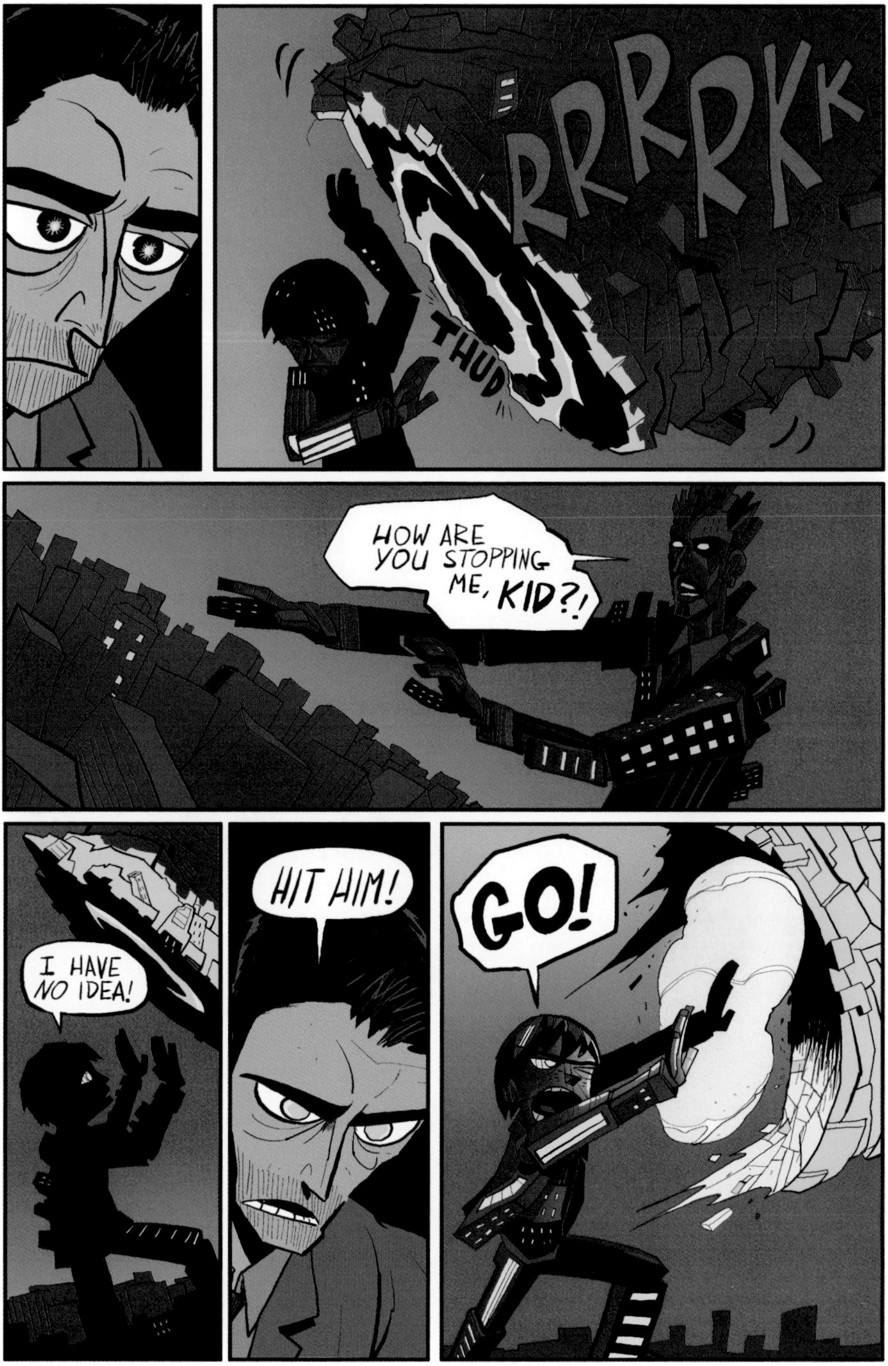
RRRRKK
THUD
HOW ARE YOU STOPPING ME, KID?!
I HAVE NO IDEA!
HIT HIM!
GO!

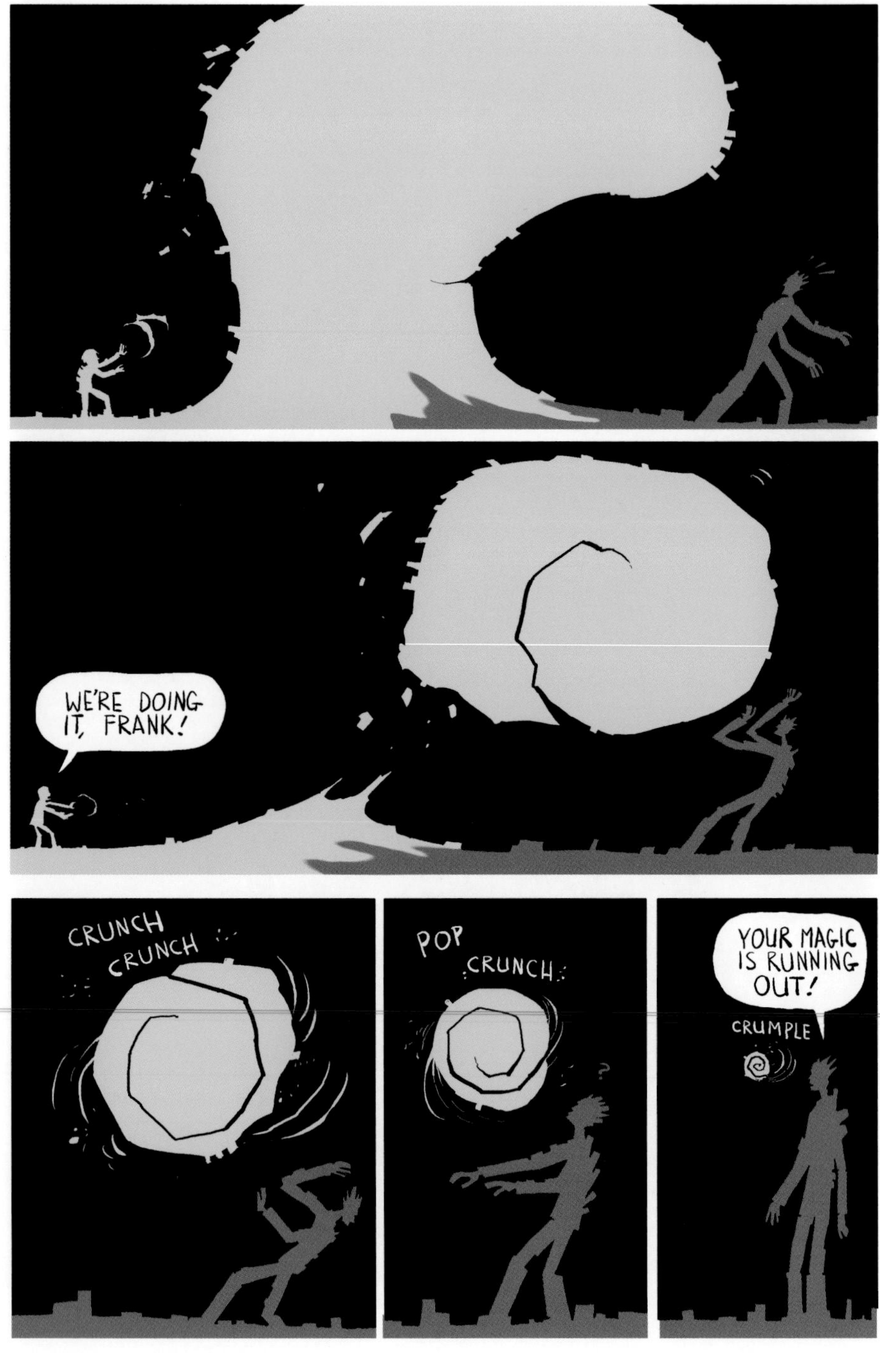
WE'RE DOING IT, FRANK!
CRUNCH
CRUNCH
POP
CRUNCH
YOUR MAGIC IS RUNNING OUT!
CRUMPLE

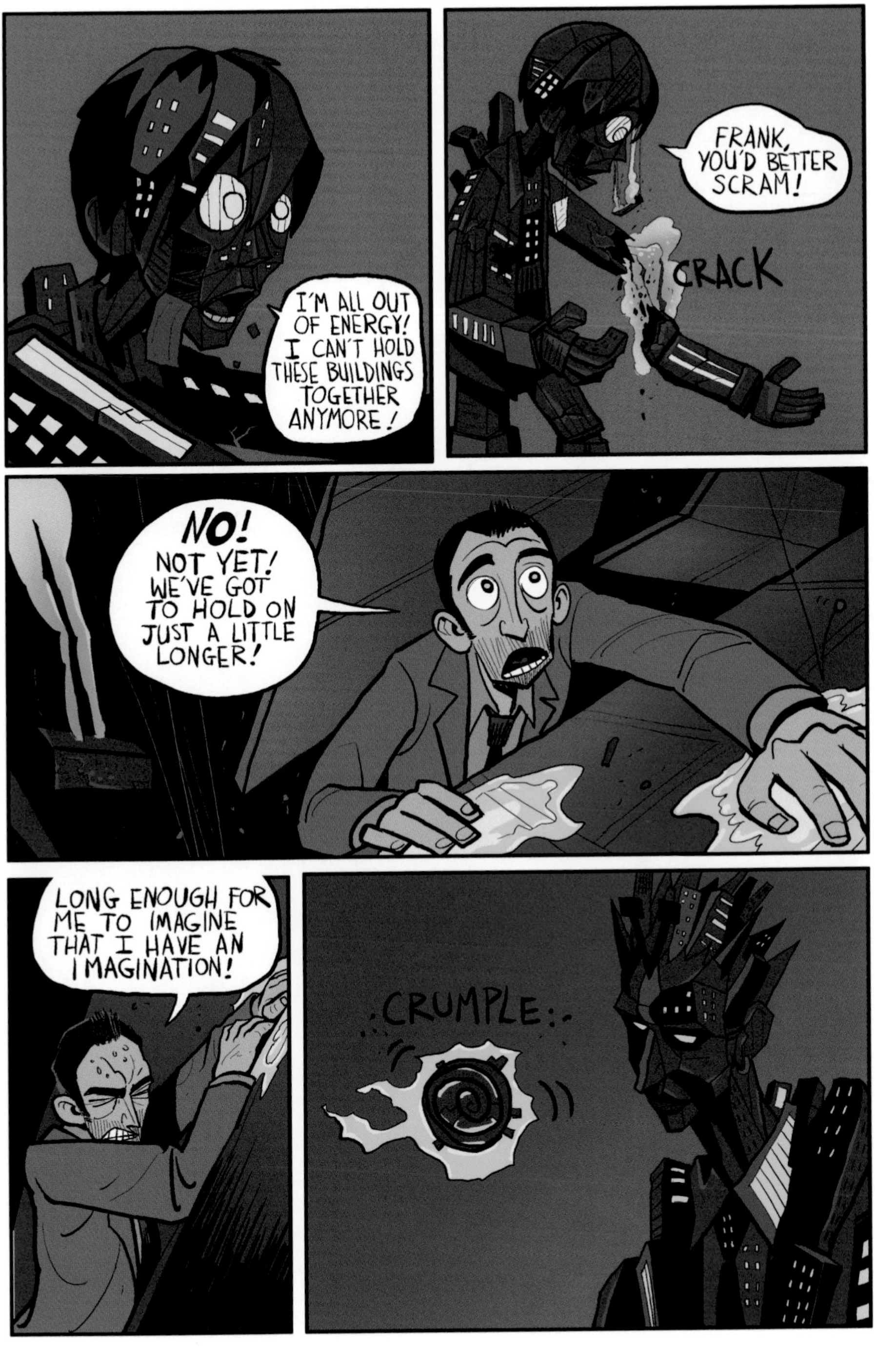
I'M ALL OUT OF ENERGY! I CAN'T HOLD THESE BUILDINGS TOGETHER ANYMORE!
FRANK, YOU'D BETTER SCRAM!
CRACK
NO! NOT YET! WE'VE GOT TO HOLD ON JUST A LITTLE LONGER!
LONG ENOUGH FOR ME TO IMAGINE THAT I HAVE AN IMAGINATION!
CRUMPLE

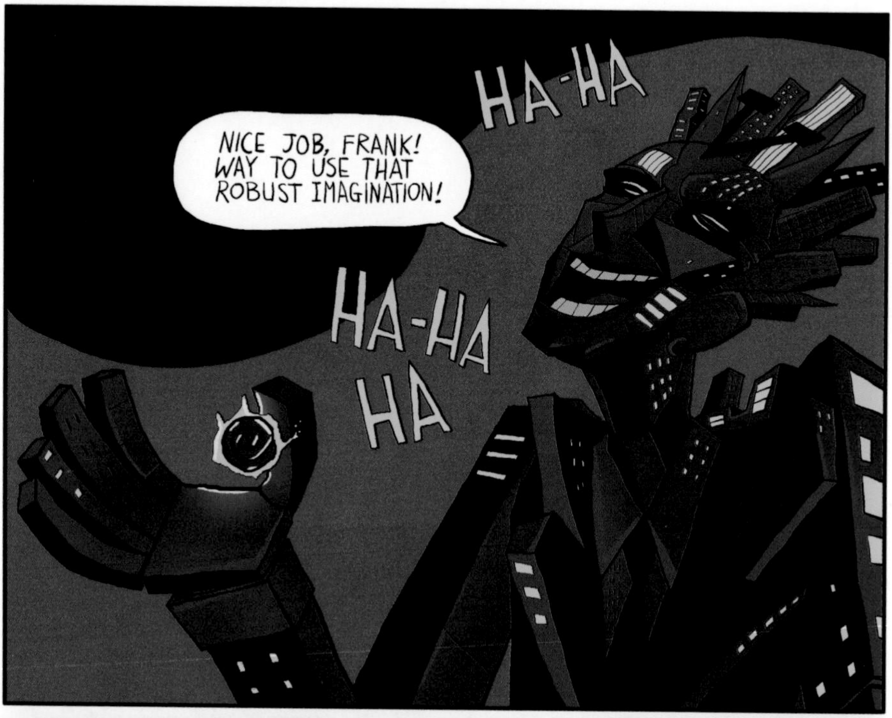
HA-HA
NICE JOB, FRANK! WAY TO USE THAT ROBUST IMAGINATION!
HA-HA HA

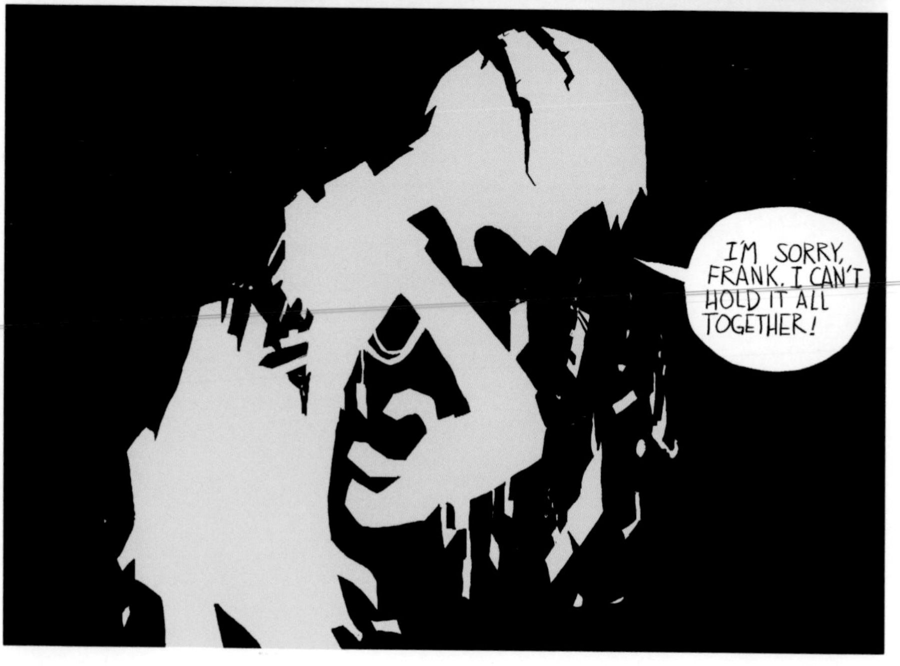
I'M SORRY, FRANK. I CAN'T HOLD IT ALL TOGETHER!

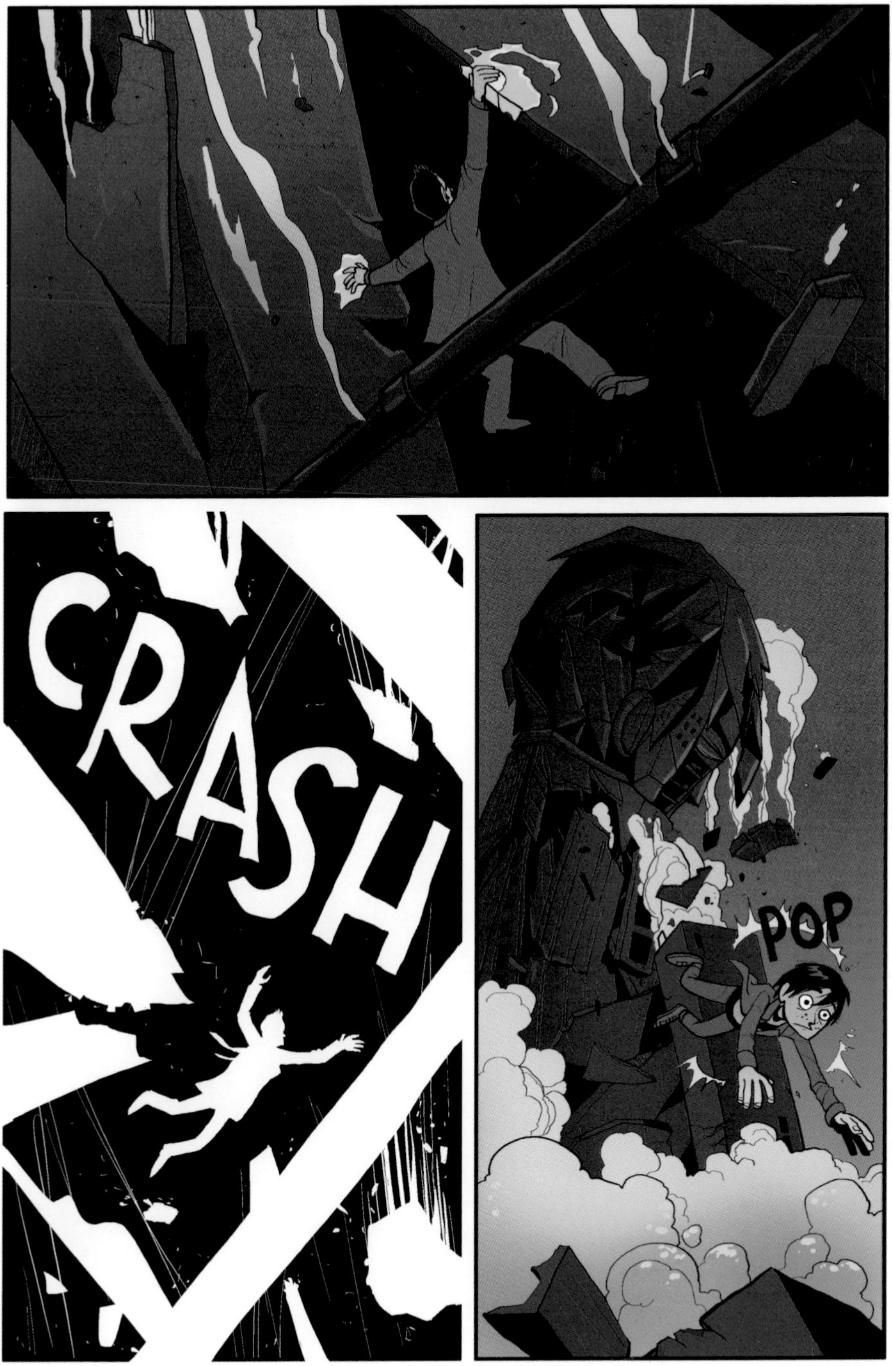
CRASH
POP

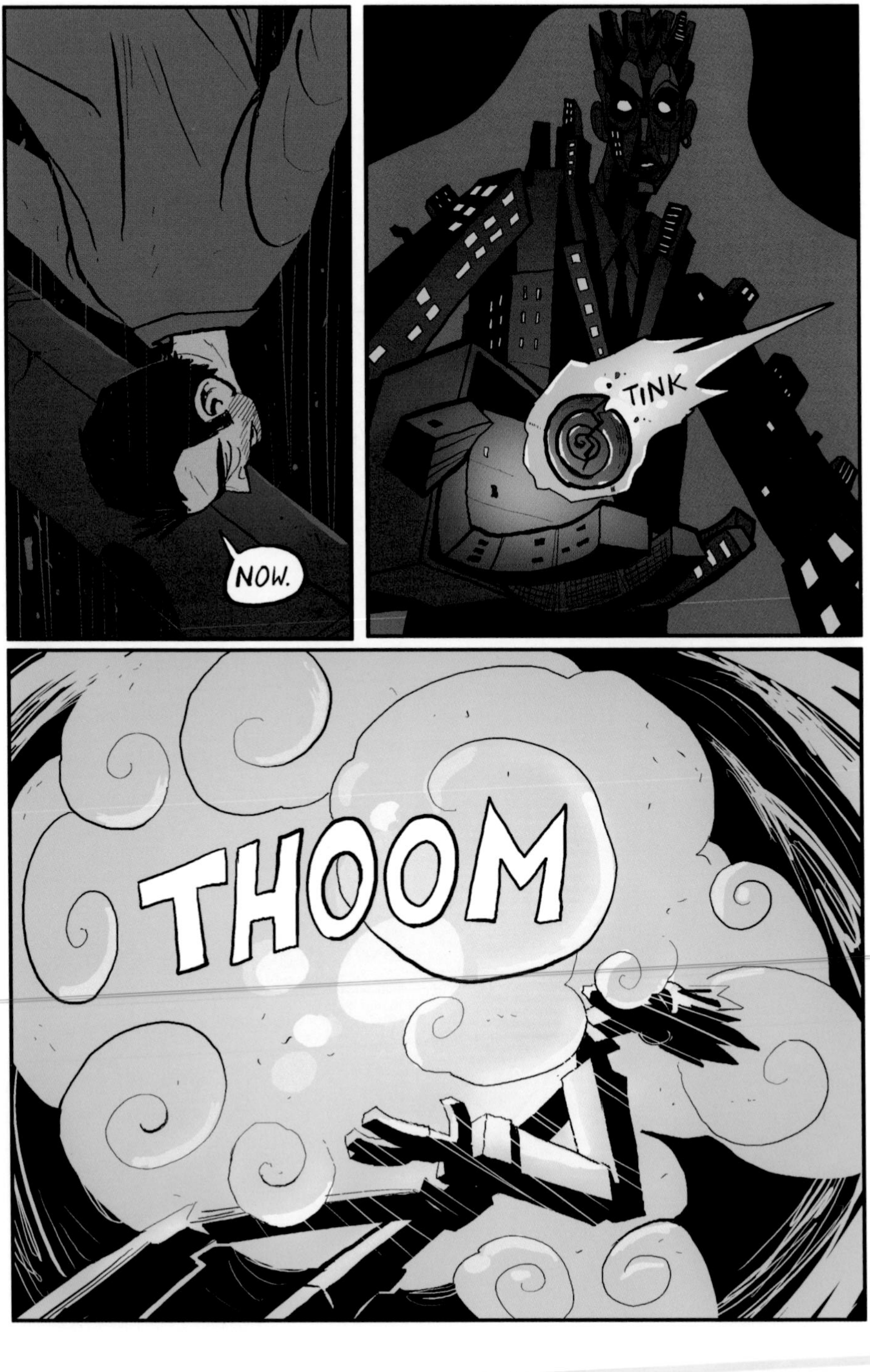
NOW.
TINK
THOOM

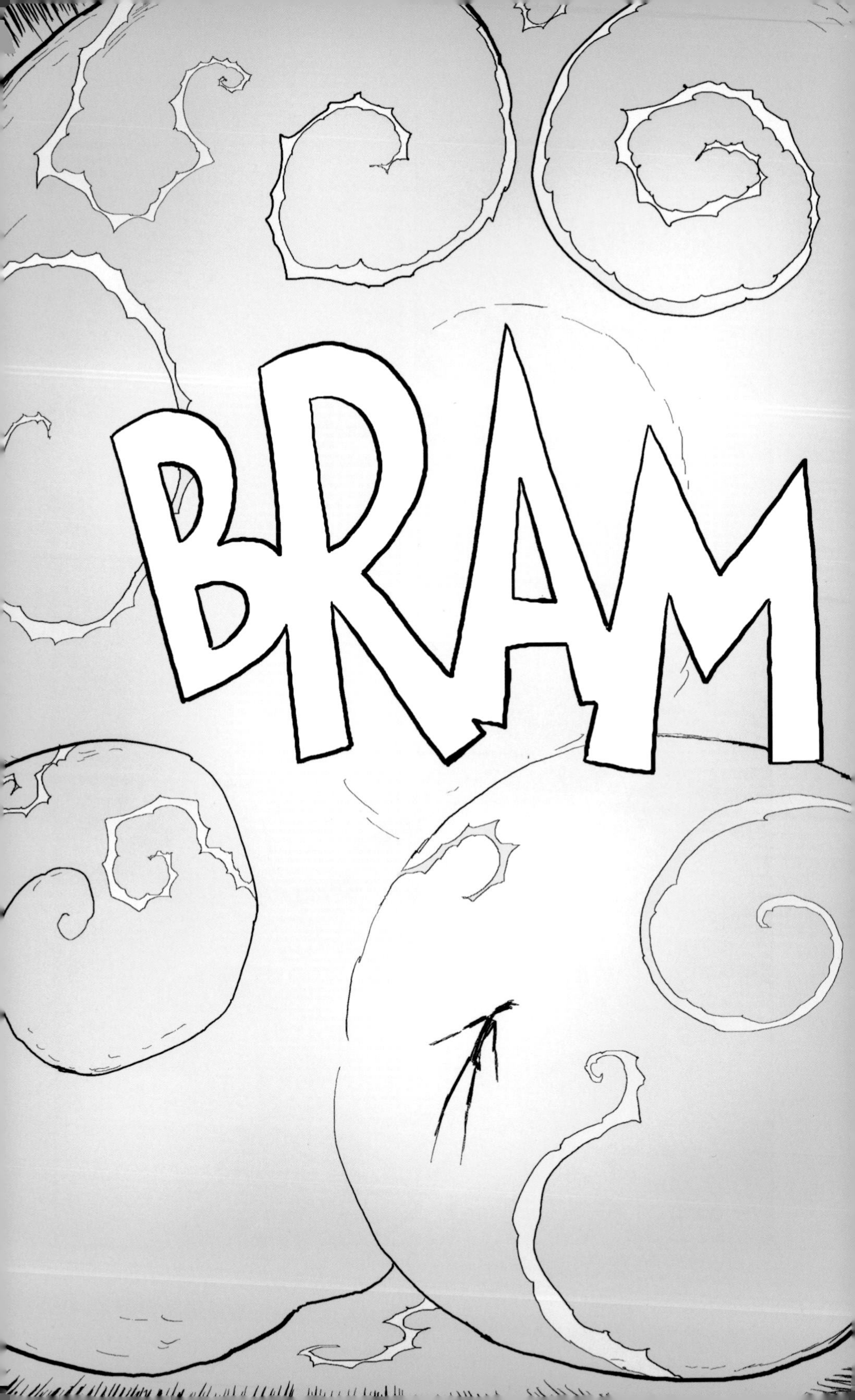
BRAM

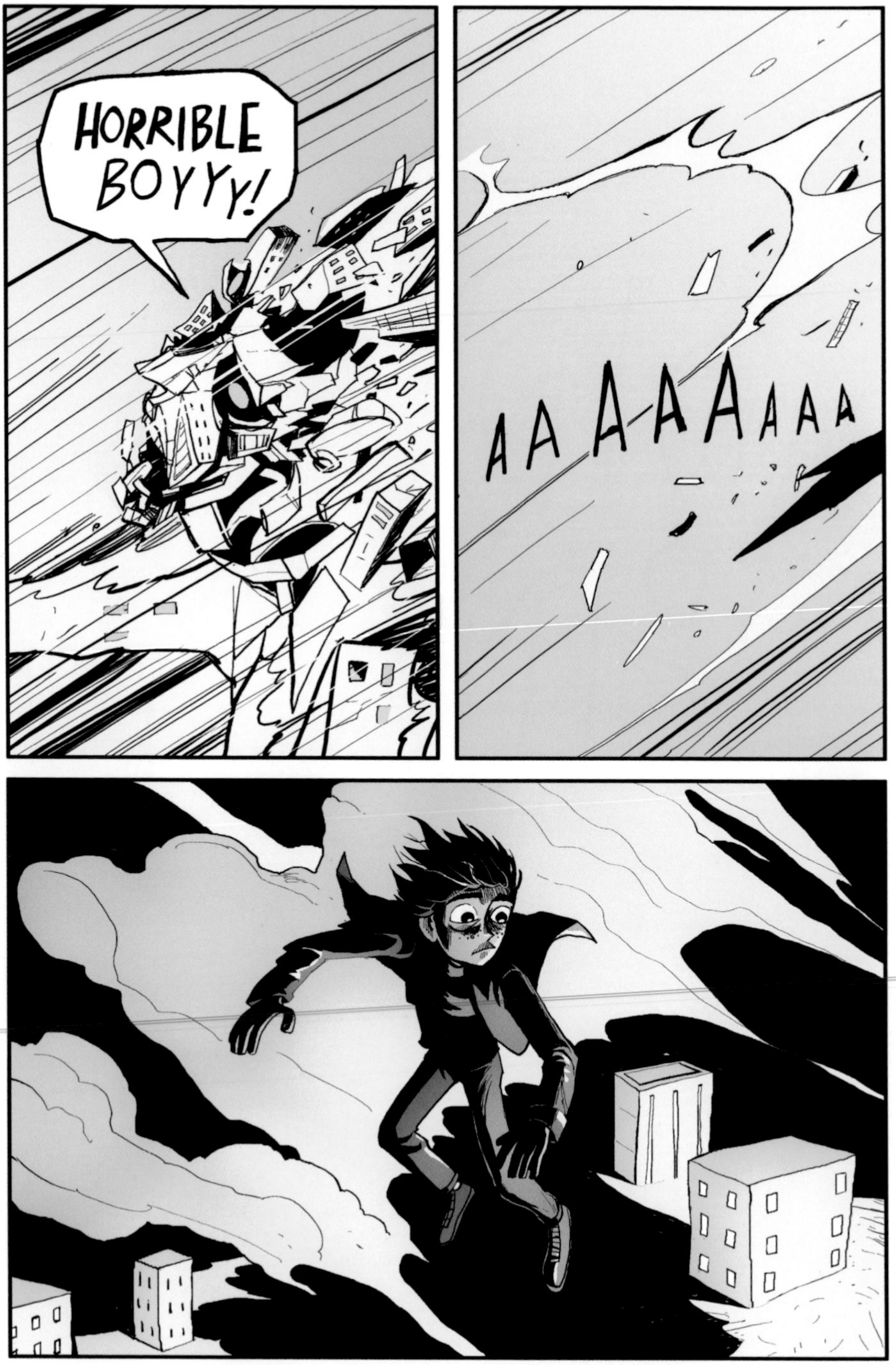
HORRIBLE BOYYY!
AAAAAAAA

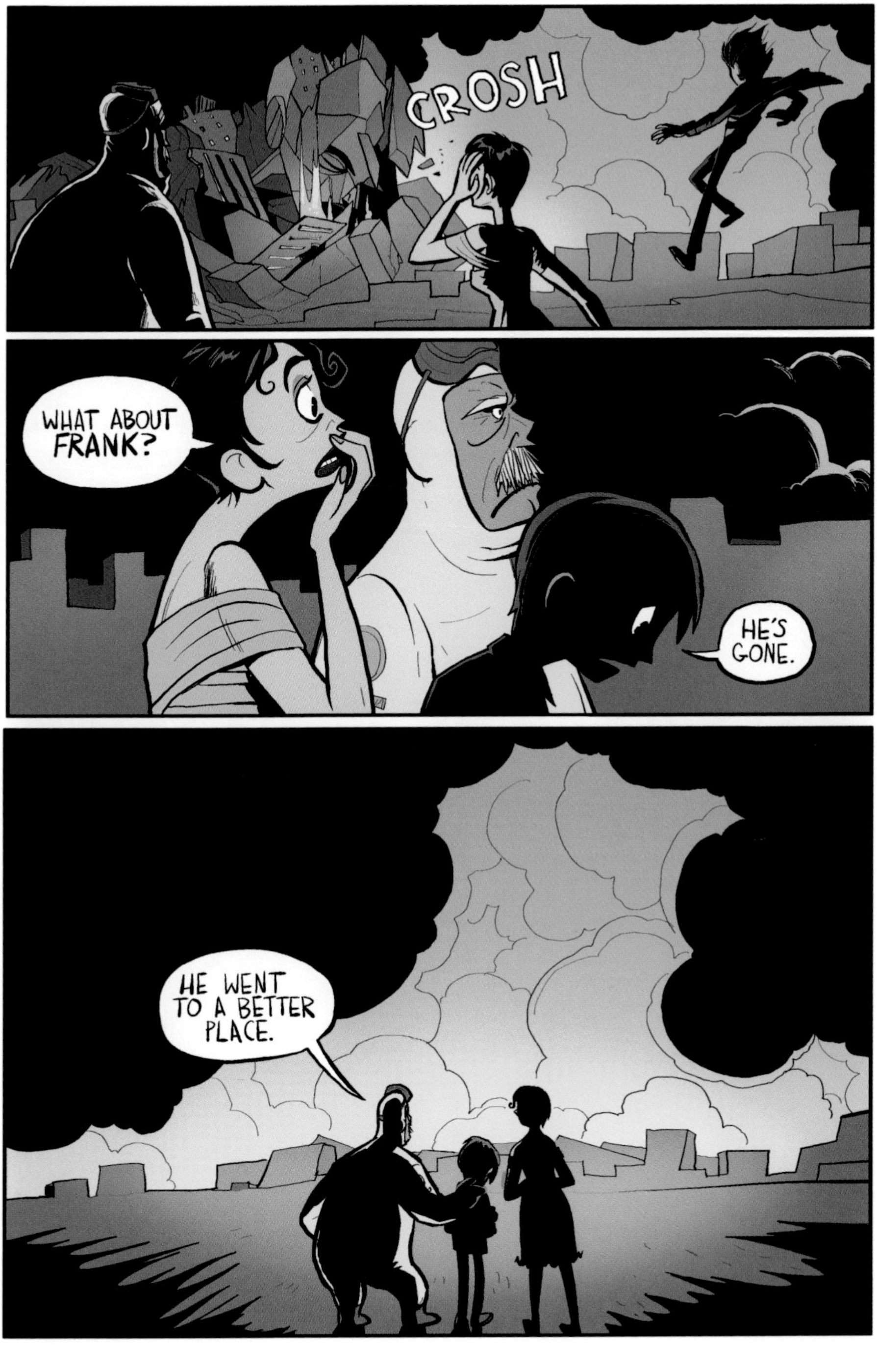
CROSH
WHAT ABOUT FRANK?
HE'S GONE.
HE WENT TO A BETTER PLACE.

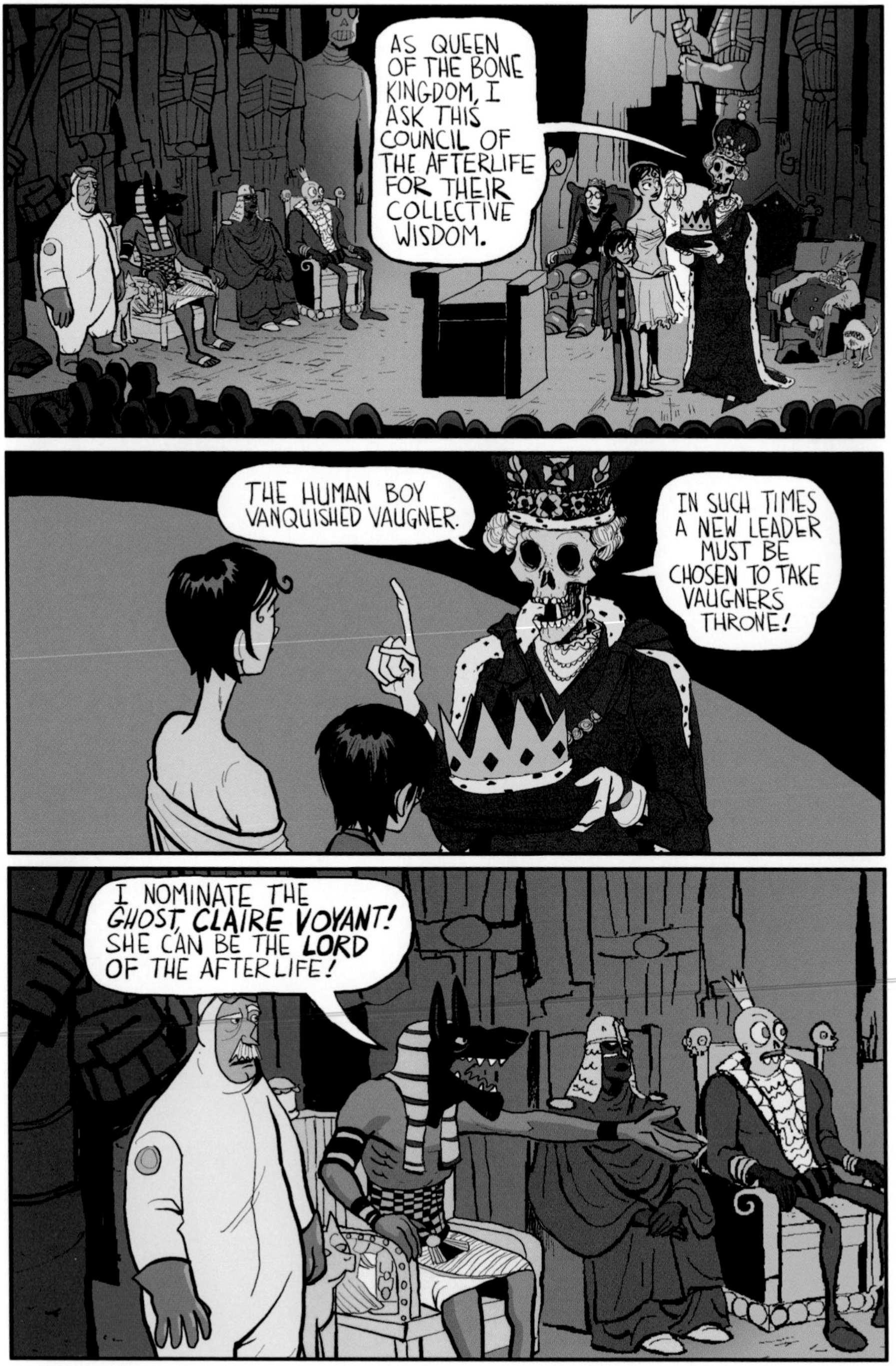
AS QUEEN OF THE BONE KINGDOM, I ASK THIS COUNCIL OF THE AFTERLIFE FOR THEIR COLLECTIVE WISDOM.
THE HUMAN BOY VANQUISHED VAUGNER.
IN SUCH TIMES A NEW LEADER MUST BE CHOSEN TO TAKE VAUGNER'S THRONE!
I NOMINATE THE GHOST, CLAIRE VOYANT! SHE CAN BE THE LORD OF THE AFTERLIFE!

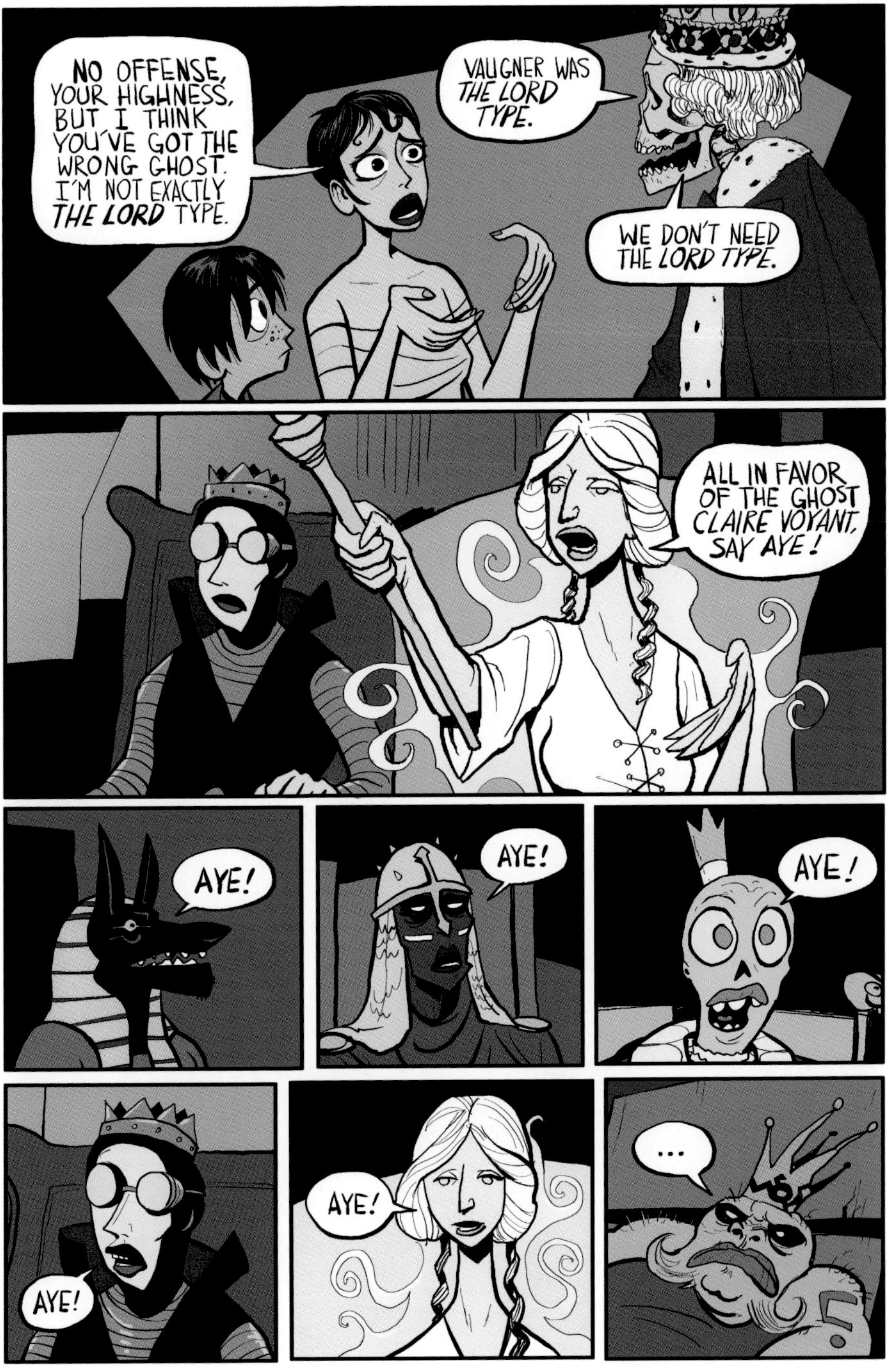
NO OFFENSE, YOUR HIGHNESS, BUT I THINK YOU'VE GOT THE WRONG GHOST. I'M NOT EXACTLY *THE LORD* TYPE.
VAUGNER WAS *THE LORD TYPE.*
WE DON'T NEED THE *LORD TYPE.*
ALL IN FAVOR OF THE GHOST *CLAIRE VOYANT,* SAY *AYE!*
AYE!
AYE!
AYE!
AYE!
AYE!
...

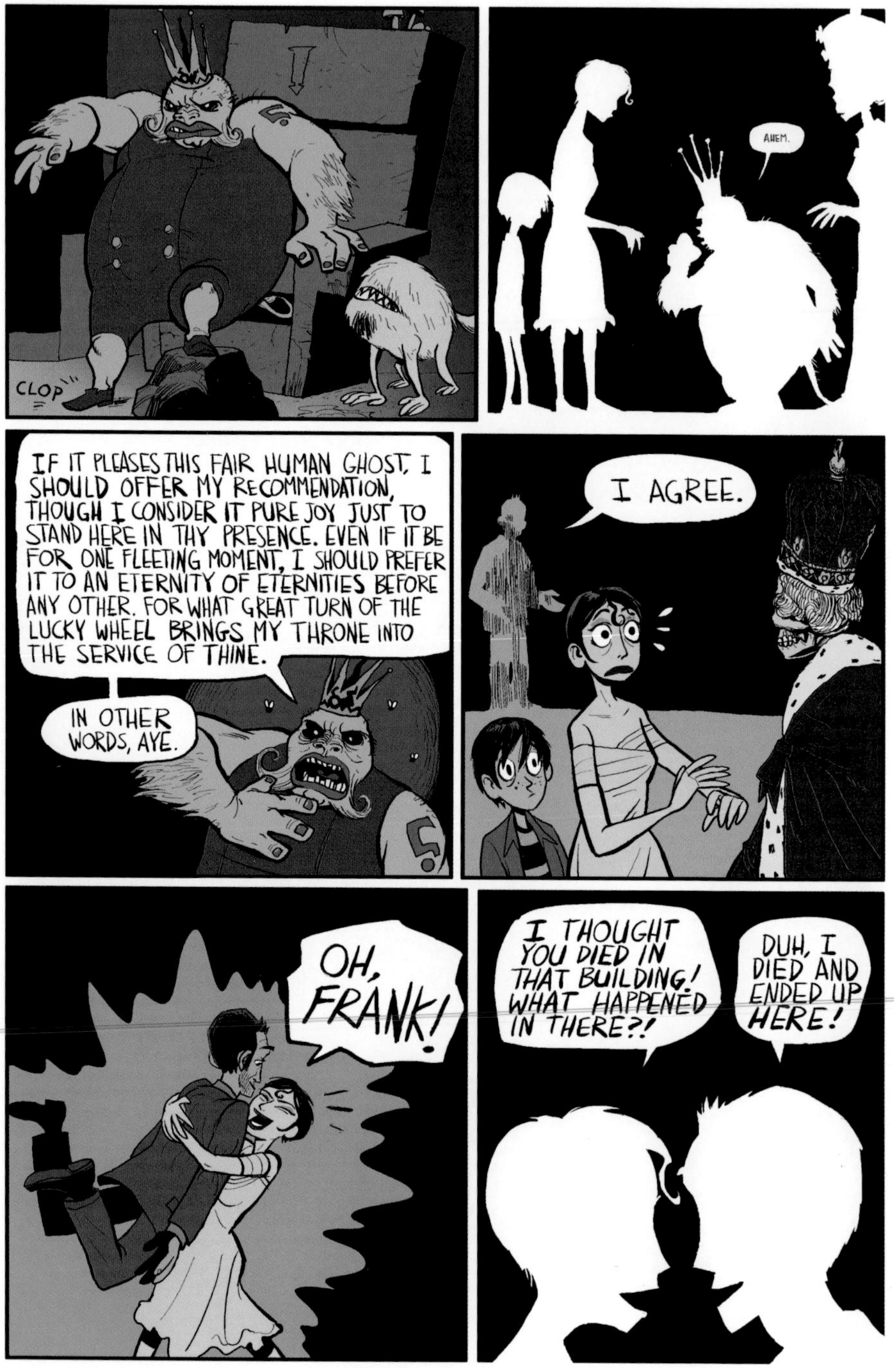
CLOP
AHEM.
IF IT PLEASES THIS FAIR HUMAN GHOST, I SHOULD OFFER MY RECOMMENDATION, THOUGH I CONSIDER IT PURE JOY JUST TO STAND HERE IN THY PRESENCE. EVEN IF IT BE FOR ONE FLEETING MOMENT, I SHOULD PREFER IT TO AN ETERNITY OF ETERNITIES BEFORE ANY OTHER. FOR WHAT GREAT TURN OF THE LUCKY WHEEL BRINGS MY THRONE INTO THE SERVICE OF THINE.
IN OTHER WORDS, AYE.
I AGREE.
OH, FRANK!
I THOUGHT YOU DIED IN THAT BUILDING! WHAT HAPPENED IN THERE?!
DUH, I DIED AND ENDED UP HERE!

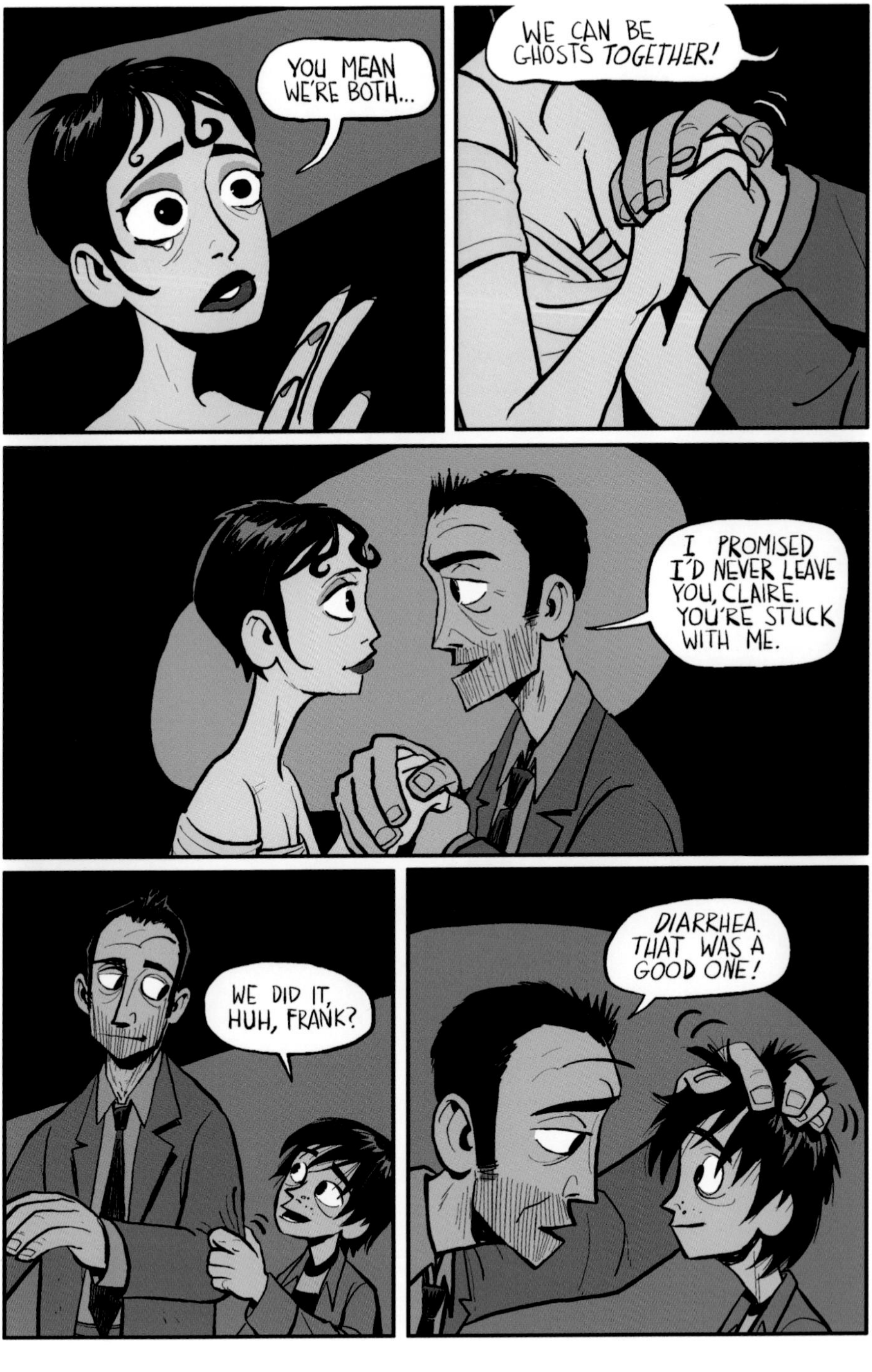
YOU MEAN WE'RE BOTH...
WE CAN BE GHOSTS TOGETHER!
I PROMISED I'D NEVER LEAVE YOU, CLAIRE. YOU'RE STUCK WITH ME.
WE DID IT, HUH, FRANK?
DIARRHEA. THAT WAS A GOOD ONE!

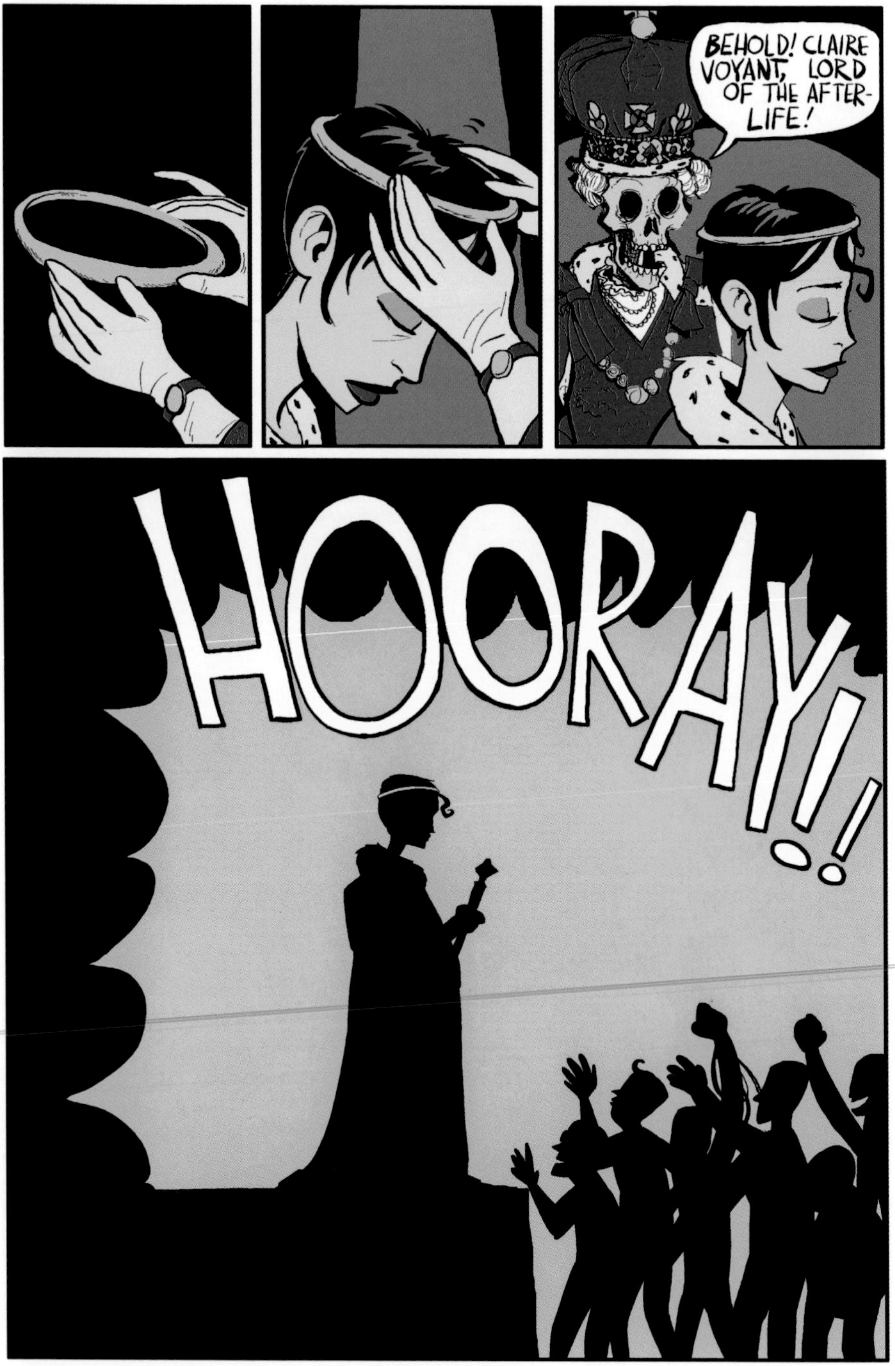
BEHOLD! CLAIRE VOYANT, LORD OF THE AFTER-LIFE!
HOORAY!!!

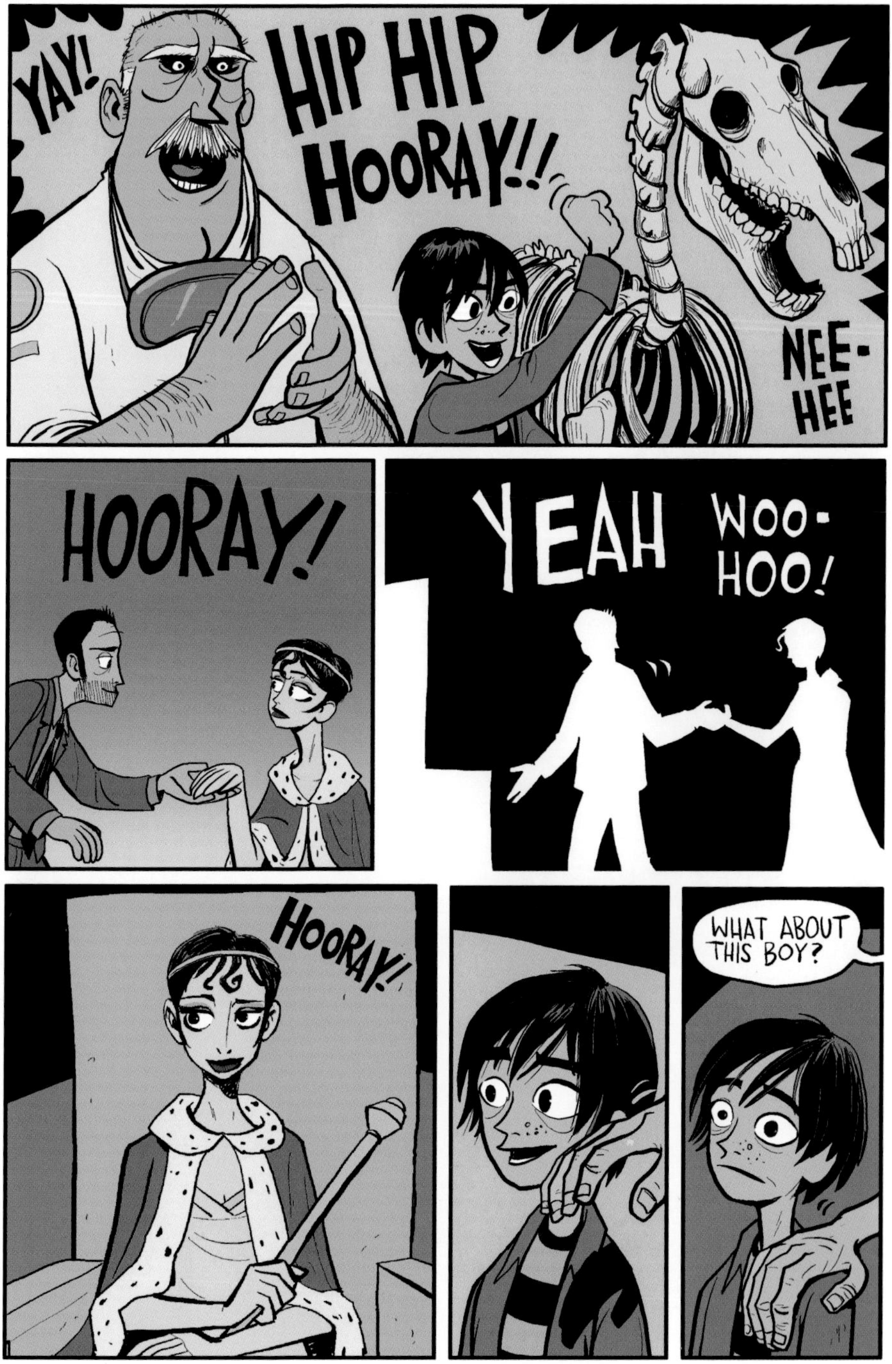
YAY!
HIP HIP HOORAY!!!
NEE-HEE
HOORAY!
YEAH
WOO-HOO!
HOORAY!
WHAT ABOUT THIS BOY?

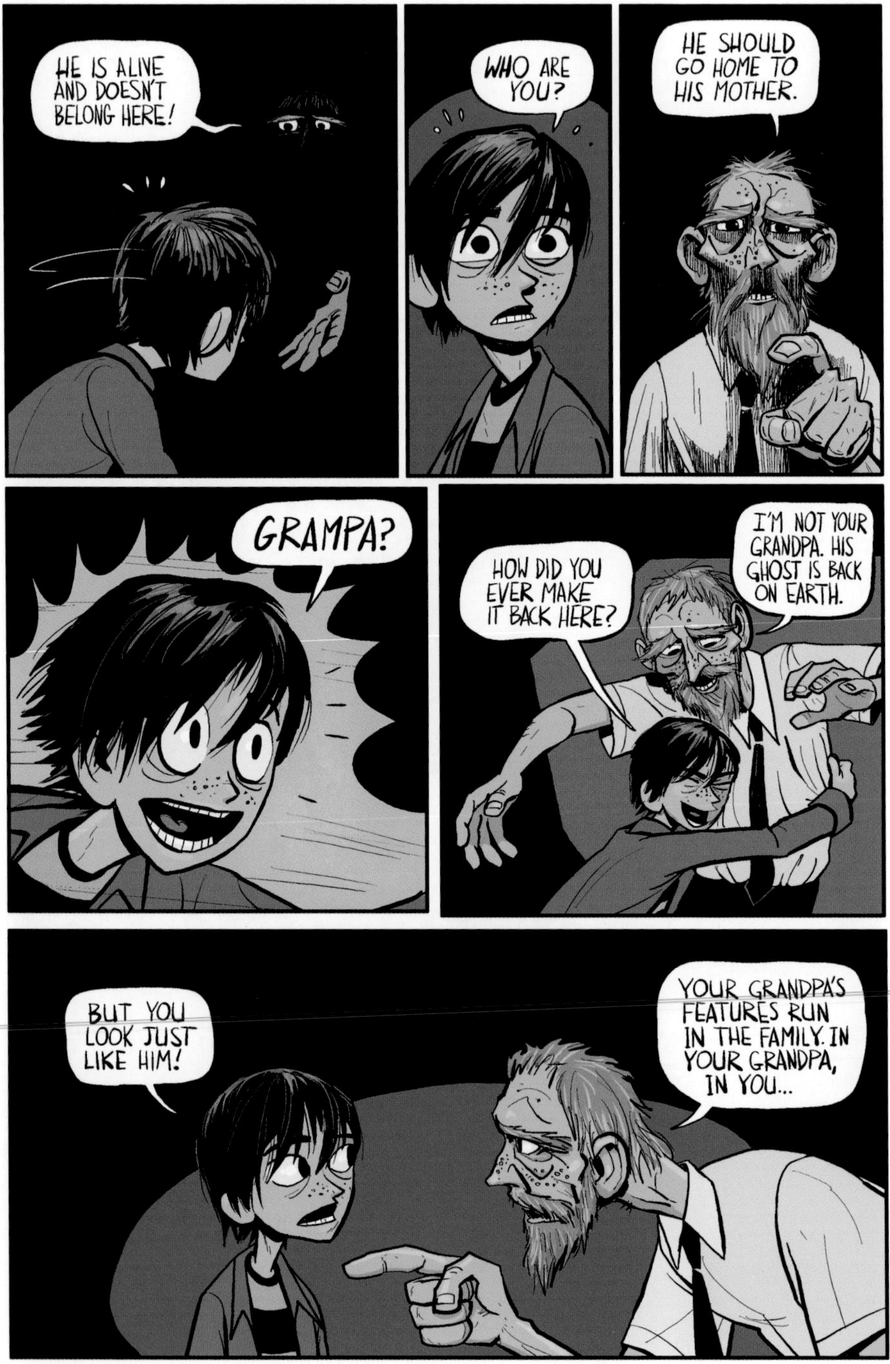
HE IS ALIVE AND DOESN'T BELONG HERE!
WHO ARE YOU?
HE SHOULD GO HOME TO HIS MOTHER.
GRAMPA?
HOW DID YOU EVER MAKE IT BACK HERE?
I'M NOT YOUR GRANDPA. HIS GHOST IS BACK ON EARTH.
BUT YOU LOOK JUST LIKE HIM!
YOUR GRANDPA'S FEATURES RUN IN THE FAMILY. IN YOUR GRANDPA, IN YOU...

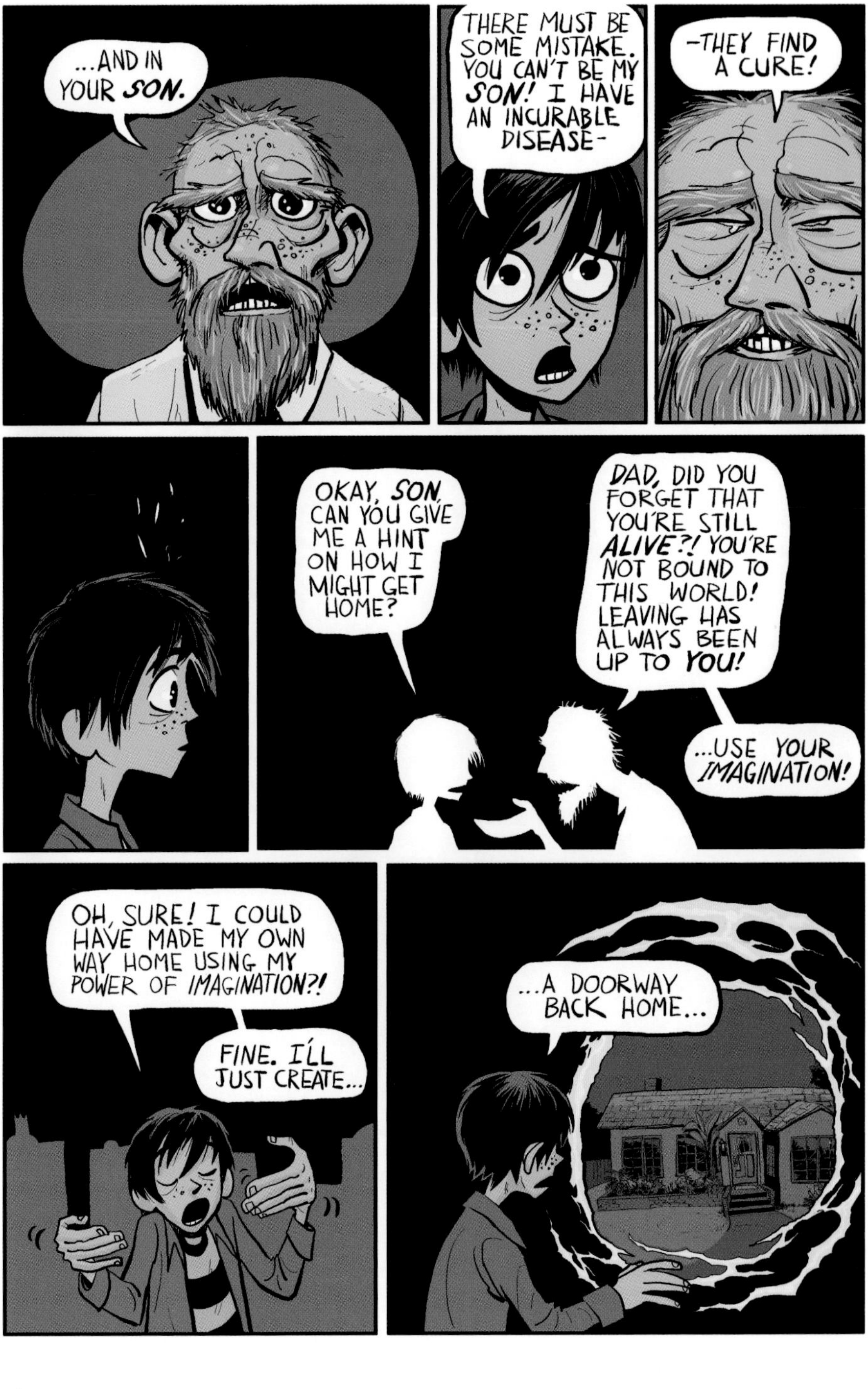
...AND IN YOUR SON.
THERE MUST BE SOME MISTAKE. YOU CAN'T BE MY SON! I HAVE AN INCURABLE DISEASE-
-THEY FIND A CURE!
OKAY, SON, CAN YOU GIVE ME A HINT ON HOW I MIGHT GET HOME?
DAD, DID YOU FORGET THAT YOU'RE STILL ALIVE?! YOU'RE NOT BOUND TO THIS WORLD! LEAVING HAS ALWAYS BEEN UP TO YOU!
...USE YOUR IMAGINATION!
OH, SURE! I COULD HAVE MADE MY OWN WAY HOME USING MY POWER OF IMAGINATION?!
FINE. I'LL JUST CREATE...
...A DOORWAY BACK HOME...

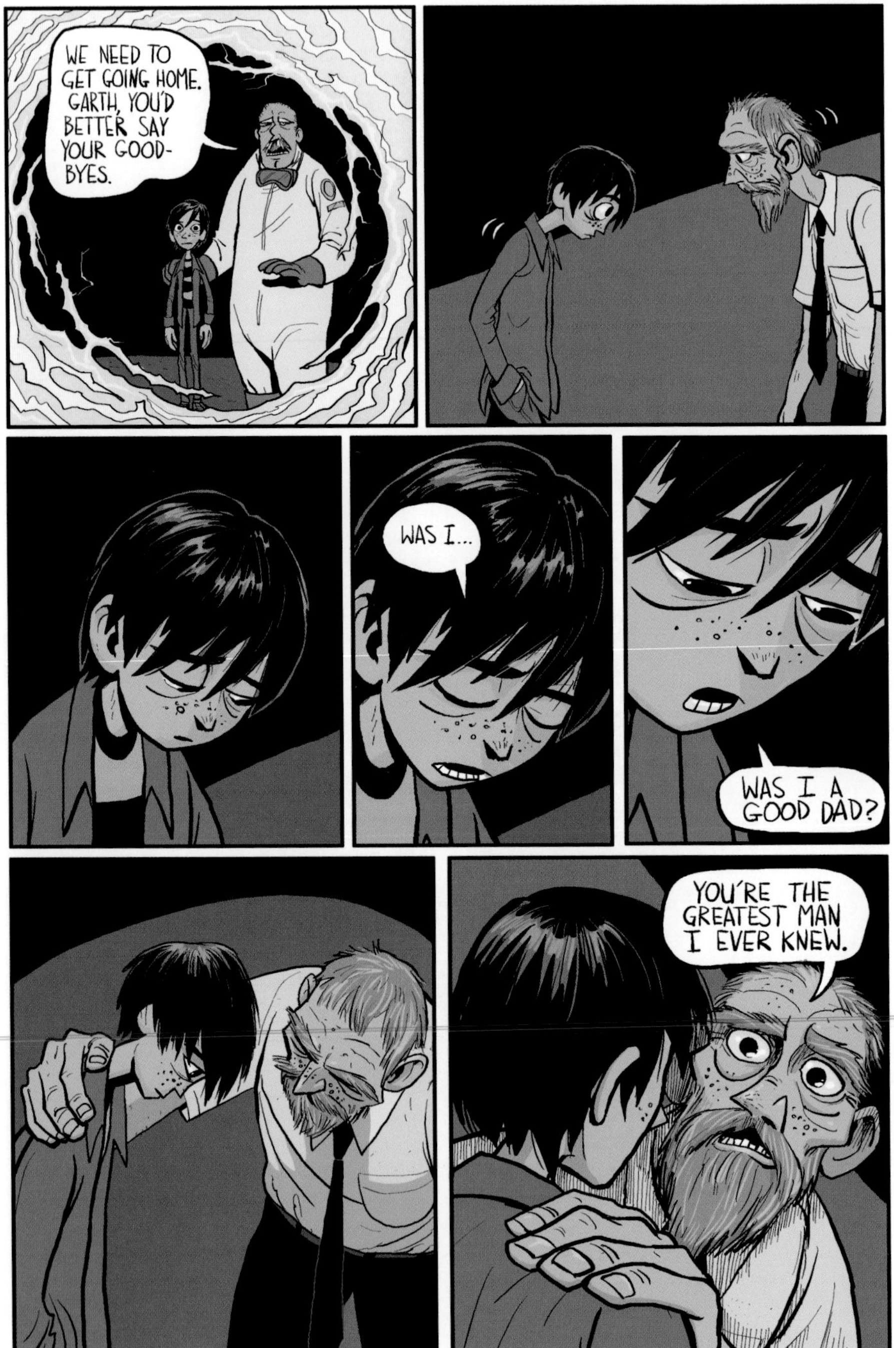
WE NEED TO GET GOING HOME. GARTH, YOU'D BETTER SAY YOUR GOOD-BYES.
WAS I...
WAS I A GOOD DAD?
YOU'RE THE GREATEST MAN I EVER KNEW.

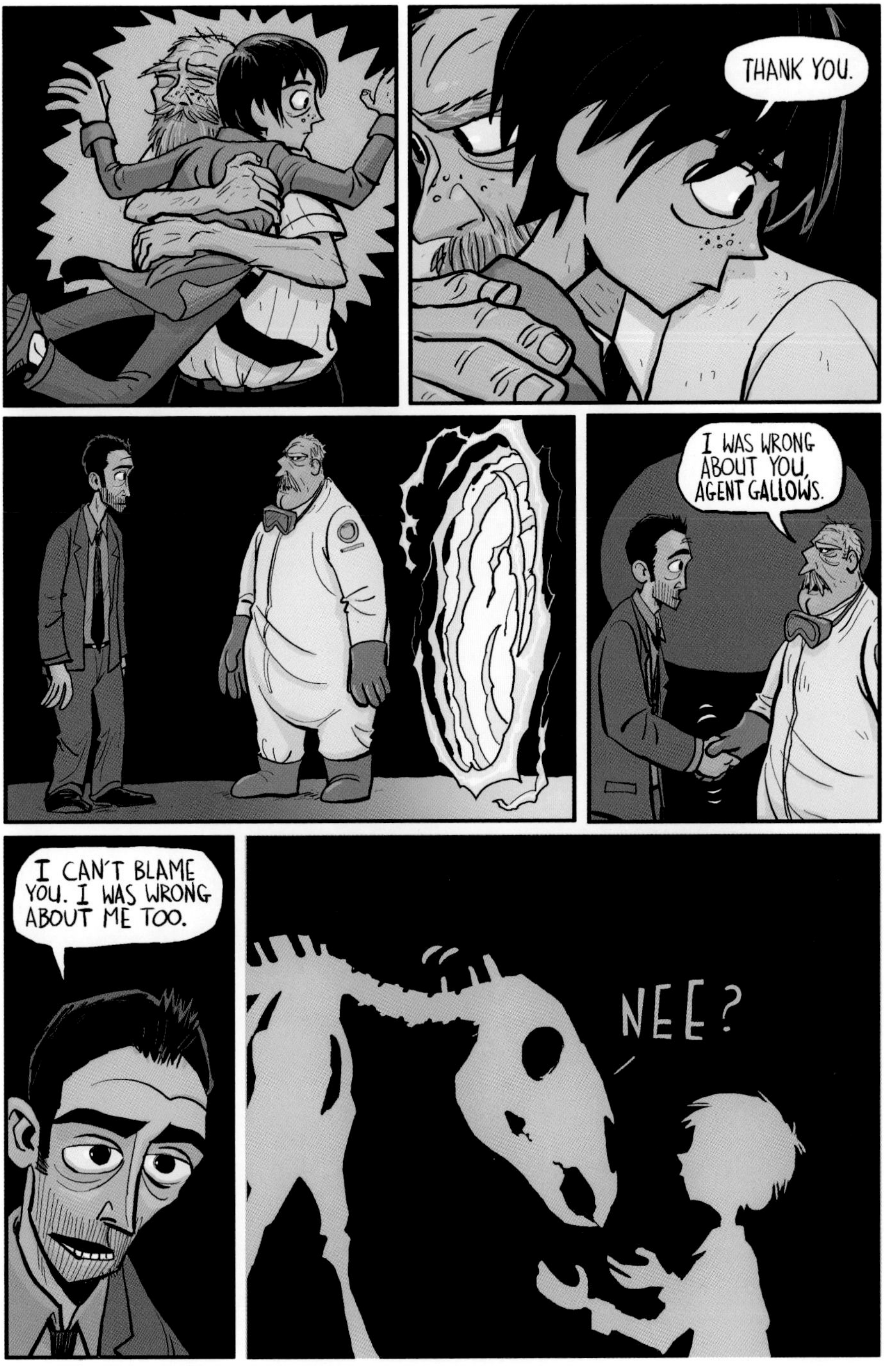
THANK YOU.
I WAS WRONG ABOUT YOU, AGENT GALLOWS.
I CAN'T BLAME YOU. I WAS WRONG ABOUT ME TOO.
NEE?

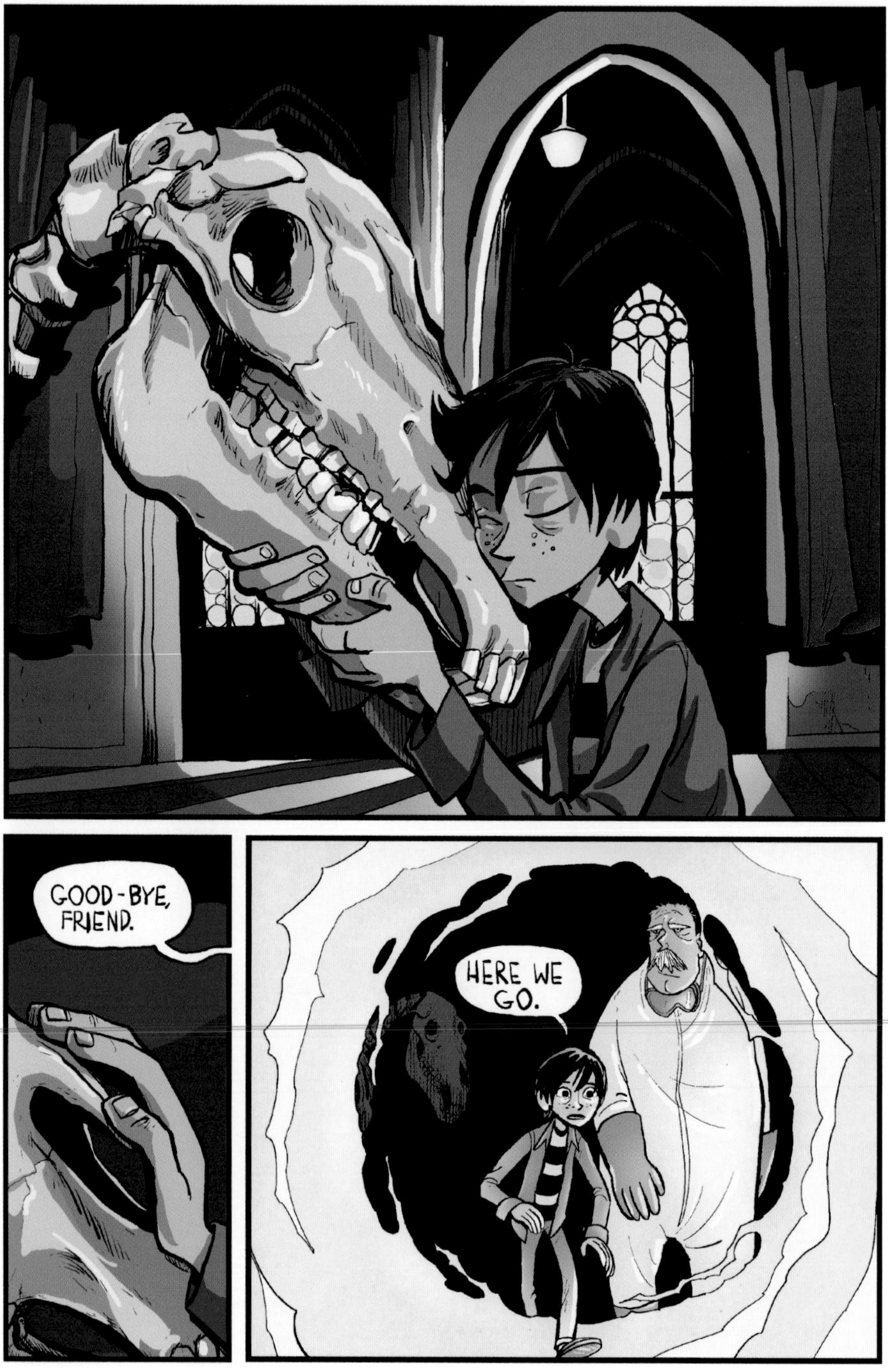
GOOD-BYE, FRIEND.
HERE WE GO.

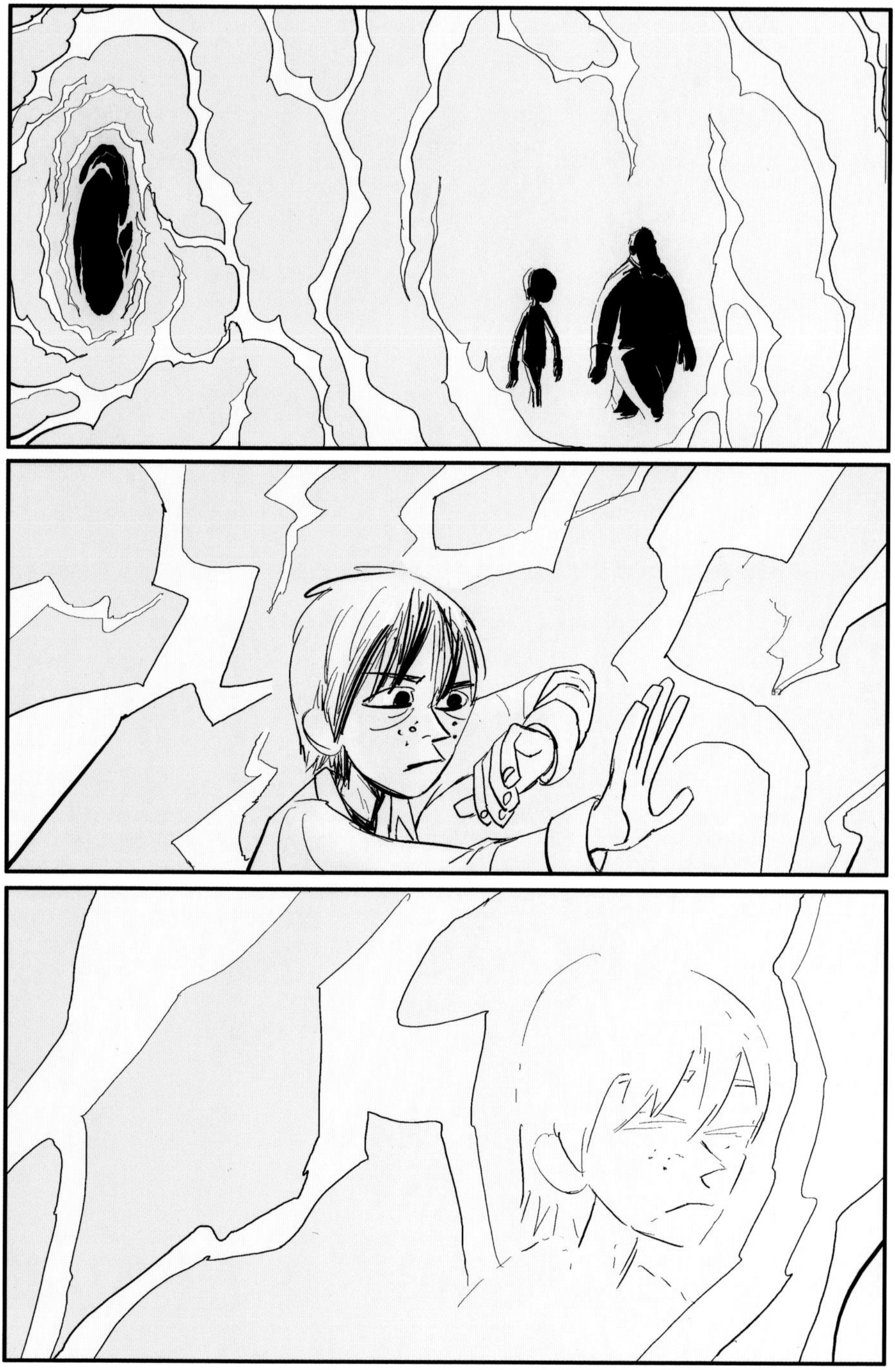

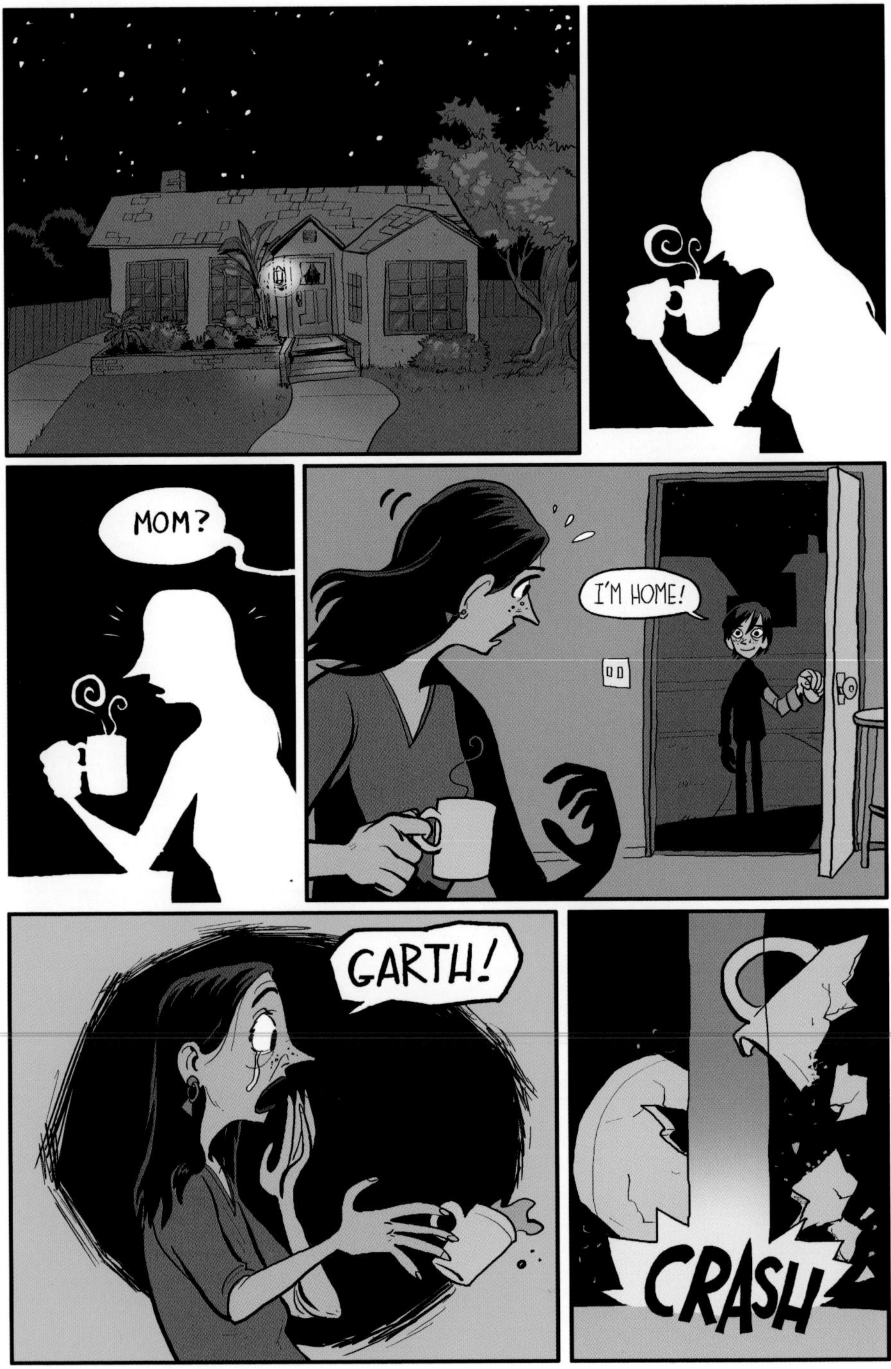
MOM?
I'M HOME!
GARTH!
CRASH

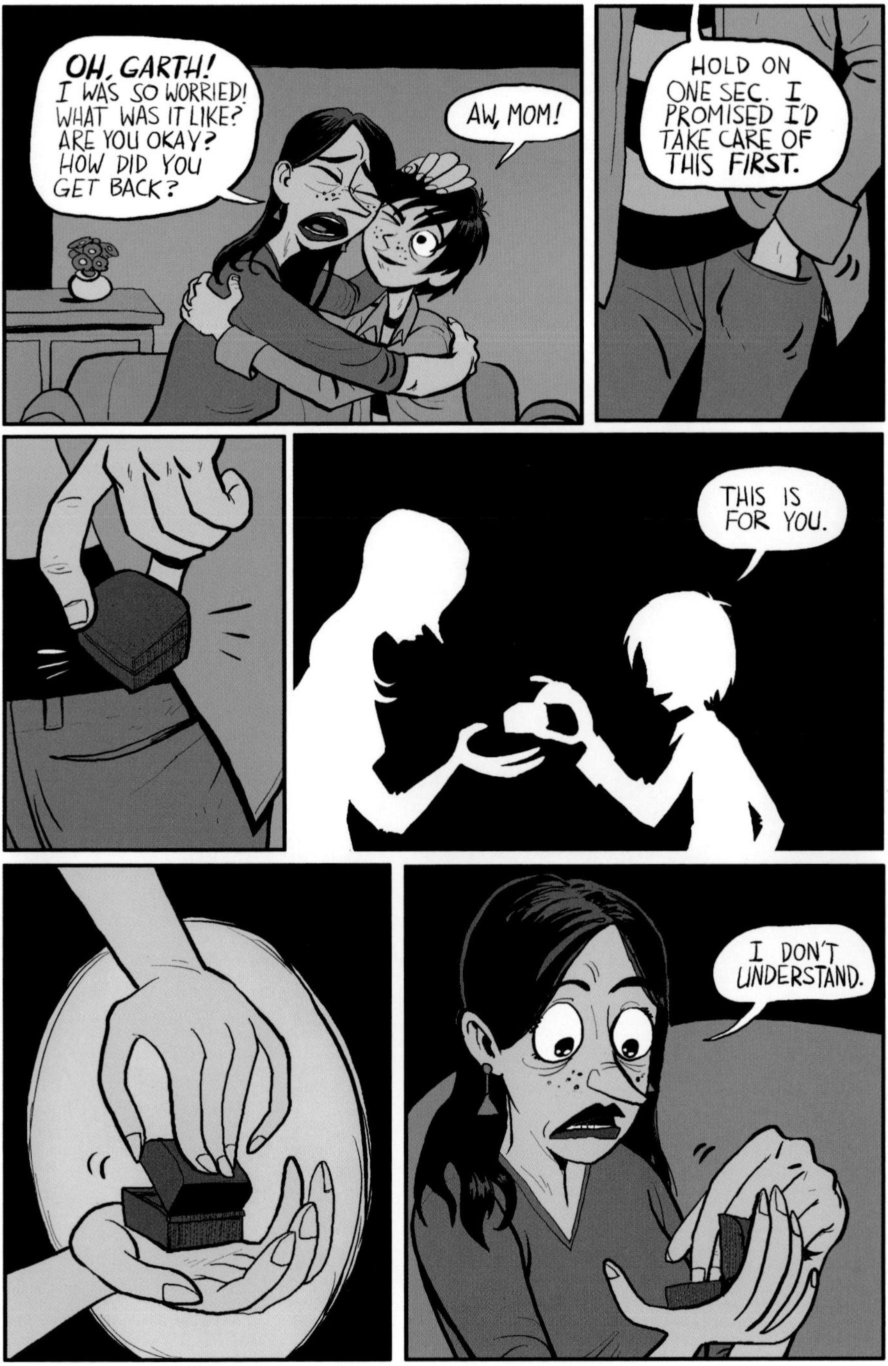
OH, GARTH! I WAS SO WORRIED! WHAT WAS IT LIKE? ARE YOU OKAY? HOW DID YOU GET BACK?
AW, MOM!
HOLD ON ONE SEC. I PROMISED I'D TAKE CARE OF THIS FIRST.
THIS IS FOR YOU.
I DON'T UNDERSTAND.

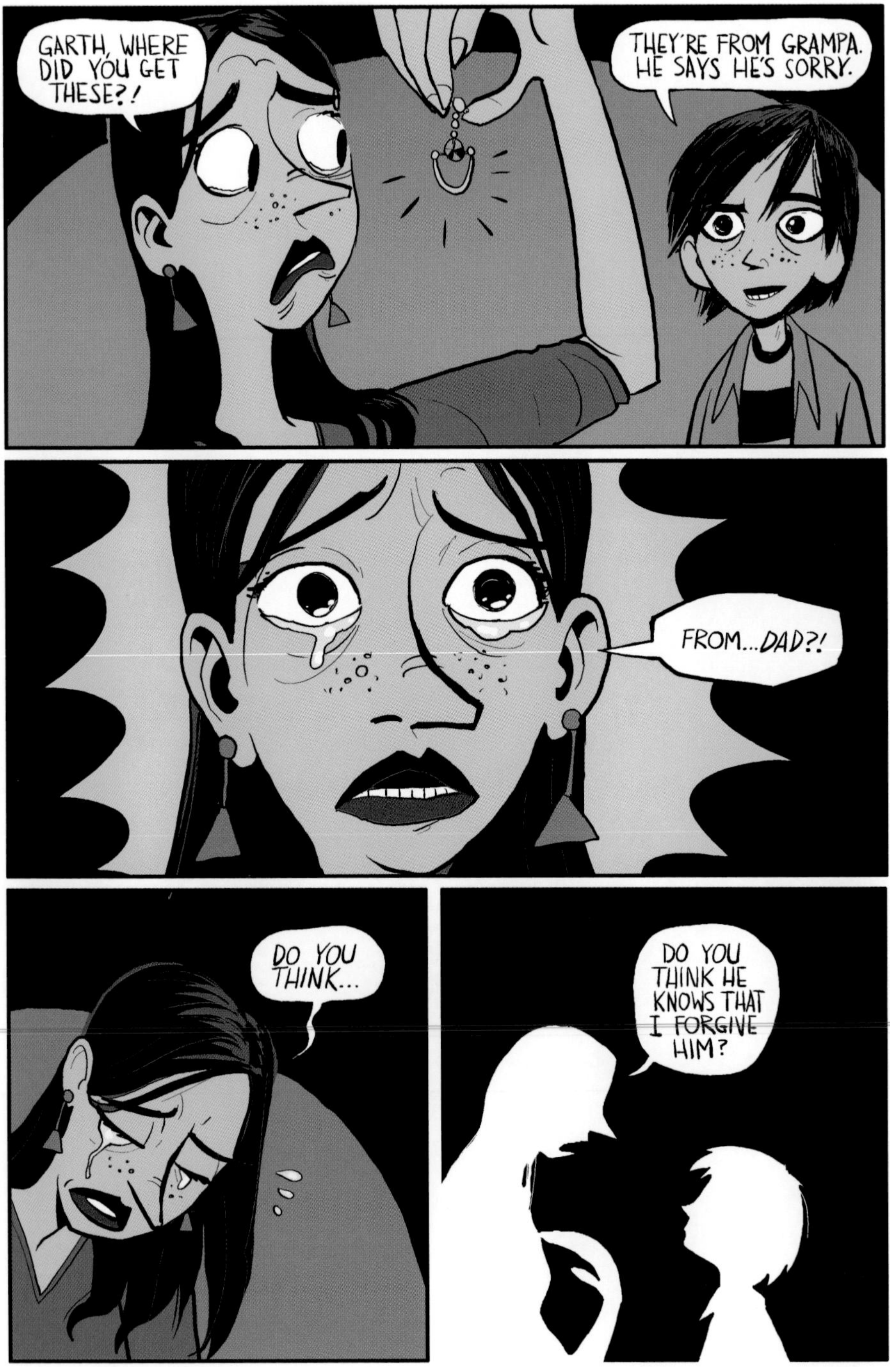
GARTH, WHERE DID YOU GET THESE?!
THEY'RE FROM GRAMPA. HE SAYS HE'S SORRY.
FROM...DAD?!
DO YOU THINK...
DO YOU THINK HE KNOWS THAT I FORGIVE HIM?

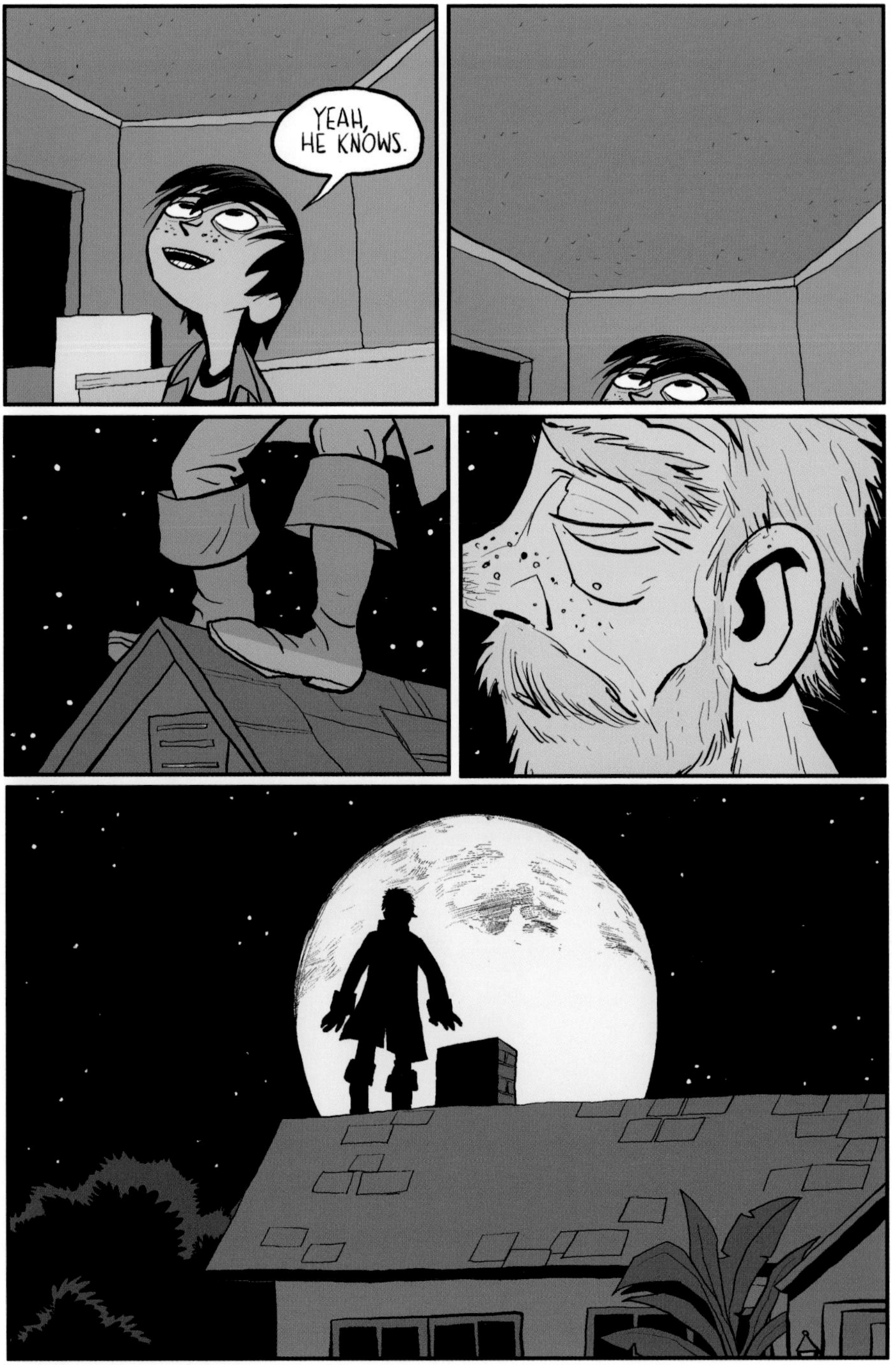
YEAH, HE KNOWS.

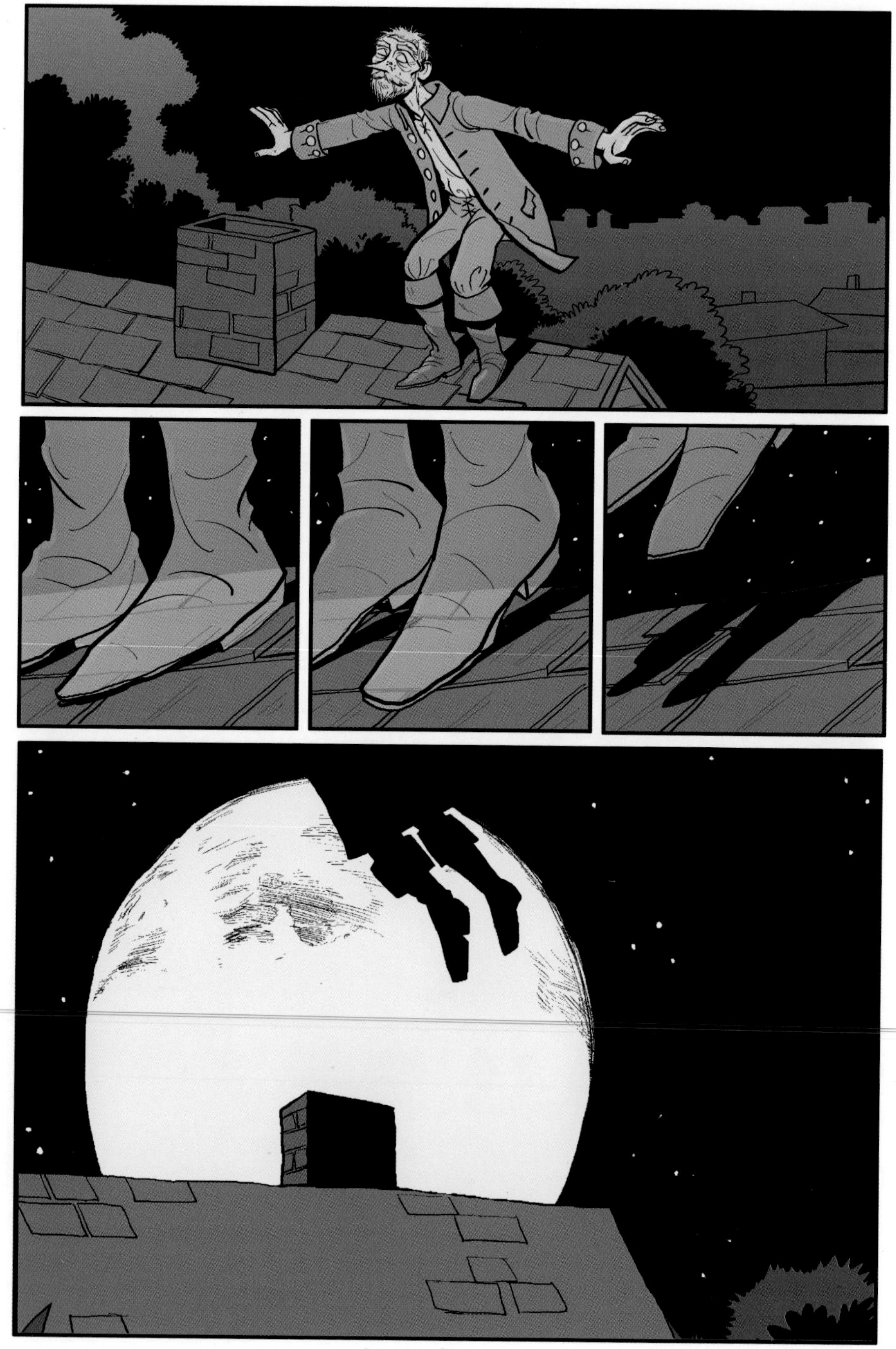

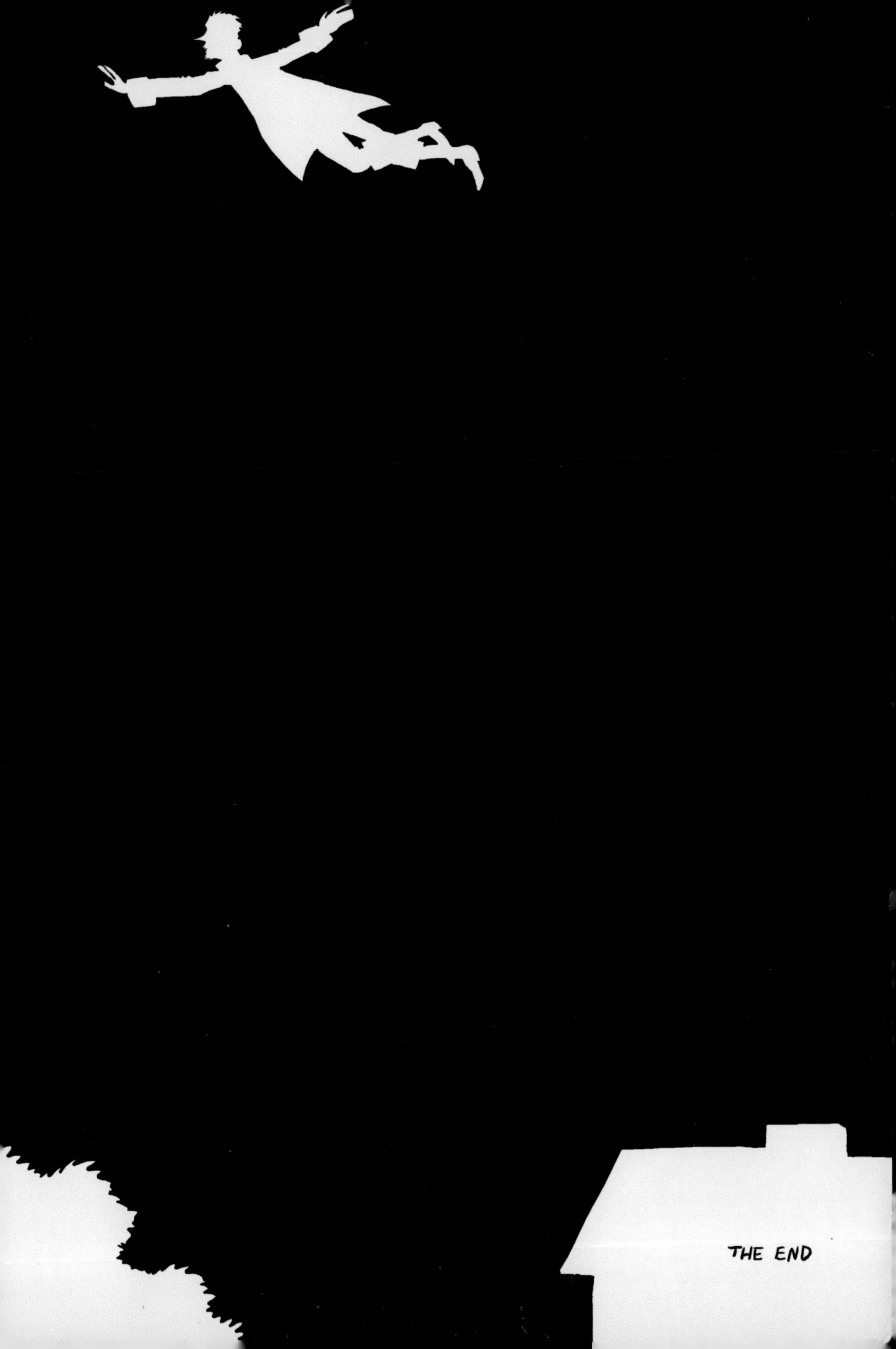
THE END

Doug TenNapel

is the author and illustrator of such acclaimed graphic novels as *Tommysaurus Rex*, *Monster Zoo*, and *Creature Tech*, as well as the creator of the popular character Earthworm Jim. He lives in Glendale, California, with his wife and four children.

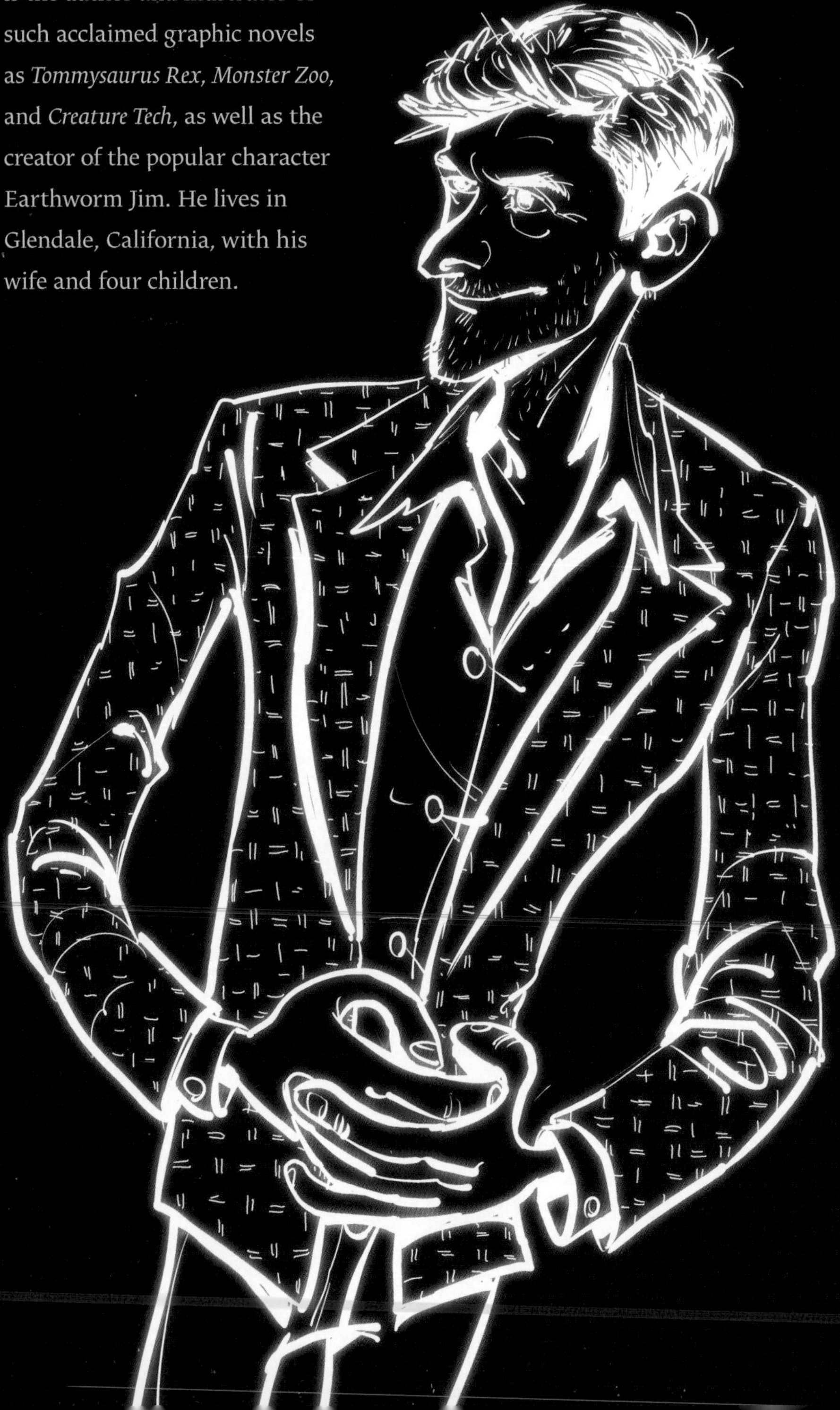